KT-178-737

OPEN A

9030 00005 9403 9

Vince Cable is the leader of the Liberal Democrats, MP for Twickenham, and also served from 1997–2015. He was the Liberal Democrat's chief economic spokesperson from 2003–2010, having previously served as Chief Economist for Shell from 1995–1997. He was Business Secretary under the Coalition Government from 2010–2015. Cable has published three non-fiction books with Atlantic to critical acclaim: *Free Radical*, *The Storm*, and *After the Storm*. *Open Arms* is his debut novel.

OPEN ARMS

VINCE CABLE

CORVUS

First published in hardback in Great Britain in 2017 by Corvus, an imprint of Atlantic Books Ltd.

This edition published in 2018.

Copyright © Vince Cable, 2017

The moral right of Vince Cable to be identified as the author of this work has been asserted by him in accordance with the Copyright, Designs and Patents Act of 1988.

All rights reserved. No part of this publication may be reproduced, stored in a retrieval system, or transmitted in any form or by any means, electronic, mechanical, photocopying, recording, or otherwise, without the prior permission of both the copyright owner and the above publisher of this book.

This novel is entirely a work of fiction. The names, characters and incidents portrayed in it are the work of the author's imagination. Any resemblance to actual persons, living or dead, events or localities, is entirely coincidental.

10 9 8 7 6 5 4 3 2 1

A CIP catalogue record for this book is available from the British Library.

Paperback ISBN: 978 178 649 1732
E-book ISBN: 978 178 649 1725

Printed and bound by Novoprint S.A, Barcelona

Corvus
An imprint of Atlantic Books Ltd
Ormond House
26–27 Boswell Street
London
WC1N 3JZ

www.corvus-books.co.uk

OPEN
ARMS

LONDON BOROUGH OF WANDSWORTH	
9030 00005 9403 9	
Askews & Holts	22-Mar-2018
AF THR	£7.99
	WW17020464

CHAPTER 1

THE BODY

Reuters, 7 June 2019:

Indian sources report a border incident on the Line of Control in Kashmir. Several Indian jawans (soldiers) and infiltrators were reported dead. A defence ministry spokesman said that terrorists from the militant group Lashkar-e-Taiba had been intercepted crossing the border. He warned that under India's Cold Start doctrine, Pakistan could expect a rapid military response if its government was found to be implicated.

The stinking rivulet was part bathroom, part laundry, part sewer and part rubbish tip, servicing the needs of a city

1

within a city. But for Ravi it was an aquatic adventure playground. Those not acquainted with the sights and smells of the baasti would have grimaced at the tannery waste and turds and dead dogs of this slum. But he was endlessly absorbed by the stately progress downstream of his flotilla of boats made from twigs, cans and bottles on their way through swampland to Mumbai harbour and thence to the Indian Ocean.

That morning his mother had risen early to be ahead of the queue performing their bodily functions and washing at the stream. There was a healthy flow swollen by heavy overnight rain and Ravi's attention was caught by a bundle of clothes trapped under a fallen tree, brought down by the rainstorm. This time of year produced a rich haul of driftwood, cans and plastic bottles to augment his merchant navy. He saw the potential of fabric for his sailing ships and with the help of a stick he managed to free the clothes until they floated closer to his harbour, a broken plastic frame that had so far escaped the attention of the boys scavenging for material to recycle. As he pulled on his catch he realised that it was bulkier than a bundle of clothes, and belonged to a man. This wasn't his first corpse but this one lacked hands and feet and the gaping eyes carried, even in death, the look of terror. His scream had the early morning bathers rushing to examine his discovery.

Had Deepak Parrikar been interested in these happenings a little over a mile away he could have seen them with the help of a telescope from the top floor of Parrikar House where he was fielding an early morning round of calls.

Dharavi, with its million or more inhabitants, can claim to be Asia's largest slum and it sits wedged between a major highway to the east, serving downtown Mumbai, and the seafront residences of Mahim Bay to the west, with fashionable Bandra to the north and the even more fashionable hilly area to the south where Parrikar House was located. But it was a place of which Deepak knew little and had never visited. And of the township of thousands of slum dwellers, where Ravi and his mother lived, between Dharavi and the middle class suburb of Chembur further to the east, he knew absolutely nothing. Yet this corner of Mumbai had a distinction: the World Health Organization had designated it one of the most polluted places on earth. Such a status was earned not just by the organically rich collection of bacteria in its water courses – for which any prize would have to be shared with many other sites in the city – but by a uniquely toxic soup of airborne, inorganic matter, a blend of traffic-generated particulates and the vaporised by-products of an ancient chemical plant, which Deepak's father owned.

Deepak had long been able to filter out of his conscious-ness the sights, sounds and smells of India's poor. It had once been necessary to apologise to overseas business visitors for the unpleasantness of the drive from the

3

airport. But a new highway, partly built on stilts across the sea from downtown Mumbai en route to the new international airport, bypassed the more sordid and congested districts. He was able to concentrate single-mindedly on his business and the web of interlocking interests that he had spun, stretching from California to Singapore via London, Munich and Tel Aviv. The only smell drifting across his desk was the perfume of his PA, 'Bunty' Bomani, bought for her on a visit to Paris and now intermingling with his own expensive aftershave. Outside the large windows the sky had cleared after the monsoon storm the previous evening and the usual cloud of dust and smoke had dissipated to reveal the endless townscape of what, on some measures, was the world's biggest city. The only sight to upset Deepak in the panoramic view was the grotesque, vulgar, multi-storey block of luxury apartments erected by one of his family's main rivals, breaching every known principle of planning, let alone aesthetic design.

'A call from your father, sir,' said Bunty. He lay back in his comfortable office chair, legs on the desk, tie askew, and in his shirtsleeves, with the jacket of his exquisite, hand-sewn suit lying on the floor. 'How's Mummy-ji?' he asked, switching to Hindi for his father's benefit. 'How's her sciatica? Have you got rid of that good-for-nothing doctor yet? Charges you the earth. Useless. Quack. Absolutely hopeless. Ancient Tamil remedies! Nonsense! I told you to try the physiotherapist at the clinic on Dr Merchant's Road.

He has sorted out a lot of our friends' back problems.' And so on, for the statutory five minutes until his father switched the conversation to politics, then business, or the other way round, since they usually came to the same thing.

'I spoke to my old friend Vikram, number three in the ruling party High Command,' Parrikar Senior explained. 'Sensible man, like the PM. Not one of these fanatics. He thanked me for our generous contribution to party funds. They know I used to back Congress and was close to Madam herself. But we are no longer outcasts. The PM likes the sound of our avionics operation, also. He may visit your factory to see India's high tech manufacturing. He understands that the country needs to develop with our overseas partners. The government knows all about the technology being developed in Pulsar, our partner company in the UK, and is keen to bring it to India. No more stupid "Swadeshi" talk about "self-sufficient" India, reinventing the wheel.'

'But Daddy-ji, where are we with this air force contract? We keep being promised. In the press ministers continue to say India has finally agreed to buy aircraft from the French – Dassault – not Eurofighter. Our British business partners are saying that India can only get access to the UK avionics technology if the air force buys Eurofighter.'

'I know. Vikram says don't believe what you read in the press. The PM understands. He has to respect procurement rules after all that fuss around the Congress party and Bofors, and other scandals. He wants clean government.

Things have to be done by the book. So it will take some time to change things. However, the British are sending a ministerial delegation to negotiate in Delhi. They may come here also to visit the factory. Check us out. The British have left Europe and want to trade with us. The PM thinks they are beggars who can't be choosers.'

The deal centred on the growing reputation of Deepak's company, in India and abroad, in the world of radar-based detection systems, used in the latest generation of jet fighters and in India's embryonic anti-missile defence shield. The company's origins lay in a century-old British firm, Smith & Smith, which had made weapons for the British Army in India. Several takeovers later it had become Pulsar but the link remained with its former Indian subsidiary, now renamed Parrikar Avionics after a burst of Indianisation by Mrs Gandhi in the 1970s. Parrikar Avionics added lustre to India's new image of sophisticated technology companies in IT, pharmaceuticals, precision engineering and aerospace. It had been built up by Deepak over the last decade. But the inspiration, as well as the capital behind it and the original acquisition of a majority stake in the clapped-out engineering plant, came from Ganesh Parrikar, his father.

Parrikar had started life as a street urchin in what was then Bombay in newly independent India. It was literally a rags to riches story. His family, landless, low caste Hindus, were starving in one of Bihar's periods of drought and, aged ten, he was packed off to a distant relative in Bombay. He never found the relative and had to survive on the streets. He did survive thanks to the kindness of strangers, a streak of ruthlessness and the immense good luck of sharing a pavement with another Bihari who was making his way in the world running errands for a developer building cheap housing for the expanding population north of downtown Bombay. Ganesh ran errands for the errand boy and acquired a tiny foothold in an industry in which he was to make his fortune. He progressed within half a century to becoming one of the city's dollar billionaires. A few years earlier his wealth would have placed him in the exclusive pantheon of India's business deities alongside the Birlas and Ambanis. But there were now dozens of billionaires, in so far as it was possible to measure wealth that was often hidden from the tax authorities and jealous relatives, dispersed internationally and embedded in family trusts of Byzantine complexity.

Ganesh Parrikar's energy, guile and unfailing instinct for property market trends and turning points were only part of his success. No one could succeed, as he had done, without being integrated into the network of corrupt officials and politicians that operated at city and state level. Nothing could be achieved without the right palms being greased. Nor could he operate without the muscle of gangsters who, for a consideration, would clear a site of unwanted occupants and ensure that rents were fully paid on time. But as a good father and patriotic Indian, Parrikar then diversified into productive and legitimate businesses to secure a legacy for his three children.

He made a berth for his eldest, Deepak. Deepak had been sent, aged thirteen, to an expensive school in England followed by engineering at Cambridge and a PhD at Imperial, and from there to Harvard Business School and several years' practical experience in the aerospace industry on the west coast of America. When he returned he was charged with building up a high-level tech business in civil and military aircraft electronics. This he had done successfully, starting with a collaboration to adapt Russian MiGs to Indian conditions and then improving quality management to become part of the supply chain of Boeing and Airbus. The company's British partner, Pulsar, was also an invaluable source of technology and marketing contacts, though the Indian offshoot was beginning to outgrow its former parent.

In truth, Parrikar Avionics made little money, though it added lustre to the family's image and India's reputation for world class manufacturing. It also advertised good corporate governance, since Deepak was a crusader for the kind of wholesome, caring, visionary company advocated by his friends in California. But the reality behind the opaque family business accounts was less wholesome: the balance sheet depended on the inflating price of land, much of it acquired by dubious means, and the cash flow was boosted by rentals from innumerable shacks of the kind occupied by Ravi and his family.

Inspector Mankad was settling into a pile of paperwork, which flapped in the gusts of air from the fan on his desk, when the call came in that a body had been found in suspicious circumstances. He was required immediately. He groaned. The pile of paper would continue to grow and the call also required venturing out into the muggy, oppressive heat until another monsoon downpour gave some relief. A possible murder in one of the most squalid, fetid, overcrowded and volatile of Mumbai's innumerable patches of slumland was not a glamorous assignment.

He straightened out his khaki uniform in front of a small mirror that nestled among his display of family photos; twirled his impressively long moustache modelled on a heroic Bollywood crime fighter; tightened his belt a notch or two to disguise a little better his prodigious paunch; and collected his even more overweight assistant, Sergeant Ghokale, to head for the waiting jeep. Both carried revolvers but they were ancient and probably didn't work. Rather, the officers' badge of authority and legitimate force was a thick bamboo cane, the lathi stick, which, from colonial times, had been used to intimidate crowds and dispense instant justice to troublemakers.

When they arrived at the scene of the crime, Inspector Mankad and Sergeant Ghokale pushed their way confidently through the swelling crowd towards the inanimate lump by the edge of the stream, now covered by a dirty cloth. The faces were suspicious, fearful: poor people who knew all about police beatings and extortion.

They parted meekly for the officers, whose peaked caps radiated authority and whose stomachs, bulging over their belts, suggested a prosperous career in law enforcement.

The four-year-old Ravi who had made the discovery pointed to the body and Sergeant Ghokale tried to ingratiate himself with the crowd by patting the child on the head and hailing him as a budding policeman. But no one understood his Marathi language. So he turned to his superior officer, and said, after a very quick inspection of the mutilated, bullet-ridden corpse, 'Sahib, gang killing. One less goonda to chase.'

'I don't know the face,' replied his boss. 'I know all their mugshots. Nice clothes. Businessman? Maybe a money man; managing their loot? Look in his pockets.'

Sergeant Ghokale did as he was told. Inspector Mankad was a good boss, shared out any pickings, looked after his team. Ghokale fought back nausea from the stench around him and expertly picked his way over the wet, bloodstained clothes. 'Nothing, Sahib. Clean. No ID.'

This could be awkward. Gang killing of unknown businessman. Kidnapping? Extortion? No one had been reported missing that fitted this man, as far as Mankad knew. He had survived and flourished in the Maharashtra police by bagging a regular crop of minor villains; generously sharing out any glory and financial rewards with superiors and subordinates; and knowing which cases to avoid, the political ones. Mankad calculated the risks. Gangland killings were dangerous. The top villains had friends in the state assembly and administration. Cases were mysteriously terminated. Police officers who showed too much curiosity could find themselves transferred to some fly-blown, poverty stricken country district. Now, with new faces after state elections, was especially dangerous. Mankad would have to be very careful.

But he was also a professional police officer. He may have played the game of brown envelopes and learnt how to swim in the shark infested seas of police politics. But he also had a medal for gallantry, and several highly commended awards, for doing his duty confronting armed criminals and protecting his team. He loathed the idea of gangsters going free.

As the officers moved to leave, Sergeant Ghokale grabbed hold of Ravi's father who was standing protectively next to his celebrity son. 'You. Witness. Come with me. Make statement.' The man cowered and pleaded with the police officer not to take him: 'Know nothing, Sahib.' His Telugu language was totally incomprehensible to the policeman but the ripple of anger through the crowd gave the officer pause. They knew what would happen. The man would be taken to the police station, beaten and detained. His family would lose their meagre income: the two hundred rupees (three dollars) a day he earned from dangerous and exhausting labour on a building site, whenever there was work available. They would be told they needed to pay for food at the police station, to stop the beatings and then to stop a false statement being filed and then again

11

to get him released. Every last rupee, and the limit of what the money lender would advance, would be squeezed out of them. And if they didn't pay he would be charged as an accessory to the murder and the police station would be able to maintain its impressive hundred per cent clear-up rate for serious crime. Either way, the family would be destroyed and return to the bottom of the ladder, back into the extreme poverty from which they had just begun to ascend.

The tension was broken by a bark of command: 'Ghokale. Leave it. We have work to do.'

As the officers retreated to their jeep, Mankad took a long look at the site. He tried to ignore the flies, the stench from the sewage pit and the curious crowd of children who were following them. He let his police training take over. One thing he noticed out of the ordinary was the pukka building on elevated land a quarter of a mile away, upstream from where the body had been found. Parked outside was a smart SUV that was unlikely to belong to the slum dwellers. And the flags flying from the building belonged to an extreme Hindu nationalist outfit that, in the heyday of its founder, ran the city and was blamed for much of the sectarian violence that plagued Mumbai. It was still a considerable political force where its cadres, operating from branch offices like the building nearby, were able to whip up communal feelings against outsiders: southerners, especially Tamils; northerners; Muslims. But all power corrupts and the pursuit of ethnic purity had long since taken second place to the spoils of extortion, smuggling, prostitution and other flourishing rackets. Mankad ordered Ghokale to drive the jeep a little further to make a note of the SUV's registration number. But not too close.

CHAPTER 2

THE CANDIDATE

One year earlier: August 2018

Kate Thompson yawned with relief. The annual summer fete had produced record takings. Over five thousand pounds. The elderly ladies who made up the backbone of the Surrey Heights Conservative Association clucked with satisfaction. They disagreed, however, as to whether the big money spinner had been Kate's Indian textiles, heavily discounted from her shop, or Stella's cupcakes. The former verdict would align them with the glamorous wife of the local party's sugar daddy. Loyalty to the latter would protect them from being flayed by the malicious, razor-edged tongue of the longstanding local party agent.

Appearances defined these respective factions. Kate was exceptionally tall, with long, comfortably unruly and naturally blonde hair; proud of her well-honed physique;

and always shown to advantage in fashionable and expensive clothes. Stella's army of elderly volunteers, with permed grey and white hair, were uniformly attired in dresses that reflected M&S fashions of a decade earlier.

Kate had never really felt she belonged to or understood the party, though her matching blue outfit and diligent work for The Cause might suggest otherwise. Her well-heeled, middle class parents – her late father had been a successful surgeon; her mother a pillar of the WI – had always voted Tory out of habit, though their broadly liberal views had sat uncomfortably with the content of their morning *Telegraph*. Kate had actually voted for Tony Blair in the noughties and at the last general election had turned up at the polling station sporting a large blue rosette and voted for the Lib Dem who seemed so much more interesting than the useless local MP. She had been further alienated by the Brexit vote, which she regarded as a disaster, one caused in part by the likes of Stella terrifying the pensioners of Surrey Heights by telling them that eighty million Turks were on their way. But a competent Prime Minister had arrived just in time to keep her in the party.

Still, she asked herself why on earth she was spending time here rather than with her daughters, her friends or her business. She had a seriously rich husband and what were rich husbands for if not to sign large cheques? His annual cheque to the association was worth at least ten times the amounts raised at this fundraiser, which had been planned over three months with as much detail as the Normandy landings. Unfortunately, he also had a tendency to treat his trophy wife as part of his successful property portfolio and had volunteered Kate's services to the association without her knowledge or approval, leading to a considerable row in a marriage increasingly characterised by lows rather than highs.

Kate realised that money wasn't really the point. The event was all about bonding, and nothing bonded the activists together more closely, short of an election, than gossip. An audible buzz rose and fell as Stella moved around like a bumble bee sucking nectar on its journey from stall to stall, while also injecting a little poison along the way. Stella was over fifty, blue rinse and twinset in imitation of her idol. She had a fathomless collection of stories from the highest sources – 'absolutely true' – about gay orgies, paedophile rings and fraud involving everybody she disliked. Kate had a firm policy of not being bitchy about other women, but those with acute hearing would have heard her mutter: 'What an absolute cow.'

This year Stella was almost out of control, such was the pitch of her excitement. The rumour mill was working flat out, fed by the story that the veteran MP, Sir Terence Watts, was about to step down. His appearances in the constituency were infrequent and embarrassing. Today he had opened the fete, not an onerous feat, but had muffed his lines, got the name of the village wrong and thanked the wrong hostess for the loan of her beautiful garden. Perhaps he was distracted by the recent press revelations that he had seriously overclaimed for his parliamentary expenses, including three properties, one in Jamaica. He would be unlikely to survive the weekend.

Kate had never understood how he had managed to cling on like a limpet through a quarter of a century of inactivity. Her husband explained that the whips valued his uncritical loyalty and many older voters liked his military bearing and beautifully tailored three-piece suit worn in all weathers. Moreover, Stella had provided him with a formidable Praetorian Guard. Her devotion may have been grounded in an ancient passion but he was also the source of her local power. Now her loyalties had moved on and she was telling her geriatric army that the party of Mrs Thatcher, with the new female PM, needed more mature women MPs and fewer 'bright young men'. Her profile of the ideal MP fitted herself perfectly. But had she been better at interpreting body language she would have realised that her enthusiasm was not widely shared.

The name on everyone's lips was Jonathan Thompson, Kate's husband: very rich, very handsome in a louche way, clever, capable, personable and well connected, a man who would inexorably rise to the top. Knowing her husband better than the party faithful, Kate could have added to the list of his attributes an insatiable appetite for serial philandering, a major deficit in emotional intelligence, and political convictions that mainly centred on the sanctity of his private property, particularly the parts of the property market that generated his fortune. She had, however, learnt to balance the bad with the good. But when she heard herself being addressed as the MP presumptive's wife, something inside her rebelled.

She flushed with annoyance and struggled to concentrate against the competing claims of fussy customers, securing change for depleting floats, polite repartee and approaching rain clouds. Although she had never publicly articulated the thought, she had long felt that she would be a far better MP than many of the men she saw, and encountered, trying to do the job, not least the useless Sir Terence. The material comforts of life with Jonathan and family duties had dulled her ambition. But there was an ambitious woman waiting to emerge and this afternoon had stirred up what she had long suppressed. Her incoherent thoughts were crystallised when she was approached by one of the few local Conservatives she actually liked. Len Cooper was a long-serving county councillor, now the leader of the council. He was highly competent, unpretentious and modest: a successful local businessman in the building trade who believed in public service and practised it. They enjoyed a good friendship, uncomplicated by any emotional undertones. Her only discomfort was that at six foot without heels she towered over his small and totally spherical body. This didn't seem to faze him; he was a man comfortable in his own skin and especially comfortable in the company of his equally spherical wife, Doris. As they started to talk they soon got around to the runners and riders and the short odds being offered on Jonathan. Len Cooper was non-committal but, after a long pause, said: 'I am surprised that you haven't considered standing yourself.' Since Len didn't do flattery, she took the comment seriously and was pleased as it reinforced a thought that had already crossed her mind.

It hadn't crossed the mind of her husband, however. They had a rare evening at home together that night, as the girls were staying with family friends while competing in a gymkhana. Over dinner he set out the pros and cons of his own candidacy and various alternative scenarios in none of which Kate featured. He saw himself as the ideal candidate but had done the maths. They had three daughters at expensive schools; horses and paddock; a 'cottage' (actually a small château) in Burgundy; Kate's Land Rover and his Maserati; the annual pilgrimage to the ski slopes at Klosters; membership of an exclusive golf club; and that was after cutting out some of the luxuries. An MP's salary would reduce them to wretched poverty if he was forced into being a full-time MP – as the party High Command was now demanding – and to hand over the property business to his partners. Kate reminded him of the contribution she made from the profits on her business and could see a 'p' word forming on his lips – 'pin money' or 'peanuts' – before he stopped himself. He had a better idea: 'The High Command is keen to find a bright young man. Ex-Oxford. Special adviser to the Foreign Secretary.

The next David Cameron. Surrey Heights would be perfect.'
He – and possibly the High Command – seemed not to have
noticed that posh boys were no longer the darlings of local
constituency associations.

By now Kate was becoming seriously irritated. 'If you
don't want the seat, why are you spending your money
and my time bailing out the local Tories?' she asked.

He thought for a while, hurt by his wife's cynicism.
'Because I care. The Labour Party has been taken over by
Marxist-Leninist revolutionaries. If they get into power at
the next election our heads will be on spikes. They hate
us. The politics of envy.'

Kate shared the more conventional view reflected in the
polls that the chances of Labour winning were roughly
comparable to Elvis Presley being found on Mars. But this
passionate outburst reminded her that while she and her
husband agreed on some things – Remain being one –
they disagreed on most others. She was privately relieved
that her husband wasn't going to be her next MP.

She then braced herself for a difficult exchange.

'It may surprise you, Jonathan, but my name also came
up in the chatter this afternoon.'

'Who from?'

'Never mind who. It did. And I am thinking about it.'

She knew him well enough to know that the words
'don't be ridiculous, woman' were forming in his mind,
but he knew her well enough not to utter them. He opted
for soft soap instead.

'You are a brilliant mother. Don't the girls need our continued attention?' (But apparently not his!) 'Your business is doing well. Are you going to let it go?' (This from someone who prided himself on not getting out of bed for a business deal worth under a million pounds.) And then the coup de grâce: 'We have had our differences but you have been a wonderfully supportive wife. I need you.' She cursed her lack of foresight in not having set up a tape recorder.

She kept going. 'The children are no longer babies. There is a commuter train from the station down the road. I have a plan for my business. I can cope. And it might help you with your business to have an MP for a wife, close to the centre of power.'

He grunted in acknowledgement. 'OK, you have a point. Let's think about it.' With that he disappeared to attend to his emails. Kate called after him: 'I take that as a "yes". Thank you, Jonathan.' There was no reply. The 'thank you' was sincere. She would win the hearts and minds of the local association only as part of a happy, smiling family. And she would need Jonathan's money.

The following morning, she rang Len Cooper. 'I have been thinking about your suggestion. The answer is positive. Jonathan isn't wild about it but he's on board.' Len expressed no surprise but took her through the practicalities. First, shortlisting by the executive committee. He would speak to Stella and assure her that her job was safe, but insist that she drop her ridiculous candidacy.

He would tell HQ that after a quarter of a century of an absentee MP there had to be a strong local candidate. The 'next Cameron' should try elsewhere. And could they suggest a few other names of aspiring MPs who wanted experience of a selection meeting? 'Then you have the hustings meeting in front of three or four hundred members. It will be a bit of an ordeal. Our Brexit militants will be out in force. You must put on a good show, but I know you will. A few of us will prep you properly.'

Reassured, Kate started to think about what she was letting herself in for. The girls were not babies, but not adults either. She had firmly resisted pressure from Jonathan to pack them off to a 'character building' boarding school (like his). She took mothering seriously, and it showed; the girls were close to each other and to her. Kate assembled them when they had returned from the gymkhana and had calmed down after telling her about their heroics in the saddle. When she explained her plans their faces lit up with excitement and they were soon texting their friends to tell them Mum was going to be the next Prime Minister. A good start.

Then there was her business: the product of twenty years' hard work and a lot of emotional investment. On the surface it was just a fancy clothes and fabrics shop on the high street specialising in high-end Indian fashion. But it also housed a strongly growing internet sales operation. And behind it all was a small army of Indian suppliers: maybe a hundred women, mainly widows, whose livelihoods depended on being able to sell their beautiful, handcrafted embroidery to Yummy Mummies in Surrey. But as a Yummy Mummy herself she understood the market better than her competitors. Jonathan had been dismissive early on, seeing her shop as a hobby business to keep her out of mischief. But to be fair to him, he had put up some cash to help her acquire the freehold. And he had pulled some effective strings when an inflexible local bank manager tried to put her out of business during the credit crunch.

It had all started when she went off to India aged eighteen, with her girlfriend, Sasha, to 'see the world' in a gap year between leaving St Paul's Girls' School and going on to study medieval history at Oxford. Her parents were nervous but reassured that they were travelling as a pair. Shortly after arriving in India Sasha was laid low by Delhi Belly, which turned out to be a severe case of amoebic dysentery, and flew back home. Kate lied to her parents and told them she had teamed up with another girl and would stay. The truth was that she was utterly captivated by India. Walking around Old Delhi constantly assailed by new sounds, sights and smells, she felt as if a door was opening up to an utterly different world she needed to explore.

Kate's academically stretching but chaste education at St Paul's had equipped her with an impressive understanding of dynastic politics in the Plantagenet era but hadn't educated her in the various species of predatory men. In Delhi's coffee shops, in Connaught Circus frequented by Westerners, she bumped into a friendly Australian, Jack (or as she discovered later, he had contrived to bump into her). He was seriously scruffy with a tangled beard and unkempt long black hair and clearly hadn't washed for some time. But beneath the grime he had an open, welcoming smile and a reassuring, generous manner. He listened sympathetically to her anxieties and adventures and offered – without, he hastened to add, any obligations – to let her tag along with him. Travelling would be safer. He explained that he was in search of true enlightenment, discovering his transcendental soul, and was finding in the poverty of India a genuine richness of spirit. His spiel was thoroughly convincing and Kate was entranced.

Needless to say, his search for enlightenment soon led to her bed, in the cheap and dirty hotels they passed through along the Gangetic plain. The experience was neither physically nor emotionally satisfying but Kate was persuaded that she was getting ever closer to her inner being. He also introduced her to pot, which made her violently sick and provided none of the mystical wonders she had read about. They finally parted company when he took her to an ashram presided over by a naked sadhu, His Holiness the Guru Aditya, who preached the renunciation of bodily needs but actively solicited sexual favours and money from his Western acolytes. Kate fled back to Delhi, alone.

She could hardly wait to get on the next plane home. But before leaving she headed into Delhi's profusion of handicraft emporia to buy presents for family and friends. She was attracted to a modest stall offering exquisitely embroidered garments and furnishings – at modest fixed prices. She spent her remaining money and, as she left, the owner, Anjuli, ran after her in some distress explaining that she had accidentally overcharged. This novel experience led to a conversation and an invitation to visit her workshop, a room off an alley nearby, where a dozen women worked, barely pausing to greet her. An idea began to form that was later to become the basis for Kate's business. The pair exchanged addresses; Kate placed an advance order for goods to sell to her friends; they worked out how she could send the money to India. Two decades later, she had established a flourishing high street and internet business on the back of Anjuli's crafts, which never failed in quality, quantity or delivery. They won other customers including a leading UK fashion brand. And when Kate had last seen Anjuli she was a little greyer but, by now, a leading social entrepreneur whose network of cooperatives was an obligatory feature of development agency reports. Together they had achieved something. Kate was now ready to hand the running of her business to others and move on to a new challenge.

The Conservative Association hired a large hall to accom-modate the five hundred members who wanted to attend the selection hustings. Kate had never spoken to a big meeting before and was extremely nervous despite inten-sive preparation and the presence of Jonathan and her daughters in the front row. She sensed that the meeting was cheering her on, though some of the questions were hostile. 'What are you going to do about immigration?' '... standing room only... overcrowded island... swamped' etc. She struggled to reconcile these questions with the local village of five thousand souls whose immigrant population consisted of Mr Shah and his family at the post office and the largely invisible owner of the Chinese restaurant. She had been advised, however, not to appear too condescending but to show, at least, a willingness to listen to heartfelt concerns. Her unsound social liberalism on gay marriage lost a few votes. But it didn't matter. She was overwhelmingly adopted on the first ballot.

Three months later the party machine swung into action for the general election, which the Prime Minister called early when her Brexit programme ran into serious trouble in parliament and before rising unemployment dented her popularity. Since the constituency had returned Conservatives with massive majorities, even in 1945 and 1997, there was little basis for anxiety.

Kate was required only to put in a few days' work shaking hands and being photographed. The Tory machine did the rest. The sole ripple of controversy in the campaign was her initial refusal to put her family in front of the cameras when she worried that this old-fashioned public display of traditional family values might prove a hostage to fortune. Stella led the opposition, arguing that the members would not countenance such a display of metropolitan liberalism so soon after the demise of Sir Terence.

Such interest as her campaign excited centred on her appearance. Her height and figure would have qualified her to be a professional model. Her face was very handsome rather than conventionally beautiful, and with her naturally blonde hair, she had the classical good looks of a well-bred, upper middle class English family whence she came. All of this would have been reserved for the electors of Surrey Heights, had an earnest Labour shadow minister not chosen to enliven the election campaign with an attack on the 'objectification of women' by the right-wing media deterring talented young women from coming forward into public life. The press, which had been bored to death by the opposition leader's lectures on the evils of capitalism, at last had a serious subject to get their teeth into. The *Sun* retaliated with a headline and two-page spread. Prominently featured was a photo of Kate taken half a lifetime earlier when she had tried modelling in her gap year, posing in a minimalist bikini. She was one of several 'Gorgeous Girls' who would be banished to an appalling Gulag if Manchester's Madame Mao and her Loony Left Labour friends got within a million miles of Downing Street. Kate was rather relieved that the *Sun* was not more widely read in Surrey Heights.

<hr />

8 June 2019

Air conditioning was an essential of life for Deepak Parrikar. Without it, office and home were intolerable. For his father it was an uncomfortable, alien distraction. His small office, downtown in the bazaar area around the old fort, relied on a noisy overhead fan. Bits of paper flapped under their weights as the fan revolved – that is, when it worked, downtown Mumbai being subject to 'brownouts' from time to time, the symptom of India's creaking infrastructure. And the noise of the fan was competing with the cacophony outside: the rattling, squeaking, banging and scraping of vehicles being loaded and unloaded; the constant hooting of horns by moped, motorcycle and car drivers and, in a deeper register, from the boats plying the harbour; the barking of dogs; the cawing of crows; the plaintive whining of the beggars; and the shouting of street hawkers and hustlers. The senses were further assaulted by a heady cocktail of smells: richly scented garlands on the wall, diesel fumes, rotting food in the street, cooking oil, human waste, spices.

None of this could be heard or smelt in Parrikar House but this was where Parrikar Senior preferred to work. It wasn't sentiment that kept him there. It was here, and in the chai shop on the corner, that his network of informers and confidants, business contacts and friendly officials could slip in and out quietly, like a colony of ants ferrying gossip, rumours and inside knowledge back to the nest. The stock exchange, the bullion market and the municipal offices were all nearby. Here he could keep up with, or ahead of, the markets in which he operated.

This morning, one of Parrikar Senior's oldest associates was in his office: Mukund Das, flustered and sweating profusely in a safari suit that was at least one size too small.

'We have a problem, Parrikar Sahib. Our Mr Patel has gone missing. He didn't come home yesterday evening.'

'Girlfriend?'

'More serious, Sahib. A few days ago he had a visit from a couple of goondas. I recognised them: shooters; the Sheikh's men. People we don't mess with. Trouble. I asked what they had come about. Patel said: "Nothing. The usual shit. I told them to fuck themselves." He didn't want to say more. But I knew the reason: these goondas want protection to cover potential "accidents" on the site. We normally pay. No problem. But not Patel. He has high principles. Then, next day, he said he had had late night calls. Some goondas threatening him. He was frightened, very shaken. He planned to come and talk to you. Now he has gone. Mrs Patel telephoned to say he did not come home last night.'

The mystery did not last long. Parrikar Senior's PA brought in the morning newspapers. On the front page of *Bharat Bombay* was a picture of a body. Unmistakably Mr Patel.

'Exclusive' is a valid claim for Mayfair's Elizabethan Hotel. It is tucked away down a quiet, cobbled mews and never advertises, relying instead on a reputation for tasteful luxury and absolute discretion of the kind demanded by those among the world's super-rich and powerful who prefer to stay out of the limelight. These qualities were especially valued by the Chairman of Global Analysis and Research when he needed to convene a meeting of his directors.

He was sprawled across a soft leather armchair in a private room in the bowels of the hotel sipping occasionally at the large tumbler of neat whisky beside him and giving his captive audience of three the benefits of his geopolitical world view. The lecture was delivered in the slowest of Cajun drawls and he could have been chewing the cud on the verandah of his eighteenth-century French mansion overlooking the swamp-lands of Louisiana. But his associates were careful not to let their attention wander too far. The Chairman's brain moved a lot quicker than his speech. And there were crocodiles in his swamp.

'Good news, colleagues. History is on our side. Good friends of our company are now in charge in the US and Russia. Islamic terrorists are in retreat. More and more customers are queuing up for our anti-missile technology and we are now the dominant supplier in parts of that market. Our external shareholders are delighted with the thirty per cent return we are giving them. And I hope you are all pleased with the size of your Cayman accounts. Let us drink to the future of Global.' There was a growl of approval and glasses clinked.

'Now, let us get down to business. Reports on our next project, please. Admiral?'

'I am lining up the British company we have researched. No problems. My contacts in government will play ball.'

The Chairman paused, sensing overconfidence and seeing that the Admiral was rather flushed. He had brought class and an impressive contacts list to the company. But he was too fond of rum.

'Are you sure? I need to be sure.'

After an awkward silence, the burly, crew-cut Orlov spoke up for his old friend. 'The Admiral always delivers. Ever since we worked together in St Petersburg twenty-five years ago he has been as good as his word. And he is the only Britisher I have met who can drink Russians under the table.' His belly-laugh proved infectious.

The Chairman swallowed his doubts. Orlov was a thug. But a reliable thug. And a man with almost unprecedented access to his old KGB chum in the Kremlin.

One member of the group remained silent and unsmiling. Dr Sanjivi Desai was slowly making his way through his favourite tipple: apple juice. He was a small man with a neat moustache, greying hair, a look of great intensity and a beautifully tailored suit of Indian design. His English was impeccable with slight Indian cadences and traces of an American accent. 'There are uniquely promising opportunities in India. A competent government aligned with our values. Badly in need of what we have to offer.'

The Chairman had known Desai for a long time and trusted his judgement. 'Good. Let us know how you get on.

'Now, I have some news of my own. On medical advice I have decided to appoint a deputy Chair. Another American. Colonel Schwarz is recently retired from the Pentagon. Their top man on anti-missile defence. Close to the Trump people. A find. None of us are indispensable, including me.'

CHAPTER 3

THE GUARD

Twitter, 8 June 2019:

President Trump's tweet after the regular six-monthly meeting between the Presidents of the US and the Russian Federation:

'Good meeting with #Putin. Sorted #Europe and #MiddleEast. Biggest nuclear war risk India and Pakistan. nice people. #SAD!'

The dead of night was very dead. For the night watchman, sitting in a cubicle outside the front entrance of the factory, the challenge was to stay awake and carry out the few tasks he was paid the minimum wage to perform. In the months since Mehmet had been given the night shift outside the Pulsar factory he had seen a variety of urban foxes and stray dogs, two tramps, an illegal fly tipper and several couples doing what couples do in the back of cars when they think they are alone in a quiet corner of a sleeping industrial estate away from the neon lights. Silence was broken only by the distant hum of the M1.

It was a job nonetheless. Not quite the intellectual stimulus of his earlier job as professor of mathematics at the Eritrean Institute of Technology. But he was grateful to have been allowed to stay and work in the UK after he had escaped the mindless carnage on the battlefields separating Ethiopia and his native Eritrea and, then, as a disabled war veteran, and known dissident, had abandoned a harsh and insecure life under the dictatorship. As he surveyed the nocturnal tranquillity of the estate he endlessly replayed in his mind the events that had led him to this life of safety and excruciating boredom.

After being conscripted into the army and surviving a pointless war that left a hundred thousand dead on both sides, there followed a long trek, familiar to asylum seekers from the Horn of Africa, through Sudan and Egypt, the journey on a leaking, dangerously overcrowded boat across the Mediterranean followed by the trek to Calais, a month's agonising wait in the Jungle and, after numerous attempts, entering the UK clinging to the chassis of a lorry. He had then been accepted as a refugee seeking asylum.

Tedium and poor wages were now a small price to pay for freedom. Eventually he would get his Indefinite Leave to Remain and he had sketched out a long term route map, requalifying through the Open University, teaching and being reunited with his family.

Little was asked of him at work beyond monitoring CCTV footage of the perimeter, protected by a formidable fence with razor wire. He was also to check that the premises were empty before switching off the main lights and locking the entrance at 10pm. Occasionally research staff stayed late and he was to ensure that they were signed out and accounted for. The purpose of the factory was never explained to him – the supervisor had simply said Pulsar did 'hush-hush' things, something to do with the military. There was a secure area from which he was barred – only accessible by lift to a small number of pass holders. In an emergency he had access to a panic button; back-up security staff would arrive within five minutes. In his six months, alternating shifts with a Nigerian, it had not been needed.

At 2am that night he needed the toilet, which was beside the reception area. As he left the building he spotted a faint light under one of the doors to the main building: torchlight perhaps? He unlocked and opened the door. There was a brief, faint scuffling sound and then silence and darkness. Mehmet looked carefully in all the rooms accessible from the door. But nothing. He rechecked the ledger. No one officially in the building. He kept a careful eye on the building until morning – but no one appeared. He signed off in the morning: 'Investigated possible intruder but no one found. Decided not to raise alarm.' He looked back through the log book and saw that Osogo, the Nigerian, had made a similar note a few weeks earlier. He asked to speak to the head of security, who laughed it off: 'Ghosts! You Africans have a very vivid imagination.' Mehmet resented the security chief's patronising manner and the rather phoney bonhomie he had displayed since their first meeting at the job interview. But he was not going to compromise his job or his immigration status by picking a quarrel. So he smiled deferentially, agreeing that Africans were indeed people with small brains and childlike fears.

×××××××××××××××××

While Mehmet left after his night duty and his encounter with ghosts, the CEO, Calum Mackie, was already in his office, preparing for an early morning call, looking over the papers from his safe first, and checking the relevant emails.

Mackie was a technological genius whose world-beating research in ultra-high frequency radio waves had found both commercially profitable and militarily useful applications. He had taken over Smith & Smith, the once great manufacturer of military equipment, when it ran aground. Renamed Pulsar, it retained a highly skilled workforce, some valuable patents and an excellent network of export outlets and overseas investments dating from the days of Empire. Calum rebuilt the business, strengthened by his inventions, and over the last ten years massively expanded exports to NATO countries and others for which he could get export licences. Like other successful British technology companies, his had struggled to raise capital to expand and he had been tempted to sell out to US competitors who were only too keen to get their hands on his technology. Indeed, the MOD was very anxious that the latest smart adaptations to his aircraft-borne missiles did not fall into the wrong hands. Fortunately for their peace of mind, and his, he had secured some American private equity investors who were willing to commit substantial sums, long term, without interfering, on expectation of exceptionally good returns, which he had, so far, delivered.

On the other end of the phone was his well-established link to government: Rear Admiral Jeremy Robertson-Smith, a military hero, UK plc's arms salesman extraordinaire and now a freelance consultant operating on the blurred boundaries of business and state. A legend promoting UK defence sales (much of it made by his former employer), his fingerprints were all over a decade of successful defence deals, and many British companies, including Pulsar, were in his debt (as he was not slow to remind them).

His soubriquet, the Red Admiral, appeared to have originated during a secondment by the MOD, via NATO, to help the Yeltsin government sort out the chaos in the former Soviet navy whose formidable military assets, some of them highly dangerous, were rusting in port or being stolen. The Red Admiral ensured that the equipment was put out of harm's way and managed, in two years of operating out of St Petersburg, to negotiate some lucrative deals including one that saw India, through a brilliant official called Desai, who was familiar with Soviet kit, acquiring a state of the art aircraft carrier and other vessels on the cheap. The Russians ensured that the Red Admiral was well rewarded, a fact not reported to HMRC or the MOD.

'Things are now moving fast,' said the Red Admiral. 'My friends in government have already sounded you out on a possible collaboration with India. I have been asked to brief you on the big picture. We both know some of the key players. The deal is this: the UK is still trying to prise the Indians away from Dassault, their chosen bidder for a new fighter. We are offering the Eurofighter. I don't need to tell you that there are thousands of jobs in the UK supply chain if we can swing it. What the Indians really want is your little toy, the MRP3, strapped onto the wings.'

'Why the MRP3?' Mackie asked. 'There are other airborne missile systems.'

'They know that. The reason you are the key is this technology you have developed for using high frequency electromagnetic waves for simulating the after-effects of a nuclear blast, when all electronic systems are disabled within a radius of several miles. They believe that if the pulsar mechanism can be incorporated into the MRP3 it can be used to disable missiles in flight. You see where I am going?'

'Sure.'

'The Indian military establishment has nightmares worrying about extremists getting their hands on Pakistani nuclear weapons and firing them off at Indian cities. India has a powerful second strike capability, which is an effective deterrent to rational military men and politicians in Islamabad. But a deterrent can't work with people who belong to a death cult. India is desperate for an anti-missile shield of the kind the US has, and Israel. They have done a lot of work already and have good lines into Washington and Tel Aviv. They have been trying for almost a decade to develop an anti-missile defence system to cover, at least, Delhi and Mumbai. They have tested an interceptor missile – the Prithic – several times and it works for high altitude ballistic missiles. But critics think it will take another decade, perhaps longer, to develop a half-effective system with all the paraphernalia of ground radar, telecommunications and data links. Meanwhile, the Pakistanis are acquiring M-11 missiles from China and the technology to help fool anti-missile defences. The Indian government is getting anxious. They are already talking to the Israelis about purchasing their successful David's Sling system and the present lot don't have hang-ups about dealing with Israel.

'Britain isn't big in this whole area of anti-missile defence. But we have you. And you in turn have your Indian partners, Parrikar Avionics, which makes the issue of getting access so much easier. And preliminary discussions between our military attachés in Delhi and the Indians suggest that they are very – repeat very – interested.

'Their boffins think your technology could help them cut corners. Very smart people. But they need our help. The Americans are keen that we should offer it. Trump's people see the Indians as "good guys" taking on militant Islam and the Chinese too. The PM is keen as well. The post-Brexit export drive. And as a sweetener the Indians are dropping hints that if we give them access to the technology they want, they will also take off our hands the second of those bloody aircraft carriers that Gordon Brown ordered and we can't find any use for.'

Calum was used to the Red Admiral's style: orders from the bridge; debate not encouraged. But he had to intervene. 'Look, this is way beyond my pay grade. I'm just a wee techie. You're getting carried away, man. There is a vast amount of work to be done, testing, refining, software development.'

'Well, you can divvy up the work with your Indian opposite numbers. I believe they are very smart.'

'Well, may be, may be. Don't forget I have a company to run and investors who won't want me straying outwith our core business activities. They don't know much about India – believe it involves a lot of dirty politics. Religious headbangers. Backhanders flying everywhere. They have been trying to encourage me to sell off our investment in Parrikar Avionics. And, to be frank, I am tempted. So far it hasn't made us much money.'

'Surely they understand that India is a coming power. We have to be there. And their best people are world class. Anyway, think about it, Calum. We want to send a delegation to India, soon, led by a minister, to talk to the key people about this package. You are essential. I believe the Indians have been told you are coming.'

'You bastard, Jeremy!'

'Yes, but my friends also keep you in business, Calum. Sorry! But I had to drop that in.'

'OK, but the detail, and the money, has to be right.'

After the call Mackie felt a sense of relief. Notwithstanding the bluster, the company's order book was dangerously low. Defence cuts in the UK and USA had hurt. He had lain awake at night for weeks, preparing himself for difficult conversations with shareholders and the workforce. Maybe he was now off the hook.

His thoughts switched to how the workforce could absorb a big new contract on a very tight schedule. Calum Mackie was a gifted inventor and scientist and a shrewd businessman. But people management was not his thing. His private life was reclusive and monastic – bed, work, bed, work. He hated face to face confrontation and had no feel for the subtleties of personal relationships. He preferred to operate at one remove from his staff, working through the very small number of people whom he trusted and who could penetrate his moods and his accent. He was also, privately, a committed socialist from his Clydeside days, a Labour donor and a believer in trade unions.

Pulsar worked as a harmonious, flexible unit because of the close, symbiotic relationship – the personal chemistry – between the boss and the Unite chief shop steward, a charismatic, ambitious, thirty-year-old senior technician called Steve Grant. They had a shared experience of the University of Life, having both left school at sixteen to work, and a similar set of political ideals. But physically they were very different. Calum was small, wiry, tense – a chain smoker – and he regarded clothing as a necessary chore, rarely dressing, even in the office, in anything other than torn jeans and a hoodie. Steve was tall, well proportioned, smart, carefully manicured and, outside of work overalls, as expensively dressed as his wages and family commitments would allow. Appearances were so deceptive that a casual visitor might think Steve the boss and Calum the office boy. And cynics at the factory would say that appearances weren't so deceptive after all.

If Calum's American shareholders knew quite how much the firm relied on a former militant and, now, aspiring Labour politician to deliver their dividends, they would have run for the exit. But they didn't. And any questions about the labour force could be answered with an impressive roll call of achievements: a decade without a strike; cooperation over part-time working in the depths of the financial crisis; new shift patterns; Japanese-style quality control led by the workers. All approved by the shop stewards' committee at their weekly meeting behind the Red Lion.

Steve, the architect of this industrial relations miracle, prepared to leave home, as usual, at 7am. Recently divorced, the quiet of the morning without his kids was something he still hadn't got used to. Arriving at work, he was summoned from the shop floor to the CEO's office for an urgent meeting of the management team, which he attended as the workforce representative. To get there he had to pass through the finance and office services department, the only part of the building where women were visible in any numbers; elsewhere, the traditions of British engineering ensured that women were to be found only in advanced stages of undress on the calendars on the walls. The women in finance had launched a feminist counter-offensive in the form of a calendar with a generously endowed black male model whose masculinity was only partly concealed by a hand performing the role of a fig leaf. The ringleaders, Sam, Sharon and Cilla, styled themselves the Three Witches, and enlivened the office with cheerful banter about their exploits with booze and sex on a Saturday night and on the annual pilgrimage to Magaluf. They were not as dumb as they appeared, however. They had respectable accounting qualifications and more than once they had rescued Calum Mackie from the consequences of his rather cavalier approach to company accounts. The fourth member of the finance team, Shaida Khan, differed from her colleagues in her stunning looks and a detachment that may have been aloofness or shyness and was probably both. She differed too in seniority. She had arrived at the company four years earlier as a graduate trainee but had quickly established her exceptional talent, leading to a recent promotion, which meant that she now had an office of her own.

Shaida's father, Ashgar Khan, was a key member of Pulsar's engineering team, an important man in both Unite and the borough Labour Party where his ability to mobilise many of the town's Kashmiri Muslims had been crucial to Steve Grant's rapid ascent in the local party. Indeed, Steve had made sure that his daughter had got the trainee job. Mr Khan rarely talked about personal matters and had never before asked Steve for a favour but he had felt he had to explain his painful dilemma, torn between his role as a model British citizen – with an OBE for his contribution to community relations in the town – and the demands of his Islamic faith and the traditions of the Kashmiri district from where many of the local community originated. 'I want my daughter to have an education, to have a career. She is too young for marriage, children. Shaida is becoming a proper accountant. She passes her professional exams and learns here also. Maybe she will be chief finance officer in a company like this. Inshallah!' A quiet word with Calum Mackie and Steve had delivered. Four years later she was indeed chief finance officer.

Steve's interest in his protégé had evolved from the professional. The more he saw of her the more he contrasted his messy and unsatisfying domestic life – a bitter divorce from his childhood sweetheart and the mother of his three young children – with the potential offered by this Asian princess of his fantasies. The fantasy was fuelled by her habit of wearing expensive-looking but traditional clothes with a Muslim headscarf, though everything else about her – her speech, her animated eyes, her poise, her walk – suggested a thoroughly confident, modern woman. The antennae of the Three Witches had picked up the vibrations and he had to endure the embarrassment of loud comments whenever he passed through: 'Your fan club's arrived, Shaida', or, 'Sorry, lover boy, can't you see she's busy'. Shaida always worked on in her office and showed no sign of welcoming the attention.

———

That day the chief finance officer had swept into the car park very early, maintaining her record of being first to work. Her diligence and capacity for hard work were major factors in her promotion. She made her way to her office, a glass room in the middle of an open plan office: sufficiently public to see and be seen; sufficiently private not to be overheard when she had a confidential conversation. It was tidy: methodical, like her life, with clearly defined priorities and no loose ends. Her personal filing system separated out family, then career, then self, in that order.

She adored her father, who worked on a high precision machine tool in the factory workshop and was now approaching retirement. Only one of Shaida's three brothers was still at home, Mohammed, a troubled young man who had fallen into bad company at school, had never managed to find a proper job after graduating in 'business studies' and who hung around with groups of Pakistani and Somali men consuming cannabis and qat. Shaida's escalating salary had enabled her family to move to a smarter detached house in a largely middle class, white, area of town, which had separated Mohammed from his friends somewhat, but increased her mother's isolation. Shaida was the emotional, as well as financial, prop that kept the family together.

Regarded as a confirmed spinster by her extended family who expected their womenfolk to produce babies at regular intervals after the age of fifteen, Shaida was sufficiently acclimatised to the British society into which she had been born to see that at twenty-five she had plenty of time to find a settled, loving relationship of her own and the family that might follow it. Meantime, she would enjoy being single.

She noticed that Steve was also in the outer office, for no very obvious reason. She didn't mind. She found him engaging and attractive; and he talked intelligently and interestingly about the politics in which he was involved, refreshingly different from the speak-your-weight machines she saw on television, trotting out the party line. She wasn't very political, but curious: voted Lib Dem as a compromise between her father's tribal loyalty to Labour and her own more business-minded and liberal instincts. She could see, however, that Steve didn't view her as a political project. He was obviously besotted with her and she enjoyed the sense of power she derived from being an inaccessible, goddess figure. In a different context he would have been a good date. If only he knew.

<hr />

At 10am Calum convened a meeting of the executive team, who arrived in his office in a state of trepidation. They knew how bad the financial position was and were expecting gallows humour from the boss following a tale of woe from the chief finance officer who, at her first meeting, had chilled them all to the bone with her forensic analysis of the near insolvency of the company.

The problem lay in the inherent riskiness of the business: the need to spend large sums on R&D to keep ahead of the field technologically, based on Calum's hunches and nods and winks from the MOD. At the same time orders were unpredictable, based on the passing enthusiasms of politicians for fancy new toys, the more or less austere disposition of other politicians who approved controversial arms export licences, and the mood of the Treasury. Calum's genius, his patient long term investors and a helping hand from the Red Admiral had kept the company afloat. But the faces that morning anticipated bad news, particularly the recently appointed head of security, Justin Starling. But to their collective relief, Calum was in an expansive mood.

'Guys, the Indian contract is happening. Could keep us in business for years. Just heard the good news from the Red Admiral who, as you know, has been a valuable friend to us and is close to the action even if no longer in government. But it is a big project. It will stretch us to the limit on both the research and production side. And, of course, this is very hush-hush.'

Starling's scepticism was clear. 'I know this is a sensitive issue', he said, looking directly at Shaida, 'but I can't be the only person in this room who is worried about taking on a highly confidential Indian military contract when we have a largely Muslim, and Kashmiri, workforce. I know the workers who need to be involved have been security cleared but... politics...'

He was met by an embarrassed silence and Shaida felt a rising sense of anger that her loyalty was being questioned.

This wasn't the first time Starling had crossed her; she had discovered that he objected to her promotion. She would have been angrier still if she had known that Starling himself was a dubious appointment; there had been unexplained holes in his CV and Calum had accepted him only after receiving a glowing recommendation from the Red Admiral based on his work at the MOD.

Steve came to the rescue. 'I have absolute confidence in my workmates. They have always been committed to this company. They are good, hard-working British people whatever their origins. They will cheer for Pakistan at the Oval like Irish and Scots sports fans do for their countries when they play England: that doesn't make them disloyal. Mr Starling – who has only recently joined the company – may not be aware that we have done business with the likes of Israel, Egypt and India before. Politics didn't come into it.'

'I hope you are right,' Starling snapped back. But Calum wanted to press on with other news.

'You all know how much I love politicians, especially Tories. Well, it seems that as our importance to the country is being recognised – at last – we are getting a ministerial visit.'

'Who is he?'

'It's a she.'

Kate's early parliamentary career was as anonymous as her arrival in Westminster. She was underwhelmed by parliament and parliament was underwhelmed by her. She got off to a reasonable start with an early, workmanlike speech generously praising Sir Terence's skeletal contributions to the local community, as custom demanded, and, for the benefit of the local press, promising to die in the last ditch fending off the horrors that disturbed her Conservative voters, notably a long mooted social housing scheme and fracking, which was improbable given the local geology, but aroused deep fears. She was momentarily buoyed by the praise lavished on her speech until it was pointed out that convention demanded it. She settled into the rhythm of parliamentary life, asking questions now and then, speaking very occasionally in debates to an empty chamber late at night, voting with the government on every sub-clause of obscure pieces of legislation, and signing lots of letters to constituents reassuring them that she was on their side fighting human rights abuses in North Korea and Iran, opposing the docking of dogs' tails and supporting the ban on fox hunting.

One morning she received a request – which amounted to a summons – to visit the chief whip in his office. She was curious, since in her year or so in parliament she had never defied the party whip, had an exemplary attendance record and responded willingly to requests to sit through the excruciating tedium of hours in primary and secondary legislative committees on the off-chance that the depleted and demoralised opposition might call a vote. She had even stooped so low as to ask obsequious questions, handed out by the whip's office, inviting ministers to acknowledge the government's brilliant record. She persuaded herself that she was not naturally so craven but merely wanted time to understand the arcane mysteries of parliament, to work out whom to trust and to build up a reputation locally for being 'loyal, conscientious and competent': adjectives that Stella was now deploying on her behalf. At some point she was determined to rebel against what she saw as the ghastly, male-dominated, pompous, antiquated, inefficient, ineffectual, dysfunctional club. But not yet.

Her sense of irrelevance and impotence reached its peak during the 'coup'. A few months earlier the Prime Minister had called an unnecessary and disastrous election, losing seats and credibility. There was a growing sense of drift around the Brexit negotiations and the new influx of militant Brexiteers had limited patience and little gratitude. The so-called 52 Group of Tory MPs and their friends in the press demanded change. Kate ignored the plotting and was unprepared for the terse announcement that the PM had resigned on 'health grounds'. Parliament went on much as before. But there was a subtle change: the boys were back in charge.

All these thoughts churned in her brain as she walked across the modern hub of parliament – Portcullis House –

with its controlled environment and indoor trees, through into the cold, stone passages that led to Speaker's Court and then to the corridor behind the Speaker's Chair and alongside the library. There was a distinctive, and reassuring, aroma of wood polish and dusty books with an occasional whiff of yesterday's dinner from the kitchens below. At that time in the morning the place was largely empty except for gnome-like figures, the clerks, who scuttled quietly in and out of offices. Then, down to the Members' Lobby, where a politically balanced selection of busts of twentieth-century giants – Lloyd George, Attlee, Churchill and Thatcher – looked down on the pygmies beneath them.

The whips' offices led off from the lobby and Kate had previously ventured inside her own only to collect messages. Now she was shown into the inner sanctum: the chief whip's office. She took in at first glance the walls covered in press cartoons that lampooned the chief whip but also advertised his importance; a capacious drinks cabinet, open and clearly in frequent use; and various pieces of expensive communications equipment that were covered in dust and obviously not used. And then she turned her attention to the large, ruddy, friendly face behind the mahogany desk. His skills in managing political power had become legendary: a survivor; a servant of three Prime Ministers; a totally uncompromising loyalist to the Prime Minister of the day until the time came to switch sides. His power was his knowledge. He knew far more about the strengths and especially the weaknesses of the four hundred-odd MPs in his charge than any of them imagined.

Kate's political apprenticeship labouring quietly in the parliamentary salt mines had not gone unnoticed. The chief whip had already put a question mark against the name of many of her contemporaries for displaying excessive independence of mind or unseemly haste to climb up the greasy pole or backing the wrong side in the coup. Kate Thompson's record was unblemished. Tom Appleby was a Devon farmer who understood human nature almost as well as his beloved horses. This Kate Thompson was a goer, a smart filly who would do as she was told, sail over the fences and manage the heavy going. A good-looker too. His political hero, John Major, would have approved. He explained he had called her in for a friendly chat after being asked by the PM to put up a list of promotable talent, with attractive women as a priority.

'I won't bullshit you,' he said. 'There are a lot more talented, hard-working and worthwhile people in this place than you.' Tough love was his preferred method of breaking in promising ponies. 'Some of your colleagues would give their right arm for a chance to be the lowest form of ministerial pond life. I have dozens of them banging on my door every day begging for jobs, even to be an unpaid parliamentary private secretary—'

She butted in: 'Chief Whip, I don't know why you have called me in but I am not complaining about lack of promotion. I'm still getting to know how this place works.'

'Not so fast. That was just my way of introducing you to some good news. You are in favour. Don't want it to go to your head. Let me explain. The PM is rattled by constant criticism that there aren't enough women in serious jobs in the government. The coup, deposing a respected woman Prime Minister, has left us open to the charge that we have a problem with women. To be very frank with you, he wants some photogenic women around him – and you are near the top of the eye candy league table… at least on our side of the House.'

'Chief Whip, Tom—'

'Sorry, I am just being straight with you. You probably think I am some kind of Neanderthal man. But that's the way it is. All those people who read the *Mail* and the *Express*, and vote for you, are more interested in how you look than what you say. I am sure I don't need to tell you that. Where I am concerned you have a spotless record. That is why I put you forward. No more, no less. I also saw that excellent interview you gave on *Newsnight*; you stuck to the line and didn't screw up, unlike that bird-brain we put up three months ago, now on her way out.

'That's it. Just a friendly word of advice. A lot of MPs will hate your guts for jumping the queue. Be careful. Watch your back. And don't waste your chance.'

She thanked the chief whip and fought back a powerful urge to puncture his self-importance and his obvious pleasure at dishing out patronage by declining his offer.

The chief whip's head of office told her to go immediately to the Prime Minister's parliamentary suite where he was waiting.

It all happened very quickly. She was ushered into the gloomy set of rooms behind the Speaker's Chair by one of the young men in the outer office. The PM looked up from the papers on his desk but clearly did not recognise her and thought she was a civil servant who had come to brief him. The speaking note in front of him put him right. He gestured to her to sit down and she had a few seconds to take in the famous face in front of her, more lined than revealed on television or in Prime Minister's Questions, but otherwise undistinguished and unmemorable.

'Kate, thank you so much for making time to come and see me. You have made such an impact since you came into the House. The tea room' (which he never visited) 'is singing your praises. Your *Newsnight* interview has become a legend – I have suggested that we use it as a master class for training wannabee MPs. How about it?'

She nodded appreciatively – feeling that although the PM was a notorious flatterer, and she was susceptible to flattery, he was getting beyond parody.

'And an entrepreneur too! Too many bloody researchers, communications consultants and special advisers. Don't you agree?' She agreed. But not too enthusiastically since she recalled that he had been all three in his time.

'I have given a lot of thought to this and have decided to fast-track you to Minister of State level. Trade. Should suit you with your outstanding business background. And deep knowledge of India. Priceless. One of our main challenges, post-Brexit, will be to land an ambitious trade agreement with the big non-EU economies. As you know, the negotiations we launched last year are coming to a climax. We are not getting much change out of the EU so we absolutely must deliver on our promises to open up other markets to British exporters. India is top of our list. But it's proving very, very difficult. We need someone who can unlock the vast potential there. You are just the person.'

Kate desperately wanted to shrink these ludicrously inflated expectations. But she could see he was in transmit, not receive, mode. She also noticed that he had a problem looking her in the eye and was gazing anywhere but. He seemed to be one of those men who struggled to engage with self-confident, attractive women. Then she remembered all those stories from years back about young men in Turkish baths and made a connection with the good-looking young men in the outer office. 'Stop it, Kate,' she said to herself. 'This is the Prime Minister.' And he was, as far as was publicly known, in a long and happy, if childless, marriage.

'Best of luck. I expect great things from you. Don't let me down. The big trade deal with India. It could be your legacy – and mine. But I will leave it to your new boss, Jim, to brief you.' A wave of the hand ended the interview.

Kate set off to start her new job as Big Ben was striking noon and ducked and weaved through the traffic, walking across the front of Westminster Abbey to where she thought the department lay. She had been offered a car by one of the PM's young men but felt the idea of taking a lift in bright sunshine for a two-hundred-yard journey was beyond parody of the ministerial lifestyle. She wasn't yet the Prime Minister, or the Queen. Leaving nothing to chance, however, the young man had arranged for her to be met by her private secretary as soon as she arrived. Unfortunately, things did not go well. She soon realised that her hazy idea of where the department lay, somewhere behind the Abbey and Methodist Central Hall, led her to the Department for Work and Pensions where baffled receptionists sought to help a lost Minister of State they hadn't expected or even heard of.

Eventually she found the right department and an extremely agitated private secretary who looked as if he was about to call the police missing persons' line. 'Sorry, I got lost in the London maze, I'm just a country bumpkin. Next time I'll take a compass.'

He didn't do humour. 'Minister, I would advise you, in future, to stick to the recognised route if you insist on not utilising the ministerial car. My name is Edwin Thoroughgood. I am your private secretary.'

She groaned inwardly at the thought of being looked after by this young fogey who was emaciated and stooped and acted as if he already had one foot in an old folks' home. His spotty and unhealthily grey face hinted at a life spent in front of a computer screen. She thought he resembled a hermit released from a lifetime of monastic contemplation who had just been confronted by his worst nightmare: a woman with attitude. The journey to the top floor took place in silence and his eyes sought refuge in the lift carpet. When they reached the ministerial corridor she was led through an expanse of open plan offices with adjacent rooms for three ministers of state and three parliamentary under-secretaries and their staff. All were regarded as unexceptional ministerial ballast, except for the most junior, a hereditary peer who owned much of Scotland but was here to promote food and drink exports, especially spirits. The Secretary of State had a grander office with a view.

Kate's office was smart, bright and functional but horribly disfigured by a dark, brooding, giant oil painting in the style of Landseer featuring a large stag and slavering bloodhounds: no doubt a masterpiece but utterly incongruous in this setting. Kate's first executive decision was to instruct Edwin to get rid of it.

'But, Minister, these things are not straightforward. There is a process. I will, however, speak to someone from the government art collection to investigate the possibility of making a change. Your predecessor, I should say, loved the painting and he was a man of good taste.'

'Please, Edwin, just get rid of it. Now.' This relationship was not going to last long.

When Mehmet sat down in his cabin for the night shift he had largely forgotten the episode two weeks ago when he sensed, or perhaps imagined, an intruder in the factory. Nothing untoward had happened since.

He had enrolled for an Open University course and had learnt to divide his attention between the CCTV monitors, the entrance area of the factory and maths problems that he found easy but at least kept his brain alive. At 3am there was absolutely nothing to disturb the peace. He set off for the entrance area for his mid-shift visit to the toilet. He had discovered that splashing water on his face helped him to keep his concentration, and the short walk was a welcome break from the tedium.

It was, however, very dark, no moon, and he had a tremor of anxiety leaving the secure cocoon of his cabin. As he unlocked the front doors, he thought he heard a sound from the inside of the building. Then silence. He decided to open the main door that led to the design office, which in turn opened out into the main production area of the factory. The office was in semi-darkness, as it should have been, but he noticed a fading glow on one of the PC screens and, nearby, the illuminated panel of the lift showed it to be in use. The lift led to the basement, the secret area to which he had no access.

He knew that something untoward was going on: someone had been using a computer and had taken refuge in the basement to which only a dozen or so high-level staff had access. He made a note of the terminal that had been in use and returned to his cabin. Perhaps someone had put in some overtime and had hidden when they heard him entering, perhaps believing him to be an intruder? That didn't seem likely. But if a senior, trusted, member of staff was engaged in something subversive inside the building, he had little or no concrete evidence. Anyway, would he be believed, an asylum seeker from Africa paid a minimum wage to sit in a hut outside? Back in his cabin he watched the monitors carefully but no one emerged from the building. When the shift ended and the first workers arrived in the morning he had a dilemma about what to put in his security report. His first report of a suspected intruder had been laughed off. This time they would think he was a fantasist or a troublemaker. But, if something was going on, and if it was exposed, why hadn't the security guard reported what he had seen?

Steve arrived for work as usual. He used to look forward to a day on the machine where his carefully honed skills made him an outstandingly productive worker. But these days his mind wandered. His work schedule would be broken up by a union meeting on the new shift patterns proposed by management and he had to prepare himself for a difficult evening meeting he was chairing at the council on budget cuts.

He had, as it happened, arrived early and on an impulse decided to make the detour through the finance department. He realised he was being ridiculous but the prospect of seeing Shaida Khan was a bigger draw than a chat before work with the lads about the weekend football results.

The room was empty except for Shaida, seemingly engrossed in work in her glass cubicle. No Witches. He couldn't hide under the comfort blanket of their office banter. He couldn't easily retreat. And he had no good reason to be there. But this was an opportunity to have the conversation he had rehearsed for some time.

The object of his fantasies was well aware that Steve was in the background. She had designed her office in such a way that through reflections in the glass she effectively had 360-degree vision. Forewarned she had time to prepare her defences against someone whose demeanour did not suggest that he anticipated a seminar in accounting. She had developed a Miss Brisk persona to impose her authority on such occasions. She turned sharply.

'Good morning. Are you here to discuss the group finances?'

'Well, actually, we've seen a fair bit of each other at meetings but I've never really introduced myself properly – I'm Steve, Grant.'

'I know exactly who you are, Steve. My dad told me

about you. Actually he is a fan of yours – he seems to think you may be a Labour Prime Minister someday. And I believe you helped secure my job. I guess I'm indebted to you... Unless there is anything else? It's a busy day and I need to get on with my work.'

Thoroughly discombobulated, he struggled to continue. He realised he had never chatted up a woman before; not beyond politics and union business. With his ex-wife he had never had to. But those big brown eyes seemed to send a different, more welcoming, message than the abrupt voice. 'Er... how do you like it here? These girls here... maybe not your cup of tea?'

'What do you mean? They are lovely. Trouble is, you men think "these girls" are only interested in shagging and booze. They're usually having you all on. Sam, the cheeky one who goes on about black blokes, spends her spare time looking after her disabled sister. Sharon, the tall one, came top in the region in her professional exams. And Cilla is seriously competitive at Taekwondo. They're kind and good fun and we have an excellent team.'

'Sorry, I didn't realise. They wind up the lads on the shop floor no end.' He started to look nervously at the clock and the stairs behind him. It was now or never. 'But you... do you fancy a drink sometime?'

'You mean you want to take me out on a date?'

'Yes... but... only...'

'Ah, the "but"... I don't want to be snide, but this conversation is quite inappropriate. We both have senior roles in this company and our relationship is professional. Besides, I am the only Asian woman here and you're a well-known face. Word gets around. And you are a bit obvious, you know, fancying me.'

He looked desperately crushed and she judged that he was a sensitive man who wasn't used to this situation. So she decided to soften the blow.

'Let me explain. My mum and dad want me to have my freedom. But even they want to line up the right kind of husband for me. They have kept the family together despite all the bad things that happen here. Somehow I have to find a way to do my own thing without breaking their hearts. That means I stay clear of trouble. This is work, not a dating agency. Do you get it?'

He mumbled a 'yes', not having expected the rebuff or the eloquent speech that she must surely have prepared in her mind. And she hadn't finished.

'So, there is no question of a date. But if you want to be a friend as well as a colleague, I have an idea. My brother and his friends are worrying my family. Radicalisation and all that. They won't talk seriously to us. My dad and I have tried to talk politics to them but they won't listen. They think the Muslim councillors in the town are a joke. Just operating a vote bank for Labour. They see you as different. They might listen to you. Will you come and chat to them?'

He didn't get a chance to say more than yes, to say what he felt: utterly besotted but with a deeper undercurrent of anxiety. There was a scramble up the stairs and Sharon emerged first: 'Ah, caught in the act!' He made himself scarce, muttering something about being on his way to see the boss.

⨯⨯⨯⨯⨯⨯⨯⨯⨯⨯⨯⨯⨯⨯⨯⨯⨯

On Steve's way to the shop floor he reflected on how he had got into this situation. He remembered the events – eight years ago? – that were the making of him, thanks to Mr Khan, but could have been a disaster. He was then a headstrong, ambitious shop-floor worker in his early twenties who had already built up a following in the union and the party. People loved the way he spoke, with the accent and idiom of his working class contemporaries but with the fluency and vocabulary of those clever, educated people who seemed to run everything including working class organisations.

One day, Calum called in the union reps for a 'frank chat'. The company was 'up the creek without a paddle', as he put it. The financial crisis was in full swing. Orders had dried up. Banks had turned nasty: wanted their money back, pronto. Big defence cuts in the US and the UK had killed the goose that laid the golden eggs for defence contractors. Over half the workforce would have to go – then, five hundred people – plus subcontractors. The rest could stay to finish contracts or do maintenance work. 'Sorry, guys, I did my best.'

But the guys didn't think much of his best. Steve, the militant, started to capture the mood of his mates and dominated the discussions in the canteen. He demanded a strike to force the management to think again by putting the rest of the business at risk. He could also see that in the absence of a strong workers' response the labour force would fracture along racial lines. Not too many years ago Pulsar, like many industrial companies, operated a colour bar confining Asian newcomers to unskilled jobs and it had taken a strong stand by the Asian workers, led by Mr Khan, to break it. But the shared jokes and sex magazines in the canteen created a fragile illusion of solidarity. Now the mood was turning ugly again with rumours that 'the Pakis' were being favoured (or discriminated against according to the audience) and BNP leaflets were circulating in the factory.

After a particularly bitter meeting, Mr Khan took Steve aside and proposed a Plan B; what was, in effect, a pay cut to save the plant and the jobs. The company would have a year to drum up some new business with a guarantee of earlier worker bonuses if profits returned. He had done the maths and it worked. Steve immediately grasped that something along these lines was necessary; he could see that militancy was no answer to this particular crisis and had no wish to become a doomed Arthur Scargill figure. When he sounded out the workforce there was support on the basis that this was the least bad option.

Mr Khan was able to mobilise the Asian workers and a branch meeting agreed, on a show of hands, to present the plan to management. Calum was relieved and promptly rang his leading investors who were so impressed that they agreed to put in more cash. Then a stroke of luck: a competitor had gone bust, couldn't deliver and Pulsar was asked to fulfil its outstanding contracts.

Soon the word got around and reached the ears of government ministers and union bosses that, in the depths of a plunging economy, here was a turnaround story, under union leadership: flexible but hard-headed, pragmatic but tough. A model for British industry. The TV cameras and print journalists needed an articulate spokesman and they found it in Steve, while Mr Khan retreated into the background, his natural modesty reinforced by his reluctance to use his heavily accented English. The local, then the national, Labour Party seized upon the new Messiah: a genuinely working class moderniser; a union man but not a Luddite, articulate but not a party wordsmith, recycling half-understood ideas from textbooks; a man who talked about 'British working families' from experience and not as if they were a tribe in Papua New Guinea.

In the years that followed Steve had progressed, and believed he now had the choice of a safe seat in parliament or progression to the leadership of his union. He had remained close to Mr Khan who could help mobilise the ethnic vote in party and council elections. He had reciprocated where possible and had cemented the friendship by prevailing upon Calum to take Ms Khan into the company, ignoring the CVs of dozens of other applicants for the job. Now he was hopelessly, and dangerously, in love with Mr Khan's daughter.

There was no way that Shaida could show any sign of reciprocating these feelings. But she had definitely taken a liking to Steve Grant, who, she had noticed, was pleasant looking and, when out of his overalls, snappily dressed. Had he been an aspiring US politician his tall, slim, athletic physique and flashing smile would have been a passport to success. But in both the industrial and political wings of the Labour Movement good looks, of men and women, were regarded with deep suspicion: indicating vanity or narcissism or, worse, a sign of reversion to the days of the traitor Blair when image and the ability to cut a dash in the Tory press enjoyed more weight than socialist substance. Shaida had so far taken little notice of such matters. But this morning's conversation had stimulated her interest. And she could see how a carefully managed friendship could be of value to them both.

CHAPTER 4

THE MINISTER

The Hindu, 23 June 2019:

The Indian government has announced that it has successfully completed the ninth test of its anti-missile defence programme. A spokesman stated that the test has been a success and that the government is on track with its plan for a missile shield for Mumbai and Delhi. However, Rtd Major-General Aggarwal of a Delhi defence think-tank cast doubt on the success of the tests and said that, with current technology, India is 'many years' away from a successful missile shield.

After a few days in the job, Kate had her first meeting with the Secretary of State who had just returned from his overseas visit drumming up business for the UK. James (Jim) Chambers was a big man: physically, politically and commercially. The Prime Minister had climbed to power on his shoulders and depended heavily on him. Out of favour under the PM's predecessor, he had come back with a vengeance to head up post-Brexit trade promotion and negotiations and was, in effect if not in name, the deputy Prime Minister. His voice had a twang of Geordie, which gave him that touch of northern authenticity so prized in his party for its scarcity value.

He was also very wealthy, a self-made millionaire many times over. Precisely how he had made his millions was the subject of numerous pieces at the back of *Private Eye*: the consumer credit company that fleeced hapless purchasers who hadn't read the small print carefully enough; the insurance claim after a conveniently timed warehouse fire; the lucrative land deal involving MOD property that could, plausibly, have only been achieved with the help of an inside source. But the mud didn't stick. He was now a TV guru on business; widely admired for his support for children's charities; while his generous donations to the Conservative Party and individual MPs had bought him political influence and, now, power.

Although several inches shorter than his new ministerial colleague, his big, shaven, bull-like head and powerful physique established a dominant presence in the room, but he was charming and solicitous, anxious to make her feel at home. His piercing blue eyes sought hers and held her gaze: a man thoroughly confident with women, as suggested by his reputation. 'Well, Kate, settling in all right?' he chortled. 'How are your Overheads?' When she looked blank, failing to get his joke, he explained that 'Overheads' was his word for civil servants. 'You and I are wealth creators. We are the profit line in UK plc's P&L. They, the public sector, consume the wealth: the debit side. We mustn't let them forget it.' The civil servant in the room, his principal private secretary, looked into the middle distance pretending not to hear, having been on the receiving end of this 'joke' many times before.

For Kate, this unorthodox introduction gave her an opportunity to broach the first awkwardness she had encountered in the department. 'Actually, I do have a problem on that front. Can we have a private word?' Jim indicated to his principal private secretary that she should leave. 'I would be grateful for your help in reshuffling my private office, Secretary of State.'

'I prefer you to call me Jim.'

'Jim, if I am to do this job I need to work with people whom I trust and have confidence in…' She explained her problem without mentioning Edwin's appearance and irritating manner: a private secretary who seemed to be devoted to her predecessor, an obscure man of mind-numbing mediocrity but who did exactly as he was told. The private secretary's style, she explained, was to advise his minister that everything he – now she – wished to do was fraught with legal, financial, reputational, organisational or presentational risk. If the case for action was overwhelming, he would invoke the Doctrine of Unripe Time to argue that the Minister should delay making a decision: 'The longer you delay, Minister, the more facts you will have on which to base your decision. Now is too soon.'

'I cannot work with this man,' she explained. 'His deputy isn't any better. He spends his time gazing at my chest and then rushes to open the door for me or help me to sit down. Where do they get these people from?'

'Kate. Absolutely right. That's what I like to hear. No nonsense. I will speak to the chief Overhead and ask him to line up some genuine talent for you. But I also want to talk to you about something else: this India thing. The PM wants you to go out there. Big deal for your first job. He thinks you will charm them. I have asked the team to come up to brief you, if you are ready.'

The civil servants trooped in: Parsons, the permanent secretary; Caroline, the principal private secretary, parked on a sofa behind the meeting table; a fierce-looking, grey-haired lady from the MOD whose label read 'Ms Kidlington'; a tall distinguished man with a military bearing who was introduced as 'the Admiral: he advises me and the Defence Secretary'; and a man in his forties who announced himself as 'Liam – security'.

'Right, ladies and gentlemen. Our new Minister, Kate Thompson, has been asked by the PM to go to India to advance the discussions on the arms contract. She doesn't need to know too much detail. The High Commissioner will fill her in and hold her hand when she gets there. But she needs to know roughly what this is about – why it matters – and what her role is. In general, she has to look beautiful – not difficult I'd say! – and speak as little as possible. But it is a bit more than that. Ms Kidlington?'

Ms Kidlington started to read from her notes, which, Kate observed, were worryingly long. 'Minister, years of patient negotiation have got us almost to the point of agreement. But the Indians are difficult negotiators and their coalition politics is complex. Buying arms from Britain, and the USA, goes against the grain with a lot of nationalist MPs and with the lefties in their parliament. But Delhi is committed to it because there is a crucial piece of equipment and associated software only we can offer them.

'Put simply, the Indians are frightened – and under-standably so – about the possibility of a Pakistan nuclear attack. They have a deterrent that could blow Pakistan to smithereens several times over. But that isn't protection against a first strike, launched by a rogue element, such as religious fundamentalists. The Indians have a "no first use" strategy as we had with the Soviets. But the Pakistanis have been unwilling to reciprocate.

'We – and they – think the risk is low but it is sufficient to build a defensive shield as best they can. Now we hear the Chinese are "giving" Pakistan an upgrade to their missile. Remember President Reagan and Star Wars? That was over thirty years ago. Technology has moved on. A shield, or a partial shield, is now possible, though the use of decoys means that missile defence is at best partial. Nonetheless, the US has a system mainly to counter rogue states like North Korea. So have the Israelis, and others are being developed. It turns out that one of the key pieces of kit is a machine that destroys the navigation systems of missiles, and aircraft, in flight. Correctly deployed it could stop, or at least minimise, a nuclear attack. Are you with me?'

Ms Kidlington paused and looked around to ensure that her lecture was still being followed. She sought to engage with Kate's eyes in order better to communicate her passion. Experience had taught her that ministers were, in general, rather ignorant about these high-level security issues and not very interested.

'Now, the bad news – the British company that has developed this technology is run by a maverick Scottish socialist, from an industrial estate north of London. His company is called Pulsar. He is a loose cannon but a genius. Frankly, MOD would prefer a more orthodox supplier but he always delivers on time and on budget, and he is British. The Indians would much prefer to deal with a recognised name, a BAE Systems or a Rolls-Royce. The American Defense Department and MOD will vouch for Mackie, but the Indians want more reassurances. We understand that, since this is a sensitive subject. They don't want the wrong kind of publicity.

'The clinching argument for Pulsar is that as a result of an old Indian connection, they have a part-owned Indian partner called Parrikar Avionics, which will make sure the technology is transferred to India and stays there. The Indians won't take our stuff off the shelf. We have done some due diligence. Family company. Old man Parrikar, the founder, is a bit of a scoundrel, but the son, Deepak, who runs the avionics company, is squeaky clean – which we need under our anti-bribery legislation.'

'Bloody Coalition government. Bloody Liberals,' broke in the Secretary of State. 'They brought in this anti-corruption crusade, crippling our businesses. Politically correct nonsense. My friends tell me they can't even buy their overseas customers a drink or they'll be sent to Wormwood Scrubs for twenty-five years.'

'Secretary of State,' interrupted the permanent secretary, who was used to his political master getting the bit between his teeth and galloping over the horizon, 'I am sure the Minister would like to know a little more about her role.'

'Yes, of course.' Chambers took over the briefing, deciding that Ms Kidlington had already had a long enough innings. 'Kate, the Indians need to be convinced that we are fully committed – politically – to this technology transfer stuff and have got a firm grip on the British supplier. If the PM or myself were spending time hobnobbing with modest-sized companies, questions might be asked about what they do. We don't want that: don't want to stir up the

Pakistanis or the arms trade protesters for that matter. A middle ranking minister will do fine. Our chaps will give you a bit of a boost in the Indian media – rising star; the next Mrs T; all that – and push to get you in to see the Indian PM. I have asked the Admiral, here, to join your party. He knows the background and is well connected in India.

'And you will like Parrikar Junior. Very handsome – one magazine called him the Indian George Clooney – not that I look at other men, unlike some I could mention. Ha.' The permanent secretary desperately tried to hide his laughter in a grotesque rictus, knowing that it would not do to appreciate a joke at the expense of the Prime Minister but equally understanding that it was career-enhancing to be amused by the Secretary of State's sense of humour.

'So Kate, smile sweetly and don't do anything I wouldn't do. And impress them with your knowledge of India. As well as your business connections, I understand you travelled around the country many years ago.'

Kate's heart sank. This was definitely not on her CV. She had erased it from her memory. That appalling Australian, whom she had fallen for. His story about spiritual enlightenment that seemed so plausible at the time. The ashram… Oh my God! They know it all!

The hitherto silent Liam interjected: 'We have you down as travelling there for four months during your gap year.'

'Actually, I spent most of my time in India on the hotel loo with amoebic dysentery. Didn't see or do much. Best ignored.' Everyone smiled understandingly.

She left the meeting rather dazed. She had never before been entrusted with confidences beyond her girlfriends' love affairs or her husband's rather obscure business deals. Now there were Star Wars, spooks and an Indian George Clooney. And people who seemed to know everything about her, even things she had managed to forget. Try as hard as she could to be calm and sensible she looked forward to this mission with a mixture of excitement and grave apprehension.

CHAPTER 5

BHARAT BOMBAY

BBC World Service, 30 June 2019:

The Pakistani Prime Minister, Imran Khan, has reshuffled his cabinet, introducing three ministers closely aligned to religious parties. They include a junior defence minister who is reputed to have been a volunteer with Al Qaeda-linked anti-Assad forces in Syria and to have been involved in training Kashmiri rebels. The Indian press has reacted furiously to a 'terrorist sympathiser' having a key position in the Pakistan government.

Inspector Mankad sat in a corner of his favourite café munching Mumbai street food and drinking mango lassi.

He liked to spend time here clearing his mind. The police station was not conducive to quiet reflection: a hive of activity, most of it not very productive.

The case of Mr Vijay Patel troubled him. He had found lots of leads and he knew he would have no difficulty finding the people who had committed the grisly murder. But he knew that there was a lot more behind the men who pulled the trigger and disfigured the corpse. They were almost certainly hired hands, minor criminals who would carry out a 'job' for a few thousand rupees. The issue was who was paying them and why.

One of his first interviews had been with the 'slumlord', the unofficial head of the community where the body was found. Within twenty-four hours of the body's discovery, Mankad's slumlord had been able to provide details of how a vehicle had arrived at the ultra-nationalist group's hut in the early hours of the morning and a group of men had emerged, one with a sack over his head. There had been muffled cries from the hut, shots were heard and shortly afterwards a heavy object, presumably the body, had been dragged outside and thrown into the stream then flowing strongly after a monsoon storm.

Mankad sent a detective, disguised as a scavenger, to nose around the site when the hut was empty and he observed footmarks and blood stains that were consistent with the account. Mankad also pulled rank to enable one of his officers to go through the records of the traffic department where the SUV could be traced back to a brother of the Corporator who was, in turn, a known associate of a powerful member of the Maharashtra Legislative Assembly. This was exactly the kind of connection that set the alarm bells ringing in Mankad's head. Especially as the killers had made few serious efforts to dispose of the body or cover their tracks: either they wanted to be traced or calculated that the police would not pursue the case.

Separate enquiries established that Vijay Patel was a law abiding project manager who had acquired a reputation for refusing to pay protection money and was widely regarded as an innocent abroad in the construction industry: unlikely to survive long. More confusingly, Patel worked for Parrikar Senior, a well-known property developer whose reputation as a survivor did not encompass innocence.

What Mankad really wanted was a good look at the Parrikar connection. Something odd there. Old man Parrikar had a reputation for being very shrewd and for keeping out of the limelight. There was a juicy scandal somewhere.

In a darkened corner of the lounge of a five star hotel in Mumbai a thin, ascetic, prematurely grey and distinguished-looking Indian was trying to direct a rambling conversation with one of his country's political class. The object of his attention was a very large, fleshy, supremely self-confident man sinking contentedly into the soft furnishings, his discursive wanderings fuelled by the bottle of whisky in front of him.

Desai preferred water. He despised such people utterly: the crude corruption advertised by the gold necklace and Swiss watch; the political promiscuity (the man had arrived at his present destination via four other parties); the bovine slow-wittedness overlaying animal cunning; the vulgarity and absence of elementary manners. But Desai had learnt to hide his contempt for such people; they could be useful. And this man was a powerful political figure in the city and the state. He was well connected to the criminal underworld that controlled much of the money on which political parties depended and had invaluable intelligence networks.

Desai had flown down from Delhi to meet this man encouraged by his associates in the intelligence and security community. They had picked up reports of heightened Pakistani activity leading, perhaps, to another major terror raid. In all probability they would try to use the gang networks, especially those with loose, ancestral ties to Pakistan. Money trumped religion in this murky world, but 'conviction criminals' were particularly dangerous and not all were under lock and key. And Desai had his own private interests to pursue.

When the politician was three quarters of his way through the bottle, Desai judged that this was the time to raise sensitive issues. 'One group that worries the government in Delhi is the criminal group around the so-called Sheikh. His brother was involved in the 2008 terrorist raid on Mumbai. We need your help in dealing with him.'

'And why should I do this? I am now a senior, respected member of the state administration. I don't get involved with such people.'

Desai rolled his eyes, suppressing his irritation that the man felt it necessary to pretend. 'Our Prime Minister has specifically asked for your cooperation and I know we can rely on you. I am not a politician; merely an adviser. But I know that the ruling party will look after you and your associates in the Assembly.'

'This Sheikh: not a problem.'

'Not a problem?'

'He cooperates with my friends these days.'

'I need more than that.'

'You don't need to know more. He is under control. Leave the details to me.'

'I understand that he is close to old man Parrikar, no?'

'No more. The old man is finished.'

'What about the son? We worry about him.'

'He is clean. Not involved in goonda business.'

'We think he is unreliable. National security concerns.'

'What're you saying? Do you want the help of my friends? My friends are expensive.'

'We can pay... I think we understand one another.'

The politician celebrated his understanding with a loud

belch, which echoed above the gentle cadences of the hotel's Muzak, and then drained the whisky bottle before demanding another.

Desai congratulated himself on a job done. He reflected on the juggling of patriotism, politics and personal enrichment in which he also indulged, though in a more cerebral and sophisticated way than this nasty piece of Mumbai low life.

CHAPTER 6

THE VISIT

The Statesman, 1 July 2019:

The Indian Defence Minister made a speech yesterday telling the Pakistani government 'not to mess with India'. Mr Subramanian Iyer is a recent appointment, the former Chief Minister of Rajasthan and known to have been active in the nationalist R.S.S., like other prominent members of the government: a 'hard liner' on communal matters and on relations with Pakistan. Mr Iyer referred to a recent escalation of incidents on the Line of Control and blamed this on a 'more aggressive anti-Indian stance by the Pakistani High Command'. He expressed particular concern over the delivery to Pakistan of M-11 missiles from China as 'an aggressive move'. He said: 'India is ready. There will be no weakness.'

Kate and her entourage touched down in Mumbai in the early afternoon. She hadn't slept much but had dutifully immersed herself in the encyclopaedic briefs prepared by the department and the High Commission, tried to memorise the bewildering collection of names of ministers and other VIPs she would meet, rehearsed a few words of Hindi and taken to heart the long list of 'elephant traps' and 'subjects to avoid'. She had even boned up on the current test series – India versus Australia – as part of her planned small talk, suppressing her memories of the mind-numbing tedium of days spent at the Oval when her husband wanted her to help chat up clients in the hospitality suite. She felt greatly reassured now that she had, in Susan, her new private secretary, a bright and warm-hearted young woman who had understood, on first acquaintance, that her job was to bring solutions rather than problems. Any tricky questions could be left to the High Commissioner. There was also the Red Admiral, whose role she couldn't quite work out and whose status as a 'consultant' somehow enabled him to travel first class while she, her civil servants and business delegation were more modestly seated.

She was whisked through the VIP arrivals and within minutes was in the High Commission Jaguar whose sporty exterior disguised the armour plating, evident only when it became necessary to open the unnaturally heavy doors. She had hoped to soak up some of the atmosphere of India; she had never been to Mumbai and was keen to explore it. But she was unable to take in very much, flashing through the suburbs with a motorcycle escort and trying, with the help of High Commission staff, to do some last minute cramming for her first meeting in the Arctic air conditioned business suite of the Taj.

It was all happening very fast: a blur of faces and voices. But she was able to take on board that a meeting had been fixed with the Indian PM, to the pleasant surprise of the High Commissioner whose extensive schmoozing with the PM's advisers and staff at his residence had paid off – or so he thought, being blissfully unaware of the role played behind the scenes by the Red Admiral and his contacts. They would all fly up to Delhi tomorrow, the only time the PM was free, double up with a call on the Defence Minister and come back to Mumbai for the rest of the visit. She protested, mildly, about the time pressures, and the onset of jet lag, but it was gently pointed out that our PM had recently 'done' India in a day and then China in a day; her two and a half days for Delhi and Mumbai was really quite leisurely.

There was to be an evening reception for her business delegation to meet the Mumbai business community: then, yes, she could change and have thirty minutes to herself and work on her address to the gathering. But first there was official business, a formal meeting chaired by her Indian opposite number. In the official hierarchy he was a junior trade minister, a very small fish in the Indian political ocean. He had been given the job to placate a sub-caste with a lot of votes in an important state and knew nothing whatever about trade, or the UK, or any of the subjects on the agenda.

In the absence of content or controversy the meeting finished very early and, after elaborate exchanges of goodwill and thanks for an invaluable discussion, most of the participants disappeared rapidly to be early in the queue for food. The High Commissioner saw the opportunity to effect an introduction between Kate and Deepak Parrikar. Her brief told her she could usefully exchange a few pleasantries, which she had memorised from her 'line to take' drawn up by officials who assumed she had never met anyone from India before: the weather in London (awful); the test score (eight wickets by Ashwin); the state of Anglo-Indian relations (excellent as always); our common history (but avoid controversy) and other inanities. Mr Parrikar was largely unknown to the High Commission having avoided social events and being closer to the Americans. The father was known to be the power behind the family company and spoke little English.

The pleasantries weren't needed. Her carefully rehearsed Namaste was aborted by the offer of a handshake. He cut short her halting introduction. He seemed to know everything about her: Oxford friends, most of the British Cabinet, her husband's business partners, all on a Christian name basis. When she had recovered from the welcoming blast she started to appraise the man described as the Indian

George Clooney. He wasn't remotely like him but extremely handsome nonetheless: tall, with very dark, almost black, skin that highlighted his large, dazzling smile; enormous brown eyes radiating warmth, engagement and sympathy.

Disregarding the private secretaries and various flunkeys hovering around the room, he took her by the elbow to the window. They looked down on the Gateway of India where the King Emperor had alighted over a century earlier and, to the right, the entrance to the Taj.

'I wanted you to see this before we sit down and talk about the deal and the equipment your country is selling us through the two linked companies, one of which I own. That, over there, is the old India when white-skinned people ruled over us and when India had its own hierarchy of privilege that for centuries confined my ancestors to the dirtiest and most menial tasks. I am from the new India where businesses like the one my father built up have broken through and where we increasingly have technology as advanced as yours.

'And over there,' he continued, pointing to the hotel entrance, 'is a symbol of the main threat to this new India. Back in 2008 a group of Islamic militants, organised by Pakistani intelligence, and helped by one of the Mumbai mafia clans, stormed the hotel. Hostages were taken. Many people were killed in cold blood – a hundred and twenty-five. This was Mumbai's 9/11.

'Our enemies are also uncomfortably close-by. We have fought four major wars since you lot left India, three against Pakistan. We face two nuclear powers, allied against us, one an almost-failed state close to being overrun by jihadis who would happily take us to Paradise with them so they can enjoy screwing all those virgins to eternity. Sorry, I am not being politically correct, am I? But I am telling you what most Indians feel.'

Kate leaned towards him, fascinated by the frank explanations which were so different to the usual political correctness.

'I believe in Indian democracy, secularism, religious tolerance – I don't do religion myself – but I recently broke the habit of a lifetime and voted for the lot we have in power at the moment. There's a lot of religious nonsense, but they are also about making the country strong. That is why I am here, and why you are here. I'm sorry,' he apologised again, 'I wanted you to understand my position before we started talking about technical and business things.'

'Don't apologise,' Kate replied. 'I am not here to judge. I have been to India a few times but I am always overwhelmed by the scale and variety of the place. I simply don't know enough about your country to have a sensible answer. I just have a job to do.' But his outburst had flicked a switch inside her. She was used to charming, handsome, articulate men, to being pursued and flattered by them and to diverting any incipient feelings into harmless channels. But this passion and intensity was new, and troubling; and also very attractive.

She knew she should stick to her – excruciating – brief and its 'line to take'. But curiosity –and something stronger – took over. 'You obviously know more about me than I know about you. I don't like to be at such a disadvantage. So tell me more about your family and yourself.'

The coughing and spluttering behind them was becoming uncomfortable, from those who had overheard snatches, like the Red Admiral who had somehow crept up to within hearing distance, or who simply wanted to get on with proceedings. The High Commissioner himself stepped forward to take the two into a side room where there was a discussion with the business delegation about their itinerary and a visit to the Parrikar factory. Kate struggled for a while to keep pace with the detail and was clearly flagging, but encouragement from the big brown eyes across the table kept her going until she was able to make a dignified exit to enjoy the promised thirty minutes of rest and recuperation. She saw the same pair of eyes following her to the door.

XXXXXXXXXXXXXXXXX

In another part of the city, altogether less salubrious than the environs of the Taj, there was an unexpected and unwanted visitor to the office of Deepak Parrikar's father. He arrived in a black Mercedes with darkened windows. Out stepped an elderly but distinguished-looking bearded man in dark glasses wearing the white cap and gown of someone who had recently left prayers at the mosque.

The Sheikh had been visiting his friend for half a century but the frequency of the visits had declined as the trajectories of their businesses had diverged. The borderline between legitimate business and organised crime was very unclear in Mumbai but Parrikar had leaned, albeit uncertainly, towards the former and the Sheikh to the latter. Parrikar had drawn the line at narcotics and guns while the Sheikh and his brothers had embraced them, accumulating great wealth and a fearsome but unsavoury reputation in the process. The family now mainly operated out of the Gulf, of necessity in the case of one of the Sheikh's brothers who, reputedly, had financed and provisioned the terrorist raid on the Taj and was high on India's 'most wanted' list.

The Sheikh had not been invited but, then, the length and depth of their friendship had always transcended formality. When he entered his friend's office, there was a chill beneath the effusive welcome and customary exchange of family news. Parrikar was acutely aware that the visit, if witnessed, would attract curiosity and criticism and he worried that the Sheikh, knowing that perfectly well, had decided to come regardless.

They conversed in the street patois of their joint upbringing, a mixture of Marathi and Hindi. When they had exhausted the pleasantries, the Sheikh got to the point. 'Brother, I hear that you are having troubles with the Versova development. There are some bad, bad people in the city these days; not the respect we once had. Greed has taken over. When we were working together there was much less violence. Shocking what happened to your project man.'

'Yes. Patel. You have good sources.'

'I read the press. But nothing much happens without my being told. My friends say that Patel was not paying what had to be paid for services. Showing lack of respect.'

'Patel was a good man. An honest man. My son wanted him to rise in the business.'

'So what are you doing about this killing?'

'The police…'

'That pile of turds is useless. We both know that CID stands for "Criminals in Disguise". If they know anything they will be involved.'

'You would know, my friend.'

'Come, let us not play with each other. I can help you. I can stop this.'

'There is a price, no?'

'There is no price. We are old friends. We trust each other. I want to see your business make good money. Like mine. Otherwise the gangsters get to run this city.'

'And?'

'I have a small favour to ask. A very small favour.'

'How much?'

The Sheikh shifted in his seat. 'This isn't about money. I have a nephew, a very well-qualified engineer. First class degree. PhD in America. He is ideal for your son's company. But he is a good Muslim and we know what will happen: the security people will find reasons for losing his application. Can you please speak to your son?'

'My son doesn't work like this. No caste or cousins. No backhanders. Professional hiring, and security vetting. The new India, like the West.'

But the Sheikh knew that his old friend belonged to the old India, not the new. There was a long pause and then the Sheikh started to leave. 'Thank you, my friend, I know that you will try to please me. I know we can work together again.'

He was right. Parrikar and he had grown apart but deeper bonds united them. They owed each other their lives. Parrikar had given the Sheikh's family sanctuary a quarter of a century earlier when religious fanatics ran amok in the streets of Mumbai and Muslims were being hacked and beaten to death. Many years earlier, in a violent skirmish between street children, the young Parrikar had been surrounded by knife-wielding teenagers from the Sheikh's clan. The Sheikh had pulled him to safety, then protected him and become a partner in crime and property development.

The few seconds between the Sheikh leaving the building and entering his chauffeur driven limousine was enough for a mobile phone, held by a young man standing in the shopfront opposite, to capture the event for his newspaper. And he wasn't the only person to observe and monitor the visit. India's counter-terrorism team, having received maximum cooperation from the local gangsters in the wake of Desai's meeting at the five star hotel, were also represented in the crowd outside the office.

×××××××××××××××××

Parrikar slept badly after the Sheikh's visit. He saw trouble ahead. The ground was shifting underneath him. The old certainties were going. Parrikar had been trying to manoeuvre from his original, less legal and decidedly underground, business into a professional legacy for his children. But the question of how to complete the transition increasingly preoccupied him. He had never explained to his children the complex accounting behind the Mumbai operations, much of which did not exist on paper, let alone on computers. Had they known how much of their shiny factories and luxury condominiums had been financed on the back of Mumbai slum dwellers and revenue defrauding scams they would have been seriously alarmed. But the Patel murder, and the unsolicited visit from the Sheikh, had now persuaded him to open up rather more to his family. Breakfast with Deepak was to be the start.

They sat outside the family bungalow set in extensive gardens where fountains played and peacocks flaunted their plumage on the carefully manicured lawns tended by a small army of servants. The setting, along the ridge of Malabar Hill looking down on Chowpatty beach, framed the most expensive real estate between Hong Kong and Monaco and it was one of Parrikar's early business coups to have acquired it cheaply.

Starting with elaborate, convoluted, childhood reminiscences to ease himself in, he soon lost Deepak's attention, which was torn between the exchange rate risk on the Pulsar contract, the stunning British Minister he had met the previous evening and the cricket commentary from Melbourne emanating from the servants' quarters. His multi-channel reverie was interrupted when his father started to talk about the disappearance and murder of Patel. Deepak had identified him as a talent but they were in different areas of the Parrikar empire. They hadn't been in touch for several weeks and Patel had given no indication of the pressures he was under. The murder hadn't been reported in the English language newspapers and none of Deepak's staff had known enough to brief him on the murky goings on in the Mumbai underworld.

His father described, haltingly, some of the background, skirting around the problems that Patel had created for himself by his attempts to be honest. He was, he said, being blackmailed by a man who knew of some irregularities in the business – without divulging the long, unedifying, history of collaboration with the Sheikh. He had initially ignored the blackmail. Patel had been the casualty. Of course the matter was now with the police but Deepak needed to understand that the blackmailer could no longer be ignored and was making fresh demands, including the posting of a 'nephew' in Deepak's factory. Otherwise more killings could follow.

Deepak took the news calmly. While he had never probed his father's dealings too closely, he had long since realised that Daddy-ji didn't belong to the Mother Teresa school of ethical business. The fact that his father had made moral compromises in his rise from poverty did not diminish Deepak's love and respect for him. He just didn't want or need to know the gory details.

'Daddy-ji, you have got to look after your staff and your family first of all. No heroics. No need to take risks. I will take on this young man. I will keep a close eye on him. But not obviously. We will make it look as if you are complying with demands. You will have to make sure your project people do what is needed to keep out of trouble.'

'Thanks, son. I knew you would understand. Things are changing in India. It isn't easy to find your way. These politicians talk about "clean hands" and pass new laws on corruption. Then they increase "commission". The goondas and the politicians are the same. And some are involved in this Muslim terrorism. Maybe even this "nephew"?'

'We can handle that. In our technology business there are always people snooping and spying. We know and we manage the risks. This country is corrupt and incompetent in lots of ways, like the clowns in the police, but high tech businesses like mine know what they are doing. Don't worry about it. Just tell your gangster friend that you will do as he asks. And that I am playing ball. And then, please, get out of this dirty property business as soon as you can.'

The old man listened for a while, and then tears appeared in his eyes. There was a long silence broken only by the cawing of the crows along the hill where the Parsees had their Tower of Silence, where the birds disposed of the flesh of the dead.

<hr/>

Shaida arranged to meet Steve, with her brother, in the old part of town where she had grown up and where most of the town's Muslims lived. She hoped he would better understand the environment in which Mo and his friends were now being radicalised, though she was aware that online recruitment was just as important as peer pressure. Indeed, in one of their angry exchanges at home he had admitted surfing the internet for material on 'our fighters'. This revelation made her desperate to find a sympathetic third party who could help her stop her brother drifting towards disaster. Mo had agreed, reluctantly, to come along.

Even as one of the town's civic leaders, Steve was unfamiliar with this area and struggled to find the café. The district was full of cheap terrace housing once occupied by the white working class, who had been moved to council housing or fled to a different part of town – the one he represented – to escape the Pakistani influx. Despite being a fully paid-up multi-culturalist Steve felt uncomfortable, the only white face in the street where many women were shrouded in black, some with veils, and many of the older men had dyed orange beards, flat woollen hats and the loose pyjamas of their homeland. The café, he had been told, was in the middle of a shopping arcade. He wandered, fascinated, past halal butchers, kebab restaurants, shops selling gold jewellery and fashionable but religiously sanctioned women's clothes, newsagents advertising cheap flights to Lahore and cheap phone calls anywhere and open-air greengrocers with stalls overflowing with coriander and ginger, onions and garlic, okra and brinjal, mangoes and papayas.

Eventually he found the café, brilliantly lit by neon lights, with shiny Formica tables and a large picture of Mecca advertising the owner's Haj. A table of five young men was waiting for him, with Shaida who was, conspicuously, the only woman in the place. At the other tables, men stopped their conversation when he entered and looked suspiciously at the group he joined.

Shaida introduced them: Mo, Ibrahim, Ikram, Abdullah and Rafaaq ('Tubby'). Her brother Mo looked sullen and suspicious and completed the stereotype of a disaffected Muslim youth by sporting a beard and a white cap advertising his devotional commitment. The others were more welcoming but shy and polite, and, unlike Mo, they wore Western dress and were clean shaven. The conversation was halting and uncomfortable at first, but they were determined to tell their stories. All very similar: second generation – fathers factory workers, school at the local comprehensive, aspirational families pushing them to get good grades. Then degree courses at unfashionable universities within commuting distance from home, in subjects their families had judged to be useful and leading to good careers: accounting, business studies, law. But now frustration: no jobs, apart from pizza delivery or serving in cafés, scrounging for tips, or doing something menial in a distant relative's shop.

Steve responded: 'Young people everywhere are struggling to get into work. The local council and the union do what they can. The Labour Party has been campaigning against these zero hours contracts and dead-end jobs and to get this Tory government to invest in jobs for young people.' It sounded lame and tediously party political and he knew it. He dared to glance at Shaida for support – she had a proper job – but she was signalling detachment and was clearly on the side of the young men.

Mo, who had retreated into taciturn contempt, spoke at last. 'The trouble is, you people don't respect us. If I put in for a job with "Mohammed" on the application it goes straight in the bin, or they hit the delete key. You know that. Why give us all this crap about "jobs for young people"?'

Steve took a different tack. 'All I can say is that at our company – where Shaida and your dad work – we have no discrimination. One third black and Asian. Management and shop floor. But you need a proper trade like electrical or mechanical engineering. Did they never tell you that at school?'

Mo shifted the angle of attack. 'What exactly do you do at Pulsar? I hear you make weapons – is that right?'

Steve looked nervously at Shaida.

'Sure. Among other things. We supply the armed forces. Do you have a problem with that?'

'I have a problem with killing Muslims.'

'We don't.'

'Israel?'

'No.'

'India?'

'I don't know anything about that.'

'What a joke! I can't believe we know more than you do. Everyone in town is talking about this big contract coming your way.'

The conversation was taking a turn Steve hadn't anticipated and was becoming seriously awkward. Shaida's eyes were fixed firmly in the middle distance as if to disclaim responsibility for having lit the fuse that had led to this explosion.

The mild-mannered Tubby tried to help out, steering the conversation on to less controversial topics, and the ways that Steve could realistically help. When the time came for Steve to go, Abdullah asked if he would come back, perhaps to see a bigger group. 'There's a meeting room in the cultural centre behind the mosque. Would you be happy coming there?' It was agreed but, before Steve left, Abdullah asked if they could have a group photo. Even Mo was persuaded to shuffle into the corner of the picture. Shaida mumbled a 'thank you' to Steve on his way out and flashed a smile, her first of the evening.

Despite the smile Steve felt some unease as he left. The meeting had shaken some of his earlier belief that the good community relations enjoyed in the factory were reflected more widely in the town. The Asian councillors in his group had always exuded a breezy self-confidence, telling their colleagues that they had 'their own people' safely tied up. Their comfortable majorities seemed to bear this out. Or so he'd thought.

Kate touched down at Mumbai for the second time in three days, returning from Delhi for another round of meetings before leaving for London. Jet lag and constant travel were playing havoc with her metabolism; night and day fused into a vague, timeless, sleepy blur. But she had a warm feeling of satisfaction from a programme that seemed to be going well and the prospect of meeting again the anonymous texter who had sent the message 'You were brilliant' after her first round of meetings in Mumbai. She had a shrewd suspicion who it was and her cynical side dismissed it as the work of a charmer who was employing the technique of telling a woman how clever she is rather than how pretty. But it had aroused her interest, whatever the motivation.

The schedule of meetings had included a brief visit to the Indian PM, a rare honour for a minister some way below Cabinet rank. There were platitudes all round but the important thing was that the meeting had happened, and favourable reference made to the prospective arms contract. She had caught in his eyes a glint of the political steel that had taken him from poverty and a career starting as a tea boy to leadership of the world's biggest democracy. He had in turn been fascinated by the article in a leading Indian daily – and planted by the High Commissioner through a friendly journalist – describing her as the rising star of British politics.

There was, however, one aspect of the meeting that troubled her, and the High Commissioner even more so. The Prime Minister anticipated all of her questions and interventions and, when discussion turned to the potential contract and collaboration and the capabilities of the technology to be supplied from the UK, he seemed to know considerably more than was in the public domain. She and the High Commissioner both noticed that as he discussed these subjects he periodically turned to the thin, ascetic-looking man behind him as if for confirmation that he was on the right track.

An alert first secretary who sat at the back of the meeting had identified him as Sanjivi Desai, who had been a prominent member of the National Security Adviser's team in the days of the previous BJP administration. He was, apparently, known at the time as brilliant but ideological. Desai had since left India for a university in the USA. There he had electrified the foreign policy community with an academic article that argued the case for nuclear weapons as part of an offensive military strategy rather than simply for deterrence. The article had since been largely forgotten and India had adopted a 'no first use' strategy (while Pakistan had not). The High Commission team was clearly taken aback by Desai's resurrection but unable to cast more light on it.

Back in Mumbai the ministerial party would stay in a hotel near the international airport for the early morning flight back to London. For the rest of the day, they would travel to the Parrikar factory, located in the city outskirts, for an inspection visit.

Kate hadn't been a minister long enough to have seen many factories and her vision of an Indian factory was that it would be – well – Indian: noisy, dirty and teeming with people. Parrikar Avionics proved to be as far from that world as it was possible to be: full of computer controlled machines and robots; industrious, uniformed staff busying themselves purposefully; a factory floor so clean you could have eaten off it; a quiet hum permitting normal conversation; and odourless beyond the smell of fresh paint. It resembled what she imagined factories to be like in Japan or Germany.

She tried to restart the conversation with Deepak that had been cut off at the hotel.

'I believe you are an engineer by training.'

'Was. Now I try, not very successfully, to make money.'

'Can't help you there. I am a medieval historian.'

'I know. But a good way to understand politics.'

Throughout the visit Deepak stayed by her side, attentive and efficient but conveying nothing in his conversation or body language to suggest any interest beyond professional correctness. On her return to the hotel Kate was left wondering whether she had read too much into the first encounter and into that anonymous text. But, shortly after arriving back at the hotel, another text arrived: 'Farewell dinner? 8pm? Car outside. Black Bentley. D.' She had a 'wash up' with her officials and her business delegation but persuaded herself, without a great deal of resistance, that the national interest might be better served by getting to know Mr Parrikar a little better. She explained her change of plan to Susan, who reacted with customary aplomb, though the upward movement of her eyebrows managed to convey the message 'Lucky you. But be careful.'

After a bath and change of clothes, she took the lift to the hotel lobby a few minutes after 8pm. The black Bentley was waiting at the entrance. The chauffeur sped off into the night, arriving after a rather hair-raising drive at an expansive villa with a luxuriant garden. Deepak Parrikar was waiting at the door to greet her.

'This is the company's VIP guest house,' he explained. 'I stay here when I am at the factory. Sorry about the air of mystery. I thought you might prefer a private dinner here instead of the hotel restaurant with all your hangers-on.' If she had any reservations, it was too late. And, anyway, she hadn't.

He had obviously made discreet enquiries about her dietary tastes – she was an enthusiast for good North Indian cooking – and she was served the best, most subtle Mughal meal she had ever tasted: gently spiced lamb in biryani with almonds and sultanas, with aubergine and dal accompaniments. Conversation flowed.

'A little bird told me that you were quite a celebrity at Oxford. Much sought after. Modelling too.'

'Yes. I enjoyed myself. But don't believe everything you read in newspapers. How about you? And don't tell me you spent your years in London and the States in a self-denying monastic order.'

They flirted with their eyes, trying not to catch the attention of the uniformed staff serving the meal, as they talked about the visit – the deal was agreed bar the formalities, was his assessment – and went on to their large overlapping circles of friends and his favourite haunts in London. When the servants had cleared away the meal and retreated to their quarters she broached the subject that they had hitherto skirted around. 'You haven't mentioned Mrs Parrikar. I believe there is a Mrs Parrikar?'

'Yes, there is. Her name is Rose. She spends most of her time in Delhi. She is a very talented writer and does a lot of scripts for Doordarshan, like your BBC. And our children are there, with Rose and my mother-in-law. Perhaps you should tell me about Mr Thompson.'

'Where to start? You know his background: inherited wealth, property market and all that.'

'Yes, I do know all about that. I also heard that he had... or has?... quite a reputation.'

She hadn't expected to get into the intimacies quite so soon. Or so easily. But why not? she told herself. 'Let's just say that we have an excellent partnership, a grown-up marriage. Stable. Solid. We adore our girls and provide them with a good family life. We know each other's strengths and weaknesses and don't let the weaknesses get in the way.'

'Sounds interesting.'

Kate hesitated. She welcomed an invitation to take their after-dinner coffee to the veranda, listening to the unfamiliar racket of cicadas in the garden. She decided to take the plunge. 'He has a roving eye,' she answered candidly. 'Always has. At the beginning I retaliated a few times when I wanted to get even. But it made me feel guilty. And I didn't like the men much. So I have a lot to be satisfied about and leave romance to my girlfriends. And you?'

'Similar. I did the rounds in London and Harvard. A lot of nice girls but nothing special. When I came back here my energies went into building up the business that my father had asked me to run. Then – this is India – my family and friends started agitating about marriage. Late twenties and still a bachelor: a problem in danger of becoming a scandal. My parents started asking about suitable girls: a degree from a reputable college; wheaten complexion; preferably a virgin (but this is difficult to guarantee these days); a dowry (but we are rich enough not to be greedy).'

Kate was intrigued. 'I thought dowries were old hat in the Indian middle classes.'

'Among the highly educated, maybe, but not otherwise. Anyway, the real problem was to marry into a "good family", Indian-speak for caste. The people my parents mix with are mostly banias – merchants, traders. My father's parents rub along with them in the business world but when it comes to marriage they made it clear that for all our money we were not socially acceptable. My ancestors are Dalits, "untouchables". In the USA, our family's climb from rags to riches would be celebrated as the American Dream. But, here, it is a guilty secret.

'Eventually I met a beautiful Christian girl from the south – Rose – who didn't have any hang-ups about caste, or colour – she is as black as me. She was attracted, I don't doubt, to the family wealth, and perhaps even to me. We married quietly in a Christian church: no dowry; no astrologers; just a few friends and family.'

Kate was glad that she had taken their conversation into their private lives, realising that it had brought them closer. She was grateful too that he didn't crowd her, engaging her only with his eyes. They talked late into the night.

She hadn't talked so freely to a man for a long time and she was encouraged by his easy, natural, candour. She knew she was very attracted to him and sensed that the feeling was shared.

It seemed easier to stay than go. The packing and the final debrief could wait until the morning. But Kate forced herself to think clearly. She felt herself to be on the threshold of a serious affair and it would send the wrong signal to rush into it impetuously. Without the need for an explanation he seemed to read her mind and speedily summoned the driver when she, regretfully, indicated her wish to leave. Confident that she had done the right thing, she felt able to show something of her feelings.

The lingering kiss on the doorstep was not, however, as private as the two of them believed. The *Bharat Bombay* team had been staking out the guest house as well as the offices downtown since they had been tipped off that Deepak was staying there, and a mystery guest had been reported arriving some hours earlier and still hadn't left. The photographer was every bit as skilled and well equipped as his paparazzi cousins in Europe; there was adequate lighting in the porch area and he captured the moment for posterity.

Nor was he the only curious observer of the guest house. If the Minister had been naïve enough to imagine that her departure from the hotel had gone unnoticed, she underestimated the resources and resourcefulness of both British and Indian security and intelligence services. By the time Kate had arrived back at the hotel sometime after 2am, a report was on the desks of the British and Indian National Security Advisers recommending that their political masters might wish to be aware of this blemish on an otherwise flawless visit.

CHAPTER 7

THE RETURN

The Times of India, 2 July 2019:

Lok Sabha has passed legislation applying across India the cow protection law piloted in Haryana in 2016. Cow slaughter is now punishable by up to ten years in prison. A new Cow Protection police force has been established to enforce the law. Members of the ruling party argued in debate that those who refused to observe the taboo on eating beef should leave India.

Steve's second meeting with Shaida's friends took place in the cultural centre at the back of the town's main mosque, though Shaida waited outside. Steve had been to the mosque before, campaigning at election time, but he had not been the centre of attention and, this time, he felt much more self-conscious.

Looking around the room Steve saw mainly friendly, welcoming faces, but there was a small cluster that included Shaida's brother, Mo, who sat separately, dressed traditionally and affected an air of disapproval and rejection. The earlier discussion had forearmed Steve with many of their concerns and arguments, so he felt altogether better prepared. Different members of the group rehearsed their grievances – jobs, the police, Islamophobia – and he felt confident enough to throw back some challenges to them: why were no women present? Did they unequivocally condemn the sadistic cruelty of some extremist organisations? One of Mo's group tried to take him down the foreign policy route but this was outside his comfort zone. Steve contented himself with acknowledging that the Blair government had made a terrible blunder over the Iraq war and this had done great damage to the country's reputation and the party's standing with Muslims. This earned him a round of applause, and he hoped it would provide him with an exit route from the meeting. It didn't.

There was an awkward silence, only broken when one of Mo's group, dressed in a long white robe and cap, launched into a bitter and angry tirade. 'Do you know how many Muslims are assaulted and spat at, in this town that your party runs and claims is some kind of multi-cultural paradise? Did you know that women have their headscarves torn off? Called "Paki prostitutes" in front of their children? Many, many cases. But not reported.'

There was a growl of support in the room. Steve was feeling very much on the defensive and wondering how he had got into the position as a figurehead for the police, the council, the Labour Party and the other establishment bodies that these young people saw either as the enemy or as hypocritical neutrals. Sensing the weakness of Steve's position, Mo tried to raise the ante. 'What you people don't realise is that we are on the receiving end of constant biased coverage in the media. Muslims are always a threat; always to blame. We all know the reasons, don't we, boys? It's all those Jews, innit, controlling everything.'

There was a hushed silence. He had overstepped the mark, no doubt deliberately, to provoke Steve into trying too hard to be one of the boys.

'You mean all those Jews like Sadiq Khan, Mo Farah, Moeen Ali and Sajid Javid,' Steve replied.

The laughter drained the tension away. 'Serves you right, you idiot, Mo,' someone called out. Even Mo felt the need to retreat a little.

'We are not getting at you personally. At least you listen to us. But you need to take on board that some in our community are close to breaking point.'

Then, as usual, a group photo for social media. He was gratified that Mo's group – which had become a little friendlier – edged themselves into the centre of the picture, alongside him. As Steve left, Shaida nodded acknowledgement at the door and prepared to go home with her brother. Tubby, who saw himself as some kind of bodyguard and protégé of Steve, ran after him, anxious to pass on information. 'I've overheard some talk. People in the community know about this Indian contract. Some of them see everything as India versus Pakistan. They are saying this is like Blair and Bush attacking Iraq: a war on Muslims. They want to make trouble.' This report left Steve more troubled than the fire-eating rhetoric of the young radicals. There were hundreds of jobs – including his own – on the line.

As they left the mosque complex, Steve saw another incident that alarmed him. There was an angry altercation between a powerfully built, bearded man who looked like a cleric, and a few of his supporters who were confronting a larger group trying to prevent them entering the mosque. There was no violence but voices were raised in anger and, whatever the language being used, it was abundantly clear that the bearded cleric was unwelcome.

Tubby was reluctant to talk but, after being pressed, he explained that the cleric was a well-known radical. 'What the government calls a hate preacher,' he explained. 'He has never advocated terrorism and isn't in one of the banned groups like Al Muhajiroun. But he praises the "martyrs" who have gone to Syria and Afghanistan and demands stronger action by the local mosques against "backsliders", especially "loose women", and people who fratcrnise with "kafiis". Like us,' he added, giggling nervously. 'He has a growing local following. But the local mosque committees don't want trouble; so they've banned him from preaching here.'

As they walked away, Steve noticed police officers at a discreet distance and in the next street a couple of vans full of police in riot gear. One of the policemen stopped him. 'Evening, sir. I trust you and... your friend are not having any problems?'

'No, officer, we're fine.'

'OK, just checking.'

On her return to London, Kate was on a high. The department, her personal team, No. 10, the High Commission all pronounced the visit a great success. No gaffes. Everyone was impressed by her grasp of the issues and her diplomatic skills. There were no obstacles remaining to the signing of a big defence contract of which Pulsar/Parrikar was part. It only remained to secure a high-level VIP visit that would be a fitting context. And she was also able to enjoy the warm glow of reflecting on her night out and her new friend, which brought into relief the lack of emotional and physical pleasures in her married life.

India receded into the background of departmental priorities. The routine work of a department minister came to the fore. She longed for the weekend, to catch up with family news and sleep. But there was one more obstacle to negotiate: the weekly advice surgery on Friday evening. Several Tory and Labour MPs had strongly warned against such diligence. 'You only encourage the nutters and troublemakers' was the gist of their distilled wisdom. MPs in marginal seats and Liberal Democrats – she was told – set great store by surgeries but she didn't need to bother; perhaps once a month for form's sake. She decided to ignore the advice, much to the fury of Stella who would have to attend, make notes and draft letters.

Kate valued the surgeries. She learnt a lot about people and their problems, which she had been shielded from in the election campaign and throughout her protected upbringing. She came to realise that in her very prosperous constituency there was a lot of financial distress, and real poverty, made all the worse by isolation and lack of neighbourly support. And there was a growing undercurrent of anxiety about rising unemployment. Last week had produced a sad family who could have stepped out of *Jude the Obscure* and for whom everything that could go wrong had gone wrong: redundancy, repossession, children with special needs. Then there was an export salesman who couldn't travel because his passport had been mislaid somewhere in the Home Office and had lost his job; a mentally ill alcoholic who couldn't get treatment for either condition until the other had first been cured; and a hopelessly overcrowded family whom the council had deemed 'intentionally homeless' after refusing to move to a corner of a council estate infested by drug dealers. She did her best for all of them but knew that these were mostly hopeless cases.

The desperate were randomly interspersed with the self-important and selfish. This week there was a delegation protesting over the decision of the local council to grant planning permission for a large home extension, wanted by a local teacher to house his expanding family ('loss of light', 'traffic congestion', 'parking problems', 'out of character'). She explained with difficulty that planning law did not encompass their concerns about 'loss of property value'.

Then, in came a young woman with a child who had obvious learning difficulties, bearing flowers and a box of chocolates: 'I just wanted to say thank you. Freddie has got the special school you helped us find.' Kate struggled to remember how she had performed this miracle, but eventually it all came back. A struggling single mum with three children: one physically and another mentally handicapped. She remembered, with a twinge of shame, how she had initially fallen back on her stereotypical assumptions about struggling single mothers. Several fathers? Actually, no: one father, a lovely man who had been killed in an industrial accident. On benefits? Actually, no: she was working but, thanks to a recalculation of her tax credits, could no longer afford proper childcare and was having to juggle babysitters. Dependency culture? Actually, no: whenever she had spare time she helped the old lady next door. Having heard all this, Kate had written a very supportive letter to the head of the county's educational and social services departments. Maybe it had helped. Something gave way inside her when she was offered the flowers and chocolates. She burst into tears, to the embarrassment of Stella, sitting beside her, and the dismay of her constituent who left quickly, worrying about what she had done to upset this important woman.

Kate then had to recompose herself for her last visitors: a delegation from the Churches Together of Surrey Heights. Stella was convinced that they were here to deliver a blast of holy wrath after Kate's last vote in support of gay adoption. Kate was prepared to tough this one out: she had never understood what all the fuss was about. She herself preferred men to women, having tried both, but had no problem with other people's preferences. But, no, this was not what worried them.

The delegation was led by a large and cheerful young woman with a dog collar and improbably red cheeks who bore a more than passing resemblance to the Vicar of Dibley. She introduced herself and her team, saying: 'We have come to talk to you about the arms trade. We want you to use your influence in government to stop the sale of weapons to governments that abuse human rights.'

She had a long, prepared speech and Kate did her best to listen politely. But the room was overcrowded and stuffy, she was tired and desperate to get away. She looked conspicuously at her watch but the vicar and her followers had been preparing for the visit for weeks and had no intention of going quickly or quietly. Kate tried to escape.

'I have a lot of sympathy,' she explained, 'but I am new in the job and this is not my area of responsibility. And there are strict rules and processes governing arms exports.'

'But we read in the press that you have just been to India. Promoting arms exports. Shouldn't the Indians be spending their money on fighting malnutrition and illiteracy?'

'Yes. They also have a democratic government with real security concerns. And shouldn't we also be concerned about British workers and their jobs?'

An earnest member of the delegation launched into scripture –'swords into ploughshares' – and Kate could see that she could not win an argument based on textual analysis of the Bible. She managed to summon a graceful smile. 'I know how much this means to you,' she responded. 'I admire your Christian spirit. I will dig out some facts on the arms trade with India and send them to you to discuss at our next meeting.'

Stella looked aghast at this prospect. 'Time wasting *Guardian* readers. They will never vote for you whatever you say,' she muttered after the delegation had left offering Kate their prayers.

⬦⬦⬦⬦⬦⬦⬦⬦⬦⬦⬦⬦⬦

Iqbal Aziz drove his 500cc Bajaj motorcycle confidently to the entrance of the Parrikar Avionics factory. In his pocket he was carrying a letter from the head of human resources explaining that a vacancy had appeared that fitted his engineering qualifications perfectly. Please would he present himself and, subject to the necessary checks, take up a job that was waiting for him in the R&D unit?

His journey there had started a few weeks earlier. He had been at his desk in a secretive defence research institution near Islamabad. He received a summons to see the legendary General Rashid: battlefield hero, now mastermind of Pakistan's covert operations overseas and head of the Inter-Services Intelligence agency ISI. The General got quickly to the point: 'We have a job for you. India. Mumbai. Give you a chance to meet your extended family.'

This wasn't the first job the researcher had been asked to do. On business and academic visits to the US and Saudi Arabia he had been asked to obtain classified information in his field of radar linked to missile technology, beyond the limit of what their governments would release officially. Unlike most agents he had the advantage of knowing exactly what he was looking for and what was useful.

He had shown himself adept at recruiting local helpers and mastering the technologies of copying, miniaturising, storing and transmitting sensitive data. His research superiors and his handlers at ISI were both delighted with his progress: he was destined for higher things that no longer involved risky trips in the field. But here was a big job that, with his family networks and travel experience in India, he was ideally qualified to carry out.

The briefing was specific: 'There is a defence industry installation on the outskirts of Mumbai that we want to know more about. We think it is developing technology linked to their missile defence system. We need to know where the Indians have got to. The firm, Parrikar Avionics, works on the programme – we think – with a British firm and British government backing. We want you to get inside their R&D department and find out what you can.'

Several weeks later he was in India staying with cousins whose family had remained behind at Partition. They were encouraged to believe that he was a bona fide visitor with a valid Indian passport.

Aziz manoeuvred his bike to the allocated parking area amid hundreds of other Indian made mopeds and motorcycles. He had a good look around and assessed the level of vigilance. Security was visible but not oppressive. No one had checked the panniers on his bike. The man at the gate had looked at his letter but appeared to be reading it upside down. Not very impressive. The perimeter fence was high but scalable. There were a few CCTV cameras but to his knowledgeable eye there were too few and they were badly positioned. Compared to the US military industrial establishments he had visited, or even back home, it all seemed rather sloppy.

He followed the signs to the security office to submit his papers and obtain a pass. When he entered the office he was told to wait in a queue and, after fifteen minutes, was invited into a small cubicle to sit opposite a bald overweight man who was sweating profusely in his tight uniform. Behind him sat a man introduced as his assistant who was reading the sports pages of a Mumbai newspaper. The overweight man laboriously and slowly took Iqbal through the details of his original application form, checking dates and places and ensuring that all the certificates and references were in place. The questioning was thorough but pedestrian: a box-ticking exercise of the kind perfected in subcontinental bureaucracies. Iqbal panicked at one point when it was noticed that the date on one of the certificates didn't tally with the date he had cited in his CV; but this was a genuine mistake and the man grumpily accepted it. After almost an hour he was pronounced security cleared and sent off to have his photo taken for a pass.

In fact, the interrogator was far from slow but an extremely sharp, US trained head of security. And his 'assistant' had flown down from Delhi for the interview, from Indian counter-intelligence. They were both well aware that Iqbal Aziz was not who he said he was and that his CV was largely a fabrication. He was Hussein Malik who had first appeared on the radar screens of intelligence agencies almost a decade earlier when he was pursuing his PhD at Stanford, as an overseas student from Pakistan. He had showed an unusual degree of interest in some of the avionics technology being developed at that time and in the heightened post 9/11 security his curiosity was noted, especially when he later reappeared at academic conferences and business negotiations, placing him near some very sensitive material.

But he was not caught doing anything untoward and went back home to a research establishment linked to the Pakistan military where the CIA kept close tabs on him, and, at one point, tried to recruit him. Subsequently he travelled widely to conferences dealing with avionics technology, and the interest of several intelligence agencies was aroused by the fact that he sometimes travelled with a false identity. There were several visits to India on an Indian passport that the Indian authorities had monitored but not aborted, hoping to find out what he was up to. Then, a few weeks ago, he had been spotted in Dubai and, after a series of flight changes, had ended up in Mumbai, staying with what appeared to be distant extended family.

The man from Delhi felt that he and his colleague had, so far, successfully hoodwinked Iqbal Aziz. No hint had been given that the watcher was being watched. He patted himself on the back for winning the argument in Delhi against those who questioned his recommendation to let Aziz into the country and into the factory in the hope he would lead them to a network of subversive contacts working for the enemy.

CHAPTER 8

TRISHUL

Press reports, Moscow, 5 July 2019:

President Putin paid a short informal visit to India, his third. He told a press conference that Russia 'wanted to restore the excellent relations between the two countries that prevailed before the break-up of the Soviet Union'. The Indian Prime Minister, receiving him in Delhi, agreed that there was common ground in suppressing Islamic terrorism in the region. Russia will also press for India to become a permanent member of the UN Security Council and President Putin referred, without giving details, to a 'sharing of competences' in relation to nuclear technology.

Kate was in the office bright and early on Monday, refreshed after a family weekend spending time with her daughters. She was beginning to enjoy her new life and the office worked smoothly now that her excellent private secretary had established an efficient, but pleasant, routine. Susan was a find.

This morning Susan came in with some highly confidential papers. 'Kate, I'm supposed to check that you have read these papers and then take them away. Not to be left lying around,' she announced. This was Kate's first exposure to papers marked 'Top Secret' and she was mildly titillated at the thought. Fascinated, she plunged into the first document. To her amazement it was a broadly accurate account and analysis of her India visit as presented to the Pakistan Security Council. They knew all about Pulsar and Parrikar Avionics and why they were important. Someone had risked their neck for this – or whatever part of the anatomy the Pakistan authorities severed when they uncovered secret agents.

There was, however, one sentence in the report that caused her to stop and reread it several times. Her head span as she grasped the significance of what she was reading: the Pakistan intelligence assessment of the kit to be provided by Pulsar was that it would destabilise the nuclear balance by giving India the potential to knock out the electronics of any Pakistani nuclear retaliation.

'This is the opposite of what I was told,' she said to Susan.

'It isn't my job to comment on policy,' Susan replied, 'but it may explain why my equivalent in the Foreign Office was anxious that you should see the report.'

'So, what should I do?' Kate asked.

'My strong advice is to say and do nothing at this stage. You are new to the job and so am I. You can raise the matter with the Secretary of State or even the Prime Minister, but you need more than an uncorroborated opinion by an unnamed Pakistani analyst.'

Kate read a less confidential paper by the Foreign Office Research Department piecing together press and other published reports from India and Pakistan that, individually, were of no great significance and none of which had made it into mainstream Western media, but taken together led the analyst to conclude that the 'threat level' had been raised a notch or two to just short of red. Indian sources reported increased numbers of crossings of the Line of Control into Kashmir by Kashmiri separatist militant groups allegedly backed by Pakistan. Substantial numbers of Indian soldiers and infiltrators were reported dead. The Cabinet reshuffles in both India's and Pakistan's governments had brought forward ministers who were more aggressively hostile to their neighbour and with strong links to religious fundamentalists.

And a leading Pakistani newspaper, *Dawn*, reported that the Pakistan Defence Minister had flown to Beijing to discuss the deteriorating security situation in the subcontinent and to seek Chinese support for countering 'illegal' Indian encroachments on Pakistani air space. He further announced that he had authorised a military exercise in the Sind desert near the Indian border, saying: 'We need to be prepared for all contingencies.'

None of this had been flagged up as a problem to Kate during her visit to India. It had all been 'business as usual'. But clearly it wasn't.

⬛⬛⬛⬛⬛⬛⬛⬛⬛⬛

Calum called in his management team and union reps for a meeting in the boardroom.

'Good news, bad news,' he began. 'Good news: the Indian contract looks as if it is now in the bag. Due diligence has raised no problems. Our investors are happy. I have some wee financial details to sort out. Not a problem. Thanks for helping me to get the project ready for launch.

'Now, the bad news. The ministerial visit in a few days' time – it's Kate Thompson, the Minister of State who led the recent delegation to India. Bright and tipped for higher things. But you know what I think about politicians, especially Tories.

'Anyway, we have no choice. If we want MOD work in future, we have to be very nice to Mrs Thompson. Keeping Whitehall sweet. The deal is: low-key event, modest publicity – local press, regional TV only – everyone on their best behaviour; a few apprentices on parade; leave the rest to me.'

When Calum's meeting dispersed, Steve made a point of walking back with Shaida. She gave not the slightest sign of intimacy and Steve felt as if their extramural meetings had never happened. What was it all for? A beautiful young woman had taken advantage of his infatuation to pursue a personal agenda whose ultimate purpose was obscure. He had done as she asked. Now what?

She must have been reading his thoughts. As they walked through the finance department he was given a broad smile and a long look at those open, big, brown eyes rather than the usual cool detachment. He felt the gentlest of touches on his elbow.

'Thank you very much for what you did the other day,' she said. 'I can assure you it was appreciated. You may not realise how much it means to most of those lads to let off steam. They are impressionable. They have now discovered you. Last week it was Russell Brand. Before that George Galloway, Osama bin Laden – the lot. Most of them have the attention span of a goldfish but if you can help keep them out of trouble that's great.

'Mo is more serious, though. My dad and I have been really worried about my brother. Completely unable to get through to him. He blanks us or gives us an Islamist rant. But he was impressed by you and said so. It is very difficult. I felt stronger, knowing I have a friend.' After quickly checking that they were not observed, she gave him a peck on the cheek and then disappeared into her office.

Steve knew that he should be in Calum's office passing on the warning that there were elements in the community who had picked up on the India connection. But in the warm afterglow of this encounter his attention wandered.

———※———

Deepak Parrikar had inherited enough of his father's guile to be no pushover in detailed negotiations. Like Calum, he was ultimately dependent for business on the goodwill of his government. But he was capable of wriggling like an eel to squeeze a few more lakh rupees out of a contract. Now he was pushing up against the limits of patience of the babus in Delhi. He received a very testy phone call from the PM's office making it clear that if he wanted to avoid annoying the Prime Minister, personally, he should be on the next available flight to London to sort out any remaining difficulties. Before he went to pack a suitcase he had time to send a text.

Kate was in her office signing papers when her mobile registered a new message. She normally ignored them. She had got used to the endless stream of messages from the whip's office instructing the government payroll to vote on some obscure piece of legislation. This time she reached for the phone. Boredom? Instinct? It was from a D in Mumbai: 'Coming London tomorrow. Hilton, Park

Lane. Fancy nightcap?' Pleasant thoughts came flooding back. Yes, she would very much like to see D again. But how? This was home turf. She wasn't exactly famous but recognised around the Westminster village. The private office controlled her diary. She had an MP's flat in Kennington and her family were used to her absences during the week. But, no, there were other MPs in the block. Arriving late at night with a handsome Indian would be tea room, then press, chatter the next day. But, of course, she could go to his hotel. Use a taxi not the ministerial car. No one could be surprised to see a minister turning up for an evening reception at the Hilton... or leaving after a business breakfast. A few minutes later she replied: 'D, love to meet. Your hotel? K.'

<hr />

Inspector Mankad arrived ten minutes early for his rendezvous at Rita's Sunshine Bar as was his habit. He would always check out the places where he had confidential meetings. Mumbai could be a dangerous place for police officers on their own in unfamiliar areas. Mankad was a long way from his parish so the risks were fewer. But it paid to be careful. The bar was unexceptional and unmemorable, which was how Mankad liked his rendezvous locations.

The crime reporter from *Bharat Bombay* arrived on time and after a few preliminaries they thanked each other. The journalist had enjoyed a prestigious splash and Mankad had been able to keep alive a murder enquiry that his supervisors would otherwise have sat on, fearing the consequences of tackling politically influential gangsters. But they were still no closer to finding out who was behind the killing of Vijay Patel.

The journalist explained that the paper was planning a big piece on the Parrikars. A story built around their dynastic succession was falling into place. The glamorous, charming, modernising, Westernised son and the grizzled old man, with a colourful past, losing his grip. Now there was the British VIP girlfriend – a blurred picture but just about usable – and the proof of a connection with the Sheikh's family with its unsavoury links to the underworld and, at one remove, Pakistani terrorist operations. And there were lots of stories of the old man's earlier life that could be reheated: the brutal clearing of the slum dwellers from desirable sites; an infamous scam involving adulterated cement; the Backbay Reclamation corruption scandal; the numerous unpunished breaches of building and planning regulations. All of this was being run past the lawyers. And the editor, whose vision of the paper was light entertainment for the commuting masses, still had to be persuaded that this foray into investigative journalism wasn't going to result in his experiencing the fate of Mr Patel.

The policeman listened quietly. He could see the attractions of shaking the tree. But he couldn't see where the murder case was leading. His network of informers had all repeated the gossip in the bazaars that Patel had been killed by a couple of thugs from the Sheikh's clan. And the motive was Patel's refusal to pay extortion money. But something didn't add up. Parrikar and the Sheikh had been close associates and – in the one piece of useful intelligence the Inspector had gleaned from his press contact – they had been in touch again very recently. Yet an execution of this kind would have been sanctioned from the top.

And he had just heard that the body of one of the suspected killers had been found on one of the city's rubbish tips.

<hr />

As he left work, Steve was surprised to find Shaida waiting for him with her younger brother, looking sheepish and carefully studying the ground in front of him: 'Can we talk? It's important,' she said. She led the way to a patch of ground where staff came out to have their snacks in summer and kick a football around.

Once settled on a bench she explained: 'My darling brother here has a problem. Mo, tell him!' Mo wouldn't say anything so she filled in the awkward silence. 'I found him, last night, by accident, watching a disgusting video on his laptop. Not hard core. I know all about that. Sex starved boys do it. Not a problem. But this was much worse. It was from one of the jihadi groups showing what they do to their prisoners. We talked afterwards and Mo said he was given it on a memory stick by one of his friends who was at the last meeting you spoke to. Eventually the truth came out. This young man – Zuffar – is trying to organise a group to "do something for the jihad". Bombing. Or killing a policeman. Trying to get Mo involved. Come. Speak up.' Still not a word. 'We need your advice, Steve. Perhaps your help. Mo doesn't want to go along with his friends, though he agrees with a lot of their ideas and seems emotionally dependent on them. He won't shop them to the police and I worry that if the police find out they will detain him, and my dad and I could be at risk of losing our jobs. We can't tell our parents; they would go spare.'

Steve was too numb to give a reply. And Mo was no closer to communicating directly. There was a long, embarrassed silence. Eventually Steve mumbled a semi-coherent response. 'Look, I'll have to think about it. I don't have any instant wisdom. My instincts are that we have to find a way of getting the intelligence to the authorities without incriminating Mo or dragging in your family. But I don't know people in that world. The only police officer I know is the sergeant in charge of my ward community team. Or there is the security man – Starling – at Pulsar, but I don't really know him from Adam.' Shaida looked at him pleadingly. For the first time he saw not a beautiful Asian princess or a desirable woman but a frightened, vulnerable person trapped between the conflicting loyalties to her family and the country of which she was a part.

On the evening following the Pulsar staff meeting, one of the attendees prepared for a long night at the office. His usual routine was to arrive for the day by public transport so there would be no car left in the car park after the factory closed. At the end of the day he would check out, wait in the toilets near the entrance to the works and then slip quietly back inside. He had access to all parts of the building including the secret basement and so could work quickly, undisturbed, through the night, copying discs and logging into the terminals for which he had been able to obtain the access codes and passwords. He didn't understand much about the material he was acquiring but he didn't need to and his customers were well pleased with his fishing expeditions.

The nights were long but he had a makeshift bed in the basement, and by carefully timing his visits to the washroom he could be fresh, shaved and ready for work in the morning. This arrangement had worked perfectly for months, with the exception of the two nights when the night watchman had shown a worrying degree of initiative and curiosity. The scare hadn't had lasting consequences and he had a plan to eliminate the risk in future.

This evening would be tricky, however. There had been no forewarning of the staff meeting and its contents required quick action on his part. Unfortunately, he had come to work by car that day and would therefore have to cover his tracks by driving the car somewhere else and returning after dark. He knew of a back entrance, had access to a key and knew how to disable the alarm before it could go off. He did have the easier option of sending out his messages from his laptop at home but his instructions were never to leave traces of his activities on his own machine: a pristine back-up system would be his alibi if questions were ever asked about data leakage and disloyal emails. Besides, he had come to enjoy his nocturnal adventures.

As Mehmet approached the end of his shift but well before staff started to arrive for work, he needed to visit the washroom at the factory entrance. As he washed his hands and prepared to leave he noticed that one of the cubicles behind him was 'engaged'. On his way out he gave a push to the door but it was clearly locked. There was no sound, or sign, of occupation. As he left the washroom and then the building, he decided to watch the washroom entrance for a while, remaining concealed behind a pillar. A part of him reached for a rational, innocent, explanation. He also realised that if there were a less innocent explanation, he might well not be thanked for revealing it. After ten minutes he decided to return to his cabin and forget about the incident. Just as he was about to end his shift he saw a movement from the washroom. Someone he recognised emerged carrying a washbag and, after looking around furtively, disappeared into the body of the factory. Mehmet hadn't been seen, he hoped, but the knowledge he now had was potentially dangerous for the night visitor – and for himself.

✂✂✂✂✂✂✂✂✂✂✂✂✂

Inspector Mankad's careful investigation into the Patel killing was finally starting to produce some results. 'Slowly, slowly, catchee monkey' was his catchphrase, picked up from some gangland Hindi movie. He didn't waste time and energy, or arouse suspicion and envy, in hyperactive investigations. He waited for the information to come to him. And he remained detached in case the political wind was blowing too much in the wrong direction and necessitated a tactful retreat. His intelligence came from his network of carefully cultivated informers. He looked after them: never compromised his sources; ensured that, if they found themselves behind bars, there would be special privileges, segregation from their gang enemies and early release. And, in this case, a friendly journalist had also done his bit, not least in signalling to the underworld that the ever approachable Inspector was on the case.

He had established already that two of the Sheikh's more unsavoury and violent foot soldiers had been responsible for Patel's killing. They had abducted him after work at knifepoint and taken him to a van. At

135

some point he had been killed and mutilated, before or after death wasn't clear, and his body deposited into a large open drain whence it had been washed some way downstream to little Ravi's harbour by a night-time downpour. Mankad discouraged his energetic assistant, Sergeant Ghokale, from arresting these small fry, and instead awaited developments. Informers reported that one of the two, Afzal, had been flashing around unusual amounts of money, buying an expensive gold necklace and watch, gambling and drinking bootleg liquor. And he had been shouting his mouth off, trashing the Sheikh as a 'has been' and a 'nobody' and making it clear that he was moving in more elevated circles now. His body was found on a rubbish tip shortly afterwards. And the other, Taheem, had disappeared.

Then, this morning, at the police station, another breakthrough of a kind. His division had launched a sweep-up operation in one of the baastis, netting a few petty criminals and many others who were merely bystanders or in the wrong place at the wrong time. Such raids kept the politicians off their backs – demanding 'action on crime' – and occasionally, but rarely, produced a serious villain. One wretched piece of humanity, his face covered in blood and snot, was dragged into Mankad's office. Mankad disapproved of his colleagues' methods as inefficient and unprofessional but had been careful to keep his views from more senior officers and, occasionally he acknowledged, there was a tiny nugget of gold among the spillage. This man, Jadhav, he was told, had some information if he could talk to the Inspector.

Jadhav was not forthcoming and clearly terrified. Mankad gave him time to settle, allowed him to go under escort to the lavatory to clean himself up and offered him sweet tea. Eventually a few words started to dribble out.

Jadhav was at the bottom of the criminal food chain. Not clever or brave or confident enough to belong fully to a gang, let alone be trusted with a weapon, he was called in to do menial tasks and paid a few rupees for his efforts. The few rupees helped his family to survive. A few nights ago he had been called to one of the better, pukka, buildings in his baasti. There was a body on the floor, blood and bits of flesh and bone lying around. He was told to help carry the body to a van in jute sacking and then to clear up the mess. He had received five hundred rupees, much more than usual, and told to maintain his silence. This hadn't, however, withstood the police interrogation.

The description of the body and clothes fitted that of Afzal, one of Patel's killers. But Jadhav couldn't or wouldn't say anything about the people who had employed him. All he would say, over and over, was 'Trishul', meaning 'trident'. Mankad knew the names of every gang in Mumbai and every serious gangster. This was a new one: a Hindu symbol, a common sight in religious pageantry, the three-pronged trident carried by the god Shiva and used to kill every Mumbaikar's favourite deity, Ganesh. What on earth was this about?

Then he recalled when he had seen tridents in action. It was a televised recording of events a quarter of a century earlier, when a mob led by militant Hindus, some of them holy men, sadhus or sanyasis, brandished tridents, as they set about destroying the ancient building disputed between the two religions. To a modern-minded citizen of the new India, like Mankad, these displays of religious fanaticism and hatred were an embarrassing relic of the past. But he was uncomfortably aware that many Indians did not share his relaxed view of these matters. Some of them were now in powerful positions. There was surely a link between the Hindu militants of the hut and criminals who adopted the iconography of that religion. It was not a link a humble policeman wanted to explore too far. These worries almost spoilt his lunch.

━━━━━━━━

Before setting off for London, Deepak Parrikar had dinner with his father. Parrikar Senior was unusually agitated; more than Deepak could remember. Their earlier heart-to-heart, exposing the Sheikh's visit and the attempted blackmail, hadn't exhausted his soul searching.

'Your mother: a lot of health problems. She is very unhappy. Talks a lot about when she is gone, what will become of the family. She asks how I will cope on my own. Funeral preparations. I try to tell her: you have years of good life. But she doesn't listen.'

Deepak had heard the tale often enough to know that it was a preliminary to other matters.

'Then there is the business. I don't want to trouble you with small things but we have many problems in Mumbai. Construction, development, very difficult. Workers all the time threaten strikes. Greedy politicians demand more money. Tenants stop paying rent. Police are no use. Also those Hindu fanatics are strengthening their hold on the city. They don't respect me. Always problems but never so bad.'

He paused, to give himself time to eat and gather his strength for the most difficult part of the conversation.

'Now this Patel thing. We have done favours for the Sheikh but I know him; he will want more to leave us in peace. Now we are in the papers. Maybe more to come. People say I keep bad company, I'm too close to gangs. I am trying to stay clean. To keep a good reputation for you, your brother and sister. To protect the family name.'

His first real conversation with his son had released a torrent of emotions. For the first time he reflected seriously on his life and his legacy, on his own powerlessness, his inability to protect his employees, his openness to blackmail.

He tried to explain to his son his complicated feelings towards the man who had almost certainly ordered the killing of Patel and was now seeking to inveigle him into some dangerous operation. In times past he would have taken on the challenge, met muscle with muscle. He was not a squeamish man and in his younger days he had had a fearsome reputation, holding his own in an underworld where might was right and the weak were trampled underfoot. Now he no longer felt able to fight.

The Patel episode was a turning point. Parrikar told Deepak that he had come to a decision. He would quit the Mumbai property market. He would sell the land and property freeholds that he had accumulated. The tax-wallahs would take a big share – but he knew how to minimise the hit. A sizeable sum would be invested in the businesses his family would inherit. But much of the money would fund the Parrikar Foundation. This would be to India what Ford or Rockefeller was to the US. It would be bigger and grander than the Tatas' charitable arm. His head was reeling with ideas for schools and hospitals for the poor. All the details would be ready when Deepak returned from London.

'Daddy-ji, stop worrying,' his son comforted him. 'The family understand that you want to get out of this dirty business and become a respectable company. It will happen. Look, I now have to tie up this big deal. I go tonight. If it succeeds, we will have a strong business for years. It gives us good links to US and UK companies. And with the big chiefs in Delhi. Then I want to launch a capital raising issue in London and New York. You will be there: the founding father, the man who turned a small-time Mumbai company into a global business empire.'

Deepak's next meeting was in London and its purpose was far removed from the family business. Kate had come to see him at the earliest opportunity. It only needed a few seconds to establish that neither was in the mood for polite, exploratory, conversation. A dam broke sweeping away their pent-up emotional and physical restraints. It was late in the night before, exhausted, they slept a little and then talked until the morning, sharing their past and beginning to map out a possible future together.

When she caught a taxi back to the office in Victoria Street the following morning she tried to rationalise her emotions. There was no sense of guilt. No regret. But a deeper feeling, tinged with worry that she was falling in love with Deepak.

The sense of detachment and calculation she had maintained with her previous lovers, and her husband, had largely gone. She found her emotions difficult to explain and that was the point. There was something new that went beyond attraction and physical compatibility. She needed to see him again but without any clear sense of where it would lead and conscious of the risks. He had said something very similar about his own feelings.

Kate forced herself, nonetheless, to focus on the dangers. She inhabited a world where risk taking was a way of life, but also where there was little room for error. There were many politicians with lovers or mistresses, of the same or

141

opposite sex. In an increasingly secular and liberal culture such behaviour shouldn't matter. But there was also an insatiable appetite for scandal: for exposing the hypocrisy of politicians who preached family values and practised the opposite; for 'love rats' whose 'betrayals' proved that they couldn't be trusted with the nation's secrets. Or, simply, the all too understandable pleasure of powerless, anonymous people, seeing the powerful and celebrated caught with their pants down. She remembered the chief whip's warning about envious colleagues. So far she had covered her tracks well, she thought.

When she arrived at the front door of her department, her team had assembled to set off for her next visit – to the Pulsar factory. She hoped that her face would not betray too much evidence of her wonderful night.

CHAPTER 9

THE RIOT

Russia Today, 9 July 2019:

Sources in the Indian Ministry of Defence report that a Pakistani F-15 fighter was, several days ago, shot down by Indian ground to air missiles after encroaching into Indian air space. Both Indian and Pakistani official spokesmen have denied knowledge of the incident. But there are reports of a heavy Indian military presence in the desert area in Rajasthan where the fighter has allegedly been downed.

BBC World Service, 9 July 2019:

Reports by the Indian Defence Ministry state that its forces are on 'heightened alert' and there has been some movement of troops to disputed areas in Kashmir. The Pakistan military authorities and an unusually high number of reported military flights close to the border are believed to be responsible.

Kate's magic carpet sped up the M1 on the way to her factory visit. The quiet hum of the official car; the aromatic smell of the polished upholstery; the space to stretch her legs; the simple luxury of being chauffeured around by the ever obliging Denis: these were part of the ministerial lifestyle she could definitely get used to. She was tempted to daydream and there were pleasant memories of last night to daydream about.

But she also felt a nagging discomfort when she had time to reflect on where her magic carpet was heading. The breezy salesmanship of the Secretary of State and the Prime Minister had obscured, initially, what her job entailed: that and her instincts to get behind British business. Over the last few days, however, Susan's drip-feeding of confidential files had left her in no doubt. She was a salesman in an arms bazaar for technologically advanced weapons that were being sold into a dangerous and tense conflict zone.

She looked in vain in the morning papers for any evidence that the British press took the matter seriously. Her office had, however, equipped her with clippings from news agencies that showed precisely how serious the matter was. But it was too late now to have a fit of conscience. The factory was fast approaching.

At the factory, final preparations were under way for the visit: business as usual; no fuss; no one to get excited. But, naturally, everyone wanted to create a good impression. Long-serving, loyal employees like Mr Khan would have a chance to shake the ministerial hand. Steve's message to the union – forget that the Minister is a Tory; jobs are at stake – was received without dissent. He had also had a quiet word with council officials to ensure that there were no disruptive traffic works planned and that refuse lorries didn't trundle past the front door at the wrong time. As agreed, there was a low-key media presence: one TV camera for regional television and to take a pooled clip for other channels should the Minister choose to say anything significant; and a couple of journalists, school leavers sent along by the local free newspaper. There was to be a plaque unveiled by Calum and the Minister and Calum had prepared a short speech purged of any controversial references to Scottish nationalism or irresponsible capitalism.

Then, about ten minutes before the scheduled arrival, down the road came a group of demonstrators waving banners – 'Stop the Arms Trade', 'Aid Not Arms' – chanting and singing hymns. They were orderly, polite and respectful towards the two police officers deployed at the entrance to the factory. A radio message was sent to the ministerial car, alerting the Minister and suggesting a brief, courteous greeting to the protesters.

Then down the road came a much larger group, not earnest and white but angry and brown. Their placards were less polite – 'Tory Murderers', 'Stop Killing Muslims'. The Socialist Worker and Respect banners vied with green flags with Arabic script and, at the back, the black flag of ISIL. As the crowd of around two hundred reached the entrance, the ministerial Jaguar arrived. The driver, acting on the earlier intelligence, pulled up and, before he could reconsider, the car was surrounded. Kate decided to face what would be a critical but polite crowd and demonstrate character for whatever media was observing. As she left the car, it was clear that the crowd was anything but polite. 'Tory scum' was one of the kinder barbs. Eggs and tomatoes were among the objects thrown and her blue business suit and elegantly groomed blonde hair were soon streaked with red, yellow and brown. One man, his face contorted with rage, spat in her face. The police presence had been swept aside and she was largely on her own.

Nothing in her previous experience had exposed her to angry crowds and personal abuse. She was well aware that her government and party weren't universally liked but to meet hatred face to face was new. She realised with hindsight that a streetwise and courageous politician would have seized the moment, demanded to address the crowd and bravely defended free speech in the hope that posterity – and the evening news – would witness her courage under fire. But she was shaking like a leaf and thought only of reaching the safety of the entrance, which, with the help of the outnumbered policemen and a few other helping hands, she eventually managed.

By the time she had calmed down and cleaned up there was no time and little appetite for the formal business. A hastily convened meeting with Calum did not advance far beyond acrimonious exchanges about the security failure. The Minister's aides were beginning to panic over the media impact. The first images were appearing on YouTube. Twitter was trending at vertiginous rates. The TV camera intended for a tame pooled clip had captured enough to be running on the news channels. Something needed to be done.

Frantic calls back to the No. 10 press room produced confused reactions: yes, the Minister needs to be out there calming the storm and being the voice of authority; but, no, we don't want to advertise a security screw-up; we don't want speculation about what Pulsar is doing; and we don't want to advertise the fact that the black flag of ISIL has spread from Raqqa and Mosul to the streets of an English town (the holding line was that these were British anarchists). After some bad-tempered exchanges, Kate was pushed in front of the camera to address one question with a bland answer.

'A new and challenging experience for me. But we live in a free country. Critics of government have to have their say. There are some people who believe in unilateral disarmament, who don't seem to care about the British jobs that go with having a defence industry. They are entitled to their point of view but the government won't change its policy. Thank you. No more questions.'

By then the police riot teams had arrived. But too late. The crowd had already dispersed. The Minister was able to leave with more dignity than when she arrived.

The post-mortems began immediately. Calum sat with his head in his hands in the boardroom. 'Shit; shit; shit. I never wanted this fucking visit. Fucking politicians. Trouble. Now we shall be like those animal experiment people: hounded from pillar to post by single issue fanatics.'

'I don't think it's that bad,' interjected Justin Starling, the head of security. 'A one-off. Nobody mentioned the Indian contract, thank God. We can get on with business as usual.'

'I am not so sure. What troubles me is that the protesters knew exactly what was happening and when. They got under the radar. They must have an inside source.'

<hr>

Back at the department, Kate was rushed into a meeting with the Secretary of State and a number of officials responsible for the visit planning, security and media who looked as if they were preparing themselves for a public execution.

When the group had assembled, Jim Chambers paused for effect, watching the officials visibly shrink into their chairs. 'So, what the fuck was that all about? Which idiot told the local police that this was just a nice, informal, low-key visit that didn't merit any extra security? Who was the clown who managed the media operation that made our Minister a laughing stock – through no fault of her own? Absolute bloody mess. We've got the PM lined up to sign an important arms contract of which this is a key part. His people are on the phone to me asking what the hell is going on. *Grip*. The PM's favourite word. He wants to know that we are *gripping* the situation. What do we know about this company? Security?'

There was a bit more bluster from the Secretary of State and a few pointed references to the Overheads. But he had achieved his objective: to reassure Kate; to shake up the officials from their culture of buck-passing and complacency; and to be able to report back to the PM that he was, indeed, *gripping* the situation.

The main post-mortem took place shortly afterwards in the COBRA meeting room below the Cabinet Office. The PM had pulled in the heads of SIS and MI5, the Metropolitan Police Commissioner to speak for the Counter Terrorism Command, the National Security Adviser and the Secretaries of State for Defence and Business, with the High Commissioner participating via Skype from Delhi. The PM was at his best in these emergencies and opened the discussion with quiet authority.

'I want to be reassured that we are still on track for this defence contract. Pulsar is a part of a much bigger picture. Until this demo at the Pulsar plant everything seemed to be under control. I can't overestimate how important it is. Potentially billions in new work. Thousands of jobs across the UK. And crucial for us and the Americans in our efforts to get closer to the Indians.

'We don't talk much about it, but we all know that the biggest threat of nuclear war comes from the subcontinent. We have done the war games. You will have seen some of the reports on the wires in the last few days. Sabre rattling, almost certainly, but these are nuclear powers with a history of real conflict. President Trump and I are agreed that we must help India acquire the capacity to intercept a first strike. Israel is kitted out. So is NATO. India has to be.

'Yet the key technology is in a small British company run by a maverick Scottish socialist: a technological genius and a successful hustler in the funding markets, granted, but a shambolic manager who runs an operation that leaks like a rusting ship. Am I right? What do we do about it? Chief?'

The head of MI5 spoke for the domestic security services. 'We have been giving the place a thorough going over. Perhaps we should have done so sooner. The position is this. There have been the usual attempted cyber-attacks from China and Russia that all our defence subcontractors get. But the firm has the know-how to deal with them. And the bad guys don't seem to have twigged how important the company is.

'So far so good. But there are these reported break-ins. And we have established that someone has successfully hacked into some of the technical material. We suspect it is an inside job by someone who knows their way around.

We don't yet know who or why, nor what they found—'

'But tell me,' the PM interrupted, 'how did the protesters know about Kate's visit? They seemed to have access to details of the visit planning.'

'Several possibilities including loose talk by someone in the know – a departmental official, a journo, one of Pulsar's management team. We did discover that a key figure in the firm – the top union official, trusted by the CEO – is a local Labour councillor who has recently been meeting Muslim militants.'

'You must be joking!'

'No, Prime Minister. This man – Steve Grant – has met a group a couple of times that includes one of the extremists we have been keeping an eye on. That may be how the Muslim, anti-Indian, activists found out. There are also quite a number of Muslims of Pakistani origin in the factory, mostly Kashmiri, though all those in sensitive jobs have been carefully vetted, and none are known to be radical. And we still have to explain how the anti-arms trade people got their information.'

At this point the National Security Adviser, who had remained silent hitherto, interjected. 'There is another, delicate, matter that I need to mention within the strict confines of this room. We discovered that the Minister, Mrs Thompson, is having an affair with the CEO of Pulsar's Indian collaborator. When he was in London, shortly before the Minister's factory visit, she was tailed to his hotel and left the following morning. There appears to be an ongoing relationship. They try to be discreet but there is clearly an element of risk.'

'I have already been briefed on this of course,' the PM replied. 'And I am the last person to want to lecture my colleagues on personal morality. I just hope she knows what she is doing. I had hoped this issue wouldn't come up, but everyone here should know that this is another complication we don't need.'

The High Commissioner rushed in with reassurance. 'I wouldn't worry about Deepak Parrikar. Got to know him quite well. Good man. Totally straight and on side.'

The National Security Adviser agreed. 'Frankly, I am more confident about the Indian side of this operation than our own.'

In his summary the PM was able to be reassuring. 'The good news is that our media haven't cottoned on to the strategic issues. They just loved the idea of a Tory minister being pelted with eggs and tomatoes and haven't got beyond that. Our American friends haven't picked up that we have a problem. The Indian operation seems to be under control. But, obviously, we need tighter surveillance and careful management at this end. So, we proceed? Any objection? No? Thank you.'

Steve was shaken to the core when, next day, he saw the front of the *Herald*, a friendly local paper that he had slavishly provided with press releases ever since his election to the council. His full-on mugshot, making him look like a convict preparing for life in prison, appeared alongside that of a bearded militant waving a black flag. The front page had another picture – the selfie – showing him grinning among his Muslim friends. The headline, 'Local Labour Man Link to Bombers', was followed up by the 'sensational' revelation that he had held 'clandestine' meetings with local 'extremists' and is believed ('according to well-informed sources') to have 'played a key role' in managing the demonstration.

He knew he had to get to Calum quickly. His position at the factory, years of close working and trust, would be destroyed if it were believed he had put his firm's future, and workers' jobs, at risk by an act of disloyalty. When he arrived at the factory he could feel the chill. Eyes were averted. There were no greetings. He could see Shaida in her glass office huddled over her PC, while her support staff were uncharacteristically silent. Calum had the newspaper in front of him. There was also a stranger in the corner of the room who didn't introduce himself. Calum broke the ice.

'You will be pleased to hear that I don't believe what I read in newspapers. Muckrakers. But I want to know what this is all about, as does our friend here from the Spooks,' he said, pointing to the silent man.

Steve had already prepared his defence. 'I did meet a few local Muslim students. But that doesn't make them terrorists or me a sympathiser. I try to talk to all sections of the community. But the leak – absolutely not me. Nor have I said a word to them or anyone else about the confidential stuff we do here.'

Calum was easily reassured. 'I have never had any reason to doubt your loyalty to the company. I must believe what you tell me.'

The man from the security services was less easily reassured. 'If the leak wasn't from you, who do you think it was?' he asked.

'No idea.'

'Well, I do have some ideas. One possible lead is that one of the local militants, who has been on our radar for some time, was at your meeting. He happens to be the son of one of your union colleagues, a Mr Ashgar Khan, and brother of a young woman who is the chief finance officer whom I believe you also know. Could it have been them?'

'No, I don't believe it,' Steve retorted. 'They are totally loyal, honest people who would never have got embroiled in an extremist movement. I know about the son and they worry about him. But anyway, none of them had the inside knowledge to set up that demonstration.'

'So, we come back to you. You did have the knowledge. You met some of the troublemakers. All we lack is a motive. What I need from you is a detailed account of your meetings. Who was there? Who chose the participants? Who organised the events?'

So far Steve had managed to avoid mentioning Shaida and, as he saw the net closing fast, he judged silence to be the safest recourse.

'I note your silence. As it happens you don't need to implicate your – friend – Ms Khan as she came to us first thing this morning when she heard about the press story. She admitted that she set up the meetings. Like you, she denied any wrongdoing. I am inclined to believe both of you. The story of Islamic fanatics causing trouble and being abetted by soft-headed politicians is just a little too convenient. But I am recommending to the company' – he glanced at Calum whose expression betrayed total confusion and powerlessness – 'and I am sure the chief executive will agree, that you and she should be suspended pending a fuller investigation – though of course this is not my company. It may well be in your interests not to see your workmates for a while; I imagine the mood on the shop floor won't be too friendly. And if someone else is at the heart of this, it may be helpful to give him or her the impression that you are in the frame. Let's leave it there. Here is my card if you have anything else useful to tell me.'

Calum shrugged his shoulders. 'Sorry, laddie. I am sure we will be able to sort this out.'

As the conversation drew to a close Steve realised this was an opportunity to get off his chest the uncomfortably heavy weight of confidences shared. He turned to the man from MI5 – Liam, according to his card – who hadn't volunteered any information on his precise role, and said:

'I don't know if this is of any relevance to your enquiries or who exactly I should speak to. But I was told various things in confidence several days ago about some of the Muslim activists in the town.'

'Go on, I am interested.'

Steve then passed on what he had been told about Mo and the group and described the episode with the preacher at the mosque entrance. He was desperate to avoid having to admit that Shaida and her father had any knowledge of the matter, which made it appear that he had acquired the information through divine revelation.

Calum interjected: 'Stop messing about, laddie. He's got a soft spot for this young woman who heads up our accounts department. That's how he knows about this stuff,' he added in case Liam hadn't already worked this out.

'Why didn't you tell us sooner?' Liam responded. 'I would have thought someone in your position would have gone straight to a senior police officer and asked for help and advice. No matter, you were trying to protect the young woman who, I have to say, appears totally professional and uncompromised. As it happens this is not new information. I obviously can't tell you all that much. But we now know quite a lot about the local radicals. When whole families went off to Syria we knew we had a serious problem here and have been keeping tabs on worrying individuals. Ms Khan's brother Mo is just a confused and angry young man. In our view he isn't – yet – committed enough to do anything really dangerous.

Such people become a genuine concern if they fall under the sway of a powerful personality. A potential terrorist? Not really. Strapping on a suicide vest or planting a bomb requires a higher degree of motivation and organisation than he or his close friends currently have. Sounding off about the "jihad" or watching nasty videos is a real cause for alarm, and makes them potential recruits. But they are a step away from actually doing something evil.'

'Well, that's a relief. I realise I should have talked to you earlier. Sorry. But it appears no harm has been done.'

'Actually, you may have helped us – unintentionally. We have been studying the pictures taken by your friends, particularly the group photos after your mosque visit.' Liam removed a set of enlarged photographs from his briefcase.

'Look carefully at this face here. It is blurred and indistinct. He was turning away and seemingly didn't want to be caught on camera.'

Steve picked up the image and studied it. 'He looks familiar. But he didn't say anything at the meeting. I didn't really register his presence.'

'That's the point. He operates in the background. But, if it is who we think it is, we are very concerned. The name is Tariq, Tariq Ahmed. Born in Birmingham, various aliases. Became committed to the cause and terrorist methods in his late teens. We believe he has been in Iraq and Syria. He recruits. He's an organiser. Careful not to blow himself up. There are "useful fools" who can be persuaded to do that. In fact, we believe he leads a breakaway group, a mutation of ISIL, which doesn't support indiscriminate killing – for tactical rather than humanitarian reasons. Rather, he believes in targeted assassination – we think he organised the killing of that Egyptian general in London recently – and attacks on symbolically important sites, like the raid last year on the drone manufacturing plant in Lancashire that set back production for months. We think he's planning a political spectacular. He is very persuasive. Your friend Mo is the kind of impressionable young man who may be sucked into joining him.

'We want Tariq Ahmed badly. But he is elusive and doesn't leave incriminating traces. Where you can help us is trying to get your friends to talk about him: where he is, what he is doing. If at all possible, get him to one of your meetings and we can put a tail on him. No heroics needed.

'As for the preacher man – he is just a nuisance, absorbing a lot of police time and resources. But always very careful to stay inside the law. Like a fast downhill skier, he knows how to stay upright. And if he falls, there are expensive lawyers in the background who will help him to his feet. Frankly, we believe the community should take responsibility for policing people like that.'

Steve started to take stock of what he was getting into. He had been in a room with a dangerous jihadist and was now being asked to help track him down. He reflected wryly on the elusive Shaida whom he had followed into this quagmire: the reward, so far, one peck on the cheek.

'Obviously I will do what I can to help,' he told Liam, 'though I doubt it's much. Quite honestly, this is a very different world from the one I'm used to.'

For the first time Liam showed a flash of anger and Steve focused properly on this figure in the corner. Unexceptional in appearance and informally dressed, he could have been a secondary school teacher with tie askew and a well-worn jumper under his jacket. His voice rose several decibels, opening up his Brummie intonation.

'You are bloody right that you are going to help us. I would say you have an obligation to help. This is as much your responsibility as mine. You chose to get involved in the politics in this town and – as you are discovering – you can't just float above it. Actions have consequences. When we see and hear evil we have to act.'

Steve was too pulverised by the events of the last few days to think of any riposte beyond mute acknowledgement.

───────

In Mumbai, the *Bharat Bombay* investigative team received warm praise and hints of promotion from the editor for their latest splash: 'Revenge', an exclusive story based around the discovery of the body of one of the Patel killers, accompanied by a gruesome photograph of the bullet-ridden corpse that didn't leave anything to the reader's imagination. *Bharat Bombay* had now followed up the story with a weightier piece: 'Business Empire in Trouble', linking the killing – at one remove – to the Parrikar family company.

The editor swallowed hard before relegating a salacious story about Miss India to accommodate a business scandal. Although his instinct was always to avoid trouble and to give pretty girls priority over price/earnings ratios, the editor had had the Parrikars in his sights for some time. His cynical, knowing mind was irritated by the new, fashionable image of the Parrikar companies and the debonair Deepak. The editor had been around long enough to have heard most of the gossip about Parrikar Senior's exploits and knew that The Caring Corporation rested on the foundations of the less-than-caring Mumbai property business. He also knew that the best time to kick a man was when he was down and the stream of stories about the weakening grip of the Parrikars provided a safe base from which to attack. Now, thanks to his impressive young team and his squad of sleuths, there was a story and two suggestive, but usable, photos of an infamous mafia don arriving at Parrikar Senior's office and Parrikar Junior embracing an attractive female British VIP at the company's guest house. There would be no comeback. The Parrikars didn't advertise with his newspaper. And any recourse to Indian libel laws would now run into hard fact. Anyway, the courts system was bogged down in cases decades old and held few real terrors.

The editor was not the only person to see the potential

of the story. Jimmy Anderson had eked out a living as a foreign correspondent in India for many years ferreting out titbits from the Indian popular press. His translation skills and eye for a good story ensured that he was able to finance a comfortable lifestyle, at the bottom of the journalistic food chain, looking for morsels passed over by loftier members of his profession. As he made his way through the day's collection of newspapers in half a dozen vernacular languages, he spotted the *Bharat Bombay* story. It didn't take long to register that the picture of the British Minister might be of some interest in London. Within an hour he had a translation of the story and a scanned picture on their way to the political editor of the *Mail on Sunday*.

CHAPTER 10

THE SCANDAL

Press release from the Ministry of Information, Government of Pakistan, 10 July 2019:

The Pakistani government officially welcomed a visit from Prince Abdullah Al-Saud, a close associate of the Crown Prince, to discuss closer cooperation between their intelligence agencies and training for Pakistan volunteers who were fighting against anti-Islamic forces in the Middle East. He visited a battalion that had acquitted itself with distinction in the fighting against 'atheists and apostates' in the Syrian civil war. He denied claims in India that the volunteers were also being infiltrated into Kashmir in preparation for a new guerrilla offensive and terrorist attacks on Indian cities. Commenting on reports of military incidents along the Indo-Pakistan border the

spokesman quoted the Defence Minister as saying:
'Pakistan is not afraid. We are not looking for a fight but
Pakistan should not be underestimated. We have battle
ready warheads. God forbid there is to be conflict but, if
it happens, it will be, for us, a jihad.'

After the drama of the factory visit, Kate opted for a
quiet weekend at home – reacquainting herself with her
daughters and husband.

'Mum, are you OK?' enquired Tilly, the youngest, over
breakfast before pony club demanded her attention. 'We
saw that demo on YouTube. It was awful. That horrible
man who threw things at you. Those men with beards
shouting and screaming. Have they been arrested? We
thought you were really brave.'

'It's the job. We can't be liked by everyone. I wasn't
brave actually. I was quite frightened but I'm OK now.'
She turned to Penny, her middle daughter. 'Your dad tells
me that there has been some bullying at school. Penny?'

The girl burst into tears. 'You're never here. I wanted to
talk to you about it. A really horrid girl was talking about
you – said the government was full of bad, greedy people
and you were one of them. That you had taken money
from her family. And now they couldn't afford a holiday.
She screamed at me. When I argued back the teacher told
us both off.'

'I'm so sorry, darling. But you stood up for me. I am proud of you.' She gave Penny a big hug but a spasm of fear jolted through her that these girls, passing through adolescence, unsure of themselves and needing her, were becoming strangers. Being a minister of the crown was all absorbing. And now there was Deepak.

Jonathan had left early for a Saturday morning round of golf with some clients from Singapore who were placing a lot of money in the central London property market and particularly liked Jonathan's tasteful conversions. She was inwardly relieved not to have to try to act normal in his presence. She could take refuge in her ministerial box for the rest of the day and in the evening there was a dinner party: his friends rather than hers. She looked forward to it, as she would be able to hide her feelings in the hubbub of polite conversation. She was, however, dreading the return home as Jonathan was usually amorous after a few drinks and a night out. Excuses would be needed.

In the event the excuses weren't required. At 10pm, as the dinner party was starting to warm up, a light flashed on her mobile – a text: 'Emergency, ring immediately. Susan.' Kate's private secretary knew not to disturb her unless there was a real emergency, so she slipped quietly outside to return the call, full of trepidation.

'A crisis, Kate, brace yourself. I have just seen tomorrow's headlines. You are on the front page of the *Mail on Sunday* with that dishy man you went out with in Mumbai.' Hearing no reply, Susan pressed on. 'Actually, the story is pretty thin and the picture is blurred. But you won't like the headline – "Bonking for Britain". Someone, goodness knows who, has said that you were out for the night. Then, inside, there is a big feature with pictures of the family and your "betrayed" husband with an unnamed "friend" expressing incredulity that you have double-crossed such an amazing hunk of manhood. The editorial is ghastly: "Minister travelling the world at tax-payers' expense… jobs at stake… PM to blame for packing the government with under-qualified women in the interests of political correctness".'

Kate was too numb to reply. Eventually she asked, plaintively: 'What do I do now?'

'Turn off your mobile. Talk to your family before they hear about tomorrow's papers. I imagine the Secretary of State, possibly the PM, will want to speak to you in the morning. I will talk to the press office about a statement… "Minister has no comment to make on press gossip. The PM has complete confidence in her", that sort of thing. We will brief out that you are fully focused on your job, building on the success of the Mumbai visit.

'One more thing. A little bird told me that you saw Deepak, privately, when he was in London. The press don't have that. Let's hope they won't find out. Hopefully this is a one-off. Next week's chip paper.'

Kate regarded this last sally as scant consolation. She thought she had covered her tracks carefully, but she was beginning, belatedly, to understand the meaning of the phrase 'being in the public eye'. Paranoia competed with shock, embarrassment, fear and confusion. She feared above all for the impact on the girls. But the hopes she had built up for the new man in her life could also now be dashed. She thought of herself as a confident and competent person, but this was something new, and outside of her comfort zone in every way.

She somehow stumbled through the rest of the evening and there was some calming, easy-listening music on the car radio so that she didn't have to make conversation with Jonathan on the way home. When they arrived back, she sat down in the living room and said: 'Can we talk for a few minutes?' She told the story as coherently as she could. She reminded him how close they had been to disaster over a decade ago when she had learnt of his string of affairs and had retaliated. But now she had broken the golden rule: don't get caught. 'Sorry… what else can I say?'

He normally managed to sustain his urbane charm even in the most awkward situations. But he responded with a long, angry silence. He didn't do shouting, let alone domestic violence. His weapon of choice was non-communication. Eventually she could bear it no longer, and said: 'So what do you want me to do? Leave? Pack my bags?'

After another long silence he replied, very quietly: 'If you want to run, that is up to you. I wouldn't advise it. I assume you value your relationship with the girls, if not with me. I am not a saint, as you have just reminded me. But we seemed to have a marriage that worked. The problem this time is that, through your carelessness, we have become public property. I will have to run the gauntlet of supercilious bastards at the office, the golf club, the gym. I guess you have the bigger problem. I hope you have good media advisers. Tell me one thing: I take it you don't actually love this Indian guy?'

'That's the problem, I think I do.'

'You think! *I* think you need to make up your bloody mind.'

There was nothing more to add. He went up to one of the spare bedrooms. No backward glance. No banged door. She knew he would settle into an Ice Man routine for days, even weeks. There would be polite greetings: 'Yes, darling; no, darling.' Forced conversations. The ball would be entirely in her court. To stay or leave. Anxious children: 'Ask your mother.' Queries from friends, relatives: 'Everything is fine. Speak to Kate.'

She felt terribly alone. She would have to tell the girls in the morning. They would need reassuring that Mummy and Daddy weren't going to break up and abandon them. Yet that seemed a likely destination.

She couldn't sleep. When she finally dozed off as dawn was breaking, she was roused by noises outside: a car door slamming, voices, scraping, the crunching of the gravel drive. Opening the curtains to investigate she saw a young peroxide blonde woman in her drive setting up a camera tripod. One van was parked at the drive entrance and another, with a satellite receiver on top, was pulling up. Then she saw a head appearing above the garden hedge followed by a long-range camera, aimed at her. She hastily withdrew and returned to bed, shaking with a mixture of anger and fear.

Half an hour later, there was a loud knock on the door. It was just after 6.30am. She waited. The knocking continued. Soon her daughters would go down to see what was going on. So she hastily dressed and went down and opened the door. There was the young woman with a man carrying a portable TV camera just behind her: 'Good morning, Mrs Thompson. I am from Sky. Do you have any comments on the *Mail* story? Do you plan to resign?'

She felt a surge of rage, a need to release the bottled-up emotions of the last few hours; indeed the last week. 'How dare you!' she shot back. 'Get out of my garden or I will call the police.' She slammed the door. The journalists stayed put and when they knocked again, very loudly, Kate opened up to avoid waking the house.

The female reporter looked about sixteen but she had the condescending manner of a matriarch offering to help a confused adolescent in distress. 'I appreciate that we are disturbing your domestic life, Mrs Thompson. But you are a big story – coming after the factory demonstration. Either we hang around and make a nuisance of ourselves, and wake the neighbours, or you cooperate by giving me a clip that we can use during the day and we go away. I suggest that you cooperate. Why don't you put on something smarter and we will rendezvous with you on your lawn in a few minutes?'

Kate did as she was told. And she returned to the camera team prepared for the interview. She looked back at the house. She saw three puzzled young faces glued to a bedroom window. 'Minister, would you like to comment on the press story this morning?' the journalist began.

'No, I have nothing to say. I am getting on with my job in government.'

'Can you tell me something about the man in the photo?'

'He is the CEO of Parrikar Avionics – he will, I am sure, be making a statement in Mumbai.'

'Are you in touch with him?'

'No.'

'Do you plan to resign?'

'No. As long as I have the confidence of the PM I shall remain in government. That's all. Thank you.'

As good as their word, the camera crews left. But she saw that the paparazzi were still there waiting to capture anyone moving inside and outside the house. She would have to go back and explain things to her daughters.

At 8am the Secretary of State rang. 'Sorry to hear your news, old girl. Bloody reptiles. Pity we can't shoot them. I've been there myself, more than once. Just spoken to the PM. He agrees with me that, while this is a bloody mess, you haven't done anything illegal or broken the ministerial code. Saw your clip. Well done. Didn't drop any balls. Continue to stand your ground. No nonsense about resignation. We will come in behind you and the PM will be very robust on Marr at 9.30.'

As the morning wore on she felt more and more like a trapped animal: fearful about what was to come next. The girls had brought her a cup of tea and given her a hug but she didn't know what to say to them nor they to her. Then her friends called, reassuring her but furious that she hadn't shared her secret. 'Seems a very handsome man but you might have told us!' 'I bet Jonathan hit the roof. But how are the girls taking it?' 'Darling, you are a star! Top item in the news, two weeks in succession.'

She realised that she should ring India. Deepak's mobile was off, so she tried the home number he'd given her for an emergency. A woman answered, in English, with an educated Indian accent, so Kate mumbled: 'Sorry, wrong number.' Half an hour later Deepak rang back.

'I've heard about the media storm in the UK,' he told her. 'It's on the BBC website. No one here has really picked up on the picture. My wife made some comment about "your British crumpet" and I asked, in a friendly way, about her Bengali novelist. We both laughed. Seemingly, no harm done.

'The problem is my father. A really scurrilous hatchet job by one of the local papers. A lot of lies and innuendo. But they have made the connection between Dad and a serious mafioso: killer, kidnapper, general hoodlum, a Muslim with family links to Pakistani-backed terrorists – though the police have never laid a finger on him. Dad knew him years back. Did some business together. One of our good people, a project manager in Mumbai, was murdered recently and the press are suggesting that there is some gangland feud and implicating my father. He has never been under public attack like this before. He is in a really bad way. Look, when will we see each other again?'

'Soon I hope,' she replied.

'But let the storm die down first,' Deepak suggested.

Kate realised as she ended the call that she had developed a strong emotional bond with this man five thousand miles away, in marked contrast to the stranger in the next room who was making his late breakfast, humming with affected unconcern.

⸙⸙⸙⸙⸙⸙⸙⸙⸙⸙⸙

To avoid stares on the train the following morning, her private office had organised a ministerial car. When she entered the department there was the usual 'Good morning, Minister'. But no one engaged her eyes. And when she reached the ministerial office there was a big bunch of flowers from her private office staff. She threw her arms around Susan and then her deputy and felt a deep pang of gratitude to the team she had appointed.

The respite didn't last long. A message came through from the whip's office that the Speaker had allowed an Urgent Question from the opposition on Anglo-Indian relations.

The question was clearly designed to make mischief. The fact that the Speaker had allowed it owed more to the deep animosity between the Speaker and the Prime Minister than to any real urgency. The Secretary of State would field the question and her job was to sit next to him looking calm, dignified, and deeply interested in the bilateral trade balance.

The opposition spokesman was a boring man with little sense of occasion who specialised in reading out, verbatim, notes written for him by a researcher. His impersonation of a man reading a telephone directory in a dull, humourless monotone, however, merely highlighted a series of unintended double-entendres referring to the 'penetration of our market', the 'climax of our recent exchanges' and 'growing intercourse between our two countries'. The schoolboy tittering on the back benches gradually swelled to a crescendo of hysterical laughter while the spokesman ploughed on oblivious and Kate, who had always blushed, turned deeper crimson as her humiliation grew. She was no longer listening when the Secretary of State rose to his feet, easily dealt with the opposition's feeble question and calmly swatted aside others from the back benches.

Towards the end of the session, however, the Speaker called an Asian MP who had earned the nickname the Member for Islamabad East and rarely ventured into unfamiliar territory, like British politics. He read out a question, which he stumbled over and which had clearly been written for him.

'Can the Secretary of State tell the House if he has issued an export licence for missile related technology to India, for the company Pulsar?'

Jim Chambers hesitated for an agonisingly long time and then replied: 'I will have to look into the matter and reply in writing to the Honourable Gentleman.'

At the end of the session the MP stood up again on a Point of Order and said: 'The Secretary of State has refused to answer my question about the way the government is recklessly fuelling the arms race on the subcontinent. We have all heard the news stories that relations on the subcontinent are very tense. I demand a debate on the issue.'

'The Honourable Member,' replied the Speaker, 'is not making a Point of Order, as he well knows. But he has made his point, which will, I am sure, be noted.'

As indeed it was, by several listening journalists who had already made the connection with the recent demonstration. Near panic descended on the department's officials and the Secretary of State who could see their project unravelling. Kate's love life was forgotten, for the moment.

<hr/>

In Islamabad General Rashid, head of Inter-Services Intelligence, was summoned to a meeting with the Prime Minister, the Defence Minister and the military High Command. The Prime Minister sought advice on how he could respond to growing public unrest over the government's lack of response to 'Indian provocation' and, more generally, to show that, as the world's militarily strongest Islamic country, Pakistan would not let its co-religionists be 'systematically humiliated'. A decision was taken in principle to carry out an underground test of the most powerful weapon yet developed by Pakistan – with Chinese assistance. It would have the capacity to obliterate Mumbai or Delhi. The decision would be reviewed after a month in the light of international developments. General Rashid was also asked to prepare an urgent note on 'robust' options involving covert special operations.

※※※※※※※※※※※※※※※

Ganesh Parrikar had aged a decade in twenty-four hours. He had spent his business life mostly in the shadows and was close to completing his life's work: transferring a profitable but ethically dubious business empire to his family who would build a recognised, respected brand in mainstream business across India and overseas. He had, of course, worried in the past that the rumours around his business activity might be given oxygen by the press, but whenever a scandal threatened, he had had warning, and a few telephone calls, from lawyers to editors and advertisers, sufficed to close it down. This time, he had had no warning. His enemies, and the press, no longer feared him. His vulnerability was painfully apparent.

When he saw Deepak he broke down and sobbed. Deepak had never seen his father in this self-pitying state.

And, as in most Indian father–son relationships, there was a reserve, a deference of the young to the old. He didn't know what to say or how to help; he could only try to reassure him.

'Daddy-ji, that picture was nothing. It just showed that man entering your office, nothing more.'

'No, son. My reputation is now ruined. Respect has gone. What I am now is some tin-pot hoodlum.'

'Daddy-ji, I have a suggestion. You told me about your plans for a charitable trust. Apart from the Tatas, and Azim Premji at Wipro, our big business tycoons have splashed their money on lavish weddings, jewellery, gold statues and mansions. You have a vision for helping the poor. Get the press people together. Tell them what you are doing and plan to do.'

'A press conference? No idea what to do. Can you do it for me?' Deepak saw that his talent for PR and the reputation management of modern business was now needed to rescue his father. A pity the Parrikar clan hadn't gone down this road sooner.

<hr/>

After a few days, the storm in London was starting to die down. Press coverage petered out. Kate remembered the phrase about next week's chip paper. But her relationships were not so easily disposed of. She escaped tension at home by staying at her London flat, with regular calls to the girls who were confused and distressed. She sought reassurance from Deepak and, while it was clear that her feelings were reciprocated, her lover was increasingly preoccupied by his father's psychological fragility.

Then she was called in by the Prime Minister. He was in his small study next to the Cabinet Room: a cosy billet with thick carpets and settees, and a desk covered with family photos. In this misleadingly informal setting many of the key decisions affecting the country were made. When Kate entered, the grim faces of the PM, the Secretary of State and the Cabinet Secretary told her that this was likely to be a difficult meeting. The PM spoke first.

'We have a problem, Kate. Our American friends, who were going to supply the Indians with a lot of expensive kit alongside ours, are getting very nervous about this Indian deal. The President doesn't major on subtlety as you know, but he is concerned that premature disclosure could jeopardise the big plans he and his business friends have for building up an alliance with India. To cut a long story short, they are thinking of pulling out, or at least putting it on the back burner. They are very worried about the UK end of things. This company, Pulsar, seems to leak like a sieve; erratic management; an ethnically diverse – that is, Muslim – labour force; demonstrations. You know the story. Then this question in parliament that suggests that the Pakistanis grasp the significance of what is going on. Problems at the other end too. The Indian partner has had a bad press – the old man who controls the family business has been involved in some unsavoury, gangland nonsense.

'The big picture is that we and the Americans want to work with India but we don't want to burn our bridges with the Pakistani military who are important in stabilising Afghanistan, holding down the Taliban and helping with counter-terrorism. And you will have seen that there has been an escalation of military tension on the Indo-Pak border. Our assessment is that a lot of this is just rhetoric, but these countries have fought three wars already and almost fought a nuclear war not too long ago. So the advice is: kick the ball into the long grass.'

The PM was orating from his armchair, his gaze directed at the ceiling. But when it came to the difficult part of the conversation he twitched nervously, paused for an uncomfortable period and forced himself to look vaguely in Kate's direction.

'This brings us to you. You have been unlucky. But if we get into a story of cancelled contracts and lost jobs, the *Mail* and the *Sun* will have you in their sights. My suggestion is that you leave the government quietly, now, before you are chased out. You can sort out your family issues. I will pay warm tributes. The chief whip will find you something important-sounding to do on the back benches; or perhaps in the whip's office. Then, the summer recess is coming up; you can disappear for a month or so. Sorry, Kate. Politics is a cruel business.'

She left the room mumbling 'thank you'. No one else spoke a word.

✕✕✕✕✕✕✕✕✕✕✕✕✕

Kate walked back to her department through the rear entrance of Downing Street onto Horse Guards Parade. As the military personnel relaxed their grip on their submachine guns to let her through the iron gate, she attracted a friendlier grin and more rapid attention than, she suspected, her male colleagues would have done. She savoured the moment since there wouldn't be many more. She recalled the phrase about 'fifteen minutes of fame'; her fifteen minutes was up and in political equivalents it had been shorter than that. It hadn't quite been the shortest ministerial career on record but she was definitely in contention.

Up past the Treasury, down Storey's Gate and along to her department to say goodbye. Susan had been told – and when they met a few tears were shed. They hadn't worked together long but strong feelings of mutual respect and affection had developed. They sat down to exchange contact details and promises of lunch to catch up on gossip and go over the messy formalities of her departure (she smiled at the fact that, while she was there, staff from the government's art collection were moving in her choice of paintings to replace the ghastly Victorian horror).

As she was about to leave, Susan hesitated but then said: 'There are a few things I haven't troubled you with but I want you to know. I am not sure I should be telling you, but, technically, until the official announcement this afternoon, you are still our Minister.'

Kate managed to raise a smile. 'Go ahead. I'm all ears.'

'A few days ago Caroline, the Secretary of State's principal private secretary, called me in for a chat. Caroline is pure gold, a brilliant civil servant and utterly loyal to her boss. But she is a stickler for process. Would never allow anything to pass that isn't absolutely kosher. She was quite upset.

'Long story. I won't give you all the details but it concerns the export licences that are needed for Pulsar's equipment, as part of this big deal. Licensing is a separate, semi-legal process distinct from the stuff you have been doing and the licences would normally be cleared by the dedicated team of officials and, if necessary, one of the other ministers. Questions were raised both here and in the Foreign Office about what the Pulsar equipment might be used for. At first sight, it is exactly what it seems to be: part of a defence system.'

Susan paused, looking around to check that no one was listening in before continuing.

'But our technical people point out that there are other potential applications of a less wholesome nature. Powerful electromagnetic pulses that can knock out electric controls over a wide area could be misused by the wrong people. Our people think that we may be at risk of contravening the Anti-Proliferation Treaty we are signed up to. The officials are, of course, very cautious. Remember Saddam Hussein's supergun? More recently the department was given a rollicking by a select committee for approving the sale of a consignment of window cleaning fluid for Syria. Turns out that the fluid contained chemicals that have nastier uses and there was enough of it to clean the windows of Damascus for several centuries. So they recommended refusal for Pulsar.'

Kate nodded. 'All this is consistent with those secret papers you showed me, so what is the issue?'

'The issue is the so-called Red Admiral. Apparently he stormed down to where the officials sit and started haranguing them. "Obstructive jobs-worths" was among the more repeatable epithets. Claimed to be speaking on behalf of the Secretary of State and for the PM at one remove. Completely out of order. A lot of us wonder what the Admiral is doing in the department anyway. He is a "consultant", not an official or even a "special adviser". He's attached to the MOD. But the Secretary of State gave him a room over the objections of Parsons, the permanent secretary. Parsons raised the whole issue of the Admiral with the Secretary of State but he brushed it aside. He got a lecture on "Overheads" not understanding the need for an entrepreneurial culture.'

'Maybe he is just an overenthusiastic trade ambassador for UK plc?' Kate suggested.

'That's what we all want to think. But what upsets Caroline is that this isn't the first episode of this kind. A few months ago there was a controversy over licences for some advanced communications equipment from a firm in Northern Ireland. For Russia. Had all kinds of applications, including strategic military uses. Post-sanctions an absolute no-no. But the Red Admiral waded in, going on about how an American company called Global had rescued the plant from closure, turned it round, saving hundreds of jobs in an unemployment black-spot. The equipment was totally harmless, he claimed, designed to improve the safety of civil aviation. Made a big fuss. The Irish peace process would be seriously damaged, etc. I don't know exactly what happened but somehow the licence was approved.'

'What am I to do with this information?'

'I don't really know,' Susan replied, 'but Caroline and I thought you had a right to know. We'll keep in touch.'

CHAPTER 11

THE INFORMER

Financial Times, London, 12 July 2019:

City analysts at Goldman Sachs have published an analysis of trends in the defence sector. They have highlighted the growing importance of a private US group called Global Analysis and Research which has entered the global top 10 by turnover for the first time. It has recently acquired several British SMEs in the sector and there have been rumours of takeover interest in others, including the Midlands-based company Pulsar.

News that the contract was being 'put on hold' came at a bad time for Calum. His mainly American investors, who normally made a virtue out of not interfering, were becoming restless. They had taken him on trust that he could manage a complex project outside the comfort zone of NATO contracts. India, like other emerging markets, was relatively high risk with unpredictable politics they didn't understand and a reputation for corruption that would test the patience of their lawyers, worrying about US and UK legislation on overseas bribery. But, so far, assurances about a 'clean' Indian partner and political backing from the relevant governments had kept doubts at bay. Now they were being told by their contacts in the State Department and the Pentagon that the high-ups were getting cold feet. Perhaps this contract, on the basis of which they had agreed to stump up substantial amounts of capital, wouldn't materialise.

During an urgently convened telephone conference of leading investors, the man from BlackRock confronted Calum directly: 'Your Plan B? We assume you have one.'

'My Plan B is making Plan A work. The contract is a win-win: jobs, strategic fit, good news all round.'

The riposte was strong: 'Unfortunately the politicos don't see it that way. They are running scared. Wishful thinking isn't good enough.'

'Well, if the project is put on hold I will have to lay off some of our people and just keep those I need to fulfil the existing contracts. We may have to lose five hundred or so. It may cause a strike, which is why the politicians over here will do what they can to keep the project afloat.'

One of the big institutional investors chipped in: 'To be frank, we would be more comfortable if you went ahead with restructuring plans. You have shown before that you can manage the workforce and sell them necessary downsizing. We try to keep out of your way but we have been scrutinising your cash flow and it doesn't look good without this contract. I have to think about the moms and pops whose money I look after. Sorry, but you know the score.'

There was a grunt of approval around the group, though no reaction from the newest investor, a group called Global Analysis and Research, which had acquired a significant stake in the last few weeks, buying out smaller holdings. Calum worried about them: a somewhat mysterious US-based group that had built up, rapidly, a portfolio of high tech supply chain companies, not unlike his own.

※※※※※※※※※※

A few minutes later he called Steve into his office. Steve was still at the company, albeit in a state of limbo as his suspension hadn't been formalised. Calum had shelved the issue, as was his habit with difficult personnel decisions.

He explained that he had just come off the phone from his leading investors, and that there was a problem. 'I have no choice but to lay off staff who aren't needed for ongoing work. There are some short-term contract workers but there will be redundancies. I need you to explain this, and sell it, to the workforce. You haven't covered yourself with glory over the demo, laddie, but now I need you. Stop the hot heads doing anything silly. Give them hope that we may be able to turn this round, if the workforce play ball. We did this together all those years ago.' Steve was unable to do more than mumble agreement.

<hr />

Steve wandered down to the canteen. Usually he was surrounded by friendly faces: his loyal committee of shop stewards; admirers who looked to him for political leadership or personal advice. Today there was a frosty silence. One exception was a man he knew to be a troublemaker, Brian Castle, who he suspected of having links to far-right groups. Today he was brandishing a tabloid that specialised in horror stories about asylum seekers and illegal immigrants, especially Muslims. 'See this, mate. Big story about our town. Teenage terrorists. Clerics trying to impose sharia law on the rest of us. Big families ripping off benefits. Maltreatment of women.'

So that Steve wouldn't miss the point Castle thrust the paper on the table in front of him jabbing his finger at the more inflammatory accusations, which were helpfully circled in biro. 'Your bloody fault,' he said. 'Your lot let 'em in. And this isn't Bradford; it's just down the road. You should be bloody ashamed of yourself.'

In normal circumstances Steve would have seized the opportunity to stamp his authority on the canteen; put Castle firmly in his place; reunite the workforce. Today he had nothing to say but just looked blankly in front of him.

Shaida, like Steve, was thoroughly disoriented by the events of the last few days. The walls of the carefully segregated compartments into which she divided her life were giving way. Her brother's troubles had invaded her professional life. And she'd let that happen because of a weakness for a man at work. She realised that she could have sent Steve packing but had, instead, found what seemed like a good way of developing their, so far platonic, relationship by involving her family. She acknowledged to herself that she wanted the friendship to deepen but had no idea how to make this happen in a way that wouldn't compound the disaster she had helped to create.

There was one consolation. Calum had made it clear that she was essential to preventing the company capsizing. With restive investors, he badly needed someone beside him who understood the numbers and could present them in the best possible light. Her job was safe.

Then she had a visitor to her office, Liam: 'just a routine security matter'. But it was more than that.

'Your brother. We have uncovered some uncomfortable information about him. Some compromising messages he sent that could lead to his facing anti-terrorism charges.'

'But you told me when I contacted you about that article that he wasn't a threat.'

'This is new material. I still think he is a bit player. But it isn't good. And the publicity will not be good for you and your family.'

'Are you threatening me?'

'No. This is a worst case scenario.'

'So. What is a better case scenario?'

'You help me.'

'I have already helped you.'

'I think I can help to get your brother off the hook. If you are willing to work with me.'

'Meaning?'

'You help me with information. In particular material from his computer. I know you are quite a whizz in that area. Something we have in common. You should be able to get access without being traced.'

'Blackmail in other words.'

'Call it what you like. I prefer to think you will help because it is right.'

'I detest these Islamic militants as much as you do. I know the way they treat women. But spying on my own people... and my brother... I can't do that.'

Liam could sense in her slight hesitation an opening.

'I don't normally talk about myself. The Service doesn't encourage it. But let me explain. My parents were Northern Ireland Republicans who settled in England. Armchair Provos who brought me up to hate the British state: Easter Rising; Bloody Sunday; Bobby Sands. All that stuff. As a student I was on the hard end of the hard left. Drifted into anarchist groups. Violent anti-globalisation protests. I got myself arrested throwing bricks at the police. Some of my group wanted to go further. Bombs. Not to kill people but to frighten the capitalist class. Unfortunately the class warriors were inept. A young woman, a passer-by, had her legs blown off by mistake. I was already rethinking my values and that tipped me over the edge. I went to the police. Grassed on them. Put my comrades behind bars. The Service saw potential in me. Poacher turned gamekeeper. Anyway, too much about me: the moral is that when we see and hear evil we have to act. I believe you understand that.'

Shaida said nothing and he took her silence as acquiescence. 'If you are with me there is a small task that you can help me with immediately. It involves your colleague Mr Grant who definitely owes us a bit of cooperation. I want you to ask Mo to pass on the message that Steve is very keen to meet the same group again at the mosque, and others, especially those of a more jihadist bent. It is just possible that we may get a lead to one of our targets who we know to be active in the town. He has been in touch with your brother and attended one of the meetings. Can you help set that up?'

Ganesh Parrikar received a message brought by hand to the servants' quarters at his home late in the evening before he retired. It was a request from the Sheikh, dictated to a trusted intermediary, for an urgent visit to an exclusive private hospital where he lay seriously ill following a heart attack. The Sheikh might not have long to live. He needed to talk. If Parrikar followed the enclosed instructions his visit would be strictly private except for the Sheikh's immediate family, currently gathered at the hospital.

He hesitated. His old associate had betrayed and blackmailed him, organised the killing of one of his employees. Now he wanted some comfort before he met his maker. But the tone of the message contained a hint of desperation. Perhaps there was something Parrikar did not know. He summoned his driver and headed to the hospital, entering as instructed by a back entrance and reaching a floor at the top of the building by a service lift. He discreetly entered an ante-room to where the Sheikh lay. His wife and daughter were weeping silently and when Parrikar entered they rose to greet him, mumbling their thanks. The shrunken old woman with the grief-stricken face was barely recognisable from her beautiful and self-confident self of a generation ago when the Parrikars had given the family refuge. Her daughter had been a child then.

When Parrikar was ushered in to the Sheikh he saw first the panoramic view of Mumbai by night and then the inert figure on the bed fed by tubes and attached to wires, with the rhythmic clicking of the machines the only sound apart from weak, uneven breathing from the patient. Parrikar sat beside the bed and the Sheikh opened his eyes with a flicker of recognition. A clammy, trembling hand sought out his visitor's. They sat together in silence for a while until the

Sheikh tried to speak in short, rasping gasps.

'My good friend… thank you… thank you… want you to understand… They tricked me… made me… afraid… my son.'

'Who is "they"?'

The Sheikh moved his head.

'You don't know?'

'No… afraid… my son.'

'Your son Ali? Someone threatened to kill him?'

He nodded slightly but definitely.

'You had Patel killed?'

He nodded again. '… or kill Ali.'

'Who is "they"?'

'Gang?'

There was a long pause. Exhaustion? Fear?

'Trish… Trish…'

'Trishul? Is that what you are trying to say?'

There was a faint nod. The Sheikh turned away and closed his eyes.

Parrikar held his hand for a while then left him to sleep. He doubted he would see the Sheikh again. He left choked with emotion.

On the way out he gently embraced the Sheikh's wife and daughter and they thanked him through their tears. He would go over the conversation in the morning with Deepak and try to make sense of it. What he had learnt was that the Sheikh had been merely part – perhaps an unwitting part – of something bigger and more threatening.

Deepak was unable to add anything when they spoke the next day. He had never heard the term Trishul used outside of Hindu iconography. 'A gang? How would I know?' He realised that his contacts in Delhi wouldn't be able to help with this one. He had the idea of consulting Inspector Mankad. 'I don't rate him or the Mumbai police but it is his job. We can at least try him.'

━━━━━━━━━━━

Deepak arrived, feeling out of place and awkward, having been dropped off by his chauffeur at Dharavi police station where Inspector Mankad held court. To add to his embarrassment there were press photographers at the entrance who were waiting for a well-known figure from Bollywood to arrive in handcuffs and who snapped Deepak instead on the basis that he was probably a minor celebrity. Then there was a long wait as his briefcase and the contents of his pockets were examined at great length by an X-ray machine and its numerous operatives. Not satisfied, the operatives insisted on a detailed hand search of the briefcase, extracting a packet of condoms for prolonged public examination. The humourlessness and officiousness of the operation added to the hilarity of the proceedings, though Deepak was in no mood to laugh. Then he had to run the gauntlet of the dozens of shouting, jostling visitors, relatives, job seekers and hangers-on who seemed to populate the entrance to every Indian public building in contrast to the quiet, orderly, air conditioned oasis that was Parrikar House.

That, and status, was why Deepak had initially summoned Inspector Mankad to his office. But the Inspector made it clear that he was not to be summoned but might find time for a meeting at the police station. He was a different man from the diffident, and deferential, officer who had been present at the official inquest into Patel's death. Deepak had quickly pigeonholed him, without much thought, as a typical Mumbai police officer: not very bright; obsequious to his superiors and the rich and powerful; bullying to his juniors and the poor and powerless; and probably on the make.

This case and the publicity around it had, however, energised and transformed Mankad. For the first time in his career he had appeared on the front page of newspapers and he was getting closer to his dream of the day when 'Mankad catches his man' led the news. He and his journalist contact had inflated each other's reputations with a steady flow of leaks from the police enquiry. Mankad realised that the 'political' element in the case was dangerous but he had also grasped that with danger went a certain power. Everyone assumed that he would not be going public unless there was a Mr Big somewhere guarding his back. His superiors, who would normally grab any glory or forbid him from going near controversial cases, gave him a free run while wondering who Mr Big was. And as the enquiry gathered momentum, more and more little birds came bringing titbits of information to his office.

The real test had come when his sources identified the group who had been present when Patel's killer had been executed as punishment for his undisciplined loquaciousness. Two accessories to the murder had been members of the state assembly. This was in itself no great surprise. In some of the more lawless states like Uttar Pradesh or Bihar over half the assembly members had been charged with murder, rape, kidnapping and other serious offences (though only a few had been convicted and imprisoned). Those two were arrested and charged on Mankad's orders and were now sitting downstairs in what some humorist had called the 'custody suite'. They resembled caricature villains whose heavily oiled hair, long moustaches, record breaking stomachs and betel stained teeth suggested that they had styled themselves on a popular movie gangster. Their initial sense of outrage had turned to sardonic humour and threats to invoke the help of friends who, they claimed, reached to the top of government. Mankad did not allow himself to be fazed and kept them behind bars. Before long the villains had greased palms sufficiently to ensure a steady supply of luxury food and journalists who could regale the world with stories of their suffering in prison because of an over-zealous, misguided obsessive in the Mumbai police. Nonetheless, Inspector Mankad had them where he wanted them and another flock of little birds felt confident enough to bring information to his office and to his rapidly expanding team who were combing the baastis with unusual care.

Now this Deepak Parrikar wanted to see him. Mankad admired Deepak's role as a global – and seemingly honest – businessman, as well as a glamorous figure. But in their brief previous acquaintance he had come across as aloof and condescending: a Westerner patronising the natives. So he could wait. And he was required to wait for half an hour outside Mankad's office on an uncomfortable bench with a number of unsavoury characters and with no respite from the heat. When he was finally shown into Mankad's small office there was a blast of cold air from an old, rattling air conditioner turned to maximum volume and lowest temperature. The room stank of paper and cloth rotted by condensation. It felt and smelt as if fresh air had never been near the place. But the Inspector looked suitably impervious; and the walls were decorated with – now mildewed – pictures commemorating his progress through the ranks and, pride of place, his gallantry medal.

Parrikar sought to settle himself and to open the conversation but he was interrupted several times by streams of messengers and tea boys and, then, heavily laden clerks bringing in more files to add to the collection on the desk. Parrikar noticed that, despite the heaps of paper, there was also a computer on the desk but it was ancient, seemed to have no power source and was probably the result of some, brief, failed attempt by a 'new broom' to modernise. At last he secured the Inspector's attention.

'I have come to discuss the progress of the investigation into the death of Mr Patel.'

'We are making good progress. Arrests made. You will have seen in the newspapers.'

'Yes, I have. I see that the alleged killers are dead or have disappeared.'

'Yes, unfortunately. But we have arrested some people who were behind it.'

'Perhaps I have some useful information.' Deepak proceeded to pass on the account of his father's visit to the Sheikh.

'Your father is not here. Why?'

'He is not well. And badly affected by recent events.'

'Sorry to hear that. Your father made a bad mistake in dealing with this Sheikh. He is responsible for much trouble.'

'But you have never arrested him... Anyway, what about this "Trishul"?'

'I have heard of it. It's a new gang.'

'Is that all? Why would a serious mafioso like the Sheikh be frightened of them?'

'That is what my current enquiries are about.'

'Let me put a theory to you.'

'I prefer facts if you have any.'

'Please hear me out,' Deepak said patiently. 'My father and I believe that the Sheikh is just a pawn in a much bigger game. Ever since the Pakistani-inspired terrorist raid a decade ago and the Dawood gang involvement with the Sheikh's brothers, he has been something of a pariah. Other criminals are reluctant to work with his people. Although he stayed here rather than flee to the Gulf, he is weakened and struggles to hold on to his territory. Perhaps this new group – Trishul – exploited his weakness. Used threats to make him do what they wanted including the pressure on my father.'

'Theory. Short of facts. But it makes sense. It fits with the facts I have. Anything else?'

'No. Well, perhaps I should tell you what I have already told the country's security services.' He described the request to place a 'nephew' in his factory. 'As long as the Sheikh was running his own operation it made sense to imagine that he might have had some pressure through his family and its connections with Pakistan to facilitate some infiltration into the country. But how does that fit into this Trishul organisation running the show?'

'I have no idea and it is the role of our very able security services to investigate. You have told them. Not a police matter.'

Deepak struggled to extract a little more from this one-way conversation with the taciturn policeman. Perhaps he wanted money? But Mankad hadn't hinted at it and if he proved to be one of the puritanical minority of honest police officers, Deepak would be most unwise to proposition him. And, anyway, Deepak had scruples of his own about corruption. Perhaps he needed encouragement from further up the police hierarchy, but pulling rank was also a risky business and Deepak didn't know who to go to in any event.

'Thank you, Inspector. You have been very helpful. I hope you can use my information.'

'No problem. It's useful.'

'Before I go, can you give me some advice? What do I do to protect my family, my business?'

Mankad thought for some time. He was used to being patronised by people like Parrikar, but humility threw him. 'This is more than usual goonda trouble. The Trishul gang has big political friends. Maybe very big. You don't. So they squeeze your family, your company. They will keep squeezing until you join them. Or you get your own friends. It's up to you. Politics is not my business.'

⬛⬛⬛⬛⬛⬛⬛⬛⬛

Deepak did not have long to wait before the next move. As dusk settled over Mumbai harbour and with the cicadas in full voice, a group of men slipped along the lane to the Parrikar Chemicals complex. The workforce had gone for the day and the only human presence on the site was a small security detail and the skeletal staff required to keep some of the machinery in twenty-four-hour operation. The men knew their way around – they had worked in the factory until the recent cutbacks – and they headed for a shed close to the water's edge. There was a storage tank with a sign warning of the dangers of extremely hazardous substances within. But the men knew how to avoid hazards to themselves and carefully loosened a series of valves that released the contents of the tank into the sea. The liquids mixed silently and invisibly, creating a lethal cocktail that would kill any living object that imbibed it over a wide area. The men then tightened the valves, cleaned them of fingerprints and quietly disappeared into the Indian night.

Several miles away in another part of the Mumbai suburbs, Iqbal Aziz waited until the evening activity in the local bazaar had started to die down. He slipped quietly along the lanes behind the main shopping street until he came to the yard marked on a map that was now being slowly digested inside him. The gate, as he had been told, was unlocked and he picked his way through piles of building materials until he reached the door of a shed, which opened, with some difficulty, as he pushed. There was a dim light inside from a low-powered naked bulb and just beyond the sparse illumination he saw, half hidden, the outline of the man he had come to meet.

His short stay at Parrikar Avionics had been almost too straightforward. Security had been lax to the point of negligence. No one had taken any particular interest in him. The Indian staff where he was carrying out induction training were friendly and welcoming without being too inquisitive. His mission was to find out what he could about the factory's activities and to report back via coded messages left under a loose brick in a wall at the Muslim cemetery. He had so far managed to construct a detailed map of the layout of the plant, an organogram of the management hierarchy and description supported by photographs of new machine tools that were being installed. He had blended into the local scene very easily.

His Indian collaborators, part of the Sheikh's network, had organised for him a nondescript flat in a township a short bus ride from the plant. He aroused little interest as he commuted back and forth and, at night, surfed the dozens of channels on Indian TV. He felt comfortable and there was enough familiarity in language, food smells and sounds to remind him of life in the spreading suburbs of big cities back home, like Lahore. There was even a mosque nearby whose calls to prayer reassured him and which he occasionally answered. The one cultural divide he struggled to deal with was the presence of Indian women: much more visible, colourful and confident than back home. In the smarter shops and restaurants, they dressed in Western clothes, some disporting themselves in what he regarded as semi-nudity. He had been to Western cities and wasn't a stranger to the adult channels on hotel TVs. But this outward sign of secular values and female independence in an Asian society very like his own he found simultaneously repulsive and exciting.

Tonight, the routine was interrupted by the message at his drop: to meet the contact who, he had been advised, would meet him in an emergency or if there were a change of plan. There was a change of plan. No need for further intelligence gathering. He was to disable a key piece of equipment and then make a quick exit. He would be helped to escape and the network would organise his safe transport back to Pakistan.

The man who passed on these instructions remained well out of sight. He was not there, in any event, to hold a conversation but to transmit orders. Iqbal Aziz had many questions but couldn't ask them. Why abort a successful intelligence gathering operation that was just getting into its stride? Why was he to be involved in explosives, an area where he had minimal expertise? Were his activities being seen, back home, as a 'success' or 'failure' (since he was banking on this final piece of field work giving him a crucial promotion to the upper echelons of Inter-Services Intelligence)?

At the conclusion of the briefing the man handed him the 'kit' with some minimal instructions. The following night he was to carry out the operation. A bicycle would be waiting for him afterwards to bring him back to this place after which he would be sent on to a safe house before returning to Pakistan. He left the way he had come and returned, unseen, to his flat.

CHAPTER 12

ESCALATION

Reuters, 14 July 2019:

Following a massive explosion on the Delhi metro unofficial estimates of casualties are as many as 200 dead and many more injured. Leading Indian ministers have blamed the terrorist attack on Islamic militants infiltrated from Pakistan with the connivance of the Pakistani authorities. The Home Minister, normally regarded as a 'moderate' in the BJP government, has spoken of a Muslim 'fifth column' aiding and abetting terrorists. As news of the explosion spread through social media, mosques were attacked in Ahmedabad and Indore and there are unconfirmed reports of mobs attacking predominantly Muslim districts with retaliation in Hindu minority areas. The Pakistani Prime Minister, Imran Khan, has put out a statement condemning the terrorist attack, disclaiming any responsibility and expressing sorrow for the victims – noting that similar attacks have also recently occurred in Pakistan, allegedly with Indian government connivance.

It was after dark, next evening, in the factory on the outskirts of Mumbai. Iqbal Aziz (aka Hussein Malik) had stayed behind after work, hiding in the men's lavatories. His mission tonight represented a dramatic escalation of activities. He was equipped with plastic explosives and had been given instructions about where to put the packages through the perimeter fence for collection, unobtrusively, later – thereby avoiding the risk of a routine check on his bag when coming into the factory for the day. He had now retrieved them. He had also memorised the exact spot where he was required to place the explosive before detonation. This was his first mission involving violence but he was told by his Indian contact that what was being asked of him was easy and his controllers back in Islamabad considered it an essential part of his task.

He secured the explosive, as instructed, in a vent from the factory power unit and prepared the timing device. There was silence in the pitch black night. Then he heard a click behind him and turned towards a gun a few inches away from his face. Floodlights were switched on around the factory and he was suddenly illuminated like an actor on a stage. He could see that he was very far from alone. The audience was a small army of black-jacketed Indian anti-terrorist troops who had been waiting for him.

In the minutes that followed as he was spread-eagled on the ground, then strip searched, he realised that he should have seen the signs of a sting operation. Now he had to brace himself for an uncomfortable interrogation and to discipline himself to follow the instructions he had been given, even when in great pain.

General Rashid wasn't totally surprised when he saw, on the CNN newsfeed in his office, his bright young protégé Aziz being paraded across the screen by his Indian captors. He felt for Aziz, who could anticipate some very rough questioning from interrogators who may well have learnt their trade from the Russians, just as his own had benefited from US expertise. He noted that the Indians had been smart enough to equip Aziz with explosives – even though he had no clue how to use them – qualifying him to be a 'terrorist' rather than a mere agent. This enhanced status carried the prospect of hanging or, more likely, a higher price if he was exchanged.

But the risks had been explained to Aziz. And since General Rashid suspected that his networks were compromised, he had prepared Aziz for what would follow. Not to be too courageous. Hold out for a while and then talk. Give the Indians lots of information. Ninety per cent of it correct, which the Indians already had; the other ten per cent new, plausible and wrong. That ten per cent could prove very useful if the current skirmishing and sabre-rattling got out of control and a fourth war broke out between the two neighbours.

Aziz hadn't picked up anything useful in his brief snooping expedition. But something more valuable perhaps? The group on the TV screen clustered around the hapless, bound Aziz contained some interesting faces. One he recognised. Sanjay? Sanjivi? Desai. What was he doing there? Some research for the boys.

With this, and the bomb in Delhi, there would be a busy day ahead.

⊠⊠⊠⊠⊠⊠⊠⊠⊠⊠⊠⊠

Steve had a very difficult two days as the redundancies were trailed and he urged moderation. The company needed time to work out the various options. Nothing was gained by rushing into industrial action. Even those who bought the arguments for a measured approach were surly and resentful, since his indiscreet behaviour was generally believed to have contributed to the company's problems and the (apparently) lost order. At a time when unemployment was rising to levels last seen a decade earlier in the wake of the banking crisis, there was little tolerance for carelessness with people's jobs.

His reputation in the local party, and the council, had also taken a nosedive: no longer the unblemished hero and hope for the future. In any event, the leftist move of the party's national leadership and the influence of new members meant that the brand of politics that Steve represented was no longer fashionable.

He received an abruptly phrased summons to the office of the council leader, Councillor John Gray. John was a retired lecturer from the town's further education college: liked, if not respected, by his colleagues as a decent, safe, uncontroversial man who kept the peace between the endlessly feuding factions and over-sized egos. The borough council had several longstanding Lib Dem wards. Another, which had once been represented by the BNP, now had a trio of community independents, who maintained the tradition of white, working class hostility to the town's Asian population. But, these apart, the council was overwhelmingly Labour.

Maintaining discipline required keeping two of the big beasts of the council tolerably happy. One was Les Harking, the regional organiser of Steve's union, Unite, who had a hard left background on Merseyside and whose permanent sense of grievance was only partly appeased by being put in charge of the town's planning, as well as a seat on the union national executive. Councillor Mirza made sure that the three wards with a large Asian vote delivered the right result, without too many questions being asked about the size of the postal vote. He had responsibility for social services and there were growing mutterings in the town about the abysmal standards in several residential care homes owned by various members of the Mirza extended family. Steve's political career had flourished thanks to the patronage of John Gray and the grudging acquiescence of the others he had managed, so far, not to alienate.

The final member of the panel worried Steve the most. Bill Daniels was the Labour group's oldest and longest serving councillor. He had been first elected in the dawn of political pre-history when Harold Wilson was Prime Minister and sometime before Steve was even born. His political contribution was negligible. He never spoke in the council or council committees and he performed no obviously useful function. But his very antiquity gave him status. Like a long surviving veteran of the Battle of Britain he regaled his colleagues with accounts of his dog-fights in the class struggle over Bedfordshire. Until recently his reputation had been sustained by the belief that 'old Bill' knew everyone in his ward and solved all their problems through assiduous casework.

This reputation had taken a severe beating in the last municipal elections. The Lib Dems had decided to fight the ward seriously – the first real contest for decades. Their simple weapon was a voters' questionnaire. The answers told them that hardly anyone in the ward knew who 'old Bill' actually was and no one could recall anything he had done. The Lib Dems buried the ward in campaigning Comments and came within two votes of unseating Bill when there was a swing from Lib Dems to Labour elsewhere in the town. Since his near humiliation, Bill had launched his own personal crusade against the Lib Dems, generating a degree of tribal passion never previously seen in his almost forty-five years on the council. One of Steve's biggest political mistakes had been to let slip in a group meeting that he felt there was quite a lot of common ground with the Lib Dems and that the party's interests might be served by letting the Lib Dems have a clear run in the leafier suburbs and rural areas where Labour stood no chance. For this terrible heresy, in the eyes of Bill Daniels, mere burning at the stake would be compassionate.

As a senior figure in the Labour group, Steve would normally be at the top table, setting the agenda. On this occasion he was placed at the end of a long table, which required him to look deferentially at his interrogators: his four senior colleagues. He saw that on the wall behind them were photographs of party leaders going back to Kier Hardie but, he noticed, excluding the traitor Blair.

Gray clearly had little appetite for the proceedings and looked, embarrassed, into the middle distance. Les Harking, however, was keen to get down to business. He had spent a lifetime intimidating college-educated managers and making an example of union 'scabs'. Cutting down tall poppies in the party was another speciality and here was one in front of him. 'Comrade,' he began, 'the party's regional executive has asked us to investigate your conduct. We have been informed that there are to be substantial redundancies at your company. We want to know about your role in this disastrous state of affairs. Some of our Brothers are not sure whether you are acting in their interest, the bosses', those of a group of pacifists or religious fundamentalists. They say you were a good rep but have fallen into bad company. They say you encouraged a demonstration against your own industry. And now you are telling our members that they have to accept redundancies imposed by the people who control your firm: private equity barons and hedge funds in America. The suggestion is being made that you are bringing the Labour Movement into disrepute.' Bill Daniels grunted his agreement.

Before Steve could answer, Councillor Mirza wanted to have his say. 'Steve, my people are angry. They are good, loyal people. They work. They pray. They give no trouble. They support our party. Now they say you are making friends with some dangerous people; troublemakers, militants. I speak for the community. They say to me: "Why does this councillor interfere and not respect you?"'

By this time Steve had woken up to the fact that he was on trial in a kangaroo court. He realised that he was sweating uncomfortably, and his heart started to race. His union experience told him, however, not to get into a brawl when he was outnumbered but to insist on due process. His prosecutors clearly didn't like him and had their own agendas. They almost certainly resented his reputation as a moderniser in the workplace and in the party. No point arguing the toss with them.

'Colleagues, I have very good answers to these charges. They are ridiculous. But I want to know what is the constitutional basis for this meeting; that it is properly constituted.' Harking and Daniels protested vehemently and Steve stood up, preparing to walk out.

This intervention gave John Gray the opportunity to pour oil on troubled waters.

He intercepted Steve on his way to the door and put his hand on his shoulder. 'Steve, calm down. We are not accusing you of anything. We all value your political and union work. We just want you to know that some of our colleagues are concerned. This town has enough problems without divisions in our own ranks. You are a good colleague, Steve. You have done excellent work for the Movement. Let us forget this meeting happened. Just take on board the worries of your colleagues.'

Despite the reprieve, Steve felt angry at the pettiness and spitefulness of colleagues with whom he had worked together to run the town for the last few years. He reflected that his effortless rise had so far shielded him from some of the uglier realities of Labour politics.

Preoccupied by these thoughts, he failed to notice a half-familiar figure loitering at the entrance as he left the town hall. But the man was determined to see him and followed. Steve initially panicked as he thought he was being tailed but then was able to put a name to the face: Mehmet, the night watchman. He paused and Mehmet asked if they could go somewhere private for a conversation. Steve was reluctant; life was already complicated enough. But there was a hint of desperation in the man's eyes. They found a coffee bar nearby.

'It is union business,' Mehmet started.

'I haven't anything to add to what I said about redundancies at the branch meeting. Sorry. Nothing I can do about that.'

'It isn't about that. I have been dismissed. I am not entitled to anything. I am an asylum seeker. I was sacked for misconduct. They said I was asleep on duty. Lies. The reason is that I know bad things are happening at the factory.'

'You know about "unfair dismissal"?'

'Yes, but I don't qualify. Not working here long enough. I came to you because you are a fair man. And you fight for the workers. Maybe you can't help me, but you must know about the bad people there.' The man was patently sincere and in distress.

Steve was now sufficiently engaged to let Mehmet tell his story, from the university classrooms of Asmara, to the battlefields on the border of Eritrea, the nightmare journey across Sudan and Libya, the terrifying experience under a lorry crossing the Channel, months in crowded bedsits around London, scraps of jobs, mostly illegal, and now –

after his papers came through – permission to work and this job on an industrial estate. He was not stupid, he insisted. He knew when things were not right. His reports on night-time visitors in the factory: ignored. And then early one morning observing the head of security clearly up to no good. Shortly afterwards he was dismissed and told that he would be well advised to disappear quietly. Any stories he told would not be believed and the company had influential contacts in the government who would ensure that he was returned to Eritrea. But rather than disappear, he wanted someone to know.

Steve wasn't sure how all this fitted into the bigger picture but there was enough to demand a proper investigation. So he rang Calum with the intelligence he had gleaned. And he remembered that he was still carrying the card of the man from MI5 – Liam – and called him too.

✕✕✕✕✕✕✕✕✕✕✕✕✕

The following day Steve had a call from his boss. Calum and Liam had confronted the company's head of security, Justin Starling, that morning. Calum had already started to have doubts about Starling's competence and had remembered the holes in his CV, which he had overlooked on the basis of the Red Admiral's character reference. The intelligence from Mehmet confirmed existing suspicions that not only was he not doing his job very well, he was actively working against the company and, perhaps, the country. A threat of criminal sanctions and the Official Secrets Act persuaded him to come clean about his activities on the basis that charges would not be pressed.

Sometime ago Starling had been approached by a US company called Global Analysis and Research that was stalking Pulsar and wanted, in due course, to make a takeover bid. In the meantime, he was to pass whatever confidential information he could gather about Pulsar's intellectual property. And to help soften up the company for a cheap takeover, he was to help destabilise it. For that reason, he had passed on in advance all the details of the Minister's visit to the anti-arms trade group and the Islamic militants. He had the run of the place at night with access to a full set of security codes, and a large, if unquantifiable, amount of Pulsar's proprietary anti-missile technology was now in the hands of a rival company in Louisiana. That company happened to be the same large minority shareholder that Calum had, belatedly, realised had Pulsar in its sights for an aggressive takeover.

It had been difficult to establish Starling's motives beyond a generous enhancement of his package if the takeover materialised. Eventually, cross-questioning established that Starling had a guilty secret. Some years ago he had been suspected of, and charged with, indecent behaviour with children. But the evidence had been inconclusive and the case had been dropped. He had no criminal record but Global had obtained information that had eluded Calum's checks. They could control him.

All it had required was a glowing reference from the Red Admiral to get him installed at Pulsar.

British intelligence had no great interest in pursuing the matter further. The damage was primarily in the form of intellectual property theft from Pulsar, a private enterprise. And an American company with apparently close links to the Pentagon could hardly be treated as if it were Chinese or Russian. If Calum wanted to take action it was up to him. He did want to take action but the lawyers would move slowly, at best, and, in the meantime his company faced an existential threat from Global's expanding shareholding. He needed political support, soon.

Steve was the first call he made, lifting the suspension with immediate effect. Calum had a guilty conscience, in any event, that Steve had taken the rap for the demonstration and had a reputation to rebuild. When the problem was explained, Steve immediately saw both the threat and the opportunity and started making calls to his high-placed Labour and union contacts and journalists to whom he had fed good material in the past. Shaida was involved in the discussions and given the job of trawling the internet for references to Global and its finances. This was a covert operation she was altogether more comfortable with than snooping for Liam.

What she found was not reassuring. The company was founded and chaired by a somewhat reclusive American called Aaron Le Fevre. He had been a very senior if somewhat murky figure in the Pentagon with Donald Rumsfeld and then on the staff of Vice-President Cheney. Shortly after 9/11 he left government to establish Global, which had expanded rapidly on the back of Defense Department orders. As Shaida dug through the press references she picked up a couple of articles based on blogs from a – now deceased – investigative journalist in Seattle, Lee Wright. Wright worried about Global's rapid expansion, taken in conjunction with Le Fevre's political history. He spoke to the CEOs of a couple of companies Global had taken over and, while the two businessmen were reluctant to talk, they said enough to leave the strong impression that dirty tricks were involved. Global seemed less interested in the health of the companies it was taking over than in getting its hands on their proprietary technology. In each case, the companies specialised in anti-missile defence, or missile technology more generally. Wright died shortly after in an unexplained shooting incident. Then Shaida found the link to the company in Northern Ireland making advanced communications equipment, and which Global took over and turned around.

She was also able to piece together a consistent pattern from an analysis of share prices and company valuations. All of the companies taken over had experienced a major crisis leading to a sharp drop in their share price. At that point Global stepped in to 'rescue' them: a white knight for companies in distress. Data on Global itself was patchy but it showed prodigious growth and profits. Global was not yet in the Premier League with the likes of Lockheed

Martin but it soon would be. More detail, however, proved hard to find. The full company accounts could not be traced any further as they were lodged in various offshore holding companies based in the Cayman Islands.

The name Aaron Le Fevre also cropped up in a different context, as a member of a group of US businessmen, security insiders and Republican congressmen called the Crusader Knights who were preoccupied with confronting the threat of militant Islam in all its forms. In a speech reported in a newspaper in Le Fevre's native Louisiana, he had advocated an 'alliance of civilisations': the Christian West and Russia, Israel and Hindu India, with Islam the common enemy. This kind of talk had gone down well with the Trump people, and press cuttings showed him at various Trump Tower events.

※※※※※※※※※※※※※※※

Islamic radicals were also the subject of conversation at the finance department's coffee machine where Steve was waiting to discuss his next rendezvous at the mosque. When Shaida arrived she anticipated the question.

'Your heroics won't be needed after all,' she explained. 'Apparently there was a police raid last night in the town. Some jihadists were caught. And lots of incriminating stuff: an arsenal, in fact. Guns. Explosives. It appears, however, that the main target, Tariq Ahmed, got away. Some of this was on local radio – you must have missed it – and Mo had picked up the news on social media. His reaction worried me – he was overjoyed that Tariq Ahmed had escaped.'

Shaida hesitated, not sure how much of what she had already shared with Liam as informant she could now share with her friend.

'I haven't discussed these things much with you recently, Steve. But Mo has become incredibly difficult to talk to. Secretive. He's started locking himself in his bedroom and goodness knows what he's doing and looking at on his computer. On the odd occasions he communicates at meal times he starts ranting about how the British are to blame for all the violence in the subcontinent: the history of divide-and-rule, Partition, all that. Now the British are to blame for supporting India and not understanding the suffering of our people in Kashmir. My mum and dad and I are "deluded". Coconuts he calls us: brown on the outside, white on the inside.'

<hr>

Back in Mumbai, the Parrikars were also anxious, waiting for the next blow to land. They experienced several days of bad publicity after the pollution spillage from their chemicals plant came to light. Another example of the company's 'irresponsible capitalism'. There would be one official enquiry by the Environment Agency and another by the state government. Villagers were being mobilised by people who claimed to be environmental NGOs to demand compensation. There would be big fines. A speech Deepak had made recently on the 'Greening of the Planet' had become the subject of newspaper cartoons and a source of ridicule among the English-speaking intellectuals.

And then one of Parrikar Senior's most loyal project managers had received threats similar to those made to Patel. He was speedily given leave of absence to head off a similar fate. Disruption of the defence contract was, for the moment, forgotten.

The telephone rang in Parrikar Senior's downtown office. His PA came through to tell him that there was an urgent call from the Prime Minister's office in Delhi: Santosh Joshi, the PM's private secretary. 'Highly, highly confidential, Sahib, I will connect you.'

'Joshi here. The Prime Minister has asked me to speak to you on a serious matter.'

'Of course. It is an honour.'

'Let me get to the point. The PM is concerned about the defence contract. There are serious problems in London, and America – they are saying the contract may be delayed, even stopped. It would be a disaster if that happens.'

'But you stopped this plot. Clever operation.'

'No thanks to sloppy security in your son's plant. And your family is a big part of the problem. Your dirty business has alarmed the Americans and your son isn't satisfied with our local prostitutes; he has to show off this English woman in front of the cameras. It's created a scandal in the UK.'

'Sahib, we only want to do good for India. We will do what is needed.'

'You will need to put in more cash. The Avionics plant must be fully tooled up and ready to start work once the contract is sorted out.'

'That is difficult. There's no other work for the factory at present. Banks will not lend without the contract being agreed.'

'That is your problem, Mr Parrikar. Your Mumbai businesses have plenty of cash. The Revenue Department tells me that they are thinking about investigating your tax affairs. If you don't want them on your back, you had better cooperate.

'We also want to sort out your son's amateurish operation. We could nationalise Parrikar Avionics but we don't operate that way. We are pro-business, not like Congress and their Communist friends. So, we will work with you to strengthen the executive team. We have someone in mind. You may know of Sanjivi Desai, a highly talented engineer who now advises the PM on national security issues. He is also well connected and respected in the US, so he ticks a lot of boxes. He will be parachuted in to give your son advice.'

'We will discuss this.'

'No, you will do it. The Prime Minister wants it. He also thanks you for your help with the last election – your donation was well received. He doesn't want to lose the respect he has for you.'

'Yes, Sahib.'

Desai soon started making himself at home. With perfunctory notice he arrived at the Parrikar Avionics site with a coterie of 'experts' and 'advisers', mostly Americans of Indian origin whom Global had recruited from Californian high tech businesses and had been rapidly given visas to operate in India. A PhD from MIT or Caltech seemed to be the minimum qualification.

When Deepak arrived at the factory, the visiting team had already thoroughly intimidated security and his personal staff, and had taken up residence in his office. Before Deepak could protest, a distinguished-looking man in a beautifully tailored Nehru suit leapt up from an armchair, a hand outstretched in greeting.

'Good morning, Mr Parrikar, you won't be surprised to see us. Forgive the invasion but we came early to get down to business. The Indian government has suggested that my team can help upgrade your operation so that it can meet the tough specifications required by our Defence Ministry and by the US and UK partners. The current security situation with Pakistan is a reminder of why this project is important. To be frank, our political masters have been none too impressed by the lax security and some of the unprofessional operations here. This is too important to be just a vanity project for your family. I am here to help. Global Research and Analysis is at your service. Let me introduce the team.'

None of this surprised Deepak. In the last few days, since he first heard of Desai's proactive role, he did the rounds of his friends in business, politics and the media who broadly shared his world view: essentially patriotic Indians, but outward looking, cosmopolitan and secular. Several of them gave him anecdotes and titbits of information. Desai was a senior, if rather obscure, figure in the first BJP – Vajpayee – government operating in the interstices of politics and administration, part of the national security apparatus that was built up after India's drubbing in the border war with China, and he was now a major force. His origins were obscure but he was identified in leftist magazines as one of the more fanatical products of the RSS, the ideological and paramilitary arm of the ruling party in Delhi that included the Prime Minister among its alumni.

When Congress came back to power, with its secular allies, Desai disappeared to the US, building up his already impressive qualifications in electronic engineering. US citizenship followed. Then he worked with right-wing Republican think tanks and published several pieces disseminated on Alt-Right websites about a Muslim 'fifth column' in both India and the USA. He met Le Fevre at a fundraiser for the – successful – Republican gubernatorial candidate in Louisiana, 'Bobby' Jindal, one of the new breed of Indians making it big in America. Desai and Le Fevre wove together their respective conspiracy theories, an ideological marriage made in heaven, and before long Desai was on the board of Global. Now, through his business, he straddled the two worlds of US and Indian politics.

One of the advantages of Deepak's Western education and US experience was that he was not easily intimidated by the likes of Desai. He decided that attack was the best form of defence.

'Thank you for the offer of help,' he replied. 'But I didn't ask for it and I don't believe I need it. We have never had complaints before in all our years of supplying the Indian armed forces. And let me be clear; this is our family business. It will remain so whether I or one of my siblings runs it.'

Desai smiled his killer-shark smile. 'We'll soon see who calls the shots here!'

Deepak tried to understand how Desai fitted into the recent tribulations of his family company. He went over in his mind the pieces of the puzzle. A gang called Trishul appeared to be targeting the business. And if the police were right, it was linked to politicians from one of the extreme nationalist parties that were powerful at state level. The Sheikh had been involved in the Patel murder and also in helping place the Pakistani agent in Parrikar Avionics. At first sight these seemed totally disconnected events. But perhaps they were connected after all.

It was odd that a man with the Sheikh's pedigree was allowed to function unobstructed by the authorities and had surfaced at such a convenient time. Perhaps he had been turned, blackmailed, by the people who now controlled the secret parts of India's increasingly sectarian state in which Desai was an important player. A Muslim gangster would be a good foil, and easily deniable.

But this was surely paranoia: conspiracy theory run riot. The theory had a coherent logic, but conspiracy theories often did. Like the internet fantasy stories peddled by dangerous cranks about 9/11 being orchestrated from Tel Aviv. But, then again, Mr Le Fevre was one of those people on the American extreme right who were reported as believing and promoting the story that, although Hitler was a bad man, the Holocaust was really the creation of the grand Mufti of Jerusalem and the Islamists.

What persuaded Deepak to believe the worst of the people threatening his family firm was the reaction of his father, who had sunk into self-pitying despair after his public humiliation in *Bharat Bombay*. But when Deepak had hesitantly set out his theory, his father sprung to life, finding it totally believable and exactly the kind of stunt that could have been pulled in the smaller universe of Mumbai slumland. He knew from experience that the frenzied religious massacres that occurred every generation or so owed far more to political manipulation than to any real difference or division. He had seen the religious militant nationalists increasing their power in Mumbai and believed them capable of anything. Fortified by this insight, his father's street fighting instincts resurfaced. They decided to stand and resist rather than capitulate to the people trying to control their company. And that involved following the advice of the policeman. They needed political friends.

Kate had returned to her constituency routine. She declined the very junior ministerial role she had been offered, a sop to her pride, but such a minor sop that leaving the government seemed more dignified. She was welcomed with open arms into the club of the dismissed, overlooked, angry, mischievous, disloyal and congenitally rebellious who occupied a corner of the tea room. She enjoyed her first experience of defying the whips.

Her constituency surgeries swelled in size, she suspected, because her brief notoriety had attracted the curious as well as the needy. Coming to the end of a long and tiring session a man came into her office with a pretty Asian woman, who looked vaguely familiar, to discuss what he had described when making the appointment as a planning problem. When they sat down he said, looking at Stella: 'We would like to see the MP alone. We have something highly confidential and political to discuss.'

'Planning?' Kate asked.

'No, when you have heard what we have to say you will understand the need for privacy.'

'This is very irregular. I am not sure I wish to have such a conversation.'

But Stella, her sense of affront getting the better of her curiosity, was already on her way to the door. When it was closed the man began. 'Let me come clean. I gave a false name and I am not a constituent. In fact, I am a Labour councillor. My colleague here is chief finance officer of Pulsar, the company you visited recently.'

'I could hardly forget,' Kate replied. 'But, look, I really think you should leave. You are completely out of order.'

'Please hear me out. What I have to say has a direct bearing on your departure from the government and, also, on your friend in India – if the newspapers are right about that. I am the union man at Pulsar.'

'So I can thank you for the eggs and tomatoes, can I?' Kate said, still bristling with annoyance at the invasion of her advice surgery on false pretences.

At this point Shaida endeavoured to steer the conversation towards the reason for the visit. 'We briefly met after you were manhandled by that mob. We have come to show you these.' She took out her bundle of documents and talked Kate through the Global story as quickly and clearly as she could.

Kate listened with mounting incredulity, and then anger. 'If all this is true, we have been well and truly done over. But it is history; water under the bridge. I don't know about you but I am trying to move on.'

Steve insisted: 'No, it isn't history. This American operation is closing in on Pulsar; probably on your Indian friend's company too for all we know.'

'Well, in that case, why come to me? Why not take it to the press? Your Labour people can publicise it; raise it in parliament.'

'Yes, I could do that. I could take it to the *Guardian*.

They would have a lot of fun with the story: right-wing extremist American destabilising and taking over British high tech company. I could also take it to our front bench people who would no doubt make hay with it and demand that the government use its powers to block takeovers where national security is involved. But, as you know, our politics is tribal. Grandstanding is satisfying but it is less likely to get results than working on the inside.

'We have come together because we are not just concerned for ourselves – but with the people I have represented in the factory. We genuinely believe that this Global outfit is sinister and needs to be stopped. You have contacts in government that I don't have and they, in turn, have contacts in the US. You also have direct access to people at the Indian end.'

'I think you overestimate my influence,' responded Kate. 'I am not exactly flavour of the month at the moment. As you know I am now on the back benches and persona non grata with the people you wish me to influence.'

Steve felt they had done enough to press her. 'All we can ask is that you do your best. I suggest the following. I understand that there is an important debate in parliament on Monday. You will get a chance to corner your former boss, Jim Chambers, at the division, even if he won't see you before. Tell him what is going on. I will try to line up some press publicity for the Wednesday that might prompt a question in PMQs or could be the basis of an Urgent Question. Ideally, you could raise it. But that is for you – I am not an MP and not sure how these things operate. The key point is that all of this will come out. Let's work together to make sure it comes out in a good way.'

<hr />

Kate drove home trembling with fear, excitement and nervous exhaustion and had to pull in to a layby to compose herself. She had been through the most difficult and traumatic few weeks in her entire, admittedly rather cosseted, existence and, just as she was coming to terms with her stalled career, she was being thrown back into the maelstrom.

She was, as the Prime Minister had suggested with heavy sarcasm, spending more time with her family. It was proving an ordeal. She had come to loathe her husband's twin-track campaign of angry silence and icy politeness. She had been called 'darling' more frequently than ever before in the sixteen years of their marriage but he somehow imbued the word with accusation and malice. He had made it clear that he wasn't going anywhere and he was waiting for her to produce the white flag of unconditional surrender and an abject, grovelling, apology. The girls weren't much help. After an initial display of solidarity with Mum, they had all retreated into adolescent sulks, making clear their embarrassment with their parents and their refusal to try to understand the world of adult emotions, let alone politics.

The house was quiet so she rang Deepak, who tried to be supportive and as sympathetic as the intermittent mobile reception would allow.

'I would like to be there with you. And I miss you,' he said tenderly. 'Things aren't as bad for me but my father's mental state is brittle and my mother's health has taken a turn for the worse. How are you feeling?'

'I am coping. Jonathan is insufferable. The girls are tricky. But, otherwise, I think the crisis is bottoming out. For the British media I am already ancient history. And this evening I learnt a lot more about the political background. About this company and what it is up to here and in India.'

'Their man Desai is much in evidence here. I am beginning to see a way forward.'

'Me too. Talking to you gives me more confidence. With luck, we'll be together again soon.'

━━━━━━━━━━━━━━━

She decided to act quickly rather than wait until Monday. She had kept the Secretary of State's home number and, to her surprise, he was both in and willing to take her call. The bonhomie was almost overwhelming.

'My dear Kate, how are you coping? I am so sorry things turned out badly. It must be awful. How is your lovely family? I am sure it will all work out for the best and we will have you back in government before long.' Even if she applied a high discount factor for his natural bombast and insincerity it was clear that, up to a point, Jim cared. Perhaps a guilty conscience that she had come to grief on his watch, on his project. And it was part of his character to enjoy being the saviour of damsels in distress.

What she thought was a dispassionate account ran, however, into a wall of scepticism: 'A Labour councillor…? That hopeless Scottish socialist trying to run the business… Eritrean asylum seeker…' As she went on she realised that her list of witnesses for the prosecution making accusations against a well-connected US company was far from convincing. She hadn't even got as far as the young British Pakistani woman. While he didn't say so explicitly, she could imagine him formulating the obvious questions: 'Are you on the brink of a nervous breakdown?' and 'Have you been reading too many spy thrillers?'

She was able to keep his attention by referring to the documents about Global and Le Fevre that the two had given her and which she undertook to scan immediately. When he rang off, he gave little indication that he was persuaded of the need to take the matter further. But she knew him well enough to know that the one thing that would have got through to him was the threat of an ambush in parliament, and bad press, and that she had done the right thing by warning him.

The Secretary of State never rang back, but then, she hadn't asked him to.

Other telephones were, however, ringing furiously. In his Sloane Square flat the Red Admiral was busy trying to retrieve a situation that was in danger of slipping out of control. All thanks to the carelessness of Starling, interfering politicians and some wretched African asylum seeker who would soon be back on his way to the jungle if he, the Admiral, had anything to do with it. So: favours called in across the Pond, in the Pentagon; Whitehall contacts alerted and suitably briefed; his friends among defence correspondents given the correct spin for when the story got out; and then, reassurance to his old friend, Jim Chambers, and his associates in Louisiana that everything was under control.

Meanwhile, Kate waited on tenterhooks for several days until the story appeared in the *Guardian* as Steve had planned and predicted. It was backed up by an editorial that had the flavour of an anti-American rant and was, she judged, unhelpful. The piece was placed low down on page seven, having been bumped off the front page by a Labour 'split' story. There was no traction. The rolling news channels and social media took little interest.

What did gain traction, however, was a powerful front page lead in the *Telegraph* under the headline 'Asylum Seeker Betrayal'. Readers were told that 'sources close to No. 10' had given the paper exclusive background on 'an act of treachery' at one of the country's important, high tech defence companies. 'An African asylum seeker with a mathematics background' had managed to hack through the security codes of the company where he was employed and was passing valuable information, for money, to commercial rivals. He had also stirred up trouble at the plant by informing Muslim militants and Marxist groups about an impending ministerial visit, leading to a violent demonstration. The article noted that the plant had a history of union militancy and Muslim extremism among the labour force.

Fortunately, the *Telegraph* reassured its readers that 'quick action by the company's head of security and by the country's intelligence services had contained the damage'. The Home Secretary was investigating how such breaches of security could be prevented in future, by ensuring that those foreign nationals who were allowed to work were excluded from sensitive sites.

Talks were taking place, encouraged by the UK and US governments, to develop a 'partnership' with a leading US company, Global Analysis and Research, to 'secure the long term future of the plant and ensure that Britain's leadership in a key area of military technology is fully protected'.

No one noticed that the *Guardian* story related to the same set of events, so different was the account.

Kate had, as recommended, put down an Urgent Question but it wasn't called. Instead, the Labour MP in whose constituency Pulsar was based raised the matter with the Prime Minister, who replied with a carefully drafted statement:

'I am aware of these accusations and the government is studying them carefully. There is a suggestion that criminal activity may have been involved concerning an asylum seeker and it will be dealt with firmly and quickly by the appropriate authorities. I also want to reassure the House that the government has been in contact with the US administration and with the Indian government and the contract is proceeding as planned. Furthermore, we are in contact with the Pakistani government and have reassured them that the contract is purely for defensive equipment.

'I wish to reassure the House that the US company that is acquiring a controlling interest in the company has given the government a set of written undertakings to protect jobs at the factory. Demonstrating confidence in Britain's future outside the EU, it has committed itself to establish a major new development facility close to the existing site, potentially employing several hundred scientific personnel. Britain is, truly, open for business. This is good news for jobs in the Honourable Member's constituency and underlines this government's commitment to jobs and to the defence industry. We are, after all, the Workers' Party.' (Jeers, hoots.)

Calum called in Steve to brief him on the latest developments. Steve saw the empty tumbler on Calum's desk and caught a whiff of the products of a Highland distillery. Calum normally never drank in the office, but today his face was flushed and looked seriously agitated.

'Well, laddie, you came out of this OK. The *Guardian* story. Now there is the local paper: "Zero to hero". The journalist who stitched you up a few weeks ago now has you as "the man who saved the plant". Your lads have secure jobs, for now, that's for sure. And, if you did half of what you are said to have done, I guess you deserve a medal. But this whole thing stinks. I have been completely fucking shafted. We have been taken over by a dodgy American company run by some right-wing ideologue, and this is supposed to be a great victory for our brilliant fucking government – and you for that matter. These people now have access to all our IP, or the bits they hadn't already nicked. That fucking Admiral, who I trusted and who brought in that pervert to spy on us, now – believe this – has us under his fucking chairmanship.

'They want me to stay and manage a handover delivering this contract. But – after my golden goodbye – I have to work out how to spend my early retirement. Can't spend more time with my family: I don't have one. Any ideas, Steve?'

Steve had never encountered Calum in this morose, self-pitying, semi-alcoholic state. Their relationship had worked because it was not a friendship. Calum was the boss; Steve the worker who wore overalls and collected his pay cheque like the other workers. There was mutual respect but distance. Now, it was clear, Calum wanted to unburden himself. He unearthed a bottle of whisky from a cupboard, poured himself a full glass, neat; then remembered that Steve was in the room and offered him a drink, which he declined.

'I realise now just what a bunch of fucking wankers we have running this country. Useless. PR men. Snake oil salesmen. Never done a proper day's work in their lives. Probably never been inside a factory; certainly never worked in one.'

He paced around the room gesticulating, spilling half the contents of his drink on the floor. But he was in full flow, absorbed in his own, drunken, eloquence. 'What have those idiots done for our manufacturing? I go to my engineering dinners. Poor sods from Rolls-Royce and BAE. They've got bean counters at their elbows. Cut this. Cut that. Shareholders on their back the whole time. No interest in making anything any more: design, development – the things we used to be good at. Before long Rolls will be bought out by Ning Ping fucking Inc if the Yanks don't get there first. Post-Brexit export drive? What a fucking joke.'

Steve would normally agree with all of that. But he was desperate to leave as he saw Calum downing two more large glasses of whisky. 'I know you want to go,' Calum said as he put down his empty glass. 'Just one word of advice. I've seen you eyeing up the Khan lassie. Her people don't like us messing with their women. They'll have your balls off if you're not careful. Fighters. Once wiped out a British army.'

'That was the Afghans.'

'Same difference. Stick to your politics.'

At the factory, Steve's reputation was largely rehabilitated. He had been puzzled by the differing interpretation of events in the *Telegraph* and the *Guardian*. But these were not papers read by his workmates. Their jobs were safe. Expansion was on the way. The local paper and the local MP claimed it was a great outcome. Calum and Steve didn't want to pour cold water on a good news story, just yet.

The conversation with Calum had worried Steve more than he let on at the time. He was unlikely in future to have the intimate, trusted role he currently enjoyed. The new owners would presumably know of the part he had played in trying to expose their dirty tricks. Jump or be pushed?

He would not be short of things to do. He had recently been voted onto the national executive of his union. And the ancient and anonymous local Labour MP had recently decided to stand down, creating a vacancy. He would start as favourite for the succession.

As for the prospect of emasculation to protect the honour of a woman from the North West Frontier, that all seemed rather academic. Shaida had given little encouragement. Even on the trip to visit that MP in Surrey Heights, which she had managed to sell to her parents as essential for the benefit of Pulsar, she had remained aloof and rebuffed any sign of familiarity.

So he was unprepared for their next encounter at the coffee machine. Shaida smiled as she walked up to him. 'Good news,' she said. 'I plucked up the courage to tell my dad I was planning to go on a date with you. Told, not asked. There was no response. No fatwa.'

He was, as always, several steps behind her, and he struggled to find a suitable reply. 'Maybe you can come and help me deliver some Labour leaflets,' he said tentatively.

She laughed – she wasn't sure if he was being serious or had a nice line in humour. 'That sounds really exciting. Maybe my brother can come along as chaperone.' Then her long, deep chuckle told him what he needed to know. She really did care for him.

In another part of town, where the more sordid bedsits were interspersed with gap sites for housing parking lots and illegal businesses operating unlicensed taxis and distributing qat and hashish, a police van sat waiting for orders. There had been a tip-off about someone described as an illegal asylum seeker. The Home Office wanted him removed, and quickly. The police were on hand in case Border Agency staff encountered serious resistance. There was no reply at the door so the police were summoned to break it down.

The flat was empty. Signs of a hurried exit were evident. The only sign left of the former occupant was a photo found under the bed of an African-looking woman and young children photographed in happier times.

The occupant was, in fact, watching the raid from behind the curtains of a nearby flat belonging to a friend. Unlike his former workmates at the factory he actually read the British broadsheets. And, when he read that article in the *Telegraph*, he realised that he had been betrayed, though by whom and why wasn't clear. Anticipating that the authorities would come after him he had quickly moved in with his friend, stayed off the streets and awaited developments.

Being a refugee was not a new experience. He had survived before and would survive again. But he felt a bitter anger at a country that had taken him in and given him hope and then spat him out again. It was a long time since he had prayed to Allah. But Allah would guide him to do what was right.

CHAPTER 13

THE ABDUCTION

Associated Press, 25 July 2019:

The official Chinese news agency Xinhua has reported that a flotilla of Chinese warships has made a 'goodwill' visit to friendly countries in the Indian Ocean. The vessels passed close to the Indian Andaman Islands en route to Dacca; sailed around the Indian coast to Karachi as part of a visit hosted by the Pakistan navy, before 'rediscovering the maritime silk route'. Indian sources are said to be investigating claims that the Chinese vessels had strayed into Indian territorial waters and have insisted that India would meet the 'maritime threat'. President Trump tweeted that China was 'again demonstrating aggressive and expansionist tendencies and aggravating the risks of nuclear confrontation in the subcontinent'.

The events in the subcontinent rippled through the respective communities in Britain. The governments in Delhi and Islamabad, prompted by their allies overseas into a belated disavowal of collective suicide, were seeking to maintain a sufficiently belligerent position to satisfy their hot-blooded militants in politics, and the military, while simultaneously trying to turn down the temperature dial. But it took a while for their acolytes to get the message. There were continuing reports of sectarian mobs running amok. Funerals for the first round of casualties fuelled demands for revenge, feeding another round of attacks. Politicians on both sides reflected on the fact that it had been easier to inflame bigotry than to put out the fires. Hate-filled speeches continued to resonate with the faithful and were amplified in the retelling and in the diaspora.

Muslim communities in Britain were mobilised for a protest demonstration denouncing the Indian government. Cooler heads at the local mosque cautioned against it: the militant cleric would demand to be heard; the black flag wavers might appear and dominate the media coverage; the factory where hundreds of local Muslims worked would again be at the centre of unwanted attention; the English Revival – a virulent, post-Brexit, nationalist group – might organise a counter-demonstration that could produce violence. The police also expressed concern and strongly advised cancellation.

The police advice was not heeded. A lot of people felt the need to let off steam and exercise their democratic rights. About a thousand of them gathered near the town hall. Their numbers included many of the same characters who had marched on the factory but, mercifully, not the black flag wavers. About a hundred English Revival protesters turned up, too, separated from the Muslims by a thick blue line. These activists – almost all young men with shaven heads, bulging muscles, bare torsos and tattoos – were clearly not here for a political seminar. The political descendants of Mosley's blackshirts, the NF, the BNP and EDL, were enjoying an upsurge in their fortunes and here was a perfect platform to demonstrate their contempt for foreigners in general and brown-skinned Muslims in particular. Tucked away around the corner were a substantial number of police riot vehicles in the event of trouble.

Steve observed all of this from the window of his office in the town hall and saw that he was not the only watcher. Plain clothes officers with cameras were filming the event, capturing faces for posterity, a fact that had registered with a significant number of demonstrators whose faces were masked. Steve did, however, notice a few familiar faces from his meetings, one of which was Mo.

The organisers lined up a series of speakers including a well-known MP and a Muslim peer who were politely received, and, then, less celebrated but more animated, there was a man in traditional Kashmiri dress who had honed his oratorical skills on the street rather than in the Palace of Westminster. The political heat rose perceptibly and it was approaching boiling point when the preacher whom Steve had seen at the mosque clambered onto the rostrum. He started slowly, switching between heavily accented English and an Asian language familiar to his audience. As he picked up speed he held up a picture of the Indian Prime Minister leading to outraged shouts and chants of 'Pakistan Zindabad. Pakistan Zindabad. Allahu Akbar. Allahu Akbar.' As he concluded his peroration and prepared to leave the stage, his supporters at the front grabbed the picture and set fire to it, waving the blazing poster in front of a conveniently placed TV camera. A choreographed outburst of spontaneous anger.

The controlled nature of the demonstration was not understood by the police officer commanding the line who saw arson as a prelude to anarchy and instructed his men to intervene. By advancing into the crowd they inadvertently created a bridge-head for the English Revival to charge into. Before long, fists were swinging and heavy boots were finding tender flesh. Although small in number relative to the size of the crowd, the Revival had a vast superiority in street fighting skills. They cut through the crowd flailing fists as they went, before orchestrating a well-planned tactical retreat by which time the police had re-established their line. As the troops from English Revival marched off in triumph down the nearest street, chanting slogans and waving captured banners, the Muslims counted their wounded. Steve could see from his vantage point that his group of friends had borne the brunt of the attack. Mo was clutching his face and his white tunic was covered in blood, the badge of martyrdom.

ⵜⵜⵜⵜⵜⵜⵜⵜⵜⵜⵜ

The demonstration was captured, too, on network television and YouTube. Scenes of Muslims in Britain being beaten by white racist thugs, while (mostly) white police officers milled ineffectually in the background, provided further evidence for millions in the Middle East, Africa and Asia, already inclined to believe that Western countries were involved in a crusade against Islam. Taken in isolation, the British news was bad enough. But the bulletins also had dramatic coverage of gruesome massacres carried out by Assad's forces, accompanied by Russian advisers, 'mopping up' the last centres of radical Islamic resistance at the end of the Syrian civil war; a revival of hostilities in Gaza; and reports of brutality in the 'concentration camps' established in several European countries to hold suspected Muslim militants. Le Fevre's dystopian and self-fulfilling narrative found a perfect echo in the Muslim world. And that world included many millions in India and Pakistan following the news on Al Jazeera or social media.

ⵜⵜⵜⵜⵜⵜⵜⵜⵜⵜⵜⵜ

In Pakistan, a Cabinet meeting was reconvened to which the military High Command, including General Rashid, were invited. It was decided that the military would press ahead with preparations for a 'worst case' scenario, including an underground nuclear test to demonstrate Pakistan's preparedness.

In Mumbai, the atmosphere was tense. From the top of Parrikar House Deepak could see several columns of smoke from some of the densely populated slums where sectarian violence had broken out. He received strong advice from his management team to work from his apartment. But he was determined to have a presence at the factory to face down Desai's uninvited 'advisers'.

He set off as usual from his apartment block with the added precaution of an armed security guard alongside the driver. The roads were eerily quiet but not in any way threatening.

But as the Bentley approached the main highway to join the stream of traffic to the north, a transit van pulled out in front of it from a concealed drive. Deepak's car screeched to a halt. And then another van pulled up behind, blocking it in. Armed men in hoods jumped from the two vans and converged on the car. Deepak was pulled out of the back; as he resisted he heard several shots in the background as the guard fired at the assailants and they fired back.

Within seconds he had been bundled into the back of the van, his legs tied with cord, his arms bound behind him and tape stuck across his mouth. The van drove off at speed onto the main road. It had all happened in less than a minute.

Lying in extreme discomfort on the rattling metal floor of the transit van, with two hooded men pointing guns at him, Deepak struggled to make sense of what had happened. His bodyguard presumably dead? Driver? Probably also dead. He was still alive; and had his captors wanted him dead, they had had ample opportunity already. Kidnap was the obvious explanation; there had been several cases in the past of Bollywood stars and rich individuals, or their children, being abducted in this way. He was certainly worth a lot more alive than dead. Or, conceivably, they had something seriously unpleasant in store for him, like the late Mr Patel.

After a journey of fifteen minutes or so – still well within the city limits, he reckoned – they turned onto a rougher track. Judging by the hubbub of human noise and the smells, savoury and unsavoury, penetrating the vehicle, they were trundling slowly into the heart of a crowded slum. Eventually the vehicle came to a halt. Deepak was blindfolded, then dragged out of the back and brought into what he judged by the echo to be a substantial building with a concrete floor, set aside from the main part of the community. His blindfold was removed and he was thrown into a side room, on the floor, still bound.

His captors – he guessed half a dozen – slammed the door and left him, bruised and terrified, in the dark.

Kate's mind was in turmoil. She hadn't slept on the overnight flight to India and she filled the time watching films, not really concentrating. She had received a call from Deepak's sister Veena very early in the morning, explaining that a few hours earlier Deepak had been abducted. The police knew where he was and had a building surrounded. Negotiations were taking place. But his captors were violent and irrational. No one could say when the crisis would come to an end. Veena knew how Deepak felt about Kate and wanted her to be properly informed. Kate decided on the spot to go out to India and booked the evening flight. She then had a tense conversation with Jonathan, explaining that there was an 'emergency', unspecified, and she would be gone for several days; he would be in charge of the girls. An indignant Stella was told that she would have to cope with the weekly advice surgery on her own. Polly, the researcher, was entrusted with the job of tactfully fielding other queries and manufacturing excuses.

As she tried to compose her thoughts, she was prepared for the fact that Deepak might be dead when she arrived in Mumbai. Another part of her toyed with the idea of a successful rescue and a future in India: the life behind her was a mess, both her marriage and her short political career. In front of her was the possibility at least of real love allied to useful work with her business associates. But she had her daughters and the umbilical cord was long and strong. Nor did she really want to run away from failure. Now, altogether more alarming outcomes seemed more plausible than a romantic ending.

On arrival she went to the airport information desk where Mr Parrikar's driver would collect her. When she arrived at the desk she was approached by an attractive but tearful young woman who introduced herself as 'Bunty' Bomani, Deepak's PA. She spoke very quickly, full of emotion, and tried to explain the sequence of events of Deepak's abduction. Kate was to come to the family residence where the rest of the Parrikars were assembled.

The driver, whom she had last met on her late night tryst, was uninjured and had recovered sufficiently to drive her there. The morning traffic was no worse than normal and they made reasonable time. But Kate was not remotely interested in the passing scenery. This was the latest big emotional shock in a few weeks – the riot, the discovery of her affair, her departure from government, now this – the worst of all.

Her first four decades of life had been largely free of trauma. She had lost her father in her twenties but he had been a rather distant figure and when he, metaphorically, disappeared beneath the waves, the waters had closed over him remarkably quickly. There was childbirth, yes, but compared to some of her friends, it had been smooth and uncomplicated. No major illnesses. Healthy, normal, children. A love life, until very recently, satisfactory if nothing much more, or less. She realised that she would need to pull herself together when she met Deepak's family. But in the car she let herself go. Bunty took her hand and they wept together. It seemed obvious that Bunty also had an attachment beyond the professional but Kate did not need or want to probe.

When they arrived at the Parrikar home on Malabar Hill, the drive was full of cars and there were a couple of police vans and uniformed and armed men standing around or communicating through walkie-talkies. A crowd of on-lookers was gathering at the gate: people who sensed, from the activity, that something untoward was taking place. She saw in the gardens the incongruous but remarkable sight of a peacock in full display: a timeless courting ritual rather wasted on the preoccupied human audience.

Kate was ushered into the house, a luxurious bungalow overlooking the city and bay below. She had remembered enough of her visit preparation to offer a Namaste to the elderly couple in front of her whom she took to be the parents: a shrunken, crumpled, unshaven, toothless man in pyjamas and an equally diminutive elderly lady in a cotton sari who insisted on trying to stand to greet her despite obvious pain and frailty.

Kate had discussed at some length with Deepak, in happier times, how she should be introduced to the family; but of course he wasn't here. There was an awkward silence and, then, a pretty woman in a sharp Western business suit stepped forward. Veena, the sister. She took command of the situation switching effortlessly between cut-glass English, which would only have come from an expensive private school education in the UK, and the language understood by her parents. She introduced Kate to the other people in the room including a rather silent brother and took her to a side room – 'operational HQ' – where a policeman was simultaneously fielding several mobile phone calls while his two assistants waited for instructions.

'This is Inspector Mankad,' Veena explained. 'He is helping us and understands the background to Deepak's abduction. There is a SWAT team surrounding his place of captivity but the Inspector is liaising with us on a ransom demand.'

Veena steered Kate by the elbow to a quiet corner of the big room where the parents and others were gathered. Kate had time to notice the beautiful, thick, handwoven carpets and the stunning artefacts of brass and wood that would have cost a fortune in a London gallery. No one was in a mood for conversation but Veena offered to explain what she could of the background.

'I don't know how much Deepak has told you?'

'A bit,' Kate responded. 'The murder of this Patel. Exposure of the family's business secrets. Then the trouble at the factory. An American company called Global and a man… Desai? There is a link with Global in the UK where it has been trying to take over the company that was to be Deepak's business partner. I had a rather exciting visit there, which you may know about. But, to be frank, I have only a hazy understanding of what is going on here and Deepak seemed too preoccupied to give me the full story.'

Veena began her explanation. 'You have the bare bones. There is a shadowy organisation, basically a criminal gang, in Mumbai called Trishul. Has its roots in the murky world where the militant, more fanatical nationalists and religious fundamentalists, who are now a big force in politics, and growing, overlap with the criminal underworld. Politicians and criminals have always fed off each other in this city, as they often do in other countries, but the sectarian element is particularly poisonous now. Goondas – as we call them – think that, if they wave a saffron flag, they will get immunity. Perhaps they are right.

'Our friend the Inspector – who is actually a lot smarter than he looks – has a handle on how the Trishul gang or gangs work. They have been muscling in on several well-established companies like Daddy-ji's making demands for protection money. Control over land and property gives them leverage and the construction industry is notoriously corrupt. This, in turn, attracts the politicians who need money for elections. The Trishul gang has been building up its network of political friends from an extreme Hindu nationalist party in this part of India, and related groups:

some of them religious extremists. One clever ploy, however, was to work through the Sheikh, a Muslim who was vulnerable to pressure because of his family connections in Pakistan and was also close to Daddy-ji.

'But there is another level to the Trishul operation that lifts it beyond the mafia-type outfits we are used to. There is some kind of link up with like-minded people at a national level, in politics, the armed forces and the intelligence services. The extremists have been hard at work in the last few weeks fanning the flames of Indo-Pak conflict – you have seen the news, and read the papers. One of the key figures is the man called Desai who is at the centre of a web of these political, intelligence and military people in Delhi. He is also involved in that US company, Global. This group dreamed up the idea of using the Sheikh's connections to bring in and set up a Pakistani agent leading to the exposure of a "sabotage plot", raising tension between our countries another notch. Deepak was in their way and – anyway – these people despise his secular, liberal, Western values.

'Deepak alerted his friends in Delhi – there are a lot of them already alarmed by the drift in Indian politics. They made the mistake of placing too much faith in the leading family. "Madam", like your Mrs Thatcher, was tough as old boots but her grandchildren and their hangers-on are absolutely clueless. Some of them are deeply corrupt. Deepak was one of a group of businessmen financing a secular "front"' to mobilise opposition. His own experiences in Mumbai were featured in a big exposé in the weekly *India Today*. He said too much; mentioned Desai; implied that the Pakistani spy was set up. There are some things you don't say even in a democracy like ours. Now this... which we think is connected but aren't sure.'

Veena hadn't paused for breath. But, for the first time Kate could see how the pieces of the jigsaw fitted together including her own small corner. Veena turned away but Kate could sense that she was trying to compose herself to maintain the front of business-like conversation. But it was clear, from the way Veena clenched her fists and dug her fingernails into the palms of her hands, that the calmness was a façade that might soon crumble. After a deep breath, Veena took up the story again.

'Deepak was seized by an armed gang yesterday on his way to the factory. The gang who took him have been tracked down to a slum area quite near here and are surrounded. Inspector Mankad's working theory is that it is a group related to the gang who killed Mr Patel and also linked to the extreme ultra-nationlist party. He knows where they hang out and, sure enough, the gang were seen there unloading a bound man from a van. It seems to have been a thoroughly clumsy operation or perhaps they didn't expect to have a competent and honest police officer on the case. Anyway, a team of paramilitaries has taken over and we are praying that they get Deepak out alive.'

Kate could see that Veena was now close to breaking point and they lapsed into a long silence, broken only by the shuffle of servants and the clink of glasses as tumblers were refilled with an inexhaustible supply of lime juice. An hour passed. Two. Then as evening approached on the second day of the crisis Inspector Mankad emerged from his room. 'Something is happening soon,' he announced. 'Our men are surrounding a building where he is. I want someone from the family...' Kate realised that he could mean identification of a corpse. She wasn't sure she had the stomach for what was coming. But when Veena stepped forward and announced that she would go with the police, Kate insisted on joining her.

The procession of police vehicles made its way through the city led by motorcycle outriders. The journey was nonetheless infuriatingly slow through streets jammed with pedestrians, cycles, motorbikes, rickshaws, mopeds, buses, cars and animals. The sirens and flashing lights of the police helped a little but they were just part of the urban cacophony and kaleidoscope and the crowds parted only slowly and reluctantly.

After what seemed an eternity they arrived on a road surrounded by a sea of shacks spreading to the horizon in each direction: the townscape of Dharavi and the neighbouring slums. There was a helicopter hovering a hundred yards away with a searchlight penetrating the gathering dusk and the fog of woodsmoke. And people everywhere with police trying and failing to marshal them behind an official-looking tape. Kate could see the excitement on the faces of the adults and the wide-eyed wonder of the children: better than the cinema, and free. And unlike the communal troubles of recent days, this drama could be watched in safety.

Kate and Veena were told to stay with their police car and not to come close to the action. Tension grew with the crowds building up, the noise level rising. Then, suddenly, there was the dull thud of an explosion, a brief crackle of gunfire and a plume of smoke rose from somewhere beneath the probing light of the helicopter. The crowd gaped and then cheered, but whether supporting the police or the putative villains wasn't clear.

After a few minutes a senior police officer beckoned to them to follow him into the settlement. They passed through narrow lanes, trying to step over rather than into the open sewers and avoiding the mangy dogs, chickens, pigs and children. When Kate recalled these events long after, one image stuck in her mind: passing a fetid rivulet, a storm drain, and seeing a little boy, totally indifferent to the chaos and excitement around him, poking with a stick at his imaginary navy and in particular steering a large paper boat, the flagship of his fleet.

Eventually they came to a more open area on raised ground and in the middle was an extensive single storey building – a meeting hall? perhaps a school? – with smoke rising through its roof. They were directed inside where police and paramilitary officers with automatic weapons were examining several corpses splayed on the floor. No Deepak.

Kate saw that there was a side room, with a half-open door guarded by a policeman, and pushed her way inside. There was a body on the floor, inert, facing away from her, with blood covering the ears and the back of the head. She knew immediately who it was, or had been. She turned the corpse towards her to look at the familiar face and gazed at it. Then, an eyelid started to quiver. She heard the rasp of a breath. She screamed for help and heard the clatter of boots coming up behind her.

<hr>

Deepak Parrikar managed a smile through the bandages covering his head. Several times in the last few days, spent mostly unconscious, with concussion, his doctors had feared for the worst. But he came through. His injuries were still severe but no longer life threatening.

He was gradually coming to understand what had happened. In the chaotic shoot-out, a bullet had entered his body causing severe blood loss and damage to bone and muscle but missing his vital organs. The greatest damage had been done not by the bullet but by a metal rod when one of his captors had seen him try to wriggle to safety. The surgeons had nonetheless been able to heal the skull fracture and contain the swelling of the brain.

It would take some time yet for him to comprehend his new celebrity status. The raid had a television audience of millions. The narrative was stripped of its complexities: Deepak was a champion of secular values, almost killed by extremists embedded in the world of gangland. The politics of the abduction, the exposure in the national press of the links between the extremists and organised crime provided a catalyst for attempts to bring together the various secular parties and factions in a common front to fight the 2019 general election. Deepak was deified somewhat prematurely by those imagining that his soul had already ascended from its earthly capsule.

The Prime Minister, no less, had seen the value of distancing himself from his party's more violent and extreme elements and their unsavoury allies like the ultra-nationalists. He sent a message of sympathy and support to the family. The abduction and attempted murder of a leading industrialist, supposedly for political ends, outraged opinion formers in a way that casualties of recent riots and the daily suffering of countless Dalits, Muslims and Christians in village India had not. The more pragmatic elements in the ruling party had drawn the conclusion that a show, at least, of inclusive secularism was a necessary requirement to staying in office. The Prime Minister had concluded his handwritten note with a tantalising comment, that he was considering a proposal that he would shortly make to Deepak 'to play a major role in India's political life'.

The drama had affected some of the other actors too. Mr Desai had withdrawn back into the shadows. There would be time again to exploit his particular skills, his links with the Mumbai underworld and his influential American friends, But, for the moment, what was needed was a blander, more emollient face.

Inspector Mankad was lauded for his efforts even though the attempt at negotiation was confused and the wild firing of the police was responsible for several deaths and at least some of Deepak's injuries. Instead of being despatched, as he feared, to some fly-blown police station in the rural depths of Maharashtra he was rapidly promoted to Superintendent within his current command, albeit on the clear understanding that his Trishul enquiry would be limited to some of the more egregiously venal and less elevated politicians involved.

All of this and the other missing details of the last few weeks were explained to Deepak by the two women who had moved to the centre of his life. With his parents no longer able to function effectively and deeply scarred, psychologically, by recent experiences, control of the family company had effectively passed to Veena with the consent of her other, less assertive, brother, Manu. She had prised out of her father's tenacious grip most of the financial secrets of the property empire and had set about restructuring it on more conventional business lines, as well as establishing the charitable trust for her father, albeit less generously endowed than he envisaged.

Parrikar Avionics already had a strong senior management team capable of operating, at least for a while, without their CEO and without Mr Desai's unsolicited advice.

Sitting next to her was Kate who, in a short but intense period of mutual need, had become a close friend and confidante. Both the family and nursing staff insisted that her presence had led to a measurable step forward in Deepak's recovery. The same was not said of the more reluctant, dutiful, visit from Delhi of Rose Parrikar. There were months of gradual rehabilitation ahead but full recovery was now probable rather than merely possible.

***

Kate's visit to India was an item on the agenda of an emergency meeting of the executive committee of the Surrey Heights Conservative Association. 'I hesitate to raise this difficult issue,' said the Chairman, Sir William Beale, non-executive director of several companies and, once, a powerful figure in the City, a former Lord Mayor of London. 'But several of you have asked me to put it down for discussion. I recognise that there is a lot of feeling in the association about the behaviour of our MP in recent months. We all had such high hopes of her, especially when she became a senior figure in our government. Who would like to speak?'

Most of the members present put up their hands. 'I am absolutely disgusted,' said one, 'we might as well have a

Lib Dem or a socialist as our MP.' 'She campaigned for Remain. Just shows the contempt those people have for decent British values,' interjected another. The discussion centred initially on her wayward, rebellious voting record since she had left the government – 'sacked' insisted one of the members – and a variety of strange causes she had taken up far removed from the interests and prejudices of Surrey Heights. There was the series of parliamentary questions she had asked about a missing asylum seeker from Eritrea: 'I ask you... where the hell is that?' 'It's some rat-hole in Africa, for God's sake.' 'How many people want more asylum seekers anyway?' Then there was the infamous debate on social housing where she admitted she had been wrong to oppose more of it in her constituency: 'I suppose she wants to bring every single mother in Britain to live here.'

But these were merely the hors d'oeuvres. The main course was 'the Indian boyfriend', or 'the coloured gentleman' as one of the elderly members preferred to call him. 'I don't have anything against them myself. But I didn't expect to see our MP chasing one of them to India like some silly school girl.' 'And what about her lovely family? I have been told she now spends her time – when she is in the country – at her flat in London, not at home.'

One brooding figure had not yet spoken. Stella was still simmering with resentment after being relieved of her duties as Kate's casework officer (and the associated remuneration). She had had to make way for a bright young woman called Anne-Marie. She had started to produce letters to constituents for the MP to sign that made some sense, answered the questions asked and were not padded out with party propaganda. For this, Kate had been profoundly grateful, since Stella's letters – which Kate had given up trying to improve – had become a source of ridicule in the correspondence columns of the local press. But Anne-Marie's faultless spoken English was delivered with a French accent, the product of her childhood, and this reinforced the sense that, thanks to the MP, 'bloody foreigners' had penetrated deep into the inner sanctum of the local party at a time when Britishness was being rediscovered and continental miscegenation was being discouraged.

Stella served up her dish of revenge with icy venom. 'I think I can claim to know Mrs Thompson better than any of you. I have worked... tried to work... with her since she was elected, which some of you may remember I masterminded. She has some good points, of course, but I speak for all of us when I say I am deeply, deeply, disappointed. I felt particularly let down – actually, betrayed is what I felt – when for the first time in many, many years the MP did not turn up for our annual fete. She was, I believe, in India.' Gasps of disapproval followed.

'We can sit here and complain. Or we can do something about it. I have taken the liberty of exploring with party HQ the procedure for deselection. You may recall that, a few years ago, one of our Yorkshire MPs was deselected for not carrying out her constituency duties as she should. I have established what the procedure is and,' with a final, triumphant, flourish, 'we should *do* it.'

The nods and grunts of approval were taken by the Chairman as assent. But there was a belated objection from one of the local councillors who remembered how much enthusiasm there had been for Kate when she was first adopted. He could also claim to speak for the under-eighties in the local party and had a job – as an estate agent. 'I think we should be careful. There will be more bad publicity. The other parties will exploit it. Mrs Thompson hasn't done anything illegal or abused her expenses. Her visit was in the summer recess when other MPs were on holiday. And my wife tells me that her friends admire her for being broad-minded and an independent thinker.'

This novel thought threw the Chairman off his stride but Stella moved quickly to close the rebellion down. 'The mood of the executive is clear. I suggest we vote on a motion to convene an extraordinary meeting of members with a resolution of no confidence in our Member of Parliament.' Agreed thirteen to one, with one abstention.

A few weeks later parliament reconvened and the National Security Council was summoned to a special meeting in the COBRA room under the Cabinet Office where Cabinet ministers, intelligence and service chiefs consider matters of exceptional sensitivity. There was one item on the agenda: aircraft carriers. The Prime Minister opened proceedings.

'Some of you were here when we last considered the future of our two new aircraft carriers, the *Queen Elizabeth* and the *Prince of Wales*. It was a mess then and it is now a bigger mess. Thanks to our dear friend Gordon Brown, whose legacy this was, we have an unnecessary, unwanted pair of white elephants. The project was designed to create thousands of new jobs not a million miles from his constituency, to keep the Scots loyal to Labour – what a joke! – and keep the Admirals happy – sorry, Chief, not you, you were probably still commanding rowing boats at the time.' Prolonged laughter followed.

'When we last looked at this, during the Coalition, some of us,' he said, looking at the then Chancellor, 'wanted to scrap the programme. We flunked it. The Scottish referendum was in the offing. The *Telegraph* ran a big campaign, prompted, I suspect, by the top brass in the navy, to keep the carriers. How could we save the Falklands again without them? A lot of wishful thinking about how the carriers could be adapted to carry the F-35 (which, of course, we hadn't bought and couldn't afford). And the frigates we would need to protect the carriers could also be built on Clydeside to provide more jobs for the Scots.

'You can guess what has happened since. All the warnings about the difficulties of adapting the F-35 to fly off the carriers proved to be spot on. The costs have escalated out of control. Then, we have had a series of own goals. The bloody Commies in Unite have been working to rule to make the job spin out longer. Then we had to agree to use British steel to avoid a scandal over our using cheap Chinese steel for the navy. Almost doubled the cost. Now, the Chancellor tells us that he can find no more money down the back of the sofa. His borrowing targets are looking worse by the week. There is no more money left.'

The Chancellor nodded in agreement while pulling a face to signal his annoyance at having his failures of financial control given such prominence.

'We will have to make some difficult choices. What I am absolutely clear about is that we cannot compromise Trident. Going ahead with the full replacement was the best decision we made after getting those wretched Lib Dems off our back. Within these four walls Trident is a complete waste of money, isn't independent and isn't a deterrent for our main enemy, the terrorists, and belongs to a bygone age. But the public and our friends in the press love it. It keeps us on the UN Security Council. And it has helped us to stuff the Labour Party.

'But, of course, it is costing us a bomb.' (Nervous laughter.) 'We thought the four subs and missiles would cost twenty billion pounds back in 2010; now we will be lucky to get away with a hundred billion. Unless we decide to abolish the army as a fighting force or put the air force back into World War Two aircraft, we have to choose: Trident or the carriers.'

The PM turned to Jim Chambers. 'Jim, I asked you to help us set out the options. What do we do?' The Business Secretary had little background in defence but enjoyed the Prime Minister's confidence. The Defence Secretary smarted at the snub but he knew he could lose his job if it emerged that he had been sitting on the cost escalation numbers for months and had done nothing about the issue; so he nodded deferentially, while Jim Chambers spoke.

'As you say, Prime Minister, it is a bloody mess. If this had happened in my businesses, heads would have rolled by now.' He looked very pointedly at the Chief of the Naval Staff, Admiral Cooke-Davis. 'But let me give my honest assessment of what we can do. Well, first, we could throw money at the project to finish it as quickly as possible and get the ships into service. We could pay for them by jettisoning not just the planes but also surface ships to defend them. Fill the decks with helicopters or something else to use the space. But, big buts. The naval people say that without planes or protection the carriers will be as much use in a fire-fight as cruise liners. We shall be slated by our own chaps on the back benches and in the press. And we shall have revolting Scots telling us we have stabbed them in the back over the frigates. So, no go.

'Second, we could pull the plug completely. Park the damn things in the Cromarty Firth with all those oil rigs. But we have gone too far for that. Her Majesty has already blessed the *Queen Elizabeth*, and the *Prince of Wales* is half built. Portsmouth is already kitted out to maintain and service them. Revolting Scots are one thing. We can't have south coast marginal seats also put at risk. And the navy and its friends in the media would crucify us. No go.

'So my recommendation is that we press on with the programme as best we can – finish equipping, build the destroyers and the frigates, buy some jets for appearance's sake. But sell the second carrier rather than keep it.'

'Who on earth will buy a carrier that we don't want and can't afford?' piped up the Scottish Secretary who hadn't been kept in the loop.

'Ah! Our people in Delhi have been talking to the Indians about this for several years,' Chambers replied. 'The Indians have a carrier building programme like us – two vessels and also horribly behind schedule and over-budget. One, the *Vaishal*, is in service; the other, *Vasant*, is years away. There is a lot of national pride involved in building their own. But the recent trouble with Pakistan has seriously rattled them. They need money to press on with missile defence. They also have the Chinese in the background with a new naval presence in the Indian Ocean. An extra carrier delivered quickly from us (at a discount!) would be timely – and they can put their converted MiGs on it, I believe.'

'Brilliant, Jim. Spot on,' the Prime Minister crowed. 'And after your recent success with the Indian missile defence project – now up and running again, I am glad to say – I have every confidence we can carry it off.'

'We did have some casualties.'

'Yes, the gorgeous Kate, poor girl. But she will get over it. You might try to use her Indian contacts – you know who I mean…'

The Chief of the Naval Staff set out all the reasons why the export proposal was a terrible idea and why the Treasury should pay for the full programme of naval modernisation. But his service colleagues pointedly declined to endorse spending commitments that would impinge on their own budgets.

It was left to the Foreign Secretary to warn of unintended consequences. 'Sorry, colleagues. Someone has to spoil the party. Even assuming the Indians want the wretched thing and can afford to pay for it – I assume we are not giving it away – we need to think about the wider implications. India and Pakistan have been involved in a confrontation that has been perilously close to war. Things are still very tense.

'Now the Chinese are involved. At Pakistan's request they have a flotilla of vessels including their own aircraft carrier circling India. We hear they may have strayed into Indian territorial waters. The Americans are seriously alarmed; this is the first time the Chinese have ventured militarily west of the Malacca Straits, in strength, since

Admiral Zheng-He went to Africa in the fifteenth century. If we get involved in fuelling an escalating naval arms race in the Indian Ocean, it could be highly destabilising. Please think again.'

'Thank you, Foreign Secretary,' the PM said with a nod. 'But I am going to have to overrule you. The rest of us are agreed – aren't we? No more Boy Scouts. It's "export or die". Post-Brexit, India is our best hope of breaking into big non-European markets. We have to get our priorities right. So, gentlemen, we are agreed. But hush-hush. I don't want to read about this meeting in the press. The Cabinet has been leaking like a paper boat recently. It must not happen again.'

It did not take many minutes for the report of the National Security Council to reach the Red Admiral. And as soon as he could organise a secure line, calls were placed to Louisiana, Delhi, Tel Aviv and Moscow.

The Admiral's stock was already high with his business colleagues and his expected commission would go a long way to paying for the ocean-going luxury yacht now on order. The Pulsar contract, if not the bigger aircraft deal, was now agreed and waiting for a formal signature. Now a big naval project offered tantalising opportunities for Global Analysis and Research and its network of associates. The carrier would need protection against attack from aircraft and missiles and the Pulsar/Parrikar Avionics technology would be invaluable. The carrier could also take adapted MiGs, and friends in Moscow could perhaps come up with an offer the Indians would find irresistible. The flourishing, but very secret, cooperation between India and Israel could find new possibilities in upgrading India's rather antiquated naval communications system. The Admiral had learnt from experience not to get too excited or to over-promise. For that reason, he thought it better not to tell his colleagues about the progress he had made in getting Global established as a leading Tier 1 Supplier in the UK's new Trident replacement programme. But the possibilities were mouth-watering.

⬛⬛⬛⬛⬛⬛⬛⬛⬛⬛⬛⬛

Steve and Shaida had their first row. The 'date' had proved less fulfilling than Steve, at least, had imagined: a drink after work in the chaste and discreet environment of a local coffee house. She had exaggerated her father's endorsement. She knew he would never countenance a relationship with someone who, however admired, was not merely from a different cultural tradition but was divorced, with young children. She knew that at some point she would face an awful choice, a fork in the road, that would affect her destiny for ever. She also loved her family and dreaded the thought of having to choose.

Not just that: her emotional energy was absorbed in steeling herself to snoop on her brother and his friends for the plausible, but demanding, Liam. And her mind was absorbed in unravelling the algorithms guarding Global's secrets. Even for someone as self-disciplined and capable as Shaida the strain was beginning to show.

Besides, Steve had become more distant. Since his election to the national executive of his union there had been growing numbers of absences on union business: meetings around the country as well as in London. He had explained that he was sinking under the weight of union responsibilities, the council and the local party. The meetings at the mosque had petered out: lack of time. She understood, but part of her resented being in a lengthening queue for his attention.

Then, he had proposed that she accompany him on a visit to Glasgow where he was meeting the Scottish shipyard workers.

'And what is my role? Researcher? Secretary?' Shaida asked pointedly.

'Well, I just wanted your company.'

'So, this is a double room at the Grand Central?'

'If you like.'

'As your date?'

'Well – I suppose… yes, isn't that what we both want?'

'God! Have you thought what this means? How do I explain it at home? Where do I go afterwards? Do you really know what you are asking of me?'

'I understand… sorry… I should have thought.'

'Yes, you should! I do want to come, but this is an impossible thing to ask of me.'

She could see that their relationship was fizzling out thanks to her distractions and his impatience. She decided on a make or break move: total candour.

'The truth is that you don't begin to understand what makes me tick. I think you have this idealised picture of an exotic Asian female, probably a virtuous virgin, just waiting to be set free. You couldn't be further from the truth. I am tempted to shatter your illusions.'

'Try me.'

'OK. But you won't like what you hear.'

'I'll risk it.'

'Where do I start? Well, at school I was gifted and marked out for higher things: a girl who loved maths. The trouble began when I wanted to be a normal British teenager. Fooled around with my girlfriends. Experimented. One night I got totally plastered. Somehow got to bed avoiding my parents. Then boys. Had my first sexual encounter at – what? – fifteen, maybe less. Then one day on my desk at school there was a Pakistani newspaper with a picture of a girl, my age, disfigured by acid burns. Someone had written across it in red ink "SLAG". Someone from my community had been spying on me.

'My parents got to hear about some of this and I was on the next plane to Pakistan to find a husband. One of my uncles tried to marry me off to a disgusting old man with dyed ginger hair who spat all over the place. My dad – bless him – took pity on me and I was allowed to come back on the strict understanding that I stuck to my books. I did. Got a place at Cambridge. But the family thought this was too high a risk so I finished up doing accounting at the local uni.

'Didn't stop me. I had a series of affairs. Very discreet. A group of Asian girls worked together to organise safe rooms and generally help each other. The nearest thing I had to a proper relationship was with a post-grad Israeli, a soldier with a family back home. I got used to living dangerously and enjoyed the thrill of it. Aren't you shocked?' Shaida looked challengingly at Steve, who knew it was now his turn to open up.

'A different world from mine. I left school at sixteen to care for my dying mother. Never went to university. Then married my childhood sweetheart. When you were discovering yourself at college I was helping – or usually not helping – bring up three toddlers. I lost myself in politics and union work, not affairs.'

'It gets worse,' Shaida replied. 'When I left uni and came here I wanted – needed – to continue my double life. A friend told me about internet dating. Sex without strings. So whenever I feel like it, I ask for permission to go to a "seminar" or "training course" in London and meet a man. Some bad experiences; mostly OK. I enjoy the control. At home I am a meek, submissive female lacking only a husband. I realise this can't go on; deep down I am not a

cold person. But I must have turned you off completely?'
Shaida studied Steve's face closely for his reaction.

'No. I suspected there was a lot more to you than meets
the eye. And since my marriage broke down I haven't
exactly been celibate either.'

'That's a relief.' They smiled at each other, glad that they
had shared their personal stories at last.

That night Shaida did not sleep: not just because of her
own conflicts of loyalty and identity, which had led to this
crisis point in her personal life, but because of growing
worries about her brother's slide back into the clutches
of his militant friends.

***

Steve's mind was also in turmoil after this exchange. He
adored her still, but her coquettish playfulness, alternating
between Miss Brisk and her affectionate teasing, so that
she was always just out of range, had become deeply
frustrating. And while he thought he could live with
the newly revealed Shaida it would require a degree of
emotional maturity he had never achieved before. He
could see that, short of a dramatic break with her family,
nothing would ever happen and the love affair would
gradually burn itself out, unconsummated.

There was frustration on other fronts too. The union
election was initially very satisfying: a recognition of his
talents on a national stage. But the sudden switch from

being a big fish in a small pond to swimming in the sea of national union politics was proving exceptionally difficult.

His brushes with Brother Harking should have warned him that his youth, moderate Labour politics, south of England accent and manufacturing background put him in a small minority. The General Secretary was a hardened militant who had built up a fearsome reputation for skilful organisation and bloody-minded negotiating techniques. This 'young lad', closer to Mandelson than Marx, was not exactly welcome.

And the talk around the table about the problems of nurses, council officers, bus drivers and Whitehall civil servants meant very little. He had one soulmate and he was dying of cancer: the gaunt figure of Kevin Dubbins, the legendary negotiator for the car industry whose guile and pragmatism was a key factor in attracting and keeping investment in Britain. All this, his tiff with Shaida, his ex-wife's demands, and, now, another decision that was looming: whether to pursue the vacancy for a parliamentary candidate to replace the retiring local MP, a window of opportunity that might not be open in future.

To clear his head, he decided to walk downtown after supper. He instinctively headed to the part of town where Shaida lived, one of the middle class, increasingly Asian, districts with well-tended, detached and semi-detached houses and expensive cars. Perhaps in his subconscious he hoped he would see Shaida and be able to signal his continuing commitment to her. He saw the house ahead and stopped, realising that his presence, if seen, would be difficult to explain to her parents. As he waited a familiar figure left the house, head covered by a shawl, and made off in the opposite direction.

Curiosity as well as animal magnetism drew him after her. After ten minutes of fast walking she headed towards an unlit piece of open ground and sat on one of the benches. A figure emerged from the shadows and sat down beside her. A man who looked, from a distance, vaguely familiar. He saw them in close conversation until they stood up to go. She handed over a small package and then they walked off in opposite directions. Sexual jealousy was in danger of dominating his emotional response especially after what he now knew of her private life. But the couple showed no signs of affection and his attempt to fit the shape of the man into his database of physical profiles came up with a name that suggested something quite different from romance: Liam, the MI5 officer. This was something that hadn't formed part of her full and frank disclosure.

CHAPTER 14

REHABILITATION

Reuters, 3 September 2019:

There are uncorroborated reports of a major explosion having taken place several weeks ago in the naval shipyards in Kerala. Commentators speculate that, if there has been disruption to the aircraft carrier building programme, it would help to explain the rumours that the Indian navy is looking at overseas options for a new carrier, regarded as essential to counter the build-up of Chinese as well as Pakistani forces in the Indian Ocean theatre. Commentators have also linked the reported explosion to the Iqbal Aziz trial, warning that Pakistani terrorist cells are still active in India.

The Prime Minister summoned the National Security Council to hear a report back from the High Commissioner, via Skype, on his round of discussions in Delhi about the aircraft carrier.

'We are here to brainstorm,' said the PM. 'Unless we crack this we are left with some pretty gory alternatives. Secretary of State? You came up with this idea in the first place.'

'Well,' Jim Chambers replied, 'we can obviously cut the price or throw in some sweeteners, give them an offer they can't refuse. In effect, give the carrier away.'

The Chancellor and the Defence Secretary both grimaced. The former spoke first. 'We can't be too cavalier. The Public Accounts Committee will be all over us like a rash. I can see the terrible headlines at this distance. And I have to balance the books – there will be a serious hit on the MOD budget.' The Chiefs of Staff also grimaced.

'Jim, back to you.'

'I have had one idea for trying to shift the debate in India. That man Parrikar who was the conduit for the last deal is now a big player. I don't know if you have been following events there but Parrikar has become some kind of hero. Shot up by a gang with connections to the extreme nationalist politicians. Now in hospital recovering from his injuries. If he were to endorse the deal, appeal to his secular friends not to embarrass the government, it might help. High Commissioner? I believe you have market-tested this idea in Delhi and it plays well.'

'Yes, Secretary of State. But the man is in a bad way. Out of danger but still in intensive care. Not sure if the family will welcome dragging him back into controversy.'

'There we have an ace card,' Chambers responded. 'Our Mrs Thompson. Currently giving our whips hell and threatened with deselection. She can reach the parts that others can't.' Jokes were not common currency in the National Security Council but he had made his point. 'We can give her a political lifeline. Back to her former glory, serving the country. Back to being Minister of State? Special envoy? Trade ambassador? Foreign policy Tsar? Whatever.'

The Prime Minister didn't look convinced. 'It's a bit weak. Clutching at straws. But I guess we don't have too many other options. Can I leave this to you, Jim? You know the girl better than I do.'

Steve had agonised for several days about how to raise with Shaida her link to the British intelligence services. He didn't want to acknowledge that he had been following her, late at night, around the town. That would appear distrustful and he found it impossible to explain to himself, let alone her, what had taken hold of him that night. He thought back to the violent clashes he had seen from his office window in the town hall, which could give him a reason to talk to her at their next lunch break.

'Has Mo fully recovered now? He looked a bit of a mess after that demo.'

'Looked worse than it was. But the experience has radicalised him further. "Why didn't the police protect us?" he asks. He genuinely didn't go to make trouble and he could see that the agitators were deliberately winding up the crowd. But being kicked in the head by British "patriots" in a peaceful demonstration has brought him closer to his radical friends. It is a pity you're no longer taking an interest in him,' Shaida said, looking Steve straight in the eye.

'Yes, I am sorry. I could and should have done more. And I promise I will. But can he not see that he is heading for disaster? His card has already been marked by the authorities – who, incidentally, were filming the demo. After the recent wave of arrests, he is only one or two moves from joining them. I haven't told you this, but a man from the security services, Liam, approached me for information about Mo and his group. I believe you contacted him after that article, to clear Mo's name. I was wondering whether he has been on to you or your family since then.'

She hesitated before answering. 'Since we confide in each other and – hopefully – still trust each other, I can tell you what I am not supposed to divulge even to my nearest and dearest. That man Liam told me that if I wanted to keep the family out of trouble, especially Mo, I should keep in regular touch and inform him of anything I pick up. I don't enjoy being a sneak but it is something I have to do.'

Her words understated the pain she felt. Until now, she had successfully juggled her different identities without ever having to really choose. Now she was being forced to, and it hurt.

'Is there anything happening I should know about?' Steve asked.

'Nothing much you don't know already. But please understand: I can't say any more. I have probably said too much already.'

He held her hand for a few minutes before heading back to his work station, but before he left she added: 'Sometimes I think he is right.'

'You mean Liam?'

'No, not Liam. Never mind. Let's leave it.'

✕✕✕✕✕✕✕✕✕✕✕✕✕

Kate received a handwritten letter from her former Secretary of State – 'My dearest Kate… Yours affectionately, Jim' – asking if she would drop by his parliamentary office for a 'catch up'. Having settled into the mind-set of a fully paid-up and thoroughly alienated rebel she was naturally suspicious. And their last serious encounter bore all the hallmarks of his political cynicism: the scapegoating of the innocent night watchman, now disappeared; the backdoor takeover of Pulsar by an American company with some very questionable connections; the side-lining of the talented if idiosyncratic Scottish CEO; the cheerful disregard for the wider consequences of throwing more fuel onto a smouldering Asian fire. Still, the tone of the letter suggested that he wanted something from her: much the safest position to start from. And she was curious.

She went to his office after the last vote of the evening, along the gloomy ministerial corridor where Cabinet ministers held court when not at their departmental desks. Away from the prying eyes and twitching ears of civil servants, this was where the serious, political business of government got done.

'Oh my dear! I am so sorry. How have you been?' Chambers rushed up to plant a kiss on both cheeks, which she accepted before retreating to a safer distance.

'Actually, I am quite enjoying being myself and getting to know something about the interesting characters in this place,' she answered truthfully.

'But I know you have been through hell, Kate. Problems at home. Your Indian friend shot and badly injured. I hear your local association has been making your life difficult too. The awful press.'

'I am coping. But I'm sure you didn't invite me here to offer a shoulder to cry on. I get a sense that you want something.'

'Well, just let's say I think we can help each other.'

She grimaced rather than smiled, and hoped he was taking in her cynical detachment.

'My last experience of helping each other ended with you smelling of roses and me face down in the dung heap.'

'Not quite. But I realise I do owe you. Let me tell you what I can do to help you and then I will tell you what you can do for me.'

'Sounds suspicious. But I'm all ears.'

'For a start, I can get the local Tories off your back. I know Beale, your chair. Not the sharpest knife in the drawer. And a bit past it. But a decent cove. We can help him steer any motion against you into a procedural cul-de-sac.'

'Not sure I care any more.'

'That's silly. You have real talent. People instinctively like and trust you; not many politicians have that. You speak well. Look good. I don't want you to go to waste. And the PM agrees; if we try to rehabilitate you, he will do whatever is needed. And there is something else, more personal.'

Curiosity was beginning to overcome her defensiveness. She waited a few seconds to suppress any sign of eagerness and then encouraged him to go on. 'Such as…?'

'Look, I don't know what the situation at home is. None of my business. Whether you go back to your husband, John, isn't it?'

'Jonathan.'

'Yes, of course, Jonathan. Or ditch him for your Indian friend. It's for you to decide. I am not a marriage guidance counsellor. But I can sense that he is an angry man. Humiliated. Any bloke would be. Maybe we can make him less angry. It would help in any settlement you reach. Money. Access to the children, that kind of thing.'

'I know you have great political skills, Jim. But how on earth do you propose to perform a miracle of anger management on my estranged husband?'

'The Honours System.'

Kate laughed. 'Jonathan is quite vain and status conscious but I can't see an OBE or MBE meaning much to him.'

'I was thinking more of something else. The Lords. I understand that he has been a party donor – not premier league, but generous. And we need people to restore political balance. All those Lib Dems after the Coalition. Then we hoped that when the hard left took over the Labour Party they would stop demanding more. Not so. Every time there is a threatened strike on the tube or the trains we are told that some Fred Bloggs has to be given a peerage. They see it as a rest home for the Labour aristocracy. So, we need more credible Tories. Jonathan, as far as I know, isn't gaga, isn't a certified crook and isn't a foaming-at-the-mouth nutter. We should be able to line this up. Would it help you if it was made clear, privately, that this was all your doing, fighting his corner?'

'I suppose I shouldn't be shocked any more,' Kate answered. 'And I suppose I should be grateful that you have taken the trouble to research what is needed to get me on board. What exactly is it you want me to do?'

'India again. Continuation of what you were doing. This time an aircraft carrier. You are our emissary – we can call you whatever you like including your old role, or some posh new title. Make it clear that you are thoroughly rehabilitated.'

'That's a bit sick, isn't it? Palming off our unwanted weapons like that. I take it you read the newspapers – about how close the subcontinent has been to a new war.'

'Now, don't go all moral on me. We have to earn our living like any other country. The Indians are grown up. Not a colony any more. A big power these days.'

'I know all that. I am not a sentimental pacifist and I know everyone else does it. But—'

'Look, Kate,' Jim interrupted, 'this country became great on the back of trade in slaves and opium. We shouldn't have a fit of conscience about what we are doing.'

'I'm not. But let's get back to what you want of me. Just another visit to make the case for our ships?'

'Not quite. Your friend has a role too.'

'How? He was – if you remember – almost killed. Still on the danger list, if no longer critical. His sister, Veena, is actually running the company.'

'Well, when he is able to communicate, we would like him to signal his support for this contract. His stock, I understand, is very high at the moment. Also, encourage his secular friends in the opposition not to oppose too vigorously. The technical stuff we can handle through the High Commission; we now have answers to most of the tricky questions. It's the politics we have to get right. There will be quite a lot of work coming his way as well.'

'When I last saw Deepak he was a long way from anything taxing. I hope this proposition isn't time specific.'

'There is a decision point in a month. But I am sure we can be flexible.'

Kate thought for a moment. 'And if I come back, even as a trade envoy rather than a minister, do I get my old private office team? I was just getting used to them and I trusted them, until you lot decided to get rid of me.'

'Won't happen again. Promise you. And, of course, your team. We'll find a way round the rules and regulations. Parsons will do the necessary.'

'I am also concerned about what happened last time. The way that Eritrean night watchman was made the scapegoat. The way the dodgy American company finished up running the show.'

'Ah! I knew you would ask me about that. Your contacts, whoever they were, got the wrong end of the stick. I asked the Admiral to look into it. He knew the set-up there. Knew the people.'

'I'm not sure I find that completely reassuring. The Admiral gives me the creeps. Up to no good.'

Jim shook his head. 'My dear girl, you have got him all wrong. A bloody hero. Not just in the navy. His salesmanship – getting the armed forces of the world fitted out with British kit – has created more jobs than all the theories of John-bloody-Maynard Keynes put together. But I know he ruffles feathers. I have already made him apologise to the civil servants. And I'd tell him to keep out of your hair.'

She stood still for a while, taking in how far she had retreated in a few moments from her initial show of cool indifference. Chambers had a special talent, she grudgingly admitted to herself.

'This is a lot to take in. Both what you are offering and what you are asking me to do. Let me sleep on it.'

'That's fine. I half expected you to walk out and slam the door. Can't ask any more, my girl.'

She stiffened but decided not to take the bait.

***

Even before she left the room Kate knew what her answer would be. Part of her detested the squalid, amoral world she was still part of. If she was a Christian or a socialist she would be indignant, walk away and campaign for a better, nicer world. But she wasn't and couldn't be, either. Or she could quietly disappear back to her family, her friends and her Indian textiles business, perhaps even her lover, a little older, a lot wiser, and put her recent experiences behind her.

But the stronger part of her had no intention of escaping. She had been hurt and humiliated but it was through her own naïvety and clumsiness – and bad luck. 'Don't get mad, get even' was a slogan she approved of. She would get even. Show she wasn't a loser, a weak woman.

To make a success of the second coming she needed a Praetorian Guard that would watch her back and prevent the wrong people getting too close. Susan was crucial. She also needed someone who could deal with the media, do the spinning that high-minded people disapproved of but was what communication was all about.

Then there was the couple from the factory – or perhaps they weren't a couple. The union and Labour man. She would need a line into the opposition and the labour force. And the Asian accountant. As someone usually described as 'handsome' or 'attractive', she had been conscious of being in the presence of a genuinely beautiful woman. And she had been taken with her poise and sharp intelligence: more than the man, she thought, who was given to using five words where one would do, like many politicians. Kate wasn't going to be blind-sided again by not knowing enough about Deepak's British business partners. She would set up meetings with them before the formalities kicked in.

When Steve arrived at Calum's office for a debrief, his way was barred by a formidable woman, large and loud, with a mid-Atlantic accent.

'May I ask you what you are doing here?'

'I have come to see the CEO.'

'Do you have an appointment?'

'We agreed that I would call in first thing this morning.'

'Not in the diary. Your name?'

'Steve Grant. And may I ask who you are?'

'Gill Travers. I am part of the new Global executive team. And you are?'

'Gill. My union represents the workforce here and I still have regular access to Calum.'

'The company is considering whether and how consultation with employee organisations will take place in future. The new owners may wish to change things. We have generally managed without unions in our other operations. Can I also point out, Mr Grant, that you are not wearing a name badge? As from the beginning of this week company policy is that name badges should be worn at all times; by employees as well as visitors.'

'And Mr Mackie? Is he free?'

'No, he is busy. But I can text you with a meeting time. You should in the meantime go to the HR department to collect your name badge and complete a security questionnaire.'

'Security questionnaire? I have been here for over a decade.'

'I understand that there were some serious security issues here. You will know that better than me. We have now introduced the same rigorous procedures we employ in the rest of the group.'

Steve could see that his role as union representative might be in jeopardy with a company unsympathetic to unions. He reminded himself that the reason why he had progressed so rapidly and enjoyed such esteem was the patronage of his boss – now outgoing, it seemed. Pulsar was an enclave of unionism in a private sector increasingly characterised by short-term employment contracts and tokenistic employee participation schemes. He would have to tread carefully.

And in his short absence, he had also found himself in the middle of an impending national storm. He had gone to meet union representatives and organisers in the defence industry in Scotland. As one of only two delegates on the national executive with an engineering background – the other being the ailing Kevin Dubbins – he had been given a rapid immersion in a potentially toxic issue. Rumours were flying about that the aircraft carrier programme reaching its end in Rosyth and the linked frigate programme on the Clyde were in trouble: that the government was thinking of pulling the plug on some or all of it. When he had arrived to meet his union colleagues in Edinburgh and Glasgow there had been an acrid atmosphere, full of suspicion and accusation with cross-cutting themes of Scottish nationalism and socialist militancy. He realised that he badly needed advice. And Calum Mackie, now on his way out and surrounded by gatekeepers provided by his successors, was the obvious source of good advice. But those gatekeepers stood in the way.

He completed the checks he needed to qualify for his name badge – conducted by an earnest young woman who stuck religiously to her script and treated him as if he had just walked in off the street. Then, he took the familiar route through the finance department. Shaida was in her office, clearly not concentrating and in some distress. He invited himself inside the, now familiar, glass office.

'What is it?' he asked with concern, discreetly taking her hand.

'Mo. He has gone. Didn't come back home last night. He took a knapsack and a few personal things. Vanished. No message. Nothing.'

'Who knows about it?'

'I notified Liam on an emergency number he gave me. No one else. Oh my God! He has gone off to fight. Do something mad. I know it.'

Steve wanted to embrace her, but with the Three Witches in the background itching with curiosity and Gill Travers waiting in the wings, he could do nothing to comfort her.

The latest domestic crisis had distracted Shaida from what had become a difficult and complex but satisfying task: integrating the accounting systems of Pulsar and Global. The old saw that Britain and America were divided by a common language applied, in spades, to accounting. Superficial similarities masked a wide variety of different conventions and standards. She realised also that the Americans were much less casual about data security. The endless checking of passwords was tiresome but the opening up of blocked passages started to give her a bigger picture of how the group operated. She had been playing with computers and solving mathematical puzzles pretty much since she had left her cot, and it wasn't long before she was able to walk round the secret gardens that the top US management had designed for their own private convenience. Liam, who really understood these things, would be very impressed.

CHAPTER 15

THE TRADE ENVOY

Press Association, 10 September 2019:

At a US State Department press conference, the Secretary of State produced satellite photographs showing what appeared to be movements of troops and carriers of short-range missiles with what could be battlefield nuclear weapons at several points along the Indo-Pak frontier. He appealed to both sides to step back from a 'dangerous confrontation'.

China's President Ji has also offered to mediate. Reaffirming his support for Pakistan's 'historic claims' in relation to Kashmir, he also expressed support, for the first time, for India's 'fully justified stance against

---

Steve was leaving parliament after a lobby of MPs on behalf of his industry, faced with a new round of defence cuts. He felt a pat on his arm. It was that Tory MP – Kate what's-her-name. She gave him a slight, conspiratorial smile and said: 'I think we need to talk.'

'How did you know I was here?'

'Never mind. Not important. Just follow me.'

She signalled to him to follow her up a spiral staircase to the upper floor where she found an empty committee room. Its pervasive sense of gloom, like many rooms on the parliamentary estate, was deepened by a dark Victorian portrait of MPs – all men and seemingly all bearded – engaged in debate.

'Sorry about the cloak and dagger,' Kate began. 'But I am back in government and I need to talk to you, strictly off the record. Our last meeting had mixed results for both of us. I realised then that there is something seriously fishy about the company Global. It has now, as you know, taken over your firm and seems to be spreading its tentacles everywhere. I expect to be dealing with them again in my new role.'

'But how can I help?' Steve asked. 'Global seems to be firmly in charge now and they have the blessing of government. They don't want me. I am on the way out.'

'I don't know how you can help. Maybe you can't. But I need to have one or two people outside government whom I can trust and to whom I can turn for advice and perhaps help. I also want to make contact with your colleague Shaida Khan. Perhaps you can help me set that up.'

'OK. But meeting is difficult. How do I get through your ministerial defences?'

'We can't meet publicly. I have learnt from painful experience that in a high-profile political job I am under more scrutiny than I thought possible. And, however much we have in common, you know that, in both our parties, the greatest crime is fraternisation with the tribal enemy. But there is a way. My private secretary, Susan, has your contact details and these are hers.' She handed over a note. 'Let's keep in touch.'

Steve was left to find his own way out of the parliamentary labyrinth. But if all went to plan he would soon be here in his own right.

———

Kate landed in Delhi the following morning on the mission agreed with the Secretary of State. It was clear, soon after arrival, that this would be a difficult visit. The High Commissioner was bristling with irritation that he had been misrepresented in London by ministers looking for a way of lessening the pain of defence cuts. Yes, he had said that a carrier sale was 'possible'; but his many qualifications and negatives had been studiously ignored. He was hardened by three years of battering on the Indian door for big arms contracts that had delivered little. Kate Thompson, Indian Trade Envoy, would have to discover for herself that the warm Indian words and friendly reminiscences about life in the UK were usually a prelude to disappointment.

And so it proved. The Prime Minister, the Finance Minister, the Commerce Minister and the Defence Minister were all busy. But, since Mrs Thompson was such an important and valued visitor, a key government adviser, Dr Sanjivi Desai, would be able to see her. She had heard from Deepak about Desai's extreme nationalist and anti-Muslim views, and his seemingly sinister role in Deepak's company. She was intrigued.

His office was Spartan and small by ministerial standards. There was none of the clutter and endless coming and going she was becoming used to. Everything was spotless and meticulously organised: neat and fastidious like its occupant.

'Dear Mrs Thompson – Minister?' Desai began.

'Trade Envoy.'

'Much more important. Delighted to have you back in the country. I am told you cut quite a dash with my colleagues on your last visit.'

'It was certainly a successful visit. Paved the way to an agreement that will hopefully strengthen your anti-missile defences and provide the UK with valuable exports.'

'Absolutely. But tell me more about how things are in the UK. As you will know I was an engineering student at Cambridge before I went to the US. Always go up to the alma mater whenever I can.'

'I was at the other place.'

'Poor you. But no hard feelings. What can I do for you?'

'Aircraft carriers.'

'Ah yes. I was warned that you would raise this issue. The High Commissioner already knows where things stand. Our philosophy is "buyers' navy to builders' navy". But the building of the second of the new class of Indian carriers – the *Vaishal*, a nuclear-powered, state of the art ship – is delayed. Because we feel threatened by the rapid build-up of the Chinese navy, as well as our old friends in Pakistan, we want to plug a gap in our defences, quickly.'

'I think that is where we can help.'

'Help from our British friends is always very welcome. But let me take you through our options. First, the Americans: now that India is an economic, political and military superpower we have developed a close relationship with the superpower that most closely aligns with our national interests: the USA. The Americans understand the Chinese threat in a way that – with respect – you may not; we keep reading about Britain's close friendship with President Ji and his Communist regime. The Americans have a clear-headed view about the threats posed by China and also about the threats posed by militant Islam. I know Western intellectuals make fun of President Trump. We don't. We admire his clear thinking. And the Americans now have a production line of carriers following *Gerald R Ford* and *John F Kennedy*, very much along the lines of our requirements.

'And if that doesn't work, we have our longstanding Russian friends. Never let us down – Soviet or post-Soviet. I don't want to be rude, Mrs Thompson, but your country has a less than stellar record when it comes to supplying us in our hour of need. And we respect Putin. Proud of his country. Good man. Taught those Chechens a lesson. We, of course, are a proper democracy and can't deal with Kashmiri subversives in that way. I should add that the Russians also have surplus carriers that can take MiG-29s, our fighters of choice.'

Kate was wilting under the barrage and the High Commissioner was, conspicuously, leaving it to her to defend her near-impossible brief.

'I think you will find we can more than match whatever the US and Russia can offer,' she began. 'But why don't you come and see for yourself? The *Prince of Wales*, the carrier we are talking about, will be in Portsmouth – where the carriers will be based when in service – in a few weeks' time. There is to be a big ceremony. Perhaps the Royal Family will be there. We would be delighted if you could come as one of our guests of honour. We believe you may well be in London at around that time with your Minister for the big defence sales exhibition?'

'Yes, that is the plan. But *Prince of Wales*? Can't have an Indian ship called the *Prince of Wales*! The Empire is over; though I know some of your countrymen want to bring it back now that you are no longer in Europe. So it would need a proper Indian name. We have *Vikrant* and *Vaishal*. Why not *Trishul* – Trident – a good maritime name?' He laughed loudly at his own joke, perhaps, she thought, too loudly, as if there was more in the joke than was initially apparent.

On the way out she reassured herself by suggesting to the High Commissioner that 'at least the invitation got a good response'.

'I would be careful what you wish for, Mrs Thompson,' the diplomat replied. 'He's a notorious Muslim baiter and will not be universally well received back home.'

The search for Mo intensified. The police and intelligence services had mugshots, mobile numbers and email access codes to intercept. But there was silence. The distraught Khan family turned to the mosque and community groups for help and in particular to Steve. The worst case scenario had him travelling to Libya, Afghanistan, Yemen or some other ISIL stronghold to train and prepare for battle. A more optimistic view was that he was holed up with friends, perhaps in London, waiting to make the next move. Either way there was no news.

Shaida and Steve decided to convene a meeting at the mosque, bringing together the earlier group to seek their help. The mood was not good. There was still simmering anger over the protest demonstration. Steve's lack of sustained interest was criticised, as was the failure (for which he was blamed) of the council leadership to put out a statement supporting the demonstrators and condemning the police and Indian government provocation. There was angry condemnation of 'traitors' in the community who were 'grassing' to the police, leading to complaints of police harassment of several local Muslim women. They did, however, agree to meet every couple of days to pool information; Mo was, after all, one of their friends and seemed likely to do harm to himself and to others.

At the second meeting there was a modest breakthrough. One of Mo's friends who was monitoring jihadi websites – and was something of an apologist for them – reported a video featuring five masked young men, one of whom had a physique similar to Mo's. The video dealt not just with the usual enemies of Islam but featured in particular the 'atrocities' being committed by anti-Muslim Hindu 'fascists' in India. The video had been shot rather carelessly and showed in one corner a window opening onto a British townscape and what someone claimed was – or perhaps was not – Waltham Forest town hall. But at least they – whoever they were – were in the UK.

Kate arrived in Mumbai at a bad time for the Parrikars. The press stories around the spill of poisonous chemicals still featured prominently in the newspapers: 'Environmental Disaster at Parrikar Chemicals'. The main casualties were fish, not that many were left in the highly polluted waters around Mumbai. But the spillage had also occurred as the tide was rising and carried poisons into a village upstream where the poorer residents washed their clothes and themselves. There were reports of serious inflammation of the skin and damage to eyes. No fatalities, at least yet. But Indian reactions were coloured by the still outstanding damages claims and political toxicity from the Union Carbide Bhopal disaster in 1984 that had killed thousands and injured thousands more. Even a limited chemical disaster was capable of making big political waves.

All of this was explained to Kate when she had barely had time to reacquaint herself with her convalescing lover in his hospital bed. Veena took her into a side room to reveal another major development.

'Kate, I am not a politician like you. But I am learning the hard way that politicians can make or break businesses like ours.'

'That isn't unique to India by any means.'

'No, but we have this link between family businesses, political parties and – to a degree – organised crime that you don't have. It is a bit like Italy, or the US in the Wild West.'

'So what has all this to do with me?'

'A few days ago Deepak had a group of visitors from the ruling party. Seriously big hitters. He hasn't recovered and didn't take it all in. But they were offering him a "ticket" for the next general election in a seat they expect to win.'

'But I thought he couldn't stand these nationalist, religious types. He always describes himself as secular.'

'True. But he did vote for them. Our father gave money last time round. Deepak likes the pro-business bit. And the Prime Minister is – apparently – wanting Deepak to be a champion of his New Industrial Policy. He sees Deepak as part of his efforts to improve his party's image – make it more inclusive: what you call a "big tent".'

'But Deepak isn't in a fit state to embark on a political career or even make decisions about it.'

'That is true. But he understands the importance of protecting his family and the company, which are under siege. He has to have political allies. And he has little time for the opposition: hopelessly divided and still revolving around the leading family, discredited though they now are by corruption and general incompetence. That is why he asked me to advise him; decide what is best for the family. And you are, for me, part of the family.' Veena reached out and took Kate's hand.

'I am, really, very touched by that,' Kate answered, the gesture of solidarity prompting a hint of tears. 'It is the nicest thing anyone has said to me for quite a while. My feelings for Deepak are quite simple. I love him and I think he feels the same. But I am painfully aware that marriage or living together is out of the question. We both have families at opposite ends of the earth. Political career apart, I am not going to abandon my girls to come and live here. So I am reconciled to the idea that there will be occasional, snatched, moments when I visit India or he is in London. Not ideal. But better than nothing.'

Veena nodded. 'That makes it easier to tell you what I plan to tell Deepak. He should take it. Do as they ask. You have a British expression: if you can't beat 'em, join 'em. That is where we are. I really don't know how far all these incidents are connected – the gangland killings in Mumbai, the attack on Deepak, this latest sabotage of our plant; lots of other things you don't know about. I am not a believer in conspiracies but because we are outsiders, because we have no protection, we are vulnerable.

'The family is under terrible strain as a result: my father is broken: my elder brother – next door – has barely survived; my younger brother is becoming an alcoholic; I am really struggling to cope. I have a lovely husband and two small children, and I am failing them, worrying twenty-four hours a day about the company. If Deepak becomes an MP for the ruling party, it won't solve all our problems but it gives us a shield. One thing Deepak will hate is seeing his factory slipping back under the control of that man Desai and his associates – it was made clear that, under the deal with the ruling party, Desai and his cronies will back off. And Deepak can, I am sure, find a way to promote his ideals.'

'Yes, I think I understand,' Kate replied. 'Very few of us are cut out to be great or heroes, taking on the world: a Mahatma Gandhi or a Mandela, or for that matter a Mrs Gandhi or a Mrs Thatcher. I am also a small fish in the big sea of Conservatism in Britain. I detest a lot of the people I have to deal with. Cynical and nasty. I don't even like the party all that much; I drifted into it. But they seem likely to be running the country for the next generation, so I want to stay where I am and do a few small good things. I guess we have both come to the same conclusion in our different countries for much the same reasons.'

The shared intimacy and frankness were infectious. Kate was eager to find out more about the man she loved; his childhood, the things about him that she could only discover second hand. Veena, for her part, was able to shed the fears and responsibilities of recent weeks, and forget, for a while, that she was now the family matriarch. After sharing some of the funnier family secrets, the time came for Kate to leave. She felt that she had found a true friend.

━━━━━━━━━

Deepak Parrikar wasn't the only budding politician whose fortune was being mapped out by the women around him. The future Lord Thompson of Surrey Heights was pleasantly surprised to discover that his wayward wife had been scheming to get him a peerage. He was already daydreaming about making a big hit in the Lords and a quick move to a ministerial post, preferably in the Treasury where his well-developed views on freeing up market forces in the property sector could be put to use. Not, he believed, that his appointment was undeserved. Had it not been for the disparity between his salary and bonuses on the one hand and the pathetic pauper's pay enjoyed by MPs on the other, he would now be the local MP. Kate would be doing what he thought she was best at: small talk at social gatherings and charming the old dears at the annual fete. After months of quiet bitterness and recrimination he could see his way to forgiving her, just.

And so, when she returned home, the 'dears' and 'darlings' were not delivered with quite such venom. She discovered that it was possible to have a cordial coexistence: lacking in love or even affection but perfectly pleasant. The girls sensed the change of mood. They had become withdrawn and resentful of their parents: Maggie had taken to teenage rebellion, and to the fury of her father had dyed her hair bright orange. The other two hid behind their iPads in endless typed chatter with their friends. Now, as they picked up the more relaxed atmosphere around the breakfast table, they gradually opened up to talk to their mum again about the things that loomed large in their lives: the preparations for next month's gymkhana, the agonies of GCSE maths, the love affair between the lesbian chemistry teacher and the head girl, the prospect of a skiing holiday. In reality they were enormously proud of their mother and greatly relieved that she was still with them and spending less time at her MP's flat and more time at home.

⨉⨉⨉⨉⨉⨉⨉⨉⨉⨉⨉⨉⨉⨉⨉

Shortly after returning from India Kate was called in to see the Secretary of State, the man responsible for the sudden turnaround in her personal and political life. She was surprised that he had moved so soon to deliver his side of the bargain when she had delivered so little.

'My dear Kate,' Jim said as she entered his office, opening his arms wide in greeting. 'Back from communing with our friends in the subcontinent. How are you? How did they treat you?'

'Thanks, Jim. You will have heard from the High Commissioner that we didn't make any headway on the carrier issue. I tried.'

'To be frank I didn't expect you to get far on that one. Other options are beginning to emerge including a joint Anglo-German project now that Berlin are getting over their hang-ups over Brexit. They want to be involved with us in the Med and the Gulf. Very hush-hush. Please don't talk about it. But the PM and the German Chancellor are enthusiastic and we may no longer need the Indians. What you did – brilliantly as always – was to get the powerful Desai interested in the UK. He is keen to follow up on your invitation for whatever reason.'

'I appreciate that you moved very quickly on the promises you made to me. Even though you've never met my husband, you seem to understand him better than I do: after one of your people dropped a hint about the peerage he has been like a little boy with a new train set.'

Jim gave a snort of laughter. 'Good. And you will also find that there is no more nonsense about deselection. The next step is to have you back in a proper, senior, job in the government.'

Kate saw her opportunity. 'Provided I can do something worthwhile,' she countered. 'I am not interested in simply having a job, I want to do something useful. I thought social housing. As a constituency MP I see some of the havoc in the lives of ordinary people because of sky-high rents and the cost of buying.'

'No, no, no. Far too left-wing. The party hates social housing. We are trying to get rid of it. We want the peasants to own their own huts – sorry! My sense of humour is getting the better of me, again. No, definitely not. Let us stick to our priorities. The PM is clear. Our top priority is the female vote: being on the side of aspirational women. What I had in mind was getting you into one of the departments where we don't normally see many women: Defence perhaps, or the Treasury.'

Kate was inwardly annoyed at his casual dismissal of her ambition to do something she cared about. But she found his brutal cynicism easier to deal with than the mealy-mouthed hypocrisy of most of their colleagues.

She also suspected that he put on something of an act for her benefit. Try as she would, she found it hard to dislike the man.

'Can I think about it?'

'Yes, of course. Perhaps I can help you think about it over a nice dinner at my favourite restaurant.'

'Mmm...'

'OK, agreed. I will set it up.'

Kate's readmission to the fold by the leadership of the party was quickly followed by reaffirmation of her status at local level. The motion to be put before a meeting of association members to proceed with deselection became, at the stroke of a pen, a motion to support reselection. The Chairman's Damascene conversion was quickly followed by the rest of the party executive whose moments of blinding light consisted, variously, of a promise by the Foreign Secretary to speak at the association's annual dinner, an offer by the Prime Minister of the unbeatable prize of 'tea at No. 10' for the fundraising auction and a generous financial contribution from Mr, the future Lord, Thompson: all predicated on the assumption that the current MP remained the party's candidate.

Although the better part of Kate winced inwardly at the party's unerring instinct for the baser qualities of human nature, she also enjoyed the benefits. Being chauffeured around in a political Rolls-Royce undoubtedly had its attractions and she lacked the streak of self-denying Puritanism required to decline the ride. The only bump felt through the suspension was the announcement by Stella that she was resigning from the party to join UKIP because of 'a decline in traditional moral values'. Her resignation was made more significant by the fact that she also took with her twenty years of membership and canvass records and minutes of party meetings including the recent executive no confidence vote in the MP.

The political Trabant that was the modern Labour Party offered a much less comfortable ride, as Steve Grant discovered when he put forward his name for selection as prospective parliamentary candidate for the town's safe Labour seat. It had been assumed for most of the last decade that he was the Dauphin waiting only to be anointed at the coronation. That assumption was soon shown to be dangerously wide of the mark.

Local party membership had more than doubled since the 2015 general election and as rumours spread of an impending selection, numbers surged again in a spasm of socialist zeal. As a former champion recruiter, Steve was no shrinking violet and he signed up many of his union colleagues at Pulsar who, in recent years, had allowed their membership to lapse. To his delight, Ikram, one of Mo's friends he had met at the mosque, had now joined the party. He had emerged as a brilliant organiser, doing prodigious work boosting membership among young

Muslims. And, despite the family's preoccupation with the missing Mo, Shaida had joined in too, enlisting the Three Witches and a dozen of her other girlfriends.

But when Steve sat down with the membership list, once closed, it became clear that he was in trouble. John Gray, the council group leader, had taken on the role of coordinating his campaign and, as they sat together in Gray's council office, analysing the numbers, they found it difficult to identify solid support from more than a third of potential voters. They had conducted a quick telephone canvass of new members and were shocked by the findings: a substantial majority had joined to elect and support the national leadership; few had a party background and many were former Greens or Socialist Workers; their issues reflected the concerns of university staff and students rather than the shop floor; and few had heard of Steve or, if they had, thought favourably of him. Most spontaneously expressed support for Steve's main opponent, Dr Liz Cook, a lecturer in the Social Anthropology Department of a new university in North London where she lived. Ms Cook was head of a university research unit specialising in War, Capitalism and Women and her expertise in this field had led to her becoming one of the architects of the party's new defence policy. She had also been a Paulina and Oxford contemporary of Kate Thompson but these inconvenient facts were kept well away from her CV.

Councillor Gray didn't beat about the bush. 'You've

got a problem, lad. If you want to win, you are going to have to fight. No more Mr Nice Guy.' He raised the possibility of resurrecting the local party's Attack Unit, which was established to fight off a Lib Dem offensive several years earlier. Its task was to destroy opponents using every tactic known to political man, short of those that would lead the candidate to be disqualified, the agent imprisoned and the party bankrupted by libel damages. That still left quite a lot of scope.

Any qualms Steve might have had were swiftly removed when Ms Cook's supporters struck the first blow with a social media blitz attacking the 'Establishment Candidate' for 'lobbying on behalf of multinational companies in the arms trade'. They had also unearthed a grainy but recognisable photo of Steve shaking hands with the then Secretary of State, Peter Mandelson, which told its own grim story of spin and betrayal. Councillor Bill Daniels's complaint about Steve's advocacy of tactical cooperation with the Lib Dems was further proof of unreliable SDP tendencies.

The Attack Unit was soon at work preparing a counter-offensive. One of their young researchers – a student intern – unearthed a copy of the *British Journal of Social Anthropology* with an article summarising Ms Cook's PhD thesis: 'Manifestations of Penile Aggression in the Military Industrial Complex: A Multi-Disciplinary and Multi-Cultural Perspective'. 'Boys toys', in other words, giggled the young woman who had excavated this gem. But after a round of laughter the team agreed that humour was likely to be counter-productive. Some of the membership might be impressed by the long words and a candidate who wrote learned articles about an Ology.

Gray had concluded that a better tack would be to work on two key power brokers: Councillors Les Harking and Mirza. Both had been hostile at the aborted disciplinary hearing but that issue had gone away and both had worked well with Steve in the past. They each had a solid block of support that might, together, get Steve over the finishing line. But they were old pros whose support would come at a price.

Councillor Mirza was the easier nut to crack. He had no real disagreements with Steve, merely a badly wounded ego that required tender massage. Steve was capable of the necessary dissimulation, much as he disliked it. And as he piled on compliments about the Mirza clan's stellar contribution to civic life, he had echoing in the back of his mind the jibes from Brian Castle and others in the works canteen about 'your corrupt Paki friend on the council' whose family was 'ripping off the council with those horrible, squalid, care homes'. The coup de grâce, however, was delivered by the Attack Unit, which sent to Councillor Mirza and his supporters a YouTube recording of a radical feminist rally at which Liz Cook had been a – not very prominent – speaker. Someone in the crowd waved a placard with a cartoon of the Prophet and the words 'male chauvinist pig'. It mattered little that the rally was a long time ago, pre-*Charlie Hebdo*, and that the organisers including Liz Cook issued a cringing apology. The verdict was: guilt by association. Steve pocketed the Muslim vote almost to a man and woman.

Councillor Harking held court in the Red Lion, savouring every second of his political courtship.

Steve sat down at his table with a pint of beer. 'Evening, Les, how are you?'

Les made it clear he was not impressed. He had a copy of the *Morning Star* in front of him and pointedly ignored Steve as he studiously worked his way through it. Steve tried again.

'Sorry, Les, you must know why I want to talk to you. I hope I can count on your support in the selection.'

'Not so fast, young man. Why do you think I would do that?' He was already into his second pint and looking forward to a long evening of drinks 'on the house'.

'We have worked together a long time. Speaking up for the local working class.'

'Sometimes. Anyway you're slow off the mark. This Liz Cook has already been in touch. Impressive. Said I would think about supporting her.'

'You know she isn't your cup of tea. Never been near the town before. A carpet bagger.'

'But I like the politics. For the first time since Michael Foot was leader we are calling ourselves socialists without being ashamed.'

'A fat lot of good that did us at the last election.'

'Maybe different next time. The young people are with us.'

'Some of them. And they don't vote. You know the story.'

'I've been around the block a lot longer than you. I was part of the struggle when you were in nappies. We need our principles back – which your friends in New Labour trashed.'

'You know as well as I do that all this academic waffle from Liz Cook and her ilk isn't taking us anywhere. Working class people are completely turned off. We'll be stuck with the Tories for ever.'

'Don't talk us down, lad. That's all the right-wing media. Can't give in to Murdoch, the *Mail* and the rest of 'em. Stick up for what we believe in.'

They had been round the houses, exhausting these arguments many times before. Les was in no hurry. He was in his element: power broker, career maker and breaker; the grizzled veteran of The Struggle passing on the wisdom of the tribe. He knew, and Steve knew deep down, that as fellow alumni of the University of Life and fully qualified operators of the town's political machine they had far more in common with each other than with the newly ascendant leadership in the party. But before consummating the relationship Les would have to extract serious political concessions. He was willing to be bought but only at a suitably high price. Before the end of the evening, Steve had refused to endorse UK withdrawal from NATO and the restoration of free tuition for students, but had signed up to full nationalisation of the banks and support for a campaign of civil disobedience against the new trade union legislation. His wallet was also lighter after meeting the bar bill.

Steve now had a somewhat incongruous – and fragile – alliance, but an alliance nonetheless, between the party's Muslim supporters and the traditional working class members. And at the public hustings he was at his eloquent best, speaking without notes, and skilfully used his local and working class credentials. But he sensed, from the audience reaction, a bristling anger and rejection of who he was and what he stood for. He was jeered and heckled. By contrast, his opponent read, badly, a tedious script full of clichés and jargon and she was seemingly unaware of which town she was in. But the audience was mostly on her side and whenever she used words like 'neoliberalism', which were not part of Steve's vocabulary, there was fervent applause.

When the votes were counted things looked bleak for Steve, until the postal vote arrived, which he won hands down. There had clearly been some successful exhumation of the dead in Councillor Mirza's kitchen. Steve was home by two votes, in the overall count. It wasn't a glorious victory but he had won. Quite what victory meant in a changed and hostile party only time would tell. For the time being victory was enough. He was still a player.

Shaida introduced herself to Susan in Caffè Nero in the town centre. She was dressed traditionally and modestly and had taken to wearing the hijab when she was on view in public places, demonstrating conformity if not piety. Susan had tried to dress down, in sweater and jeans, but her demeanour was that of the smart, tidy, official that she was.

'Kate has asked me to liaise with you,' Susan explained. 'I do need to stress that I am a civil servant. There are rules. I am not political and here essentially as a messenger. But I know something about the background and my line manager is comfortable with my being a conduit. Kate's message is that any inside information you have on Pulsar, under the new owners, would be very helpful. As you know she believes something seriously irregular is going on there. Any evidence would be better used than when you last approached her.'

'I already got a message indirectly through Steve and my other government contact who I want to help,' Shaida acknowledged. 'I don't like what I've seen of the new owners one little bit. But I need to be careful. They're very security conscious. But in a very mechanical, box-ticking, kind of way. I get to see a lot of email traffic between senior managers that even Calum, the CEO, is excluded from and, to do my job, I see the important money flows. I am also quite good at finding my way around security protocols and passwords. They don't yet seem to have cottoned on to the fact of my brother going missing or my joint activities with Steve and your Minister. But they will, and then doors will close.'

Shaida reached into her bag and brought out a file of documents, which she handed to Susan. 'I've brought along a few copies of interesting-looking financial transactions and I've highlighted a few names – Kate will recognise their significance. There is a lot more. This is just a sample. But, as I said, I am on borrowed time.'

'Kate will be very pleased. Thanks for these. Let me know when you have more.'

'One more thing,' Shaida added. 'There has been some talk of a big exhibition in London in the next month. They want me to be on the company stand. One of the new people – an American – wasn't very subtle: they think a brown female face will help to present the right kind of inclusive image. And the top brass will be coming over and holding a board meeting to coincide with the exhibition.'

'Ah yes. I know all about this event. Every two years Britain hosts the world's biggest arms bazaar. It is theoretically private but the government is heavily involved. We're gearing up for it: lots of VIPs from the defence sales world. A kind of Davos for arms dealers. I imagine Kate will be on parade with the Secretary of State. Useful info about your company; I'll feed it back.'

CHAPTER 16

THE TRAINEE

Dawn (Lahore), 20 September 2019:

It is reported from sources in the Pakistan military that the mooted nuclear test has been postponed and that efforts are being made through intermediaries to de-escalate the 'war of words' between India and Pakistan. Senior figures in the Pakistan army are reported to have expressed alarm at the way civilian 'hotheads' have been allowed to set the agenda.

He had little idea where he was. The van had no windows and his companions didn't wish to talk. When he asked where they were going the answer was 'Better you don't know.' The night journey by motorway – he assumed the M1 – had lasted about an hour. Then ten minutes on a side road and, briefly, a rutted track. Now, a big house surrounded by trees. There was a distinctive smell – pigs, silage? He was too much of a town boy to tell. And there was the occasional distant sound of aircraft far overhead. He could be anywhere.

When they arrived, three bearded men – Asian or Arab, they didn't introduce themselves – provided hot soup and bread and spelled out the rules: no one to leave the house except under supervision; no attempt to communicate with friends or family (mobiles were collected in – 'secure' phones would be issued in due course); and a daily roster of duties, education and prayer. Then into the room came the man who had inspired him, Tariq Ahmed, and who was clearly in charge of this operation. Tariq Ahmed gave him a short nod of acknowledgement.

Mo was allocated a room in the attic and spent the rest of the night awake, wondering whether he had made the right decision when he had said yes to the friend who challenged him to say if he was ready and sufficiently committed to fight for the cause. There was a Holy Quran by the bedside but he didn't open it.

He discovered the following morning that there were six of them: a couple of Asians from Bradford, one from Stoke, a white convert from Birmingham and an African who was from the same town though they had never met. It soon became clear that he and the African had a different motivation from the others who were totally devout; assiduous in the rituals; seemingly entranced by the prayer. Mo's family had pride in their Muslim identity but religion played only a minor and occasional part in their life. As with his Christian school friends, religion surfaced at weddings and funerals and was experienced through feasting rather than fasting.

Mo was more engaged by the political sessions that Tariq Ahmed led and particularly the videos that dramatised the hurt and discrimination suffered by fellow Muslims: the suffering of helpless children during the siege of Aleppo; footage of the Iraq war; the men of Srebrenica being led off to execution; the humiliation of Palestinians at Israeli checkpoints and the bombing of Gaza; the burnt bodies lying beside a rail track after a massacre in Gujarat; torture victims in profusion; Guantanamo. Mo's beating by a group of racist thugs and several experiences of 'stop and search' didn't quite match those horrors but a shared sense of victimhood reminded him why he was there.

Mo felt confident enough to air his doubts: his lack of religious conviction; his disquiet at some of the gruesome practices of ISIL; and his secular views on the role of women. Tariq Ahmed was not fazed. His branch of fighters was comfortable with intelligent doubt; respected ISIL's achievements but not their methods. Mo would be called on to show courage but there was also a role in less demanding work: providing safe houses or storage for weapons; organising protests in support of the cause; disciplining informers; collecting information on potential targets; recruiting in colleges and universities: part of the penumbra of terrorism rather than its core.

But the recruiters had spotted in Mo some spark – created from anger, intelligence, determination – that was the basis of a good fighter. The next big mission did not require suicide from its perpetrators but basic competence and discipline with careful planning and skilful execution using firearms.

Mo was taken to an outbuilding, perhaps once a barn, where a shooting range had been constructed. The structure was well insulated for sound and no one passing nearby would be aware of its purpose. There, Mo was taught to use semi-automatic weapons and small arms as a back-up. He had never handled guns before, but, once he had learnt to suppress the rush of adrenalin and master the action, proved to be the most adept of the group.

Mo also bonded better with the others and joined in the prayers with more conviction. Too much conversation and intimacy was, however, not encouraged. The instructors revealed little about themselves and kept discussion at a general and practical level. If the recruits were interrogated at some point in the future, the information they gave up would be of dubious value.

Then, without warning, the instruction came to pack their small collection of personal possessions and to prepare to leave for a safe house, nearer the planned action, where final detailed instructions would be given.

✕✕✕✕✕✕✕✕✕✕✕✕✕✕✕

Steve was concentrating on union work. And this currently involved representing the union on a trip to Portsmouth to celebrate a major milestone in the dockyard's history. The process of transforming the Portsmouth dockyards from a shipbuilding centre to a base for servicing the navy's two new carriers and other warships had been industrially and politically difficult. But his union had been credited with a tough but pragmatic, rather than disruptive, approach that had borne fruit in a minimum of redundancies, and deadlines being met. There would continue to be a role for the skilled craftsmen and engineers who made up his union's membership at the base.

He had never been to this city before and on arrival at the harbour station was struck by the force of the naval presence: Nelson's *Victory*, a symbol of past glories, and the giant Spinnaker Tower, a powerful and optimistic statement of belief in a maritime future. He wandered around the city centre where seamen had drunk, eaten, boasted, brawled and womanised for centuries before looking for his Premier Inn. His allowance permitted something a little more luxurious but he had already discovered that even relatively minor public figures lived under scrutiny. After unpacking he went in search of an evening meal.

By the time he left the restaurant, the city centre was filling up with young people, some of them already quite far gone with alcohol. Despite the cold evening many of the boys wore nothing more warming than T-shirts, the better to display tattooed arms, and the girls had flimsy tops and ridiculously short dresses. Lack of inhibition gave vent to some raucous but good-natured singing and shouting. Steve felt a twinge of sadness that his early marriage, caring duties and night school had circumvented this stage of growing up. But his isolation had also fuelled his ambition, the hunger to succeed, that had lifted him above his contemporaries.

As he moved away from the centre he saw a group of young Asian men gathered on a street corner. Most were slumped inside oversize jackets, hoods up, hands in pockets, and there was an edginess and awkwardness quite different from their white contemporaries a few hundred yards away. Street lighting was poor and the darkness masked whatever it was they were doing. But something caught Steve's eye in a brief exposure to reflected light. The profile of one of the youths looked very familiar. The more he looked, the more he became convinced that he knew who it was.

Steve sternly reminded himself that there were tens of thousands of Asian men in the UK of roughly the same age and appearance and the probability of one of them appearing in the same city as him at the same time was slim. Unless, of course, it was not a coincidence. His mind raced with possibilities. An obvious one was that there were a lot of VIPs in town. But he prevaricated.

He wanted to talk to Shaida about the episode but then realised that there was little concrete to go on. A half-baked story about, maybe, sighting her brother would simply agitate her without helping. He hovered, watching the group from a distance. He was tempted to go across and present himself. Then the young men broke up, embracing each other before departing in different directions. The object of Steve's attention slipped away into the darkness of a side street. But his suspicions hardened into near certainty when he saw a characteristic hand gesture in the seconds before the youths disappeared into the gloom.

Who should he contact? He realised that he had other options apart from Shaida. In his phone he had the number Kate Thompson had given him in the Commons. He decided to ring. He was surprised to discover that she was in the same city for the same reason, albeit in the rather more comfortable Marriott. In explaining the call, he introduced a sufficient number of caveats to make her irritated.

'Is this an emergency or not?' she said tersely. 'If you are asking me to alert the security guys, I need to be clear that this is serious. Yes, or no?'

'Yes.'

'In that case I will alert the people who need to know.'

Until she was interrupted by the telephone call, Kate had been preparing for an uneventful day as part of the supporting cast. She was there to represent her department and support the Secretary of State for Defence who was to visit the city and tour the naval base and to thank the navy, the base commander and his staff, the workforce, and the city fathers for their work in getting the base port ready on time for the arrival of the first of the carriers. And, no doubt, to tell local voters, through the national media, that the government should get the political credit.

Someone in Whitehall had joined up the dots and realised that a lot of senior overseas visitors would be in London for the biennial DSEI, the defence and security equipment exhibition. Wouldn't it be a good idea to show some of them around the naval base and some of the fighting ships in part? Make them feel important as esteemed guests of Her Majesty's Government?

Kate's mentor, Jim Chambers, let it be known that her presence would be expected in her capacity as Trade Envoy, since among the visiting VIPs was India's Dr Desai. She wasn't expected to do much as the Red Admiral would act as his chaperone. Kate's job was the usual: 'Smile sweetly and look pretty... not difficult, my girl. Just make the Indians feel at home.' And besides ('and very much for your ears only'), 'The PM has said that in the next reshuffle you will have a big job in the government. You are now one hundred per cent on board.' She let the blandishments wash over her; she had decided to go with the flow and not to think too deeply about the motives of the men who were, for the moment, inclined to give her a helping hand.

Had she been fully briefed on Desai's recent activities she might have found a good excuse not to be there; but the ripples hadn't yet reached her. Following her visit, the Indian Prime Minister had asked Desai to carry out a wide ranging review of India's defence procurement practices, and this responsibility further pricked the interest of the UK High Commissioner in Delhi and the MOD and Department of Business back in London. They made sure that the grand tour of major prospective suppliers – the US, Russia, France – had a good slot reserved for the UK and, fortuitously, the dates coincided with this splendid opportunity to show off the best of the British navy, along with a shopping trip at the defence exhibition.

Mr Desai started his tour with the USA and, while there, agreed to speak at a seminar at America First, the new think-tank close to the Administration, and sponsored by his associates from Global. The subject was 'The Military and Political Threat of Islam' and fellow speakers included the President's Director of Strategy, who predictably scooped the headlines by letting the audience know what the President really thought about Muslims. Almost as much attention was given to an Israeli Cabinet minister from an extreme settlers' party who had advocated requiring all Muslims, including Israeli citizens, to wear green crescent badges at all times to identify them for security purposes.

The British broadsheets picked up on both stories and reported them with suitably outraged comment.

Much less attention was paid to the speech of an unknown Indian functionary who made a largely impenetrable presentation around a series of demographic projections that purported to show, for those who could follow, the convergence of the populations of Hindus and Muslims in India. Later in his speech he referred favourably to an aspect of Mrs Gandhi's emergency in the 1970s when her son Sanjay had embarked upon a campaign of mass sterilisation, voluntary in theory but often compulsory in practice. The programme had been concentrated on poorer people (who had larger families) including Muslims, and the potential of such a programme for 'stabilising India's demographic profile' was explored by the speaker and what was left of his audience. One listener, a young Muslim journalist who had got into the seminar under an assumed name, was paying particularly close attention and he ensured, through social media, that the speech was promptly reported in the subcontinent. Before long the reports, which had bypassed the British press, were reflected back into the diaspora communities in the UK.

The outraged response might well have burnt itself out had an alert junior diplomat in the Pakistani High Commission in London not spotted that the British government's list of official visitors included the self-same Desai. Questions were put down in parliament, predictably, by the Member for Islamabad East. The ethnic press became excited even if the mainstream press didn't, and for militant Islamists this became yet further evidence of the complicity of the British state with Islamophobes. Something would have to be done. But, except for a few boffins in the security services tracking political noise on the internet, there was little sense of threat.

The Portsmouth visit got under way smoothly. The Secretary of State for Defence was on time for a 9am start. Security checks were heavy but the cluster of senior officials, naval officers and VIPs, including the delegation from India, were waved through and headed for the ships at anchor. The crisp early autumn morning, with a cloudless sky, was a perfect backcloth to a modern naval pageant. Everyone expressed themselves massively impressed by the carrier whose grey bulk loomed over them: the largest naval vessel by far that the Royal Navy had ever operated.

The VIPs were feeling peckish by 10.30 and the procession was directed to the gardens at the rear of the base commander's residence where a marquee had been erected for morning refreshments, and a microphone gave warning of speeches and thank-yous to come. The group spread out over the lawn, soaking up the morning sun and finding, in companionable conversation over coffee and cakes, some relief from the barrage of facts and figures directed at them during the tour. There was an armed security presence in the background but it was unobtrusive and modest.

After exchanging Oxbridge banter with Dr Desai, Kate did the rounds of Sheikhs and African generals and a group of suited, dapper, Asians who she discovered, through a translator, were from the Vietnamese politburo. She then found herself in conversation with the Lib Dem council leader who introduced her to his husband and she reflected how far the country had travelled in recent years so that such encounters were perfectly normal and drained of prurient interest. Desai was at the centre of a group of industrialists who were unsubtly peddling their wares, while the guardian Admiral was trying to moderate their shameless pitch for business. The Secretary of State moved towards the microphone and extracted his speaking notes before addressing the small crowd.

After an eternity spent clearing his throat and tapping the microphone, the Defence Secretary began his speech and the platitudes reserved for such occasions poured out in thick profusion. Then there was a loud bang and a scream from the back of the refreshments tent. Within a split second a security detail dragged the politician off the microphone, while soldiers in battle fatigues appeared from nowhere and pushed the distinguished visitors to the floor. Kate and the Lib Dem council leader managed a synchronised dive. Then a group of commandos advanced on the rear of the tent, guns poised. When they rounded the corner, ready to fire, they encountered two naval ratings flat on the floor. One of them had managed to knock over a pile of metal containers causing the apparent sound of detonation that had caused the panic.

When order was restored, the VIPs required some reassuring that this was a false alarm. The story quickly spread among the visitors that they had been rescued from a terrorist attack by a brilliant, rapid-reflex response from the UK military security. They were grateful and impressed and Kate for one was happy to allow the fiction to settle.

As Steve left he saw Kate standing next to Liam, his presence a product of Steve's phone call the evening before, and an officer who appeared to be responsible for the security operation. 'Mr Grant, I assume?' the officer said. 'I believe we have you to thank for the tip-off. As you see, we countered the terror threat.' The officer had a perfectly straight face but Steve sensed that the joke was on him.

'We are all indebted to your men and women for their vigilance,' he replied, chastened. 'I'm sorry but I can't explain the sighting yesterday evening.'

'I think I can. Overnight we checked out the ISIL operatives you identified, using local witnesses and CCTV footage. It turns out that they were a local five-a-side football team, celebrating in town after a tournament.'

Deepak Parrikar decided to launch his entry into high-level politics with a symbolic event. He would commemorate the death of his protégé, the unfortunate Patel, by launching his father's Parrikar Foundation on the site where the body had been found. The Foundation would commit to a scheme of community development in the baasti: improved sanitation, a primary school, a health clinic. Those who harboured doubts about the political colours Deepak now stood under would be reassured that he was a force for enlightenment, committed to helping the poor regardless of caste or religion.

When the big day came, the Maidan in the centre of the baasti was transformed. A stage had been erected and decorated with gaudy bunting. The stage was packed with chairs for the VIPs, sheltering from the sun under a canopy. The VIPs threatened to outnumber the slum dwellers: they included the Parrikar family, relatives of the murdered Patel, the local politicians from the council and the state assembly, a police delegation led by Superintendent Mankad, various functionaries from the city council who (for a small consideration) would ensure that the promised improvements would be made, and assorted businessmen who had decided to match-fund the Parrikar Foundation, judging that this was a politically significant new force they would do well to join.

Deepak had succeeded in persuading his father and mother to forsake the seclusion of their home in order to celebrate the Foundation launch, and even Rose, on one of her rare visits to Mumbai, had agreed to come, concealing her distaste behind her largest sunglasses. The real organisational triumph, however, had been the intense diplomacy that had resulted in the frail, tottering Sheikh to arrive, supported by his old friend. His freshly dyed beard and white robes advertised his religious identity, and few of those present were aware of his colourful CV.

The slum dwellers initially numbered around fifty and the elected council man, who had been instructed to ensure maximum attendance, was beginning to feel rather uncomfortable. His trusted local representative, the slumlord, would have some explaining to do. But the crowd swelled as it became clear that the police were not here to make arrests or launch a tax collection, and the whiff of cooked food started to drift across the encampment. Tables were set out with savouries and sweetmeats that the slum dwellers encountered, if at all, only on special occasions like weddings or as leftovers scrounged or stolen from local hotels. As the more adventurous, or hungrier, residents tucked into the feast it soon became clear that the organisers had miscalculated. Those at the front of the queue positioned themselves to return for several helpings and scooped as much food as possible into their clothes to ensure that their families could eat well for the coming week. The late arrivals at the back of the queue seemed likely to miss out and scuffles broke out. Sergeant Ghokale had to deploy his two constables to restore order and calm was re-established with a loudspeaker announcement that more food was on its way; there would be enough for everyone.

After fresh consignments of food arrived from a nearby shopping centre and all had had their fill, a troupe of dancers and musicians performed for the crowd, which was now in an altogether happier and less suspicious mood. Unfortunately, Deepak Parrikar had chosen the performers who reflected his classical tastes. The Bollywood hits the crowd had been waiting for failed to make an appearance. Before long the refined rhythms and delicate phrasing of the ragas could be heard only in the best seats and the crowd was again becoming restive.

Deepak was advised by the organiser to proceed at once with the speeches and dedication and after much fiddling with the sound system he was able to begin, but only following a lengthy introduction from the council man. He expressed deep gratitude for the generosity of the Parrikars in terms of such obsequiousness that even those familiar with the style of such occasions winced inwardly. Deepak was used to public speaking in English but decided to speak in Marathi, the language of the state that he judged to be the lingua franca of the crowd. He noticed that his clap lines elicited applause from the authority figures on the platform but most of the crowd simply looked puzzled. In this polyglot community five or six different languages were spoken, and for those recently arrived from impoverished villages in other parts of India, Hindi, Telugu or Tamil would have been more accessible.

Even if the crowd had fully taken on board the sweep and scale of the urban transformation Deepak envisaged, they would not have been easily impressed. The community already boasted the disused shell of a primary school promised after a visitation by a Scandinavian aid agency: the community worker left to supervise the project had pocketed the funds required to run it and disappeared. At the last general election, a new latrine had been promised in return for votes, had been half-dug and then abandoned. The Parrikars were made of sterner stuff but the crowd did not yet know that.

The climax was to be a ceremonial digging of the ground to lay the foundation stone of the promised new school with a blessing from a Hindu priest, accompanied by the release of helium balloons that had been distributed among the children, who then howled with anguish when their new toys had to be released into the sky. Ravi, the now forgotten hero who had discovered Patel's body, took the precaution of holding on firmly to his new red plaything.

Then there were fireworks, which spread delight and terror in equal measure. Superintendent Mankad instinctively reached for his revolver as the firecrackers exploded around him. He was nervously watching the three goondas in dark glasses standing by the hut on the hillock nearby where the murder was committed and where his rescue of Deepak Parrikar had been effected. Following Deepak's political baptism, the Trishul gang and its political mentors had achieved a state of coexistence with their improbable new ally. But the Superintendent knew the difference between a truce and a peace and was taking no chances. Deepak and the leading VIPs were bundled into a van and driven off to greater safety.

As they drove back into downtown Mumbai, Deepak reflected on the awkwardness of the occasion: the many things he needed to learn before he could call himself 'a man of the people'. He contrasted the discomfort he felt among his own people – he had almost thrown up on the platform, nauseated by the stench of the slum – with the easy, warm familiarity he enjoyed with his British lover who now seemed so very far away.

He needn't have worried. The High Command in the ruling party were delighted with their new recruit and the media exposure he generated. *Bharat Bombay*'s coverage, like that of other popular papers, focused on national and family unity and the generosity of the Foundation. No one noticed, or was inclined to point out, the half-completed latrine, the disused shell of a school, the scramble for food and the unsavoury gang of goondas watching from the hillside nearby. Together with other occasions around the country featuring India's eclectic mix of colours, castes and creeds, the Prime Minister's slogan for the forthcoming election – Inclusive India – took shape. It tested well with focus groups. It remained only to arrange, through intermediaries, a gesture of reconciliation with Pakistan, which would calm down worrying talk of war and enable him to proclaim: Blessed are the Peacemakers.

CHAPTER 17

THE EXHIBITION

Statement by the Metropolitan Police Commissioner, 1 October 2019:

A group of suspected recruits to an Islamic terrorist group is active in the UK. They are of Pakistani origin and may be seeking targets with an Indian connection in the light of recent confrontation and riots in the subcontinent. Extra guards have been placed around the Indian High Commission in London, offices of Air India and major temple complexes in Southall, Slough and Neasden.

Shaida's missing brother was nearer than either of them realised. His group arrived at its destination in the early hours of the morning. The van slowly made its way up a dark alley and moved quickly and quietly through a yard at the back of a three storey terraced house.

The group split up once inside the house. Each was given a room and told to wash, change and prepare himself for a briefing shortly after dawn. There were only a few dimmed lights in the room Mo occupied, but it seemed to be a child's bedroom, with a few soft toys piled beside the bed and a scooter in the corner. A reassuring, familiar smell of Asian cooking seeped through from the kitchen below.

He lay on the bed and tried to sleep. His brain, however, was in overdrive with memories flashing past: his parents, his brothers and sister in episodes of his generally happy childhood; the embarrassing, awkward, unfulfilling encounters he had had with girls; the horrific images he had seen of Muslim suffering around the world; the day when he had been allowed time off school to go to Buckingham Palace to see his father receive a medal – when his parents glowed with pride and happiness; then the demonstration and the look of hatred in the eyes of the racist thug in the seconds before his face felt the force of the man's blow. He felt mounting excitement and anticipation but also fear and a nagging, sinking feeling of doubt that he could not, despite his best efforts, totally suppress. In his semi-conscious state he could still hear every sound in the house: a snore from somewhere; a whispered, animated conversation somewhere else.

When the first signs of morning light appeared he forced himself to follow the routine he had been given. He washed and changed into the clothes that were waiting for him: what seemed to be a waiter's suit, which fitted almost perfectly. He tiptoed downstairs past the open door of a room inside which one of his group was kneeling and whispering his prayers. The lounge gradually filled and there was fruit juice and bread to break the fast. Tariq Ahmed stood at the back and left the floor to a burly man in black T-shirt and jeans who stood before them with a large chart taped to the wall. Mo noticed that one of their number was not present and he broke the silence by asking about him. The man was brusque and clearly didn't wish to discuss the matter: 'He has been allocated to another task.' He then took the group carefully through the morning's programme and the instructions they were to follow once they had been delivered to their – unspecified – destination up to the point that they were to open fire on their target: a group of mainly American businessmen who were supplying arms to the enemies of Islam. The rest of the group seemed drugged – with sleep or some sort of hypnosis – and did not share Mo's curiosity to know more. After being rebuffed several times, he was unable to pluck up the courage to ask the question nagging at him: what do we do after the shooting? The instructor read his thoughts but was studiously vague: 'Allah will protect us. You will be shown the way out of the building and return to continue our struggle.'

The weapons on which they had trained were distributed and checked. Then the group made its way back through the yard to the van. Mo was surrounded by his fellow warriors and two of the instructors who eyed him much as they would have done a prisoner in custody. If he had any second thoughts, it was too late. In the van he sat next to the African from his hometown whom he had wanted to get to know better but had never had the chance. The African smiled at him, an open, almost loving, smile, put his arm around him and said: 'You'll be fine, son.'

<hr/>

The top floor of the tower in Canary Wharf provided a good vantage point overlooking Docklands. Tariq Ahmed had come up here with the help of a sleeper from his organisation to understand better the distribution of security around the exhibition.

What was unfolding in front of him amazed and delighted him. There were flashing blue lights and police sirens everywhere. In front of him, on the roof of the O2, a group of nocturnal protesters had painted, in large luminescent orange letters, 'STOP THE ARMS TRADE'. He could just make out a cluster of people on the public steps to the top of the building gesticulating, no doubt working out how to conceal this embarrassing welcome to the world's largest and best-attended defence equipment exhibition.

At the nearby City Airport, police helicopters hovered over the runway and there were scores of ambulances and police cars. According to the radio commentary, a group of twenty to thirty protesters were lying down on the runway having adopted the successful technique from their road blockage of the previous DSEI event in 2017. It would take several hours to clear them – perhaps longer since another group had apparently landed by dinghy from the waterway alongside the airport. In the air, a growing number of aircraft were circulating and a leading member of the Saudi Royal Family had already been diverted to Stansted, with his London-based entourage fighting their way through the traffic to get to the M11 in order to greet him.

The Metropolitan Police were expecting trouble. Thousands of extra officers were on duty. With forty thousand visitors expected, including delegations from some of the world's least savoury regimes, the attraction for protesters was obvious. And unlike at previous DSEI events, where protests had been small and limited to dedicated pacifist and human rights groups, this time there was plenty of advance publicity. Television programmes featured torture equipment, cluster bombs and landmines allegedly being sold, illegally, on British soil, in a privately run exhibition heavily patronised by the British government as part of its global export drive.

Moderate opinion was outraged. The kind of people who marched against the Iraq war but generally disdained public protests started to say 'something must be done', and those within travelling distance headed off to join hastily assembled demonstrations. Docklands does not have the public gathering places like Trafalgar and Parliament squares through which protest could be channelled, and policed. So the impact was chaotic. The DLR became dangerously overcrowded and had to be suspended. Key access routes, through the Blackwall Tunnel and Thames Gateway, became hopelessly blocked preventing emergency vehicles getting through. At the ExCeL entrance itself, a long thin blue line held at bay thousands of protesters, and delegates struggled to get through.

All of this was witnessed with mounting satisfaction by the watcher in the tower. He had played no part in organising the chaos below but it made his own job easier. He had long admired the self-restraint, discipline and humour of Britain's peaceful mass protesters and had seen the same techniques used with good effect in the subcontinent. But they lacked the impact of violence: the shock, the terror that even a few people could create. Personal experience, as well as theory, had led him into this, more brutal, kind of politics. And like moths drawn to a flame, the media would always amplify the violence and ignore the worthy and well intentioned.

Today was the biggest venture he had attempted. The arms exhibition was a perfect target. And meeting the African, now a committed recruit to the cause, had given him the idea of concentrating the attack on the Global operation. The propaganda value of taking on a company with links to rabidly anti-Muslim forces was potentially huge… if the attack was a success.

Success today did not depend on the tens of thousands of protesters but the team of young men who had been well prepared for their task. Their first big obstacle had been the security screen around the exhibition centre. But the obstacle proved to be scalable. The scrutiny devoted to searching the bags of visitors did not extend to the comings and goings of staff serving Michelin Star meals to VIPs and VVIPs, nor to their food containers. It had not been unduly difficult to find a willing helper who was able to obtain a set of security passes for a chef and a serving team, doctored to accommodate new faces and names. The only anxiety was whether the congestion below would prevent certain guests arriving.

※※※※※※※※※※※※※※

Tariq Ahmed need not have worried. A block booking at the O2 InterContinental, near the exhibition, had secured penthouse suites and a comfortable, secure business meeting room for the board of Global. The evening before the exhibition opened, all were comfortably ensconced and unaware that they were the object of so much interest. The company had a prominent display to advertise its arrival in the big league of weapons makers and distributors and a list of potential customers or partners had been drawn up for board members to cultivate. It was also an opportunity for the board to meet, to hear the Chairman set out his strategic vision and, hopefully, discover that their services would continue to be very well rewarded.

The Chairman convened a meeting of directors and was in good form. Since their last meeting in London the Chairman had secured a one-to-one meeting at Trump Tower and had been given the names of key people in the Pentagon who the President guaranteed would be helpful. Not only that: the British acquisition had come through – well done, Admiral! – though it was a pity about the unhelpful publicity. Desai, for once, was on the defensive explaining the complex politics of India; but it would be sorted. A pity Orlov couldn't be here; the British had refused his visa: 'tiresome Cold War politics'.

The Chairman was, however, in an expansive mood. The heightened tension in East Asia over North Korea and China's increasing assertiveness was creating a big market for Global's products and services in South Korea, Japan and, above all, Vietnam. Global's new Vice-Chairman, ex-Pentagon Colonel Ted Schwarz – would lead that work. 'I will ask Ted to say a few words in a minute. He has just come back from Ho Chi Minh City, which he last saw as a teenage marine.'

He then explained his next big play: the opportunities that had opened up as a result of meetings Orlov had arranged in the Kremlin. Russia would pay very well indeed for access to the most sophisticated Western military technology that wasn't available through conventional channels. The White House had been kept informed and wouldn't make a fuss. Once Desai had cleared away 'obstructions', the Pulsar/Parrikar Avionics partnership would be the main conduit for equipment officially exported to India, but then diverted to other lucrative destinations, including Russia. Board colleagues, he concluded, could look forward to a 'bumper Christmas bonus'.

Elsewhere in the same hotel a couple of old adversaries met for their regular exchange of information. The mere fact of their meeting would, were it known, lead to demands for their court martials and exemplary execution. In fact, they were both passing to their mutual enemy information on nuclear missile deployment that no ordinary spy could have obtained. Yet they were not traitors or spies but deeply patriotic – indeed, nationalistic – soldiers whose loyalty could never be doubted. One was General Rashid, the architect of the 2008 Mumbai raid and the more recent, and less successful, adventure at Parrikar Avionics. The other was General Balbir Singh, known as the Snowman for his exploits fighting on the Siachen Glacier where extreme cold rather than Pakistani bullets had claimed several fingers and toes.

They were not friends exactly. Indeed, they spent much of their time working out how to destabilise each other's countries through disinformation, terror raids and military action short of outright war. Their family histories during Partition matched each other in horror. Neither had ever visited the other's country, though they shared a common language and history. But their acquaintanceship had engendered camaraderie and they exchanged presents: Cuban cigars for the Snowman; the best Glenlivet for Rashid who was obliged to curtail his drinking habits back home. And they both had a soldier's contempt for their respective politicians: venal, self-serving, lying hypocrites whose endless pandering to popular prejudices had, more than once, taken their countries perilously close to a nuclear exchange.

The events of the last few weeks had underlined just how important it was to be able to control these idiots in an emergency. And each could speak with confidence knowing that in a safe back home there were letters from their chiefs of staff, and Prime Ministers, authorising the meeting. At the end of it, they had exchanged enough information to be sure that nuclear war could not start by accident – or misunderstanding – and without trip wires to ensure that the politicians on both sides had a clear, unambiguous understanding about what Mutually Assured Destruction could mean.

When the business was complete they settled down to a companionable drink and an exchange of news about their families. Then they wished each other well and looked forward to a good day shopping for 'toys' in the exhibition.

Steve was on his way to London, to the exhibition for which he had been given a pass and time off for 'union duties'. He didn't much like the idea of an arms fair but he could no more disown it than a fisherman could reject the sea. The union expected him to be there, visiting the stands of Rolls-Royce, BAE Systems, Westland and the rest, including Pulsar, for a photo and reassuring words with the bosses and their prospective customers.

When he reached the underground he saw the signs advising that the DLR to ExCeL was closed, for reasons unspecified. Chatter on the station platform established that public and private transport was immobile. No problem: it was early; he would walk. He hadn't realised quite how far it was. But there was the entertainment, and mounting excitement, of endless flashing blue lights from police motorbikes, helicopters overhead and crowds moving in his direction.

It then took an age to get through the crowds milling at the entrance, the pass check and then the bag check. Either the organisers were utterly incompetent or there was something seriously untoward going on. Overheard conversation from people glued to their phones filled in the story: the demonstrations; the sit-in at the airport; the protesters' message on the O2. He could see that at the next Labour Party meeting Ms Cook's friends would have plenty to say when they discovered that he had been abetting the sale of weapons to a miscellany of visiting tyrants.

Once through security he headed for the main hall. He had a list of company stands to visit but his first port of call wasn't the exciting new drone at BAE as the list suggested but to attend to the woman he loved. Shaida was greeting guests at the entrance to an impressive, expensively designed marquee devoted to the products of Global and its various subsidiaries, of which there were many after the recent spurt of acquisitions. Today she was not the Asian princess he so admired but an impeccably smart woman in a fitted, perfectly tailored navy blue suit, white blouse, stiletto heels and glossy coiled hair. It was a style he hadn't seen before but had clearly caught the eye of the line of men waiting patiently for her to introduce them to the world of laser-bearing missiles.

When she saw Steve in the background she gave him one of her most welcoming smiles and asked him to come back in the lunch break. 'As you see, I am auditioning to be an air hostess. Company dress code. Suits only. No hijabs here. It should be quiet when the VIP guests are eating.' What she didn't tell him was that this was how she liked to dress on her private trysts in London. They were getting closer, more comfortable. But she didn't want to assume too much too soon.

The last twenty-four hours had opened Shaida's eyes to the kind of company she now worked for. The firm wanted her to be available to lubricate the socialisation of top management. Duty No. 1 was to be present at a drinks party after the board meeting the previous evening. She was one of two young women in addition to the waitresses and when she entered the room she sensed that more was expected of her than looking pretty and making small talk.

She gradually fitted names to faces. The Chairman was a larger-than-life, fleshy man – over twenty stone she reckoned – with a garish mustard suit and uncoordinated tie. His loud Deep South drawl could be heard above every conversation introducing his new 'catch': a top Pentagon official, recently retired. She could also see that his eyes were not fixed on the man from the Pentagon but on her or, at least, her body. Having heard the gossip about his reputation, rather similar to that of his friend and sometime business associate Donald Trump, she kept her distance and avoided eye contact. She experienced a brief moment of panic when she was introduced to the Israeli director who bore a striking similarity to her old flame; but it wasn't him.

By carefully avoiding the eyes and arms of the Chairman, she found herself embraced by the tentacles of another octopus: the Red Admiral, rather the worse for wear after several glasses of rum. When she disentangled herself she was struck by his handsome, weather-beaten face, the intense blue – if somewhat bloodshot – eyes and the rich, baritone voice. She could have warmed to him but his intentions were so crudely obvious that she made her excuses and headed for the other Asian in the room: a silent, stone cold sober Indian sipping apple juice in the corner. This was presumably the Desai she had heard about and seen reference to in the communications she had been channelling to Kate.

Although he was no conversationalist, she managed to extract from him the information that he had been badly shaken by a 'security incident' in Portsmouth earlier in the week. He was travelling back as soon as a flight could be found and would miss the rest of the exhibition. That provided Shaida with an excuse to leave, 'to help our Indian colleague with his travel'.

But that last conversation and in particular the description of the 'security incident' reminded her what she was trying to blot out of her consciousness: her missing brother.

Liam sat in front of his computer screen, puzzled and worried. He looked around the room for inspiration, at the several dozen bowed heads absorbed in their own unresolved puzzles and at the silent screens on the wall offering a variety of news channels. The owners of the bowed heads, like him, had once thought of themselves as incarnations of Bond; but that was not how the Service worked. It had headed off attacks since 7/7 through meticulous intelligence gathering and data analysis. Boring. Sedentary. Necessary. No one wanted to be the person who missed something.

Liam's problem was that his intelligence sources had dried up. Mo had disappeared from the face of the earth, seemingly, as had other young men from around the country known to have an anti-Indian agenda. Mo's sister had been as helpful as she could and his friends were convinced he was still in the country. Nothing else. The consensus among Liam's colleagues was that 'something big' was being planned, by people who were well organised and had unusually secure communications.

A couple of days ago the mystery seemed to have been solved: the call from the Tory MP and Trade Envoy passing on what seemed to be strong intelligence based on a sighting in Portsmouth. His bosses trusted his judgement and mobilised help. Then, the farcical 'terrorist attack'. Sniggering all round. Liam's five-a-side triumph. His colleagues spent their lives hunting for needles in haystacks and weren't impressed by people who became overexcited at the first sighting of a shiny object.

The screens on the wall were showing the enveloping chaos in the Docklands area. Liam got up from his seat for a closer look: the drama at City Airport filmed from a helicopter hovering above; the lengthening queues and restless crowds at the ExCeL; the static traffic for miles around.

Shaida had already told him that she would be there representing Pulsar. Thinking of Shaida prompted other thoughts. The company board. They and a lot of other VIPs from pretty unsavoury places. A controversial industry bash that some highly motivated people found threatening or offensive. An obvious target. But the Met were all over it. Months of risk assessment and contingency planning. Judging by the unfolding drama on the screens, there were risks and contingencies the clever boys and girls at Scotland Yard hadn't factored in. The company Global?

He wanted to be on the safe side. So he rang the number he had been given of the officer in charge of security at the exhibition. Assistant Commissioner Maggie Brown. He didn't know her, but she was highly regarded. She ranked well above him but would listen to someone from the Service. She answered immediately: calmness personified. He explained his concerns about the suspected terrorist cell: 'Sorry, nothing more concrete. Just a hunch. May need some extra security.' She wasn't fazed: 'You can see we have our hands full. But we will check it out. American company; Global, you say? Consider it done.'

<hr>

The cavernous halls of the ExCeL were packed with stands advertising every conceivable mechanism for killing, maiming or hurting fellow human beings that our species' ingenuity could devise. The professionals, the military men and their civilian masters or servants eyed up the potential on offer and tried to match it to their budgets. Businesses from the biggest to the smallest practised their sales pitch. The halls gradually filled up as the police cleared a way through the demonstrators outside and celebrity spotters could identify the President of the DRC, the Saudi Defence Minister – a regular spender but reportedly short of cash this year – a couple of UAE ruling heads, and large posses of Chinese, Japanese, Koreans and Vietnamese preparing for mutual hostilities. The demonstrators outside would also have been alarmed to see how many delegations spent time among the stalls of the ingenious entrepreneurs offering a variety of novel techniques for disrupting demonstrations. Undoubtedly the stars of the first morning were the Presidents of Egypt and Nigeria who had each arrived with a long and expensive shopping list, albeit without a clear indication of who would pay for them.

The Global stand faced stiff competition but the beautiful Asian woman welcoming visitors was a pull for the overwhelmingly male delegates. At noon the Chairman was due to give an address, according to the programme, to an enclosure of invited guests, in a space set aside within the area of the stand. He would speak alongside the Secretary of State for Business. The defence correspondents of *The Times*, the *Telegraph* and the BBC had been invited to ensure that an announcement on the latest dollop of public spending on the Defence Industrial Strategy was given appropriate coverage. Then the guests would settle down to a sumptuous lunch provided by the catering arm of a top London restaurant, no expense spared. Board members would each host a handpicked table at which conversation would flow in the direction of Global's latest offerings. Apart from a couple of security guards with walkie-talkies and bulging pockets, this was to be a relaxed, convivial, corporate event that could as easily have been transplanted to the Chelsea Flower Show or the hospitality suite before an international at Twickenham. As noon approached, however, it was becoming clear that all was not going to plan.

Kate Thompson could see from the rolling news on her office TV that something untoward was happening at the ExCeL where she was due for lunch with her Secretary of State and the board of Global. After the excitement and false alarm at Portsmouth she wasn't sure whether to be concerned or amused by the drama on the screen. She expected the event to be cancelled in any case since traffic was at a stand-still and Jim Chambers would never dream of using public transport. But after she settled to her files, Susan came in to say that she had just received instructions to take Kate to the helicopter pad on the MOD roof. It was late but they could still make the lunch.

The two women quickly made their way to Whitehall and Kate was in a cheerful mood; this was much more fun than being a rebellious back bencher. Chambers was waiting for them in the helicopter with Caroline, his principal private secretary, and he was altogether less cheery. 'Bloody anarchists,' he grumbled. 'Time we sorted them out. Britain can't be "open for business" when a few troublemakers can hold the capital city to ransom, like this.' Kate tuned out of his rant as the helicopter revved up and headed off across London. This was her first time in a helicopter and she was totally absorbed in the scenery and, as they approached their destination, the signs of chaos on the ground. The rude welcoming message on the O2 triggered another burst of indignation from the Secretary of State above the crackle of the intercom; but Kate was full of admiration for the protesters' nerve and creativity, and exchanged conspiratorial smiles with Susan. There was, however, a reality check as they landed next to the ExCeL: a serious warning from the security services. Should they go back? No. Just be careful.

Led by a couple of security staff, the ministerial group made their way through the exhibition hall, late but just in time for lunch. They went straight through the crowds of delegates to the Global stand and Kate noticed Shaida, stunning in unfamiliar Western dress, receiving guests at the entrance. They arrived just as the Chairman was about to launch into a welcome speech, looking greatly relieved that his chief guest had made it with his entourage to fill some of the embarrassing number of empty chairs.

Kate was struck by the Chairman's appearance: a rather gross man with remarkable coiffed hair in the style of his soulmate Trump. He was dressed in what Susan called, in a whisper, 'cowboy chic' missing only the Stetson hat. Kate recognised his accent, from the Mississippi delta in Louisiana, but his warm words scarcely disguised his irritation that British 'communists' were depleting his audience and delaying lunch. She had expected someone thoroughly sinister but found his folksy manner and cartoon-like appearance rather endearing. The Secretary of State responded with an off-the-cuff, charming and witty speech of the kind he had perfected on the Tory rubber-chicken circuit but with a few scripted lines for the journalists.

Lunch commenced. Kate was seated alongside a taciturn American, Colonel Schwarz, who had a military bearing, cold grey eyes and a severe crew-cut. He didn't do small talk and her attention wandered to the rest of the gathering. She recognised the Red Admiral entertaining what sounded like East European or Russian businessmen and he winked when he saw her looking in his direction. She had been told to expect a group of Indians, including Desai, but there were empty seats where they should have been. She couldn't help noticing the waiters, mostly Asian, who seemed remarkably awkward and inexpert as if they were serving a meal for the first time.

⨯⨯⨯⨯⨯⨯⨯⨯⨯⨯⨯⨯⨯⨯⨯⨯

Shaida was watching events from the back of the stand, irritated that it hadn't occurred to Global's organisers that the woman who had charmed dozens of visitors to the stand might merit a lunch. Nonetheless, she was able to locate Steve and they found a good vantage point where they could see and not be seen. They had a laugh at the mannerisms of the strange American they now worked for. But, then, they noticed that there were more disturbing oddities.

A group of armed men silently filled the back of the stand around them and one of them indicated to them to stay where they were and remain silent. Then they noticed the strange behaviour of the waiters whose clumsy unprofessionalism was in marked contrast to the sophisticated food they were serving. One of them managed to spill a soup bowl over one of the guests. Next, Shaida saw that one of the waiters looked familiar: an African; she knew she had seen him before. Then, to her shock, she saw her brother. Instinctively she stepped forward, out of the shadows, towards him. He didn't see her. But a moment later one of the waiters dropped a tray of glasses and, as everyone looked at the offender, the other waiters drew weapons from under their jackets.

Firing started. There were screams and shouts. Mo raised his weapon but then froze when he saw his sister in front of him. They stared at each other, fixed to the spot. Then he crumbled under a fusillade of bullets.

The firing stopped almost as quickly as it had begun, though the screams and cries for help continued along with a fire alarm that someone had activated. Shaida's first thought was for the body in front of her. She embraced her brother, whispering words of hope and encouragement. Steve rushed to join her to try to revive Mo, who was clearly critically injured and bleeding from the mouth. But it was hopeless. As more security men, police, medics and voyeurs descended on the scene, Steve led her away, shaking and too stunned to speak.

The carnage was, however, less serious than initially suspected. Kate and most of the other guests had found refuge under the tables, though several appeared to be injured and at least one, a Korean, was dead. A passer-by, a waitress at a neighbouring hospitality event, had been hit in the head by a stray bullet and was also dead.

One of the assassins had failed to fire a shot after his weapon had jammed and he was pinioned to the floor by a scrum that included Jim Chambers and the Red Admiral. Another, described as African in appearance, managed to flee in the mayhem leaving his white jacket and gun behind. Two others, one a white convert, were unambiguously dead. And the fifth was found, mortally wounded, being cradled by his sister. There was one other body: Chairman Le Fevre. His corpse was unscathed, however; he had died of a heart attack.

As the news channels and, later, the newspapers sought to interpret these events, the initial focus was inevitably on another terrorist outrage in parallel with those on the Continent and in the USA. Several terror groups claimed credit – not that there was much credit to claim. The biggest peaceful demonstration in recent years, and its cause, largely disappeared from the news. As the journalists hunted for a human interest angle, the first target was the waitress, an innocent bystander. But she turned out to be an illegal migrant from Moldova; no one knew her backstory; even her name, Irma, was probably false. The image that dominated the story was the photo taken from a mobile phone and distributed on social media, of the beautiful young woman holding her dying brother. Divided family; divided allegiances; here was a modern parable for the country to debate.

<hr>

The funeral took place several days later in the corner of the municipal cemetery where the town's Muslims buried their dead. It had taken a few days to get Mo's body back from the authorities, while they investigated the plot. It was a cold wet day: the first real sign of coming winter. Steve had come to join the mourners, but he soon realised that he was the only non-Muslim in the gathering crowd and judged from facial reactions that he was unwelcome. So he retreated to a copse of trees and watched from a distance. Even there he was caught up in the mood of the ceremony. At the sight of Shaida, in the front row of women relatives cradling her mother, he felt, for the first time in years, warm tears running down his cheeks and he sobbed to himself quietly. He was distracted from his grief by the sound of several men moving through the trees behind him and when he turned he recognised Liam among them. He assumed that they were here to watch the mourners rather than to mourn.

After the funeral crowd dispersed, he waited and then stepped forward bearing the red carnations that he judged were suitable. He placed them on the freshly dug soil covering the grave and then stood for a long time contemplating. Not since the death of his mother had he been to a funeral and that was a rather antiseptic, badly attended event in a crematorium, drained of emotion. He was more profoundly moved by this young man in the earth in front of him, who had shown little beyond hostility but who had helped to send his own life in a new direction. He was at the point of leaving when he heard a rustle of clothes behind him and then felt a hand slip under his arm. It stayed there and a head rested against his shoulder.

A week later Deepak Parrikar passed through London on his way to the USA. There was a joyful reunion with Kate in his hotel. They had both survived near-death experiences and had much to share. Kate and he knew that their paths were diverging but they were reconciled to the reality and were able to savour each other's company as it came, for the moment, as if each encounter were to be the last. They had not been truly alone together for weeks, and longed to express their passion for each other. At last, their physical desires satisfied, they lay entwined and talked in the warm glow of shared contentment through much of the night with an easy fluency and depth of understanding that neither had ever had with anyone else.

They explained to each other how they managed their roles as accidental politicians whose family circumstances and events had moulded them rather than career and ambition. They shared, too, their awkwardness as outsiders; not part of the tribe; not anchored by rigid ideology; used by but also learning how to use the system. Neither was a saint nor even particularly idealistic but both had a basic sense of decency and a nose for detecting evil. They marvelled at the fact that the dividing lines between them of convention, colour and country mattered so little.

As Kate prepared for an early morning departure she took a folder from her briefcase and gave it to Deepak. She explained the role played by the unlikely couple: the British trade unionist and Labour MP in waiting and his courageous and beautiful friend (she had never established what precisely the relationship was). Shaida's researches had established a trail of nefarious activity across several continents. The folder compiled by Shaida detailed Desai's activities within Global. There was almost certainly enough – the offshore accounts, the lavish tax-free payments, the involvement with political figures on the American extreme right – to have Desai ejected from the inner circles of government, and from Parrikar Avionics. The Indian ruling party valued the appearance, at least, of probity and the threat of bad publicity was a powerful inducement with an election approaching.

<hr />

When the drama of the terror attack had passed, Kate organised an appointment to see the Secretary of State. She arrived with a fat folder.

'Well, Kate, I hope you are none the worse for our little adventure. Terrible business. I hope it will silence all those hopeless, wishy-washy liberals who want to go soft on Muslim terrorism.'

'I guess we owe a big debt to Liam and the security people. They were ready and casualties were minimised. Your rugby tackle helped too!'

Jim guffawed. 'I was just doing my bit for UK plc. A pity we didn't have more time at the exhibition. It was a superb, professional, show. Inevitably we lost some business in all that fuss, but I am told by the defence sales chaps that we still had record turnover. But let's get down to business. The Prime Minister has asked me to confirm that the job we have promised you is coming through in a reshuffle in a few weeks' time. Have to keep it under wraps, but probably a big job at the Treasury. Next step the Cabinet! And he also wants you to take on an inter-ministerial task force on diversity as someone who has empathy for our ethnic minorities, as well as being a champion of women.'

Kate smiled in acknowledgement. 'Actually, I wanted to talk to you about something else. Global. The Red Admiral.'

'He's fine. Tough as old boots.'

'He isn't fine. He's a crook.'

'Oh Kate, really. Not that again. I do hope you haven't been encouraging the Overheads to tell tales out of school.'

'Nothing to do with the civil servants.' She put down her folder on Jim's desk. 'This file is made up of documentation from inside the company. If you want to look at the sections I have highlighted, it points to the fact that he has been involved in illegal arms smuggling, corrupt payments to officials in overseas governments, tax evasion, sanctions busting and unhealthily close links with a Russian associate whose enemies have a habit of disappearing. Liam and the permanent secretary will confirm what I am telling you.'

The Secretary of State maintained his composure remarkably well. 'That's quite a charge sheet. If you leave the file with me, I will consider what can be done.'

'I should say, Jim, that there are several copies. I think you should ask the Red Admiral to clear his desk immediately and pass the papers to the police. Otherwise I may not be able to restrain the people who gave me this material from going straight to the press.'

For the first time since she had known him he was totally lost for words. Eventually he recovered enough to speak. 'Well, Kate, I take my hat off to you. You have learnt how to survive in the political jungle, and more. I can see that I shall have to ditch my old friend the Admiral. Pity. Basically a good man fallen into bad company.'

'That isn't quite all, Jim. There is one very large payment that looks as if it could only be to one person. You. You should check if the bank details correspond to your own. If they don't, I apologise for jumping to conclusions.'

She was taking a risk. In fact, she had no proof, merely a suspicion. If he called her bluff, she would be in difficulty.

He looked at her for a long time, calculating the odds, she thought. 'Actually, you are right. It is me. But the money went to the party. I didn't keep a penny.'

'I suppose you think that makes it OK. Sorry, Jim. No go.'

With that she left the room.

<hr>

The Sloane Square flat felt bigger and emptier than he could ever remember. He looked again at that photo with his men, taken before they set off for the Falklands. The open, trusting, confident smiles. That picture often produced tears. But tonight the tears were of self-pity.

The two policemen had been quietly and respectfully spoken: almost gentle in their questioning. But it was painfully clear where they were leading: the lucrative, undeclared, conflicts of interest; the secret accounts; the national secrets passed on for a financial consideration. When it was clear that he could not save himself he tried not to implicate others like the Secretary of State but the officers knew too much already and he finished up dragging his friends down with him under the waves.

When it was all over he picked up the phone to speak to the only people he had left. But Louisiana didn't want to take the call. The acting Chairman, Colonel Schwarz, was busy. An underling, a new voice, told him that an exit payment was being arranged to his Caymans account. The acting Chairman had decided that, in view of terrorism risk, lax security, embarrassing publicity and the police interest, Britain was no longer a good place to do business. There were big opportunities opening up elsewhere. European operations would be handled in future out of Paris by retired General de Massigny, formerly of the French Defence Ministry and Dassault.

He tried St Petersburg but it was very late, even for an old friend in distress. Orlov yawned: 'Sorry, Comrade.'

He remembered that he had kept his service revolver locked in the desk drawer.

Author's Note and Acknowledgements

My biggest debt is to my wife Rachel, who acted as literary critic, moral support and typist in the early stages of the book and who also suggested the title.

Joan Bennett did a large amount of work typing and amending the manuscript.

I am grateful too to friends like Pippa Morgan and the Oakeshott family who read early drafts and gave me both encouragement and the benefits of constructive criticism.

Those sections describing British political life, and the civil service, draw on my own experience of politics, parliament and my years in the Cabinet. But any similarity between the characters in this book and real people is entirely accidental.

The sections on India draw on over half a century of visits to that country, and to Mumbai in particular, as part of the extended family which had my late wife, Olympia, at its heart. I also had many professional visits, of which several were as a minister promoting British exports, including arms.

The scenes depicting slum life in Mumbai rely not just on personal observations but on fictional and non-fictional accounts as in Suketu Mehta's *Maximum City*; Katherine Boo's *Behind the Beautiful Forevers*; Gregory David *Roberts' Shantaram*; and Vikram Chandra's *Sacred Games*.

The book can be traced back to my first serious experience of British politics as a Glasgow city councillor, over four decades ago, and the conflicting demands of jobs for Clyde-side workers, political idealism and the requirements of the arms trade. I then found myself in the Diplomatic service for a period, charged, among other things, with promoting British arms exports to Latin America. In opposition I challenged the corruption involved in some of our arms exports business. And then, as Secretary of State, I had ministerial responsibility for arms export licensing. The companies and individuals described in this book are however wholly fictitious.

The particular contract I describe, related to the creation of a shield against a nuclear strike, is based on what is publicly known about Indian and Pakistani defence policy. I am grateful for advice I received from Professor Michael Clarke at the Royal United Services Institute.

The book was made possible by the excellent team at Atlantic Books: Will Atkinson, Karen Duffy, Susannah Hamilton, Sara O'Keeffe and Margaret Stead. And, as ever, I benefitted enormously from the encouragement and advice of my literary agent, Georgina Capel.

EYEWITNESS TRAVEL

CUBA

DK

KT-197-186

LONDON, NEW YORK,
MELBOURNE, MUNICH AND DELHI
www.dk.com

PRODUCED BY Fabio Ratti Editoria Srl, Milan, Italy

PROJECT EDITOR Giorgia Conversi
ART EDITOR Paolo Gonzato

EDITORS Carla Beltrami, Barbara Cacciani,
Fernanda Incoronato, Alessandra Lombardi

MAIN CONTRIBUTOR
Irina Bajini

OTHER CONTRIBUTORS
Alejandro Alonso, Christopher Baker, Miguel A Castro Machado,
Andrea G Molinari, Matt Norman, Marco Oliva, Francesca Piana

PHOTOGRAPHERS
Heidi Grassley, Lucio Rossi

CARTOGRAPHERS
Laura Belletti, Oriana Bianchetti, Roberto Capra

ILLUSTRATORS
Marta Fincato, Modi Artistici

ENGLISH TRANSLATION
Richard Pierce

Dorling Kindersley Limited
EDITOR Fiona Wild
CONSULTANT Emily Hatchwell
DTP DESIGNERS Jason Little, Conrad van Dyk
PRODUCTION Joanna Bull

Printed and bound by South China Printing Co. Ltd., China

First published in Great Britain in 2002
by Dorling Kindersley Limited,
80 Strand, London WC2R 0RL

14 15 16 10 9 8 7 6 5 4 3 2

Reprinted with revisions 2004, 2007, 2009, 2011, 2013

Copyright © 2002, 2013 Dorling Kindersley Limited, London
A Penguin Company

ALL RIGHTS RESERVED. NO PART OF THIS PUBLICATION MAY BE
REPRODUCED, STORED IN A RETRIEVAL SYSTEM, OR TRANSMITTED
IN ANY FORM OR BY ANY MEANS, ELECTRONIC, MECHANICAL,
PHOTOCOPYING, RECORDING OR OTHERWISE WITHOUT THE PRIOR
WRITTEN PERMISSION OF THE COPYRIGHT OWNER.

A CIP CATALOGUE RECORD IS AVAILABLE FROM THE BRITISH LIBRARY.

ISBN 978 1 40938 644 5

Front cover main image: Vintage cars outside Capitol Building, Havana

MIX
Paper from
responsible sources
FSC
www.fsc.org   FSC™ C018179

**The information in this
DK Eyewitness Travel Guide is checked regularly.**
Every effort has been made to ensure that this book is as up-to-date
as possible at the time of going to press. Some details, however, such
as telephone numbers, opening hours, prices, gallery hanging
arrangements and travel information are liable to change. The
publishers cannot accept responsibility for any consequences
arising from the use of this book, nor for any material on third
party websites, and cannot guarantee that any website address in this
book will be a suitable source of travel information. We value the
views and suggestions of our readers very highly. Please write to:
The Publisher, DK Eyewitness Travel Guides, Dorling Kindersley,
80 Strand, London WC2R 0RL, UK or email: travelguides@dk.com.

CONTENTS

HOW TO USE THIS
GUIDE **6**

Ídolo de Tabaco, Museo
Montané, Havana *(see p101)*

INTRODUCING CUBA

**Primary school children in
Santiago de Cuba**

◁ **A house in Trinidad with characteristic iron grilles; in the insert, the bust of Hatuey at Baracoa**

The beach at Guardalavaca, one of the best-known resorts in Cuba

Guava paste and cheese

Dancing at the Casa de la Tradición in Santiago de Cuba

Museo de la Revolución *(see pp88–9)*

HOW TO USE THIS GUIDE

This guide will help you to get the most out of your visit to Cuba by providing detailed information and expert recommendations. *Introducing Cuba* maps the island and sets it in its historic, artistic, cultural and geographical context. *Havana* and the four regional sections describe the most important sights, with maps, floor plans, photographs and detailed illustrations. Hotels and restaurants, together with night spots and shops, are described in *Travellers' Needs*, while the *Survival Guide* offers tips on everything from transport to phones and local currency.

HAVANA
AREA BY AREA

The centre of the city is divided into three areas, each with its own chapter. The last chapter, *Further Afield*, covers peripheral sights. All the sights are numbered and plotted on the *Area Map*. The detailed information for each sight is easy to locate because it follows the numerical order on the map.

Sights at a Glance lists the sights in each chapter by category: Churches, Museums and Galleries, Streets and Squares, Historic Buildings, Parks and Gardens.

All pages relating to Havana have red thumb tabs.

A locator map shows where you are in relation to the other areas of the city.

1 Area map
All the major sights are numbered and located on this map. Those in the historic centre are also listed in the Havana Street Finder (see pp118–23).

2 Street-by-Street Map
This gives a bird's-eye view of the most important areas in each chapter.

Stars indicate the sights no visitor should miss.

Suggested routes are shown in red.

3 Detailed Information
The most important monuments and sights in Havana are described individually. Addresses, phone numbers, opening hours and information concerning guided tours and taking photos are also provided.

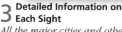

1 Introduction to the Region
The landscape, history and character of each region are described here, showing how the region has developed over the centuries and what it has to offer to visitors today.

CUBA REGION BY REGION
Apart from Havana, the island has been divided into four regions, each with a separate chapter: Western Cuba, Central Cuba – West, Central Cuba – East and Eastern Cuba.

2 Regional Map
This shows the road network and provides an illustrated overview of the whole region. All the interesting places to visit are numbered in the same order in which they are described, and there are also useful tips on getting around the region by car and by public transport.

Each region can easily be identified by its own colour coding.

3 Detailed Information on Each Sight
All the major cities and other top sights are described in detail. They are listed in order, following the numbering on the Regional Map. Within each town or city there is detailed information on important buildings and other sights.

The Visitors' Checklist provides all the practical information you will need to plan your visit.

Boxes provide further information on the region: leading figures, legends, historical events, local flora and fauna, curiosities, and so on.

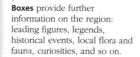

4 Cuba's Top Sights
These are given two or more full pages. Historic buildings are dissected to reveal their interiors, while museums have colour-coded floor plans to help you locate their most interesting features, which are shown in photographs with captions.

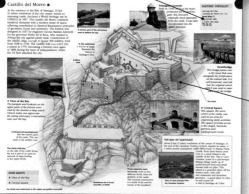

INTRODUCING CUBA

DISCOVERING CUBA

Cuba is a fascinating island nation. Its lively capital city, Havana, is rich in attractions and steeped in atmosphere. Western Cuba has a dramatic mountain chain, with lush forests and fertile valleys planted with fields of tobacco. Charming Colonial cities are plentiful in Central Cuba, with important wetland habitats

Classic car in Havana

on the Caribbean shores in the West, and a string of beach-rimmed isles along the Atlantic seaboard in the East. The rugged mountain terrain of Eastern Cuba is combined with several ancient cities endowed with a strong African heritage. These pages give a brief overview of the distinctive highlights of each region.

Exuberant carnival scene in the streets of Havana

HAVANA

- **Fascinating museums**
- **La Habana Vieja**
- **Captivating nightlife**
- **Evocative fortresses**

A vibrant, once cosmopolitan capital city teeming with historic buildings and irresistible allure, Havana boasts dozens of sights of interest, a vibrant nightlife and carnivals. Many sights are concentrated in **La Habana Vieja** *(see pp60–77)*, the compact old city centred around cobbled plazas and characterized by Hispanic-Andalusian architecture. The Plaza de la Catedral is surrounded by 18th-century aristocratic buildings and the elegant cathedral, while the Plaza de Armas has a strong Colonial feel.

Centro Habana *(see pp78–95)* includes the area around the Parque Central with the

intriguing **Museo de la Revolución** *(see pp88–9)* and the well-stocked **Museo de Bellas Artes** *(see pp92–5)*.

Taxis are useful for exploring **Vedado** *(see pp96–105)* and **Miramar** *(see pp108–9)*, sprawling regions full of Beaux Arts, Art Nouveau and Modernist buildings. The **Hotel Nacional** *(see p98)* is a must-see, as is the **Plaza de la Revolución** *(see p102)*.

On the outskirts of the city, the beaches of **Playas del Este** *(see p113)* and the **Finca La Vigía** *(see p115)* – Ernest Hemingway's Cuban home – are well worth a visit, as is the Parque Histórico-Militar Morro Cabaña in the **Castillo del Morro** *(see p110)*.

WESTERN CUBA

- **Superlative scenery**
- **Valle de Viñales**
- **Lush tobacco fields**
- **Islands and beaches**

With spectacular landscapes, tobacco fields and charming towns that evoke a sense of

nostalgia for past times, mountainous Western Cuba invites leisurely exploration. A short distance west of Havana, the **Sierra del Rosario** *(see p136–7)* forms a magnificent setting for Cuba's prime ecotourism resort – Las Terrazas – while westward the Sierra de Órganos are studded with *mogotes* – fantastic limestone formations centered on the **Valle de Viñales** *(see pp142–5)*. Also a centre of tobacco production, this valley offers the most quintessential of Cuban landscapes.

María la Gorda *(see p146)*, at the western tip of Cuba, is a prime dive site. Off the coast are the isles of the Archipiélago de los Canarreos, shimmering with gorgeous beaches. Here, the best diving in all Cuba awaits off the southwest tip of the **Isla de la Juventud** *(see pp148–51)*, while **Cayo Largo** *(see pp152–3)* draws visitors with its stunning sands and turquoise waters – the only place in Cuba to allow nude sunbathing.

The fertile Valle de Viñales with limestone *mogotes* in the background

◁ Mural on the corner of Calle Heredia and Calle Clarín, Santiago de Cuba

The enchanting *casco viejo* (historic core) of Trinidad

CENTRAL CUBA – WEST

• **Parque Nacional Zapata**
• **Revolutionary museums**
• **Famous resort of Varadero**
• **Fireworks battles in Remedios**

With the country's top beach resort and largest national park, plus important museums honoring revolutionary heroes, this region is Cuba at its most varied. With a glorious beach, **Varadero** *(see pp162–3)* makes a fine base

Pink flamingos at the Parque Nacional Zapata

for watersports enthusiasts and for exploring the towns of **Matanzas** *(see pp158–9)* and **Cárdenas** *(see p161)*.

Nature lovers are enticed to the **Península de Zapata** *(see pp164–7)*, part of which has been designated a national park, good for spotting crocodiles and colourful birds, and for sportfishing for bonefish in shallows. Playa Girón (setting for the 1961 Bay of Pigs battle) is off-limits to

visitors but has an evocative museum on the CIA-sponsored invasion. **Santa Clara** *(see pp174–6)* claims another fascinating revolutionary museum, while close by, the colonial town of **Remedios** *(see p177)* is best visited at Christmas for its *parranda* (fireworks battle). With a strong French heritage, **Cienfuegos** *(see pp168–71)* features unique architecture.

CENTRAL CUBA – EAST

• **Gorgeous beaches**
• **Trinidad's historic centre**
• **Flamingos at Cayo Coco**
• **Lush Sierra Escambray**

Fringed to the north and south by offshore isles, this region claims the most attractive beaches in Cuba. Coral reefs and walls edge the isles, providing tantalizing opportunities for diving and top-notch sportfishing. **Cayo Coco** *(see pp198–9)* is the most developed isle, with a wide choice of luxury all-inclusive hotels.

The beautifully preserved town of **Trinidad** *(see pp182–90)* is the loveliest of Cuba's Colonial cities, its *casco viejo* (historic core) full of cobbled streets. The immediate area is replete with attractions, from steam-train rides to hiking and birding in the **Sierra del Escambray** *(see p173, 191)*.

The main highway, the Carretera Central, links three provincial capitals of modest appeal – **Sancti Spíritus** *(see pp194–5)*, **Ciego de Ávila**

(p196), and **Las Tunas** *(p207)* – and a fourth – **Camagüey** *(pp200–3)*, with restored colonial plazas that are redolent of yesteryear.

EASTERN CUBA

• **Carnival in Santiago de Cuba**
• **Basílica del Cobre**
• **White sands of Guardalavaca**
• **Pre-Columbian sites**

Birthplace of both the independence and revolutionary movements, Oriente (as this region is known) abounds in monuments and museums. Many are in **Santiago de Cuba** *(see pp222–31)*, the most African of Cuban cities, with inspiring architecture and a vivacious spirit, best experienced during July's exciting Carnival.

Visitors are also drawn to Cuba's main pilgrimage site – **Basílica del Cobre** *(see p221)* with its statue of the black Madonna – and to **Parque Baconao** *(see pp234–7)*, a UNESCO biosphere reserve that also contains an unusual range of attractions, from dolphin shows to an antique car museum. Cuba's best pre-Columbian site is located here too, near the resort of **Guardalavaca** *(see p215)* with its crescent-shaped beach and in **Baracoa** *(see pp242–3)*, the country's oldest city, which enjoys a spectacularly lush setting.

The **Sierra Maestra** *(see p220)*, the setting for Castro's guerrilla headquarters, is a beautiful national park.

The glorious white sand beach of Guardalavaca – a major resort

Putting Cuba on the Map

Washed by the Atlantic Ocean, the Caribbean Sea and the waters of the Gulf of Mexico, Cuba is the largest island in the Greater Antilles, situated just south of the Tropic of Cancer. It lies only 180 km (112 miles) from Florida and 210 km (130 miles) from Mexico, while Haiti and Jamaica are slightly less than 80 km (50 miles) and 140 km (87 miles) away, respectively. Cuba is not a single island, but a varied archipelago with a total surface area of 110,922 sq km (42,815 sq miles). Lying on an east-west axis, the main island, the elongated Isla Grande, is about 1,250 km (776 miles) long and 100 km (62 miles) wide on average. Around it are five archipelagos: Colorados, Sabana, Camagüey, Canarreos and Jardines de la Reina, consisting of thousands of *cayos* (keys and small islands). The largest minor island is Isla de la Juventud. Cuba has about 11 million inhabitants, 2,500,000 of whom live in Havana, the capital.

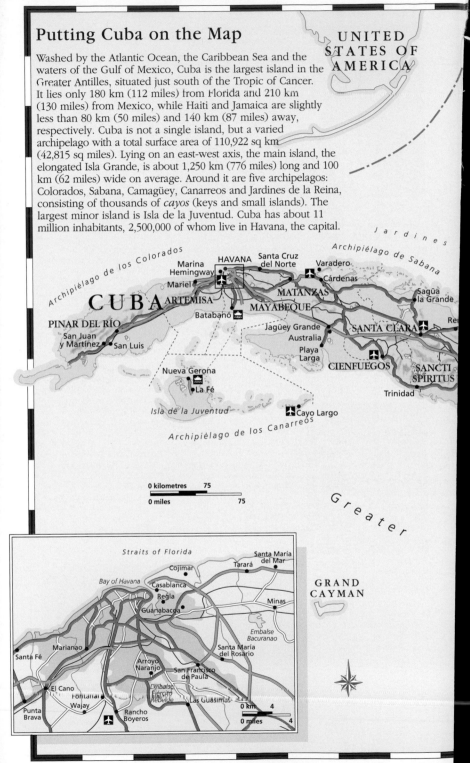

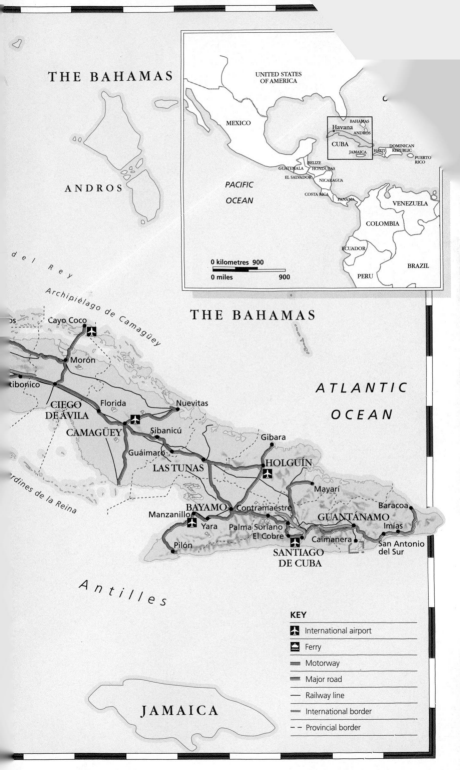

THE BAHAMAS

ANDROS

Inset map

UNITED STATES OF AMERICA

MEXICO

Havana
CUBA
JAMAICA

BAHAMAS
ANDROS

HAITI
DOMINICAN
REPUBLIC

PUERTO
RICO

PACIFIC
OCEAN

GUATEMALA
EL SALVADOR
BELIZE
HONDURAS
NICARAGUA
COSTA RICA
PANAMA

VENEZUELA

COLOMBIA

ECUADOR

PERU

BRAZIL

0 kilometres 900
0 miles 900

Main map

del Rey

Archipiélago de Camagüey

os

Cayo Coco

Morón

tiboníco

CIEGO
DE ÁVILA

CAMAGÜEY

Florida

Sibanicú

Guáimaro

LAS TUNAS

THE BAHAMAS

Nuevitas

Gibara

ATLANTIC

OCEAN

HOLGUÍN

Mayarí

Baracoa

rdines de la Reina

BAYAMO

Manzanillo

Pilón

Yara

Contramaestre

Palma Soriano
El Cobre

GUANTÁNAMO

Imías

Caimanera

San Antonio
del Sur

SANTIAGO
DE CUBA

A n t i l l e s

JAMAICA

KEY

✈	International airport
⛴	Ferry
▬	Motorway
▬	Major road
—	Railway line
—	International border
- -	Provincial border

A PORTRAIT OF CUBA

I mages of Cuba show hot sun and fields of sugar cane, tall palm trees and deep, clear blue sea. Cuba is indeed all these things, but it is also a country with a deep-rooted, complex culture in which old traditions and new intellectual developments co-exist. It is a young and vital island, a place of music and colour, which despite severe economic difficulties has held on to its unique identity.

Cuba's identity owes a great deal to the fact that it is surrounded by sea as well as to its geographical position. It is sometimes called the "key to the gulf" because of its strategic location between North and South America at the entrance to the Gulf of Mexico, and the island has been a crossroads since the beginning of the colonial period. As a result, the island's early population consisted of European settlers, a few native Indians who had survived struggles against the invaders, imported diseases and hard labour, and thousands of black slaves, brought over from Africa. Up to the abolition of slavery in 1886, the dominant culture was that of the

The crest of Cuba, "key of the gulf"

conquering Spanish, with some influence from the sailors and travellers who had stopped in Cuba. However, by surreptitious means, the African slaves managed to preserve their songs, musical instruments and dances, introduced new spices and tastes to the local cuisine, and continued to worship their Yoruba gods *(see pp22–3)*.

The result of this cross-fertilization is a surprising ethnic mosaic of whites, blacks, people of mixed race and Asians (a Chinese community grew in Havana in the 19th century). The same mosaic characterizes Cuban culture too: the bringing together of vastly different traditions has produced a unique blend.

Chatting outside the front door, a typically Cuban habit

Students outside their school, illustrating the diverse ethnic mix of the Cuban population

Playing dominoes, a national past time

THE LIFESTYLE

In general, Cubans are outgoing, talkative and sociable. The doors of their houses are always open, a glass of rum or a cup of coffee is there for anyone who passes by to say hello and chat. There is no clear-cut boundary between home and the street: people talk to one another from their balconies, or from the steps or pavement in front of their house.

A trio of musicians playing in the street

The whole day can be spent outside, thanks to the perennial tropical summer. People spend a lot of time outdoors, chatting, playing dominoes, flirting, cycling around the streets buzzing with colour, voices and sounds, or simply sitting. Music is everywhere and is the soul of the island. Melodic thanks to the Spanish heritage, and dynamic due to the hypnotizing rhythm of Afro-Cuban percussion, religious and passionate at the same time, music is a vital part of daily life, like dance. Even the smallest Cuban town

has a Casa de la Trova, now a Cuban institution, where local bands play and young and old alike go to dance. Indeed, there is no single designated venue for dancing in Cuba, and any excuse is good enough to improvise a party. One of the official celebrations is the debut in society of 15-year-old girls, who are dressed up like brides for the occasion. Besides this lively, fun-loving side, Cubans have an equally strong domestic one, and love to spend time at home with the family, in front of the television or chatting from the ever-present rocking chairs.

THE POLITICAL SYSTEM

The present Constitution of the Republic of Cuba, approved by 97.7 per cent of voters (in Cuba people can vote at the age of 16), was promulgated in 1976. In 1992 various amendments were introduced, including guarantees for foreign investments, some flexibility in foreign trade, more religious freedom, and the introduction of direct election by universal suffrage of deputies to the National Assembly. The Constitution states that Cuba is a socialist republic whose supreme

A 15-year-old girl preparing for her debut in society

Fidel Castro, the Líder Máximo, during a rally in Plaza de la Revolución

governmental body is the National Assembly of People's Power (the equivalent of Parliament), elected by universal suffrage every five years. The Assembly in turn elects the State Council, the Council of Ministers, and the president of the State Council, who is the head of state and of the government, as well as the judges of the Supreme Court. There are also the Provincial and Municipal Assemblies of the People's Power (Poder Popular), through which the population expresses its wishes. Since the only political party is the Cuban Communist Party, which by law cannot propose candidates, the citizens directly elect their candidates. Lastly, there are many social organizations, to which most of the citizens belong. These groups are for young people (UJC), children (UPCJM), women (FMC), students (FEEM and FEU), trade unions (CTC) and small private farmers (ANAP). The largest of these groups consists of the Committees for the Defence of the Revolution (CDR), founded in 1960 to watch over neighbourhoods and tackle social issues.

In spite of the severity of the Castros' government, national pride is quite strong, partly thanks to the continued embargo imposed by the US. Fidel Castro (although no longer president) is still a charismatic figure for many, and there is general awareness and appreciation of the social reforms achieved since the revolution. It remains to be seen how the introduction of Western affluence will affect the country in the long term.

Billboard with political propaganda along the Carretera Central

EL PARTIDO ES HOY
EL ALMA DE LA
PCC
REVOLUCION CUBANA

THE ECONOMY

The most important factor in the Cuban economy is tourism. Since 1980 the island has been open to foreign tourists, which has meant that the traditional flow of citizens from Eastern European countries has been

Waving Cuban flags at a rally

Varadero, one of the most popular resorts for international tourism

replaced by the arrival of tourists from western capitalist countries – the only people who can bring strong currencies into the country. The decision to make more of the nation's rich natural and architectural heritage to produce some degree of wealth was crucial for the economy. However, it has also created major changes in the social relationships, habits and customs of millions of people, who after 30 years of semi-isolation have begun to measure themselves alongside Western Europeans, Canadians and embargo-defying Americans. The uneasy dual economy of the Cuban *peso* and the

A popular toy made of wood and three wheels

convertible peso, the result of the boom in tourism, is still a problem to be resolved. Another important item in the local economy is sugar cane: Cuba is still one of the world's leading exporters of sugar, with 156 extraction centres.

EDUCATION AND CHILDREN

José Martí, who was a poet and man of letters, and became a hero of national independence *(see p45)*, stated that the only way to be free was to be educated. The Cuban Revolution has not forgotten this motto and has staked much on fostering free public education. Thanks to the massive literacy campaign of 1961 *(see p52)*, illiteracy was almost completely eradicated within a short time. Today most of the island's people, half of whom are under 30 – that is, born since the Revolution – can read and write the official language, Spanish, and are also taught foreign languages. Throughout the country Casas de la Cultura, or cultural centres, act as venues for exhibitions, performing arts and even dance evenings. Child care is an important component of the

Machines used to harvest sugar cane

nation's educational policy: the government has invested a great deal of effort and funds in the younger generations and is particularly keen on protecting children, who are safeguarded from the exploitation and sweatshop labour so common in many Latin American and Third World countries. Children are well looked after in Cuba: they have the right to attend nursery schools and day-care centres and to education, physical education and recreational activities. All these services are free for everyone and generally of good quality.

HEALTH

The achievements of the government in the field of health have raised the country to the level of the world's most industrialized nations. A great deal has been invested in providing hospitals and medical consultants throughout the island, in free medicine, and in concentrating on prevention (the nationwide vaccination of infants and children has virtually eliminated diseases common on the American continent) and medical research. Cuba has the lowest infant mortality rate and the highest life expectancy rate in Latin America. The health service, which is free for everyone, is good despite restrictions imposed by the economic crisis. The presence of highly trained Cuban doctors and the reduced costs of therapy and hospitalization have made the island a centre for "health tourism"; patients from many countries come here for specific treatments, especially for skin and stress problems.

Javier Sotomayor, the gold medallist in the high jump in the 1992 Olympics at Barcelona

SPORTS

Physical activity has always been encouraged by the government via a mass physical education programme and numerous specialist schools that offer talented youngsters the chance to make a name for themselves. As a result, sports standards are high, and Cuba has many Olympic champions. Baseball is the national sport (the Cuban team is one of the best in the world), and athletics, volleyball, basketball and boxing are also popular. Leading figures in sport include boxer Kid Chocolate (1910–88), successful in the US before the Revolution, high-jump champion Javier Sotomayor, Ana Fidelia Quirot, the 800m world champion in 1995 and 1997, and Ivan Pedroso, gold medallist in long-jump in Sydney 2000 and Edmonton 2001.

Boxing training in a Havana gym

Landscape, Flora and Fauna

A land crab, a marsh inhabitant

The Cuban poet Nicolás Guillén once likened his native island to a green crocodile with eyes of stone and water. An aerial view would show the island stretching out in the Caribbean Sea and indeed covered with vegetation and patterned with rivers. Small islands and coral reefs lie just offshore in the sparkling blue sea. In the interior, the landscape is very varied, from plains of red earth to the *mogotes* outcrops of Viñales, from desert cactus to tropical forest. Protected reserves make up 22 per cent of the national territory. There are numerous species found only on Cuba, but no poisonous creatures.

Coral reefs, with their own distinct ecosystem *(see p147)*

MOUNTAINS

The most important ranges are the Sierra de los Órganos to the West, the Sierra del Escambray in the centre and the Sierra Maestra to the southeast. The latter is Cuba's principal range and includes Pico Turquino (1,974 m/ 6,475 ft), the highest peak in the country. The slopes are covered with forests of deciduous trees, pines and tropical plants, and by coffee and cocoa plantations.

PLAINS

Areas of plain occur throughout the island, but are particularly prevalent in the central regions – the provinces of Matanzas, Sancti Spíritus and Camagüey – and in the Pinar del Río area. The land is fertile and planted with sugar cane, palm trees, mangoes and citrus fruit, or left as grazing land for cattle.

Carpintero *(carpenter) is the Cuban name for the woodpecker, which nests in tree trunks.*

The cartacuba (Todus multicolor) *is an endemic species only a few centimetres long. It has highly coloured plumage.*

The tiñosa, *or turkey vulture, with its unmistakable red head, flies the plains in search of carrion.*

The cattle egret *follows grazing cows and feeds on insects, both those disturbed by ploughing and others on the cows' hides.*

The tocororo (Cuban trogon) is the national bird. The colours of the flag of Cuba were inspired by its feathers.

The so-called gulf fritillary *is one of 190 species of butterfly in Cuba, about 30 of which are endemic to the island.*

FLORA

The Cuban landscape is characterized by the many varieties of palm tree *(see p173)*, together with the pine in the mountainous areas, and the ceibas in the plains. The *yagruma*, with large dark green and silvery leaves, is also widespread. Three important hardwoods are mahogany, cedar and *majagua*. Splashes of colour are added to the luxuriant green vegetation by flowering hibiscus, bougainvillea and *flamboyán* (royal poinciana). Numerous species of orchid grow here, as well as mariposa, Cuba's national flower.

A *flamboyán* (royal poinciana)

The ceiba tree, sacred to Pre-Columbian peoples

The mariposa, the national flower

MARSHLANDS

The southern part of the island in particular has many lagoons and marshlands, often distinguished by mangrove swamps, and is rich in birdlife. The most important area is the Ciénaga (swamp) de Zapata, in the province of Matanzas *(see p166)*.

TROPICAL FOREST

The Sagüa-Baracoa mountain range in Eastern Cuba, under the influence of northeast trade winds, is one of the most biologically diverse areas in the Caribbean. Here, the heavy rainfall produces thick vegetation.

The tiny *zunzuncito*, *the smallest hummingbird in the world, lives in protected or wooded areas like the Península de Zapata.*

Pink flamingoes *live in areas of brackish water from Cayo Coco to Zapata.*

Buteogallus anthracinus gundlachi *is an endemic hawk that feeds on crabs.*

The black anolis *lizard, a forest reptile, reacts to disturbance by inflating the white part under its throat.*

Mangroves *develop an intricate root system under water. This habitat suits a diverse range of birds and fish.*

The *Polymita picta*, *an endemic species of snail that lives only in the Baracoa area, has a brightly coloured shell and feeds on plant parasites.*

Santería

Different religions co-exist in Cuba as the result of its history. Both the Roman Catholicism of the Spanish conquerors and the practices imported by the African slaves have survived. The most widespread of the African faiths is Santería, also called Regla de Ocha. In order to be able to worship their gods despite the persecution of the Spaniards, Yoruba slaves, originally from Nigeria, merged their gods' identities with certain Roman Catholic saints. Over the years the two religions have almost become blended. Pure Roman Catholicism today is not a widespread religion in Cuba, while Santería is so strongly felt that it is an important part of the national identity.

The batá, *three conical drums of different sizes with two skins, accompany the most important Santería ceremonies.*

The crown of Changó, the king of the *orishas*

Rituals *are almost always performed in a domestic context (Santería has no temples as such). Rites are inspired by animistic spirituality, although there are elements that share similarities or even merge with Roman Catholicism.*

Fresh fruit, including bananas, Changó's favourite

Santeros and babalawos, *the Santería priests, foretell the future, the former by means of seashells, the latter through a complex system of divination that makes use of stones, seashells, seeds and coconut shells.*

Agogó (traditional rattles), maracas and bells are played while greeting the gods.

AN ALTAR FOR CHANGÓ

Altars are set up by Santería initiates on feast days, such as their "saint's birthday" (the initiation anniversary), and decorated with the attributes of the god to whom they are dedicated. They also contain elements belonging to other *orishas*, such as cloth, devotional objects, flowers, fruit and other special foods.

THE *ORISHAS*

The main Santería god is Olofi, the creator divinity, similar to the God of Christianity but without contact with Earth. The gods who mediate between him and the faithful are the *orishas*, who listen to the latter's prayers. Each *orisha* has his own colour and symbols, as well as a ritual characterized by its type of dance, music and costumes: Oshún, for example, wears yellow clothes and loves honey, pale soft drinks and violins.

Obbatalá, *a hermaphrodite god, is the protector of the head as well as the chief intermediary between Olofi and humankind.*

Oshún, *the goddess of love, lives in rivers, and corresponds to the Virgen del Cobre (see p221).*

The aspiring priest (santero) *has to undergo a week of intense initiation ceremonies, and for an entire year has to dress in white and adhere to strict rules of behaviour.*

Various objects – *Christian, secular or even personal items – are set together on Santería altars. Here, three Madonnas are placed alongside plastic horses.*

The double-edged axe and sword are Changó's two warlike attributes.

The *batea* is a wooden receptacle containing natural elements in which the spirit of the god resides. Only the *santero* may open it.

The *pilón* is the large wooden mortar on which the *santero* sits during the week of initiation, and it is preserved as an object of worship.

Eleggúa *is the first god to be greeted during ceremonies. He is represented by a stone made to look like a face, with two shells as eyes, and is usually placed behind a believer's front door.*

Fresh flowers are always placed on the altars of the *orishas*: red ones for Changó, yellow ones for Oshún, and white ones for Obbatalá.

Candles

A basket of offerings is on display during ceremonies. The money is used to buy objects of worship.

OTHER AFRO-CUBAN RELIGIONS

Among the African cults practised in Cuba, two others are also significant: Palo Monte (or Las Reglas de Congo), in which herbs and other natural elements are used for magical purposes, and Abakuá, more of a mutual aid secret society, for men only. The former, introduced to Cuba by Bantu-speaking African slaves from the Congo, Zaire and Angola, is based on the cult of the dead. The faithful, called *paleros*, perform rites that are sometimes macabre and even verge on black magic. A region between Nigeria and Cameroon was the birthplace of the Abakuá cult. In celebrations the participants, disguised as little devils (*diablitos*), dance and play music. The *diablito* has become part of Cuban folklore.

Yemayá, *sea goddess and mother of orishas, wears blue. Capable of great sweetness and great anger, she is linked with the Virgen de Regla (see p112).*

Changó *is the virile and sensual god of fire and war who adores dancing and corresponds to St Barbara.*

An Abakuá *diablito* **with his typical headdress**

Architecture in Cuba

Formal architecture in Cuba began in the colonial period. For the entire 16th century all efforts were concentrated on building an impressive network of fortresses; then came the first stone-built *mudéjar*-style houses, which replaced simple wooden dwellings with tiled roofs. The 18th century was a golden age of civic architecture, characterized by the Baroque style imported at a late stage from Europe, which in turn made way for Neo-Classical buildings in the 19th century. The mixture of styles typical of the *fin de siècle* was followed, in 1900–30, by Art Deco, a forerunner of the 1950s skyscrapers. Ugly prefabricated buildings mainly characterize the post-1959 era.

The courtyard was a typical feature of colonial architecture and the centre of domestic life. Above, the Conde de Jaruco's Havana residence (see p76).

THE 17TH CENTURY

The tropical climate, with high temperatures and heavy rain, influenced the local architecture. Many private homes had thick walls, tiled roofs and windows protected by shutters.

Balconies with slender wooden columns

Sloping roof of terracotta tiles

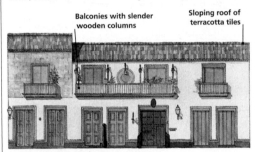

A typical wooden ceiling at Calle Tacón 4, in Havana

The house at Calle Obispo 117–19 (p72), *with its characteristic central courtyard and wooden balconies, shows a clear Spanish influence in the structure itself and in the building techniques used.*

THE 18TH CENTURY

More rooms were added to houses with a central courtyard, more houses were built, and some wonderful examples of civic architecture were created. Three highlights of light Cuban Baroque in Havana are the Palacio de los Capitanes Generales (*pp70–71*), Palacio del Segundo Cabo (*p66*) and Havana Cathedral (*p64*). Trinidad also has many 18th-century colonial buildings.

The mezzanine, a structural element introduced in the 1700s

The arcade on the ground floor, which was the external equivalent of the inner courtyard, was an 18th-century innovation. As trade increased, mansions like this housed growing numbers of servants, who lived in the lower part of the building.

Stained-glass windows

Arches supported by columns and pilasters distinguish 18th-century buildings.

Limestone façade

Palacio de los Capitanes Generales *is a typical Cuban Baroque mansion, with thick stone walls, an abundance of arches, columns, porticoes and balconies, and a large central courtyard with dense vegetation.*

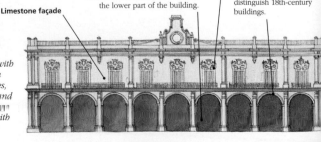

An elegant arched *mediopunto* window

MEDIOPUNTO

These half-moon, stained-glass windows were created in the mid-18th century to protect houses from the glare of the tropical sun. They became popular in the 1800s, when mansion windows were decorated with glass set into a wooden frame. The original geometric motifs were later replaced by others drawing inspiration from tropical flora and fauna.

THE 19TH CENTURY

The widespread use of porticoes with columns and lintels, wrought iron and decoration inspired by Classical antiquity or the Renaissance, is the distinguishing feature of 19th-century Cuban Neo-Classical architecture. Grilles across windows and shutters helped air to circulate inside (previously the central courtyard performed this function). Buildings that best represent Cuban Neo-Classicism are the Palacio de Aldama in Havana *(p84)* and the Teatro Sauto in Matanzas *(p158)*.

Wrought- or cast-iron grilles

Shutters and *mediopuntos* protected rooms from bright light.

Ionic pilasters

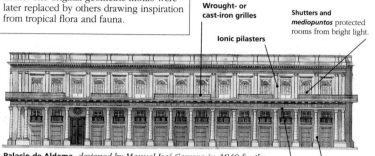

Doric columns

In the portico the arch is replaced by the lintel.

Palacio de Aldama, *designed by Manuel José Carrera in 1840 for the wealthy Don Domingo de Aldama, is the most important Neo-Classical building in Havana. Rejecting Baroque exuberance, it echoes the austerity and purity of line of Classical architecture.*

BRIDGING THE 19TH–20TH CENTURIES

The architectural value of many Cuban cities derives from the mixture of different styles. This is seen in buildings such as the Neo-Moorish Palacio de Valle in Cienfuegos *(p170)*, the Capitolio in Havana *(pp82–3)*, and at Paseo and Calle 17, Havana's so-called "millionaires' row", with splendid mansions such as the Casa de la Amistad, built in 1926 *(see p99)*.

Detail of the façade of the Palacio Guasch, Pinar del Río *(p136)*

Palacio de Valle *in Cienfuegos, designed by the Venetian architect Alfredo Colli in 1912 for Acisclo del Valle, combines Moorish and Venetian Gothic elements with references to Beaux Arts forms – a typical example of the eclectic style's use of a range of prevailing architectural motifs and elements.*

THE 20TH CENTURY

The early 20th century saw the construction of a few examples of Art Nouveau and Art Deco buildings, paving the way for the major urban development that took place in Havana in the 1950s. This period witnessed the building of some very tall, modern skyscrapers and hotels such as the Riviera and the Habana Libre (then called the Habana Hilton, *p98*). In parallel with this came the rise of a style that was reminiscent of Rationalist architecture.

Edificio Bacardí *(1930) in Havana, designed by E Rodríguez Castells, R Fernández Ruenes and J Menéndez, is a splendid example of Art Deco. It is clad in granite and limestone, with enamelled motifs.*

Painting in Cuba

The history of Cuban painting can be divided into three basic stages. The first began in 1818 with the foundation of the San Alejandro Fine Arts Academy, run by Jean-Baptiste Vermay, a French Neo-Classical painter. The second began over a century later, in the 1930s, when, thanks to great artists such as Wifredo Lam, René Portocarrero and Amelia Peláez, a movement influenced by the European avant-garde created a universally comprehensible idiom that expressed the unique essence of Cuban identity. Thirdly, after 1959, as part of a programme of art education that promoted avant-garde artists, the National School of Art and the Institute for Advanced Art Studies were founded. Cuban painting has always brimmed with vitality and painters of recent generations have achieved international recognition, helped by shows like the Havana Biennial.

Víctor Manuel García, *one of the fathers of modern Cuban art, created the archetypal* Gitana Tropical *(1929).*

Wifredo Lam *(1902–82), lived for a while in Europe and worked with Pablo Picasso in Paris. He developed a new pictorial language that went beyond national boundaries. He painted extraordinary pictures such as* La Jungla *(The Jungle), now in the Museum of Modern Art, New York,* La Silla *(see p93), and* The Third World *(1966), seen here, which cast a dramatic light on the elements in Cuban religions.*

Amelia Peláez *(1897–1968) blended still life motifs with the decorative elements in Cuban colonial architecture such as stained glass and columns, as seen here in* Interior with Columns *(1951).*

René Portocarrero *(1912–86) expressed the essence of Cuba through a Baroque-like vision of the city, painting domestic interiors and figures of women, as in* Interno del Cerro *(1943). He made use of bold colour and was influenced by the European avant-garde and Mexican mural painting.*

Raúl Martínez *(1927–95)
and Guido Llinás were
leading exponents of the
abstract art movement
that came to the fore
in the 1950s–60s
and later adopted
the Pop Art style in
representions of
current-day heroes, as
exemplified by* Island 70
*(1970) by Raúl
Martínez, seen here.*

Alfredo Sosabravo *(b. 1930) – a painter, illustrator, engraver
and potter – tackles the themes of nature, man and machines
with an ironic twist. A leading figure, he has been active since
the 1960s, together with Servando Cabrera Moreno, a Neo-
Expressionist, Antonia Eiriz, a figurative artist, and Manuel
Mendive, whose subject is Cuba's African heritage.*

Flora Fong *(b. 1949) –
along with Ever Fonseca,
Nelson Domínguez, Pedro
Pablo Oliva, Tomás
Sánchez and Roberto
Fabelo – represents a
strand of 1970s painting,
which tended towards
abstraction without quite
losing sight of objective
reality. Her* Dimensiones
del Espejo *is
seen here.*

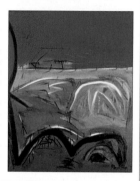

GRAPHIC ART

Graphic design, which first flourished during the
Colonial period, when it was used in the sugar and
tobacco industries, with time became an independent
art form, with the creation of prestigious periodicals
such as *Social*. During the 20th century the growing
importance of marketing produced different types
of graphic art. In the 1960s, in the wake of the
enthusiasm for the
victorious revolution,
well-designed graphic
posters became a
natural part of the
main political and
cultural campaigns,
and designs
became ever more
sophisticated. Use
of graphic art is still
very visible in Cuba's
towns and cities and
at the roadside all
over the island.

**Poster by Alfonso Prieto
for July 26 celebrations**

CERAMICS

In 1950, the Cuban ceramicist
and former physician Juan Miguel
Rodríguez de la Cruz brought
together a group
of leading
painters,
including
Wifredo Lam,
René Porto-
carrero and
Amelia Peláez,
in Santiago de
las Vegas, near
Havana, so that
they could all
work on ceramic
designs. This
marked the
beginning of a new artistic genre in
Cuba that today ranges from crock-
ery to sculpture, and also includes
installations and works for home
interiors. Wonderful examples of
Cuban ceramics can be found in
the Hotel Habana Libre *(p98)*.

**Decorated plate,
Havana Ceramics
Museum**

Cuban Literature

A frequent theme in the literature of Cuba has always been the question of national identity, and the genre has evolved with a marked interest in social problems and questions about reality. The works of the great 20th-century Cuban authors are regarded as classics, and younger authors are beginning to attract attention on the international scene. The Revolution was a golden era for publishing, because production costs for books were very low. However, the trade was plunged into sudden crisis in the early 1990s and many publishers are only now slowly regaining their former status. Every year Havana plays host to an International Book Fair, a major literary event involving authors and publishers from all over the world.

An expressive portrait of the great Cuban poet Nicolás Guillén

THE 19TH CENTURY

The birth of Cuban literature is usually dated from *Espejo de Paciencia*, an epic poem written in the early 1600s by Silvestre de Balboa, originally from the Canary Islands. However, truly national literature only began to emerge in the 19th century, with the call for an end to slavery and for Cuban independence from Spain.

Félix Varela, writer-philosopher

Among the literary figures of that time, various names stand out. Father Félix Varela (1787–1853) was an eclectic philosopher and patriot who wrote a pamphlet extolling the "need to stamp out the

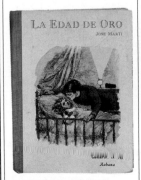

La Edad de Oro, José Martí's children's periodical

slavery of the blacks on the island of Cuba, which would also be in the interests of their owners". José María de Heredia (1803–39) was a romantic poet who introduced the American landscape into New World literature and was forced to live in the US and Mexico because of his nationalist stance. Gertrudis Gómez de Avellaneda (1814–73), another romantic, lived for a long time in Spain and defended the black population in her novel *Sab*. Cirilo Villaverde (1812–94) was a patriot and author of *Cecilia Valdés*, a famous abolitionist work which was made into a *zarzuela* (operetta) in the 20th century by the Cuban composer Ernesto Lecuona.

However, the towering figure in the 19th century was the great José Martí (1853–95), an intellectual, journalist and author who expressed his nationalist ideas in elegant literary form (*Ismaelillo* and *Versos Sencillos* are his best-known works), and became a leading exponent of Latin American modernism.

Another figure in this movement was Julián del Casal, a decadent, symbolist writer. The premature deaths of these two brought the development of innovative literature to a halt.

THE 20TH CENTURY

The leading interpreters of 20th-century Cuban literature were the poet Nicolás Guillén (1902–89) and the novelist Alejo Carpentier (1904–80), both of whom were sent into exile because of their opposition to Gerardo Machado's regime and their fierce criticism of Batista's dictatorship.

Guillén, who was of mixed race, spoke for the black population, exposing among other things the brutal working conditions of the *macheteros*, the labourers who cut sugar cane on the plantations. After Castro's victory, Guillén was proclaimed as "national poet" and asked to head UNEAC, the Cuban writers and artists' union. Taking as his starting point the rhythms of dance and traditional musical genres such as *son (see p30)*, grafted onto the classical Spanish octosyllable, Guillén's stylistic studies gave rise to bold experiments as early as 1931 in works like *Songoro Cosongo, poemas mulatos.*

Alejo Carpentier, an architect, musicologist and writer acutely

José Lezama Lima

aware of the realities of Cuba's situation, was one of the most original and innovative authors in 20th-century world literature. Using a blend of irony and respect, he gave voice to the myths of his country, anticipating the destructuring of the post-modern novel. Among his major works are *The Kingdom of This World*, *The Lost Steps*, *Concierto Barroco* and *The Age of Enlightenment*.

Two other leading figures of the same period are the dramatist Virgilio Piñera (1912–79), a reformer, who had a marked taste for experimental theatre, and José Lezama Lima (1910–76), a poet of elegance, also a novelist and chief editor of the magazine *Orígenes*. From 1944 to 1956 this leading periodical printed works by the best Cuban writers and artists of the time. It became one of the key publications in Latin America. Lima is internationally known as the author of *Paradiso* (1966).

Alejo Carpentier
CONCIERTO BARROCO

A famous novel by Alejo Carpentier (1974)

In general, the literary scene in revolutionary Cuba has been characterized by creative fervour, in poetry and in novel-writing. Among the "veterans", people who lived through the experience from the outset, mention should be made of the poets Eliseo Diego, Cintio Vitier, Pablo Armando Fernández and Fina García Marruz; and the novelists Félix Pita Rodríguez, Mirta Aguirre, and Dulce María Loynaz. The works of Loynaz were not published in Cuba until the late 20th century, just before her death.

These authors were followed by the younger writers Miguel Barnet, Antón Arrufat, López Sacha and César López, committed writers in favour of the revolution.

Among the anti-Castro authors writing in exile, the leading name was the late Guillermo Cabrera Infante (1929–2005), whose works include *Infante's Inferno* and *Three Trapped Tigers*.

Author Dulce María Loynaz, pictured in her twenties

CONTEMPORARY WRITERS

Present-day authors worthy of mention include Abel Prieto, former Minister of Culture, a brilliant and perceptive author of several novels, including *The Cat's Flight*. Another name is Abilio Estévez, a dramatist and novelist of extraordinarily expressive intensity, with a lyrical and visionary tone. Marylin Bobes and Mirta Yáñez both write from the feminist angle. Senel Paz wrote the story that inspired the film *Strawberry and Chocolate*; and detective-story writer Leonardo Padura is known abroad for a quartet of mystery novels set in Havana.

CUBAN CINEMA

The founding of the Instituto Cubano del Arte y la Industria Cinematográficos (ICAIC) in 1959 virtually marked the birth of cinema in Cuba. The aim of this institution was to disseminate motion picture culture throughout the country, and thus encourage the formation of Cuban directors, to work on documentary films in particular. Fostered by the revolutionary government, Cuban cinema experienced a golden age in the 1960s and has been evolving ever since. Today Havana is the capital of new Latin American cinema thanks to the annual film festival organized by ICAIC. Gabriel García Márquez, winner of the Nobel Prize for Literature, is president of the Fundación del Nuevo Cine Latinoamericano, which also runs the Escuela Internacional de Cine film school, based in San Antonio de los Baños. Among Cuba's many directors, who include Julio García Espinosa, Manuel Octavio Gómez and Pastor Vega, there are three outstanding names: Santiago Alvarez, who has made fine documentaries; Humberto Solás, the late director of the classic *Lucía* and of *Cecilia*; and the late Tomás Gutiérrez Alea, who found fame abroad in 1993 thanks to *Fresa y Chocolate (Strawberry and Chocolate)*, which he made with Juan Carlos Tabío, which courageously dealt with the themes of homosexuality and dissent.

Symbol of the ICAIC

Poster for the film *Strawberry and Chocolate*

Music and Dance

Anything can be used to make music in Cuba: two pieces of wood, an empty box and a tyre rim are enough to trigger an irresistible rhythm, anywhere and at any time of day, on the bus, on the beach or in the street. There are top classical music composers and interpreters, but it is popular music, a fusion of Spanish melodies and African rhythm, that is the very essence of Cuba. The success enjoyed by mambo and cha-cha-cha in the 1950s was followed by the worldwide popularity of *son*, rumba and salsa. Dance, too, is an essential part of life here. No one stays seated when the music starts: feet and hands start to move with the rhythm, and bodies sway and rock.

Compay Segundo (1907–2003), the famous *son* singer and songwriter

Salsa *is dance music which maintains the rhythmic structure of* son *while adding new sounds borrowed from jazz and other Latin American genres.*

The guitarist is often also the accompanying voice, while the solo singer plays a "minor" percussion instrument such as the maracas or *claves*.

Traditional maracas are made from the fruit (gourd) of the *güira* tropical tree.

Bongo

Double bass

Tres

SON

This genre is a type of country music that originated in Cuba in the 19th century, a blend of African rhythm and Spanish melody, which then greatly influenced Latin American music as a whole. In around 1920 *son* began to be played in towns in Eastern Cuba, where, along with other genres, it produced the *trova tradicional*, a ballad-style song with guitar.

THE MUSICIANS

Ernesto Lecuona

Three great 20th-century composers and musicians are pianist Ernesto Lecuona (1896–1963), Ignacio Villa (or "Bola de Nieve"), and Pérez Prado, in whose orchestra Benny Moré sang *(see p171)*. In the 1920s there was the star Rita Montaner and the Trío Matamoros, the top *trova* band in Santiago. Others were Nico Comp, a bolero writer, and César Portillo de la Luz, a founder of *feeling* music in the 1960s. Contemporaries include the *salsero* Issac Delgado and Afro-Cuban jazzman Chucho Valdés.

Bola de Nieve *(1911–71),* or "snowball", *is the stage name that Rita Montaner gave to her pianist Ignacio Villa. This husky-voiced musician also wrote and sang very moving love songs.*

Dámaso Pérez Prado *(1922–89), the king of mambo, achieved international success with his orchestra in the 1950s.*

Guaguancó, a fast rumba, enacts a breezy battle between a man and woman who tries to parry his insistent advances. In effect, this dance is a thinly disguised simulation of the sexual act.

A *batá* **covered with canvas and seashells**

Tumbadora **or conga**

The voice was the original element of the rumba, which began as song. The percussion instruments, the basis of this musical genre, were added at a later stage.

CUBAN MUSICAL INSTRUMENTS

Claves

Tres

Güiro

There are several exclusively Cuban musical instruments. Among the stringed instruments are the *tres*, a small guitar, always used in *son* bands, with three pairs of metal strings, and the *requinto*, another small, high-pitched guitar that is used in trios to play melodic variations.

Typical Cuban percussion instruments are the *tumbadora*, a tall wooden and leather drum played with the hands, which is used in all musical forms, including jazz; the *bongó*, two small round drums; the *claves*, two wooden cylinders played by striking them against one another; the *güiro*, the gourd of the güira fruit which is stroked with a small stick; and the *marímbula*, a rarely used small piano.

RUMBA

The African soul of Cuban music, the rumba originated in the warehouses of Matanzas as a voice of rebellion against slavery and segregation. It then became a form of political satire and social criticism, as well as the poignant expression of an unhappy love affair. *Columbia* is country-style solo dance, while *yambú* and *guaguancó* are the urban varieties, with dance rhythms that are sensual and dynamic, or sad and slow.

Los Van Van *have dominated the Cuban musical scene for over 30 years and are world-famous for their new rhythms and sounds (they invented a new genre, the* songo*).*

Silvio Rodríguez, *a singer and songwriter who defends the ideals of the Cuban revolution, founded the Nueva Trova with Pablo Milanés (right) in the late 1960s, revitalizing the style and repertory of the* trova, *a rural musical genre.*

Buena Vista Social Club, *Wim Wenders' film (1998), brought into the limelight traditional* son *interpreters over 80 years old, such as the late guitarist and singer Compay Segundo, the late pianist Rubén González, and the late singer Ibrahim Ferrer.*

Cuban Cigars

The cigar is an inextricable part of Cuba's culture, history, and even, for some, its essence. It is known that cigars were used by the native Indians. After Columbus's voyage, tobacco, regarded in Europe as having therapeutic qualities, was imported to Spain. However the first smokers were imprisoned, because people believed that cigar smoke produced diabolical effects. Even so, tobacco grew in popularity and was later exported to other European nations, where government agencies were set up to maintain a monopoly over the product. After the revolution, the US embargo had a serious effect on the international sale of cigars *(puros)*, but since the 1990s the fashion for cigar smoking has given a boost to sales.

Tobacco (cohiba) *was used by Cuban Indians during religious rites to invoke the gods. They either inhaled the smoke through a tubed instrument called a* tabaco, *or smoked the rolled leaves.*

The *tripa* is the inside, the "core" of the cigar with the filler leaves. In handmade cigars, the *tripa* consists of tobacco leaves which have been selected in order to obtain a particular flavour.

The *capa* is the wrapper leaf on the outside of the cigar. It gives it its smooth, velvety look as well as its colour.

The head (or top part of the cigar) is cut off before smoking.

Foot

The *capote* is the binder leaf that holds the inner part together and keeps it compact.

THE PARTS OF A CIGAR
Cigars can be either handmade or machine-made. With handmade cigars the inside consists of whole tobacco leaves, while machine-made cigars are made up of leaves that are blended and then shredded.

BRAND NAMES
There are 33 brands of Cuban cigar on the market today. Below are four, each represented by a *marquilla*, or label, which is placed on the cigar box to identify the brand. Some designs have not changed since first marketed.

Montecristo (1935)

Cohiba (1966)

Cuaba (1996)

Vegas Robaina (1997)

The ***anillo***, *the band that goes around the central part of the cigar and bears its brand name, has a curious history. It is said that in the 18th century, Catherine the Great of Russia, a heavy smoker, had her cigars wrapped with small bands of cloth so they would not leave stains on her fingers. Her eccentricity soon became fashionable. The first commercial cigar band was produced in 1830 by the manufacturers Aquila de Oro. Above is a band produced by the Cuban cigar-maker Romeo y Julieta in 1875.*

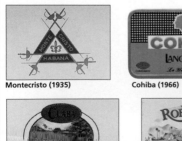

HOW CIGARS ARE MADE

Cigar manufacturing is a real skill that Cubans hand down from generation to generation. This sequence of photographs shows how Carlos Gassiot, a highly skilled *torcedor* (cigar roller), makes a cigar, from selecting the loose tobacco leaves to the final touches.

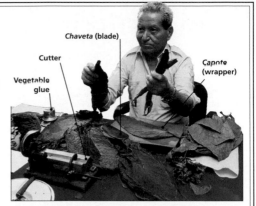

Chaveta (blade)

Cutter

Capote (wrapper)

Vegetable glue

1 *Having placed the* capote *(wrapper leaf) on the tablet, the* torcedor *chooses the filler leaves he wants to use for the core of the cigar: three leaves from different parts of the plant –* seco, volado *and* ligero *(see p139).*

2 *He begins to roll (*torcer *in Spanish, hence the term* torcedor*) the leaves. The* capote *is wrapped around the filler leaves selected for the* tripa, *which in turn is covered by the* capa, *which is smooth and regular. This determines the appearance of the cigar.*

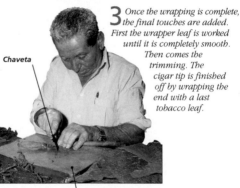

Chaveta

3 *Once the wrapping is complete, the final touches are added. First the wrapper leaf is worked until it is completely smooth. Then comes the trimming. The cigar tip is finished off by wrapping the end with a last tobacco leaf.*

Tableta (tablet)

Gauge

4 *Once the cigar is finished, the* torcedor *checks its diameter with a special gauge stamped with the various standard sizes established for every kind of cigar. The same instrument is also used to measure the pre-established length, after which the cigar is cut to this size using the cutting machine.*

THE SHAPE AND SIZE

Cigars are made in different sizes (heavy, standard or slim ring gauge) and shapes (they may be regular or tapered, *figurado*). Fatter cigars tend to have a fuller flavour, which connoisseurs prefer. The best hand-rolled Cuban cigars benefit from ageing, like fine wine.

Cuaba Exclusivo, *figurado* cigar

Trinidad Fundador, regular-shaped cigar

CUBA THROUGH THE YEAR

Because of its tropical climate, Cuba does not really have a high or low season, although officially, peak season is from December to the end of March and in July and August, when hotel rates are higher and flights are packed. Except for the peak of summer, when temperatures can be searingly hot, and September and October, when hurricanes are most likely, any month is suitable for a visit. It is warm at the beach even in winter, because the *frentes fríos* (cold fronts)

A Carnival outfit

generally last only a couple of days and even then the temperature hardly ever drops below 10°C (50°F). The cooler, drier months from November to March are the best for sightseeing. Thanks to the climate, and the Cubans' love of music and cultural events, there are open-air concerts, festivals, and religious and folk festivities all year round. However, the most interesting and eventful months are July, during Carnival, and December, when the festivities in Remedios and Havana's famous cinema festival takes place.

SPRING

During this season there is an escalation of dance and theatre performances. The beaches are crowded, but mainly with visitors – the Cubans usually go to the seaside only in summer.

MARCH

Festival Internacional de la Trova Pepe Sanchéz, Santiago *(Mar)*. A celebration of Cuban *trova* music in all its forms. This festival attracts both Cuban and international performers.
Bienal de Danza Contemporánea del Caribe *(Mar–Apr)*. Attended by representatives from countries across the Caribbean, this event brings together dancers, choreographers and directors.

APRIL

Taller Internacional de Teatro de Títeres, Teatro Papalote, Matanzas *(Apr)*. Performances by leading puppet theatres, with seminars, conferences and workshops. Other workshop spaces include the Teatro Sauto and Galería Provincial de Artes Plásticas "Pedro Esquerré". See www. atenas.cult.cu/titeres.
Fiesta Internacional de la Danza, Santa Clara *(Apr–May)*. The best local dancers perform in the towns of this province. The fiesta ends with a great celebration in Santa Clara.

A batá player

MAY

Primero de Mayo *(1 May)*. Rallies, marches and parades in every city in Cuba. The

most important one takes place, of course, in Havana, where the citizens gather in Plaza de la Revolución for speeches and patriotic songs.
Romerías de la Cruz de Mayo *(3 May)*. The townsfolk of Holguín process up to La Loma de la Cruz, a hilltop that dominates the northern end of the town. A mass is held at the wooden cross, followed by a lively party.
Feria Internacional del Disco Cubadisco (International Record Fair), Pabellón Cuba, Havana *(mid-May)*. Records on display and for sale; conferences and concerts.
Festival de Raíces Africanas "Wemilere", Guanabacoa *(May)*. A festival of folk events, with a closing prizegiving ceremony.
Bienal de la Habana *(May–Jun)*. A highly respected art fair (next staged in 2014) welcoming local and international artists. In 2012, more than 100 artists from 45 countries congregated in Havana. The city was enlivened with workshops, performances and exciting gallery shows. See www. bienalhabana.cult.cu.
La Huella de España, Gran Teatro and other venues, Havana *(May Jun)*. Celebrating Cuban culture of Spanish derivation: concerts, classical dance, flamenco and theatre.

The First of May Parade in Plaza de la Revolución, Havana

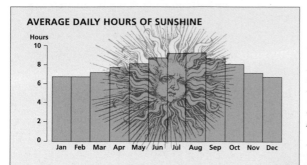

AVERAGE DAILY HOURS OF SUNSHINE

Hours: 10, 8, 6, 4, 2, 0

Jan Feb Mar Apr May Jun Jul Aug Sep Oct Nov Dec

Sunshine
This chart shows the average daily hours of sunshine in Cuba. In the winter the days are short: at 6pm the sun has already set. In the summer the sun is strong and you should protect your skin and wear a hat and sunglasses, even if only taking a short stroll in town.

SUMMER

There are various festivals and festivities during the summer months, especially in Havana and Santiago. Almost every evening there are open-air concerts along the Malecón in Havana, particularly in the square known as the Piragua, which is transformed into an open-air dance floor (free of charge). If you plan to include the Carnival in your visit, book accommodation well in advance in Santiago.

JUNE

Ernest Hemingway International Billfishing Tournament, Marina Hemingway, Havana *(early Jun)*. Fishermen compete for trophies in this annual tag-and-release event.
Festival Boleros de Oro, Santiago, Morón, Havana *(mid-Jun)*. String of concerts by the best Cuban and international performers of bolero songs plus various lectures.

Walking on stilts in Morón during the Fiesta del Gallo

Encuentro de Bandas de Concierto, Plaza de la Revolución, Bayamo *(Jun 1–15)*. Outdoor concerts by national and international bands; lectures, workshops.
Fiesta del Gallo, Morón *(end of Jun)*. A parade through the town based on the theme of the cockerel, which is symbolic here.
Jornada Cucalambeana, Encuentro Festival Iberoamericano de la Décima, Las Tunas *(end of Jun)*. The most important festival of Cuban rural culture. Includes concerts and performances by poets, musicians and *repentistas* (improvisers). Lectures and literary meetings, exhibits of local handicrafts and theatre also feature.

JULY

Fiesta del Fuego, Santiago de Cuba *(first half of Jul)*. Annual festival celebrating the music, poetry, figurative art, religions and history of the Caribbean nations. Meetings, shows, exhibits, concerts, poetry readings and festivities throughout the city, culminating on the last night with the *Quema del Diablo* – the burning of an effigy of the Devil.
Havana Carnival *(Jul–Aug)*. A parade of floats in the city streets, going from the Hotel Nacional to Calle Belascoaín, and live music performances by *comparsas* (processional groups who prepare all year long) in various parts of the city. At weekends, free concerts are held at the Piragua. The parades can be viewed from a grandstand.

A group of dancers from a Havana comparsa

Santiago Carnival, Santiago de Cuba *(week leading up to 26 Jul)*. Parades along the city streets and live music performed by *comparsas*. For the most important parades there is a grandstand for spectators. Afternoons are filled with children's parades; adult floats start parading at 10pm. During the day, food and drink stalls are set up in various *repartos* of the city such as Sueño and along La Trocha, where *"peso* beer" is doled out to the crowds from giant vats.
"26 de julio" *(held every year in a different city)*. The official commemoration of the attack on the Moncada barracks *(see p230)*, with a speech by president Raúl Castro and other political leaders in the main square of a Cuban city, accompanied by concerts and by children who recite poetry.

AUGUST

Symposia de Hip Hop Cubano, Casa de la Cultura de Plaza, Calzada and Calle 8, Vedado, Havana *(third week of Aug)*. Performances and workshops of Cuban hip hop.

AVERAGE MONTHLY RAINFALL

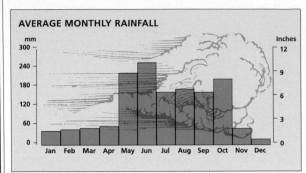

Rainfall
In Cuba, the dry season (from November to April) alternates with the rainy season, when brief but heavy showers fall. In the Baracoa and Moa area at the eastern tip of the island, rainfall is heavier because the mountains block the Atlantic winds.

AUTUMN

After the August heat, when everything to do with work seems to slow down, life starts to pick up again. In autumn the schools reopen and work returns to a normal rhythm. The number of tourists – Europeans in particular – decreases.

SEPTEMBER

Fiesta de la Virgen del Cobre, El Cobre, Santiago de Cuba *(8 Sep)*. On the feast-day of the Virgin there is a surge in the regular pilgrimage to this site from all parts of the island. The statue of the Virgin is borne in procession through the streets.

Festival de Teatro de Camagüey, Camagüey *(Sep)*. A national theatre competition dedicated to Gertrudis Gómez de Avellaneda *(see p28)*, with the added participation of various foreign companies. **Matamoros Son**, Santiago *(Sep)*. A biennial festival given over to *son (see p30)*.

OCTOBER

Days of Cuban Culture, countrywide *(10–20 Oct)*. Cubans celebrate their history and Cuban and Afro-Cuban culture. The main day is October 20th, in commemoration of the first day that the national hymn was sung in Bayamo.

Alicia Alonso performing at the Teatro García Lorca

Literature, children's shows, film, arts and music all play their role.
Fiesta de la Cultura Iberoamericana, Holguín *(second half of Oct)*. A festival given over to Spanish culture, with concerts, exhibitions, festivities and lectures.
International Fishing Tournament Jardines del Rey, Marina Cayo Guillermo *(mid–late Oct)*. A fishing tournament in Cayo Guillermo, a favourite fishing ground of author Ernest Hemingway. Anglers can win prizes in exchange for caught sailfish and blue marlin. Contact Naútica Marlin Jardines del Rey, tel (33) 301 323.
Festival Internacional de Ballet de La Habana, Gran Teatro and Teatro García Lorca, Havana *(Oct–Nov, biennial)*. A wide-ranging survey of classical ballet, organized by the Ballet Nacional de Cuba headed by Alicia Alonso. Famous international artists take part as well. The next staging of the festival is in 2014; see www.balletcuba.cult.cu.

NOVEMBER

Festival de Teatro de La Habana, Havana *(Nov)*. This biennial theatre festival features a wide range of performances, including opera, dance, puppet theatre, street shows and pantomime. Theoretical aspects of theatre are also discussed.

HURRICANES

Hurricanes form when masses of hot air with low central pressure move upwards in a spiral, pulling cold air in towards the centre from the surrounding atmosphere. They cause high tides, extremely strong winds, and very heavy and persistent rainfall resulting in floods. The areas most vulnerable to these storms are the coasts, areas with little surface drainage, the valleys, the mountain areas and the cities. Most of the natural disasters in Cuba in the last 100 years have been caused by these storms. In 2008, Hurricanes Gustav and Ike hit the island eight days apart. Over three million people were evacuated and thousands of homes and crops were destroyed, making them the costliest hurricanes to ever hit Cuba. September and October are the most likely months for Caribbean hurricanes to occur.

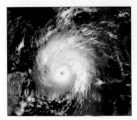

Satellite photograph of Hurricane Gustav over Cuba

AVERAGE MONTHLY TEMPERATURE

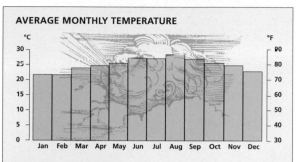

°C: 30, 25, 20, 15, 10, 5, 0
°F: 90, 80, 70, 60, 50, 40, 30
Jan Feb Mar Apr May Jun Jul Aug Sep Oct Nov Dec

Temperature
The chart covers the entire island. In practice, Eastern Cuba, especially the Santiago area (except for the mountainous zones) is hotter. On the cayos the annual temperature range varies little. The humidity level goes from 81 per cent in summer to 79 per cent in winter.

A dancer performs in traditional Afro-Cuban costume

Festejos de San Cristóbal de La Habana *(Nov)*. Festivities and concerts to commemorate the foundation of Havana.
Festival Cuba Danzón, Teatro Sauto, Matanzas *(second half of Nov)*. Performances by *danzón* orchestras and dancers, courses and conferences.
Baila en Cuba, Havana *(late Nov)*. Dance classes, workshops and seminars on the Cuban casino style of salsa.
Festival Internacional de Música Contemporánea de La Habana, Havana *(late Nov)*. Contemporary classical, choral and electro-acoustic music as well as the work of young Cuban composers. Concerts, world premières and lectures. See www.musicacontemporanea.cult.cu.

WINTER

The most active season of the year from a cultural point of view, with many top conferences and festivals, the majority held in the capital. The events calendar is not generally disrupted by the holiday season; although Christmas has been an official holiday since 1998, it is

in fact little celebrated. New Year's Day is usually celebrated at home with the family or with close friends, rather than being the focus for public events.

DECEMBER

Festival Internacional del Nuevo Cine Latinoamericano, ICAIC, Havana *(first half of Dec)*. This is the most important cinema festival and competition of the year, attracting famous international guests. The main cinemas in the capital present screenings of the Latin American films in the competition, as well as retrospective Cuban and international filmmakers.

The Feria Internacional del Libro logo

Fiesta a la Guantanamera, Guantánamo *(first half of Dec)*. Performances of, and lectures on, Afro-Cuban religion. Visits to the French *cafetales* (old coffee plantations) and the stone zoo.
Día de San Lázaro, Santiago de Las Vegas, El Rincón

Festival Internacional del Nuevo Cine Latinoamericano poster

(17 Dec). The faithful and the sick come on pilgrimage to the church of Rincón; many come from Havana on their knees.
Parrandas de Remedios, Remedios *(8–24 Dec)*. Cuba's most popular folk festival begins with a children's parade and ends with floats, fireworks and exuberance on Christmas Eve *(see p177)*.
International Jazz Festival *(mid-Dec)*. The great and the good in world jazz celebrate alongside organiser Chucho Valdés.
Feria Internacional de Artesanía, Pabexpo, Havana *(Dec)*. Handicrafts fair. Stands from different countries; meetings and lectures.

FEBRUARY

Feria Internacional del Libro, Fortaleza de San Carlos de La Cabaña *(Feb–Mar)*. Book fair featuring a different nation each year. New Cuban and foreign publishing initiatives presented and sold. Round tables, poetry readings, events and concerts.

NATIONAL HOLIDAYS

New Year's Day/ Liberation Day (1 Jan)

Labour Day (1 May)

National Rebellion Day (26 July)

Start of First War of Independence (10 Oct)

Christmas Day (25 Dec)

THE HISTORY OF CUBA

irst inhabited in Pre-Columbian times, Cuba was later conquered by the Spanish, who ruled here for four centuries. The island gained independence in 1899, only to come under the virtual control of the US, with the help of dictators Machado and Batista. The revolution headed by Fidel Castro and Che Guevara, who defeated Batista on 1 January 1959, was a turning point for the country. The new political system achieved major social results and Cuba is now finally emerging from decades of isolation.

Before the arrival of the Spanish, Cuba was inhabited by three Amerindian ethnic groups: the Guanajatabey, Siboney and Taíno. The first were gatherers who lived in caves. The Siboney, hunters and fishermen, left behind the most interesting Pre-Columbian rock paintings in the country, more than 200 pictures in the caves of Punta del Este on Isla de la Juventud (see p151). The Taíno were farmers and hunters thought to be from present-day Venezuela, and their culture, the most advanced of the three, achieved a primitive form of social organization.

Indo-Cuban find, Museo Bani (see p215)

On 28 October 1492, Christopher Columbus landed in Cuba during his first voyage of discovery in the New World (see p214). He named it "Juana" in honour of the king of Spain's son, but the natives continued to call it "Cuba". From 1510 to 1514 Diego Velázquez de Cuellar, upon commission from Columbus's son, set about annexing the island to Spain. This proved to be a straightforward enterprise, because the Indians put up little resistance, with the exception of a few episodes. The chief Hatuey led a rebellion in 1511–12, but was taken prisoner and burnt at the stake (see p219).

Diego Velázquez then turned to colonization. He founded the city of Baracoa, first capital of the island, in 1511; San Salvador (present-day Bayamo) in 1513; San Cristóbal (the original Havana), Santísima Trinidad (Trinidad) and Sancti Spíritus in 1514; and Santiago de Cuba and Santa María del Puerto del Príncipe (present-day Camagüey) in 1515. The native population was decimated despite vigorous defence by Friar Bartolomé de las Casas, so-called "Protector of the Indians", and the Spanish soon had to import slaves from western Africa to fulfil the need for labour. Later, dissatisfied with the lack of gold in Cuba, the Spanish began to use the island both as a base from which to conquer other American territory, as well as a port of call for ships taking the riches of the New World back to Spain.

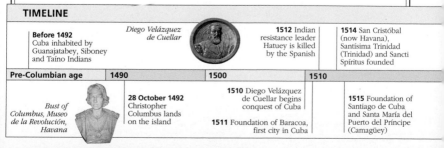

TIMELINE

Pre-Columbian age	1490	1500	1510
Before 1492 Cuba inhabited by Guanajatabey, Siboney and Taíno Indians	*Diego Velázquez de Cuellar*	**1512** Indian resistance leader Hatuey is killed by the Spanish	**1514** San Cristóbal (now Havana), Santísima Trinidad (Trinidad) and Sancti Spíritus founded
Bust of Columbus, Museo de la Revolución, Havana	**28 October 1492** Christopher Columbus lands on the island	**1510** Diego Velázquez de Cuellar begins conquest of Cuba **1511** Foundation of Baracoa, first city in Cuba	**1515** Foundation of Santiago de Cuba and Santa María del Puerto del Príncipe (Camagüey)

◁ Detail from the painting *Siempre Che* (Che Forever) by Raúl Martínez

PIRATES AND BUCCANEERS

By the mid-1500s the population of Cuba had dwindled considerably because the native Indians had been virtually annihilated by forced labour and diseases, and the Spanish had left for other parts of the New World in search of gold. However, the island was still important, strategically, as one of the defensive bastions of the Spanish colonies in America against the expansionist policies of France, Britain and the Netherlands.

Havana, the chief dock for vessels transporting treasure from America to Spain, soon drew the attention of pirates, who were plying the Caribbean Sea by the second half of the 16th century. In 1555, the French buccaneer Jacques de Sores sacked and burned Havana, triggering the construction of an impressive fortification system. Pirate raids became more and more frequent in the 17th century. The first buccaneers were French, then came the turn of the British (including Francis Drake and Henry Morgan) and

Henry Morgan, the British buccaneer

the Dutch, who attacked Spanish galleons loaded with treasure as well as the Cuban ports.

In order to deprive Spain of her colonies, France, Britain and the Netherlands joined in the "corsair war" – essentially state-sanctioned piracy – by financing attacks on Spanish merchant ships. The Spanish crown took several measures to defend its possessions, but to no avail. In 1697 the Ryswyk Treaty signed by Spain, France and Britain finally put an end to this unusual war in the West Indies.

In the meantime Havana had become the new capital of Cuba, thanks to its well-protected bay, and the constant ebb and flow of men and precious cargo imparted a vitality unknown to most of the other cities in the New World. However, the rest of the island was isolated from this ferment, even though agriculture was developing rapidly as the Spanish encouraged the large-scale cultivation of sugar cane and tobacco, which soon became desirable commodities in Europe (see p32). Cuba, a major hub of maritime traffic, was compelled to trade only with the parent country, Spain. Within a short time the island became a haven for smuggling, which was a boost for the island's economy, stimulating the exchange of Cuban sugar and tobacco for the products of the Old World.

THE BRIEF BRITISH DOMINION

Although in the 17th century the Cuban population, concentrated around Havana, had increased with the arrival of Spanish settlers and African slaves, in the early 18th century the island was

The French buccaneers led by Jacques de Sores sacking the city of Havana

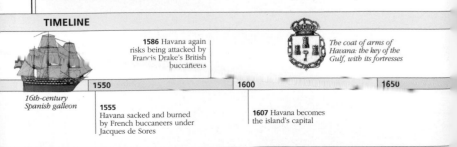

TIMELINE

1586 Havana again risks being attacked by Francis Drake's British buccaneers

The coat of arms of Havana: the key of the Gulf, with its fortresses

1550

1600

1650

16th-century Spanish galleon

1555 Havana sacked and burned by French buccaneers under Jacques de Sores

1607 Havana becomes the island's capital

The British fleet taking Havana in the summer of 1762

still a minor colony. In the summer of 1762 Havana was conquered by the British under the leadership of George Pocock and Lord Albemarle, who ruled for about a year. However, even in this short period the British occupation changed the economic and social organization of the island. The trade restrictions imposed by Spain were abolished, and Cuba began to trade openly with British colonies in North America. The slave trade intensified with Africans being used as labourers on the sugar cane plantations. As a result of the Treaty of Paris, drawn up in 1763, Havana was returned to the Spanish in exchange for Florida.

THE RISE OF NATIONAL IDENTITY
The 18th century marked the birth of a Creole aristocracy. These people, Cuban-born of Spanish descent, commissioned the fine buildings which can still be seen today, and led a colonial lifestyle based on a combination of local, Indian and African traditions. At the end of the century, a cultural

movement promoted by the intellectuals de Heredia, Varela and Villaverde *(see p28)* aimed at establishing a Cuban national identity. In the early 19th century, Spain, forced to recognize the independence of other American colonies, granted some freedom to Cuba, but then gave the island's governors dictatorial powers. Years of revolts, which the Spanish subdued mercilessly, then ensued. However, the new Creole middle class no longer had vested interests in the Spanish crown, and was determined to gain independence for the island.

The new Havana middle class taking a carriage ride

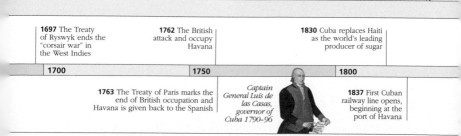

1697 The Treaty of Ryswyk ends the "corsair war" in the West Indies

1762 The British attack and occupy Havana

1830 Cuba replaces Haiti as the world's leading producer of sugar

1700   **1750**   **1800**

1763 The Treaty of Paris marks the end of British occupation and Havana is given back to the Spanish

Captain General Luis de las Casas, governor of Cuba 1790–96

1837 First Cuban railway line opens, beginning at the port of Havana

Sugar, Slaves and Plantations

At the beginning of the 19th century the Cuban sugar industry was booming, thanks to the growing demand for sugar in Europe and America. The growth of the industry was made possible by the labour of slaves brought from Africa in their greatest numbers from the late 18th to the early 19th centuries. About one million men and women were brought to Cuba, and by around 1830 black Africans, including slaves and legally freed slaves, made up more than half the population of Cuba. The island became the world's leading sugar manufacturer, overtaking Haiti, and the industry continued to thrive after the abolition of slavery. Life on the sugar plantations therefore became a key feature of the island's history and life.

Bells *marked the daily routine of life in the* ingenio: *at 4:30am the Ave Maria was played to wake the workers; at 6am the assembly marked the beginning of work proper. At 8:30pm the last bell sounded to announce bedtime.*

Cimarrones *were runaway slaves who hid in the mountains or forests to avoid the* rancheadores, *whose job it was to find and capture them, dead or alive. These fugitives organized frequent revolts, which were almost inevitably suppressed with bloodshed.*

Storehouses, stables and cattle sheds were built around the *ingenio* area.

The sugar refining area stood in the original core of the sugar factory, the *trapiche* or mill.

The first stretch of railway on the island, which actually preceded the introduction of trains in Spain, was inaugurated in 1837 to transport sugar cane to the port of Havana.

Slaves were used *in all phases of sugar manufacture, and not only as field labourers. This old illustration shows the sala de las calderas, where the cane juice was boiled before being refined.*

Carlos Manuel de Céspedes, *the owner of an estate near Manzanillo, freed his slaves on 10 October 1868, thus triggering the Cuban wars of independence. In his manifesto he asked for the abolition of slavery.*

The dances and music *that are thought to have given rise to the rumba (see p31) were performed in the* ingenio, *accompanied by the drumming of* cajones, *wooden boxes used to transport goods. Every year on 6 February the plantation owners allowed their slaves to celebrate their origins by dancing in the streets dressed in traditional costumes.*

The *barracones* (the slaves' dormitories) were rectangular buildings divided into small rooms and with only one grilled door.

THE *INGENIO*

The sugar factory *(ingenio)* was in reality an agro-industrial complex, in the middle of which stood the owner's house. This was usually an elegant building, often embellished with arches and wrought-iron grilles. The sugar factory owner would stay here during the long inspection periods. The *batey*, an Amerindian term used to describe collectively all the buildings on an *ingenio*, included a sugar cane mill, refinery rooms, a distillery, an infirmary, stables and cow sheds, vegetable gardens, storehouses, and the slaves' *barracones*, or sleeping quarters.

los negros esclavos

Fernando Ortiz

The ethnologist Fernando Ortiz *(1881–1969) was the first person to seriously analyze the social condition of the blacks in Cuba, emphasizing the cultural bonds with African traditions.*

A CULTURAL MELTING POT

Symbol of the Abakuá religion

The *ingenio* was a place where landowners, farmers and slaves, white and black, men and women, had to live and work together. The African slaves came from different ethnic groups and spoke different languages, but they managed to keep their religious practices alive by meeting in the *cabildos* (mutual aid associations), where they continued to pray to their gods, "concealing" them in the guise of Roman Catholic saints *(see pp22–3)*. The Spanish themselves ended up assimilating elements of the very traditions they had been trying to suppress. Present-day Cuban music and dances were widespread in the *batey*, and the original songs and literature constantly refer to the *ingenio*, since it was here that the cultural crossover, typical of Cuba, evolved.

THE TEN YEARS' WAR
AND THE ABOLITION OF SLAVERY

On 10 October 1868, at his La Demajagua estate *(see p219)*, the landowner Carlos Manuel de Céspedes launched the *grito de Yara* (war-cry from Yara), calling upon his fellow Cubans to rebel against Spanish rule. After conquering Bayamo, the rebels set up a revolutionary government and chose Céspedes as President of the Republic. On that occasion, the Cuban national anthem was sung for the first time. The new republic, however, was short-lived. The Spanish came back with a vengeance and the rebels – known as *mambises* (villains) – responded with the famous "machete assaults". In the meantime, the struggle had spread to other provinces, but differences among the rebels certainly did not help the cause.

Máximo Gómez

The Ten Years' War – during which the first Cuban constitution was written (1869) – ended in 1878 with the Treaty of Zanjón, at which the rebels capitulated. Some revolutionaries rejected this agreement; one was General Antonio Maceo, who was forced into exile. There followed the so-called *"guerra chica"*, a brief conflict that resulted in the official abolition of slavery in 1886 (slave trade had in practice been prohibited since 1880). Cuba was the last American colony to abolish slavery. It was in this period that trade relations with the US developed.

General Maceo, who was exiled in 1878

RESUMPTION OF HOSTILITIES
AND THE END OF THE WAR

Towards the end of the 1800s, despite the rebellions, living conditions on the island had remained basically the same and none of the promised reforms had been enacted. In 1892, the Cuban intellectual José Martí (1853–95), in exile in the US, made a major contribution to the struggles that would follow: he founded the Partido Revolucionario Cubano, which united the Cuban forces in favour of independence.

The war against Spanish repression resumed on 24 February 1895. The leading figures were Martí – the real author and coordinator of Cuba's struggle for independence, who died in battle on 19 May, Máximo Gómez (recruited by Martí himself, who went to Santo Domingo to meet him) and Antonio Maceo. These last two had already distinguished themselves in the Ten Years' War. There was an escalation in the war and Spain sent reinforcements, but the situation was already out of control. Gómez and Maceo extended the war from the east to the west, gradually liberating the island. Not even the arrival of the Spanish general Valeriano Weyler, who was granted extraordinary powers, did any good: the war had taken a decided turn for the worse for the Spanish.

On 15 February 1898, when the Cubans had practically won, the American cruiser *Maine*, officially sent to the bay of Havana to protect US citizens and property in Cuban territory, exploded mysteriously, causing the death of about 250 marines. The US accused Spain of being responsible for the tragedy and, with public opinion

---

TIMELINE

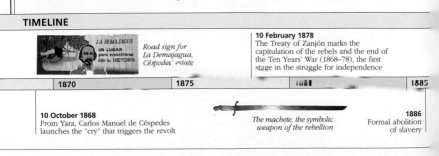

Road sign for *La Demajagua, Céspedes' estate*

10 February 1878
The Treaty of Zanjón marks the capitulation of the rebels and the end of the Ten Years' War (1868–78), the first stage in the struggle for independence

| 1870 | 1875 | | 1885 |

10 October 1868
From Yara, Carlos Manuel de Céspedes launches the "cry" that triggers the revolt

The machete, the symbolic weapon of the rebellion

1886
Formal abolition of slavery

The US battlecruiser *Maine* in Havana Bay in 1898, with the Castillo del Morro on the right

on their side at home, intervened in the war. On 3 July the US Navy defeated the Spanish fleet, with the obvious intent of taking part in the peace treaty. On 10 December the Treaty of Paris – which involved Spain and the US, but not Cuba – marked the end of Spanish colonial dominion in America. On 1 January 1899 the last Spanish governor, Jiménez y Castellanos, officially handed the keys of Havana to US general John Brooke. From this point onwards, Cuba became inextricably linked with the United States.

US SUPERVISION

In February 1901 the Constituent Assembly approved the first Cuban constitution and Tomás Estrada Palma was elected president. However, the delegates were forced to accept the Platt Amendment, formulated by US senator Orville Platt and added to a bill in Congress. Officially this provision aimed at safeguarding peace on the island, but its underlying purpose was to sanction the right of the US to intervene in Cuban affairs and to supervise trade relations between Cuba and other nations. In addition, the US was granted the right to establish naval bases on the island, including the one at Guantánamo in Eastern Cuba, which it still leases *(see p239)*.

Although formal independence was granted to Cuba on 20 May 1902, in the years that followed American involvement in the local economy increased and, on the pretext of safeguarding their citizens and investments, the US sent marines to the island on many occasions.

JOSÉ MARTÍ

In 1895, when he died in battle at Boca de dos Ríos, José Martí was only 42. Despite this, he had had years of experience of living in exile and revolutionary struggle, besides writing a number of poems, articles and essays that would be the envy of a veteran author. Martí was born in Havana in 1853 to Spanish parents. By the time he went to secondary school he was already participating in anti-Spanish conspiracies. This activity led to his being deported in 1868, and exiled in 1878, after which he lived in the US, Spain, Mexico, Guatemala and Venezuela. As an essayist and journalist, Martí was known for his vigorous style. He was also a modernist poet *(see p28)*. He was an activist, a great politician and a sensitive interpreter of the impulses of the human soul.

José Martí, a national hero

		15 February 1898		*Tomás Estrada Palma, first president of Cuba*
	1895–8	Explosion	25 February 1901	
	José Martí heads resumption of hostilities against the Spanish	of the battlecruiser *Maine*	First constitution	

1890		1895		1900	
1892 José Martí, in exile in the US, founds the Partido Revolucionario Cubano	19 May 1895 José Martí dies in combat	7 December 1896 Antonio Maceo dies in combat	10 December 1898 Paris Treaty marks end of Spanish dominion and beginning of American control	20 May 1902 Cuba obtains formal independence	

THE EARLY PERIOD OF THE REPUBLIC

In its first 25 years, the Cuban Republic was headed by various presidents who did relatively little for the country. The second incumbent, José Miguel Gómez, who was nicknamed *tiburón* (shark), is at least to be credited for having introduced free public education and freedom of association and speech, as well as the separation of Church and State, and laws regarding divorce. In the early 1900s, sugar cane production increased to the point where sugar became virtually the only crop grown, and several new sugar factories were built. Havana, especially in the 1920s, saw the development of entire urban areas.

However, in general, independence had not really benefited the population at large, and protest demonstrations, repressed with force, began to increase. The first trade and student unions were set up, and in 1925 the Cuban Communist Party was founded. The leading figure in the party was the Marxist intellectual Julio Antonio Mella, leader of the Havana student movement and key to Latin American left-wing politics. Mella was arrested in Cuba but then freed because of the massive demonstrations that took place after he went on hunger strike; he was then sent into exile in Mexico. However, on 10 January 1929, Mella was assassinated in Mexico City by hired killers in the pay of the dictator Gerardo Machado. He became a national hero.

A popular uprising against the corrupt, inefficient government of Gerardo Machado

GERARDO MACHADO'S REGIME

In 1925 Gerardo Machado became president of Cuba, later changing the Constitution so he could rule for a further term, which he did with iron force until 1933. This period was marked by violence and tyranny; the people demonstrated their discontent by means of continual strikes, and the situation worsened with the Great Depression. A long general strike and the loss of the support of the army forced Machado to flee to the Bahamas on 12 August 1933.

After a brief period of progressive government, from early 1934 onwards there were various presidents who were little more than puppets, placed there by Sergeant Fulgencio Batista – who himself became president from 1940 to 1944. From 1934 to 1940 various social reforms came into being: the Platt amendment was revoked, women were allowed to vote, an 8-hour working day was instituted, and a new constitution was enacted.

The Marxist intellectual Julio Antonio Mella

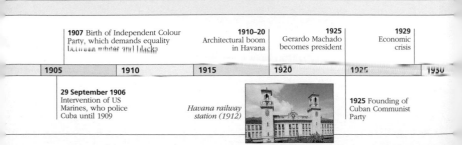

1907 Birth of Independent Colour Party, which demands equality between whites and blacks

1910–20 Architectural boom in Havana

1925 Gerardo Machado becomes president

1929 Economic crisis

1905　　　1910　　　1915　　　1920　　　1925　　　1930

29 September 1906 Intervention of US Marines, who police Cuba until 1909

Havana railway station (1912)

1925 Founding of Cuban Communist Party

BATISTA'S DICTATORSHIP

After World War II the Orthodox Party led by Eduardo Chibás became popular, supported by the more progressive members of the middle class This party might have won the election that was to take place on 1 June 1952, but on 10 March Fulgencio Batista staged a coup. Protest demonstrations followed, consisting mostly of students, which were ruthlessly repressed. The university was then closed. Batista's government, having the official support of the US, abandoned its initial populist stance and became an out-and-out violent dictatorship indifferent to the needs of the Cuban people. Vast areas of land were sold to American and British firms, and the money was pocketed. As the dictator's cronies became rich, the population became poorer, and the country more and more backward. Cuba was becoming a "pleasure island" which held an overpowering fascination, especially for Americans.

By the 1950s Cuba was famous for glamour – its music and cocktails, its prostitutes, cigars, drinking and gambling, and the sensational tropical life attracted mafiosi and film stars, tourists

Fulgencio Batista (left) with American vice-president Richard Nixon

and businessmen. However, there was a high price to pay: Cuba had not only become a land of casinos and drugs, it had also fallen into the hands of the American underworld, which ran the local gambling houses and luxury hotels, used for money laundering.

THE CUBAN REVOLUTION

After Batista's coup, a young lawyer, Fidel Alejandro Castro Ruz, an active student leader who associated with the Orthodox Party, denounced the illegitimacy of the new government to the magistracy, without effect. Since peaceful means did not work, on 26 July 1953 Castro made an unsuccessful attempt to capture the Moncada army barracks at Santiago (see p230). He was one of the few fortunate surviving rebels and was tried and sentenced to imprisonment in the Presidio Modelo, on Isla de Pinos (currently Isla de la Juventud). Thanks to an amnesty, he was freed two years later and went into exile in Mexico, where he set about organizing the revolutionary forces, and was joined by a young Argentine doctor, Ernesto "Che" Guevara. This famous collaboration proved to be decisive for the success of the Revolution. In 1959, after years of armed struggle, the island was freed from previous dictatorships (see pp48–51).

Dancers at the Tropicana in the 1940s

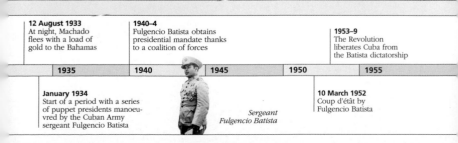

12 August 1933	1940–4		1953–9
At night, Machado flees with a load of gold to the Bahamas	Fulgencio Batista obtains presidential mandate thanks to a coalition of forces		The Revolution liberates Cuba from the Batista dictatorship

1935	1940	1945	1950	1955

January 1934		10 March 1952
Start of a period with a series of puppet presidents manoeuvred by the Cuban Army sergeant Fulgencio Batista	*Sergeant Fulgencio Batista*	Coup d'état by Fulgencio Batista

The Cuban Revolution

In exile in Mexico after the attack on the Moncada army barracks, on 25 November 1956 Fidel Castro left for Cuba on the yacht *Granma* with 81 other revolutionaries, including Che Guevara and Raúl Castro. Three days later, after landing, they were attacked by Batista's troops. Only a few escaped to the Sierra Maestra, where they began to organize their guerrilla war. The miserable living conditions of the people and ever-increasing corruption and repression lent impetus to their struggle. The rebel army, which included farmers, students, women and regular army deserters, defeated Batista's troops after two years of fighting.

The attack against the Moncada barracks *took place on 26 July 1953. The rebels took advantage of the Carnival festivities to move unseen in the crowds, but the attack ended in failure.*

KEY

– – Raúl Castro's march

– – Che Guevara's march

– – Camilo Cienfuegos' march

Havana was occupied by Che Guevara's guerrillas, while Fidel Castro entered Santiago de Cuba (1 January 1959).

Santa Clara was the scene of the battle that marked the triumph of the revolution. After the rebels' victory, Batista fled to Santo Domingo (31 December 1958).

- Havana
- Matanzas
- Pinar del Rio
- Santa Clar
- Cienfuegos

Isla de la Juventud

Sierra del Escambray was reached by Che Guevara after an exhausting march; his men were without food or shoes and extremely weary but they were victorious (October 1958).

Radio Rebelde *was the guerrillas' radio station, set up in the Sierra Maestra by Che Guevara in February 1958. Its programmes were listened to avidly all over the island.*

THE PHASES OF THE WAR

The advance of two columns of guerrillas from the Sierra Maestra – one led by Che Guevara and Camilo Cienfuegos to the west (October 1958), the other by Raúl Castro bound for Guantánamo – marked the climax of the revolutionaries' struggle. After the battle of Santa Clara and the taking of the city by Guevara's troops at the end of December, Batista escaped to Santo Domingo. On 1 January 1959 victory was declared by the revolutionaries.

The Landing of the *Granma* *in Cuba took place on 2 December 1956. Due to some problems at sea, the yacht landed on 2 December and not 30 November as planned. Three days later they were ambushed by Batista's troops. Those captured were killed, while the survivors (including Fidel and Raúl Castro) took refuge in the Sierra Maestra.*

Young women, *including Haidée Santamaría, Celia Sánchez and Vilma Espín, participated actively in the revolutionary war. After Havana was captured, they were entrusted with guarding strategic points.*

Fidel Castro entered Havana *on 8 January 1959 and on 16 February was elected prime minister. At the time the president was Manuel Urrutia, elected after Batista's escape. The revolutionary government immediately abolished racial discrimination and reduced rents and the cost of electricity.*

On the Sierra Maestra, *Cuba's largest mountain range, the rebels organized guerrilla warfare, recruiting soldiers from among the population (above, Fidel Castro recruiting farmers). The strategy was to ambush Batista's troops and take their supplies and weapons.*

• Camagüey

Holguín •

Playa Las Coloradas was where the *Granma* landed on 2 December 1956.

• Bayamo   Santiago de Cuba
• Guantánamo

The attack at La Plata, a military barracks, was the rebels' first success (17 January 1957).

In the Sierra Maestra Fidel Castro, Che Guevara and the other survivors of the *Granma* worked out a strategy of guerrilla warfare with a growing number of *barbudos*, students, army deserters and reinforcements sent by the urban branch of the Movimiento 26 de Julio.

At Santiago de Cuba the rebel movement won an important victory on 17 January 1957.

TIMELINE

October 1953 Fidel Castro condemned to 15 years' imprisonment in Presidio Modelo

30 November 1956 Bloody repression of revolt at Santiago

Che Guevara

31 August Che and Cienfuegos leave east to conquer central regions

1 January Che and Cienfuegos enter Havana; Castro, Santiago

| 1953 | 1956 | | 1958 | 1959 |

26 July 1953 Attack on Moncada barracks

15 May 1955 Fidel Castro freed, goes to Mexico in exile

Castro leaving prison

2 December 1956 Landing of *Granma*

1956–8 Guerrilla war in Sierra Maestra

24 February Radio Rebelde set up

31 December Santa Clara falls, Batista flees

8 January Castro enters Havana in triumph

The Heroes of the Revolution

The success of the revolution can be partly explained by the moral stature of the heroes who headed it, and partly by the unity of the movement – an entire population was determined to obtain freedom. After their triumphal entrance into Havana, the revolutionary leaders were entrusted with the task of realizing their objectives: the reorganization of the country's agriculture, afflicted with large landed estates and monoculture; the battle against illiteracy and unemployment; industrialization; the construction of homes, schools and hospitals. Fidel Castro became Prime Minister and Che Guevara was appointed Minister of Industry and president of the National Bank. The revolution continued, with its heroes and ideals.

Ernesto "Che" Guevara *was an Argentinian who met Castro in Mexico. Unpretentious, straightforward and ascetic, and an uncompromising idealist, he believed the Third World could be freed only through armed rebellion (see p176).*

The straw hats worn by the *barbudos* were those commonly used by farmers.

Camilo Cienfuegos, *a commander whose courage was legendary, was a direct, spontaneous person with a great sense of humour. He played a crucial role in the armed struggle, but took part in the government only for a brief period. On 28 October 1959, while returning from Camagüey in his small plane after arresting guerrilla commander Hubert Matos, who had betrayed the Revolution, Cienfuegos disappeared and was never seen again.*

Horses were the most common means of transport used by the revolutionaries.

Frank País *(seen here with his mother and fiancée), head of the Movimiento 26 de Julio, was entrusted with organizing a revolt in Santiago de Cuba that would coincide with the landing of the* Granma *on 30 November 1956. But because of too heavy in it landing the revolt was repressed. País died in Santiago during the armed revolt, in an ambush set up by the chief of police.*

Raúl Castro, *Fidel's brother, currently President of Cuba, was one of the few survivors of the landing of the Granma. He took part in the guerrilla war and became a member of the government, adopting a radical stance. As Minister of Defence he signed, with Khrushchev, the agreement for the installation of the nuclear missiles in Cuba that caused the 1962 crisis.*

Fidel Castro with Juan Almeida *(left), one of the strategists of revolutionary guerrilla warfare. Castro, a great orator and political strategist, the Líder Máximo and an uncompromising patriot, personified the Cuban state. As poet Nicolás Guillén wrote, "he accomplished what José Martí had promised". Born on 13 August 1926 in Mayarí in Eastern Cuba, the son of Spanish immigrants, he studied with the Jesuits and took a degree in law. He began to fight for the cause while at university.*

The Cuban flag, used after the wars of independence, has the colours of the French Revolution. The three blue stripes represent the old provinces of the island.

THE BARBUDOS
The rebels were referred to as *barbudos* (bearded men) because during their time in the mountains, they all grew long beards. A large number of farmers joined their famous marches. This photograph, taken by the Cuban photographer Raúl Corrales, expresses the epic and team spirit of the revolution.

Guillermo García Morales *was one of the first Cuban farmers to join the revolutionary war of the Movimiento 26 de Julio. A guerrilla in the Sierra Maestra together with Castro, he was named Commander of the Revolution for his distinguished service.*

Celia Sánchez Manduley *espoused the revolutionary cause at an early age and fought in the Sierra Maestra. Considered Fidel Castro's right-hand "man" and companion, after 1959 she filled important political positions. Celia died of cancer in 1980, while still young.*

ERADICATING ILLITERACY, AGRICULTURAL REFORM

One of the first acts of the revolutionary government was a campaign against illiteracy, initiated in 1961: thousands of students travelled throughout the countryside, teaching the rural population to read and write. Che Guevara, who during the guerrilla warfare in the mountains had encouraged his men to devote some time to study, participated in the campaign. In a short time illiteracy was eradicated.

The next step was agrarian reform, which began with the abolition of ownership of large landed estates, especially those in foreign (in particular American) hands. US landholdings were drastically reduced. This marked the beginning of hostilities between the two countries. In October 1960 the US declared an economic boycott that blocked the export of petroleum to Cuba and the import of Cuban sugar.

After nearly two years of growing tension, Cuba secured closer economic and political ties with the Soviet Union, Eastern Europe and China. In the meantime, the struggle against counter-revolutionary guerrillas in the Sierra del Escambray continued.

Marines arriving at the US naval base of Guantánamo during the missile crisis

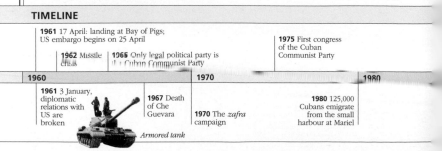

Participants in the campaign against illiteracy in 1961

against Cuba, which heralded a boycott by most other countries in the Americas (except Mexico and Canada). These countries also severed diplomatic relations with the island, as the US had done. The result was the establishment of even closer ties between Cuba and the communist world. A year later, when the US discovered the presence of nuclear missile sites in Cuba, President Kennedy ordered a naval blockade around the island and demanded that the missile installations be dismantled immediately. At the height of the crisis, with the world poised on the brink of nuclear war, the Soviet president Nikita Khrushchev ordered the missiles to be taken back to the Soviet Union.

THE EMBARGO AND MISSILE CRISIS

On 17 April 1961 a group of Cuban exiles and mercenaries trained by the CIA landed at Playa Girón, in the Bay of Pigs, to invade the island. But the attack failed because, contrary to the expectations of the US, Cuban civilians did not rise up against Castro (*see p167*). Eight days later President Kennedy declared a trade embargo

FROM THE *ZAFRA* CAMPAIGN TO THE EMIGRATION OF THE *"MARIELITOS"*

During the early stages, the government had aimed to create as much diversity in the economy as possible. However, in 1970, in order to inject life into the flagging economy, all efforts were concentrated on promoting the

TIMELINE

1961 17 April: landing at Bay of Pigs; US embargo begins on 25 April

1962 Missile crisis

1965 Only legal political party is the Cuban Communist Party

1975 First congress of the Cuban Communist Party

1960

1970

1980

1961 3 January, diplomatic relations with US are broken

Armored tank

1967 Death of Che Guevara

1970 The *zafra* campaign

1980 125,000 Cubans emigrate from the small harbour at Mariel

zafra (sugar cane harvest) campaign. A target was set of ten million tons, but in the end only 8,500,000 were harvested. In the same period some Latin American countries resumed diplomatic relations with Cuba. While the revolution had achieved a great deal in social terms, the country's economic problems had by no means been resolved. 1980 saw the emigration of 125,000 Cubans, the so-called *marielitos* – named after the small harbour of Mariel, near Havana, where they set off for Miami.

Pope John Paul II and Castro during his visit to Cuba

THE *PERÍODO ESPECIAL*
The dismantling of the Berlin Wall in 1989 and the subsequent collapse of Communism in Eastern Europe deprived Cuba of economic partners; and Castro did not conceal his dislike of Gorbachev's *perestroika* policy. The suspension of Soviet aid was a crippling blow for the Cuban economy, and triggered a crisis that the government faced by imposing a programme of austerity. In 1990 the island went through one of the most difficult phases in its history, the Período

Especial. Many sectors of industry came to a standstill due to a lack of fuel, imports were reduced, interruptions in the supply of electricity and water became part of everyday life, transport virtually came to a halt, food rations were reduced and wages were lowered. In 1991 the Soviet Union also withdrew its troops and technicians. The economic crisis continued to worsen until 1994.

INTO THE 21ST CENTURY
To counter the Período Especial the government began to encourage foreign investment, limited private enterprise was allowed and the US dollar became legal tender. A significant sign of change was Pope John Paul II's visit to Cuba in 1998. The 2000s saw a massive influx of tourism but still the economy remained precarious; the US dollar was later withdrawn. Raúl Castro replaced his ailing brother Fidel as president in early 2008 and introduced social and economic reforms, but the economy remained strained. In 2010 Raúl Castro began releasing political prisoners incarcerated since 2003, and Fidel reappeared in public after a four-year absence from the public stage. As the economy continued to sink, Raúl Castro announced that 500,000 workers would be laid off by the state, ameliorating their predicament with new self-employment rules allowing many more Cubans to work for themselves and start their own businesses – a sea change in state-run Cuba.

Empty shelves in a shop during the crisis period

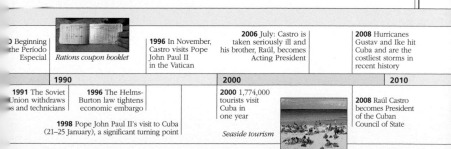

				2006 July: Castro is taken seriously ill and his brother, Raúl, becomes Acting President	2008 Hurricanes Gustav and Ike hit Cuba and are the costliest storms in recent history
0 Beginning the Período Especial	*Rations coupon booklet*	1996 In November, Castro visits Pope John Paul II in the Vatican			
1990				**2000**	**2010**
1991 The Soviet Union withdraws s and technicians	1996 The Helms-Burton law tightens economic embargo			2000 1,774,000 tourists visit Cuba in one year	2008 Raúl Castro becomes President of the Cuban Council of State
	1998 Pope John Paul II's visit to Cuba (21–25 January), a significant turning point			*Seaside tourism*	

HAVANA
AREA BY AREA

Havana at a Glance

The crest of Havana

Havana is a lively, colourful capital city, full of bustle and entertainment, with some splendid architectural gems from the colonial period and beyond, and numerous other sights. The city alone is worth the trip to Cuba. Many attractions are concentrated in three quarters: Habana Vieja (Old Havana), Centro Habana and Vedado. In the following pages Habana Vieja, the colonial centre within the old city walls, is described first, followed by Centro Habana and the area known as Prado. The western part of the city is covered in the chapter called Vedado and Plaza. For map references for major sights in Havana, refer to the Street Finder (see pp118–23).

HAVANA

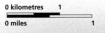

0 kilometres   1

0 miles   1

Necrópolis de Colón (see pp104–5) *is Havana's city cemetery as well as a national monument. Many famous people are buried here, often in striking tombs, and the site has become a place of pilgrimage for many.*

VEDADO AND PLAZA
(see pp96–105)

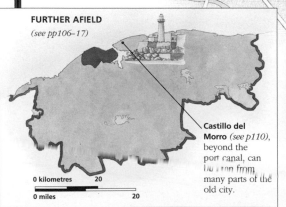

FURTHER AFIELD
(see pp106–17)

0 kilometres   20

0 miles   20

Castillo del Morro *(see p110)*, beyond the port canal, can be seen from many parts of the old city.

Martí Memorial (see p103) *in Plaza de la Revolución is one of the symbols of Cuba. The white marble statue of the great patriot forms a focal point for national celebrations.*

◁ Havana at sunset, with the dome of Capitolio rising up over the rooftops

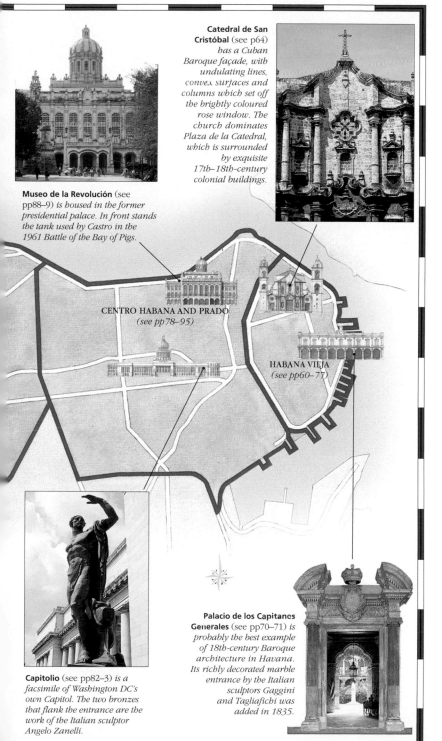

Catedral de San Cristóbal (see p64) *has a Cuban Baroque façade, with undulating lines, convex surfaces and columns which set off the brightly coloured rose window. The church dominates Plaza de la Catedral, which is surrounded by exquisite 17th–18th-century colonial buildings.*

Museo de la Revolución (see pp88–9) *is housed in the former presidential palace. In front stands the tank used by Castro in the 1961 Battle of the Bay of Pigs.*

CENTRO HABANA AND PRADO
(see pp 78–95)

HABANA VIEJA
(see pp60–77)

Capitolio (see pp82–3) *is a facsimile of Washington DC's own Capitol. The two bronzes that flank the entrance are the work of the Italian sculptor Angelo Zanelli.*

Palacio de los Capitanes Generales (see pp70–71) *is probably the best example of 18th-century Baroque architecture in Havana. Its richly decorated marble entrance by the Italian sculptors Gaggini and Tagliafichi was added in 1835.*

The Malecón

No other place represents Havana better than
the Malecón, and no other place thrills tourists
and locals so much. This seafront promenade
winds for 7 km (4 miles) alongside the city's historic
quarters, from the Colonial centre to the skyscrapers
of Vedado, charting the history of Havana from past
to present. The busy seafront boulevard is lined with
many attractive buildings, but it is the overall effect
that is striking – and the Bay of Havana looks truly
spectacular at sunset. In addition, the Malecón
means tradition and religion to the people of the
city: offerings to the gods *(see p23)* are thrown
from the parapet into the sea.

LOCATOR MAP
See Street Finder pp120–23.

① **The Caryatid Building**
*is one of the most important
structures in the first stretch
of the Malecón. Built in the
early 20th century, it was
named after the Art Deco-
style female figures that
support the entablature
of the loggia.*

② **The area between Prado
and Calle Belascoaín,** *which
has been scrupulously restored, is
known for its pastel buildings.
In the same part of the street,
at No 51, is the "Ataúd" (the
coffin), a 1950s skyscraper
whose name derives from
the shape of its balconies.*

Varied decoration

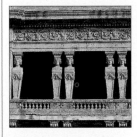

Balconies with Neo-Moorish
decorative patterns

ARCHITECTURE

The Malecón is lined with
buildings whose pastel hues
have faded in the sun and
salty air, as well as early
20th-century structures,
often with two or three
storeys and a loggia on the
upper floor, in a mix of
different architectural styles.

Edificio Focsa

③ **The Monument to
the Victims of the Maine**
*was built in 1926 in
memory of the sailors who
died when the American
warship* Maine *exploded in
the Bay of Havana
in 1898 (see p45).
It stands in one of
the wide stretches
of the avenue
on the edge
of Vedado.*

Hotel
Nacional

④ **Between Calle 23 and Calle G** *is the
stretch of the Malecón that borders the
Vedado quarter to the north. Dominated
by Havana's tallest buildings, this is
the seafront of the capital city.*

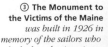

On stormy days *the waves break against the rocks and crash over the sea wall onto the street. Children love it when this happens. Storms are also a source of inspiration for followers of* Santería, *who view it as the wrath of Yemayá, the sea goddess (see p23).*

Fishing *on the Malecón is a popular pastime among the locals. Others are playing music, strolling, or simply sitting on the low wall and watching the horizon.*

ATMOSPHERE
The Havana seafront is especially magical at sunset, when the colours of the buildings are accentuated. The Malecón is at its busiest on Sundays, when the *Habaneros* who cannot get to the Playas del Este flock here.

Young people love to gather along the Malecón, to meet friends, socialize, swim, sunbathe and drink rum.

The striking setting *of the Malecón, facing the sea and with the city behind it, makes it a popular place for romantic young couples. There is also the occasional single person on the lookout for female or male companionship.*

A WALK BY THE OCEAN: THE HISTORY OF THE MALECÓN

On 4 November 1901, the US authorities then occupying Cuba planned the Malecón as a tree-lined, pedestrian promenade to begin at the Castillo de la Punta. However the strong wind and rough sea obliged the engineers to change their original project and it was an American engineer named Mead, and Frenchman Jean Forestier, who came up with a more practical plan. In 1902 the open space in front of the Prado was completed with a municipal bandstand. Hotels and cafés were built near the old city, while bathing facilities were concentrated in Miramar. In 1919 the Malecón stretched as far as Calle Belascoaín, and in 1921 as far as Calle 23. It soon became a fast link between the old and modern cities – so much so that in the 1950s it was virtually abandoned by pedestrians. Today, despite the traffic, its original function has been partly revived.

The Malecón in the early 1900s

LA HABANA VIEJA

The historic heart of Havana, which was declared part of the "cultural heritage of humanity" by UNESCO in 1982, is the largest Colonial centre in Latin America. After three centuries of neglect, restoration work under the direction of Eusebio Leal Spengler, the *historiador de la ciudad* (Superintendent of Cultural Heritage), is reviving the former splendour of this district. La Habana Vieja is characterized by

Statue of Columbus, Palacio de los Capitanes Generales

Hispanic-Andalusian architecture, vitalized by the tropical sun and lush vegetation. Time seems to stand still here but nonetheless the zone does not give the impression of being a museum. The restoration programme is not limited to monuments and major buildings, but also includes old shops and ordinary houses. The aim is to ensure the revival of both the beauty of La Habana Vieja and its original vitality and everyday activities.

SIGHTS AT A GLANCE

Museums and Galleries
Museo de Arte Colonial ❷
Museo José Martí ⓱
Museo del Ron ⓭

Historic Buildings
La Bodeguita del Medio ❹
Castillo de la Real Fuerza ❺
Palacio de los Capitanes Generales pp70–71 ❽
Seminario de San Carlos y San Ambrosio ❸
El Templete ❻

Historic Streets and Squares
Calle Obispo ❾
Calle Oficios ❼
Casa de Africa ⓫
Casa de la Obra Pía ❿
Plaza de San Francisco ⓬
Plaza Vieja ⓮

Churches and Monasteries
Catedral de San Cristóbal ❶
Convento de Santa Clara ⓯
Iglesia del Espíritu Santo ⓰
Iglesia de Nuestra Señora de la Merced ⓱

KEY
⬜ Street-by-Street map *pp62–3*
⬜ Street-by-Street map *pp66–7*
ℹ️ Tourist information
⛴ Ferry

0 metres 300
0 yards 300

GETTING THERE
The easiest way to reach this quarter is by taxi, or by *cocotaxi (see p315)*. A tourist bus also circuits the area *(see p314)*. La Habana Vieja can be easily explored either on foot or by hiring a bicycle-rickshaw or carriage. The latter can be found behind the Castillo de la Real Fuerza, at the corner of Calle Mercaderes and Calle Empedrado.

◁ **Colonial buildings in Plaza Vieja *(see p76)***

Street-by-Street: Plaza de la Catedral

Dominated by the elegant profile of its church, Plaza de la Catedral is one of the symbols of La Habana Vieja. In 1592, the Zanja Real, the city's first aqueduct (and the first Spanish aqueduct in the New World), reached the square. Water was channelled from the Almendares river, 11 km (7 miles) away. The Zanja Real was built to provide water to ships docking in the harbour, as well as to local residents. A 16th-century plaque in the square marks the spot where the Zanja Real was located. In the 18th century the aristocratic buildings and present-day Cathedral were built here. Plaza de la Catedral is an unmissable attraction for anyone visiting the historic centre, with women in colonial costume who stroll under the arcades and read fortunes, and a bar-restaurant where you can relax in the shade and listen to music.

A woman in colonial costume on the Cathedral steps

Former entrance to the seminary

Centro Wifredo Lam, housed in an 18th-century palazzo, promotes contemporary art with exhibitions and lectures.

Seminario de San Carlos y San Ambrosio
The modern entrance of this 18th-century building echoes the Baroque decorative motifs of the Cathedral ❸

Palacio de los Marqueses de Aguas Claras was built in the second half of the 18th century. In the 1900s it housed the París Restaurant and then the offices of the Banco Industrial. It is now a bar-restaurant, El Patio, with tables in the inner courtyard as well as in the picturesque square.

KEY

– – – Suggested route

STAR SIGHTS

★ Catedral de San Cristóbal

★ Museo de Arte Colonial

★ La Bodeguita del Medio

Casa de la Condesa de la Reunión, a 19th-century building surrounding a splendid courtyard, is the headquarters of the Alejo Carpentier Foundation. This well-known 20th-century Cuban writer *(see p29)* set his novel *Siglo de las Luces* here.

★ La Bodeguita del Medio
This restaurant and bar is legendary thanks to the writer Ernest Hemingway, who came here to drink mojitos ❹

LOCATOR MAP
*See Street Finder, pp120–23,
map 4*

★ **Catedral de San Cristóbal**
*The Baroque façade of this church, declared
a national monument, is considered one of
the most beautiful in the Americas* ❶

Palacio del Conde Lombillo (1746)
is now home to offices of the
Historiador de La Habana and hosts
temporary exhibitions of photographs,
paintings and lithographs.

CALLE TACÓN

CALLE EMPEDRADO

CALLE MERCADERES

PLAZA DE LA CATEDRAL

**Palacio de los Marqueses
de Arcos**, built in the 1700s,
houses an art gallery where
handicrafts and prints are
on sale. The building was
once the main post office
and the original letter box is still
visible on the outside wall.

Plaza
de Armas
*(see
pp66–7)*

| 0 metres | 40 |
| 0 yards | 40 |

CALLEJÓN DEL CHORRO

CALLE SAN IGNACIO

**The Taller Experimental de
Gráfica** (1962) holds theoretical
and practical courses in graphic
art for Cubans and foreigners, and
houses a Gallery of Engravings.

★ **Museo de Arte Colonial**
*Dating from 1720, this is one of the
city's finest examples of early Colonial
domestic architecture. It houses an exhibition of Colonial furniture and objects* ❷

Catedral de San Cristóbal ●

Calle Empedrado 156. **Map** 4 E2.
Tel (7) 8617 771. ⬤ *9am–5pm Mon–Fri, 9am–1pm Sat, 9am–noon Sun.* ✝ *6pm Mon–Fri, 3:30pm Sat, 10:30am Sun.* ⬤

Construction of the Catedral de San Cristóbal (Cathedral of St Christopher) began in 1748 under the supervision of Jesuit priests. They were, however, expelled from Cuba following conflict with the Spanish crown, meaning the church was finished by Franciscans in 1777. It became a cathedral after the collapse of the old Parroquial Mayor *(see p70)*, which was caused by the explosion of a ship in the nearby port.

In 1789, present-day San Cristóbal was consecrated as Catedral de la Virgen María de la Inmaculada Concepción, and the small square where it stands gained its current status. In 1796 it was renamed Catedral de San Cristóbal de La Habana, because, according to popular belief, from that year until 1898 it housed the relics of Christopher Columbus himself. A plaque to the left of the pulpit tells the same story, though there is no official historical record.

The architecture is in keeping with other Jesuit churches throughout the world: a Latin cross layout, chapels on the sides and to the rear, the nave higher than the side aisles. The Cuban

The austere nave of Catedral de San Cristóbal

Baroque façade is grandiose, with two large, asymmetrical bell towers and an abundance of niches and columns, which Cuban author Alejo Carpentier described as "music set in stone".

In comparison, the Neo-Classical interior is rather disappointing. Large piers separate the nave from the aisles, which have eight chapels. The largest one is the Sagrario chapel; the oldest (1755), designed by Lorenzo Camacho, is dedicated to the Madonna of Loreto and contains quaint, tiny houses used as *ex votos*.

The three frescoes behind the high altar are by Giuseppe Perovani, while the original wooden and plaster ceiling, demolished and then rebuilt in 1946–52, was the work of

Statue of St Christopher

Frenchman Jean Baptiste Vermay, who founded the San Alejandro Fine Arts Academy *(see p26)*. The high altar was created by Italian artist Giuseppe Bianchini in the 1800s. To the right is a huge wooden statue of St Christopher, carved by the Seville sculptor Martín de Andújar in 1636. The legs are out of proportion with the trunk, as they were cut in order to allow the statue to pass through the portal.

On 16 November, the saint's feast day, a solemn mass is held here, during which the faithful, who have to stay quiet during the service, file past the statue to silently ask for his blessing. This blessing is given as long as worshippers do not utter a word until they have left the church.

Pope John Paul II in front of the Cathedral

POPE JOHN PAUL II'S VISIT

Pope John Paul II visited Cuba from 21–25 January 1998 *(see p53)*. This carefully planned event was of great historical significance to Cuba and was greeted with enthusiasm not only by Roman Catholics, but by virtually the entire population. The Cuban government had shown signs of favouring dialogue with the Church and greater religious tolerance in the 1990s. The Pope's visit was broadcast on television and the government also officially recognized Christmas Day as a holiday for the first time since 1969. On 25 January the "Celebration of the Word" was held in the Cathedral, during which the Pope met Cuban priests. Journalists from all over the world attended, and the Pope also held an audience with the faithful in Plaza de la Revolución.

Museo de Arte Colonial ❷

Calle San Ignacio 61. **Map** 4 E2.
Tel (7) 8626 440. ⬤ *closed for restoration.* 📷 📹 📷 *(with charge – phone ahead for more information).*

This 18th-century mansion, built by Don Luis Chacón, governor of Cuba, has been the home of a fascinating museum dedicated to colonial art since 1969. The building is a fine example of a colonial residence and is constructed around an elegant courtyard.

The 12 rooms on the ground floor and first floor contain furniture, chandeliers, porcelain and other decorative pieces from various 18th–19th-century middle-class and aristocratic houses in Havana, in which European, Creole and colonial traditions are combined. Besides a remarkable collection of furniture made of tropical wood, the museum has an exceptional collection of stained glass windows *(mediopunto)*, typical of Cuba's Creole craftsmen *(see p25).*

There is also a 13th room where exhibitions of contemporary art and crafts inspired by colonial art are held. During the week the museum organizes tours for school children and leisure activities for the elderly in the area.

Colonial furniture in the Museo de Arte Colonial

Museo de Arte Colonial: an arched *mediopunto* window

Besides the old portal on Calle San Ignacio, built in the Churrigueresque style which was common in Spain and her colonies in this period, there is also another entrance in 20th-century Neo-Baroque style on the Avenida del Puerto. The large central courtyard is the only one of its kind in Cuba: it has galleries on three levels, the first with simple columns, the second with double columns, and the third with plain wooden piers.

The lavishly decorated inner stairway leading to the first floor has trapezoidal motifs instead of the more common arch, and fine black mahogany banisters.

Seminario de San Carlos y San Ambrosio ❸

Calle San Ignacio 5. **Map** 4 E2.
Tel (7) 8626 989. ⬤ *by prearranged visit only.* ⬤ *1 Jan, 26 Jul, 10 Oct, 25 Dec.* 📷

This building was erected by the Jesuits in the mid-18th century to house a seminary first founded in 1689. Famous Cuban patriots and intellectuals studied here. One of them was Padre Félix Varela (1788–1853), who laid down the theoretical bases for the Cuban war of independence *(see p28).*

The seminary was relocated to a new building in Guanabacoa in late 2010. The old Havana building is currently used by the Archbishop of Cuba's office.

La Bodeguita del Medio ❹

Calle Empedrado 207. **Map** 4 E2.
Tel (7) 8671 374. ⬤ *noon–midnight daily.* 📷

Standing exactly at the halfway point in a typical small street in old Havana, a few steps away from the Cathedral, La Bodeguita del Medio (literally, "little shop in the middle") has become a big attraction.

The place was founded in 1942 as a food shop. A bar serving alcoholic drinks was added, and the place became a haunt for intellectuals, artists and politicians. Today it is no longer a shop but a bustling bar at the front serving shots of rum and Cuban cocktails and a good restaurant hidden in the back offering typical Creole dishes. The walls are plastered with photographs, drawings, graffiti and visitors' autographs, including those of famous patrons such as the singer Nat King Cole, poets Pablo Neruda and Nicolás Guillén, and the writers Gabriel García Marquez, Alejo Carpentier *(see p29),* and Ernest Hemingway, who was a regular here.

La Bodeguita del Medio with its memento-covered walls

Street-by-Street: Around Plaza de Armas

The elegant, spacious Plaza de Armas is lined with
Baroque buildings, giving it a delightful colonial
atmosphere. The space overflows with tropical
vegetation and is enlivened by the stalls of the
second-hand book market *(see p69)*. The plaza
was built in the 1600s to replace the old Plaza
Mayor, the core of Havana's religious, administrative
and military life, and up to the mid-1700s it was
used for military exercises. After its transformation
in 1771–1838, it became a favourite with rich Havana
citizens and popular as an area for carriage rides.
Following years of careful restoration work, the square
now attracts throngs of visitors and locals, many of
whom simply gather here to sit and relax.

**Palacio del
Segundo Cabo**
(1776), the former
residence of the
Spanish lieutenant
governor, is now the
home of the Cuban
Book Institute.

CALLE TACÓN

★ **Palacio de los
Capitanes Generales**
*This fine Baroque
palace, now the Museo
de la Ciudad, was
built for Cuba's old
colonial rulers. A
statue of Columbus
stands in the
courtyard, beneath
towering royal
palms* ❽

Plaza de la
Catedral
*(see
pp62–3)*

CALLE O'REILLY

CALLE MERCADERES

CALLE OBIS

STAR SIGHTS

★ Castillo
de la Real Fuerza

★ El Templete

★ Palacio de los
Capitanes Generales

★ Calle Obispo

Hotel Ambos
Mundos

Former
Ministerio
de Educación

Farmacia
Taquechel

★ **Calle Obispo**
*Like an
open-air museum
of colonial
architecture, this
street is lined with
buildings of interest
dating from the
16th–19th centuries,
including old
pharmacies and
historic shops* ❾

CALLE OBRAPÍA

Casa de la Obra Pía
*This large 17th-century
mansion is well-known for its
elaborate Baroque doorway,
which was sculpted in Spain* ❿

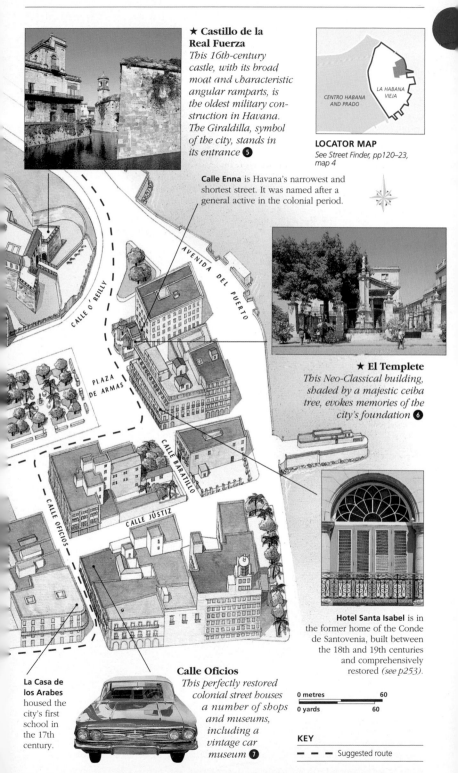

★ **Castillo de la Real Fuerza**
This 16th-century castle, with its broad moat and characteristic angular ramparts, is the oldest military construction in Havana. The Giraldilla, symbol of the city, stands in its entrance **5**

LOCATOR MAP
See Street Finder, pp120–23, map 4

Calle Enna is Havana's narrowest and shortest street. It was named after a general active in the colonial period.

★ **El Templete**
This Neo-Classical building, shaded by a majestic ceiba tree, evokes memories of the city's foundation **6**

Hotel Santa Isabel is in the former home of the Conde de Santovenia, built between the 18th and 19th centuries and comprehensively restored *(see p253).*

La Casa de los Arabes housed the city's first school in the 17th century.

Calle Oficios
This perfectly restored colonial street houses a number of shops and museums, including a vintage car museum **7**

| 0 metres | | 60 |
| 0 yards | | 60 |

KEY

– – – Suggested route

Stairway leading to the battlements, Castillo de la Real Fuerza

Castillo de la Real Fuerza **❺**

Calle Tacón e/ Calle Obispo y O'Reilly. **Map** 4 F2. **Tel** (7) 864 4490. ⬤ 9:30am–5pm Tue–Sun. 🗹 🗹 ⬤ (with charge).

This fortress *(castillo)* was built in 1558–77 to protect the city from pirate attacks, following a raid by the French buccaneer Jacques de Sores in 1555, in which the original fort was destroyed and Havana devastated *(see p40)*. But despite its moat and thick walls, the castle soon proved to be quite inadequate as a defensive bulwark because of its poor strategic position, too far inside the bay. The castle then became the residence of governors, military commanders and leading figures, as well as a safe place to store treasures brought from America and en route to Spain. In 1634, a weathervane known as La Giraldilla was placed on

---

LA GIRALDILLA

There are various theories as to the meaning of the bronze weathervane sculpted by Gerónimo Martín Pinzón in 1630–34 and modelled on the one crowning La Giralda in Seville. Some people say it is the symbol of victory, others think it is the personification of Seville, the final destination of ships going to Europe. But others say the statue represents Inés de Bobadilla, wife of the Spanish governor

The tower with its copy of the 17th-century weathervane

Hernando de Soto. According to legend, she spent hours gazing at the horizon, waiting for her husband to return from his exploration of Florida and other parts of the US (in vain, since he died on the banks of the Mississippi). This is said to be the reason why the statue was placed on the highest point of the fortress dominating the port entrance.

---

the lookout tower, which soon became the symbol of Havana. The original is on display in the entrance and a copy has been placed on the tower. In 1851, part of the fortress's façade was demolished to enable Calle O'Reilly to be extended to the waterfront. This street was named for Alejandro O'Reilly, an Irishman who became a Spanish military commander in the 18th century and who advised King Carlos III of Spain on improving Havana's defences after the British invasion of 1762.

Today, the Castillo houses a shipwreck museum with displays of artifacts, jewels and a large model of the naval ship *Santísima Trinidad.*

El Templete **❻**

Plaza de Armas, Calle Baratillo y O'Reilly. **Map** 4 F2. ⬤ 9am–5pm daily. ⬤ 1 Jan, 1 May. 🗹 🗹 ⬤ (with charge).

Small and austere, this Neo-Classical building, resembling a temple, stands on the spot where, according to legend, the city of San Cristóbal de La Habana was founded in 1599. Here, under a leafy ceiba – a tropical tree considered sacred by all the natives of Central America – the first meeting of the local government *(the cabildo)* and the first mass reputedly took place. A majestic ceiba tree still stands in front of El

View of the Castillo de la Real Fuerza: the drawbridge and entrance, the moat and the Giraldilla tower (left)

Templete, although it is not the original. Next to it is the Columna de Cacigal, a column named after the governor who ordered its construction in 1754.

El Templete, completed in 1828, was modelled after a monument in the Basque town of Guernica in northern Spain. Inside are three enormous canvases by Jean-Baptiste Vermay (see p26), depicting scenes from the history of Havana: the local authorities inaugurating the building, the first cabildo, and the first mass, which was celebrated by Bishop Juan José Díaz Espada y Land, who blessed the city as part of the ceremony.

The First Mass, one of Vermay's paintings in the Templete

Calle Oficios ❼

Map 4 F2.

This street was originally a link between the military centre of Plaza de Armas and the commercial and harbour activities centred around Plaza San Francisco. Together with Calle Obispo, this is one of the most atmospheric streets in Old Havana and should be toured slowly (don't miss the many interesting façades).

Approaching from Plaza de Armas, there are three buildings well worth visiting. The first, at No. 8, is the home of the **Museo Numismático**, built in the late 1700s and for long time the premises of the Monte de Piedad bank. According to legend it was inhabited by the ghost of a colonial lady dressed in white. It has a rich collection of coins, banknotes, old lottery tickets, medals, and Cuban and foreign bank documents.

At No. 16 is the 18th-century **Casa de los Arabes**, with displays of 18th- and 19th-century Hispanic-Arab bronzes, fabrics, rugs and furniture: the largest ethnographic display of Arab objects in Cuba, evidence of the presence of an old Lebanese, Syrian and Palestinian colony on the island. The building also houses the only mosque in Cuba and an Andalusian restaurant.

The third interesting and curious museum on the street is the **Depósito del Automóvil**, featuring vintage Cadillacs, Rolls-Royces, Packards and Fords dating from the 1930s, as well as the Bel-Air Chevrolet that once belonged to Che Guevara.

🏛 **Museo Numismático**
Tel (7) 8615 811. ⬤ 9:15am–4:45pm Tue–Sat, 9am–1pm Sun. ⬤ 1 Jan, 26 Jul, 10 Oct, 25 Dec. 🎫 📷

The Casa de los Arabes patio, with narrow balconies and a Moorish-style fountain

🏛 **Casa de los Arabes**
Tel (7) 8615 868.
⬤ 9am–5pm Tue–Sat, 9am–1pm Sun. 📷

🏛 **Depósito del Automóvil**
Tel (7) 863 9942.
⬤ 9am–5pm Tue–Sat, 9am–1pm Sun. ⬤ Mon. 🎫 📷
📷 (with charge).

THE MARKET IN PLAZA DE ARMAS

Since the early 1990s, when small businesses were officially authorized, this plaza (see p67) has been filled with colourful stalls. In the streets that surround it is a market (9am–6pm Tue–Sun) with second-hand books and periodicals of every kind, magazines published in the 1940s and 1950s, newspapers from the time of the revolution and Cuban classics now out of print. The tourist handicraft market that used to be next to the San Carlos y San Ambrosio Seminary and behind the Castillo has been moved to the Almacenes San José near the Iglesia de San Francisco de Paula, Avenida del Puerto, La Habana Vieja.

Second-hand books at the daily market in the Plaza de Armas

Palacio de los Capitanes Generales ❽

Early 19th-century marble bathtub in the bathroom

Construction of this palace, a splendid example of Cuban Baroque *(see p24)*, took from 1776 to 1791. It was commissioned by the governor Felipe Fondesviela and designed by engineer Antonio Fernández de Trebejos y Zaldívar. The Palacio originally housed the Chapter House and the governor's residence as well as a house of detention, which until 1834 occupied the west wing. The seat of the Cuban Republic in 1902, the building became the Museo de la Ciudad (City Museum) in 1967, but the original structure of the sumptuous residence and political centre has not been altered. The complex as a whole offers an overview of the history of Havana, from the remains of the old Espada cemetery and Parroquial Mayor church to mementoes from the wars of independence.

★ Hall of Flags
This hall contains objects from the independence wars, including the flag of Céspedes (see p42).

The Cabildo Maces
Considered the first major example of Cuban goldsmithery, these maces, by Juan Díaz (1631), are on display in the Sala del Cabildo, the room where local town council meetings were held in the governor's palace.

★ Christ of Humbleness and Patience
Once carried through the streets in processions, this 18th-century devotional wooden statue is, in the fashion of the time, naturalistically painted with glass eyes and real hair to increase its dramatic impact on the faithful.

Leather Cannon
Taken from the Cuban independence fighters by the Spanish army in 1873, this makeshift weapon – a lead pipe wrapped in horsehide – was loaded with whatever projectiles were at hand, from shrapnel to stones.

STAR SIGHTS

- ★ Christ of Humbleness and Patience
- ★ Hall of Flags
- ★ Salón de los Espejos

Gallery

The monumental gallery, which overlooks a large, leafy courtyard, features a collection of busts of illustrious figures, the work of the Italian sculptor Luigi Pietrasanta in the early 1900s.

VISITORS' CHECKLIST

Plaza de Armas, Calle
Tacón e/ O'Reilly y Obispo.
Map 4 E2. **Tel** (7) 8612
876, 8615 062. ☐ 9:30am–
4pm Tue–Sun. 🖼 ✔
📷 (with charge). 🚻

The White Room
has on display the
escutcheons of Bourbon
Spain and the city of
Havana, and is decorated
with 18th- and 19th-
century Meissen
porcelain.

Throne Room

Modelled on the large salon in the Palacio de Oriente in Madrid, this room was originally built for a Spanish monarch, but never used. It was restored in 1893 for the visit of Princess Eulalia of Bourbon.

The stained-glass windows brighten the grey of the *piedra marina*, a limestone encrusted with coral fossils.

The Espada Cemetery Room
has relics from the first city
cemetery, founded by Bishop
Juan José Díaz de Espada in 1806.
They include the tomb of the
French artist Vermay (*see p26*).

★ Salón de los Espejos

The end of Spanish rule was proclaimed in 1899 in this light-filled salon with its 19th-century Venetian mirrors, and in 1902 the first president of the Republic of Cuba took office here.

The portico pavement, made of *china pelona*, a hard, shiny stone, dates from the 18th century.

Casa del Agua la Tinaja, vendor of purified well water

Calle Obispo 9

Map 4 E2.

The liveliest and most characteristic street in Old Havana is like a long, narrow bridge linking the two architectural souls of the historic centre, the colonial and the Art Nouveau-eclectic. At one end is the Plaza de Armas, the Cuban Baroque heart of the old city, while at the other is Avenida de Bélgica and the famous El Floridita restaurant, which mark the start of the more modern district. The street is called Calle Obispo because in the past the city bishop *(obispo)* resided in the building situated on the corner of Calle Oficios.

Old filter, Taquechel pharmacy

Thanks to the restoration work promoted by the Oficina del Historiador de la Ciudad, headed by the charismatic Eusebio Leal Spengler, aimed at salvaging the best buildings in the old area, Calle Obispo has retained the elegance, vivacity and colours of the colonial period. Street lighting makes for enjoyable evening strolling.

A plaque on the left-hand side of the Palacio de los Capitanes Generales bears quotations made by the great Cuban patriot José Martí concerning Garibaldi's stop at Havana. Opposite is the small

shop window of the **Casa del Agua la Tinaja**, which for centuries has been selling well water purified by very old but still quite efficient ceramic filters. Next door, **La Mina** restaurant serves food and cocktails outdoors and brightens up the whole block with live traditional music *(see p276)*.

Among the most fascinating shops in this part of the street is the old pharmacy called **Taquechel**, which sells cosmetics and natural and homeopathic products, all created and produced in Cuba. Quaint shelves boast a pretty collection of 17th- and 18th-century glass and Italian majolica jars, as well as alembics and antique pharmaceutical and medical objects. No. 117–19 is the oldest house in Havana *(see p24)*.

One of the major sights in the street is the restored **Hotel Ambos Mundos** *(see p253)*. This charming, eclectically decorated hotel is rich in literary memories. The writer Ernest Hemingway stayed here for long periods from 1932 to 1939 *(see p114)*, and began writing his famous novel *For Whom the Bell Tolls* in room 511.

Towards the end of the street, near the small Obispo y Bernaza square, there are

Wooden *"azul avana"* blue doors of the Colonial house at No. 117

more modern shops offering everything from embroidered shirts to books.

Next is **El Floridita** restaurant *(see p277)*, known as "the cradle of the daiquiri". It was here, in the 1930s, that barman Constante (his real name was Constantino Ribalaigua) perfected the original cocktail mixed by Pagluchi *(see p275)*. The new-style daiquiri, a blend of white rum, lemon, sugar and a few drops of maraschino and ice, was devised with the help of Ernest Hemingway, who was a regular. Today, in El Floridita's luxurious interior, besides Constante's classic cocktails you can feast on lobster and shellfish in the company of a bust of the great novelist. It was sculpted by Fernando Boada while Hemingway was still alive.

An old letter box at No.115

Typical majolica jars on the shelves of the former Sala Museo

For hotels and restaurants in this region see pp252–6 and pp276–9

The upper gallery of the Casa de la Obra Pía, with its frescoed walls and polished wood balustrade

Casa de la Obra Pía ⑩

Calle Obrapía 158 esq. Mercaderes. **Map** 4 E2. **Tel** (7) 8613 097.
⬤ currently closed for restoration
🔲 📷

Calle Obrapía (literally Charity Street) was named after this mansion, whose own name commemorates the pious actions of Martín Calvo de la Puerta y Arrieta, a wealthy Spanish nobleman who took up residence here in the mid-17th century. Every year he gave a generous dowry to five orphan girls for them to use to get married or enter a convent. A century later the residence became the home of Don Agustín de Cárdenas, who was given the title of marquis for taking Spain's side in 1762 during the British occupation of Havana (see p40). In 1793 new decoration, and the elaborate arch leading to the loggia on the first floor, were added to the building.

La Casa de la Obra Pía is regarded as one of the jewels of Cuban Baroque architecture, and its luxurious salons were used for young noblewomen to make their debut in society.

Majolica tile street sign for Calle de la Obrapía

Many colourful legends survive concerning the building's past. It was said that incredible treasures were hidden in its walls and that wailing and weeping could be heard from one of the rooms on the upper floor.

At the corner of Calle Obrapía and Calle Mercaderes is the **Casa de México**, a cultural centre that shows the close links between Mexico and Cuba. It has a library with more than 5,000 books and a museum displaying handmade glass, silver, fabric, terracotta and wooden objects. Lastly, on the other side of the street is the **Casa de Guayasamín**, named after the Ecuadorean painter whose works are on display.

Palo Monte objects (see p23), Casa de Africa

Casa de Africa ⑪

Calle Obrapía 157 e/ San Ignacio y Mercaderes. **Map** 4 E2. **Tel** (7) 8615 798 ⬤ 9am–5pm Tue–Sat, 9am–1pm Sun. ⬤ 1 Jan, 26 Jul, 10 Oct, 25 Dec. 🔲 🔲 📷 (with charge).

Opposite the Casa de la Obra Pía is a 17th-century building that was rebuilt in 1887 to accommodate a family of plantation owners on the upper floor and a tobacco factory, worked by slaves, on the ground floor. It is appropriate that the building is now a museum containing more than 2,000 objects linked to the history of sub-Saharan Africa and the various ethnic groups that were taken to Cuba on slave ships. Many of these items belonged to the ethnographer Fernando Ortíz, a specialist in the African roots of Cuban culture. Together with the section on religion, which includes objects from the various Afro-Cuban religions (see pp22–3), there are instruments of torture used on the slaves, batá drums, and paintings of plantation life. The museum also has a well-stocked library.

Plaza de San Francisco ⑫

Map 4 F2. **Basílica Menor de San Francisco de Asís** *Tel* (7) 862 9683. ⬜ 9:30am–4:30pm Tue–Sat, 9:30am–1pm Sun. ⬛ 1 Jan, 1 May, 26 Jul, 10 Oct, 25 Dec. 🖼 📷 📷

Bordering the port, this picturesque square has an Andalusian character and evokes images of a distant age when galleons loaded with gold and other cargo set sail for Spain. In the middle of the square is the **Fuente de los Leones**, modelled on the famous fountain in the Alhambra in Granada. This work by the Italian sculptor Giuseppe Gaggini was donated in 1836 by the fiscal superintendent, Don Claudio Martínez de Pinillos, the Count of Villanueva, and for many years it supplied the ships docked here with drinking water.

The original commercial nature of the area can be seen in two buildings: the Aduana General de la República (the old customs house), built in 1914, and the **Lonja del Comercio** (the former stock exchange, 1908), with a dome crowned by a statue of Mercury, god of commerce. Restored in 1995, this building houses the offices of some of the top foreign firms now operating in Cuba.

The most important building in the square, however, is the **Basílica Menor de San Francisco de Asís**, built in

The Fuente de los Leones, Plaza de San Francisco

1580–91 as the home of the Franciscan community and partly rebuilt in the 1700s. The three-aisle interior has a Latin cross layout and contains some paintings by unknown 18th-century Cuban artists and a wooden statue of St Francis dating from the same period, again by an unknown artist. The basilica also has the remains of major Havana citizens, from the Marquis González, who died during the British siege of 1762, to José Martín Félix de Arrate, an illustrious historian of the colonial period. Because of its exceptional acoustics, this church has been converted into a concert hall for choral and chamber music *(see p125)*.

Attached to the church is a large, 42-m (138-ft) high bell

Logo of the Havana Club Foundation

tower that affords a lovely view of the city. Originally a statue of St Francis of Assisi stood on the top, but it was badly damaged by a cyclone in 1846.

In the cloister and rooms of the adjacent monastery, which dates back to 1739, is a museum of holy art with 18th–19th-century missals, a collection of votive objects made of precious metals, and 16th–18th-century majolica and ceramics.

Museo del Ron ⑬

Calle San Pedro 262. **Map** 4 F3. *Tel* (7) 861 8051. ⬜ 9am–5pm Mon–Thu, 9am–4pm Fri–Sun. 🖼 📷 📷 📷 🖥 www. havanaclubfoundation.com

The manufacture of Havana Club, the most famous brand of Cuban rum, is displayed here with visuals and models that explain the production process of the spirit described as the "cheerful child of sugar cane" by Cuban writer and journalist Fernando Campoamor, a friend of Ernest Hemingway. The organized tours begin in the colonial courtyard of the Havana Club Foundation. After watching a brief film on the history of sugar cane and its cultivation, visitors are taken through rooms with exhibits that explain the fermentation, distillation (in a room with old alembics), filtration, ageing, blending and bottling processes. In the central hall is a fascinating model of an *ingenio (see pp42–3)*, or sugar plantation, which also includes a miniature steam train. Tours end in a bar where visitors can relax and sample three-year-old rum. The street-front bar also serves excellent cocktails and often has live music; it is open from 9am to midnight. The shop sells rum, glassware and various souvenirs.

Interior of the basilica of San Francisco, now used for chamber music concerts

Cuban Rum

The history of rum dates back to the early 1500s, when an impure distillate was first obtained from sugar cane. With the arrival of Facundo Bacardí *(see p228)*, a new technique of distillation was introduced, and Cuban rum *(ron)* went on to enjoy international success. Rum is part of everyday life in Cuba: a constant companion at parties and festivities, the main ingredient in cocktails, and an offering that is frequently given to the gods of *Santería*. Rum-making begins with the main by-product of sugar, the sticky amber paste called molasses, which is diluted with water and fermented using special yeasts. The "must" thus obtained is then distilled and filtered to produce an eau de vie. Purified water and pure alcohol are then added 18 months later to produce Silver Dry, a young, clear rum.

Seal of guarantee of Cuban rum

Distillation, *which used to be effected by means of alembics (left), is now carried out by using a series of connected tubes in which the molasses vapour is channelled until it condenses and is transformed into a colourless liquid that is then aged in special barrels.*

The *mezcla* process *is carried out under the expert guidance of a master taster and consists of mixing the new rum with other rums. Once blended, the rum rests for a few weeks in special vats until the right balance of taste and aroma is obtained.*

Special oak barrels *are used for the ageing process which takes at least three years. With time the rum becomes richer in colour and more full-bodied, like the seven-year añejo. The temperature, humidity level and ventilation in the ageing cellars are carefully regulated.*

THE TYPES OF RUM

Besides Silver Dry, which is normally used in cocktails, the market offers rum aged for three years *(carta blanca)*, five years *(carta oro)*, and seven years *(añejo)*, or even longer. Old rum, which is the most highly prized, should be drunk neat and at room temperature, while *carta blanca*, which is the most commonly seen, can be used in many ways and is often drunk with ice. There are assorted brands of Cuban rum, not all of which are internationally known like Havana Club.

Silver Dry   Carta Blanca   Carta Oro   Añejo

The cloister of the convent of Santa Clara, filled with tropical plants

Plaza Vieja 🄯

Map 4 E3.

This square was laid out in 1559 and was originally called Plaza Nueva (New Square). In the 19th century, after the widening of Plaza de Armas and the creation of other urban areas, it lost its role as the city's main public square and was renamed Plaza Vieja. From the 1950s to the 90s it was a car park, but it has now been restored to its original appearance.

The plaza is surrounded by arcades and a number of historic buildings from four different centuries. The most important of these is the **Casa del Conde Jaruco**, built in 1733–37. This was the home of the Countess de Merlin, a Cuban romantic novelist who

became a French citizen and also wrote a travel book about Cuba. The house is now used for art exhibitions. The spacious salon on the first floor, with its large fine stained-glass windows or *mediopuntos (see p25)*, is well worth a visit.

Next door are two 17th-century buildings, and at the corner of Calle Muralla and Calle Inquisidor is the eye-catching Art Nouveau Hotel-Palacio Cueto. It was first built as a hotel in 1908, then later turned into apartments and is now being restored as a five-star hotel.

A fountain designed in 1796 stands in the middle of the square. It bears the crest of the city and of the Count of Santa Clara, then the city's governor. Nearby are a centre for visual arts, a photo gallery and a high-tech planetarium.

Convento de Santa Clara 🄯

Calle Cuba 610 e/ Sol y Luz.
Map 4 E3. **Tel** (7) 8613 335.
⬤ *closed for restoration.* 🎨 📷 🚻
📷 *(with charge – phone ahead for more information).*

The Convent of Santa Clara is one of the oldest and most typical colonial religious buildings in the New World. The convent occupies a considerable area of La Habana Vieja and was founded in 1644 by Sister Catalina de Mendoza from Cartagena de Indias, to offer refuge for the wealthy girls of the city.

The plain exterior, with its simple windows, makes a striking contrast to the interior, which has a colonnaded courtyard with elaborate inlaid wooden ceilings. Two of the three original cloisters have stood the test of time. In one of them, overflowing with luxuriant tropical vegetation and with an 18th-century fountain known as "The Samaritan", is the Centro Nacional de Conservación, Restauración y Museología, a body which coordinates the preservation and restoration of Cuba's historic architecture.

The second cloister is now part of a charming hotel decorated in colonial style. Parts of the building are open to the public but it cannot be seen in its entirety.

Façade of Casa del Conde Jaruco, with typical *mediopunto* stained-glass windows on the first floor

For hotels and restaurants in this region see pp252–6 and pp276–9

The nave of the Iglesia de la Merced, illuminated by small light bulbs

Iglesia del Espíritu Santo ⑯

Calle Cuba esq. Acosta. **Map** 4 E3.
Tel (7) 862 3410. ◻ 9am–12:30pm,
3–6pm Tue–Fri, 9am–3pm Sat, 9am–
noon Sun. ◙ ✚ 5pm Thu & Sat,
10:30am Sun.

The Church of the Holy Ghost
(Espíritu Santo) is of historical
importance as one of the oldest
Roman Catholic churches in
Havana. It was built in 1637
by freed African slaves. Thanks
to a papal bull and a royal
decree from Carlos III, in 1772
it acquired the exclusive right
to grant asylum to all those
persecuted by the authorities.

From an architectural
standpoint, the building's
most striking feature is the
tower, which is almost as tall
as the one on the Basilica of
San Francisco (see p74). The
church was radically rebuilt in
the 19th century, retaining its
Hispanic-Arab look only in
the characteristic double pitch
roof. The main chapel was
built by Bishop Jerónimo
Valdés in 1706–29.

The area around the church
plays host to one of the most
picturesque religious markets

in the city, in which the
yerberos, or herbalist-healers,
sell votive objects and various
herbs that are used mostly in
the local Afro-Cuban religious
rites (see pp22–3).

Iglesia de Nuestra Señora de la Merced ⑰

Calle Cuba 806. **Map** 4 E3.
Tel (7) 8638 873. ◻ 8am–noon,
3–5pm daily. ◙ ✚ 9am Thu–Tue.

Construction of this
church began in
1637 but ended only
in the following
century, while the
lavish decoration of
the interior dates
from the 19th
century. The church
is popular among
those who follow
Santería, or local
Afro-Cuban religion
(see pp22–3).
According to the
beliefs of this cult, Our Lady
of the Merced corresponds to
a Yoruba divinity known as
Obatalá, principal figure
among the gods and the

protector of mankind, who
imparts wisdom and harmony.
On the Catholic saint's feast
day, 24 September, Santería
followers come dressed all in
white – the colour associated
with Obatalá.

Museo José Martí ⑱

Calle Leonor Perez 314, esq. Egido.
Map 4 E4. **Tel** (7) 8613 778.
◻ 9:30am–4:30pm Tue–Sat,
9:30am–12:30pm Sun. ● 1 Jan, 1
May, 26 Jul, 10 Oct, 25 Dec. ◙ ◙
◙ (with charge).

This modest 19th-century
building in the Paula quarter
became a national monument
thanks to the special historic
importance attached to José
Martí (see p45), who is the
object of great patriotic veneration. The author and national
hero, who died in combat on
19 May 1895 during the wars
of independence against the
Spanish, was born here in
1853. After his death, his
mother Leonor Pérez lived
in the building, and when
she died it was rented to
raise money to bring up her
grandchildren. In 1901 it was
purchased by the municipality
after city-wide fundraising,
and was turned into a museum in 1925, but government
funding only became sufficient
with the advent of Fidel Castro.

The house has been
restored beautifully, and
visitors can view furniture,
paintings, and first editions of
the writer's works. There are
also objects of great historic
value such as the
inkpot and ivory
pen used by
Generalissimo
Máximo Gómez and
José Martí to sign
the Manifesto de
Montecristi, which
officially marked
the beginning of the
war against Spain.
Everyday objects
are also on display,
such as the pen-
knife Martí had in
his pocket when he died, and
the album with dedications
and signatures from friends
during his wedding to
Carmen Zayas-Bazán.

Portrait of José Martí
by Herman Norman
in the museum

CENTRO HABANA AND PRADO

Centro Habana has the air of an impoverished aristocrat – a noble creature whose threadbare clothes belie a splendid past full of treasures. This varied quarter developed beyond the city walls (which ran parallel to present-day Avenida Bélgica and Avenida de las Misiones) during the 1800s and was initially built to provide houses

Remains of the old walls

and greenery for the citizens. Most construction took place after 1863, when the walls began to be demolished to make more land available. The work was finally completed in the 1920s and 30s, when French architect Forestier landscaped the area of the Paseo del Prado, the Parque Central, the Capitolio gardens and Parque de la Fraternidad.

SIGHTS AT A GLANCE

Historic Buildings
Capitolio pp82–3 ❸
Castillo de San Salvador
   de la Punta ❽
Hotel Inglaterra ❶
Palacio de Aldama ❻
Real Fábrica de Tabacos
   Partagás ❺

Historic Streets and Plazas
Avenida Carlos III ⓯
Callejón de Hammel ⓰
City Walls ⓱
Parque de la Fraternidad ❹
Paseo del Prado pp86–7 ❼

Quarters
Barrio Chino ⓭

Theatres
Gran Teatro de La Habana ❷

Churches
Iglesia del Ángel Custodio ❿
Iglesia del Sagrado
   Corazón ⓮

Museums
Museo Nacional de Bellas
   Artes pp92–5 ⓬
Museo Nacional de la Música ❾
*Museo de la Revolución
   pp88–9* ⓫

KEY

  Street-by-Street map *pp80–81*

🚃 Railway station

GETTING THERE
The easiest way to get to this quarter is by taxi, and the best way to explore it is on foot. When map reading, bear in mind that the commonly used names of the streets differ from the official ones *(see p118).*

Estación Central

0 metres   800
0 yards   800

◁ Classic American cars line up outside the Gran Teatro, Centro Habana *(see p82)*

eet-by-Street: Around the Parque Central

Lying on the border of the old city and Centro Habana, between the Capitolio and the Prado promenade, the Parque Central was designed in 1877 after the old city walls were demolished. A statue of Isabella II was put in the middle of the square but was later replaced by one of José Martí. The park is surrounded by 19th- and 20th-century monumental buildings and adorned with palm trees, and is the heart of the city centre, a popular meeting place. Towards evening, when the air is cooler, people gather here to talk until the small hours of the night about baseball, music and politics.

★ Gran Teatro de La Habana
With one of its rooms named after the great Spanish poet, García Lorca, who stayed in Havana for a few months in 1930, the theatre is a mixture of influences with slender, angular towers ❷

Real Fábrica de Tabacos Partagás
This elegant red and cream-coloured building is home to a prestigious cigar factory ❺

Parque de la Fraternidad
The park was laid out in 1892 to celebrate the 400th anniversary of the discovery of America ❹

CALLE SAN MARTIN (SAN JOSÉ)

CALLE INDUSTRIA

CALLE DRAGONES

PASEO DE MARTÍ (PRADO)

CALLE BRASIL

The Cinema Payret, Cuba's first motion picture theatre, opened in 1897, a year after the Lumière brothers presented their invention in Paris.

STAR SIGHTS

★ Capitolio

★ Gran Teatro de La Habana

★ Hotel Inglaterra

★ Paseo del Prado

★ Capitolio
The dome of one of the most imposing buildings in Latin America towers over the urban landscape of Havana ❸

★ Hotel Inglaterra
This historic hotel has retained its 19th-century atmosphere. Despite the British name, the architectural elements and decoration are clearly Spanish-inspired ❶

LOCATOR MAP
See Street Finder, pp120–23, map 4

Calle San Rafael, known as *Boulevard*, is a narrow street for pedestrians only. Up to the 1950s it was famous for its luxury shops and boutiques.

The Hotel Parque Central is relatively modern but its style and decor blend in well with the surroundings *(see p254).*

★ Paseo del Prado
This avenue, the locals' favourite for strolling, is lined with lovely buildings with carefully restored arcades ❼

The statue of José Martí, Cuba's national hero, was sculpted in Carrara marble in Rome by José Vilalta y Saavedra and inaugurated on 24 February 1905 by Generalissimo Máximo Gómez.

CALLE NEPTUNO

RQUE CENTRAL

CALLE SAN RAFAEL

0 metres   100
0 yards   100

KEY

– – – Suggested route

The Manzana de Gómez, a 19th-century building, was once a major commercial centre, and gradually shops are returning here.

The Hotel Plaza, built in the 19th century as a private residence, became a hotel in 1909. It was frequented by great artists of the time, from Isadora Duncan to Enrico Caruso and Anna Pavlova *(see p254).*

The Centro Asturiano, with the characteristic towers on its corners, was designed by Spanish architect Manuel del Busto and opened in 1928. It is home to the Museo de Bellas Artes' international art collection *(see pp92–5).*

Hotel Inglaterra ❶

Paseo de Martí (Prado) 416, esq. a San Rafael. **Map** 4 D2. **Tel** (7) 860 8594. See p254.

Although this hotel is built in the style of late 19th-century Havana Neo-Classical architecture, its soul is *mudéjar* (Moorish): the fine ochre, green and gold majolica tiles of the interior were imported from Seville, the foyer is decorated with Andalusian mosaics, and the wooden ceilings are reminiscent of Moorish inlay. Plus, one of the columns in the *salón-café* bears a classical Arabic inscription: "Only Allah is the victor". The Hotel Inglaterra dates from 1875, when a small hotel merged with the lively Le Louvre night spot and its adjacent ballroom. The pavement outside the hotel, known as the "Louvre sidewalk", was an animated meeting point for Havana liberals. It was here that the young José Martí *(see p45)* advocated total separation from Spain, as opposed to more moderate liberal demands for autonomy. General Antonio Maceo, a hero of the wars of Cuban independence, prepared plans for insurrection in this hotel.

Among many illustrious guests were the great French actress Sarah Bernhardt and the Russian ballet dancer Anna Pavlova.

Gran Teatro de La Habana ❷

Paseo de Martí (Prado) y San Rafael, Central Havana. **Map** 4 D2. **Tel** (7) 861 3077. ⬜ 10am–4pm Mon–Fri. ⚫ 1 Jan, 1 May, 26 Jul, 10 Oct, 25 Dec. 🎦 🎟 📷 (with charge).

One of the world's largest opera houses, Gran Teatro de La Habana is part of the monumental Palacio del Centro Gallego (1915), designed by Belgian architect Paul Belau to host the social activities of Havana's large and affluent Spanish community.

The magnificent façade is decorated with four sculpture

The staircase of honour, originally reserved for MPs

Capitolio ❸

A symbol of the city, the Capitol (Capitolio) combines the elegance of Neo-Classicism with Art Deco elements. Inaugurated in 1929 by the dictator Gerardo Machado, it is a loose imitation of the Washington DC Capitol, but is even taller. It stands in an area once occupied by a botanical garden and later by the capital's first railway station. The home of government until 1959, the Capitol has seen major historic events: in 1933 the police fired on a crowd gathered here during an anti-Machado demonstration. Today the magnificent building houses the Ministry of Science, Technology and the Environment. It is currently closed to the public while it undergoes a major restoration.

National Library of Science and Technology

Chamber of Deputies
The Chamber still has its original furnishings and is decorated with bas-reliefs by the Italian artist Gianni Remuzzi.

STAR SIGHTS

★ Salón de los Pasos Perdidos

★ Dome

Façade of the former Centro Gallego building, now home to the Gran Teatro

groups by the Italian sculptor Giuseppe Moretti, depicting Charity, Education, Music and Theatre. The building lies over the foundations of the Teatro Nuevo or Tacón. From 1837 to the early 20th century this was the venue for performances by world-famous artists, including the Austrian ballet dancer Fanny Essler, who made her debut here on 23 January 1841. In the mid-19th century Antonio Meucci, the inventor of the "talking telephone", worked here as a stagehand, and his invention was patented in the US, thanks to the support of the Gran Teatro's impresario.

The theatre was inaugurated on 22 April 1915 with a performance of Verdi's *Aida*, and became a stage for great dramatic occasions. Sarah Bernhardt performed here in 1918, and the pianist Arthur Rubinstein the following year. Cuban composer Ernesto Lecuona and the great Spanish guitarist Andrés Segovia have also appeared.

In 1959 the Gran Teatro, though continuing in its role as a concert hall and theatre, became the "home" of Alicia Alonso, the great Cuban ballet dancer. She founded the Ballet Nacional, which is the dance company and school known for organizing a famous biennial ballet festival (*see p125*).

★ **Dome**
Almost 92 m (300 ft) high, the dome was the highest point in the city until the 1950s.

Parliament

VISITORS' CHECKLIST

Paseo de Martí (Prado) esq. a San José. **Map** 4 D3.
***Tel** (7) 861 5519.*
◐ *closed for restoration.*
🖼 📷 🎒 📷 *(with charge).*

★ **Salón de los Pasos Perdidos**
This sumptuous hall, with fine marble floors and gilded lamps, takes its name ("Hall of Lost Steps") from its unusual acoustics.

A copy of a 25-carat diamond
is embedded in the floor beneath the dome. The original belonged to the last Tsar of Russia and was sold to the Cuban state by a Turkish jeweller. It was stolen and, mysteriously, later turned up on the President's desk.

Statue of the Republic
This work, cast in Rome and covered with 22-carat gold leaf, stands 17 m (56 ft) high and weighs 49 tons. It is the third tallest statue in the world.

Parque de la Fraternidad ❹

Map 4 D3.

The spacious area of greenery behind the Capitol was called Campo di Marte (Parade Ground) in the 19th century, because it was near the Paseo Militar, used frequently for army drill. As the Parque de la Fraternidad (since 1928), it commemorates Cuba's common roots with the other people of the Americas, with monuments to major figures such as the Argentine José de San Martín, the Venezuelan Simón Bolívar, and US president Abraham Lincoln.

In the middle of the park is a gate with a plaque bearing an exhortation by José Martí: "It is time to gather and march together united, we must go forward as compact as the silver in the depths of the Andes. Peoples unite only through bonds of friendship, fraternity and love." Beyond the gate is a monument to American friendship and solidarity: a large ceiba – a tree sacred to both the Amerindians and the African slaves taken to the New World – planted here around 1920.

In front of the square is a white marble fountain, sculpted in 1831 by Giuseppe Gaggini. The fountain is known as the "Fuente de la India" or "La Noble Habana" – an allegorical representation of the city.

Nowadays the Parque de la Fraternidad is usually full of old American cars, most of which operate as private taxis.

The Fuente de la India symbolizing Havana

Façade of the Partagás cigar factory with its prominent pediments

Real Fábrica de Tabacos Partagás ❺

Calle Industria 524. **Map** 4 D3. **Tel** (7) 862 4604. ⬤ *closed for restoration; call for more information.* 📷 🏛 📷 🖥 🚫

Cuba's largest cigar factory, with its Neo-Classical façade, is a good example of 19th-century industrial architecture. It was founded in 1845 by the ambitious Catalan businessman Jaime Partagás Ravelo. However, he never revealed the sources of his tobacco leaves or how they were processed. The only information that survives is that he was the first person to use wooden barrels to ferment the leaves in order to heighten the aroma.

With the profits made from his high-quality cigars, Partagás bought a plantation in the province of Pinar del Río. He wanted to oversee all aspects of the cigar-making process personally, from growing the plants to the placing of a wrapper leaf around the filler and binder leaves rolled by the *torcedor (see p33)*. However, Partagás was assassinated in mysterious circumstances

Neon sign at the Partagás cigar factory

and the project failed. His factory was then purchased by another shrewd businessman, Ramón Cifuentes Llano.

Dozens of people work in the aroma-filled interior. Nowadays, there is no longer someone reading aloud to alleviate the monotony of the work by entertaining and educating the workers, as was the case in the 19th century (Partagás himself introduced this custom to Cuba).

However there is a loudspeaker that alternates reading passages with music and news on the radio. Connected to the factory is La Casa del Habano, an excellent shop with a back room that is used for sampling cigars.

Palacio de Aldama ❻

Avenída Simón Bolívar (Reina) y Máximo Gómez (Monte). **Map** 4 D3. ⬤ *to the public.*

This mansion *(see p25)* was designed by Manuel José Carrera and built in the middle of the 19th century, having been commissioned by the rich Basque industrialist Domingo de Aldama y Arrechaga. He had to depend on his influential friends in order to obtain permission to build his residence in front of the Campo di Marte, or Parade Ground, which was reserved for military and administrative buildings. The monumental grandeur of this Neo-Classical building, considered the finest example of 19th-century architecture in Cuba, is still striking. The mansion is now the seat of the Instituto de Historia de Cuba. Sadly, it is not officially open to the public, but upon request the porter allows visitors to go into the courtyard to admire the impressive marble staircases, Baroque arches, splendid wrought iron with Imperial motifs and the two inner gardens with fountains made of Carrara marble.

The monument to General Máximo Gómez

Paseo del Prado **7**

See pp86–7.

Castillo de San Salvador de la Punta **8**

Malecón y Paseo de Martí (Prado). **Map** 4 D1. *Tel* (7) 8603 196. ⬤ *closed for restoration.* 🖼 🗚

A modest fortified block on the west bank of the port entrance, this fortress *(castillo)* makes an ideal setting for political speeches and concerts because of its elevated position near the road. In the past it played a crucial role in the defence system of the capital but today it is a naval museum. Designed by Giovanni

Bautista Antonelli, Juan de Tejeda and Cristóbal de Roda and built in 1590–1630, it was part of the city's first line of defence, together with the much larger Castillo de los Tres Reyes del Morro on the other side of the bay.

A large floating chain of wooden and bronze rings, an ingenious device added by the Italian engineer Antonelli in the late 16th century, connected the two fortresses. It was stretched tightly as soon as an enemy ship was sighted, to block access to the port. In the open space in front of the Castillo are the three cannons to which the chain was tied.

The adjacent forecourt has several monuments that are more important historically than artistically. In the middle is the equestrian statue of Generalissimo Máximo Gómez, the hero of the wars of independence, by Italian sculptor Aldo Gamba (1935). Behind this, a dilapidated chapel is used daily for stamp exhibitions and history lectures. It originally belonged to the Real Cárcel prison, where José Martí was kept for 16 years for subversive activities against the Spanish crown. Some cells still stand, as does a section of the wall against which some medical students were executed on 27 November 1871 as punishment for rebelling against Spanish rule. A cenotaph in their honour stands in the Columbus cemetery *(see p104).*

The Museo de la Música, an example of eclectic architecture

Museo Nacional de la Música **9**

Calle Capdevila 1, e/ Habana y Aguiar. **Map** 4 E1. *Tel* (7) 8619 846, 8630 052. ⬤ *closed for restoration; call before visiting.* 🖼 🗚 🗚

The building (1905) that houses the National Music Museum is a mixture of different styles, a perfect example of 20th-century eclectic architecture. It was the residence of a family of opera lovers, whose guests included such illustrious figures as the great Italian tenor Enrico Caruso and the Spanish poet Federico García Lorca.

The museum was founded in 1971, and contains the largest collection of traditional musical instruments in Cuba, gathered by the ethnologist Fernando Ortiz, a pioneer in the study of Cuba's African roots. Besides the most complete collection of African drums in the world, there is the piano of singer and composer Bola de Nieve *(see p30)* and 40 guitars used by legendary figures of 20th-century Cuban music, such as the Trío Matamoros and Sindo Garay. Also on show are gramophones and phonographs, photos and famous composers' original manuscripts. In the foyer is a music stand with the score of the Bayamo, the Cuban national anthem. Visitors can consult specialist Cuban and foreign periodicals, as well as the archive of rare musical documents.

Castillo de la Punta ramparts and the Morro fortress behind

Paseo del Prado ⓪

The most picturesque boulevard in Havana is popular in
the daytime for a gentle stroll and gossip in the shade
of the trees, and at sunset is one of the locals' main
haunts. The Marquis de la Torre had the Paseo laid out
in 1772 outside the city walls, and it rapidly became the
favourite spot for city aristocrats to take their carriage
rides. Bands were positioned in five spots along the
boulevard to play for their enjoyment. The Paseo
was used for military and carnival parades in the
19th century, when the paving was redone. In 1927
the French architect Forestier designed the Prado
as we see it today: it was widened and lined
with bronze lions and marble benches.

Lions
*Eight imposing bronze lions,
symbolizing Havana, were
added to the boulevard in
1927, together with the
marble benches.*

Neo-Moorish Building
*The building at the
corner of Calle Virtudes,
richly decorated and with
mudéjar arches, shows
many architectural
influences and is
typical of Havana.*

Casa del Científico
was the residence of
José Miguel Gómez,
second President of the
Republic of Cuba.

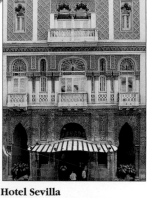

Hotel Sevilla
*This historic hotel opened in
1908 and a ten-storey tower was
added in 1917. It is a homage to
Moorish architecture: the façade
and hall decoration are mudé...
(see p24) in style.*

Palacio de los Matrimonios
*Named after the civil weddings celebrated on
the first floor, this Neo-Baroque building was
inaugurated in 1914 as the Casino Español.*

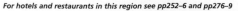
For hotels and restaurants in this region see pp252–6 and pp276–9

Children playing in the shade during school break

Home of Dr Carlos Finlay, who discovered that mosquitoes spread yellow fever.

```
0 metres        60
0 yards         60
```

The Teatro Fausto was built in 1938 over the foundations of an old theatre of the same name.

Restored Buildings
These porticoed buildings were built along the avenue in the late 19th to early 20th century as private homes. They have been carefully restored, and the original bright pastel colours have been brought back to life.

Street Lamps
Elegant wrought-iron street lamps were added in 1834, together with the multi-coloured marble pavement.

Iglesia del Ángel Custodio ⑩

Calle Compostela 2, esq. Cuarteles.
Map 4 D2. *Tel* (7) 8610 469.
🕙 8:30am–6pm Mon–Fri,
8:30am–noon Sun. 🕕 6pm Tue
& Thu; 9am Sun.

Built in 1693 on the Peña Pobre or "Loma del Ángel" hill as a hermitage and then transformed into a church in 1788, today the Neo-Gothic Ángel Custodio looks rather too white and unreal as a result of vigorous "restoration".

Standing in a key position between the former presidential palace (now the Museo de la Revolución) and the old town, it exudes literary references. The 19th-century Cuban novelist Cirilo Villaverde *(see p28)* used the Loma del Ángel hill as the setting for his story *Cecilia Valdés* about the tragic love affair between a Creole woman and a rich white man.

Félix Varela *(see p28)* and José Martí *(see p45)* were both baptised in this church.

The bell tower and spires of the church of Ángel Custodio

GRAHAM GREENE IN HAVANA

The classic espionage thriller *Our Man in Havana* (1958), by the English author Graham Greene, is an excellent description of Havana at the eve of the Revolution. In the book Greene narrates the adventures of a vacuum cleaner salesman who becomes a secret agent against his will. The novel is imbued with a dry sense of humour, and is set against an intriguing environment filled with casinos and roulette wheels, New York skyscrapers and decadent Art Nouveau villas, cabarets and prostitution. The Hotel Sevilla is a constant presence in the background.

Graham Greene (1904–91)

Museo de la Revolución ⑪

The idea of putting the Museum of the Revolution in the former presidential palace of the dictator Fulgencio Batista was clearly symbolic. Designed by the Cuban architect Rodolfo Maruri and the Belgian architect Paul Belau, the building was inaugurated in 1920 by Mario García Menocal, and it remained the residence for 25 other presidents until 1965. The building has Neo-Classical elements, and was decorated by Tiffany of New York. It contains works by the leading Cuban decorators of the early 1900s and by sculptors such as Juan José Sicre, Esteban Betancourt and Fernando Boada. The museum features documents, photographs and memorabilia presenting an overview of the Cubans' struggle for independence, from the colonial period on, but focusing in particular on the 1959 Revolution, from the guerrilla war to the Special Period in the 1990s.

Statues of Che Guevara and Camilo Cienfuegos
These life-size wax statues depict the two heroes in combat.

The third floor contains photos and memorabilia from colonial times to 1959.

The side wing of the palace was home to Batista's office.

GRANMA MEMORIAL

The large glass and cement pavilion in the tree-lined plaza behind the museum contains the yacht *Granma* (named after its first owner's grandmother). In 1956 this boat brought Fidel Castro and some of his comrades from Mexico to Cuba to begin the armed struggle against Batista *(see p48)*. There are also objects and vehicles relating to the invasion of the Bay of Pigs (1961), remains of an American spy plane shot down in 1962 during the missile crisis, and the delivery truck that was used by revolutionaries to attack the palace in 1957.

The remains of a plane

STAR FEATURES

★ Salón de los Espejos

★ Main Staircase

The Dome

The inside of the dome, visible from the staircase, consists of multicoloured ceramics. It includes four panels, decorated by Esteban Valderrama and Mariano Miguel González, against a gold leaf background.

VISITORS' CHECKLIST

Calle Refugio 1, e/ Avenida de las Misiones y Zulueta.
Map 4 D2. **Tel** (7) 862 4091.
◯ 10am–6pm daily.

The second floor displays the President's desk, the Council of Ministers and memorabilia from 1959 to the present day.

★ **Salón de los Espejos**
Lined with vast mirrors (espejos), the reception hall of the former presidential palace has ceiling frescoes by Cuban painters Armado Menocal and Antonio Rodríguez Morey.

The tall windows are similar to those in the Gran Teatro de La Habana, and were designed by the same architect, Paul Belau.

The terrace opposite the Salón de los Espejos has a fine view of the Bay of Havana.

Entrance

★ **Main Staircase**
The monumental staircase, which leads to the first floor, still bears marks of the bullets shot here on 13 March 1957, during an attack by some revolutionary university students on a mission to kill Batista. The dictator managed to save his life by escaping to the upper floors.

Museo Nacional de Bellas Artes ⑫

See pp92–5.

Barrio Chino ⑬

Map 3 C3.

The Chinese quarter of Havana, the Barrio Chino, which now occupies a small area defined by Calles San Nicolás, Dragones, Zanja and Rayo, developed in the 19th century. In its heyday, in the early 1900s, there was a cultural association performing plays and operas, and a casino. The colourful streets were full of vendors of fritters and other Asian specialities, and people came to buy the best fruit and freshest fish in the city.

Today, all the Chinese shops are concentrated in the so-called Cuchillo de Zanja area (the intersection of Zanja and Rayo), a mixture of the oriental and the tropical; the architecture, however, is not particularly characteristic, except for the quarter gate,

The austere interior of Iglesia de la Caridad

which has a pagoda roof. Another, much more impressive Ming and Ching-style portico was erected in 1998 at the corner of Calle Dragones and Calle Amistad. It is almost 19 m (62 ft) wide and was donated to Cuba by the Chinese government.

The Barrio Chino is also home to the **Iglesia de la Caridad**, dedicated to Cuba's patron saint *(see p221)*. The church also has a popular statue, a Virgin with Asian features, brought here in the mid-1950s.

THE CHINESE COMMUNITY IN HAVANA

The first Chinese arrived in Cuba in the mid-1800s to work in the sugar industry, and they were treated like slaves. The first to gain their freedom began to cultivate small plots of land in Havana. In one of these, near the present-day Calle Salud, they grew Cuba's first mangoes, which were an immediate, spectacular success. Chinese restaurants began to appear in the area after the second wave of Chinese immigrants arrived from California (1869–75), armed with their American savings. Without losing any of their cultural traditions, the Chinese community has become assimilated into Cuban society, accepting and sharing the island's lot. A black granite column at the corner of Calle Linea and Calle L remembers the Chinese who fought for Cuban independence.

Entrance gate to Barrio Chino, the Chinese quarter in Havana

Iglesia del Sagrado Corazón ⑭

Avenida Simón Bolívar (Reina) 463. **Map** 3 B3. **Tel** *(7) 8624 979.*
◯ *7:30am–noon, 3–6pm daily.*
✚ *8am, 4:30pm Mon–Sat, 8am, 9:30am, 4:30pm Sun.* 🖼 📷 ⏺

With its impressive bell tower, 77 m (253 ft) high, the Church of the Sacred Heart can be seen from various parts of the city. It was designed in the early 1900s by the Jesuit priest Luis Gorgoza and consecrated in 1923, and is a rare example of the Neo-Gothic style in Cuba.

Dominating the façade is a figure of Christ resting on three columns decorated with a capital depicting the parable of the prodigal son. The interior has elaborate stained-glass windows narrating the life of Christ and a wealth of stucco-work and pointed arches. A Byzantine-style Sacred Heart with sculptures of saints and prophets is on the high altar.

Entrance to the Iglesia del Sagrado Corazón, with its statue of Christ

Avenida Carlos III ⑮

(Avenida Salvador Allende) **Map** 3 B3.

Laid out in 1850 during redevelopment under the supervision of Captain Miguel de Tacón, this boulevard (official name Avenida Salvador Allende) was designed to allow troops and military vehicles to go from the Castillo del Príncipe – built on the Aróstegui hill in the late 1700s – to their parade ground in the present-day Parque

Callejón de Hamel, famous for its exotic and colourful murals

de la Fraternidad. The middle section of the boulevard was reserved for carriages, while the two side avenues with their benches, trees and fountains were for pedestrians. First named Alameda de Tacón or Paseo Militar, it was renamed Avenida Carlos III in honour of the Spanish king who encouraged Cuban commerce and culture in the 18th century.

One of the most curious buildings on the street is the Grand National Masonic Temple, with a world map on the roof, built in the mid-1900s.

Callejón de Hamel ⑯

Map 3 A2.

This street in the working-class Cayo Hueso quarter is a curious open-air Afro-Cuban sanctuary. Its name derives from a legendary French-German resident called Fernando Hamel, a wealthy arms dealer-turned-merchant, who took the entire quarter under his wing. The colourful, 200-m (656-ft) mural here, for which the street is now famous, is the work of native painter Salvador González. He wanted to

Representation of Oshún, the goddess of love

pay homage to his varied cultural roots by representing all the religious cults and movements of African origin that are still active in Cuba, hence the many symbols, writings, and images of African gods and Abakuá devils *(see p23)* He began this enormous project in 1990.

This alley has everything: from small shops selling hand-crafted religious objects to a *Nganga*, the large cauldron-like pot which forms the basis of Palo Monte, the religion of former Bantu slaves from the African Congo. On Sundays Callejón de Hamel becomes the venue for rumba shows, popular with the locals and tourists alike.

City Walls ⑰

Avenida del Puerto **Map** 4 D5.

The old colonial city of San Cristóbal de La Habana was encircled and fortified by a 9-m (30-ft) high wall with nine bastions and a moat. Construction began in 1671 and took over a century to complete, finishing in 1797.

Once finished, the gates were closed every evening and access to the bay was blocked by a chain. Cannon shots were fired every night from a ship anchored in the bay, informing the inhabitants that the gates were closing. By the early 19th century, the city was expanding so fast that finally in 1863 the walls had to be torn down. Today, the best remaining sections are opposite the Museo de la Revolución and by the train station.

Remaining section of the old City Wall near Estación Central

Museo Nacional de Bellas Artes ⑬

The National Fine Arts Museum was founded on
23 February 1913 thanks to the efforts of the architect
Emilio Heredia, its first director. After frequent moves,
the collections eventually found a definitive home in
the block once occupied by the old Colón market. The
original design was changed when the arcades of the
building were demolished and in 1954 the new Palacio
de Bellas Artes was inaugurated, a Rationalist building
with purely geometric lines designed by the architect
Rodríguez Pichardo. The museum is now divided
between two buildings: the original palacio dedicated
to Cuban art, and the Centro Asturiano, by the Parque
Central, dedicated to international art.

LOCATOR MAP
See Street Finder, p123, map 4

Virgin and Child
*This triptych by Hans Memling
(1433–94) exemplifies the vivid
style and masterful spatial
construction that made
this artist one of the
great masters of
Flemish painting.*

Sagrada Familia
*The Holy Family by
the Spanish artist
Bartolomé Esteban
Murillo (1618–82),
who enjoyed great
fame during his
lifetime, is a calm,
meditative scene.*

**CENTRO
ASTURIANO**
*European painting
and sculpture, together
with the collection of
ancient art, are on display
in the Centro Asturiano,
designed in 1927
by the architect
Manuel del Busto.*

STAR SIGHTS

★ La Silla
 by Wifredo Lam

★ La Habana en Rojo
 by René Portocarrero

★ Panathenaean
 Amphora

★ **Panathenaean Amphora**
*This terracotta amphora in the black
figure style is one of the most important
pieces in the museum's collection of
ancient Greek vases, which once
belonged to the Count de Lagunillas.*

★ **La Habana en Rojo (1962)**
Havana in Red *is part of a long series that René Portocarrero dedicated to the capital. This painting in particular expresses the passionate Baroque spirit that characterizes all of Portocarrero's work.*

VISITORS' CHECKLIST

Palacio del Centro Asturiano, San Rafael, e/ Zulueta y Monserrate. **Palacio de Bellas Artes**, Calle Trocadero, e/ Zulueta y Monserrate.
Map 4 D2. **Tel** *(7) 861 0241.*
◯ *9am–5pm Tue–Sat, 10am–2pm Sun.* ● *1 Jan, 1 May, 26 Jul, 10 Oct, 25 Dec.*

The permanent collection is displayed in chronological order on the first and second floors.

Entrance

PALACIO DE BELLAS ARTES
The Palace of Fine Arts is entirely given over to Cuban art. Sculptures line the perimeter of the central courtyard, which houses service rooms for cultural education, the auditorium and the library. The two upper floors feature galleries divided into three sections: Colonial, academic and 20th-century art (divided into decades from the 1930s to the 1990s).

Form, Space and Light (1953)
This marble sculpture by Rita Longa, at the museum entrance, is characterized by a fluid concept of volume. Two male figures create a harmonious counterpoint.

★ **La Silla (1943)**
One of several fine works in which Wifredo Lam combines Cubism and Surrealism and adds a distinctively Cuban stamp: a Cubist chair with a vase on it is set in the magical context of the jungle.

Exploring the Museo Nacional de Bellas Artes

During the reassessment of many of Cuba's cultural institutions after 1959, a large number of works were added to the original museum collection – the result of the confiscation of property that had been misappropriated. The collection was divided into two sections: Cuban and international art. The first consists of paintings, prints, drawings, and sculptures; the second has paintings, sculptures and drawings primarily from Europe, the US and Latin America, with some works dating from the Egyptian to the Roman age.

Clotilde en los Jardines de la Granja by Joaquín Sorolla

CENTRO ASTURIANO (INTERNATIONAL ART)

The building, designed in 1927 as the home of the collection of international art, has maintained its original architectural elements, with furnishings, iron grilles, stained-glass windows and chandeliers. Besides the gallery, the place also has communal areas for the public, study rooms, a book shop, café, a video room and an auditorium.

The collection of international art comprises paintings and sculptures displayed in specific sections. These include the Middle Ages, Italy, Germany, Flanders, the Netherlands, Great Britain, France and Spain. There are also works from various European schools, the United States and Latin America.

Head of the god Amon, ancient Egyptian sculpture

Among the finest works in the collection are the Flemish paintings and the 19th-century Spanish pictures, including one by Joaquín Sorolla: *Entre Naranjos* (1903). In this the artist depicts a banquet in the countryside, using the play of the figures, light and shadow to create an Impressionist-like atmosphere. The same can be said of the movement of the water and the garden in the background in *Clotilde en los Jardines de la Granja*, which is a portrait of the artist's wife. Other Spanish artists represented are Murillo and Zurbarán. Then there are works by Constable, Bouguereau and Van Mieris.

The Italian collection includes a group of landscape paintings, including one by Canaletto: *Chelsea College, Rotunda, Ranelagh House*

and the Thames (1751), in which the painter brilliantly renders the atmosphere of London. There is also a scene of Venice by Francesco Guardi, *The Lagoon in front of the Fondamenta Nuove*, a youthful work with the delicate rendering that characterized his later production. Other Italian works are *St Christopher* by Jacopo Bassano (ca. 1515–92), *Alpine Landscape with Figures* by Alessandro Magnasco (1667–1748), and *The Spinstress* by Giovanni Battista Piazzetta. *The Reception of a Legation* by Vittore Carpaccio (1490) has a rigorously symmetrical composition.

The ancient art section is also fascinating: Greek, Roman and Egyptian works, as well as Mesopotamian, Phoenician and Etruscan finds. The 5th-century BC Greek amphora and the Fayoum portraits are especially interesting.

PALACIO DE BELLAS ARTES (CUBAN ART)

The permanent exhibition of 18th–21st-century Cuban art offers a complete overview of works by individuals and schools, and highlights the leading trends in each period. The temporary exhibition of prints and drawings, as well as of paintings, adds variety and

One of the many views that Canaletto painted of London

For hotels and restaurants in this region see pp252–6 and pp276–9

richness to the permanent collection, which has works by the great masters of contemporary Cuban art.

Two of the major figures are painter Wifredo Lam (*La Silla*, 1943) and sculptor Agustín Cárdenas, who were both influenced by the European avant-garde and African art. The free play of volumes in the wooden sculpture *Figure*, less than 1 m (3 ft) high, expresses to the full the African-derived sensuality that informs Cárdenas's style.

Cuban art in the 19th century, characterized by its technical skill, is represented by the portraits of Guillermo Collazo, an academic and painter, and landscapes by the Chartrand brothers. Other artists with an academic background are Armando García Menocal and Leopoldo Romañach, a painter and lecturer at the Academy.

The pioneers of modern Cuban art are particularly interesting. One of these is Víctor Manuel García, an exceptional landscape painter who conveys peaceful atmospheres with silently flowing rivers and figures with sinuous movements. García is the creator of the "mestizo" archetype: *Gitana Tropical* (Tropical Gypsy, 1929) includes a figure of a woman

El Malecón by Manuel Mendive, an extraordinary Naive painting

Figure (1953) by Augustín Cárdenas

against the background of a barren landscape, which has become a symbol of Cuban painting *(see p26)*. There are several works by Amelia Peláez, who revived the still-life genre by merging Cubism and specifically Cuban motifs; among these are *Naturaleza Muerta sobre Ocre*, executed in 1930 in Paris, and *Flores Amarillas*, a mature work that marks a return to more simple compositions after a "Baroque" period.

El Rapto de las Mulatas (1938), by Carlos Enríquez, is a dream-like "tangle"of human figures, horses and landscape that echoes the classical theme of the rape of the Sabine women. It is considered emblematic of Cuban painting and of this artist's oeuvre. The sensuality of the human bodies and the tropical atmosphere in this work provide a key to the interpretation of the motifs of traditional art.

The chronological display of works illustrates the development of Cuban art. In the 1950s there was a move away from figurative art, as seen in the work of Guido Llinás and Hugo Consuegra.

After the victory of the revolution in 1959, Cuban art embraced extremely varied styles. Servando Cabrera first took guerrillas as his subject and then made an erotic series. Antonia Eiriz was a particularly powerful Neo-Expressionist, and Raúl Martínez began with abstract art and then absorbed elements of Pop Art.

Another renowned contemporary artist is Manuel Mendive who, in embracing Cuba's African heritage, searches for the hidden depths of existence. *El Malecón* (1975), one of his most significant works, depicts the city's famous promenade as if it were an almost sacred site where people mingle with African gods. The style here is at once naive and sophisticated.

Of the leading artists of the 1970s there are works by Ever Fonseca, Nelson Domínguez, and the unique style of illustrator Roberto Fabelo. Among the younger artists (all graduates of the historic San Alejandro Academy and Escuela Nacional de Arte), Tomás Sánchez, with his archetypal landscapes, and José Bedia, with his bold installations, stand out. The artists who continue to emerge on the Cuban art scene – thanks to the Biennial Show – exhibit their works in the many temporary shows.

Of the considerable number of works in its possession, the museum now exhibits many paintings, drawings, prints and sculptures.

Flores Amarillas (1964), a still life dating from Amelia Peláez's mature phase

VEDADO AND PLAZA

The unusual grid plan of Vedado was the design of the engineer Luis Yboleón Bosque in 1859. It called for pavements 2 m (6 ft) wide, houses with a garden, and broad straight avenues. The name Vedado ("prohibited") arose because in the 1500s, in order to have full view of any pirates approaching, it was forbidden to build houses and streets here. In the late 19th and early 20th century the quarter was enlarged, becoming a prestigious residential

Sculpture at the corner of 23 and 12 Street

area for many of the city's leading families. Vedado has two different roles. It is Havana's modern political and cultural centre, with the city's main hotels, restaurants, shops, theatres, cinemas, offices and ministries; and it is also a historic quarter with a wealth of gardens and old houses with grand Colonial entrances. Plaza de la Revolución, the venue for major celebrations, is the political centre of Havana and the whole of Cuba, as well as a highly symbolic place.

SIGHTS AT A GLANCE

Museums and Galleries
Museo de Artes Decorativas ❸
Museo Napoleónico ❺

Historic Buildings
Casa de las Américas ❷
Quinta de los Molinos ❻
Universidad de La Habana ❹

Monuments
Memorial José Martí p103 ❽

Streets and Squares
Plaza de la Revolución ❼

Cemeteries
Necrópolis de Colón
pp104–5 ❾

Walks
A Walk through
Vedado
pp98–9 ❶

KEY
⬛ Walk pp98–9
🚌 Coach station

GETTING THERE
This area is huge, but getting around on foot can be a rewarding experience if you have time. Otherwise, the best alternative is to go by taxi. In order to orientate yourself you will need to know how the street names work (see p118).

0 metres   1000
0 yards   1000

◁ The end of the Malecón in Vedado with the mouth of the Río Almendares

A Walk through Vedado ❶

This walk takes in the broad avenues which are typical of Vedado, providing a taste of the district's odd architectural mix of ugly 1950s high-rises and crumbling Neo-Classical mansions. There is only one museum on this route (Vedado has few conventional attractions), leaving you free to simply stroll and look around. Calle 23, modern Havana's most well-known street, is the main reference point for the walk. The most famous section is the first few blocks, known as La Rampa.

The Hotel Habana Libre, with the mosaic *La Fruta Cubana* (1957)

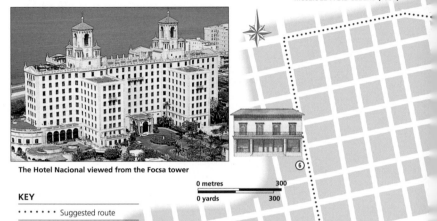

The Hotel Nacional viewed from the Focsa tower

KEY

• • • • • • Suggested route

0 metres 300
0 yards 300

Malecón

The stretch of the Malecón where this walk begins is dominated by the headland occupied by the Hotel Nacional ①. This gem of Art Deco architecture opened in 1930 *(see p255)*. Many famous guests have stayed here including Winston Churchill, Fred Astaire, Buster Keaton and Walt Disney. The hotel park offers lovely views across the bay.

La Rampa

Head briefly south to reach La Rampa (the first rising stretch of Calle 23 between the seafront and Calle N). Modern and lively, lined with offices, restaurants and bars with old-fashioned neon signs, La Rampa would pass for a typical 1950s street were it not for the façade of the Ministry of Sugar (or Minaz) with its revolutionary mural

and the "futuristic" Pabellón Cuba, which hosts exhibitions. This part of the walk is accompanied by the unmistakable profile of the Edificio Focsa ②, a skyscaper built in the 1950s.

This route also takes you by a small open-air crafts market and the Centro de Prensa Internacional, which caters to foreign journalists.

Calle 23

In the middle of the park the corner of Calle 23 and L is the Coppelia ice cream parlour ③, a large glass and metal building (1966). This classic location in Havana was made famous by Tomás Gutiérrez Alea's film *Strawberry and Chocolate (see p29)*.

Coppelia is the most popular ice-cream parlour in the city (hence the queues).

On the other side of Calle 23 is the impressive Hotel Habana Libre *(see p255)*, with a tiled mural by renowned Cuban artist Amelia Peláez. The hotel first opened in 1958, and a year later was requisitioned from the Americans and became Fidel Castro's headquarters. Inside are two mosaics by Portocarrero and Sosabravo *(see pp26–7)*. At the intersection with Calle J is the Parque El Quijote ④, a tree-filled area with a modern statue of a nude Don Quixote on horseback by Sergio Martínez. Further along Calle 23 the buildings lessen in height and are more varied in style.

The statue of Don Quixote by Sergio Martínez (1980)

ITINERARY

Hotel Nacional ①
Edificio Focsa ②
Coppelia ③
Parque El Quijote ④
Museo de la Danza ⑤
Casa de la Amistad ⑥
ICAIC ⑦

The constant queue for the Coppelia ice-cream parlour

VISITORS' CHECKLIST

Departure: Hotel Nacional.
Arrival: corner of 23 y 12.
Length: 3.5 km (2 miles).
Where to eat: Coppelia
ice-cream parlour, Casa de la
Amistad, one of the bars at the
corner of 23 y 12. Plan stops
and museum visits for the (hot)
middle of the day.
Museo de la Danza Tel (7)
831 2198. ◻ 10am–5pm
Tue–Sat. ● 1 Jan, 1 May, 26 Jul,
25 Dec. ▨ ✎ ◙

Avenida de los Presidentes

The tour continues by turning right at Calle G (Avenida de los Presidentes), a wide, tree-lined avenue with luxurious 19th- and 20th-century French-style buildings. In the middle of the street are benches and flower beds. Behind the statue of Simón Bolívar is the junction with Calle Línea.

Calle Línea

The first street to be laid out in the Vedado quarter owes its name to the tramline *(línea)* that once ran from here to the historic centre. Calle Línea also has many French-style buildings as well as colonial houses with stained-glass windows.

The restored building at the corner of Calle G is the Museo de la Danza ⑤, run by the legendary ballerina Alicia Alonso, founder of the Ballet Nacional *(see p83)*. The only dance museum in Latin America, it has mementoes of

Alicia Alonso's shoes, Museo de la Danza

famous dancers who have visited Cuba, drawings of stage sets, historic photos, and works by contemporary artists.

Paseo

Continue along Calle Línea to the junction with one of the loveliest streets in Havana: Calle Paseo, which is like a long, thin park running up to the Plaza de la Revolución *(see p102)*. It is lined with elegant buildings with splendid gardens: mostly ministries and public administration offices. The Casa de la Amistad ⑥, at No. 406 between Calle 17 and 19, is a cultural centre with a bar and restaurant, and part of a lavish Art Deco building given by the wealthy Pedro Baró to his mistress Caterina Lasa, grande dame of Havana high society. They were forced to flee to Europe by the scandal caused by their affair, but returned in 1917, when Lasa managed to get a divorce from her first husband.

23 y 12

Continue on Calle Paseo back to Calle 23, six blocks away from the busy central intersection where this walk ends. A plaque declares that on 16 April 1961, on the eve of the American invasion at the Bay of Pigs *(see p167)*, Fidel Castro announced that the Cuban Revolution was Socialist.

At Calle 23 y 12 there are restaurants and bars, shops, and cinemas like the Chaplin Cinematheque and the Cuban Institute of Cinematographic Arts and Industry (ICAIC) ⑦ *(see p29)*, with an art gallery featuring contemporary artists.

The permanent poster exhibition in the ICAIC building

The Art Deco building that is the home of the Casa de las Américas

Casa de las Américas ❷

Calle 3ra, esq. G. **Map** 1 C1. *Tel* (7) 838 2706, 838 2707. ☐ 10am–5pm Mon–Fri. ● 1 Jan, 1 May, 26 Jul, 10 Oct, 25 Dec. ✍ www.casa.cult.cu

On the Malecón, beyond the Monument to the Victims of the *Maine (see p58)*, there is a kind of secular temple, with a bell tower but no cross. This is the Casa de las Américas, a cultural institution, which was built in just four months after the triumph of the Cuban Revolution. Haydée Santamaría, one of the heroines of the struggle, founded the Casa with the aim of promoting exchanges among artists and writers on the American continent.

The centre features Arte Nuestra América, the most comprehensive collection known of Latin American painting and graphic art from the 1960s to the present.

Museo de Artes Decorativas ❸

Calle 17, 502. **Map** 2 D2. *Tel* (7) 8309 848. ☐ 10am–5pm Tue–Sat. ● 1 Jan, 1 May, 25 Dec. ✍ ☒ ☒ (with charge). ☒

The wonderful Museum of Decorative Arts is housed in the former residence of one of the wealthiest Cuban women of the 20th century: the Countess de Revilla de Camargo, sister of José Gómez Mena, the owner of

the Manzana de Gómez *(see p81)*. The mansion was built in 1927, and is well worth a visit for its French Rococo-Louis XV furnishings, as well as for the inner gardens.

The collection reveals the sophisticated and exotic tastes of the ruling classes and wealthy collectors of the colonial period. Major works of art here include two paintings by Hubert Robert, *The Swing* and *The Large Waterfall at Tivoli*, and two 17th-century bronze sculptures in the foyer.

The main hall on the Louis XV-style ground floor has 18th-century Chinese vases, Meissen porcelain, a large Aubusson carpet dating from 1722 and paintings by French artists.

A bedroom on the ground floor holds a collection of Chinese screens, while the Countess's room features a secretaire that once belonged to Marie Antoinette.

Last but not least is the pink marble Art Deco bathroom, which should not be missed.

Chinese porcelain, Museo de Artes Decorativas

Universidad de La Habana ❹

Calle 27 de Noviembre (Jovellar) y Ronda. **Map** 2 F2. **Museo Antropológico Montané**, Felipe Poey Bldg, Plaza Ignacio Agramonte. *Tel* (7) 8793 488. ☐ 9am–2pm Mon–Fri. ● 1 Jan, 1 May, 26 Jul, 10 Oct, 25 Dec. ✍ ☒ ☒

The University of Havana was founded under the auspices of a papal bull in 1728 and was initially housed in the Dominican monastery of St John Lateran, in the heart of La Habana Vieja. In 1902, a few days after the proclamation of the Cuban Republic, it was transferred to the Vedado area to a site which had been utilized as an explosives store in the colonial period.

The new university, housed in various buildings, was built between 1906 and 1940. In front of the main entrance, now the venue for political demonstrations and concerts, is the Alma Mater, the symbol of Havana

The Neo-Classical foyer of the Museo de Artes Decorativas

The austere façade of the University of Havana, with the statue of the Alma Mater at the top of the staircase

University. This statue, of a woman with her arms outstretched in a gesture of welcome, was cast in 1919 in New York by the Czech sculptor Mario Korbel. It was installed at the top of the broad granite stairway that forms the entrance to the complex in 1927. The student entrance to the university is in Calle San Lázaro, which broadens out into an open space where the ashes of Julio Antonio Mella *(see p46)* are kept, before sloping upwards.

In the Science Faculty, the Felipe Poey Museum of Natural History is open to visitors. Of much greater interest, however, is the **Museo Antropológico Montané**, in the Mathematics Department. Founded in 1903, this museum has exceptional pre-Columbian archaeological finds from Cuba, such as the Idolo del Tabaco found on the eastern tip of the island, the Idolo de Bayamo, one of the largest stone sculptures in the entire Caribbean area, and the Dujo de Santa Fe, a wooden ceremonial seat.

The oldest building on the hill is the Great Hall, with an austere façade behind which are allegorical paintings by Armando Menocal. The hall itself contains the old University of San Gerónimo bell, used to convene the professors, and the remains of Félix Varela *(see p28)*, brought to Cuba in 1911 from Florida, where the Cuban intellectual had died.

Idolo de Tabaco, Museo Montané

Museo Napoleónico ⑤

Calle San Miguel 1159, esq. a Ronda. **Map** 2 F3. *Tel (7) 8791 412, 8791 460.* ☐ *9:30am–5pm Tue–Sat, 9:30am–1pm Sun.* 🏛 🗓 📷 *(with charge).* 📷

The surprising presence of a Napoleonic museum in Cuba is due to the passion of a sugar magnate, Julio Lobo. For years he sent his agents all over the world in search of Napoleonic mementoes. In 1959, when Lobo left Cuba, the Cuban government bought his collection.

Every room in this curious museum contains fine examples of imperial-style furniture as well as all sorts of surprising Napoleonic memorabilia, including one of the emperor's teeth and a tuft of his hair.

There are two portraits, one by Andrea Appioni, painted in Milan during Napoleon's second Italian campaign, and another by Antoine Gros. There is also his death mask, cast two days before Napoleon's death by Francesco Antommarchi, the Italian physician who had accompanied him to the island of St Helena and who later settled in Cuba.

The restored mansion itself was built in the 1920s by Oreste Ferrara, counsellor to the dictator Gerardo Machado, who furnished it in a Neo-Florentine Gothic style.

Quinta de los Molinos ⑥

Avenida Carlos III (Salvador Allende) y Luaces. **Map** 2 F3. *Tel (7) 8798 850.* ⬤ *closed for restoration.*

A typical 19th-century villa in the Vedado quarter, the Quinta de los Molinos was built as the summer residence of the captains-general in 1837. The villa stands in a leafy area with two tobacco mills *(molinos)*.

The rambling grounds around the villa were filled with tropical vegetation from the Botanical Garden, which was then in the Capitol area but was dismantled after the Parque Central was enlarged. The park is popular among local musicians, who come here to practise.

In 1899, General Máximo Gómez, Commander in Chief of the Cuban liberation army, stayed here, which is why it is now a museum dedicated to this distinguished hero of the wars of independence *(see p44)*.

A stained-glass window in the Quinta de los Molinos

A parade in front of the Ministerio del Interior, Plaza de la Revolución

Plaza de la Revolución ❼

Map 2 E5.

Plaza de la Revolución has been Cuba's political, administrative and cultural centre since 1959. The square was designed in 1952 under the Batista regime, and most of the buildings visible today also date from the 1950s. What had been known as the Plaza Cívica was renamed Plaza de la Revolución following Fidel Castro's victory in 1959.

Though it does not distinguish itself by its architecture or design, the square is nonetheless an important place to visit because of its historic and symbolic importance. It was the venue for the first mass rallies following the triumph of the revolution and of the festivities for the campaign against illiteracy in 1961.

Since 1959, military parades and official celebrations have often attracted crowds of more than a million people. During these events the area fills with people, and the speakers take their place on the podium next to the statue of José Martí, at the foot of the obelisk.

On the morning of 28 March 2012, Pope Benedict XVI celebrated mass from this podium together with thousands of worshippers.

⚏ Ministerio del Interior
Calle Aranguren.
The façade of the Ministry of the Interior, which stands directly opposite the statue of Martí, is almost completely covered by a huge bronze wire sculpture of Che Guevara, which was completed in 1995. (The guerrilla fighter had his office in this building in the early 1960s.) This striking and symbolic image was inspired by the world-famous photograph taken by the press photographer Alberto Korda *(see p176)*. Under the bust are the words: "Hasta la victoria siempre" (keep striving for victory). The façade is illuminated at night.

⛫ Museo Postal Cubano
Ave Rancho Boyeros y 19 de Mayo.
Tel (7) 881 5551. ◯ *8am–5:30pm Mon–Fri.* ● *1 Jan, 1 May, 26 Jul, 10 Oct, 25 Dec.* 📷 ⚏ ◯ *(with charge).*
This fascinating postal museum has occupied a small corner of the Ministry of Communications since 1965. Through the medium of stamps, it illustrates the last two centuries of Cuban history, from the end of the Colonial period to the years following the fall of the Berlin Wall, including the wars of independence, and figures like Machado, Batista and Che Guevara.

The most curious item on display is a fragment of a "postal missile". In 1939, a group of Cubans decided to use a missile for "express airmail deliveries" from Havana to Matanzas, but the crude device exploded a few minutes after "take-off".

The Teatro Nacional seen from Martí's memorial

⚏ Palacio de la Revolución
Calle Martí.
The former Ministry of Justice (1958) behind the Martí Memorial now houses the offices of the Council of State, the Council of Ministers and the Central Committee of the Communist Party. It was here that Fidel Castro received Pope John Paul II on 22 January 1998.

The elegant wooden card-index files in the Biblioteca Nacional

⚏ Biblioteca Nacional José Martí
Plaza de la Revolución.
Tel (7) 855 5442. ◯ *9am–5:30pm Mon–Sat.* ⚏
The José Martí National Library has over two million books and is particularly strong in the humanities. The United States embargo, plus the Special Period crisis, have slowed the development of a library computerization programme, but all services are being modernized.

🎭 Teatro Nacional
Paseo y 39.
Tel (7) 879 3558.
Built with a striking convex façade, the National Theatre is Cuba's most important cultural complex. It was inaugurated in June 1959. There are two auditoriums: the Avellaneda, with a seating capacity of 2,500, and the Covarrubia, which seats 800 and has a mural by Cuban artist René Portocarrero *(see p26)*. Theatre programmes include lectures, courses, theatre festivals, guitar and jazz concerts, and ballet. There is also a *café cantante* and a piano bar with live shows *(see p124)*.

Memorial José Martí ⑧

Work on this monument in the middle of the Plaza de la Revolución began in 1953, on the 100th anniversary of the birth of Cuba's national hero. The memorial was finished in 1958. It consists of a 109-m (358-ft) tower representing a five-pointed star and is built of grey marble from the Isla de la Juventud. At the foot stands a huge statue of José Martí in a meditative pose. The actual Martí Memorial is in the interior of the base, which also houses the Sala de Actos, an auditorium used for concerts, lectures and poetry readings.

★ **Panorama**
On clear days, the mirador on top of the tower, the highest point in Havana, affords a view of the entire city. The panorama shown here stretches from the Ministerio del Interior to the sea.

A lift goes to the top of the tower, which reaches a height of 139 m (458 ft) – the monument stands on a hill 30 m (100 ft) above sea level.

★ **The Memorial**
Two rooms contain manuscripts, portraits and mementoes of Martí; the third room describes the history of the monument and the square, while a fourth puts on contemporary art exhibitions. The mural in the lobby features the patriot's thoughts.

VISITORS' CHECKLIST

Plaza de la Revolución.
Map 2 E5
Tel (7) 859 2347.
🕐 9am–4:30pm Mon–Sat.

Statue of José Martí
The 18-m (59-ft) high, white marble statue, carved on site by Juan José Sicre, is surrounded by six half columns.

STAR FEATURES

★ Panorama
★ The Memorial

Necrópolis de Colón ❾

Havana's monumental Columbus Cemetery is one of the largest in the world, occupying an area of 56 ha (135 acres) with 53,360 plots, where some two million people have been buried. It was designed in the 1860s by the Spanish architect Calixto de Loira, who based the layout on the rigorously symmetrical plan of Roman military camps. It was built between 1871 and 1886. Because of its many sculptures and monuments in different styles – from eclectic to the boldest expressions of contemporary art – the Necrópolis has been proclaimed a national monument. However, although it is full of fascinating funerary art, it is still the cemetery for and of Havana's citizens. People come here to visit their loved ones or simply to stroll around.

The Osario General, the ossuary built in 1886, is one of the cemetery's oldest constructions.

La Milagrosa

Mártires del Asalto al Palacio Presidencial
This avant-garde memorial (1982) honours the students killed during their attack on Batista's Presidential Palace in 1957.

The Pantheon of Catalina Lasa *(see p99)* was commissioned by her second husband, Juan Pedro Baró, who had her embalmed and brought from Paris to Havana.

★ **La Piedad de Rita Longa**
This delicate marble bas-relief pietà adorns the black marble tomb of the Aguilera family, which was built in the 1950s.

Chapel of the Six Medical Students

★ **Main Entrance**
The statue in Carrara marble of the three theological virtues, Faith, Hope and Charity, was sculpted in 1904 by the Cuban artist José Villalta de Saavedra in "Neo-Romantic" style.

JANUA SUM PACIS

Tomb of the author Alejo Carpentier (1904–80)

Entra

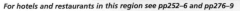

Fuerzas Armadas Revolucionarias Monument (1955)
This pantheon houses the heroes of the Revolutionary Armed Forces.

VISITORS' CHECKLIST

Calle Zapata esq a Calle 12.
Map 1 C5.
***Tel** (7) 832 1050.*
🕗 8am–5pm daily.

Panteón de los Prelados

Capilla Central
Built in the late 1800s in the middle of Avenida Colón, the cemetery's main avenue, this chapel contains frescoes by the Cuban artist Miguel Melero.

The Falla Bonet Pantheon
is a truncated grey granite pyramid with a statue of Christ by the Spanish sculptor Mariano Benlliure.

★ Monumento a los Bomberos
This monumental homage to the 25 fallen firefighters of a fire that occurred in 1890 in the Isasi hardware store was designed by Spanish architects Agustín Querol and Julio Zapata.

Tomb of Generalissimo Máximo Gómez *(see p44)*

STAR SIGHTS

★ Main Entrance

★ La Piedad de Rita Longa

★ Monumento a los Bomberos

A mother placing flowers on the statue of La Milagrosa

LA MILAGROSA

"The Miraculous One" is the tomb of Amelia Goyri de la Hoz, who died in childbirth in 1901, along with her baby. She was only 24. In keeping with the custom of the time, she and the child were buried together. According to popular legend, a few years later the tomb was opened and she was found intact, holding her baby in her arms. This "miracle", and the fact that the bereaved husband went to her tomb every day and never turned his back to it, made Amelia a symbol of motherly love. She became the protector of pregnant women and newborn children, and her tomb is a pilgrimage site for future mothers, who ask for her blessing and leave without turning their back to the tomb. The statue placed at the tomb in 1909 is by José Villalta de Saavedra.

FURTHER AFIELD

Beyond the city of Havana, sights of interest are rather more scattered. The Miramar quarter lies to the west of the city, and the Castillo del Morro and Fortaleza de La Cabaña defence fortresses, evidence of Havana's strategic importance, are physically separated from the city, to the east, but linked to it historically.

Cubans are enthusiastic beachgoers and the long golden beaches at Playas del Este, east of Havana, are especially popular at the weekend. Among the sightseeing highlights are the favourite haunts of Ernest Hemingway, including Finca La Vigía, the villa where he wrote some of his best novels, and the fishing village of Cojímar.

SIGHTS AT A GLANCE

Museums
Finca La Vigía ⑩

Monuments and Churches
Castillo del Morro ③
San Carlos de La Cabaña ④
Santuario de San Lázaro ⑬

Parks and Gardens
Jardín Botánico Nacional ⑫
Parque Lenin ⑪

Beaches
Playas del Este ⑨

Towns and Suburbs
Casablanca ⑤
Cojímar ⑧
Guanabacoa ⑦
Regla ⑥

Historic Places
Tropicana ②

Walks
*A Walk through Miramar
(pp108–9)* ①

KEY

▨	Historic centre
▢	Built-up area
✈	Airport
⛴	Ferry
═	Motorway
━	Major road
═	Minor road

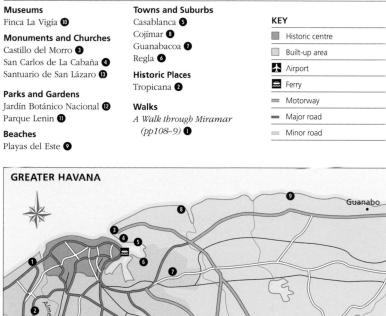

GREATER HAVANA

A Walk through Miramar ❶

Miramar is the most elegant part of Havana – as it was before the Revolution, when the city's richest inhabitants lived here. Life in this quarter revolves around the Avenida 5, a broad, tree-lined avenue flanked by splendid early 20th-century villas that are now home to embassies and institutions. Administratively, Miramar belongs to the municipality of Playa, as does the adjacent Cubanacán quarter, where many foreign embassies are located.

Looking down Avenida 5, the main avenue in Miramar

The compact Fuerte de la Chorrera

Arriving from Vedado

This walk begins at the Fuerte de Santa Dorotea de la Luna en la Chorrera fort ①, a national monument. The fort, designed by Giovanni Bautista Antonelli and built in 1645, was crucial to the city's defence system

(see p110) for over 200 years. Opposite the fort is the 1830 ②, a salsa venue and restaurant in a house that once belonged to Carlos Miguel de Céspedes, Minister of Public Works for President Machado.

Along Avenida 5 (Quinta Avenida)

From here, follow the northernmost tunnel under the Almendares river to reach Avenida 5, a broad, tranquil avenue with shrubs and benches in the middle. On both sides of it are large, imposing mansions built in

the early decades of the 20th century and many Art Deco and eclectic-style houses, most of which were abandoned by their owners after Fidel Castro took power. The Cuban government has turned many of these buildings into ministries, embassies and even orphanages (an example is the residence of the former President of the Republic Grau San Martín at the corner of Calle 14). Further down the Avenida, at the corner of Calle 26, is the modern Iglesia de Santa Rita ③, with three

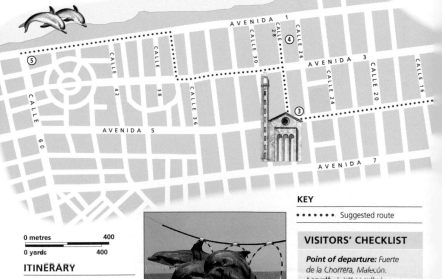

KEY

●●●●●● Suggested route

Dolphins performing at the Miramar aquarium

ITINERARY

Fuerte de Santa Dorotea de la Luna en la Chorrera ①
Restaurante 1830 ②
Iglesia de Santa Rita ③
Maqueta de La Habana ④
Acuario Nacional ⑤

0 metres   400
0 yards   400

VISITORS' CHECKLIST

Point of departure: Fuerte de la Chorrera, Malecón.
Length: 5 km (3 miles).
Stops: Mesón La Chorrera, Calle Calzada 1252, before the tunnel; Bar Dos Gardenias, Ave 7 y Calle 28, *Tel* (7) 204 2353.

distinctive tall arches on its façade. Pop in to see the statue of St Rita by Cuban sculptress Rita Longa, to the left of the entrance. Walk up Calle 28 to Avenida 3 *("tercera")*. In the block above is the fascinating Maqueta de La Habana museum ④, a detailed model of Havana measuring about 10 sq m (108 sq ft), with different areas colour-coded according to construction date, showing how the city developed from colonial times onwards. Continue the walk along Avenida 3, taking in the stylish architecture, and then turn right to walk one block up to Avenida 1.

Statue by Rita Longa, Church of Santa Rita

The Seafront

Avenida 1 *("primera")* lacks the liveliness and fascination of the Malecón, but the water is clear and there are peaceful spots for sunbathing, such as Playita 16 (at the end of Calle 16). At the corner of Calle 60 is the unmistakable pale blue building housing the Acuario Nacional ⑤, the city aquarium. Here, large saltwater tanks reproduce an assortment of Caribbean and ocean habitats. About 3,500 specimens represent 350 different species of sea fauna. The most spectacular section is the tank of *Tursiops truncatus* dolphins, more commonly known as bottle-nosed dolphins. Dolphin shows are also performed here at regular intervals. The aquarium complex is open from 10am to 6pm every day except Monday.

The model of Havana: in the foreground, Castillo del Morro, behind, the Malecón

RÍO ALMENDARES

The Almendares river is no longer crystal-clear, but it must have been cleaner in the past, because in the 17th century a Spanish bishop called Almendáriz came to Havana in bad health and fully recovered after a stay along its banks. The river's name was changed from Casiguaguas to Almendares

Thick vegetation in the Parque Almendares, Havana's "forest"

in the bishop's honour. Along its west bank, by the Calle 23 bridge from Vedado, is the Parque Almendares, an area filled with tropical plants and vegetation.

The early 20th-century Fountain of the Muses at the Tropicana

Tropicana ❷

Calle 72 e/ 41 y 45, Marianao.
Tel (7) 267 1010.

The most famous nightclub in Cuba, America and perhaps the world is located in the outskirts of Havana, in the Marianao district. Many legendary figures of the 20th century have performed here, including Josephine Baker, Bola de Nieve, Rita Montaner and Nat King Cole.

The Tropicana was originally a farm estate belonging to Mina Pérez Chaumont, the widow of a wealthy man named Regino Truffin. In the 1930s she transformed her property into a vast nightspot with a restaurant and casino featuring extravagant floor shows with lavish costumes. The nightclub opened on 31 December 1939.

Perhaps surprisingly, given the change of regime, the Tropicana is still alive and kicking. Fortunately, the trees in the original estate were left intact, so that today the Tropicana stands in the middle of an extraordinary tropical forest. At night, floodlights illuminate the palm trees, partly hidden by clouds of artificial smoke. A reminder of the Tropicana's golden age is the enormous "Bajo las Estrellas" ballroom. With its capacity of 1,000 it is one of the largest of its kind.

At the main entrance is the Fountain of the Muses (1952). The garden's statue of a ballet dancer, by Rita Longa (1952), is now the symbol of the club.

Aerial view of the Castillo del Morro, situated on a rocky headland at the entrance to the bay of Havana

Castillo del Morro ❸

Carretera de la Cabaña, Habana del Este. *Tel* (7) 863 7063. ◯ 8am–8pm daily. 🈳 🗹 🖬 🍴 🚻 🛗 🚻

Construction of this fortress, which was designed by the Italian military architect Giovanni Bautista Antonelli, began in 1589 at the request of the governor, Juan de Texeda. The function of the Castillo de los Tres Reyes del Morro (its full title) was to detect the approach of any enemy (pirates especially). Various treasures of the New World were periodically concentrated in the port when ships were docked in Cuba on their voyage to

The old lamp in the Morro lighthouse

Spain, and it was necessary to protect them.

The original lighthouse on the "Morrillo", the highest point of the hill, was rebuilt several times, until General Leopoldo O'Donnell ordered a new one to be built in 1845. This still stands today. It is made of stone, and has its original lamp, the rays of which shine for a radius of 30 km (20 miles). Today the fortress and the neighbouring La Cabaña fortification *(see below)* form the **Parque Histórico-Militar Morro Cabaña**. Many tourists and locals come here to admire the outlook, as the fortress affords a magnificent view of the city and port of Havana.

Access to the castles is through an impressive gallery,

where plaques indicate the spot where the British opened a breach in 1762, allowing them to take the Morro and all of Havana after a 40-day siege.

On the northern side of the complex is the Plataforma de la Reina, with defence walls and a flight of steps leading to the upper terrace. From here visitors can gain an overall view of the fortress.

San Carlos de La Cabaña ❹

Carretera de la Cabaña, Habana del Este. *Tel* (7) 862 0617. ◯ 10am–10pm daily. 🖬 🍴

After the British conquest of Havana in 1762, it was 11 months before the Spaniards regained the capital. The bitter experience of foreign occupation convinced them of the need to fortify the hill

HAVANA'S DEFENCES

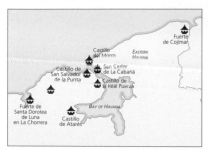

Havana was the most important port in the New World in the 1700s. It was a highly prized target for enemies and pirates because of its extremely favourable strategic position in the Caribbean, and it was also the most fortified city in any Spanish colony. Beyond the maritime canal affording access to the Bay of Havana were the two large fortresses of Morro and Cabaña. These two, together with the castles of Real Fuerza, Punta, Atarés and Príncipe and the city walls, constituted for centuries the city's impressive defence and attack system. From the outlying forts of Cojímar and La Chorrera, to the east and west respectively, any enemy approach could be sighted.

For hotels and restaurants in this region see pp252–6 and pp276–9

dominating the port in a more effective manner, so, on 4 November 1763, construction work began on the new Cabaña fortress. No fewer than 4,000 men laboured on the project, including Mexican and Indian prisoners transported from the Yucatán peninsula in conditions of semi-slavery.

The new fortification cost 14 million pesos, a sum so large that, according to an old legend, when King Carlos III of Spain was informed of the expense, he asked for a spyglass and reputedly commented: "Such an expensive construction should be visible from Madrid."

La Cabaña, which extends for more than 700 m (2,300 ft) along the entrance canal of the bay, is a huge 10-ha (25-acre) polygon designed in keeping with the principles of French military schools, but with detailing by the Spanish engineer Silvestre Abarca. With its crown-shaped plan, it is considered a fine example of a bastion-type defence fortification.

A visit to the fortress offers a variety of experiences. The fortress's central thoroughfare leads up to the Baluardo di San Ambrosio bastion and the

Entrance to the de La Cabaña parish church, which stands in the fortress parade ground

Terraza de San Agustín, where the poet Juan Clemente Zenea was executed for his separatist ideas in 1871. In the same area some Soviet nuclear missiles, left over from the 1962 Cuban Missile Crisis *(see p52)*, are on display.

The **Museo Monográfico** illustrates the history of the fortress through documents and photographs. The **Museo de Armas y Fortificaciones** is a military museum.

However, the one museum not to miss is the **Comandancia del Che**: on 3 January 1959 the *barbudos* (as Castro and his bearded revolutionaries were known) occupied La Cabaña and set up their head-quarters in the 19th-century building that was once the residence of the Spanish military governor. Today it is a museum containing various items that belonged to Che Guevara, including his weapons, glasses and camera. The revolutionary's original office, which has been left intact, is also open to visitors.

Casablanca ❺

Regla (Havana). 🚢 *from Muelle de Luz, La Habana Vieja, every 30 mins.* ***Tel*** *(7) 860 8506.* 🚉

This fishing village was built in the 1700s on the other side of the Bay of Havana from the city. Casablanca is best known for the huge Cristo de la Habana, an 18-m (60-ft) tall white marble statue of Christ, which looms over the village. The work of the Cuban sculptress Jilma Madera (1958), it was commis-sioned by President Batista's wife, Marta. She had made a vow that she would finance a large statue of Christ if her husband survived the attack by students on the presiden-tial palace in 1957, during which he risked his life. The statue was completed a week prior to the Revolution. It can be seen from many parts of the city and is familiar to all Cubans.

The colossal Cristo de La Habana

THE CAÑONAZO

Every evening, at 9pm exactly, the picturesque "Cañonazo" ceremony is held in the La Cabaña fortress. On the hour, a volley of cannon shots is fired by a group of young soldiers of the Revolutionary Armed Forces, dressed in 18th-century uniforms. This theatrical ceremony is interesting from the historical point of view: in the colonial period, a volley of cannon shots was fired at the end of each day to tell citizens that the city gates were closed and access to the bay had been blocked by a chain *(see p85)*.

The Cañonazo ceremony, a commemoration in historic costume

Regla ❻

Havana. 🏚 47,000. 🚢 from
Muelle de la Luz, Habana Vieja, every
30 mins; (7) 977 473.

Regla lies on the east coast
of the Bay of Havana, a few
minutes by ferry from Muelle
de la Luz. The town was
founded in 1687 and over
the years grew in economic
importance as a fishing port
and centre for huge sugar
warehouses. In the 19th
century freed slaves settled
in Regla, and there is still a
strong Afro-Cuban culture
here today.

The church of **Nuestra
Señora de la Virgen de
Regla** was built here in 1687.
A modest structure, it stands
on a small hill from which
there are scenic views of
the bay. The humble interior

**Interior of the Regla church with its
ornate high altar**

includes an ornate golden
altar into which is incorporated the figure of the dark-
skinned Virgin.

The Liceo Artístico y
Literario was opened by
José Martí in 1879 with a
famous speech on Cuban
independence.

Guanabacoa ❼

Havana. 🏚 100,000. 🚢

After its foundation in
1607, this town became
an obligatory port of call
for the slave traffic,
which explains its fame
as a city associated with
Afro-Cuban culture.
Its name, of Indian
origin, means
"land of many
waters": there
are several
springs in this area   **The Mano Poderosa in**
which at one time   **the Guanabacoa**
encouraged wealthy   **Municipal Museum**
Habaneros to build
homes here. Today,
Guanabacoa is proud of its
colonial houses and of having
been the birthplace of three
leading 20th-century Cuban
musicians: pianist and
composer Ernesto Lecuona,
singer Rita Montaner, and
chansonnier Ignacio Villa,
better known as Bola de Nieve.

Guanabacoa has several
interesting churches. Of
these, the **Ermita de Potosí** in
particular is well worth a visit.
Built in 1644, it is one of the
oldest and most original
colonial period churches.

The interesting **Museo
Municipal de Guanabacoa**,
located in a well-restored
colonial house, illustrates the
history of the town.

The dominant figure is
that of Pepe Antonio,
the local hero in the
struggle against the
British in the 18th
century. The museum
places particular
emphasis on the
Santería and Palo
Monte religions and
on the rituals of
the Abakuá cult
(*see p23*). An
impressive piece
in this section is
the *Mano Poderosa*,
a multicoloured
wooden sculpture
that stands approxi-
mately 1 m (3 ft) high.
According to legend, the
sculpture belonged to
a woman who was able to
make contact with the dead.
Traditional Afro-Cuban
events are sometimes held
in the courtyard.

🏛 **Museo Municipal
de Guanabacoa**
Calle Martí 108, esq. Versalles.
Tel (7) 797 9117. 🕙 10am–6pm
Tue–Sat, 9am–1pm Sun. 🈲 💷 📷

Cojímar ❽

Havana. 🏚 20,100.
ℹ Hotel Panamericano Resort,
(7) 766 1010.

A charming village with one-
storey wooden houses –
often with a garden, small
porch and courtyard at the
back – Cojímar was once
inhabited only by fishermen.
Now there are also many
elderly people, including
writers and artists, who have
chosen to leave the capital
for a more peaceful life.

In the 1950s however, there
was only one author to be
seen on the streets of Cojímar:
Ernest Hemingway. Many of

LA VIRGEN DE REGLA

The Virgin of Regla has been the
patron saint of fishermen and
Havana since 1714. The Neo-
Classical sanctuary dedicated
to her contains an icon of a
dark-skinned Virgin holding a
white child that the faithful
call "La Negra". The icon's
origins are not known but one
legend suggests it acquired its
colour while being taken
across the Black Sea. The
statue was brought from Spain
by a hermit in 1696, and in the
1900s was watched over by a
certain Panchita Cárdenas,
whose modest home next to   **La Virgen de Regla, the**
the church is now open to   **protector of fishermen**
worshippers. For followers of
Santería the Virgen de Regla is also Yemayá, the patroness
of the sea and mother of all men, to whom food, flowers,
candles and sweets are offered. On her feast day (8 Sep) the
icon is borne through the town.

The 17th-century fort at Cojímar

the local fishermen were his friends and he liked to play dominoes and drink rum while listening to their stories. He made this village the setting for his famous novel *The Old Man and the Sea*.

In the small square named after Hemingway there is a monument featuring a bust of the author – a faithful copy of the one in El Floridita *(see p72)*. It is here thanks to the author's fishermen friends, who donated anchors, hooks and tools to pay for the casting.

Nearby, on the seafront, is a small fort, which was built as the easternmost defence point of Havana in 1646. It was designed by Giovanni Bautista Antonelli, architect of the Castillo del Morro *(see p110)*.

Cojímar is also the home of Hemingway's favourite restaurant, La Terraza *(see p278)*. It is still as elegant and well-run as it was during Hemingway's time. The cocktail lounge has a splendid wooden bar and is an ideal spot to enjoy a drink.

Playas del Este ❾

Havana.

Havana is one of the few cities in the world to have sizable beaches only a 20-minute drive from the city centre. The Playas del Este consist of a stretch of about 50 km (31 miles) of fine sand and crystal-clear water, easy to reach via a good, fast road, with hotels, villages and tourist facilities of every kind. The beaches can offer a good compromise for people who want to spend some of their holiday at the seaside during

their visit to Havana. Bear in mind, however, that this area is also a popular haunt of *jineteros (see p300)*, though in places security guards have been drafted in to deter them.

Arriving from central Havana, the first beach is **Bacuranao**, a peaceful spot and a favourite with families. However, the loveliest place on the riviera is **Santa María del Mar**. It has the best beach, lined with pine and coconut trees, as well as a good choice of hotels and sports, and is therefore very popular with tourists. **Guanabo** is more traditional, with small houses, restaurants and shops; at weekends this is the liveliest place along the coast when Habaneros arrive by the hundred. The Bajo de las Lavanderas, close to the shore, is a delight for scuba and skin divers, and deep-sea fishing trips can be arranged at the **Marlin Punto Náutico** kiosks on the beaches.

A small island, **Mi Cayito**, lies at the mouth of the Itabo river. There are fine views from Mirador Bellomonte.

One of the Playas del Este beaches popular with Havana residents

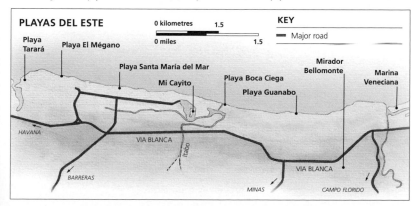

PLAYAS DEL ESTE

0 kilometres 1.5

0 miles 1.5

KEY

— Major road

Playa Tarará

Playa El Mégano

Playa Santa María del Mar

Mi Cayito

Playa Boca Ciega

Playa Guanabo

Mirador Bellomonte

Marina Veneciana

HAVANA

VIA BLANCA

Itabo

VIA BLANCA

BARRERAS

MINAS

CAMPO FLORIDO

Ernest Hemingway in Cuba

Period print of the Ambos Mundos hotel

The great American author fell in love with Cuba on his first visit in 1932, attracted initially by the marlin fishing. It was not until 1939, however, that Hemingway decided to move to the island, initially settling down in the Ambos Mundos hotel in Old Havana *(see p253)*. Having decided to stay on, he found a quiet villa outside the city in which to write, Finca La Vigía, where he lived at first with journalist Martha Gellhorn (whom he married in 1940). His bond with Cuba lasted 20 years, through the Batista period and the beginning of the Revolution, and longer, in fact, than his relationship with Martha Gellhorn. Hemingway's last wife, Mary Welsh (married in 1946), joined the writer in Cuba and lived with him at Finca La Vigía. The villa is now a museum *(p115)*. He eventually returned to the US in 1960, a year before his suicide.

A lover of cocktails, *Hemingway was a regular at La Bodeguita del Medio (see p65) and El Floridita (see p72). Both bars were a stone's throw from his room on the fifth floor of the Ambos Mundos Hotel. The writer helped to invent the daiquiri.*

Hemingway wrote *his most famous novels in Cuba. He was at Finca La Vigía in 1954 when he found out that he had received the Nobel Prize. "This prize belongs to Cuba, since my works were created and conceived in Cuba, with the inhabitants of Cojímar, of which I am a citizen." With these words, Hemingway placed the prize at the foot of the Virgen del Cobre (see p221).*

A marlin fishing tournament is held every year at the Hemingway Marina.

Gregorio Fuentes

Ernest Hemingway

Martha Gellhorn

THE SEA AND FISHING

Hemingway loved the sea and was passionate about swordfish and marlin fishing. He practised the sport with great commitment and courage – not on a luxury yacht, but on a small fishing boat, the *famous Pilar* together with a fisherman, Gregorio Fuentes, who also became a good friend. The boat was moored at the picturesque village of Cojímar.

PILAR

Finca La Vigía ⑩

Calle Vigía y Stheinhard, San Francisco de Paula, Havana. 🚍 *San Francisco de Paula*. **Tel** (7) 691 0809. 🕙 10am–5pm Mon–Sat, 10am–1pm Sun 🖼 🎫 📷 *(with charge)*. 🛗 💻

At San Francisco de Paula, on the outskirts of Havana, is the only residence Ernest Hemingway ever had outside the US. He lived here, in the periods between his various foreign trips, for almost 20 years.

The villa, built in 1887 to a design by Catalan architect Miguel Pascual y Baguer, was bought by Hemingway in 1940. It was made a public museum in 1962, as soon as news of the writer's suicide in the US reached Cuba. To protect the interior, visitors are not allowed inside, however the rooms can be viewed through the windows and doors to the garden, which are thrown open but roped off, except on rainy days.

Everything in the villa is in the same meticulous order it was in when Hemingway lived here. There is his library with its more than 9,000 books; various hunting trophies from African safaris hanging in the living room; personal possessions, such as his weapons and typewriter, and valuable artworks, including a ceramic plate by Picasso.

Two curious features in the garden are the pet cemetery (Hemingway had about 50 cats during his lifetime), and the *Pilar*, the author's fishing

The façade of Finca La Vigía, surrounded by tropical vegetation

boat, which was transferred from Cojímar to the museum and placed in a specially built pavilion in the former tennis court. The *Pilar* was a comfortable and fast boat made of black American oak, and the author loved ploughing through the waves on fishing expeditions with his friend Gregorio Fuentes. During World War II he used it to patrol the sea north of Cuba,

on the lookout for Nazi submarines that were trying to sink ships laden with sugar intended for the Allied troops.

Environs

Near Hemingway's villa is the village of **Santa María del Rosario**, founded in 1732 by Count Don José Bayona y Chacón on the estate of his large sugar factory. A real gem here is the church of the same name (it is also known as Catedral de los Campos de Cuba), notable for its splendid *mudéjar* ceilings.

The church was designed in 1760–66 by architect José Perera. The austere façade is reminiscent of the Spanish missions in the western US, while the interior contains some unusually lavish elements, such as the extravagantly gilded high altar, and paintings attributed to Nicolás de la Escalera, one of Cuba's early artists.

The living room of Hemingway's villa, with hunting trophies on the walls

For hotels and restaurants in this region see pp252–6 and pp276–9

Parque Lenin ⑪

Calle 100 y Cortina de la Presa,
Arroyo Naranjo, Havana. *Tel (7) 644
8880.* ◯ *10am–5pm Wed–Sun.* 🖼
🍴 🎫 ExpoCuba *Tel (7) 697
4252.* ◯ *9am–6pm Wed–Sun.* 🖼
Parque Zoológico Nacional
Tel (7) 643 8063. ◯ *9:30am–
3:15pm Wed–Sun.* 🖼

The impressive monument to Lenin designed by Lev Korbel

Lenin Park, 20 km (12 miles)
south of Central Havana,
occupies an area of 1,840
acres (745 ha). It was created
in the 1970s as an amusement
park for children and an area
of greenery for a city in
continuous expansion.

In the same period, thanks to
an initiative by Celia Sánchez,
Castro's personal assistant during the Revolution, the Russian
architect Lev Korbel designed
the vast monument honouring
the Soviet leader. The statue of
Lenin, which weighs 1,200 tons
and is 9 m (30 ft) high, was
completed in 1982 under
the supervision of Antonio
Quintana Simonetti, who
also designed the park.

The most enjoyable way of
getting around Parque Lenin
is to take the narrow-gauge
train which follows a route of
9.5 km (6 miles) in 45 minutes,
making several stops. The
train's old steam engines were
used in previous years by
Cuba's sugar factories to
transport sugar cane. Open
carriages allow passengers to
admire the scenery. The park
is popular with Habaneros,
who love to walk among the
palm, cedar, pine and araucaria
trees. There is also a freshwater
aquarium, stables, outdoor
cinema, art gallery, swimming
pools, café and the Las Ruínas
restaurant. The latter occupies
a 1960s building that incor-
porates the crumbling walls
of an old plantation house.

Environs

Near the park, among gardens
and tree-lined paths, is the
largest exhibition centre in
Cuba, **ExpoCuba**, which stages various exhibitions and
shows all year round. In
autumn the pavilions are
occupied by the famous Feria
Internacional de La Habana,
which offers an overview
of Cuba's economic and
socio-political life. From
Parque Lenin it is also easy to
reach the 840-acre (340-ha)
Parque Zoológico Nacional,
where animals live freely in
various natural habitats, often
without cages. The savannah
area is populated with zebras,
hippopotamuses, giraffes and
antelopes. Another area is the
habitat of lions.

Jardín Botánico Nacional ⑫

Carretera del Rocío km 3, Calabazar,
Arroyo Naranjo (Havana). *Tel (7) 697
9364.* ◯ *8am–4pm Wed–Sun.*
● *1 Jan, 26 Jul, 25 Dec.* 🖼 🎫 🖼

This enormous 1,500-acre
(600-ha) botanical garden, set
in an area of woods and
cultivated fields, contains

The tranquil Japanese Garden, part of the Jardín Botánico Nacional

plants from all over the world. These are on display to the public and are also studied by specialists. The huge gardens are divided into geographical zones – Cuba, America, Africa, Asia and Oceania. The Caribbean section, which takes up one-fifth of the garden, has 7,000 flowering plants, half of which are unique to Cuba. There are also curiosities such as the Archaic Woods and the Palmetum. The former has plants descended from species that thrived in ancient geological eras, such as the *Palma corcho*, a fossil species that can still be found in the Pinar del Río region. The Palmetum has a large collection of palm trees from all tropical latitudes.

A must is the cactus area near the entrance. However, the most interesting part of this rather sparse park is the Jardín Japonés, a Japanese garden with artificial waterfalls and a pond with a gazebo. It was donated to Cuba by the local Asian community in 1989.

Another fascinating sight here is the orchid garden, with numerous varieties.

The Sanctuary of San Lázaro at El Rincón

Santuario de San Lázaro ⑬

Calzada de San Antonio km. 23, El Rincón, Santiago de las Vegas (Havana). *Tel* (7) 683 2396.
🔘 7am–5pm daily. ✝ 10am Wed, Fri, 9am Sun. 🎏 Feast Day of St Lazarus, 17 Dec.

This sanctuary, dedicated to St Lazarus, the patron saint of the sick, lies in the small village of El Rincón, outside Santiago de las Vegas, next to an old lepers' hospital (now a dermatological hospital).

In Afro-Cuban religions Lazarus corresponds to Babalú Ayé. Both saints are represented in folk iconography as old men in tatters and covered with sores. In the case of the African saint, the skin disease was supposedly punishment from Olofi, the father of all the gods *(see p22)*, for the saint's adulterous and libertine past.

On 17 December, the simple white sanctuary welcomes thousands of worshippers, who flock here to make vows or ask the saint to intercede for them. Before the high altar, or in front of the image of St Lazarus (who is called *milagroso* or "the miraculous one"), at a side altar, pilgrims light candles, leave flowers and make offerings.

The water from the fountain to the right of the sanctuary, considered miraculous by believers, is used to cure diseases and ease pain.

ITALO CALVINO AND CUBA

Santiago de las Vegas, most famous for its San Lázaro sanctuary, was also the birthplace of the great Italian novelist Italo Calvino (1923–1985). His father Mario was an esteemed agronomist who went to Cuba in 1918, following his appointment as director of the Estación Experimental de Santiago de las Vegas. This experimental field station covered 123 acres (50 ha) of land and employed 100 university graduates and 63 office workers. While in Cuba, Mario Calvino found ways of making genetic improvements to sugar cane and introduced new plants, including pumpkin and lettuce. He also worked on tobacco, corn and sorghum, while his wife Eva wrote articles exhorting Cuban women to emancipate themselves and acquire new dignity through education and training.

When the Calvino family returned to San Remo in Italy, they took not only a son who would become a great writer, but also mango, avocado, flamboyant, cherimoya and even sugar cane seeds, which they cultivated at the San Remo Experimental Agriculture Station. In 1964 Italo Calvino was named a member of the jury for the Casa de las Américas prize *(see p100)* and visited Cuba, where he returned to his birthplace and also met Che Guevara.

Author Italo Calvino, born at Santiago de las Vegas

The altar of St Lazarus with flowers left by worshippers

HAVANA STREET FINDER

The page grid shown on the *Area by Area* map below shows the parts of Havana covered by maps in this section. All map references in this guide refer to the maps in the *Street Finder* section. Addresses are indicated in keeping with the system used in Cuba so that people will understand your requests

Street sign, corner of Calle 13 and Ave de los Presidentes

for information. The street name (and sometimes house number) is followed by either "e/" (*entre*, or "between") and the names of the two streets between which the address you want is located, or "*esq.*" (*esquina*, or "corner") followed by the name of the street on the crossroad where the address is located.

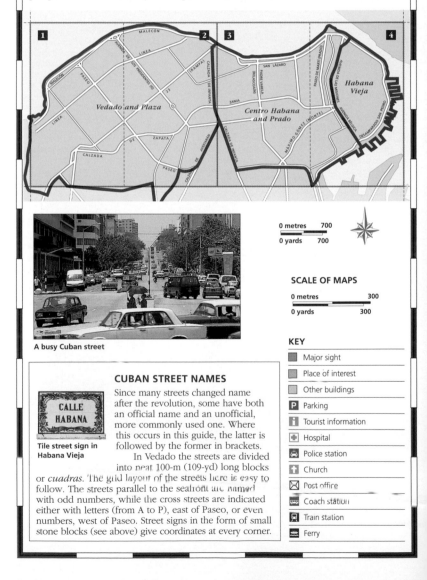

A busy Cuban street

0 metres   700
0 yards   700

SCALE OF MAPS

0 metres   300
0 yards   300

KEY

■	Major sight
■	Place of interest
■	Other buildings
P	Parking
ℹ	Tourist information
✚	Hospital
🚓	Police station
✝	Church
✉	Post office
🚌	Coach station
🚆	Train station
⛴	Ferry

CUBAN STREET NAMES

Tile street sign in Habana Vieja

Since many streets changed name after the revolution, some have both an official name and an unofficial, more commonly used one. Where this occurs in this guide, the latter is followed by the former in brackets.

In Vedado the streets are divided into neat 100-m (109-yd) long blocks or *cuadras*. The grid layout of the streets here is easy to follow. The streets parallel to the seafront are named with odd numbers, while the cross streets are indicated either with letters (from A to P), east of Paseo, or even numbers, west of Paseo. Street signs in the form of small stone blocks (see above) give coordinates at every corner.

Street Finder Index

Calle 1	1 B2		Campanario	3 C2
2	1 B2		Cañongo	3 C2
3	1 B2		Capricho	4 D1
4	1 B3		Cárcel	4 D1
5	1 B3		Cárdenas	4 D3
6	1 B3		Carlos III	2 F4
7	1 B3			& 3 A4
8	1 B3		Carlos M de Céspedes,	
9	2 D1		Avenida	2 D5
10	1 B3		Carmen	3 B4
11	1 A2		Carpinetti	4 F2
12	1 B3		Castillejo	3 A3
13	1 A4		Castillo	3 B5
14	1 B3		Catedral, Plaza de la	4 E2
15	1 A4		Cerrada del Paseo	3 B3
16	1 A3		Chacón	4 E2
17	1 A4		Chávez	3 B3
18	1 A4		Churruca	4 F2
19	1 A5		Cienfuegos	4 D4
19 de Mayo	2 E4		Clavel	3 A5
20 de Mayo, Avenida	2 F5		Collado	2 F4
21	1 A5			& 3 A4
22	1 A4		Colón	4 D2
23 (La Rampa)	1 C4		Colón, Avenida de	2 D5
24	1 A4		Compostela	4 E2
24 de Febrero	2 F5		Concepción de la Valla	3 B4
25	1 A5		Concordia	2 F2
	& 3 A2			& 3 A2
26	1 A5		Conde	4 E4
27	1 C4		Condesa	3 B4
27 de Noviembre	2 E3		Consulado	4 D1
28	1 A5		Corrales	3 C4
29	2 D4		Crecherie	1 C4
30	1 A5		Crespo	3 C2
31	2 D4		Cristo	4 D3
33	2 D4		Cruz del Padre	3 A5
35	2 D5		Cuarteles	4 E1
37	2 D5		Cuba	4 E2
39	2 D5		Cuchillo	3 C3
41	2 D5		Curazao	4 E3

A
A	1 B2
	& 1 A5
A Alvarez, Pasaje	3 B4
Acosta	4 E3
Agramonte	4 D2
Aguacate	4 E2
Aguiar	4 E2
Aguila	3 C2
Aguire	2 F3
Alambique	4 D4
Almendares	2 F4
Amargura	4 E2
Amenidad	3 A5
Amezaga	2 F5
Amistad	3 C2
Angeles	3 C4
Animas	3 A2
Antón Recio	3 C4
Apodaca	4 D4
Aponte (Someruelos)	4 D3
Aramburu	2 E5
	& 3 A5
Arbol Seco	3 A4
Arroyo (Manglar), Avenida	3 A5
Ayestarán, Calzada de	2 F5

B
B	1 C2
B, Pasaje	3 B4
Baratillo	4 F2
Barcelona	3 C3
Barillo	4 F2
Basarrate	2 F3
Bayona	4 E4
Belascoaín	3 B2
Bélgica (Egido), Avenida	4 D2
Bellavista	2 D5
Benjumeda	2 F4
	& 3 A4
Bernal	3 C2
Bernaza	4 D3
Blanco	3 C2
Brasil (Teniente Rey)	4 E3
Bruzón	2 F4

C
C	1 C2
C Protestantes	2 D5

D
D	1 C2
Damas	4 E3
Desagüe	2 F4
	& 3 A4
Desamparado	4 E4
Diaria	3 C5
División	3 B4
Dragones	3 C3

E
E	1 C1
Economía	4 D3
Egido	4 E4
Empedrado	4 E2
Enrique Barnet (Estrella)	3 A4
Escobar	3 B2
Espada	2 F2
	& 3 A2
Espada (Vives), Avenida de	3 C5
Esperanza	3 C4
Estévez	3 B5

F
F	1 C1
Fabria	2 F4
Factoría	4 D3
Figuras	3 C4
Flores	3 B5
Florida	4 D4
Franco	3 B4

G
G	2 D2
Galiano	3 C2
General Aguirre	2 F5
General E. Núñez	2 F5
General Suárez	2 E5
Genios	4 D1
Gervasio	3 B2
Gloria	3 C5
Gregorio	3 B5

H
H	2 D1
H Uppman	2 F3
Habana	4 E2
Hamel	3 A2
Holguín	3 C4
Hornos	3 A5
Hospital	3 A1
Humboldt	2 F1
	& 3 A1

I
I	2 D1
Indio	3 C4
Industria	4 D2
Infanta, Calzada de	2 F2
	& 3 A4
Inquisidor	4 F3

J-K
J	2 D1
Jesús María	4 E3
Jesús Peregrino	3 A3
Julia Borges	2 D5
Jústiz	4 F2
K	2 D1

L
L	2 E1
Lagunas	3 B2
Lamparilla	4 E2
Lealtad	3 B4
Leonor Pérez (Paula)	4 E4
Linas, Pasaje	3 B4
Lindero	3 B5
Línea	1 A3
López	4 F2
Luaces	2 F4
Lucena	3 B2
Lugareño	2 F4
Luz	4 E3

M
M	2 E1
Malecón	1 A2
	& 3 A1
Maloja	3 A4
Manglar	3 D5
Manrique	3 C2
Marina	3 A2
Marino	2 D5
Marqués González	3 B2
Marta Abreu	2 F5
Masó	2 F5
Matadero	3 B5
Máximo Gómez (Monte)	3 B3
Mazón	2 F3
Mercaderes	4 E2
Mercado	3 B5
Merced	4 E3
Misión	3 D4
Misiones, Ave de las (Monserrate)	4 D2
Montero Sánchez	1 D4
Montoro	2 F4
Morales	3 A4
Morro	4 D1
Muralla	4 E3

N
N	2 E1
N López	4 F2
Neptuno	2 F2
	& 3 A2
Nueva	3 A5
Nueva de Pilar	3 B4

O
O	2 F1
O'Reilly	4 E2
Obispo	4 E2
Obrapía	4 E2
Oficios	4 F2
Omoa	3 B5
Oquendo	3 A2

P
P Laccoste	2 F5
P Vidal	2 F5
Panorama	2 D5
Panchito Gómez	2 F5
Pasaje 21	1 B2
Paseo	1 B2
Paseo de Martí (Prado)	4 D2
Pedroso	3 A5
Peña Pobre	4 E1
Peñalver	2 F4
	& 3 A4
Pereira	2 F5
Perseverancia	3 C2
Pirota	4 E3
Plasencia	3 A4
Pocitos	3 A3
Porvenir	4 A3
Pozos Dulces	2 F4
Presidentes, Ave de los	1 C1
Príncipe	2 F2
	& 3 A2
Progreso	4 D2
Puerta Cerrada	3 C5
Puerto, Avenida del	4 D5

R
Rancho Boyeros, Avenida de	2 E5
Rastro	3 C4
Rayo	3 C4
Reina	3 L3
Refugio	4 D1
Requena	2 F4
Retiro	3 A4
Reunión	3 C4
Revillagigedo	4 D4
Ronda	2 F3

S
Salud	3 A3
San Antonio	2 D5
San Antonio Chiquito	1 B5
San Carlos	3 B4
San Francisco	3 A3
San Ignacio	4 E2
San Isidro	4 E4
San Joaquín	3 A5
San José	3 B5
San Lázaro	2 F2
	& 3 A2
San Martín	2 F5
	& 3 A5
San Martín (San José)	2 F3
	& 3 A3
San Miguel	2 F3
	& 3 A3
San Nicolás	3 C2
San Pedro	4 F3
San Rafael	2 F3
	& 3 A3
Santa Clara	4 F3
Santa Marta	3 A5
Santa Rosa	3 B5
Santiago	3 B3
Santo Tomás	3 A4
Santo Tomás, Pasaje	3 B4
Sardinas	2 F5
Sitios	3 A4
Sol	4 E3
Soledad	3 A2
Suárez	4 D4
Subirama	3 A4

T
Tacón	4 E1
Talla Piedra	4 D5
Tejadillo	4 E2
Tenerife	3 C4
Territorial	2 E5
Tetuán	3 B3
Trocadero	4 D2

U-V
Universidad	2 E3
	& 3 B5
Valle	2 F3
	& 3 A3
Vapor	2 F2
	& 3 A2
Venus	3 A2
Vieja, Plaza	4 E3
Villegas	4 D2
Villuenda	2 F5
Virtudes	3 A2

X-Z
Xifré	3 A4
Zanja	3 A3
Zapata, Calzada de	1 B4
Zulueta	4 D2

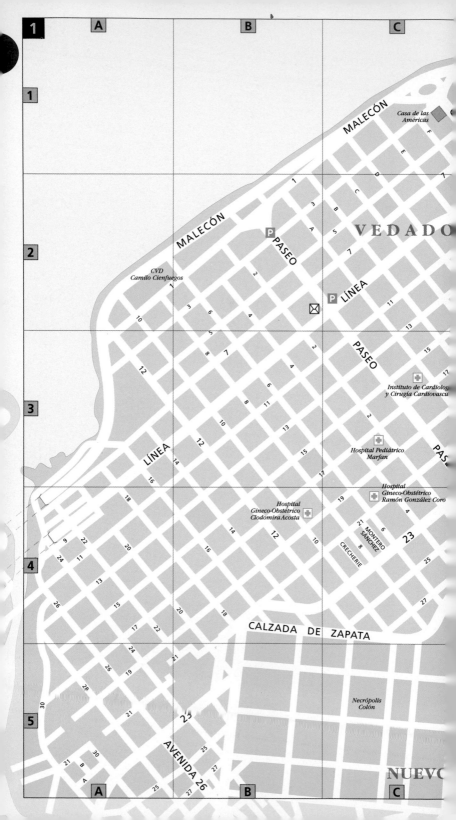

1

A   B   C

1

MALECÓN   Casa de las Américas

F
E
D
C
B
A   7

2

MALECÓN

PASEO

V E D A D O

1
3
5
7

CVD
Camilo Cienfuegos   1

LÍNEA

10   3   6   4   2

11

13

3

5   8   7   PASEO   15

8   6   4   17

Instituto de Cardiolog
y Cirugía Cardiovascu

12   8   11   2

10   13

LÍNEA   12   15   Hospital Pediátrico
Marfan   PAS

14   17

16   Hospital
Gineco-Obstétrico
Ramón González Coro

18   19   4

22   14   Hospital
Gineco-Obstétrico
Clodomira Acosta   12   21   6   23

4

9   20   16   10   MONTERO
SÁNCHEZ   8   25

24   11   CRECHERIE   27

13

26   15   20   18

17   22   CALZADA DE ZAPATA

24   21

26   19   Necrópolis
Colón

28   21

5

30   25

21   30

B

A   25   AVENIDA 26   25

A   27   B   27   **NUEVC**   C

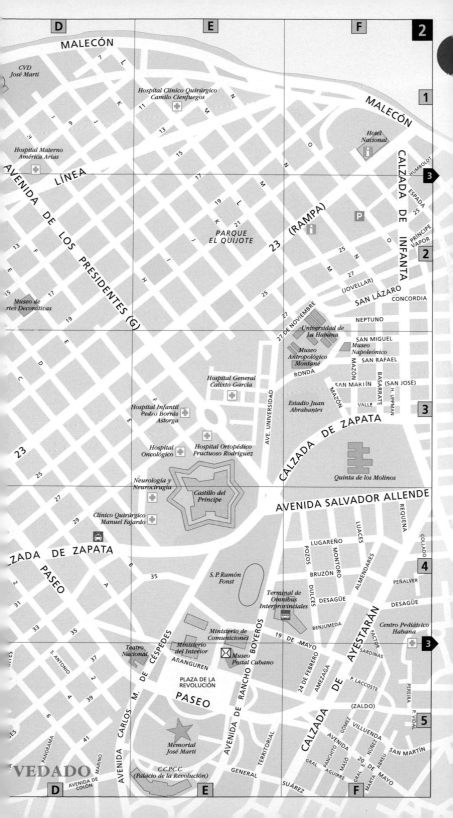

MALECÓN

D   E   F

2

1

MALECÓN

CVD
José Marti

Hospital Clínico Quirúrgico
Camilo Cienfuegos

Hotel
Nacional

CALZADA DE INFANTA

HUMBOLDT

ESPADA

Hospital Materno
América Arias

LÍNEA

3

AVENIDA DE LOS PRESIDENTES (G)

PARQUE
EL QUIJOTE

23 (RAMPA)

P

PRÍNCIPE

VAPOR

25

2

(JOVELLAR)

SAN LÁZARO

CONCORDIA

Museo de
rtes Decorativas

27 DE NOVIEMBRE

NEPTUNO

Universidad de
la Habana

Museo
Antropológico
Montané

SAN MIGUEL

Museo
Napoleónico

SAN RAFAEL

(SAN JOSÉ)

MAZÓN

BASARRATE

H. UPMANN

RONDA

SAN MARTÍN

23

Hospital General
Calixto García

Estadio Juan
Abrabantes

MAZÓN

VALLE

3

Hospital Infantil
Pedro Borrás
Astorga

CALZADA DE ZAPATA

Hospital
Oncológico

Hospital Ortopédico
Fructuoso Rodríguez

AVE. UNIVERSIDAD

Quinta de los Molinos

Neurología y
Neurocirugía

Castillo del
Príncipe

AVENIDA SALVADOR ALLENDE

REQUENA

Clínico Quirúrgico
Manuel Fajardo

LUACES

COLLADO

ZADA DE ZAPATA

PASEO

35

S. P. Ramón
Fonst

LUGAREÑO

MONTORO

ALMENDARES

4

POZOS

BRUZÓN

PEÑALVER

DULCES

DESAGÜE

DESAGÜE

Terminal de
Omnibus
Interprovinciales

BENJUMEDA

Centro Pediátrico
Habana

3

Ministerio de
Comunicaciones

19 DE MAYO

FACTOR

SARDINAS

Teatro
Nacional

Ministerio
del Interior

Museo
Postal Cubano

BOYEROS

24 DE FEBRERO

AMEZAGA

P. LACCOSTE

PEREIRA

P. VIDAL

ARANGUREN

PLAZA DE LA
REVOLUCIÓN

AVENIDA DE RANCHO BOYEROS

(ZALDO)

5

CARLOS M. DE CÉSPEDES

PASEO

CALZADA DE AYESTARÁN

Memorial
José Martí

TERRITORIAL

GRAL

PANCHITO
GÓMEZ

AVENIDA
MASÓ

VILLUENDA

20 DE MAYO

SAN MARTÍN

VEDADO

C.C.P.C.C.
(Palacio de la Revolución)

AVENIDA DE
COLÓN

AVENIDA

GENERAL

SUÁREZ

AGUIRRE

GBAL. E

MARTA ABREU

NÚÑEZ

D   E   F

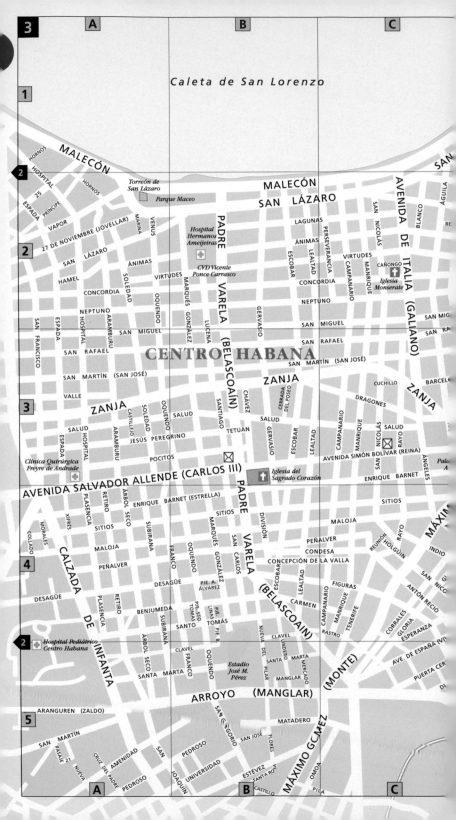

ENTERTAINMENT IN HAVANA

The lively, pleasure-loving capital of Cuba offers entertainment to suit visitors of all ages and tastes. Theatres, cinemas and concert halls are active year-round, while the city's annual ballet, cinema and jazz festivals draw admirers from afar. Havana has the biggest and best nightclubs in the country, offering all kinds of music from salsa and jazz to bolero to rap. The cabaret scene

Ballet Nacional de Cuba dancer

is world-class. You can dance 'til dawn in the discos, while those who prefer more traditional entertainment can investigate the neighbourhood Casa de la Trova or Casa de la Cultura. The bar scene is somewhat desultory, and many venues that pre-date the revolution are rough around the edges, but this adds atmosphere to Havana's sense of a *temps perdu*.

The National Symphony performing in Havana

INFORMATION

The airport, hotels and travel agents all distribute information brochures. The elusive *Cartelera*, a biweekly newspaper, and the online *Cuba Absolutely* events publication provide addresses of nightclubs and other venues, with details of shows. The *Granma* daily lists major events, which are also broadcast on Cubavisión (channel 6) on Thursdays at 10:25pm. Visitors can tune in to Radio Taíno (93.3FM), which broadcasts in Spanish and English. Havana's thriving underground scene requires seeking out. The corner of Calles 23 and L (outside Cine Yara) is a good spot to find out about impromptu parties and shows – especially for the gay scene. Consult http://promociones.egrem.co.cu for all Casas de la Música.

BUYING TICKETS

To avoid long queues for festivals and other major events, visitors can purchase tickets

in advance from the venue's ticket office, from tourist agencies in the hotels or through **Paradiso: Promotora de Turismo Cultural**.

Tickets for cabaret shows at the world-famous Tropicana nightclub and Cabaret Parisien can be obtained at the tour bureaus of any tourist hotel. For smaller shows and events, you will need to stand in line on the day or night of the performance.

THEATRE

Theatre has a long and illustrious tradition in Havana, though the range of offerings has been severely curtailed for political reasons since the Revolution. The *Festival Internacional del Teatro*, held every two years, offers both traditional and experimental theatre, and some companies, such as El Público, have their own venues. Havana's most important and active theatres are located mostly in the Vedado quarter and are presented exclusively in Spanish.

The Teatro Nacional de Cuba, a complex with several auditoriums (*see p102*), often hosts major international companies, while the Teatro Karl Marx seats 5,500 and puts on the city's biggest events. The **Teatro Hubert de Blanck** specializes in contemporary drama, while the **Teatro Mella** has a more varied programme. The **Teatro Trianón** and **Teatro El Sótano** are committed to presenting experimental theatre. The **Café Teatro Brecht** shows alternative plays.

Cuban comedy tends towards bawdy slapstick. The best venues are **Casa de la Comedia**, offering shows at weekends, **Teatro Fausto** and **Café Teatro Brecht**.

CLASSICAL MUSIC & OPERA

There are two main classical music venues in Havana. The restored **Teatro Amadeo**

The impressive exterior of the Gran Teatro de la Habana

Roldán is home to the National Symphony Orchestra, while the Gran Teatro de la Habana *(see p82)*, which has excellent acoustics, hosts opera and other productions.

The lovely Basílica de San Francisco de Asís *(see p74)* is an atmospheric venue for choral and chamber music concerts. The Agrupación Anfitriona de Música Antigua "Ars Longa" puts on Renaissance and Baroque concerts in the beautiful **Iglesia de San Francisco de Paula**.

BALLET

Classical dance is popular in Cuba thanks to the promotion of the **Ballet Nacional de Cuba**, founded by the international ballet star Alicia Alonso. This institution organizes a biennial international ballet festival and promotes specialist courses for foreign dancers. Performances take place in the Gran Teatro de la Habana *(see p82)*. Visitors are often shocked to discover many performances featuring taped music. The **Teatro Mella** hosts occasional ballet shows.

La Zorra y El Cuervo – a popular and crowded jazz venue

FOLK & TRADITIONAL MUSIC

Traditional Cuban music covers a broad range of styles including rumba, *guaguancó, son, danzón,* bolero and *punto guajiro (see pp30–31)*.

Some of the best performances are based on Afro-Cuban forms, as perfected by the **Conjunto Folklórico Nacional**, which performs an open-air rumba every Saturday and hosts lessons for Cubans and foreigners. Similar performances are hosted on Sundays

A traditional *son* band performing on the street

at the **Asociación Cultural Yoruba de Cuba**, and at **Rumba del Callejón de Hamel** in Centro Habana, one of the city's most popular weekend venues. Thursdays at the **Cabaret Nacional** also feature rumba.

HIP HOP, ROCK & JAZZ

Hip hop is very popular in Cuba. An international festival is held every August in Vedado *(see p35)*, where the **Casa de la Cultura de Plaza** hosts live performances, as do the **Teatro América** in Centro Habana and **La Madriguera** in the botanical gardens.

The **Teatro Karl Marx** is the main venue for big-name rock and pop stars. Rock music is also played and danced to in Playa's **Salón Rosado de la Tropical**, usually referred to as La Tropical. **Río Club** was the most famous rock venue in Havana in the 1970s, when it was called Johnny Club. People still use its old name.

Cubans love jazz, and Cuba's leading jazz musicians are popular the world over. An annual jazz festival is held in venues throughout Havana. Among the best of these is **La Zorra y el Cuervo**, a cramped and smoky basement bar. Cuba's top performers, such as Chucho Valdés, play the spacious **Jazz Café**.

Other music venues include **El Sauce**, which puts on everything from salsa to Cuban indie rock, and the basement of the Café Teatro Brecht, which plays host to groups such as Interactivo, a collaborative Cuban jazz-funk band. The intimate bar of the **Centro Asturiano** hosts up-and-coming singer-songwriters.

NIGHTCLUBS & DISCOS

Salsa is the staple of nightclubs and discos. Havana's hottest salsa venues are the twin **Casas de la Música** in Centro Habana and Miramar, where nightly events don't warm up until after midnight. **1830 Club**, located next to the tunnel to Miramar, is a very popular al fresco salsa venue on Thursday and Sunday nights. The **Café Cantante**, in the Teatro Nacional, has regular live bands. The **Salón Turquino**, on the top floor of the Tryp Habana Libre hotel, is the classiest salsa spot. As with many Cuban nightclubs, foreigners are likely to be approached by potential partners hoping to have their entrance paid.

Café Concierto Gato Tuerto is famous as home of the blend of Cuban and North American music called *feeling*. This small venue fills quickly, so arrive early. Fans of the *bolero* should head to **Dos Gardenias**.

A live musical performance at one of Havana's many nightclubs

CABARET

The most exotic of venues, and a long-time Cuban tradition, *cabarets espectáculos* are famous for their extravagantly – and minimally – dressed female dancers in sequins and feathers. The music is first-rate, ranging from salsa to crooners performing traditional boleros.

The most famous is the Tropicana *(see p109)* featuring more than 200 performers. Though expensive, it offers a true spectacular with grandiose choreography, lavish costumes and legendary dancers. The **Cabaret Parisien** is the most important of the hotel shows, while the **Cabaret Salón Rojo** and **Cabaret Copa Room** are among the better small shows.

BARS

The colourful bar-life of pre-revolutionary days is a mere memory today. Nonetheless, most upscale tourist hotels have classy bars (albeit filled with foreigners).

Two bars associated with Hemingway remain among the city's most colourful. La Bodeguita del Medio *(see p65)*, a cramped bar where the author popularized *mojitos,* features troubadors. Famous for its daiquiris, **El Floridita** *(see p72)* exudes a fin-de-siècle ambience. Other hip drinking spots include **El Madrigal**, Havana's only private bar, and the late-night bar at Tocororo *(see p279)*.

In Vedado, the Hotel Nacional's **Bar Vista del Golfo**

Dancers at the Tropicana, Havana's most famous and colourful cabaret

has served cocktails to the rich and famous for decades. Also in Vedado, head to the top of **La Torre** in Edificio Fosca to enjoy a cocktail and admire the incredible views out over the city.

CINEMA

Cuba has a thriving cinema industry. The annual December *Festival Internacional del Cine Latinoamericano*, a major international film festival, is organized by the **Instituto Cubano del Arte e Industria Cinematográfica** (ICAIC), which presides over the activities of the "seventh art" in Cuba *(see p29)* and also runs the **Cine Charles Chaplin**.

Most of the major cinemas are in the Vedado district. The main one is **Cine Yara**. **Cine Riviera** screens mostly Hollywood action movies, while **Cine La Rampa** shows mainly Cuban and Latin American films. Havana's largest cinema is the multi-screen **Cine Payret**, in La Habana Vieja; it has midnight shows at weekends.

CULTURAL CENTRES

For visitors interested in Cuban culture, the Casa de las Américas *(see p100)* has a good library, well-stocked book shop and a fine art gallery. It organizes literary and poetry festivals. High-level cultural events are also held at the **Fundación Alejo Carpentier**, dedicated to the work of the great Cuban writer, and the **Fundación Fernando Ortíz**, specializing in Afro-Cuban studies. The **Asociación Cultural Yoruba**, dedicated to

African-derived religions, has a library, exhibits, and lectures.

One of the most active centres is **UNEAC** (Writers and Artists' Union), which hosts musical and literary events at El Hurón Azul – the main spot for Havana's bohemians.

CULTURAL TOURS

Week-long holiday packages are available from **Paradiso: Promotora de Turismo Cultural** *(see Ticket Agencies)*. The cost includes accommodation in a "4-star" hotel, lunch and dinner in typical Cuban restaurants, transport, guides, entrance to museums and theatres, meetings with Cuban artists and visits to specialist educational centres. The *"Aché Habana"* programme focuses on a religious and cultural tour of Regla and Guanabacoa, while "Dancing the Cuban Style" features salsa classes. There are also packages tailored around the city's jazz and ballet festivals.

CHILDREN

Cubans adore children and the State takes good care of its young. However, entertainment venues for children are few. The Acuario Nacional *(see p109)* puts on dolphin shows. Donkey rides are offered at **Parque Luz Caballero** in La Habana Vieja, and at Parque Lenin *(see p116)* and **Parque Metropoliano de La Habana**. The **Teatro Guiñol** hosts puppet shows and children's theatre. The **Planetario** and shadow puppet theatre **El Arca** are also popular with families.

Bartender preparing one of the famous daiquiris at El Floridita

DIRECTORY

TICKET AGENCIES

Paradiso: Promotora de Turismo Cultural
Calle 19 560, esq. C. **Map** 2 D3. *Tel (7) 832 6928.*

THEATRE

Café Teatro Brecht
Calle 13 esq. I. **Map** 2 D2. *Tel (7) 832 9359.*

Casa de la Comedia
Calle Jústiz 7, esq. Baratillo. **Map** 4 F2. *Tel (7) 863 9282.*

Teatro El Sótano
Calle K, e/ 25 y 27. **Map** 2 E2. *Tel (7) 832 0630.*

Teatro Fausto
Paseo de Martí 201, esq. Colón. **Map** 4 D2. *Tel (7) 863 1173.*

Teatro Hubert de Blanck
Calzada 657, e/ Calles A y B. **Map** 1 C2. *Tel (7) 830 1011.*

Teatro Mella
Línea 657, e/ A y B. **Map** 1 C2. *Tel (7) 830 4987.*

Teatro Trianón
Línea 706, e/ Paseo y A. **Map** 1 C2. *Tel (7) 830 9648.*

CLASSICAL MUSIC & OPERA

Iglesia de San Francisco de Paula
Avenida del Puerto esq. Leonor Pérez. **Map** 4 F4. *Tel (7) 860 4210.*

Teatro Amadeo Roldán
Calzada y D. **Map** 1 C2. *Tel (7) 832 4521.*

BALLET

Ballet Nacional e Cuba
Calzada 510, e/ D y E. 1 C2.
7) 835 2945.

FOLK & TRADI-TIONAL MUSIC

Asociación Cultural Yoruba de Cuba
Prado 615, e/ Dragones y Monte. **Map** 4 D3. *Tel (7) 863 5953.*

Cabaret Nacional
Calle San Rafael esq. Paseo de Martí. **Map** 3 A3. *Tel (7) 863 2361.*

Conjunto Folklórico Nacional
Calle 4 103, e/ Calzada y 5ta. **Map** 1 B2. *Tel (7) 830 3939.*

Rumba del Callejón de Hamel
Callejón de Hamel e/ Aramburo y Hospital. **Map** 3 A2. *Tel (7) 878 1661.*

HIP HOP, ROCK & JAZZ

Casa de la Cultura de Plaza
Calzada y Calle 8, Vedado. *Tel (7) 832 3503.*

Centro Asturiano
Prado 309 esq. Virtudes. **Map** 3 A2. *Tel (7) 864 1447.*

El Sauce
Avenida 9na no.1201S, e/ 120 y 130, Playa. *Tel (7) 204 7114.*

Jazz Café
Avenida 1ra esq. Paseo. **Map** 1 B2. *Tel (7) 838 3556.*

La Madriguera
Avenida Salvador Allende e/ Infanta y Luaces. **Map** 2 F4. *Tel (7) 879 8175.*

La Zorra y el Cuervo
Calle 23 e/ N y O. **Map** 2 F2. *Tel (7) 833 2402.*

Río Club (Johnny)
Calle A e/ 3ra y 5ta, Miramar. *Tel (7) 209 3389.*

Teatro América
Avenida de Italia 253, e/ Concordia y Neptuno. **Map** 3 C2. *Tel (7) 862 5416.*

Teatro Karl Marx
Avenida 1ra e/ 8 y 10. *Tel (7) 203 0801.*

NIGHTCLUBS & DISCOS

1830 Club
Malecón y Túnel, Vedado. *Tel (7) 838 3090.*

Café Cantante
Paseo esq. 39. **Map** 2 E6. *Tel (7) 878 4275.*

Café Gato Tuerto
Calle O 14, e/ 17 y 19. **Map** 2 F1. *Tel (7) 838 2629.*

Casa de la Música
Galiano e/ Concordia y Neptuno. *Tel (7) 862 4165.* Avenida 35 esq 20. **Map** 3 C2. *Tel (7) 204 0447.*

Dos Gardenias
Complejo Dos Gardenias, Calle 7 y 26, Playa. *Tel (7) 204 2353.*

Salón Turquino
Calle L e/ 23 y 25. **Map** 2 F2. *Tel (7) 834 6100.*

CABARET

Cabaret Copa Room
Paseo y Malecón. **Map** 1 B2. *Tel (7) 836 4051.*

Cabaret Parisien
Calle O esq. 21. **Map** 2 F1. *Tel (7) 836 3663.*

Cabaret Salón Rojo
Calle 21 e/ N y O. **Map** 2 B2. *Tel (7) 833 3747.*

BARS

Bar Vista del Golfo
Calle O esq. 21. **Map** 2 F1. *Tel (7) 836 3564.*

El Floridita
Obispo esq. Monserrate. **Map** 4 D2. *Tel (7) 866 8856.*

El Madrigal
Calle 17, no.809 (altos), e/ 2 y 4, Vedado. *Tel (7) 831 2433.*

La Torre
Calle M esq. 17, Vedado. *Tel (7) 832 7306.*

CINEMA

Cine Charles Chaplin
Calle 23 1155, e/ 10 y 12. **Map** 1 C4. *Tel (7) 831 1101.*

Cine La Rampa
Calle 23 111, e/ N y O. **Map** 2 F2. *Tel (7) 878 6146.*

Cine Payret
Paseo de Martí 503, esq. San José. **Map** 4 D3. *Tel (7) 863 3163.*

Cine Riviera
Calles 23 e/ H y G. **Map** 2 E3. *Tel (7) 830 9564.*

Cine Yara
Calle 23 y Calle L. **Map** 2 E2. *Tel (7) 832 9430.*

ICAIC
Calle 23 1155, e/ 10 y 12. **Map** 1 C4. *Tel (7) 831 1101.*

CULTURAL CENTRES

Asociación Cultural Yoruba
Paseo de Martí 615. **Map** 4 D3. *Tel (7) 863 5953.*

Fundación Alejo Carpentier
Empedrado 215. **Map** 4 E2. *Tel (7) 861 3667.*

Fundación Fernando Ortíz
Calle 27 160, esq. L. **Map** 2 F2. *Tel (7) 832 4334.*

UNEAC
Calle 17 351, esq. H. **Map** 2 D2. *Tel (7) 832 4551.*

CHILDREN

El Arca
Avenida del Puerto y Obrapía. **Map** 4 D5. *Tel (7) 864 8953.*

Parque Luz Caballero
Avenida del Puerto y Chacón, La Habana Vieja. Avenida 47, Miramar. **Map** 4 E1.

Parque Metropol-itano de La Habana
Avenida 47, Miramar.

Planetario
Plaza Vieja. **Map** 4 E3. *Tel (7) 864 9165.*

Teatro Guiñol
Calle M, e/ 17 y 19. **Map** 2 E1. *Tel (7) 832 6262.*

CUBA REGION BY REGION

Cuba at a Glance

The lovely palm-fringed beaches of Cuba, such as those at Varadero and on Cayo Largo, are famous throughout the world, and justly so. But the interior of the island also offers a variety of unexpected experiences, from mountainous scenery to marshland and freshwater lagoons. The towns are full of interest, often with well-preserved architecture. Cuba really has two capitals. Havana is monumental and maritime, modern and colonial, and represents the most European spirit of the country. The second, Santiago, embodies the Caribbean soul of Cuba. For the purposes of this guide, the island is divided into five regions – Havana, Western Cuba, Central Cuba – West, Central Cuba – East and Eastern Cuba. Each area is colour coded as shown here.

Varadero (see pp162–3), *known for its clear sea, is a popular holiday resort with sports centres and parks such as the Parque Josone.*

HAVANA

CENTRAL CUBA-WEST *(pp154–177)*

WESTERN CUBA *(pp132–153)*

The Valle de Viñales (see pp142–3) *has spectacular natural scenery with unique outcrops called* mogotes *and many cave formations. The most significant cave is the Cueva de Santo Tomás.*

Cayo Largo del Sur (see pp152–3), *a small island with stunning white sand beaches on the shores of the Caribbean Sea, is a holiday paradise.*

Trinidad (see pp182–90) *is a beautifully preserved and restored city noted for its colonial architecture. The pastel-washed bell tower of the former Iglesia de San Francisco is the symbol of the city.*

◁ The church and monastery of San Juan de Dios in Camagüey

Cayo Coco *is a natural reserve for flamingos in the Jardines del Rey archipelago (see pp198–9). The coasts, mostly marshland, are dotted with mangrove swamps.*

Camagüey *(see pp200–203), in Central-Eastern Cuba, is full of well-preserved colonial buildings and courtyards, with fine streets and squares such as Plaza San Juan de Dios, seen here.*

Baracoa *(see pp242–3), the isolated, easternmost city in Cuba, is the only one with traces of the island's first inhabitants. Near the town are remnants of the tropical forest that covered the entire island when Columbus first landed here.*

CENTRAL CUBA–EAST
(pp178–207)

0 km   90
0 miles   90

EASTERN CUBA
(pp208–245)

Santiago de Cuba *(see pp222–31) is a fascinating town built around a bay, with its heart around the Catedral de la Asunción. Every summer Santiago plays host to the liveliest carnival in Cuba, in which the entire local population takes part.*

WESTERN CUBA

PINAR DEL RÍO · ISLA DE LA JUVENTUD · CAYO LARGO DEL SUR

The western region of mainland Cuba is characterized by swathes of cultivated fields and, at times, extraordinarily beautiful scenery. The main attraction here is the Viñales valley, where unusual limestone outcrops (called mogotes*) loom over lush fields of tobacco. Off the coast, scattered islands with stunning white beaches offer a peaceful refuge from the bustle of Havana.*

According to the inhabitants of Santiago, Pinar del Río and Artemisa provinces are the least "revolutionary" parts of Cuba. They form the island's most rural region, populated by white farmers, who have never been known for their warlike passion, although western Cuba was the scene of several battles against the Spanish in the late 1800s, and in 1958 there was a revolutionary front here.

This part of Cuba was colonized in the 16th and 17th centuries by Europeans mainly from the Canary Islands. Historically Pinar has preferred to concentrate its efforts on producing what they claim is the best tobacco in the world. Tobacco fields are scattered among the Sierra del Rosario and Sierra de Órganos ranges, which are barely 600 m (1,970 ft) above sea level – not high enough to be mountains yet tall enough to create a breathtaking landscape. Palm trees mingle with pine trees, and delicate wild orchids thrive where the conditions are right. These low mountains provide excellent walking territory. The Sierra del Rosario is now a UNESCO world biosphere reserve, as is the Guanahacabibes peninsula in the far west. In both areas, the emphasis is placed on conservation-conscious ecotourism.

Ecotourism is less of a priority on Cayo Largo, a long-established island resort with lovely sea and sand, and numerous hotels. This island forms part of the Archipiélago de los Canarreos, in the Caribbean Sea, which is made up of 350 *cayos* or keys. All of these are uninhabited apart from Cayo Largo and Isla de la Juventud (Isle of Youth), a large island with a rich history and the best diving in Cuba.

Miles of white beaches and beautifully clear water at Playa Tortuga, Cayo Largo

Bike riding in the peaceful Viñales valley; in the background is a typical *mogote*

Exploring Western Cuba

The extraordinary tranquillity and agreeable climate of Western Cuba make it a lovely area for a relaxing break. However, there is also plenty to do. Besides walking and horse riding, there is the provincial capital of Pinar del Río to explore, while tempting coral beaches are easily accessible off the north coast. More effort is required to reach remote María La Gorda, in the far west, but keen divers are attracted to this diving centre. Isla de la Juventud attracts divers and visitors interested in curious attractions, from painted caves to the one-time prison of Fidel Castro. The Valle de Viñales hotels make the best base for a stay in Western Cuba.

View of a street in Pinar del Río, "the city of capitals"

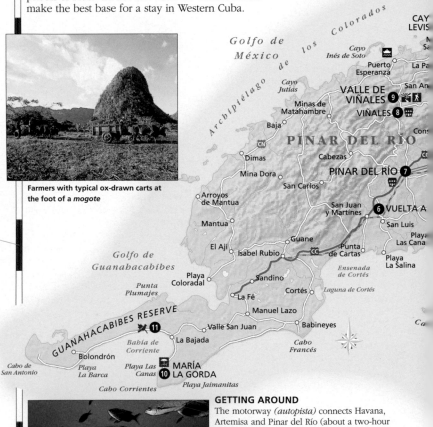

Farmers with typical ox-drawn carts at the foot of a *mogote*

Schools of tropical fish, easily spotted on the sea bed along the Los Canarreos archipelago

GETTING AROUND

The motorway (*autopista*) connects Havana, Artemisa and Pinar del Río (about a two-hour drive), and another slower, but more picturesque, road follows the northern coastline. From Pinar a road runs southwest to Guanahacabibes. There are one-day tours that start off from Havana and include Soroa, Pinar and Viñales, but not the beaches: information is available at tourist offices. The best way to get to Isla de la Juventud and Cayo Largo is by air from Havana (40 mins). There is also a catamaran service to the former from Batabanó; the trip takes two hours. Excursions can also be booked to the two islands; departures are from Havana or larger towns.

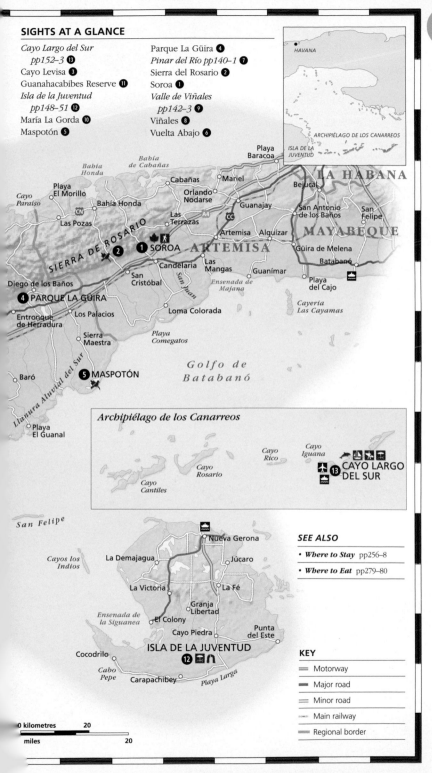

SIGHTS AT A GLANCE

HAVANA

ARCHIPIÉLAGO DE LOS CANARREOS

ISLA DE LA JUVENTUD

Playa Baracoa

Bahía de Cabañas

Bahía Honda

Cabañas   Mariel

Orlando Nodarse   Bejucal

LA HABANA

Cabañas

Cayo Paraíso

Playa El Morillo

Bahía Honda

Las Pozas

Guanajay

San Antonio de los Baños   San Felipe

Las Terrazas   A4

CC   Artemisa   Alquízar   **MAYABEQUE**

SIERRA DE ROSARIO   ② ① SOROA   **ARTEMISA**

Güira de Melena

Candelaria   Las Mangas   Batabanó

Diego de los Baños

④ PARQUE LA GÜIRA

San Cristóbal   Guanímar

Entronque de Herradura   Los Palacios   *Ensenada de Majana*

Playa del Cajo

San Juan

Sierra Maestra   Loma Colorada   *Cayería Las Cayamas*

Llanura Aluvial del Sur

Playa Comegatos

Baró   ⑤ MASPOTÓN   *Golfo de Batabanó*

Playa El Guanal

Archipiélago de los Canarreos

Cayo Rico   Cayo Iguana

Cayo Rosario

⑬ CAYO LARGO DEL SUR

Cayo Cantiles

San Felipe

Nueva Gerona

Cayos los Indios   La Demajagua   Júcaro

SEE ALSO

• **Where to Stay** pp256–8

• **Where to Eat** pp279–80

La Victoria   La Fé

Ensenada de la Siguanea   Granja Libertad

El Colony

Cayo Piedra   Punta del Este

Cocodrilo   **ISLA DE LA JUVENTUD**

⑫

Cabo Pepe   Carapachibey   *Playa Larga*

KEY

══ Motorway

▬▬ Major road

══ Minor road

‑‑‑ Main railway

▬▬ Regional border

0 kilometres   20

miles   20

Soroa ❶

Candelaria (Artemisa). **Road Map** A2. 🚉 *Candelaria.* 🏨 *Hotel Soroa, (48) 523 556.*

The valley road from Havana to Soroa crosses a peaceful area of cultivated fields and rural villages. Soroa itself lies 250 m (820 ft) above sea level in the middle of tropical forest. It was named after two Basque brothers, Lorenzo and Antonio Soroa Muñagorri, who, in around 1856, bought various coffee plantations in the area and soon became the proprietors of the entire territory. One of the estates in the valley, Finca Angerona, was in the 19th century the setting for a legendary love story involving the French-German Cornelius Sausse, who built the farm in 1813, and a Haitian girl, Ursule Lambert.

A flower in the Soroa orchid garden

Soroa, today, is a small town with a hotel (Villa Soroa) and a number of tourist attractions. The most photographed is the **Saltón**, a spectacular waterfall on the Manantiales river, a 20-minute walk from the Villa Soroa. But the major sight here is the **Orquideario de Soroa**, an orchid garden which has been declared a national monument. It has one of the largest orchid collections in the world, with more than 700 species, 250 of which are endemic, in an area of 35,000 ha (86,500 acres). The park, often visited by Hemingway, was founded in 1943 by a lawyer from the Canaries, Tomás Felipe Camacho. He had orchids sent here from all over the world in memory of his daughter, who had died at the age of 20 in childbirth, and his wife who died shortly after.

Outside the town is the **Castillo de las Nubes**, a medieval-like construction built in 1940 for Antonio Arturo Sánchez Busta-mante, the land-owner of this area. The Castillo boasts marvellous views over the Sierra del Rosario.

🌺 **Orquideario de Soroa**
Carretera de Soroa km 8. **Tel** (48) 523 871. ⭕ *daily.* 📷 📷

Bathing under the falls *(saltón)* of the Manantiales river at Soroa

Sierra del Rosario ❷

Artemisa. **Road Map** A2.
🚹 *Las Terrazas, (48) 578 700.*

This area of 61,750 acres (25,000 ha) of unspoilt Cuba has been declared a bio-sphere reserve by UNESCO. Woods consisting of tropical and deciduous trees and plants cover the Sierra del Rosario range, which is crossed by the San Juan river

---

Beaches of the North Coast

An alternative route to the Pinar region from Havana is the road that skirts the coastline at the foot of the Guaniguanico mountain range. The drive from the capital to Viñales, with fine panoramic views and scenery, takes about five hours. From the northern coast there is access to the splendid beaches on some of the small islands in the Los Colorados Archipelago. For the most part, the locals make their living by fishing, but the islands have already attracted some tourism. The sea can be rough and a general lack of facilities makes this area more suitable for visitors who love water sports rather than a place for a relaxing beach holiday.

Cayo Jutías *is still unspoilt and frequented more by Cubans than by tourists. The island is an oasis of peace and white sand, populated by many species of local and migratory birds.*

KEY

▬	Motorway
—	Major road
⋯	Minor road
⛴	Ferry

• Cayo Inés de Soto   Cayo Lev

• Cayo Jutías

Puerto Esperanza •

Santa Lucía •

Minas de Matahambre •

Around 3 km (2 miles) from Santa Lucía, whi has hotel facilities and connections, is a cau way connecting the mainland with Cayo Ju

with its small falls. The area is home to abundant, varied fauna: 90 species of bird as well as many different reptiles and amphibians. The walks here are lovely (permission is needed from the resort area), on paths lined with flowers, including wild orchids.

Most of the farmers in the Sierra live in communities founded by a government programme in 1968. The best-known is **Las Terrazas,** whose name derives from the terraces laid out for the pine trees that are now a characteristic feature of the area. The 1000 inhabitants make a living by maintaining the woods and from

ecotourism, which has increased since the building of the environmentally friendly Hotel Moka (*see p257*). The hotel makes a good starting point for guided walks in the reserve, all of which are fairly easy and take no more than two hours to cover. Also open is the restored 19th-century French coffee plantation of Buena Vista, which has a restaurant.

For birdwatching, hike along the San Juan river as far as the Cañada del Infierno, a shady pool frequented by local birds such as the *zunzún* hummingbird, the *tocororo* and the *cartacuba* (*see pp20–21*).

The **well-managed pine forest at Las Terrazas**

Cayo Levisa ❸

Pinar del Río. **Road Map** A2.
🚢 *from Palma Rubia (1 hr), departures 9am & 10am, return 5pm & 6pm.* **Excursions from Pinar del Río** 🛈 *Havanatur, Calle Osmani Arenado, esq. Martí. (48) 750 100.*

This small island, with its white sand beaches, an offshore coral reef and mangroves, is the most geared up for tourists in the Los Colorados archipelago, and the only one with diving facilities. Despite this, it is still unspoilt and is home to several species of bird and the surrounding waters have an abundance of fish, especially marlin.

The artificial pool at the heart of the Las Terrazas rural community

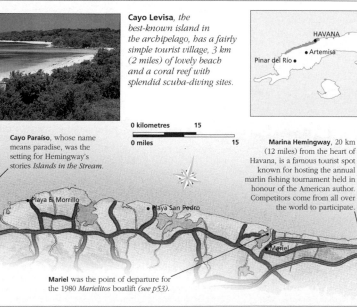

Cayo Levisa, *the best-known island in the archipelago, has a fairly simple tourist village, 3 km (2 miles) of lovely beach and a coral reef with splendid scuba-diving sites.*

Cayo Paraíso, whose name means paradise, was the setting for Hemingway's stories *Islands in the Stream.*

0 kilometres   15

0 miles   15

HAVANA

• Artemisa

Pinar del Río •

Marina Hemingway, 20 km (12 miles) from the heart of Havana, is a famous tourist spot known for hosting the annual marlin fishing tournament held in honour of the American author. Competitors come from all over the world to participate.

Ima Rubia
Playa El Morrillo
Playa San Pedro
Mariel

Mariel was the point of departure for the 1980 *Marielitos* boatlift (*see p53*).

Parque La Güira ④

San Diego de Los Baños (Pinar del Río). **Road Map** A2. 🏠 *3,000.*
ℹ *Cueva de los Portales.* ◯ *daily.* 📷

The former estate of the landowner Don Manuel Cortina, who was forced to leave Cuba in 1959, this was one of the first properties to be nationalized after Castro's revolution. The large park includes the ruins of a medieval-style residence and an English garden with a small Chinese temple and statues of mythological figures including sphinxes and satyrs.

About 5 km (3 miles) east of the Güira park is **San Diego de los Baños**, a peaceful village on the slopes of the Sierra de los Quemados, which has retained its original colonial atmosphere. The village has always been a major tourist and therapeutic centre. The springs in the area produce sulphurous water that was said to help cure rheumatism and skin diseases; they have been closed for several years.

Don Manuel Cortina also owned a nearby cave, the **Cueva de los Portales**, discovered in the 19th century. This old hiding place was used by the natives as a refuge from the massacres that were waged by the Spanish in the early 16th century. In more recent history, during the missile

The lovely gardens in Parque La Güira

crisis, the cave became the headquarters of Che Guevara, some of whose personal belongings and mementoes are on display. Plaques indicate where he played chess and slept.

Maspotón ⑤

Los Palacios (Pinar del Río). **Road Map** A3. ℹ *Ecotur, (48) 753 844.*

The best-known of the many hunting reserves in Cuba, Maspotón includes three lagoons and 61 covers. Besides the endemic birds, migratory birds also come here to escape the cold in North America. Game includes ducks, snipe, pheasants and wild guinea fowl.

Hunting and fishing at Maspotón are regulated. Open season is from October to March, and hunters may not kill more than 40 birds per session. Each day includes two sessions. The hunting lodge hires out all necessary equipment, including everything needed for hunting on horseback, and will also provide hunters with expert guides. Maspotón is a 25-km (15-mile) drive from the Pinar del Río highway by dirt road.

Ecotur also offers another hunting area in Punta de

A Hoyo de Monterrey cigar band

Palma, with better options for hunters. Only 9 km (5.5 miles) away from Pinar del Río, hunters can stay at the renovated Rancho La Guabina.

Vuelta Abajo ⑥

Pinar del Río. **Road Map** A3.

The small area between Pinar del Río, San Juan y Martínez and San Luís produces very high quality tobacco. Good growing conditions are the result of a series of factors: for example, the Sierra del Rosario protects the plants from heavy rainfall, and the sandy red soil in which the tobacco plants grow is well drained and rich in nitrogen. This is a unique environment; in fact, the former landowners who left Cuba in 1959 have tried in vain to reproduce the miracle in Nicaragua, Honduras, Santo Domingo and the US.

On the road from the provincial capital to San Juan y Martínez, the prestigious Hoyo de Monterrey plantations can be visited. Here plants are protected from the sun by cotton cloth in order to maintain the softness of the tobacco leaves. There are also curing houses, windowless storehouses where the leaves are left to dry on long poles.

The entrance to the Cueva de los Portales

For hotels and restaurants in this region see pp256–8 and pp279–80

Cuban Tobacco

The tobacco plant *(Nicotiana tabacum)* grows from small, round, golden seeds. Cuban tobacco seeds are in demand throughout the world, because their quality is considered to be so good. The plant reaches its full height in the three or four months from November to February. Like cigar-making *(see pp32–3)*, tobacco growing is the result of age-old expertise handed down from generation to generation. Tobacco plants are quite delicate, and need skilful handling. There are two types: *Corojo*, grown in greenhouses, which has the prettiest leaves, selected for use as wrapper leaves for the cigars, and *Criollo*, which grows outdoors and provides the other leaves.

Criollo leaves *are separated into three grades:* ligero, seco *and* volado. *The first, which is the best, has the most aromatic leaves, which absorb most sun and are harvested only when completely mature.*

Floating cultivation *is a technique of experimental hydroculture in which the seeds germinate ten days earlier than those grown with traditional methods.*

Poles for transport and drying

Traditional cultivation in rows

TOBACCO HARVEST
Harvesting tobacco is a delicate and laborious operation. The leaves are tied in bunches, hung on horizontal poles and then transported to curing barns. In the case of the *Corojo* plant, the harvest is carried out in various stages, at intervals of several days.

Drying *takes from 45 to 60 days. The leaves, hung on small poles in storehouses known as* casas de tabaco, *gradually turn from bright green to brown.*

Humidification *is a hydrating process carried out after the drying so that the leaves do not dry out and become brittle. Once sprayed, the bunches of leaves are suspended in order to eliminate excess water.*

By establishing a tobacco monopoly *in 1717, the colonial authorities obliged farmers to sell all their tobacco to Spain. Although the Cuban government allows private tobacco growers to have 17-acre (7-ha) plots, the state, along with the UK's Imperial Tobacco, is still the sole manufacturer and distributor of cigars.*

Pinar del Río ❼

Road Map A3. 👥 *200,000.*
ℹ️ *Cubanacán, Calle Martí 109, esq.
Colón, (48) 750 178.* 🚌 🚆 *from
Havana.*

In 1778, when the Cuban
provinces were founded, the
town of Nueva Filipina was
renamed Pinar because of a
pine grove in the vicinity, on
the banks of the Guamá river.
Nearby, General Antonio Maceo
fought a number of battles in
1896–7 that were crucial to the
Cubans' victory in the third
war of Cuban independence.

Today, the pines no longer
grow here, but the clean air
and colonial atmosphere of
Pinar del Río are unchanged.
The town has long been a
centre for the cultivation and
industrial processing of
tobacco. The most striking
aspect about the historic
centre of this small, orderly
and peaceful town is the
abundance of columns:
Corinthian or Ionic, simple or
decorated. Not for
nothing is Pinar del
Río known as the
"city of capitals".

The most important
buildings lie on the
arcaded main street,
Calle Martí (or Real).
In the **Cultural
Heritage Fund** shop,
at the corner of Calle
Rosario, visitors can
buy local crafts as well as art
reproductions. In the evening,
the **Casa de la Cultura** (at No.
125) hosts shows and concerts
of traditional music such as

A capital with bas-
relief decoration

punto guajiro (from *guajiro*,
the Cuban word for farmer),
which is of Spanish derivation,
and is generally characterized
by improvisation.

At Nos. 172, 174 and 176 in
Calle Colón, there are three
unusual buildings
designed by Rogelio
Pérez Cubillas,
the city's leading
architect in the
1930s and 1940s.

🏛️ Palacio Guasch

Calle Martí 202, esq.
Comandante Pinares.
Museum Tel *(48) 753
087.* ⬜ *9am–6pm Tue–
Sat, 9am–1pm Sun.* 🔴 *1 Jan, 1 May,
26 Jul, 10 Oct, 25 Dec.* 🎟️ 📷
This somewhat extravagant
building is a mixture of
Moorish arches, Gothic spires
and Baroque elements. It was
built in 1909 for a wealthy
physician who had travelled
widely and who wanted to
reproduce in his new
residence the architectural
styles that had impressed him
the most. In 1979 the mansion
was transformed into a Museo
de Ciencias Naturales (natural
history museum) named after
Tranquilino Sandalio de
Nodas, a well-known land
surveyor in this region. The
museum illustrates the natural
and geological history of Pinar

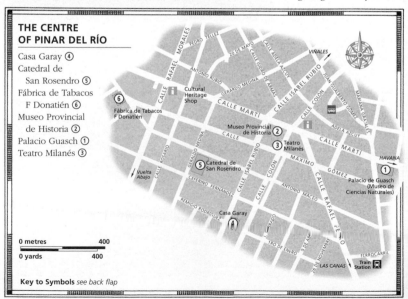

One of the three eclectic-style buildings on Calle Colón

THE CENTRE OF PINAR DEL RÍO

Casa Garay ④
Catedral de
San Rosendo ⑤
Fábrica de Tabacos
F Donatién ⑥
Museo Provincial
de Historia ②
Palacio Guasch ①
Teatro Milanés ③

0 metres   400
0 yards   400

Key to Symbols *see back flap*

The unusual façade of the Palacio Guasch, Pinar del Río

and has on display stuffed birds and animals, including the tiny Cuban *zunzún* hummingbird, and a crocodile more than 4 m (12 ft) long, as well as rare plants and butterflies. In the inner courtyard are sculptures of prehistoric animals.

🏛 Museo Provincial de Historia

Calle Martí 58 e/ Colón y Isabel Rubio. *Tel (48) 754 300.*
⏱ noon–4:30pm Mon, 8:30am–10pm Tue–Sat, 9am–1pm Sun.
⬤ 1 Jan, 1 May, 26 Jul, 10 Oct, 25 Dec. 🖼 📷 📷
This museum illustrates the history of the province from the Pre-Columbian period to the present. On display is a major collection of 19th-century arms, Colonial furniture, works by local painters, including a huge landscape by Domingo Ramos (1955), and mementoes of the musician Enrique Jorrín, the father of the cha-cha-cha.

🎭 Teatro Milanés

Calle Martí y Colón.
Tel (48) 753 871.
A Neo-Classical gem and the city's pride and joy, this theatre is named after the romantic poet José Jacinto Milanés. It started out as the Lope de Vega theatre, which first opened in 1845 and was then bought in 1880 by one Félix del Pino Díaz. He totally renovated it, modelling it on the Teatro Sauto in Matanzas *(see p158).* Its name was changed in 1898.

This simple but functional structure has a rectangular plan, a linear façade and a portico with tall columns. Its opulent, three-level, U-shaped wooden auditorium has a seating capacity of about 500.

🎭 Casa Garay

Calle Isabel Rubio 189 e/ Ceferino Fernández y Frank País. *Tel (48) 754 300.* ⏱ 8am–4:30pm Mon–Fri, Sat every other week. ⬤ 1 Jan, 1 May, 26 Jul, 10 Oct, 25 Dec. 🖼 📷
Since 1892 the Casa Garay has produced Guayabita del Pinar, a famous liqueur based on an ancient recipe. It is made by distilling brandy from the sugar of the *guayaba* (guava), which is grown in this area.

Guided tours of the small factory finish up at the tasting area, where visitors can try the sweet and dry versions of this popular drink.

🎭 Fábrica de Tabacos Francisco Donatién

Antonio Maceo 157. *Tel (48) 773 069.* ⏱ 9am–noon, 1–4pm Mon–Fri, 9am–noon Sat. ⬤ 1 Jan, 1 May, 26 Jul, 10 Oct, 25 Dec.
🖼 📷 📷
This tiny cigar factory, housed in a former 19th-century jail, is open to the public. Visitors can watch the 70 or so workers making Trinidad cigars. These and other cigars are sold in the small shop. The factory is also a training school for *torcedores* (cigar rollers).

Viñales 🟫

Pinar del Río. **Road Map** A3.
🚶 *4,000.* 🚌

Viñales, whose name derives from a vineyard planted here by a settler from the Canary Islands, was founded in 1607.

This small town, the economy of which has always been based on agriculture, is now the subject of government protection as an example of a perfectly preserved Colonial settlement. The main street, named after a 19th-century nationalist, Salvador Cisneros Betancourt, is lined with many Colonial houses with characteristic arcades, which make useful shelters from the hot sun and any sudden violent tropical rainstorms.

The town's most important architecture is in the main square, the **Parque Martí**, on which stand the Iglesia del Sagrado Corazón de Jesús (1888), and the former Colonia Española (diplomatic headquarters of the Spanish gentry). This is now the home of the Casa de la Cultura, which offers an interesting programme of cultural activities.

Viñales also boasts a minor architectural gem, the **Casa de Don Tomás**, built in 1887–8 for Gerardo Miel y Sainz, a rich merchant and agent for a shipping line. The building was blown down in the 2008 hurricane, but then rebuilt true to the original; it is now a good state restaurant *(see p280).*

The main street in Viñales, with its one-storey porticoed houses

Valle de Viñales ❾

A unique landscape awaits visitors to the Viñales Valley. The *mogotes*, the characteristic, gigantic karst formations that resemble sugar loaves, are like stone sentinels keeping watch over the corn and tobacco fields, the red earth with majestic royal palm trees and the farmhouses with roofs of palm leaves. According to legend, centuries ago some Spanish sailors who were approaching the coast thought the profile of the *mogotes* they glimpsed in the fog looked like a church organ. Hence the name, Sierra de los Organos, given to the network of hills in this area.

A *casa de tabaco* for curing tobacco near a *mogote*

Sierrita de San Vicente
is famous for its
hot springs.

San Vicente •

• Cueva
del Ruiseñor

SIERRA

DE VIÑALES

VALLE DE LA GUASASA

Mural de la Prehistoria
On the face of a mogote *the Cuban painter Leovigildo González, a pupil of the famous Mexican artist Diego Rivera, painted the history of evolution (1959–62), from ammonites to Homo sapiens. The mural, restored in 1980, makes use of the cracks in the rock to create special effects of light and colour.*

Mogote
Dos Hermanas ▲

▲ Mogote
Del Valle

KEY

▲	Peak
═	Paved road
═	Path
═	River
═	Underground river

Comunidad El Moncada
(Entrance to the Santo
Tomás Cavern)

VALLE DE VIÑALES

Hotel Los Jazmines

Pinar del

Gran Caverna de Santo Tomás
This is the largest network of caves in Cuba and the whole of Latin America. With its 46 km (29 miles) of galleries and up to eight levels of communicating grottoes, the Gran Caverna is a speleologist's paradise. In the 19th century, the Cueva del Salón was used by local farmers for festivals.

Cueva del Indio
This cave, discovered in 1920, lies in the San Vicente Valley. The first part of the tour here is on foot through tunnels with artificial lighting. Then a small motorboat takes visitors up the underground San Vicente river for about a quarter of a mile.

VISITORS' CHECKLIST

Viñales (Pinar del Río). **Road Map** A3. 🏠 30,000. ℹ️ Cubanacán Viajes, Salvador Cisneros 63b, Plaza Viñales, (48) 796 393; Infotur, Salvador Cisneros 63b, (48) 796 263. 🚌 Salvador Cisneros 63; connections with Havana, Cienfuegos, Pinar del Río, Trinidad, and Varadero.
Excursions & tours of the caves ℹ️ Centro de Visitantes, Carretera a Viñales, (48) 793 157.

Puerto Esperanza

VALLE DE SAN VICENTE

• Hotel Rancho San Vicente

La Palma

Cueva De • San Miguel

▲ Mogote La Esmeralda

▲ Mogote De Robustiano

Río Palmarito

▲ Mogote Rustico

• Viñales

• Hotel La Ermita

0 kilometres   1

0 miles   1

Viñales still has a colonial feel *(see p141)*. It is a tranquil, pleasant little town, ideal for a short stay.

Palenque de los Cimarrones
In the depths of Cueva de San Miguel, past the bar at its mouth, is a spectacular cave that was once a refuge for runaway African slaves (cimarrones). It now houses a small museum and a pleasant restaurant.

THE STRUCTURE OF A MOGOTE

The *mogotes* are among the most ancient rocks in Cuba, and all that remains of what was once a limestone plateau. Over a period lasting millions of years, underground aquifers eroded the softer limestone, giving rise to large caverns whose ceilings later collapsed. Only the hard limestone pillars, or present-day *mogotes*, were left standing. *Mogotes* generally have only a thin covering of soil, but those in the Sierra de los Organos are covered with thick vegetation. Some endemic plant species have adapted to life on their craggy crevices; these include the mountain palm tree *(Bombacopsis cubensis)*, and the cork palm *(Microcycas calocoma)*.

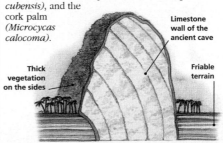

Limestone wall of the ancient cave

Thick vegetation on the sides

Friable terrain

The jetty at María La Gorda, the departure point for boats taking people to dive sites

María La Gorda ⑩

Pinar del Río. 🛈 *Hotel María La Gorda Diving Centre, La Bajada, (48) 778 131, 778 077.*

The best-known bathing spot on the southwestern coast owes its name to a sad legend. A few centuries ago, a plump (*gorda*) girl named María was abducted by pirates on the Venezuelan coast and then abandoned here. In order to survive, she was forced to sell herself to the buccaneers who passed by. The place still bears her name today.

The extraordinary beauty of the coral reefs – populated by sea turtles, reef sharks and other rare species of tropical fish – makes these 8 km (5 miles) of coastline with fine white sand and a warm, translucent sea a real tropical aquarium. The reefs are also easy to reach, lying just a short distance from the shore (the coral and fish can even be seen without swimming under water).

From the jetty opposite the diving area, a boat with a doctor on board takes divers twice a day to the various dive sites. Areas of particular interest include the so-called Black Coral Valley, a wall of coral over 100 m (328 ft) long, and the Salón de María, a sea cave at a depth of 18 m (60 ft), which is the habitat of rare species of fish.

A *cotorra*, a species of parrot seen in the reserve

Guanahacabibes Reserve ⑪

Pinar del Río. 🛈 *Estación Ecológica, La Bajada, (48) 750 366.* 🖳

The peninsula of Guanahacabibes, named after a Pre-Columbian ethnic group, is a strip of land 100km (62 miles) long and 6–34 km (4–21 miles) wide. In 1985 it was declared a world biosphere reserve by UNESCO, to protect the flora and fauna. Access to the inner zone, in the vicinity of La Bajada, is therefore limited. Permission to visit is granted by the park rangers at La Bajada, and visits to the park are made in visitors' vehicles and then on foot with a local guide.

The mixed forest of deciduous and evergreen trees contains about 600 species of plants and many animals, including deer, boar, reptiles and *jutías*, rodents similar to opossums that live in trees. Among the bird species are woodpeckers, parrots, hummingbirds, *cartacuba* and *tocororo (see p18)*.

Cabo San Antonio, the western tip of Cuba, is identifiable by the 23-m (75-ft) high Roncali lighthouse, built in 1849 by the Spanish governor after whom it was named.

Cabo Corrientes at the southern end of the Guanahacabibes reserve

◁ The Valle de Viñales with *bohíos*, farmers' houses characteristic of rural Cuba

Diving in the Caribbean Sea

The Caribbean Sea beds off the island of Cuba offer some of the most exciting coral reef scenery imaginable. The coral formations lie at a maximum depth of 150 m (495 ft), at an average temperature of about 23° C (73 °F), and never less than 18° C (64 °F). The most fascinating areas for

A scuba diver surrounded by a school of grunts

divers are situated at María la Gorda, the Archipelago de los Canarreos, Playa Santa Lucía and Jardines de la Reina. Qualified scuba-diving centres *(buceo)* take visitors on trips out to the reefs. In some areas it is possible to see tropical fish and coral simply by snorkelling *(see p293)*.

Sea plume is a type of gorgonia that looks much like a feather.

"Soft coral" results from an evolutionary process during which the hard skeleton turns into a flexible structrure.

The grouper, *with its unmistakable colouring, is one of the most common fish in the Caribbean, together with the queen triggerfish and the* Pomacanthus paru *angelfish. Other widespread species are the tarpon, with its silvery colouring, and the barracuda, with its powerful teeth. Sharks are less common.*

Sponge

The blue surgeon fish is born with bright yellow colouring that later turns blue.

Coral

THE SEA FLOOR
The coral reef is a rich and complex ecosystem. The Caribbean sea beds are home to numerous varieties of coral and a great many sea sponges and gorgonias, as well as tropical fish, sea turtles and various crustaceans.

Brain coral *is one of many types of coral common to the Cuban seas, along with black coral, iron wire coral with its rod-like structure, and elkhorn coral with its flat branches.*

Tubular sponges *vary in size, the largest ones being 2 m (6 ft) high. If they are squeezed or stepped on they emit a purple dye that will stain your skin for several days. There are also barrel- and vase-shaped sponges.*

Gorgonian sea fans (Gorgonia ventalina) *are quite widespread on Caribbean sea beds. It is possible to see splendid examples of huge proportions.*

Isla de la Juventud

Billboard welcoming visitors to Nueva Gerona

The naturalist Alexander von Humboldt *(see p185)* described this island as an abandoned place, Robert Louis Stevenson allegedly called it *Treasure Island*, the dictator Batista wanted to turn it into a paradise for rich Americans, while Fidel Castro repopulated it with young people and changed its name to the Isla de la Juventud (youth). With a surface area of 2,200 sq km (850 sq miles) and 86,000 inhabitants, this is the largest island in the Archipiélago de los Canarreos. Comparatively few tourists venture here, but there are a few interesting sights and the diving is excellent.

Nuestra Señora de los Dolores, in Nueva Gerona

Nueva Gerona

The capital of the island is a small and peaceful town. Surrounded by hills that yield multicoloured marble, Nueva Gerona was founded in 1828 on the banks of the Las Casas river by Spanish settlers who, together with their slaves, had left countries on the American continent that had won their independence.

The town is built on a characteristic grid plan (intersecting and parallel streets, with a main avenue and a central square) and the modern outskirts are in continuous expansion.

A good starting point for a visit to Nueva Gerona is **Calle 39**, the graceful main street flanked by coloured arcades. Here can be found the local cinema, theatre, pharmacy (which is always open), post office, hospital, bank, Casa de la Cultura, tourist office and bars and restaurants.

This street ends at the Parque Central, Nueva Gerona's main square, where the **Iglesia de Nuestra Señora de los Dolores** stands. First built in Neo-Classical style in 1853, this church was totally destroyed by a cyclone in 1926 and rebuilt three years later in colonial style.

South of the Parque Central, the former City Hall building is now the home of the **Museo Municipal**, or town museum. This has on display many objects and documents concerning pirates and buccaneers – the main protagonists in the island's history – as well as the inevitable photographs and mementoes of the revolution. There is another museum in town that is dedicated solely to the struggle against Fulgencio Batista's dictatorship: the **Casa Natal Jesús Montané**.

Lastly, another must for visitors is the **Museo de Ciencias Naturales**, the natural history museum. The geological and natural history of the island is illustrated and there is also a fine Planetarium, the only one in the world in which the North Star can be seen together with the Southern Cross.

The harbour at Nueva Gerona, where fishermen moor their boats

Ensenada de los barcos

La Demajagua

Atanagildo Caj..

Mina de Oro

0 km 5
0 miles 5

Hotel Colony

Ensenada de la Siguanea

Cocodrilo

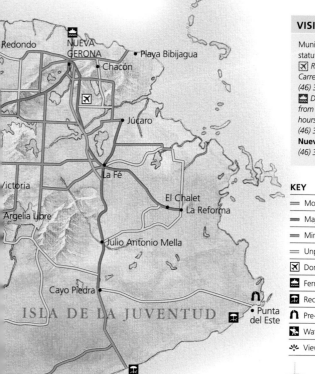

VISITORS' CHECKLIST

Municipality with a special statute. 🏙 86,000.
☒ *Rafael Cabrera Mustelier, Carretera La Fé, km 5, (46) 322 300.*
🚢 *Daily catamaran ride from Batabanó, lasting 2–3 hours. For information call (46) 324 415 or (46) 396 206.*
Nueva Gerona 🛈 *Ecotur, (46) 327 101.*

KEY

═══ Motorway

▬▬▬ Major road

▬▬ Minor road

── Unpaved road

☒ Domestic airport

🚢 Ferry

🏖 Recommended beach

∩ Pre-Columbian site

🤿 Watersports

🌿 Viewpoint

The monumental façade of the Presidio Modelo prison

🏛 **Museo Municipal de Nueva Gerona**
Calle 30 e/ 37 y Martí.
***Tel** (46) 323 791.*
⬜ *9am–5pm Tue–Fri, 9am–4pm Sat, 8am–noon Sun.* 🏷 📷 *(with charge).*

🏛 **Museo de Ciencias Naturales**
Calle 41, esq. 54, No. 4625.
***Tel** (46) 323 143.* ⬜ *8am–5pm Tue–Sat, 8am–noon Sun.* 🏷 📷 *(with charge).*

...lling along the arcades on ...va Gerona's Calle 39

🏛 **Presidio Modelo**
4 km southeast of Nueva Gerona, Reparto Delio Chacón. ***Tel** (46) 325 112.* ⬜ *8am–4pm Mon–Sat, 8am–noon Sun.* 🏷 📷 *(with charge).*
On the road that connects the capital with Playa Bibijagua, a popular beach of black sand frequented by the inhabitants of Nueva Gerona, is Cuba's most famous penitentiary. Originally built by Machado, it was modelled on the famous one in Joliet, Illinois (US) and converted into a museum in 1967. The prison consists of tiny cells in the interior of four enormous multi-storeyed round cement blocks. In the middle of each stood a sentry-box from which guards could keep a close watch on all the prisoners. Guards and prisoners never came into contact with one another. Guards circulated in underground galleries, keeping constant watch over the prisoners above.

It was in the Presidio that the organizers of the attack on the Moncada army barracks in Santiago, led by Fidel Castro, were imprisoned in October 1953. They were liberated two years later, in May 1955.

At the entrance to the first pavilion is cell 3859, where Castro, despite his isolation, managed to reorganize the revolutionary movement, starting with the defence plea he made in court, *History Will Absolve Me* (see p47).

Exploring Isla de la Juventud

Unlike other islands in the Archipelago de los Canarreos, there are no grand luxury hotels on the Isla de la Juventud. As a result it seems to have a more genuine Cuban atmosphere, and the tourist industry works alongside other island activities without pressure. The island is not new to habitation, unlike other *cayos* which have only recently seen housing development, and retains vestiges of five centuries of Cuban history. The town of Nueva Gerona and its surroundings make a good starting point for a visit, followed by the southern coast. The main hotel is in the southwestern part of the island, while the eastern tip has some fascinating ancient cave paintings by Siboney Indians.

Coral formations on the island's sea floor

🏛 Casa Museo Finca El Abra
Carretera Siguanea km 1.5
(5 km southwest of Nueva Gerona).
Tel (46) 396 206. ⬤ 9am–5pm
Tue–Sat, 9am–noon Sun. ⬤ Mon.
🖼 ▶ 📷 (with charge).

On the edge of the Sierra de las Casas is an elegant villa where, in 1870, the 17-year-old José Martí was held for nine weeks before being deported to Spain for his separatist views. Part of the building is now a museum with a display of photographs and documents relating to the national hero's presence on the island. The rest of the villa is occupied by the descendants of the original owner, a rich Catalan.

Nearby is the vast Parque Natural Julio Antonio Mella, which has a botanical garden, a zoo, an amusement park, an artificial lake, and a viewpoint overlooking the entire island. To the south the Ciénaga de Lanier is visible, a marshy area in the middle of which is the village of Cayo Piedra.

Hotel Colony
Tel (46) 398 181. 🚌 to the Centro de Buceo, daily at 9am, return trip at 4:30–5pm.

This low-rise hotel (see p257) – a landmark for all scuba divers on the island – blends in well with the natural environment. The nearby sea is green and translucent, with a sandy floor that is often covered with swathes of the submerged marine aquatic plant *Thalassia testudinum*.

The hotel overlooks Playa Roja, the large, palm-shaded beach where an important diving centre, the **Centro Internacional de Buceo**, is also located.

In the mornings a van takes guests from the Hotel Colony to the diving centre, where all kinds of diving equipment can be rented (although it is advisable to take a 3 mm wetsuit with you), and which provides boats to take visitors

A hotel sign

to the dive sites. At noon, lunch is served at the Ranchón, a restaurant on a platform on piles connected via a pontoon to a beach at Cabo Francés.

The 56 dive sites, between Cabo Francés and Punta Pardenales, lie at the end of a shelf which gently slopes down from the coast to a depth of 20–25 m (65–82 ft), and then abruptly drops for hundreds of metres. This vertical wall is a favourite with passing fish, which literally rub shoulders with divers. While dives on the platform can be made by beginners, those along the shelf are more difficult and suited to divers with more experience.

Among the most fascinating dives are: the one at La Pared de Coral Negro, which has an abundance of black coral as well as sponges as much as 35 m (115 ft) in diameter; El Reino del Sahara, one of the most beautiful shallow dives; El Mirador, a wall dive among sponges and large madrepores; and El Arco de los Sábalos, which is the domain of tarpons. At Cayo Los Indios shipwrecks can be seen on the sea bed at a depth of 10–12 m (33–40 ft).

There are also two wonderful boat trips that can be made from the Hotel Colony. One goes to the Península Francés, which is better known as **Costa de los Piratas**. This is a paradise for divers because of its wonderfully colourful and

The Hotel Colony, surrounded by tropical vegetation

View of Punta del Este beach with its white sand and crystal-clear sea

varied underwater flora and fauna. A variety of other activities can also be enjoyed here, including surfing, sailing, deep sea fishing and even horse riding.

The second excursion goes to **Cocodrilo**, formerly called Jacksonville. This traditional fishing village was founded in the early 20th century by a small community of emigrants from the British colony of the Cayman Islands. In fact, there are still a few inhabitants who speak English as their first language.

The settlers at Cocodrilo introduced a typical Jamaican dance known as the Round Dance, which, blended with a variation of traditional Cuban *son* music (the *Son Montuno*), has resulted in the creation of a new and interesting dance which is highly popular among the locals, who call it the Sucu Sucu.

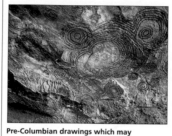

Pre-Columbian drawings which may represent a calendar, in the Cuevas del Este

Cuevas de Punta del Este

59 km (37 miles) southeast of Nueva Gerona. *Ecotur, (46) 327 101, where permits must be obtained.*
Punta del Este, on the south-eastern tip of the island, has a stunning white sand beach. It is, however, most famous for its seven caves, which were discovered in 1910 by a French castaway who took refuge here. On the walls of the caves are 235 drawings made by Siboney Indians in an age long before the arrival of Christopher Columbus.

The drawings in the largest cave – a series of red and black concentric circles crossed by arrows pointing eastward – probably represent a solar calendar. The complexity of these drawings led the Cuban ethnologist Fernando Ortíz, who studied them in 1925, to call them "the Sistine Chapel of the Caribbean". Protect yourself against mosquitoes – the caves are full of them.

HISTORY OF THE ISLAND

The corsair
Sir Francis Drake

The Taíno and Siboney peoples knew of the Isla de la Juventud *(see p38)* long before Columbus "discovered" it in 1494 on his second journey. The Spanish crown licensed the island to cattle breeders, but in practice handed it over to pirates. Because of the shallow waters, heavy Spanish galleons were unable to approach the island, while the buccaneers' light vessels could land there. This meant that figures such as Francis Drake, Henry Morgan, Oliver Esquemeling and Jacques de Sores were able to exploit it as a hiding place for booty captured from Spanish ships.

After Nueva Gerona was founded (1828), the island was used as a place of detention for Cuban nationalists, including José Martí. Its use as a prison island continued for 50 years in the 20th century; construction of Presidio Modelo began in 1926. In 1953 Batista turned the island into a free where money could be laundered. The dictator also wanted to turn it into a holiday paradise for rich Americans, but his plans failed. On New Year's night in 1958, as Castro's *barbudos* were entering Havana, a group of soldiers in the rebels' army took over the island during the opening ceremony of the Hotel Colony, and arrested the mafiosi in the hotel.

In 1966, after a devastating cyclone, the Cuban government decided to plant new citrus groves on the island which would be worked by students from Cuba and around the world. The idea was such a success that in 10 years the island's population grew from 10,000 to 80,000.

An old map of Isla de la Juventud from the Museo Municipal of Nueva Gerona

Cayo Largo del Sur ⑬

The Cayo Largo logo

This island is a wonderful holiday destination for those who love sun, sea and sand. It is 25 km (15 miles) long and has a surface area of 37.5 sq km (15 sq miles). There are no extremes of climate here. It rains very little, the temperature is 24° C (75° F) in winter and less than 30° C (86° F) in summer, the coast is flat, the sand as white and fine as talcum powder, and the sea is clear and calm. It is safe for scuba diving, and the island offers other sporting activities such as fishing, sailing, tennis and surfing. And if you prefer not to swim, you can walk for miles in the shallow water. There are no villages except those built for tourists, with comfortable hotels, as well as restaurants, bars, discos and swimming pools.

View of Playa Tortuga

Marina Cayo Largo is the point of departure for boat trips to several scuba diving sites. In shallow water there are coral gardens populated by multicoloured fish, and a black coral reef 30 km (19 miles) long. Fishing equipment can be hired in the watersports centre.

★ **Playa Sirena**
This 2-km (1.5-mile) beach is very tranquil: sheltered from the wind, the sea is calm all year round.

Combinado is a marine biology centre which is open to the public.

Isla del Sol   Las Piedras

Playa Paraíso is very secluded, making nude sunbathing possible.

Playa Lindamar is a shell-shaped beach, 5 km (3 miles) long, sheltered by white rocks, with hotels and bathing facilities.

STAR SIGHTS

★ Playa Sirena

★ Playa Los Cocos

★ Playa Tortuga

Holiday Villages
Exclusive holiday resorts, with family bungalows and cottages, are concentrated on the southwestern coast.

For hotels and restaurants in this region see pp256–8 and pp279–80

VISITORS' CHECKLIST

Archipiélago de los Canarreos
(Isla de la Juventud).
Road Map B3. 🚗 500.
✈ Vilo Acuña, (45) 248 141.
ℹ Cubatur, (45) 248 258;
Havanatur, (45) 248 215.
Excursions from Marina
Cayo Largo: departure in the
morning, return at sunset.

★ **Playa Tortuga**
*This beach in the eastern part of the island is popular with
nature lovers: it is a nesting area for marine turtles and
has become a natural reserve for Chaelonidae (species of
marine turtle), which are also raised at Combinado.*

KEY

━ Major road

━ Minor road

═ Unpaved road

✈ International airport

🏖 Beach

⛴ Ferry

**Playa
Los Pinos**

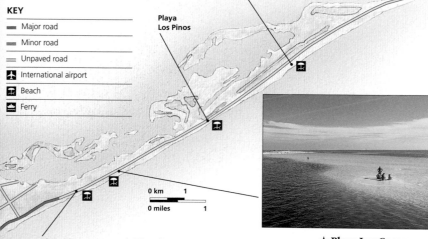

0 km 1
0 miles 1

Playa Blanca, surrounded by white
rocks, is the longest beach on the
island (7.5 km/5 miles). It is divided
from Playa Lindamar by a rocky point.

★ **Playa Los Cocos**
*The coconut palms along the shore
provide some shade here and the shallow
water makes it ideal for children. The
nearby coral reefs and shipwrecks
attract scuba divers.*

An iguana in Cayo Iguana

VISITING THE NEARBY ISLANDS

The small *cayos* nearby offer many natural attractions. Cayo
Rico, an island surrounded by brilliant green water and
fringed with beaches of sand as fine as sugar, is only a few
minutes away by boat. The sea beds, which are especially
rich in lobsters and molluscs, are fascinating and can be
admired from glass-bottomed boats. While various species
of fish abound at Cayo Rosario, which is a scuba diver's
dream, the only inhabitants of Cayo Iguana, just off the
western tip of Cayo Largo, are the harmless iguanas, which
can be as much as 1 m (3 ft) long. Cayo Pájaro is the craggy
habitat of ocean birds, while Cayo Cantiles, rich in flowers,
birds and fish, is also home to several species of monkey.

CENTRAL CUBA – WEST

MATANZAS · CIENFUEGOS · VILLA CLARA

T*he central-western provinces are the rural heart of Cuba, with cultivated fields and a gentle landscape, even where the plain gives way to the Sierra del Escambray. Apart from Varadero, the famous holiday resort, the main attractions in this region are two lively towns – Santa Clara and Cienfuegos – and the natural scenery of the Zapata peninsula and the Escambray mountains.*

In 1509, while circling Cuba, the Spanish navigator Sebastián Ocampo caught sight of a bay on the northern Atlantic coast inhabited by Siboney Indians. Their land was requisitioned almost immediately and assigned to settlers from the Canary Islands. The Indians opposed this injustice so fiercely that the city of Matanzas, which was built in that bay in the 1600s, probably owes its name to the memory of a massacre *(matanza)* of Spaniards by the natives.

Another bay, on the south coast, was sighted by Columbus in 1494. The Jagua Indians living there were later wiped out, but it wasn't until 1819 that Cienfuegos was founded by Catholic settlers from the former French colonies of Haiti and Louisiana, who were granted this territory to counterbalance the massive presence of African slaves. From the mid-1500s to the mid-1700s, both coasts in this region had to face the serious threat of pirate raids, against which the many redoubts, citadels and castles that are still visible along the coastline had very little effect. As a result, in 1689, 20 families from the village of Remedios, not far from the sea, decided to move to the interior, to be at a safe distance from the buccaneers' ships and cannons. In this way the city of Santa Clara was founded.

Santa Clara, capital of Villa Clara province, holds a special place in Cuban hearts since it was the setting for heroic acts by Che Guevara and his *barbudos*. On 28 December 1958, they captured the area after what was to be the last battle of the revolution *(see p48)* before Batista fled.

unique wooden house along the Punta Gorda peninsula, Cienfuegos

radero, extremely popular with international holidaymakers

Exploring Central Cuba – West

This part of Cuba boasts some exceptional attractions: the beaches of Varadero – perhaps the best and certainly the most well-equipped in Cuba – and the swamp *(ciénaga)* of Zapata, a nature reserve which is particularly good for fishing and birdwatching. Cienfuegos, Matanzas and Santa Clara are all appealing towns, this last a must for those interested in Che Guevara's life. A good route for a tour could begin with Matanzas and Varadero, before turning south to Cienfuegos, perhaps via the Península de Zapata. From there it is an easy ride to Santa Clara and beyond to Remedios.

Aerial view of Cayo Libertad, off the coast of Varadero

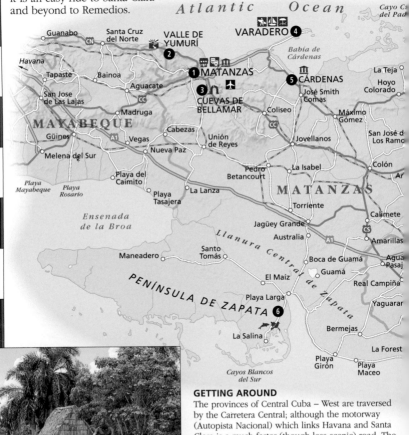

Atlantic Ocean

Cayo Cs del Pad

Guanabo   Santa Cruz del Norte   **VALLE DE YUMURÍ** ②   **VARADERO** ④

Bahía de Cárdenas

Havana   Tapaste   Bainoa   Aguacate   ① **MATANZAS**   ⑤ **CÁRDENAS**   La Teja

San José de Las Lajas   ③ **CUEVAS DE BELLAMAR**   José Smith Comas   Hoyo Colorado

Madruga   Coliseo   Máximo Gómez

MAYABEQUE   Cabezas   Unión de Reyes   Jovellanos   San José d Los Ramo

Güines   Vegas   Nueva Paz   La Isabel   Colón

Melena del Sur   Pedro Betancourt   **MATANZAS**   Ar

Playa del Caimito   La Lanza   Torriente   Calimete

Playa Mayabeque   Playa Rosario   Playa Tasajera

Ensenada de la Broa   Jagüey Grande   Australia   Amarillas

Maneadero   Santo Tomás   Boca de Guamá   Agua Pasaj

El Maíz   Guamá   Real Campiña

PENÍNSULA DE ZAPATA ⑥   Playa Larga   Yaguarar

La Salina   Bermejas   La Forest

Playa Girón   Playa Maceo

Cayos Blancos del Sur

One of the bronze statues by Rita Longa in the reconstruction of the Indian village at Guamá

GETTING AROUND

The provinces of Central Cuba – West are traversed by the Carretera Central; although the motorway (Autopista Nacional) which links Havana and Santa Clara is a much faster (though less scenic) road. The railway line connecting Havana to Santiago passes through Matanzas, Mayabeque and Santa Clara, while another links Havana and Trinidad via Cienfuegos. There are also daily return flights from Havana to Cienfuegos and Santa Clara. For visitors with limited time, it may be best to go on an organized tour. These typically cover a province or a few cities, and include visits to parks.

SIGHTS AT A GLANCE

Cárdenas ⑤
Cayo Santa Maria ⑫
Cienfuegos pp168–71 ⑦
Cuevas de Bellamar ③
*Jardín Botánico
    Soledad pp172–3* ⑧
Matanzas pp158–9 ①
*Península de Zapata
    pp164–7* ⑥
Remedios ⑪
Santa Clara pp174–6 ⑨
Sierra del Escambray ⑩
Valle de Yumurí ②
Varadero pp162–3 ④

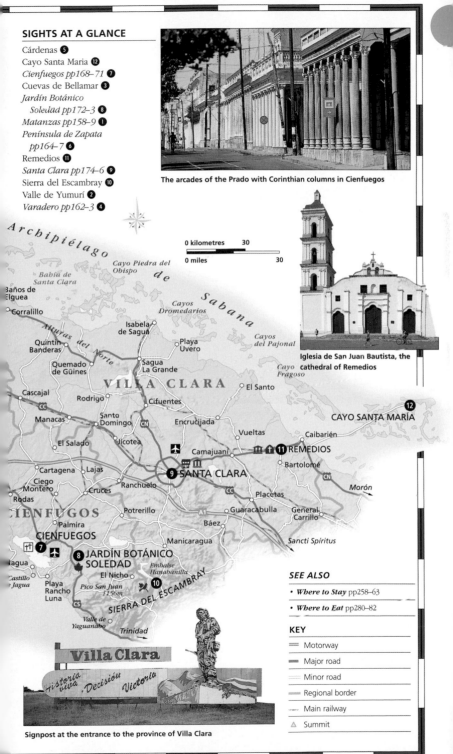

The arcades of the Prado with Corinthian columns in Cienfuegos

Iglesia de San Juan Bautista, the cathedral of Remedios

0 kilometres 30

0 miles 30

Archipiélago

Cayo Piedra del Obispo

Bahía de Santa Clara

de

Baños de Elguea

Corralillo

Cayos Dromedarios

Sabana

Isabela de Sagua

Playa Uvero

Cayos del Pajonal

Alturas del Norte

Quintín Banderas

Sagua La Grande

Cayo Fragoso

Quemado de Güines

VILLA CLARA

El Santo

Cascajal

Rodrigo

Cifuentes

Manacas

Santo Domingo

Encrucijada

Vueltas

Caibarién

El Salado

Jicotea

Camajuaní

⑪ REMEDIOS

⑫ CAYO SANTA MARÍA

Cartagena

Lajas

⑨ SANTA CLARA

Bartolomé

Ciego Montero

Ranchuelo

Cruces

Placetas

Morón

Rodas

Potrerillo

Guaracabulla

General Carrillo

CIENFUEGOS

Palmira

Báez

Sancti Spíritus

⑦ ✈

CIENFUEGOS

Manicaragua

Jagua

⑧ **JARDÍN BOTÁNICO SOLEDAD**

Embalse Hanabanilla

Castillo de Jagua

El Nicho

Playa Rancho Luna

Pico San Juan 1156m

⑩

SIERRA DEL ESCAMBRAY

Valle de Yaguanabo

Trinidad

Villa Clara

Historia viva *Decisión* *Victoria*

Signpost at the entrance to the province of Villa Clara

SEE ALSO

• *Where to Stay* pp258–63

• *Where to Eat* pp280–82

KEY

═══ Motorway

━━━ Major road

═══ Minor road

━━ Regional border

╍╍ Main railway

△ Summit

Matanzas

Stained-glass window, Triolet pharmacy

Situated on the shores of a large bay, Matanzas is the capital of the province of the same name. It is a major industrial town, with the fourth most important port in the world for sugar exports. Because of the many bridges over the Yumurí and San Juan rivers, linking the historic centre to the various quarters of Matanzas and its two suburban districts (Versalles and Pueblo Nuevo), the city has been called the "Creole Venice", a match for the no less ambitious "Athens of Cuba". These two names date back to the 19th century, when the artistic and cultural life of the city, the hub of a flourishing agricultural region, outshone that of Havana.

Teatro Sauto in Matanzas with its beautiful wood-panelling

The Centre of Matanzas

The streets in Matanzas are officially indicated by a number, but in practice their colonial names are still commonly used.

The historic centre can be seen in a few hours. A good place to start is **Plaza de la Vigía**, connected to the outskirts by the Concordia and Calixto García bridges. In the square is the statue of an unknown soldier of the wars of independence, and around it stand several of the city's key sights: the Neo-Classical fire station (1898), the Palace of Justice (1826), the Museo Provincial, the Sauto Theatre and Ediciones Vigía.

Museo Provincial

Calle Milanés, e/ Magdalena y Ayllon. *Tel* (45) 243 464. ◯ 9am–4:40pm Tue–Sat, 8:30am–noon Sun. ◯ Mon. 🖾 🗹 🞇

This museum occupies the two-storey Palacio del Junco, a bright blue porticoed building constructed in 1838 for the del Junco family. The collection includes documents and objects concerning the history of the province. The section devoted to the colonial period, with documents on slavery and sugar cane farm tools, is of particular interest. Copies of *Aurora*, the most interesting Cuban periodical of the 19th century, are also on display.

🎭 Teatro Sauto

Calle Magdalena y Milanés. *Tel* (45) 242 721. ◯ 9am–5pm daily. ◯ 15 Aug–1 Sep & 20 Dec–5 Jan. 🖾 🗹 🞇

The pride and joy of the city, this theatre was designed by the Italian architect Daniele Dell'Aglio, who was also responsible for the church of San Pedro in the Versalles district. On 6 April 1863 the auditorium was opened to the public as the Esteban Theatre, in honour of the provincial governor who had financed the construction. It was later renamed the Sauto Theatre because of the Matanzeros' affection for the local pharmacist, Ambrosio de la Concepción Sauto, a passionate theatre-goer. He was famous for having cured Queen Isabella II of Spain of a skin disease, using a lotion he had himself prepared.

A solidly built Neo-Classical structure with several Greek-inspired statues made of Carrara marble, the theatre has various frescoes of Renaissance inspiration, executed by the architect himself. The U-shaped interior is almost entirely covered with wood-panelling.

Because of its exceptional acoustics, the versatile theatre has been the chosen venue for all kinds of shows and great 19th- and 20th-century Cuban artists have appeared here. World-famous performers have included actress Sarah Bernhardt (in *Camille* in 1887), ballet dancer Anna Pavlova and the guitarist Andrés Segovia.

THE DANZÓN

In the 19th century two composers, José White and Miguel Failde, were born in Matanzas, which was at that time a major cultural centre. In 1879 the latter composed *Las Alturas de Simpson*, which introduced a new musical genre to Cuba, the Danzón. This Caribbean and Creole adaptation of European country dancing became the most popular dance on the island for about fifty years. It is still danced in Matanzas, in the Casa Amigos del Danzón, the house where Miguel Failde was born.

Period print of people dancing the Danzón

Bookbinding at the Ediciones Vigía publishing house

🔲 Ediciones Vigía

Calle Magdalena 1, Plaza de la Vigía.
Tel (45) 244 845, (45) 260 917.
⬭ 8:30am–4pm Mon–Fri. ● 1 Jan,
1 May, 26 Jul, 10 Oct, 25 Dec. ▮
This publishing house's products are entirely hand-crafted – duplicated, painted and bound – on special untreated or recycled paper. Visitors can watch the various stages of production and buy books (on poetry, theatre and history) by Cuban and foreign authors, as well as periodicals.

Parque Libertad

Calle Milanés, an important commercial street, leads to the city's other large square, Parque Libertad, where military parades were held in the 1800s. The square was built on the site of the Indian village of Yacayo. In the middle of the plaza is an impressive statue of José Martí, surrounded by some attractive buildings: the Liceo Artístico y Literario (1860); the Casino Español, built in the early 1900s; the Palacio del Gobierno; the **Catedral de San Carlos**, dating from the 17th century but mostly rebuilt in the 19th century; and, next to the derelict Hotel El Louvre, the Museo Farmacéutico de Matanzas.

🏛 Museo Farmacéutico de Matanzas

Calle Milanés 4951, e/ Santa Teresa y Ayuntamiento. *Tel* (45) 243 179.
⬭ 10am–5pm Mon–Sat, 10am–2pm Sun. 🎥 🔲 📷 (with charge).
This fine example of a 19th-century pharmacy, overlooking Parque Libertad, was founded on 1 January 1882 by Ernesto Triolet and Juan Fermín de Figueroa and turned into a museum in 1964.

On the wooden shelves stand the original French porcelain vases decorated by hand, others imported from the US, and an incredible quantity of small bottles with herbs, syrups and elixirs. The museum also has a collection of three million old labels, mortars and stills, and

VISITORS' CHECKLIST

Matanzas. **Road Map** B2.
🏯 132,050. ✈ Carretera a Varadero, (45) 247 015.
🚌 Ave. 8 y 5, (45) 292 409.
🚏 Calzada de Esteban, (45) 291 473. ℹ Havanatur, Calle Jovellanos e/n Medio y Río, (45) 253 856.

advertising posters boasting the miraculous curative powers of Dr Triolet's remedies. The façade of the pharmacy faces the square.

The shop also serves as a bureau of scientific information, with more than a million original formulae and rare books on botany, medicine, chemistry and pharmaceuticals, in several foreign languages.

The wooden shelves at the Museo Farmacéutico de Matanzas

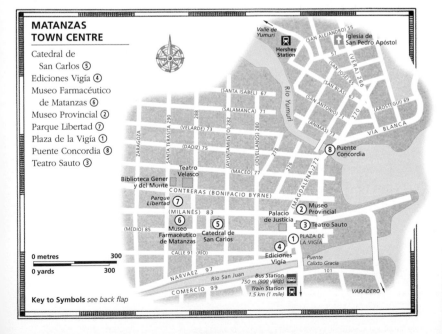

MATANZAS TOWN CENTRE

Catedral de
    San Carlos ⑤
Ediciones Vigía ④
Museo Farmacéutico
    de Matanzas ⑥
Museo Provincial ②
Parque Libertad ⑦
Plaza de la Vigía ①
Puente Concordia ⑧
Teatro Sauto ③

0 metres   300
0 yards   300

Key to Symbols *see back flap*

The Bacunayagua bridge, 110 m (360 ft) high, spanning the Yumurí river

Valle de Yumurí ❷

Matanzas. **Road Map** B2.

The Bacunayagua bridge, 7 km (4 miles) west of Matanzas, is a fine work of Cuban engineering. At 110 m (360 ft), it is the highest bridge in Cuba. Built over the Yumurí river in the early 1960s, it offers lovely views of the peaceful, wooded valley below, which can be reached via a road running parallel to the river.

This attractive area of undulating land dotted with royal palm trees is well known for its many centres and clinics specializing in treatments for stress, asthma and high blood pressure. From the Monserrat hill,

where the Nuestra Señora de Monserrat Sanctuary is located, there is a fabulous view of the bay of Matanzas.

Legends vary concerning the origins of the word "Yumurí". The most fantastic associates it with the lamentation of the Indians massacred by the

A huge limestone formation in the Cuevas de Bellamar

Spanish. Another version came in a letter written by the Swedish writer Fredrika Bremer, who visited Cuba in the late 19th century. According to her, in order to escape from slavery, Siboney Indians used to commit suicide by throwing themselves into the river while screaming "*Yo morí*" (I died).

Cuevas de Bellamar ❸

Carretera de las Cuevas de Bellamar, Matanzas. **Road Map** B2.
Tel *(45) 253 538.* ⬭ *daily.*

Discovered by chance in 1861 by a slave who was surveying the terrain in search of water, the fascinating Bellamar caves lie just 5 km (3 miles) southeast of Matanzas.

Only the first 3 km (2 miles) of these extensive caves have been explored to date, and expert speleologists say there are still many surprises in store. Access to the public, with a specialist guide, is limited to the first 1,500 m (5,000 ft) of the caves. This stretch includes caves and galleries covered with crystal formations in intriguing shapes. The temperature is a constant 26° C (79° F), thanks to the continuous seepage of the cave walls. This impressive tour (available

---

THE HERSHEY TRAIN

The small Hershey electric train

The first stretch of the Hershey rail line, inaugurated in 1916, connected the Hershey sugar factory and the village of Canasí, both near the coast west of Matanzas. The electrical system was one of the first in Cuba. In 1924 there were 38 pairs of trains, though only four covered the full distance between Havana and Matanzas. Today, the Hershey train links Casablanca *(see p111)* and Matanzas *(pp158–9)* via beautiful scenery, covering 89 km (55 miles) in 3 hours 20 minutes, with frequent stops.

daily) goes 26 m (85 ft) below sea level, and visitors can see marine fossils dating from 26 million years ago. Trained speleologists are allowed to enter a cave that is 50 m (164 ft) below sea level.

At Varadero guided tours of the Bellamar caves can be booked at the larger hotels.

Varadero ❹

See pp162–3.

Cárdenas ❺

Matanzas. **Road Map** B–C 2.
🏛 *100,000.*

On arriving in Cárdenas, 50 km (31 miles) east of Matanzas and 18 km (11 miles) south of Varadero, visitors may feel they are entering another age. This is mostly due to the gigs and one-horse carriages which circulate in the streets.

The town was founded in 1828 as San Juan de Dios de Cárdenas. In the 19th century the town thrived thanks to the sugar industry. Today, however, except for a rum factory near the port, Cárdenas offers only two possible areas of employment: work on a farm or a job in Varadero's important tourist industry.

A closer look at the squares and monuments allows visitors to appreciate the little hidden

The linear façade of the historic Dominica building at Cárdenas

gems in this town. Parque Colón, one of the two main squares, is dominated by the first statue of Christopher Columbus erected in Cuba, inaugurated in 1862 by Gertrudis Gómez de Avellaneda, the 19th-century Hispanic-Cuban author *(see p28)*.

Next to the Iglesia de la Inmaculada Concepción (1846) is a very important monument: the **Dominica** building. In 1850, when it was the headquarters of the Spanish government in Cuba, Cuban nationalist troops led by Narciso López hoisted the Cuban flag here for the first time.

In the second major square, Parque Echevarría, is a fine Neo-Classical building, erected in 1862, which was once the city's district prison. It became the **Museo Municipal Oscar**

María de Rojas in 1900, making it the oldest town museum in Cuba. It houses a collection of coins, arms, shells, minerals, butterflies and stuffed animals.

Cárdenas is also famous for being the birthplace of José Antonio Echevarría (1932–57), the revolutionary who was president of the University Students' Federation in Havana. He waged an anti-Batista campaign and was assassinated by the police. The house he was born in is now a museum.

In 1999, five-year-old Elián González was shipwrecked off Miami in a failed escape attempt by his mother. After months of legal tussles between the US and Cuba and an international outcry, Elián was repatriated to his father in Cárdenas. The **Museo a la Batalla de Ideas** is dedicated to this incident.

🏛 **Museo Municipal Oscar María de Rojas**
Calzada 4, e/ Jénèz y Vives.
Tel *(45) 522 417.* ⬜ *9am–6pm Tue–Sat, 9am–1pm Sun.*
📷 ✎ 🎥 *(with charge).*

🏛 **Museo Casa Natal de José Antonio Echevarría**
Plaza José A Echevarría.
Tel *(45) 524 145.* ⬜ *9am–6pm Tue–Sat, 9am–1pm Sun.* ⬛ *1 Jan, 1 May, 26 Jul, 25 Dec.* 📷 ✎ 🎥

🏛 **Museo a la Batalla de Ideas**
Calle Vives e/ Coronel Verdugo e Industria.
Tel *(45) 523 990.* ⬜ *9am–5pm Tue–Sat, 9am–1pm Sun.*
📷 ✎ 🎥

Cárdenas, the city of horse-drawn carriages

Varadero ④

Monument to the Indians

Cuba's top resort, which occupies the 19-km (12-mile) long Península de Hicacos, is connected to the mainland by a drawbridge, a sign of Varadero's exclusivity. When, in the late 19th century, some families from Cárdenas bought part of the land on the peninsula and built themselves summer residences on the north coast, Varadero became a fashionable beach for the wealthy. After Castro took power in 1959, the area was opened up to all kinds of people, and is now especially popular with Canadians and Europeans, drawn to the white, sandy beaches, clear blue water and good facilities.

The attractive home of Varadero's municipal museum

Exploring Varadero

The peninsula – which can be toured by hiring a scooter, classic car or one-horse carriage – is a succession of hotels, restaurants, holiday villages, bars, discos, shops and sports centres, all set among lush greenery that includes bougainvillea, royal poinciana, coconut palms and seagrapes.

The main road along the northern side of the peninsula is Avenida Primera (1ra), the eastern part of which is named Avenida Las Américas. It is here that the main luxury hotels, the major marinas and

a golf course are located. The Autopista del Sur (motorway) runs along the southern coast.

The Historic Centre

The old centre of Varadero, which has no significant historical monuments, lies around the Iglesia de Santa Elvira and the **Parque de 8000 Taquillas**, in Avenida 1ra between Calle 44 and 46. The oldest hotel of note is Hotel Internacional (at the western end of Avenida Las Américas), which was built in the 1950s, complete with a casino and extravagant swimming pool. It puts on a popular cabaret show.

🍂 Parque Retiro Josone

Avenida Primera y Calle 56.
Tel *(45) 667 228.*
◻ *daily.*
This is a beautiful park, with elegant trees, tropical flowers and plants, three restaurants and a small lake where birds gather and tourists hire rowing boats and pedalos. It was established in 1942 by José Iturrioz, the owner of the Arrechabala *ronera*, the rum factory just outside Cárdenas. He named it Josone, a combination of the first syllable of his Christian name and that of his wife, Onelia.

The park is a hit with children, who can enjoy a boat ride, among other attractions.

🏛 Museo Municipal

Calle 57 y Playa. ***Tel*** *(45) 613 189.*
◻ *10am–7pm Tue–Sun.* 🖼 📷
📷 *(with charge).*
The Municipal Museum recounts the history of Varadero both as an urban and tourist centre and also has a collection of Indian tools on display. It is interesting primarily because of the building which it occupies.

The white and blue wooden chalet with French roof tiles is characteristic of the architectural style imported from the US and in fashion in Varadero and the Caribbean area in the early 1900s.

The architect Leopoldo Abreu, the original owner of this villa, landscaped splendid gardens which visitors to the museum can still enjoy. One side of the museum faces the sea, and the balcony on the first floor offers a fine view over the splendid beach and the coastline.

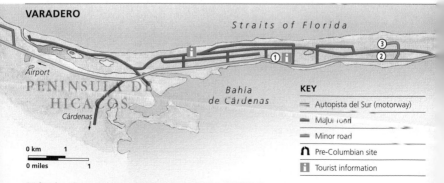

VARADERO

Straits of Florida

Airport

PENINSULA DE HICACOS

Cárdenas

Bahía de Cárdenas

① ② ③

KEY

═══ Autopista del Sur (motorway)

▬▬ Major road

▭▭ Minor road

∩ Pre-Columbian site

ℹ Tourist information

0 km   1
0 miles   1

For hotels and restaurants in this region see pp258–63 and pp280–82

A stretch of the magnificent beach at Varadero

VISITORS' CHECKLIST

Matanzas. **Road Map** B2.
🏛 27,000. ✈ 🚌 Autopista del
Sur y 36, (45) 614 886.
ℹ Infotur, Calle 13 y Ave 1, (45)
662 961; Ave 1 e/ Calle 44 & 46,
(45) 667 044.

🍴 Restaurante Las Américas (Mansión Xanadú)

Avenida Las Américas km 8.5.
Tel (45) 667 388.
☐ lunch and dinner.

During the years from 1920 to 1950 an American millionaire, chemical engineer Alfred Irénée Dupont de Nemours, gambled a great deal of money by purchasing most of the beautiful Hicacos peninsula from the heirs of the Spanish landowners. At that time there were only a few villas and one hotel here. Dupont then parcelled the land out to Cubans and Americans who, within a few years, had transformed Varadero into a centre for gambling and prostitution.

At the height of his property dealings, Dupont asked the two Cuban architects Govantes and Cabarrocas, who had designed the Capitolio in Havana (see pp82–3), to design a villa for the rocky promontory of San Bernardino, the highest point in Varadero. This sumptuous four-storey building, completed in 1929 and named Mansión Xanadú, was dressed with Italian marble and precious wood. The roof was covered with green ceramic tiles with thermal insulation. The house was surrounded by a huge garden with rare plants and features which included an iguana farm and a golf course. This extravagant construction cost $338,000, an enormous sum at the time.

In 1959, after the Revolution, Dupont escaped from Cuba, leaving the villa to the Cuban government, which, in 1963, turned it into "Las Américas", the most elegant restaurant in Varadero. It specialises in French cuisine, but can be visited without any obligation to eat there. The dining room still has its original furniture. The top-floor bar, with its wide selection of drinks and cigars, is a favourite spot for sundowners.

The golf course offers 18 holes and breathtaking views.

Upon request, golf players can book accommodation in the few luxury bedrooms in the villa.

🏞 Punta Hicacos

For those interested in wildlife, the most fascinating part of Varadero is the area near Punta Hicacos, which has become a protected nature reserve. Here you can visit several caves, including the Cueva de Ambrosio, with fossils, Pre-Columbian rock paintings, and some quiet, secluded beaches.

The peninsula is also an attraction for scuba divers, who have 23 dive sites, offering both deep and shallow dives, to choose from.

The former Mansión Xanadú, now a bar-restaurant, with its distinctive green roof

Straits of Florida

Bahía de Cárdenas

VARADERO

Península de Zapata 6

Pineapple plants, common here

This peninsula is named after the landowner who was granted the land by the Spanish crown in 1636. It is one of the least populated areas of the island, and mostly consists of a huge swamp, partly covered by forest. In the past the inhabitants made their living by extracting peat and making charcoal. Zapata is one of the most complete wildlife reserves in the Caribbean, rich in birds and animals, and one part, the area around the Laguna del Tesoro, has been designated a national park, the Gran Parque Natural de Montemar. The Caribbean coast, with its sandy beaches, attracts scuba divers and snorkellers.

A mangrove swamp, characteristic of some tropical coastal areas

STAR SIGHTS

★ Guamá

★ Playa Larga

★ Playa Girón

Corral de Santo Tomás is a refuge and observation point for migratory birds. It can only be visited with an official guide (ask at the National Park office).

Santo Tomás
Quemado Grande
Maneadero

ZAPATA

THE FAUNA OF THE ZAPATA SWAMP

This habitat supports about 150 species of bird, including the *zunzuncito (see p21)*, the Cuban Pygmy owl, the Zapata Rail, a rare type of baldicoot, waterhen, various species of parrot, and heron. Along the coast manatees can be seen (the Caribbean species is over 4 m/13 ft long and weighs about 600 kg/1,320 lbs). The beaches and roads are invaded each spring by crabs leaving the water to mate.

The Laguna de las Salinas is the winter home of many species of migratory bird from November to May.

The Cuban crocodile (Cocodrilo rhombifer) *has been protected since the 1960s.*

The Cuban Pygmy owl (Glaucidium siju) *is a small nocturnal raptor.*

The grey heron *lives in the mangrove swamps and feeds on small fish and amphibia.*

The zunzuncito (Mellisuga helenae) *is multicoloured (male) or black-green (female).*

KEY

— Major road

— Minor road

☒ Aerotaxi

ℹ National Park office

🅱 Recommended beach

✗ Nature reserve

✚ Medical centre

Central Australia
The headquarters of the Cuban Armed Forces in 1961, during the Bay of Pigs conflict, the sugar refinery office now houses the Museo de la Comandancia.

VISITORS' CHECKLIST

Matanzas. **Road Map** R?
🏠 10,000. 🚌 from Boca de Guamá to Guamá.
ℹ️ Cubanacán, Jagüey Grande, (45) 913 224; National Park office, (45) 987 249.

Central Australia

Cienfuegos
Trinidad

↑ Matanzas
Varadero

Boca de Guamá

Laguna del Tesoro

Pálpite

Soplillar
Molina

tón
Playa
Larga

La Majaqua

Los Sábalos

Caleta del Rosario

El Jiquí

Bay of Pigs (p163)

Punta Perdiz

Helechal

Playa Girón

El Polvorín

Playa Maceo

Bahía de Cochinos

★ **Guamá**
Home to a holiday resort, built on ten islands in the Laguna del Tesoro, Guamá also features the Aldea Taína, a reconstruction of a typical pre-Columbian village.

★ **Playa Larga**
With its beach and hotel, Playa Larga is a good base for exploring the swamp.

Caleta Buena, a splendid cove 8 km (5 miles) from Playa Girón, is perfect for diving and snorkelling.

0 kilometres   6

0 miles   6

★ **Playa Girón**
This beach is best known as the site of the final battle between Fidel Castro's armed forces and the counterrevolutionary army, which took place on 17–19 April 1961.

La Cueva de los Peces is a natural pool *(cenote)*, 70 m (230 ft) deep, lying along a fault line. It is an ideal spot for scuba diving and snorkelling.

Exploring the Península de Zapata

A welcome sign at the Península de Zapata

The Península de Zapata is synonymous with unspoiled nature and luxuriant tropical vegetation. It is a place where visitors can walk among lianas, mangroves and swamp plants, lie in a hammock in the shade of palm trees, observe birds with multicoloured plumage, go fishing, or row a boat on the Laguna del Tesoro. The tranquil Gran Parque Natural de Montemar attracts lovers of wildlife and untouched habitats, rather than adventure seekers. In any case, there is nothing to be feared from the wildlife – there are no ferocious beasts or poisonous snakes on the peninsula.

Statue of Manguanay by the Cuban sculptress Rita Longa, Guamá

Boca de Guamá

Arriving from the north, after passing through Jagüey Grande, which has the largest citrus groves in Cuba, and Central Australia *(see p165)*, you reach Boca de Guamá. Here a picturesque *ranchón*, a kind of rustic hut, converted into a restaurant, indicates that you are near the **Criadero de Cocodrilos**, or crocodile breeding farm. Visitors can watch and photograph the crocodiles.

Founded in 1962 to safe-guard 16 endangered species of reptile, this is the largest crocodile farm in Cuba and includes about 4,000 animals kept in separate pools according to size, age and species.

⚒ Criadero de Cocodrilos
Tel (45) 915 662. ◯ *daily.* 🖼 🍴
🍽 ◻

Guamá

This unusual holiday village *(see p260)* in the Laguna del Tesoro (Treasure Lake), measuring 16 sq km (6 sq miles), is named after Guamá, a Taíno warrior who resisted the Spanish conquistadors until he was killed in 1533.

The village consists of 18 huts standing on several small islands in the lagoon. Built of royal palm wood and thatched with palm leaves, the huts provide simple accommodation. However, they are equipped with modern amenities, including air conditioning. Make sure you take adequate supplies of mosquito repellent if you plan to stay here.

The huts are supported on stilts and are connected to one another by hanging bridges or by canoe. In fact, the only way to reach this tourist village is by boat, which takes about 20 minutes to travel along the luxuriantly fringed canal to the lagoon from Boca de Guamá.

This unusual resort also includes a restaurant, a bar, and a small museum, Muestras Aborígenes, which has on display some finds dating back to the Taíno civilization, discovered in the Laguna del Tesoro area.

Also of interest is the reconstructed Taíno village of Aldea Taína, which occupies another of the islands in the lagoon. It comprises four earth *bohíos* (typical Indian huts), a *caney* (a larger round building), and 25 life-size statues of natives by the well-known Cuban sculptress Rita Longa. The figures form the Batey Aborigen, or native Indian square, and represent the few people who lived in the village: a young girl named Dayamí; a crocodile hunter, Abey; Cajimo, hunter of *jutías* (a type of rodent, *see p146*); Manguanay, the mother who is preparing *casabe* (cassava) for her family; Yaima, a little girl who is playing; and the key figure, Guamá, the heroic Taíno warrior.

One of the 18 thatched huts in the Laguna del Tesoro

Playa Larga

At the end of the Bay of Pigs is one of the better beaches along this part of Caribbean coastline, where thick vegetation usually grows down as far as the shore. The coral reef offshore offers magnificent dive sites. Playa Larga's resort area is a popular destination with Cubans; the diving, fishing and birdwatching attract international tourists.

Near the car park, a monument commemorates the landing of the anti-Castro troops in 1961, while along the road to Playa Girón there are numerous monuments honouring the Cuban defenders who died in the famous three-day battle.

Northeast of Playa Larga is an ornithological reserve, and the Centro Internacional de Aves (International Bird Centre) of Cuba.

Cueva de los Peces (see p165), near Playa Larga, ideal for diving

Playa Girón

This beach was named in the 1600s after a French pirate, Gilbert Girón, who found refuge here. It became famous three centuries later, when it was the site of the ill-fated, American-backed landing in 1961. A large sign at the entrance to the beach reads: "Here North American imperialism suffered its first major defeat".

Situated on the eastern side of the Bay of Pigs, this is the last sandy beach in the area, ideal for fishing and diving and also equipped with good tourist facilities.

A must is a visit to the small **Museo Girón**, which covers the anti Castro invasion using photos, documents, weapons, a tank and the wreckage of aeroplanes that took part in the last battle, as well as films taken during the invasion.

🏛 **Museo Girón**
Playa Girón, Península de Zapata. *Tel* (45) 984 122. ⏱ 8am–5pm daily. 📷 🎫 📷 (with charge).

Playa Girón, the easternmost sandy beach in the Bay of Pigs

THE BAY OF PIGS INVASION

The long, narrow Bay of Pigs *(Bahía de Cochinos)* became known throughout the world in 1961. On April 14 of that year, at the height of the Cold War, a group of 1,400 Cuban exiles, trained by the CIA with the approval of the president of the United States, John F Kennedy, left Nicaragua for Cuba on six ships. The next day, six US B-26 aeroplanes attacked the island's three military air bases, their bombs killing 7 people and wounding 53.

On April 16 the group of counter-revolutionaries landed on the main beaches along the bay, Playa Larga and Playa Girón. However, they were confronted by the Cuban armed forces, headed by Fidel Castro himself, who were well prepared for the battle and had the support of the local population. The fighting lasted just three days and ended in the rapid defeat of the invaders. In order to avoid an international crisis, which could have escalated into an extremely serious situation, given the Soviet Union's support of Cuba, the US suddenly withdrew its aerial support, leaving the invading forces at the mercy of Cuban troops.

The abandoned invaders, many of whom were mercenaries, were taken prisoner and immediately tried. After 20 months in prison, they were allowed to return to the US in exchange for supplies of medicine, foodstuffs and equipment for Cuban hospitals.

The hostages released by Cuba on their return to the US

Cienfuegos 🏅

The triumphal arch (1902)

The capital of the province of the same name, Cienfuegos, a UNESCO World Heritage Site, is a maritime city with a well-preserved historic centre and one of the most captivating bays in the Caribbean Sea, which helped earn the city the name "Pearl of the South" in the colonial era. When Columbus discovered the gulf in 1494, it was occupied by Jagua Indians. In order to defend the bay from pirates, the Spanish built a fortress here in 1745. The first town, called Fernandina de Jagua, was founded in 1819 but, in 1829, it was renamed after the Cuban Governor General of the time, José Cienfuegos.

The "zero kilometre" in the Parque Martí

Parque Martí

The "zero kilometre", the central point of Cienfuegos, is in the middle of Parque Martí, the former Plaza de Armas (parade ground). The vast square, a 200 x 100 m (655 x 330 ft) rectangle, has been declared a national monument because of the surrounding buildings and its historic importance. It was here that the foundation of Cienfuegos was celebrated with a solemn ceremony in the shade of a hibiscus tree, chosen as a marker for laying out the city's first 25 blocks.

Lions on a marble pedestal flank a monument to José Martí, erected in 1906. On Calle Bouyón stands the only triumphal arch in Cuba, commissioned by the local workers' corporation in 1902 to celebrate the inauguration of the Republic of Cuba. One side of the square is entirely occupied by the **Antiguo Ayuntamiento**, now the home of the provincial government assembly, supposedly modelled on the Capitolio in Havana (*see pp82–3*).

🎭 Teatro Tomás Terry

Ave. 56 No. 2703 y Calle 27. *Tel (43) 513 361.* ⬜ *daily.*
🖐️ 📷 📷
This theatre was built in 1886–9 to fulfil the last will and testament of Tomás Terry Adams, an unscrupulous sugar factory owner who had become wealthy through the slave trade and then became mayor. World-famous figures such as Enrico Caruso and Sarah Bernhardt performed here in the early 1900s.

The theatre was designed by Lino Sánchez Mármol as an Italian-style theatre, with a splendid U-shaped, two-tiered auditorium and a huge fresco by Camilo Salaya, a Philippine-Spanish painter who moved to Cuba in the

late 1800s. The austere, well-proportioned façade on the Parque Central has five arches corresponding to the number of entrances. The Byzantine mosaic murals on the pediment, made by the Salviati workshops in Venice, represent the muses.

To the left of the theatre is the Neo-Classical Colegio de San Lorenzo, built thanks to a generous donation by the academic Nicolás Jacinto Acea to ensure that needy children in the town would be educated.

🔒 Catedral de la Purísima Concepción

Ave. 56 No. 2902 y Calle 29. *Tel (43) 525 297.* ⬜ *7am–noon Mon–Fri, 8am–noon Sat, 8–10am Sun.* 🔶
7:15am Mon–Fri, 8am Sat, 9am Sun.
The cathedral of Cienfuegos, constructed in 1833–69, is one of the major buildings on the central square. Its distinguishing features are the Neo-Classical façade with two bell towers of different heights, and French stained-glass windows depicting the 12 Apostles.

🏛️ Museo Provincial

Ave 54 No. 2702 esq. Calle 27. *Tel (43) 519 722.* ⬜ *10am–6pm Tue–Sat, 9am–1pm Sun.*
🔴 *1 Jan, 1 May, 26 Jul, 25 Dec.*
🖐️ 📷 📷 *(with charge).*
The Provincial Museum is in the former Casino Español, an eclectic-style building first opened on 5 May 1896. The furniture, bronze, marble and alabaster objects, crystal and porcelain collections, bear witness to the refined taste and wealth of 19th-century families in Cienfuegos.

The mosaic-decorated façade of the Teatro Tomás Terry

Palacio Ferrer, with its unmistakable blue cupola

🏛 Palacio Ferrer

Ave. 54 esq. Calle 25. **Tel** (43) 516 584. ◯ for cultural events.
The palacio that houses the Casa Provincial de la Cultura was built in the early 1900s by the sugar magnate José Ferrer Sirés. Enrico Caruso is said to have stayed here when he performed at the s Tomás Terry.

This building stands on the western end of the plaza and is the most bizarre and eclectic in the square. It is distinguished by its cupola with blue mosaic decoration. It is worth climbing up the wrought-iron spiral staircase to enjoy the fine views over the city.

🏛 Museo Histórico Naval Nacional

Ave. 60 y Calle 21, Cayo Loco. **Tel** (43) 516 617. ◯ 10am–6pm Tue–Sat, 9:45am–1pm Sun. ● 1 Jan, 1 May, 26 Jul, 25 Dec. 🎟 📷
A short walk northwest of Parque José Martí, on the Cayo Loco peninsula, is the most important naval museum in Cuba, featuring a series of documents concerning the anti-Batista insurrection of 5 September 1957, and an interesting display recording the history of the Cuban Navy.

VISITORS' CHECKLIST

Cienfuegos. **Road Map** C3.
🏙 407,000. 🚉 Ave. 58 y Calle 4, (43) 525 495. 🚌 Calle 49, e/ Ave. 56 y 58, (43) 518 114.
🛈 Cubatur, Ave. 56 e/ 31 y 3, (43) 551 242. 🎭 Villa de Nuestra Señora de los Ángeles de Jagua (22 Apr).

Paseo del Prado

The liveliest street in town is known for its elegant, well-preserved buildings and the monuments honouring leading local figures. It crosses the historic centre and goes south as far as Punta Gorda. It was laid out in 1922.

Paseo del Prado, the main street in the historic centre of Cienfuegos

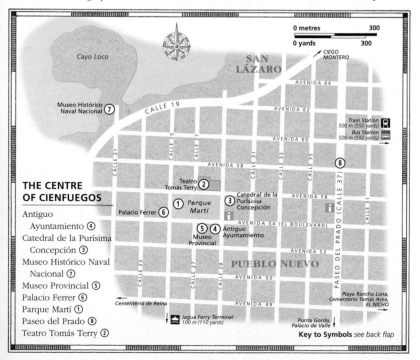

THE CENTRE OF CIENFUEGOS

Antiguo Ayuntamiento ④
Catedral de la Purísima Concepción ③
Museo Histórico Naval Nacional ⑦
Museo Provincial ⑤
Palacio Ferrer ⑥
Parque Martí ①
Paseo del Prado ⑧
Teatro Tomás Terry ②

Exploring Cienfuegos

The presence of the sea at Cienfuegos makes itself felt more and more the further you go from the historic centre towards the Reina and Punta Gorda districts, two narrow strips of land almost entirely surrounded by water. However, for a fuller taste of the sea, go to the mouth of the bay, which is dominated by the Castillo de Jagua fortress with the picturesque Perché fishing harbour. Southeast of Cienfuegos is one of Latin America's most spectacular botanic gardens.

The interior of Palacio de Valle, with its Neo-Moorish decoration

The characteristic wooden houses of Punta Gorda

Punta Gorda

At the southern tip of the bay of Cienfuegos lies Punta Gorda – the aristocratic quarter of the city in the early 1900s – which affords a lovely panoramic view of the bay. A short walk along the seafront takes you past many attractive villas. Various brightly coloured wooden houses can be seen towards the tip of the peninsula. They were modelled on the American prefabricated "balloon frame" homes that were so much in vogue in the early 20th century.

🏛 Palacio de Valle

Calle 37 e/ Ave. 0 y 2, Punta Gorda. **Tel** (43) 551 003 ext 830. ⏲ 10am–10pm daily. 🔪 🍸 📷

The most original building in the area, Palacio de Valle was designed by local and foreign architects engaged by the sugar merchant Acisclo del Valle Blanco, one of the wealthiest men in Cuba. It was built as a private house in 1913–17. This two-storey building, which is now a restaurant, is lavishly decorated with Gothic, Venetian and Neo-Moorish motifs, much in the Arab-Spanish style of the Alcázars in Granada and Seville. The façade has three towers of different design symbolizing power, religion and love. The terrace is open to the public.

🏛 Cementerio Monumental Tomás de Acea

Ave. 5 de Septiembre. **Tel** (43) 525 257. ⏲ 8am–4pm daily. 📷 📷

This impressive monumental cemetery lies in the eastern suburb of Cienfuegos. Varied in stylistic influences, it was conceived as a large garden with paths and fruit trees. The entrance is a replica of the Parthenon in Athens.

Palacio de Valle, which Batista turned into a casino, now home to a restaurant

⚱ Cementerio General La Reina

Ave. 50 y Calle 7, Reina.
⬭ daily. 📷

The municipal cemetery of La Reina is located at the western end of the city, and has been declared a national monument. Laid out in the 1830s, this Neo-Classical cemetery includes a famous funerary statue of La Bella Durmiente (Sleeping Beauty).

The statue of Sleeping Beauty in La Reina cemetery in Cienfuegos

⚓ Castillo de Jagua

Poblado Castillo de Jagua. 🚌
Tel (43) 596 402. ⬭ *9am–5pm Mon–Sat, 9am–1pm Sun.* 📷 🎫
📷 *(with charge).*

Built by engineer José Tantete, following a design by Bruno Caballero, to protect the bay and the region from Jamaican pirates, the Castillo was the third most important fortress in Cuba in the 18th century and the only one in the central region of the island. The original moat and drawbridge are still intact. According to

legend, the citadel was inhabited by a mysterious lady dressed in blue, who every night walked through the rooms and corridors, frightening the guards. It is said that one morning one of the guards was found in a state of shock while wringing a piece of blue cloth in anguish. The unfortunate man never got over this experience and ended up in an asylum.

At the foot of the Castillo is the fishing village of **Perché**, with picturesque wooden

houses, in striking contrast to the majestic military structure above. Most visitors arrive by ferry from Pasacaballos hotel (29 km/18 miles south of Cienfuegos), or from the dock in Cienfuegos.

Environs

Cienfuegos province is interesting to eco-tourists. Besides the **Ciego Montero** spa north of the capital, other noteworthy sights are **El Nicho**, to the southeast, which is famous for its waterfalls, and the conservation area of Aguacate.

However the main sight is the **Valle de Yaguanabo**, in the southern region, which is traversed by the river of the same name, which forms small waterfalls and clear freshwater pools. On the slopes of one of the mountains in this valley, populated by mammals such as boar, deer and opossums, is the entrance to the **Cueva de Martín Infierno**. This cave has been a national monument since 1990, because it has one of the largest stalagmites in the world (67 m/220 ft high) and other rare mineralogical sites such as Moonmilk and Flores de Yeso.

About 20 km (12 miles) south of Cienfuegos is **Playa Rancho Luna**, with golden sand and a hotel *(see p259)*. It is popular with tourists and local families alike.

BENNY MORÉ

A great source of pride to Cienfuegos is the figure of Maximiliano Bartolomé Moré, better known as Benny Moré, who was born at nearby Santa Isabel de las Lajas on 24 August 1919. Moré inspired many generations of Cubans and foreigners with his supple, unique voice, which enabled him to interpret a variety of musical genres. For this reason the artist was nicknamed *el bárbaro del ritmo* (the barbarian of rhythm). He was self-taught, and when still quite young performed with famous orchestras such as those led by the Matamoros brothers and Pérez Prado (see *pp30–31*). He died in the early 1960s. For some time Cienfuegos – a city with a great musical tradition and the birthplace of cha-cha-cha – has paid tribute to him with the Benny Moré International Festival. The Cabildo Congo de Lajas in his home town puts on performances of Afro-Cuban popular songs and dances.

The Cuban singer, Benny Moré

Jardín Botánico Soledad ⑧

In 1901 Edwin Atkins, owner of the Soledad sugar works 15 km (9 miles) from Cienfuegos, transformed 4 ha (10 acres) of his estate into a sugar cane research centre, and filled the garden with a great number of tropical plants. In 1919 the University of Harvard bought the property and founded a botanical institute for the study of sugar cane and tropical flora. The botanical garden has been run by the Cuban government since 1961, and is one of the largest in Latin America, with a surface area of 94 ha (232 acres) and more than 1,400 different species of plant, including 195 palms. Besides the endemic species there are also huge bamboo trees. Guided tours, made partly on foot and partly by car, reveal the exceptional diversification of the garden.

★ Garden Drive
Lined with royal palm trees, the drive borders one entire side from the entrance to the glasshouse.

Leguminous plants

Laboratory

Ticket office, library

Medicinal plants, which are grown throughout the country, can be viewed in this small plot.

Forest plants

STAR SIGHTS

★ Banyan Tree

★ Garden Drive

Protected woodland

★ Banyan Tree
Among over 50 varieties of fig in the botanical garden, perhaps the most striking is a huge Ficus benghalensis or banyan tree, a species with aerial roots (with a circumference of over 20 m/65 ft). The roots, trunks and branches form an impenetrable barrier.

Cacti
Many species of cactus are housed in this glasshouse. They are young specimens, grown after the serious damage inflicted by hurricane Lilly (1996).

VISITORS' CHECKLIST

Calle Central 136, Pepito
Tey, Cienfuegos. **Map** C3.
Tel (43) 545 115. ○ 8:30am–
5pm Mon–Thu, 8:30am–4:30pm
Fri–Sun. 📷 ✂ 🚽 📷

Water Lilies
The pool near the glasshouse is entirely covered with water lilies of different colours: bright pink, white, dark purple, violet, blue and yellow.

Mimosa
With its deeply divided leaves, the mimosa makes a very attractive ornamental plant.

Santa Clara ⑨

See pp174–5.

Sierra del Escambray ⑩

Villa Clara, Sancti Spíritus, Cienfuegos. **Map** C3. 🏨 *Hotel los Helechos, (42) 540 330.*

The Sierra del Escambray mountain range, with an average height of 700 m (2,300 ft) above sea level, covers a large part of southern Central Cuba, across three provinces: Villa Clara, Cienfuegos and Sancti Spíritus *(see p191).* In the heart of the range is the **El Nicho** nature reserve, which is of great scientific and ecological value with its abundant mountain fauna and varied plantlife. **Pico San Juan** (1,156 m/ 3,790 ft), dotted with conifers and lichens as well as coffee plantations, is the highest mountain in the Sierra.

A long steep road leads from the northern side of the mountains up to stunning **Embalse Hanabanilla**, a large artificial lake overlooked by a hotel. The Río Negro path, which skirts the waterfall of the same name, leads to a belvedere viewing point from which one can see the entire lake.

In the village of La Macagua is the **Comunidad Teatro Escambray**, an international theatre school. The school was founded in 1968 by members of the Havana Theatre, who used to rehearse here before touring rural communities.

PALM TREES

For many Cubans, palm trees represent the power of the gods. A great variety of species, many of them native to Cuba, grow throughout the island: the royal palm *(Roystonea regia),* the national tree; the bottle palm *(Colpothrinax wrightii),* called *barrigona* (pregnant one), because the trunk swells in the middle; the sabal, whose fan-like leaves are used for roofing; the local coccothrinax *(C. crinita),* with its unmistakable foliage; and the *corcho* *(Microcycas calocoma, see p139).*

Royal palm

Bottle palm

Coccothrinax palm

Santa Clara 🟊

Founded on 15 July 1689 by a group of inhabitants from Remedios *(see p177)*, who had moved away from the coast to escape from pirate raids, Santa Clara was for centuries the capital of the province of Las Villas, which included the present-day provinces of Cienfuegos, Sancti Spíritus and Villa Clara. One important historical event has made Santa Clara famous: in 1958 it was here that the last battle of the guerrilla war led by Che Guevara took place, the battle which marked the end of Batista's dictatorship. Santa Clara is now known as "the city of the heroic guerrilla". Today, it is a lively city and has several interesting sights.

Bust of Leoncio Vidal

The Teatro de la Caridad, where Enrico Caruso performed

Santa Clara's well-tended main square, Parque Leoncio Vidal

Parque Leoncio Vidal

The heart of the city, this charming square with its pristine flower beds, wrought-iron benches and period street lamps has retained its original 1925 atmosphere.

An obelisk stands here. It was commissioned by the rich heiress Martha Abreu de Estévez in honour of two priests, Juan de Conyedo and Hurtado de Mendoza. The heiress also financed the construction of the Teatro de la Caridad, the town's first four public bathhouses, the astronomical observatory, the electricity station, a hospital and a fire station.

There is also a bust of Leoncio Vidal, a colonel in the national independence army who died in battle in 1896, here in this square. There is also a fountain, and a sculpture entitled *Niño de la Bota* (child in boots), purchased by mail order from the J L Mott Company, an art dealer in New York.

Until 1894 the square was partly off limits to blacks, who could only walk along certain areas of the pavement.

🎭 Teatro de la Caridad

Parque Vidal 3. *Tel (42) 205 548.*
Built to a design by the engineer Herminio Leiva y Aguilera for the heiress Martha Abreu de Estévez, this theatre was inaugurated in 1885 and restored in 2009–10.

An antique vase in a hall in the Museo de Artes Decorativas

The theatre offered many additional services – a barber shop, ballroom and gambling room, café and restaurant – with the aim of collecting money to be given to the poor in the city (hence its name, Charity Theatre).

The building has a simple, linear façade, in contrast to the ornate interior, with its profusion of chandeliers and painted panels and a stage with all kinds of mechanical gadgets and draped curtains. The auditorium itself, which has three tiers of boxes with wrought-iron balusters, had folding seats in the stalls right from the start – something completely new in Cuba at the time.

Perhaps the best feature of the theatre is the frescoed ceiling, executed by the Spanish-Philippine painter Camilo Salaya, representing the allegorical figures of Genius, History and Fame.

🏛 Museo de Artes Decorativas

Calle Martha Abreu esq. Luis Estévez
Tel (42) 205 368. ⬜ 9am–6pm Mon–Thu, 1–10pm Fri & Sat, 6–10pm Sun. 📷 🎫 📷 (with charge).
The excellent Decorative Arts Museum, housed in a building dating from 1810, contains 17th-, 18th-, 19th- and 20th-century furniture, as well as furnishings and paintings that belonged to leading local families.

Among the objects on display here, those donated by the Cuban poetess Dulce María Loynaz *(see p29)* are particularly elegant and delightful: five fans, eleven sculptures and two Sèvres porcelain jars, the largest of their kind in Cuba.

The Tren Blindado Monument, a work by José Delarra

VISITORS' CHECKLIST

Villa Clara. **Road Map** C3. ▓
239.000. 🚉 *Luis Estévez 323.*
🚌 *Carretera Central km 2.5.*
ℹ️ *Infotur, Calle Cuba 68 e/*
E. Machado and Maestra
Nicolosa, (42) 227 557.

Also on show is the D-6
Caterpillar bulldozer that
was used by the guerrillas
to remove rails and cause
the derailment. The episode
ended with the surrender
of Batista's men.

Parque Tudury
This square, in front of the
Neo-Classical Iglesia di Nuestra
Señora del Carmen (1756), is
also known as Parque El Carmen. Here stands a monument
commemorating the founda-
tion of the town of Santa Clara.
It was erected in 1951 around
a tamarind tree, on the spot
where, on 15 July 1689, the
first mass was celebrated in
the new city. The monument
consists of 18 columns on
which are carved the names
of the first families in Santa
Clara, crowned by a cross.

🏛 Tren Blindado Monument

Carretera Camajuaní, junction with
railway line. *Tel (42) 202 758.*
🕘 *9am–5:15pm Mon–Sat.*
On 28 December 1958, with
the aid of only 300 men,
Che Guevara succeeded in
conquering the city, which
was fiercely defended by
3,000 of Batista's soldiers.
The following day Guevara
handed the dictator another
severe setback by derailing
an armoured train that was
supposed to transport 400
soldiers and weapons of all
kinds to the eastern region
of Cuba in order to halt the
advance of the rebels.
    Cuban sculptor José Delarra
commemorated this event by
creating a museum-monument
on the spot where it took
place, in the northeastern part
of Santa Clara, on the line to
Remedios. The sequence of
events is recreated using
original elements such as four
wagons from the armoured
train, military plans and maps,
photographs and weapons.

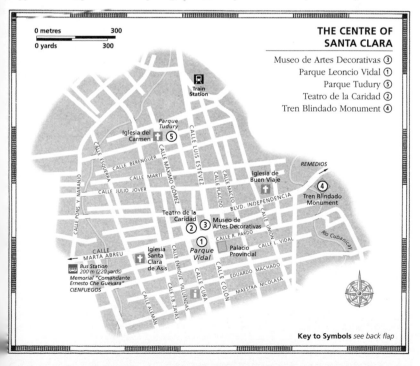

THE CENTRE OF SANTA CLARA

Key to Symbols *see back flap*

The group of sculptures in Santa Clara, dedicated to Che Guevara

🏛 Conjunto Escultórico Comandante Ernesto Che Guevara

Avenida de los Desfiles, Santa Clara. **Tel** *(42) 205 878.*
🕐 *9:30am–6:30pm Tue–Sun.*
📷 ♿ 📷 *(outdoors only).*

The monument in Plaza de la Revolución was built to commemorate the 30th anniversary of the battle of Santa Clara. It was designed by the architect Jorge Cao Campos and the sculptor José Delarra, and was unveiled on 28 December 1988.

The complex comprises a museum and memorial of Che Guevara. Dominating the monument is an impressive bronze statue of Che, with his arm in plaster (he had broken it in a previous battle). Beneath, a bas-relief depicts scenes from the battle, on which are carved the historic words that Che wrote in his farewell letter before leaving for Bolivia.

Under the monument (the entrance is at the back) is the museum, designed by the architect Blanca Hernández Guivernau, which has some of Che's personal belongings on display, together with a chronological reconstruction of his life, which clearly reveals the evolution of his revolutionary ideas.

Che's personal effects include his pistol holster, his uniform, watch, pipe, the container from which he used to drink *mate* tea, his beret and the telephone he used during the campaign of Santa Clara, along with his binoculars, camera and radio.

The newest construction is the memorial containing the remains of Ernesto Che Guevara and 38 other comrades, found in Bolivia 30 years after their death and transferred to Cuba in December 1998. The tomb is in the shape of a cave and consists of numbers of niches with ossuaries as well as a central brazier where an eternal flame burns. Cubans flock here daily in order to pay their respects.

Part of the bas-relief memorial to Che Guevara

ERNESTO CHE GUEVARA

When Ernesto Guevara de la Serna was killed in Bolivia upon orders from the CIA, he was only 39 years old. In the summer of 1997 – while Cuba was celebrating the 30th anniversary of the death of the *guerrillero heroico* – the body of Che Guevara was returned to the island. He was one of only two foreigners in the history of Cuba (the other is the Dominican

The photographer Korda with his famous portrait of Che Guevara

general Máximo Gómez) to be proclaimed a Cuban citizen "by birth". Watching his coffin being lowered from the aeroplane to the sound of the *Suite de las Américas* served to remind everyone, especially young Cubans, that Che had died and had therefore really existed; he was not merely a 20th-century legend, but a reality for millions of people who had shared his ideas. Further testimony is given by his children, his widow Aleida March, many of those who fought with him in the Sierra Maestra and in the Congo, and also Alberto Granado, with whom Che made his first trips to Latin America and who, after the Revolution, moved to Cuba on his friend's invitation. Though Che suffered from asthma, he had an iron will, loved books as well as sports, and had a great spirit of sacrifice; he could appreciate beauty and was a perfection-ist but had a sense of humour. He was a man of action who also found time to meditate on reality and to write.

Iglesia de San Juan Bautista, Remedios

Remedios ⓫

Villa Clara. **Map** C3. 🏯 16,500.
🚉 🚌 ℹ️ *Hotel Encanto Mascotte, Calle Máximo Gómez 114, (42) 395 144.* 🎭 *Parrandas (24 Dec).*

Founded around 1514 by Vasco Porcallo de Figueroa and given the name of Santa Cruz de la Sabana, this town was renamed San Juan de los Remedios del Cayo after a fire in 1578.

This peaceful place has a small, well-preserved Colonial historic centre in the area around Plaza Martí. Overlooking this square is the Iglesia de San Juan Bautista, which is considered one of the most important churches in Cuba. What we see today is the result of restoration carried out in the 20th century thanks to the rich landowner Eutimio Falla Bonet, who revived its original Baroque splendour without touching the Neo-Classical bell tower. Most striking are the lavish Baroque altar and the magnificent decorative ceiling.

Behind the cathedral is the **House of Alejandro García Caturla**. Here, the musical instruments, photographs and some personal belongings of

this talented 20th-century personality are on display. García Caturla was a composer, pianist, saxophone player, percussionist, violinist and singer, as well as a fine tennis player and rower, journalist and art critic.

Also in the square are three other noteworthy buildings. The Mascotte hotel was the site of an important meeting between Generalissimo Máximo Gómez and a US delegation in 1899. The former Casino Español, now Casa de la Cultura, and the El Louvre café, founded in 1866, also stand here.

However, Remedios is most famous for the Parrandas, the local festival documented in the fascinating **Museo de las Parrandas Remedianas**. Here, photographs, musical instruments, costumes, sketches, carriages and *trabajos de plaza* – decorated wooden structures – bring to life Parrandas past and present.

Environs
Located north of Remedios, the resort of Cayo Santa María is reached via 48 km (30 miles) of low-lying causeway known as *El Pedraplén*. The resort is made up of hotels set along stunning sandy beaches, as well as a dolphinarium, a bowling alley and a shopping complex.

🏛 **House of Alejandro García Caturla**
Calle Camilo Cienfuegos 5.
Tel (42) 396 851. ◻ 8am–5pm Tue–Sat, 9am–noon Sun. 🖼 🎥 📷

🏛 **Museo de las Parrandas Remedianas**
Calle Máximo Gómez 71, esq. Andrés del Río. **Tel** (42) 396 818. ◻ 8am–noon, 1:30–5pm Tue–Sat, 9am–noon Sun. ◼ 1 Jan, 1 May, 26 Jul, 25 Dec. 🖼 🎥 📷

THE PARRANDAS

A 19th-century print showing people gathering in the square

In 1829 the parish priest of Remedios, Francisco Virgil de Quiñones, had the idea of getting some boys to bang on sheets of tin in order to get the lazier church members out of their homes to participate in the night-time celebrations of the Advent masses (16–24 Dec).

In time this strange concert developed into a fully fledged festival, with music, dances, parades with floats and huge wooden contraptions *(trabajos de plaza)* The festivity is a sort of cross between Mardi Gras and the Italian Palio horse race, based on the competition between two quarters of Remedios, San Salvador and Carmen.

The Parrandas begin on 4 December with concerts performed with various percussion instruments, and end with a great crescendo on Christmas Eve. The two *trabajos de plaza*, one per quarter, which are made during the year, are left in Plaza Martí during the festivities. They are illuminated at nine in the evening and may have a historical, patriotic, political, scientific or architectural theme. Later on there are fireworks to welcome the entrance of the floats *(carrozas)*, which never occurs before 3am. These *tableaux vivants* move among the crowd.

The most endearing aspect of the Parrandas, enlivened by songs, polkas and rumbas, is that all the inhabitants, of all ages, take part.

Plaza Martí, the tranquil central square in Remedios

CENTRAL CUBA – EAST

SANCTI SPÍRITUS · CIEGO DE ÁVILA · CAMAGÜEY · LAS TUNAS

T his area in the heart of the island presents two different facets. One is colonial, with Spanish traits which are visible in the architecture and local customs and is best expressed in beautiful Trinidad, and fascinating, labyrinthine Camagüey. The other aspect is unspoilt nature, the coastline dotted with cayos (islands), which now attracts many visitors from abroad.

Trinidad, Camagüey and Sancti Spíritus, the main cultural centres in this region, were three of seven cities founded in the 16th century by a small group of Spaniards led by Diego Velázquez. The 17th and 18th centuries were marked by the threat posed by state-sanctioned pirates and by raids such as that made by Henry Morgan at Camagüey (then Puerto Príncipe) in 1666. At that time Trinidad had political and military jurisdiction over the whole of central Cuba, where the economy was based solely on sugar cane cultivation and the sale of sugar. The great landowners resided in luxurious mansions in these three cities.

In the second half of the 19th century, a period of crisis began with the advent of new technology, for which there was no skilled labour. Slave revolts, the first of which broke out in Camagüey in 1616, became increasingly frequent and violent, while competition from Cienfuegos was becoming more intense. In the late 19th century the major landowners left the cities and as time went on they gradually ceded their sugar factories to American businessmen, who converted them into one large sugar-producing business. Camagüey concentrated on livestock raising, an important resource in the province, while Trinidad engaged in handicrafts and cigar-making. It remained isolated from the rest of Cuba for a long time, since the railway was not extended to Trinidad until 1919 and the road to Cienfuegos and Sancti Spíritus was only laid out in the 1950s. One result of this isolation, however, is that the historic centres of Trinidad and Sancti Spíritus have preserved their colonial atmosphere.

Aerial view of the causeway linking Cayo Coco to the mainland

◁ Calle Simón Bolívar in Trinidad, sloping down towards the plain

Exploring Central Cuba – East

From a cultural point of view, the most interesting place in the area is the delightful town of Trinidad. This small town also has a lovely beach nearby and makes a good base for tours to the Sierra del Escambray or for excursions to the Valle de los Ingenios. A transit town, Sancti Spíritus can seem disappointing after Trinidad, while Camagüey is appealing both for its fascinating colonial architecture and as an authentic, vibrant Cuban city. The Atlantic coast in the province of Ciego de Ávila is good for swimming and watersports, especially at Cayo Coco and Guillermo, where there are good tourist facilities.

Playa Prohibida at Cayo Coco, fringed by sand dunes

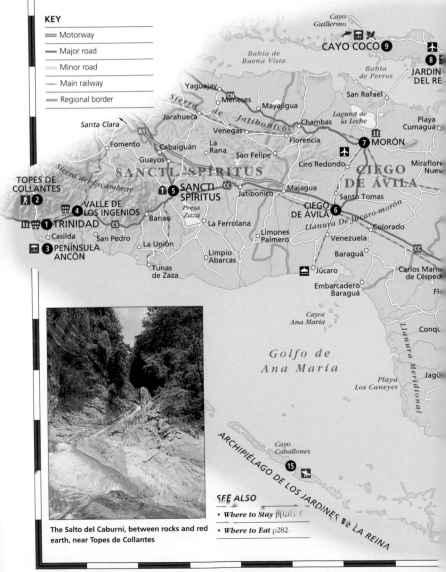

KEY

═══ Motorway

── Major road

┄┄┄ Minor road

╍╍╍ Main railway

── Regional border

The Salto del Caburní, between rocks and red earth, near Topes de Collantes

SEE ALSO

• *Where to Stay* pp263–7

• *Where to Eat* p282

One of the colonial houses around the peaceful pedestrian square of San Juan de Dios, in Camagüey

SIGHTS AT A GLANCE

Camagüey *pp200–3* **10**
Cayo Coco *pp198–9* **9**
Cayo Sabinal **13**
Ciego de Ávila **6**
Jardines de la Reina **15**
Jardines del Rey **8**
Las Tunas **14**
Morón **7**
Península Ancón **3**
Playa Santa Lucía **12**
Sancti Spíritus
pp194–5 **5**
Sierra de Cubitas **11**
Trinidad *pp182–90* **1**
Valle de los Ingenios **4**

Tours
Topes de Collantes *p191* **2**

GETTING AROUND
There is at least one domestic airport in each province. The cities are linked by road and by trains bound for Oriente, while from Trinidad the Valle de los Ingenios can be toured on a delightful small steam train. Cayo Coco can be reached by car along the cause-way, or by air. The most difficult area to travel around is the Sierra del Escambray *(see p173)*, although organized tours now include Topes de Collantes.

The Cockerel Festival at Morón, celebrating the city's symbol

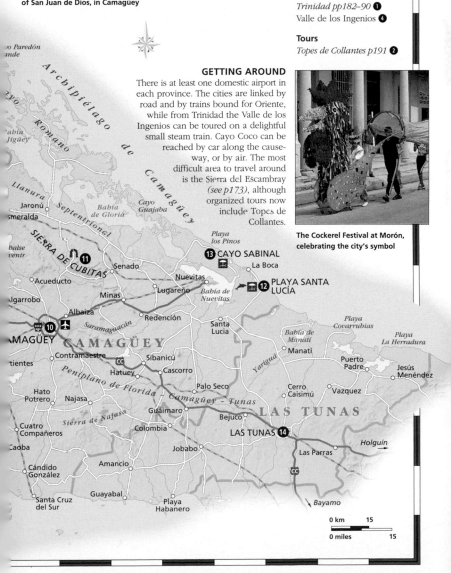

0 km   15

0 miles   15

Trinidad ❶

A cannon used as a bollard

This city was founded by Diego Velázquez in 1514, and was declared a World Heritage Site by UNESCO in 1988. The original cobblestone streets and pastel-coloured houses give the impression that time has scarcely moved on since colonial times. From the 17th-19th centuries, the city was a major centre for trade in sugar and slaves, and the buildings around the Plaza Mayor, the heart of Trinidad, bear witness to the wealth of the landowners of the time. A long period of isolation from the 1850s to the 1950s protected the city from any radical new building and the original town layout has been left largely unchanged. The historic centre has been skilfully restored, down to details like the street lights.

★ Palacio Brunet
This mansion is now the Museo Romántico, with a collection of furniture and items that belonged to the wealthiest local families (p185).

Casa de la Música

Nuestra Señora de la Popa *(see p190)*

★ Iglesia y Convento de San Francisco
The monastery is the home of the Museo de la Lucha contra Bandidos, while the church bell tower, the symbol of the city, offers fine views. The bell dates from 1853 (p189).

CALLE HERNÁNDEZ ECHERR

CALLE PIRO GUINART

SIMÓN BOLÍVAR

Canchánchara
This typical casa de infusiones, housed in an 18th-century building, is known for its namesake cocktail canchánchara, made from rum, lime, water and honey. Live music is played here.

CALLE MARTÍNEZ VILLENA

In Plazuela del Jigüe, where an acacia tree *(jigüe)* stands, Father Bartolomé de Las Casas celebrated the first mass in Trinidad in 1514 *(p189).*

The Museo de Arqueología Guamuhaya occupies an 18th-century building where the naturalist Humboldt once stayed *(see p185).*

STAR SIGHTS

★ Palacio Brunet

★ Palacio Cantero

★ Iglesia y Convento de San Francisco

KEY

— — — Suggested route

Iglesia Parroquial de la Santísima Trinidad
The church of the Holy Trinity was built in the late 1800s on the site of a 17th-century church that had been destroyed by a cyclone. It has an impressive carved wooden altar decorated with elaborate inlaid wood (p184).

VISITORS' CHECKLIST

Sancti Spíritus. **Road Map** C3.
🏠 75,000 🚌 Calle Piro Guinart 224, e/ Maceo e Izquierdo, *(41) 994 448.* 🚉 Ave. Simón Bolívar 422, (41) 993 348.
ℹ️ Cubatur, Calle Antonio Maceo esq. Francisco Javier Zerquera, (41) 996 314. 🚪 daily.

The Casa de los Conspiradores, with a wooden balcony on the corner, was the meeting place of the nationalist secret society, La Rosa de Cuba.

La Casa de la Trova, a live music venue *(see p289)*, stands almost opposite the Palenque de los Congos Reales, which also offers music and dance *(see p288)*.

Museo de Arquitectura Colonial
Housed in the beautifully restored Casa de los Sánchez Iznaga, this museum illustrates the main features of Trinidad's architecture (p184).

PLAZA MAYOR

CALLE MARTÍNEZ VILLENA

CALLE JAVIER

CALLE SIMÓN BOLÍVAR

Casa de la Cultura *(p189)*

Casa de Aldemán Ortiz
Besides being a fine example of 19th-century architecture, this building has an interesting art gallery with works by local artists, as well as handicrafts (p184).

★ Palacio Cantero
This Neo-Classical gem was built in the early 19th century and is now the home of the Museo Histórico Municipal, which recounts the history of the region. The tower has a commanding view of the historic centre (p189).

| 0 metres | 100 |
| 0 yards | 100 |

Trinidad: Exploring Plaza Mayor

The museums and buildings facing the main square in Trinidad lend historic weight and depth to the "suspended-in-time" feel of this city. It is worth stopping in the town centre for at least half a day to see the museums, relax on the benches in the shade of the palm trees, enjoy a cocktail at the bar on the steps next to the cathedral, or stroll around the stalls in the crafts market.

Decorative element in Plaza Mayor

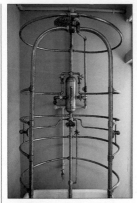

A 19th-century shower in the Museo de Arquitectura Colonial

🔒 Iglesia Parroquial de la Santísima Trinidad

Plaza Mayor.
🕐 10:30am–1pm Mon–Sat.

Completed in 1892, this austere church with a Neo-Classical façade stands at the top of the sloping Plaza Mayor.

The four-aisle interior has a fine Neo-Gothic altar dedicated to the Virgin of Mercy, with a painting by the Cuban painter Antonio Herr on the rear wall. But the real attraction of this church is an 18th-century wooden statue made in Spain, the *Señor de la Vera Cruz* (Lord of the True Cross), which is associated with a curious story. The sculpture, made for one of the churches in Vera Cruz, Mexico, left the port of Barcelona in 1731, but three times in succession the ship was driven by strong winds to the port of

Casilda, 6 km (4 miles) from the city of Trinidad. While preparing to make a fourth attempt to reach Mexico, the ship's captain decided to leave behind part of the cargo, which included the huge chest containing the statue of Christ. The locals regarded the arrival of the sacred image as a sign from Heaven, and from that time on the *Señor de la Vera Cruz* became an object of fervent worship.

The Maundy Thursday procession, which was suspended in 1959 and revived again in 1997, is dedicated to this statue.

🏛 Museo de Arquitectura Colonial

Calle Ripalda 83, e/ Hernández Echerri y Martínez Villena, Plaza Mayor.
Tel (41) 993 208. 🕐 9am–5pm Sat–Thu. 📷🎥📹 (with charge).

The front of the 18th-century mansion of the Sánchez Iznaga family, now the home of the Museum of Colonial Architecture, features a lovely portico with slim columns, a wrought-iron balustrade and wooden beams. Originally, the building consisted of two separate houses, both of which belonged to sugar magnate Saturnino Sánchez Iznaga.

The houses were joined during the 19th century.

The museum, the only one of its kind in Cuba, covers the different architec-elements seen in

Bronze knocker, Museo de Arquitectura Colonial

Trinidad and illustrates the building techniques used during the colonial period. There is a collection of various locks, latches, doors, hinges, windows and grilles, as well as parts of walls and tiles.

In one of the bathrooms facing the inner courtyard is a fine example of a 19th-century shower, with a complicated network of pipes supplying hot and cold water.

🎨 Universal Benito Ortiz Galería de Arte

Calle Rubén Martínez Villena y Bolívar, Plaza Mayor. **Tel** (41) 994 432. 🕐 8am–5pm Tue–Sat, 9am–1pm Sun–Mon.

This beautiful mansion with a long wooden balcony, reminiscent of the colonial buildings in La Habana Vieja, is evocative of the city's golden age. It was built in 1808 for Ortiz de Zúñiga, a former slave trader who later became the mayor of Trinidad. The house currently serves as an art gallery.

The first floor has paintings on display (and for sale) by contemporary Cuban artists, including Antonio Herr, Juan Oliva, Benito Ortiz, Antonio Zerquera and David Gutiérrez. Of interest in the gallery itself are frescoes, the great stair case, and, in the upper hall, a ceiling decorated with figures. From the balcony there is a fine view of the entire square.

The statue of Señor de la Vera Cruz (1731), in one of the chapels inside Santísima Trinidad

Museo de Arqueología Guamuhaya and Palacio Brunet

🏛 Museo de Arqueología Guamuhaya

Calle Simón Bolívar 457, e/ Fernando Hernández Echerri y Rubén Martínez Villena, Plaza Mayor.
Tel *(41) 993 420.* ⬤ *9am–5pm Sat–Thu.* 📷

Alexander von Humboldt

HUMBOLDT IN CUBA

The German naturalist Alexander von Humboldt (1769–1859), the father of modern geography, made two trips to Cuba (1800–1, 1804), which are recorded in a museum at Calle Oficios 252 in Havana. The book that followed, *Political Essay on the Island of Cuba*, in which he described Cuba as "the land of sugar and slaves", illustrated its geography, rivers, population, economy, government and slave system. Because of its abolitionist ideas the book was soon banned.

The building that is now the home of the Archaeological Museum was constructed in the 18th century and was purchased in the 1800s by the wealthy Don Antonio Padrón, who added a portico with brick columns and Ionic capitals.

The Guamuhaya (the native Indian name for the mountainous Escambray area) collection includes Pre-Columbian archaeological finds as well as objects associated with the Spanish conquest and slavery in Cuba, and stuffed animals, including the *manjuarí*, an ancient species of fish that still lives in the Zapata swamp.

In the courtyard is a bronze bust commemorating the German geographer and naturalist Alexander von Humboldt, who stayed here as Padrón's guest in 1801, during his travels in the New World.

🏛 Palacio Brunet (Museo Romántico)

Calle Hernández Echerri 52, esq. Simón Bolívar, Plaza Mayor.
Tel *(41) 994 363.* ⬤ *9am–5pm Sun–Fri.* 📷 📷 📷 *(with charge).*
Built in 1812 as the residence of the wealthy Borrell family, Palacio Brunet now contains the Museo Romántico. The decoration of the mansion blends in well with the objects on display, most of which once belonged to Mariano Borrell, the family

founder. They were inherited by Borrell's daughter, the wife of Count Nicolás de la Cruz y Brunet (hence the name Palacio Brunet), in 1830.

The museum's 14 rooms all face the courtyard gallery with its elegant balustrade. The spacious living room has a Carrara marble floor, a coffered ceiling, Neo-Classical decoration, furniture made of precious wood, Sèvres vases and Bohemian crystalware. There are also English-made spittoons, which reveal that the 19th-century aristocratic landowners were partial to smoking cigars. In the dining room the fan windows are a particularly attractive feature.

Other rooms of interest are the countess's bedroom, with a bronze baldachin over the bed, and the kitchen, which is still decorated with its original painted earthenware tiles.

One of the elegant frescoes decorating Palacio Brunet

The Houses of Trinidad

The historic centre of Trinidad has an extraordinarily dense concentration of old Spanish colonial houses, many still inhabited by the descendants of old local families. The oldest, single-storey buildings have two corridors and a porch parallel to the street, with a courtyard at the back. In the late 1700s another corridor was introduced

A mampara, an interior door with two leaves

to the layout. In the 19th century, the houses formed a square around an open central courtyard. In general, the houses of Trinidad, unlike those in Havana, have no vestibule or portico. The entrance consists of a large living room that gives way to a dining room, either through an archway or a *mampara*, an inner, double door.

Barrotes, small turned wooden columns, characterize the 18th-century windows.

Red tile roof

Wooden supports

Wooden beams *support the two- or four-pitch sloping roof, which is covered with terracotta tiles. Inside, mudéjar-style coffered ceilings can often be found.*

TRINIDAD FAÇADES
The façade of the typical Trinidad house has a large central door, with a smaller door (or doors) cut in it for easy access. The windows, set slightly above ground level, are almost the height of the door. They have strong wooden shutters instead of glass. This house is in Plaza Mayor, next to the Casa Ortiz.

Wrought-iron ornamental motifs

Wooden shutters

The arched windows *so characteristic of Trinidad have radiating wooden slats instead of* mediopunto *windows. These allow the air to enter but keep out the sunlight.*

The 19th-century iron grilles *replaced the wooden* barrotes *and typically have simple decoration at the top and bottom.*

The wooden front door *is sometimes framed by plaster motifs: flattened pilasters, moulding, half-columns either with simple Tuscan capitals or with upturned bowls at the top.*

Trinidad: Around Plaza Mayor

Walking along the streets leading from Plaza Mayor is a fascinating experience even if you have no particular destination. A slow stroll allows time to observe the detail of a window, a small balcony, the irregular cobblestones, or the cannons used as bollards. The historic centre is more or less free of traffic. In the evening the houses glow in the warm hues of sunset, and music fills the streets: the Casa de la Trova *(see p183)* and Casa de la Música *(see p182)* put on daily concerts by local bands.

The river cobblestones *(chinas pelonas)* used in Trinidad's streets

The frescoed entrance hall in Palacio Cantero and its Italian marble floor

血 Casa de la Cultura Trinitaria

Calle Zerquera 406. *Tel (41) 994 308.*
During the day, the spacious, well-lit vestibule is used as permanent exhibition space by local artists (some of whom also have their studios here), who sell their paintings. In the evening, performances of various kinds of entertainment are held in the rear courtyard: theatre, dance, concerts and shows for children.

血 Palacio Cantero (Museo Histórico Municipal)

Calle Bolívar 423. *Tel (41) 994 460.*
⬜ *9am–5pm Sat–Thu.* ⬛ *Fri.* 🖼
📷 *(with charge)*.
This mansion, which belonged originally to Don Borrell y Padrón – one of the major figures in local sugar production – was purchased in 1841 by María de Monserrate Fernández, the widow of a sugar magnate. A year later she married the landowner Cantero, renaming the mansion and transforming it into a sumptuous Neo-Classical residence. The building is now the Museo Histórico Municipal.

From the grand entrance hall, with frescoed arches, the route takes in the dining room, the kitchen, the court-yard and an area for domestic servants.

The history of Trinidad can be traced through exhibits, maps, and monuments related to different themes: the Cantero family, piracy, the plantations in the Valle de los Ingenios, the slave trade and the wars of independence. There is a viewing platform atop the tower.

Plazuela del Jigüe

This peaceful little square, where a spreading acacia tree offers shady respite from the sun, is rich in history *(see p182)*. El Jigüe restaurant is housed in a lovely porticoed building decorated with panels of painted tiles.

血 Iglesia y Convento de San Francisco

Calle Hernández Echerri, esq. Guinart.
Museo de la Lucha contra Bandidos *Tel (41) 994 121.*
⬜ *9am–5pm daily.* 🖼 🎥 📷
This elegant church was built in 1730 by Franciscan monks, but it was taken from them in 1848 in order for it to be used as a parish church. In 1895 the authorities transformed the monastery into a garrison for the Spanish army. Then in 1930, because of the lamentable state of the place, the monastery and part of the church were demolished. Only the bell tower was salvaged, along with adjacent buildings, which were used as a school until 1984, when the complex became the home of the **Museo de la Lucha contra Bandidos**.

The museum illustrates with documents, photographs and exhibits the struggle against the "bandits", the counter-revolutionaries who fled to the Sierra del Escambray after 1959. Fragments of a U2 plane, a boat, a militia truck and weapons are displayed in the former monastery's cloister.

The small Plazuela del Jigüe, with its handful of handicrafts stalls

Beyond Trinidad's Historic Centre

Away from the centre there are more interesting areas to explore. One spot to head for is Parque Céspedes, where locals, young and old, gather to listen and dance to live music in the evenings. Or, walking eastwards, Plaza Santa Ana draws people at all times of day. From the hill north of Plaza Mayor there are marvellous views over the valley, especially beautiful at sunset.

The Cabildo de San Antonio, with votive offerings and sacred drums

Façade of Nuestra Señora de la Candelaria de la Popa hermitage

done by a violent cyclone. The complex is being converted into the five-star French-Cuban Hotel Pansea, which is expected to open for business by 2014.

Plaza Santa Ana

A short walk from Plaza Mayor, in the eastern part of the city, this square is dominated by the 18th-century Iglesia de Santa Ana. It was partly rebuilt in 1800, and the bell tower was added 12 years later. The now decaying church is flanked by a royal poinciana tree.

The square is a popular place to gather, and is a favourite with children who come here to play ball games.

🔒 Ermita de Nuestra Señora de la Candelaria de la Popa

This small 18th-century church on a hill north of the centre is connected to Plaza Mayor by a narrow, steep street. The striking three-arch bell tower loggia was added in 1812, when work was done to the church to repair the damage

🏛 Cabildo de los Congos Reales de San Antonio

Calle Isidro Armenteros 168.
In the picturesque working-class quarter of El Calvario (Las Tres Cruces), in the northern part of Trinidad, is the Cabildo de los Congos Reales, a temple founded in 1859 for the worship of

Afro-Cuban divinities. In the 1800s Cuba witnessed the rise of many *cabildos*, cultural centres differentiated by ethnic group which aimed to preserve the spiritual and musical heritage of the slaves. This Cabildo in Trinidad, dedicated to Oggún – a warrior god whose Catholic equivalent is St Anthony of Padua – is for the followers of the Palo Monte religion *(see p23)*.

Environs

On a rise 1 km (half a mile) northeast of the centre, near Hotel Las Cuevas *(see p266)* is the **Museo Espeleológico**. Located inside a cave of 3,700 sq m (4,440 sq yds), it can be visited with an expert guide as far as the Salón de las Perlas, a smaller cave where water drops "fall like pearls". According to legend, an Indian girl called Cacubu took refuge (and died) here, escaping from the lecherous Spanish conquistador Porcallo de Figueroa. Karstic fossils gathered from caves near Matanzas are also on show.

Iglesia de Santa Ana, on the square of the same name, in eastern Trinidad

Topes de Collantes ②

The unspoilt landscape of the Sierra del Escambray *(see p173)*, where pine and eucalyptus grow alongside exuberant trees, ferns and tropical plants, offers extraordinarily beautiful scenery that can best be seen by hiking from Topes de Collantes, a steep 30-minute drive north of Trinidad. Here, two itineraries are suggested, indicated by a letter and colour. Itinerary A consists of a walk of average difficulty through the tropical forest as far as the Caburní falls. Itinerary B is longer but easier and less tiring, and includes a detour to the Batata cave.

TIPS FOR HIKERS

Departure points: *Topes de Collantes.* 🏠 *Gaviota Reservations Office, (42) 540 180.*
Length: *Itinerary A: 3.5 km (2 miles); Itinerary B: 4.5 km (3 miles).*
Stopping-off point: *Parque Codina*

KEY

— Major road
= Path
- - Itinerary A
- - Itinerary B
🅿 Parking
➕ Hospital

Hacienda Codina ④
The Codina farm has orchid and bamboo gardens, a pool with mud baths, and fine views. The route continues for 1 km (half a mile) among medicinal plants.

La Batata ⑤
This cave is traversed by an underground river, with natural pools at a temperature which never rises above 20° C (68° F).

Santa Clara
Manicaragua ↗

0 kilometres   1
0 miles   1

Trinidad ↙

Topes de Collantes ①
At 800 m (2,625 ft) above sea level and with good clean air, this spot was chosen as the location for a sanitarium for lung diseases, now used as an anti-stress centre.

Salto del Caburní ③
After a 2-hour walk you will come to a cliff with a steep, plunging waterfall. Water gushes over rocks and collects further down, forming a pool where it is possible to bathe.

The Forest ②
The path leading to Salto del Caburní crosses untouched tropical forest with curious rock formations.

La Boca beach, shaded by royal poinciana trees

Península Ancón ❸

Road Map C3.

About 10 km (6 miles) south of Trinidad is one of the first coastal areas in Cuba to be developed for tourism, the peninsula of Ancón, where foreign visitors have been coming since 1980. The fine white sand and turquoise water (not as clear here as along the north coast, though) make this promontory a small tourist resort, with a handful of hotels, bars, restaurants and watersports facilities. This area is visited by visitors and locals alike. Cubans head mainly for **La Boca**, 6 km (4 miles) from Trinidad, near the neck of the peninsula, especially on warm Sundays and in summer.

At **Playa Ancón**, 5 km (3 miles) of white sand in the southern part of the peninsula, there are comfortable hotels, a splendid beach and a diving school. From the beach by Hotel Ancón, assorted boat excursions are available to take divers to snorkelling sites out on the coral reef.

For some fascinating dive sites, divers should take an excursion to **Cayo Blanco**, 8 km (5 miles) off the coast. At the western tip of this small coral island with white sand beaches, is the largest black coral reef in Cuba, where divers can choose from a number of different dive sites. On the rocky coasts near **María Aguilar**, on the other hand, there are pools where swimmers only need a mask to easily spot a great variety of tropical fish.

As with Varadero *(see pp162–3)*, bicycles can be hired and make a pleasant way of getting around the Ancón peninsula.

Opposite the peninsula, across the bay, is the old port of **Casilda**, 6 km (4 miles) from Trinidad, where in 1519 Hernán Cortés recruited the troops that went on to conquer Mexico.

Once a prosperous port thanks to the sugar trade, Casilda has long since declined, and is now above all a place that people pass through on their way to the local beaches.

Valle de los Ingenios ❹

Road Map C3. 🚂 🚌
Excursions *from Trinidad.*
ℹ️ *at railway station, (41) 993 348; Cubatur, Calle Antonio Maceo, esq. Francisco J Zerquera, (41) 996 314.*

The bell on the Iznaga bell tower

Leaving Trinidad and heading northeast, along the road to Sancti Spíritus, one can appreciate the beauty of the fertile plain, with the green hills of the Sierra del Escambray forming a backdrop. Only 12 km (7 miles) separate Trinidad from the Valle de los Ingenios, whose name derives from the sugar mills *(ingenios, see pp42–3)* built here in the

Valle de los Ingenios, from the Mirador de la Loma: green swathes of sugar cane at the foot of the Sierra

The Iznaga estate tower, with a commanding view of the valley

early 19th century. Today, fields of sugar cane form a blanket of green, interrupted only by towering royal palms.

The valley is rich in history with ruins providing evidence of the time when the sugar industry was at its peak. These buildings also help visitors to understand the social structure that was the order of the sugar plantations. The whole zone, which has a surface area of 270 sq km (104 sq miles), includes more than 70 old *ingenios*. UNESCO has declared the valley a World Heritage Site.

A good way to visit the area is to take the steam train that, when working, departs from Trinidad and covers the entire valley. One of the places only accessible by car is the **Mirador de La Loma del Puerto** (6 km/4 miles east of Trinidad, on the road to Sancti Spíritus). This observation point *(mirador)*, 192 m (630 ft) above sea level, offers a magnificent view of the whole valley. There is also an outdoor café where you can sample the drink *guarapo*, sugar cane juice.

However, the most impressive destination is the **Manaca Iznaga Estate**, where about 350 slaves lived in the 1840s. The landowner's house

survives and has been converted into a bar and restaurant. Also still standing are the *barracones* (slaves' huts), and a monumental seven-level tower 45 m (147 ft) high. Each level is different from the next in shape and decoration: the first three are square, the top four are octagonal. The symbolic meaning of this tower is apparent. It was built in 1830 as an assertion of authority over the valley by Alejo Iznaga, a rival to his brother Pedro, who was also a major landowner and sugar producer. The tower also functioned as a lookout for supervising the slaves.

The top of the tower, which is reached via a steep wooden stairway, today offers lovely, wide-ranging views of the surrounding countryside. At the foot of the tower is the bell that once tolled the work hours on the plantation.

There are other estate mansions to be seen in this area, including one at Guachinango, which was built in the late 18th century in a dominating position over the Río Ay.

The village of **San Pedro** is an example of the urban settlements that developed in association with the sugar plantations and works.

SUGAR PRODUCTION IN CUBA

For centuries, sugar cane *(Saccharum officinarum)*, which was introduced to the island in 1512 by Spanish settlers, has been the mainstay of the Cuban economy. Sugar extraction takes place in various phases: after being washed, the cane stalks are pressed by special mills and the juice *(guarapo)* is extracted from the fibrous mass *(bagassa)*, which is used as fuel and as livestock fodder. The juice is treated chemically, filtered and then evaporated so as to obtain a concentration of dark syrup that is then heated. This produces crystals of sucrose. The syrupy mass then goes into a centrifuge. Other by-products are obtained from sugar cane, including molasses, a residue of the syrup, which still contains 50 per cent sugar and is used as the basic ingredient in the production of rum *(see p75)*.

Ripe cane *is 2–5 m (6–16 ft) tall with a diameter of 2–6 cm (1–3 in). Once cut, the plant shoots again and becomes ripe again in a year. Newly planted cane, grown from cuttings 30–40 cm (12–16 in) long, ripens in 11–18 months.*

The zafra (harvest) *takes place between December and June. Before harvest begins, the cane field is burned to remove the outer leaves, which obstruct harvesting. In the plains cutting is done with machines, while in the hills the* machete *is still used.*

Transport *has to be rapid to minimize the deterioration of the sucrose in the heat. To this end, in the late 1800s a special railway network was built and steam trains travelled between the cane fields and the sugar works. Some are still running.*

Sancti Spíritus ❺

The city of Sancti Spíritus, deep in the heart of fertile agricultural countryside, was founded by Diego Velázquez on the banks of the Tuinucú river in 1514. It was moved to its present site, near the Yayabo river, eight years later. In 1586 British pirates set fire to the town along with all the documents relating to its foundation. The political, economic and military centre of the area, Sancti Spíritus was embellished with elegant mansions throughout the 17th and 18th centuries. Today, its small, attractive colonial centre receives few visitors, despite its "national monument" status.

Statue of Christ beside the cathedral

🏛 Yayabo Bridge

Its medieval appearance and large terracotta arches make this bridge, built in 1825, unique in Cuba, and for this reason it has been declared a national monument. According to one bizarre legend, in order to make the bridge more robust, the workmen mixed cement with goat's milk.

The Yayabo bridge is an important part of the city's street network: it is the only route into town for those coming from Trinidad.

Exploring Sancti Spíritus

The central part of the city can be explored on foot in a few hours. It is pleasant to simply stroll along the attractively restored streets (many of which are for pedestrians only), where brightly coloured colonial houses with wrought-iron balconies are characteristic. The most famous approach to the town is the southern one, across the lovely old bridge over the Yayabo river. The narrow, quiet streets leading up from the bridge to the city centre are the oldest in Sancti Spíritus. They are paved with irregular cobblestones and lined with one-storey houses with shingle roofs.

Calle Máximo Gómez, which leads to the main square, Parque Serafín Sánchez, is lined with 18th- and 19th-century monuments, museums and mansions. These include the **Teatro**

The Yayabo Bridge, leading to the colonial centre

Principal, a bright blue porticoed construction built in 1876 and restored in 1980; a large 19th-century mansion that is now the Pensamiento bar; the **Casa de la Trova**; a typical bar-restaurant, Mesón de la Plaza; and the Placita, a small square with a statue of Dr Rudesindo Antonio García Rijo, an illustrious citizen.

🏛 Museo de Arte Colonial

Calle Plácido 74. **Tel** *(41) 325 455.*
⬜ *9:30am–5pm Tue–Sat, 9:30am–noon Sun.* ⬤ *Mon.* 📷 *(with charge).*

This fine 18th-century building once belonged to the Iznaga family *(see p193).* It is now an outstanding museum with crystal, porcelain, furniture, paintings and a courtyard.

Restored colonial homes, with their original colours, in one of the streets near the river

For hotels and restaurants in this region see pp263–6 and p282

The interior of the Parroquial Mayor during mass

🏛 Parroquial Mayor del Espíritu Santo

Calle Agramonte Oeste 58.
Tel (41) 324 855. ⭕ *9–11am Tue–Sat, 8–11am Sun.* 🕇 *8pm Tue & Thu, 5pm Wed & Fri, 10am Sun.*
Using money donated by Don Ignacio de Valdivia, the local mayor, the present church was built of stone in 1680, over the original 16th century wooden church that had been destroyed by pirates. It is one of Cuba's oldest churches. The simple and solid building is reminiscent of the parish churches of Andalusia, and still has its original, exquisitely worked wooden ceilings. The 30-m (100-ft) bell tower, with three levels, was added in the 18th century, and the octagonal Cristo de la Humildad y la Paciencia chapel, built next to the church in the 19th century, has a remarkable half-dome.

Parque Serafín Sánchez

The heart of the city consists of a tranquil square with trees and a charming *glorieta* (gazebo), surrounded by Neo-Classical buildings. A national monument, the park is dedicated to Serafín Sánchez, a local hero in the wars of independence, whose house is open to the public in the nearby Calle de Céspedes. In the evenings, the plaza is a popular gathering place.

The most notable buildings here are the Centro de Patrimonio, with broad stained-glass windows and Seville mosaics, the large **Biblioteca** (library), and the **Hotel Perla de Cuba**, one of the most exclusive hotels in Cuba in the early 1900s and now a shopping centre. The **Hotel Plaza**, whose bar is popular with locals, is part of a colonial building.

VISITORS' CHECKLIST

Sancti Spíritus. **Road Map** C3.
🏠 *165,450.* 🚌 *Carretera Central, km 2.* 🚏 *Avenida Jesús Menéndez.* 🛈 *Cubatur, Calle Máximo Gómez 7, (41) 328 518.*

Environs

Around 8 km (5 miles) east of Sancti Spíritus, in the direction of Ciego de Ávila, nature lovers and fans of fishing can enjoy **Presa Zaza**, an artificial lake well stocked with trout and black bass. Tours of the lake depart from the Zaza hotel, while the shores are ideal spots for birdwatching. Presa Zaza is Cuba's largest man-made lake but has suffered from low water levels in recent years. Ask at Cubatur for details.

Chatting in the Parque Serafín Sánchez in the evening, a popular pastime

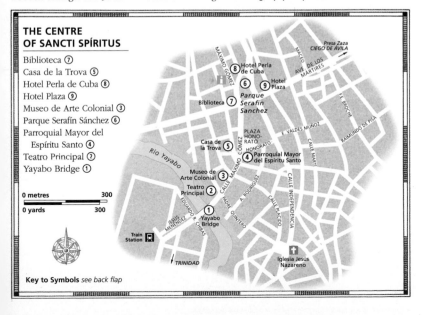

THE CENTRE OF SANCTI SPÍRITUS

Biblioteca ⑦
Casa de la Trova ⑤
Hotel Perla de Cuba ⑧
Hotel Plaza ⑨
Museo de Arte Colonial ③
Parque Serafín Sánchez ⑥
Parroquial Mayor del Espíritu Santo ④
Teatro Principal ②
Yayabo Bridge ①

0 metres   300
0 yards   300

Key to Symbols *see back flap*

Parque Martí in Ciego de Ávila, with a monument to José Martí

Ciego de Ávila ➏

Road Map D3. 🏚 *130,000.*
🚻 🚆 🚌 🛈 *Hotel Ciego de Ávila,
Carretera a Ceballos, (33) 228 013.*

When Ciego de Ávila was founded in 1538 by the conquistador Jácome de Ávila, it was just a large farm in the middle of a wood, a *ciego*. It only became a bona fide city in 1840. Today, it is a rural town with two-storey houses fronted with Neo-Classical columns, and streets filled with one-horse carriages.

The few visitors who come here are mostly on their way to the *cayos* in the Jardines del Rey archipelago.

Anyone who does stop off should visit the **Teatro Principal** (1927) and the **Museo Histórico Provincial**. This last has four rooms of documents and photographs concerning the history of the province, in particular the story of La Trocha. This line of defence was constructed in the 19th century. It was devised by the Spanish to block the advance of the Cuban nationalists *(mambises)* by cutting the island in half, from Morón, north of Ciego de Ávila, to Júcaro, on the Caribbean coast. Some surviving La Trocha towers, built about 1 km (0.6 mile) from one another, lie a short distance outside town and are open to the public.

One of La Trocha's redoubts

The multi-ethnic character of the city means that visitors can enjoy both the rural festivals of Spanish origin *(parrandas)*, similar to those in Remedios *(see p177)*, and merengue and congo dance shows, especially in the quarter where Jamaican and Haitian immigrants live. Ciego de Ávila also has a cycling school which is attended by children from all over the island. At Epiphany the town is the starting point for the month-long Vuelta, a Cuban cycle race much like the Tour de France.

THE COCKEREL OF MORON

"Be careful not to end up like the cockerel of Morón, which lost its feathers as well as its crest." This Spanish saying dates back to the 1500s, when the governor of the Andalusian village of Morón de la Frontera, who lorded it over the local farmers and was known as "cockerel" *(gallo)* for his arrogance and presumptuousness, was punished with a good thrashing and thrown out of town by the angry citizens. The event became well known and to commemorate it, a statue of a plucked rooster was set up in the main avenue. When a community of Andalusians emigrated to Cuba in the 18th century and founded a city they called Morón, to maintain their traditions they put a statue of the rooster at the entrance to the town. It was taken down in 1959, and replaced in 1981 by a bronze sculpture placed next to a tower. At 6am and 6pm daily, a recording of a cock crowing is played here.

The bronze statue (1981) of the legendary cockerel of Morón

Morón ➐

Ciego de Ávila. **Road Map** D3.
🏚 *45,000.* 🚌 🛈 *Cubanacán, Hotel Morón, Avda de Tarafa, (33) 504 720.*
🎉 *Cockerel of Morón: end of June.*

Morón lies on the road that runs north from Ciego de Ávila (a town with a long-standing rivalry with Morón). The road is known for its occupation in 1896 by nationalist rebels *(mambises)* after they had managed to breach the Spanish defence.

Morón was founded as a villa in 1869 and retains a small, well-preserved colonial centre. The **Museo Municipal** has more than 600 archaeological finds, brought to light

A street in Morón with pastel-coloured houses and arcades

Isla Turiguanó, the unusual "Dutch village" near Morón

in the 1940s a short distance from town, including a famous statuette, the Idolillo de Barro.

🏛 Museo Municipal
Calle Martí 374 e/ Antuña y Cervantes. **Tel** *(33) 504 501.*
⏰ *9am–5pm Tue–Sat, 8am–noon Sun.* ⬤ *1 Jan, 1 May, 26 Jul, 25 Dec.* 📷 📹 📵

Environs
North of Morón are two fresh-water lagoons: the **Laguna Redonda**, which owes it name to its almost circular form and is known for its great abundance of trout, and the **Laguna de Leche**. This latter is called the "Lagoon of Milk" because of its colour, caused by the limestone deposits in the water. It is the largest stretch of brackish water in Cuba, with a surface area of 67 sq km (26 sq miles). It abounds in carp and pike and is a refuge for herons and flamingos.

Immediately north of the Laguna de Leche is the **Isla Turiguanó**, a peninsula with a village of Dutch-style houses surrounded by grazing land for cattle. The animals are also Dutch, having been imported by Celia Sánchez *(see p51)*.

Florencia, about 20 km (12 miles) west of Morón, is the starting point for hikes in the small **Sierra de Jatibonico**. This range can be explored on horse-back, along the route followed by Camilo Cienfuegos's column in 1958 *(see p48)*.

The Canal Viejo de Bahamas is used

for platform fishing for large tropical fish. There are also hunting reserves: the Coto de Caza de Morón and Coto de Caza Aguachales de Fala.

Jardines del Rey **❽**

Ciego de Ávila, Camagüey.
Road Map D3.

In the Atlantic Ocean, north of the province of Ciego de Ávila, the Sabana and Camagüey archi-pelagoes, known collectively as "Jardines del Rey", include about 400 small islands, almost all of which are uninhabited.

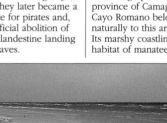

The lighthouse at Cayo Paredón Grande

They were discovered in 1522 by the conquistador Diego Velázquez, who was so struck by them that he dedi-cated them to the king *(rey)*, Carlos V. They later became a hiding place for pirates and, after the official abolition of slavery, a clandestine landing point for slaves.

A causeway 27 km (17 miles) long, built in 1988 as a link between the archipelago and mainland Cuba, makes it easy for visitors to get to the lovely beaches, the coral reef, and the beach resorts which are currently concentrated on Cayo Coco and Cayo Guillermo *(see pp198–9)*. Visitors must pass a tollgate on the causeway. Cayo Paredón Grande, 6 km (4 miles) long, is the third largest island in the Jardines. Although there are no hotels, it is worth visiting for the lovely beaches, and the coral has some fine dive sites, too.

There are good views of the distinctive black and yellow Diego Velázquez Lighthouse, built by Chinese immigrants in 1859.

Although part of the province of Camagüey, Cayo Romano belongs naturally to this archipelago. Its marshy coastline is the habitat of manatees.

The pristine white sandy beach of Cayo Paredón Grande, Jardines del Rey

Cayo Coco ❾

A boat heading out to a coral reef

With 22 km (14 miles) of white sandy beaches and 370 sq km (143 sq miles) of partly marshy land abounding in mangroves and coconut palms, Cayo Coco is an important natural reserve for marine birds. Flamingos may be spotted in the lagoon areas near the coast. The name of the island derives from another rare species of bird that lives here: the white ibis, known to Cubans as the "coco". The island is peaceful, and tourist amenities have been built and organized with environmental concerns in mind. The beaches are lovely, with fine sand washed by clear turquoise water. The warm, shallow water makes Cayo Coco particularly suitable for families with children, but the island is also popular among diving and water sports enthusiasts, who can take advantage of the modern sports facilities here.

★ **Playa Pilar**
Named after Ernest Hemingway's yacht, Playa Pilar sits at the western tip of Cayo Guillermo.

The Duna de la Loma del Puerto is a natural viewing point which can be reached via a path that goes through tropical vegetation.

Archipélago de Sa

CAYO GUILLERMO

C A

Cayo Guillermo
Linked to Cayo Coco, this small island is covered with mangroves and palms as well as mahogany, juniper and mastic trees. At Playa Pilar beach the dunes rise as high as 16 m (52 ft).

Playa Prohibida, surrounded by sand dunes reaching heights of 14 m (46 ft), is a particularly peaceful, secluded beach.

KEY

▬	Major road
▬	Minor road
✈	International airport
⛱	Recommended beach

Bahía de Perros

The Pedraplen
A major work of civil engineering, this causeway links the islands with the mainland. It has caused some concern to ecologists, since it blocks the tide and may disturb the ecosystem of the bay.

La Loma

San R.

★ **Playa Los Flamencos**
This beach, almost 3 km (2 miles) long, is regarded as one of the best on the island because of its lovely clear sea and fine sand. The shallow water is only knee-deep even 200 m (650 ft) from the shore.

VISITORS' CHECKLIST

Ciego de Ávila. **Road Map** D3.
✈ Cayo Coco, (33) 309 165.
ℹ Infotur, Aeropuerto Jardines del Rey, Cayo Coco, (33) 309 109.
⚓ Marina Marlin, Cayo Guillermo (33) 301 737.

Centro de Investigaciones de Ecosistemas Costeras
This centre for the environment studies the effects of tourism on local ecosystems. It is open to the public, and illustrates the bird species on the island, including the roseate spoonbill seen here.

Sitio la Güira, a village in traditional style, is a starting point for horse riding excursions and puts on animal shows for children.

amagüey

CO

• Bautista

0 km   5.5
0 miles   5.5

Cayo Paredón Grande (see p197)

CAYO ROMANO

The Coccothrinax litoralis palm tree
This evergreen palm tree can be found all over Cuba, but is particularly common in Cayo Coco.

Manatí

STAR SIGHTS

★ Playa Los Flamencos

★ Playa Pilar

Camagüey ⓿

This city, declared a UNESCO World Heritage site in 2008, lies in the middle of a vast area of pastureland. It is nick-named "the Legendary" for its traditions of heroism and patriotism as well as for its Neo-Classical architecture. There is a large, rich colonial-style historic centre and the city has an active cultural life. Founded in the bay of Nuevitas on the northern coast as Nuestra Señora de Santa María del Puerto Príncipe, the city was moved to the interior to escape from revolts by the Indians, who staunchly resisted Spanish domination in the 1500s, and from pirate attacks. The irregular, intricate street network that distinguishes Camagüey from other Cuban cities resulted from the need to protect itself from raids.

An example of 19th-century Neo-Classical architecture in Camagüey

Parque Agramonte: the equestrian statue and the Cathedral

Saldaña and built in 1735. In 1777 a bell tower was added, but it collapsed a year later. Since then, the church has been through phases of reconstruction, taking on its present appearance in 1864. It now has a monumental façade surmounted by a pediment, and a bell tower crowned by a statue of Christ.

Parque Ignacio Agramonte

The former Plaza de Armas is dominated by an equestrian statue of Agramonte, a Cuban independence hero, sculpted by the Italian artist Salvatore Boemi and inaugurated by Amalia Simoni, Agramonte's wife, in 1912. At the four corners of the small square stand royal palms, planted in memory of a group of nationalists executed here on 24 February 1851. As so often during the wars of independence, the palms were symbolic monuments to the rebels, as the Spanish would never have allowed real monuments to be built.

Buildings of interest on the square include the Palacio Collado (1942), Bar El Cambio, opened in 1909, a colonial building housing the Café de la Ciudad, the **Casa de la Trova Patricio Ballagas** in an 18th-century building with a courtyard, the Biblioteca Julio Antonio Mella and the cathedral. With its benches and shade

from the palm trees, the square is a natural gathering point for the people of Camagüey. During the day old people gather to watch life go by, and in the evenings the young are drawn to the square.

It is also a popular spot for tourists to see the town's famous *tinajones* (clay pots) up close.

🏠 Catedral de Nuestra Señora de la Candelaria

Calle Cisneros 168, Parque Agramonte. **Tel** (32) 294 965. ⏰ 2:30–6pm Mon–Fri (also 8–11:45am Wed), 2:30–4pm Sat, 8–11:45am Sun. 🔔 5pm Mon–Fri, 9am Sun.
Camagüey's cathedral, dedicated to Our Lady of Candelaria, the patron saint of the city, was designed by Manuel

THE CENTRE OF CAMAGÜEY

Casa de la Trova ⑪
Casa Natal de Ignacio
   Agramonte ③
Casa Natal de Nicolás Guillén ⑫
Catedral de Nuestra Señora
   de la Candelaria ②
Cinco Esquinas ⑦
Iglesia del Carmen ⑥
Iglesia de la Merced ④
Iglesia de la Soledad ⑬
Museo Ignacio Agramonte ⑨
Parque Casino Campestre ⑩
Parque Ignacio Agramonte ①
Plaza San Juan de Dios ⑧
Teatro Principal ⑤

The courtyard at Casa Agramonte, where concerts are performed

🏛 Casa Natal de Ignacio Agramonte

Calle Ignacio Agramonte 459, e/ Independencia y Cisneros. **Tel** (32) 297 116. ☐ 9am–4:30pm Tue–Sat, 8:30–11am Sun. 🌐 1 Jan, 1 May, 26 Jul, 25 Dec. 📷 🚻 🅿 (with charge).

Near Plaza de los Trabajadores, where a large ceiba tree marks the middle of the old town, is the former home of Ignacio Agramonte.

Plaque on Nicolás Guillén's birthplace

This famous local patriot died in battle in 1873 at the age of 31. The two-storey house dates from 1750 and has a beautiful inner courtyard with old *tinajones*.

The museum has documents concerning the war of independence, the hero's personal belongings, such as his 36-calibre Colt revolver from 1851, and family furniture, including the piano of his wife, Amalia Simoni, reputed to be one of the richest, loveliest, most virtuous women in the city.

A short walk away is another famous home. The **Casa Natal de Nicolás Guillén** (see p28), birthplace of Cuba's poet laureate who died in 1989, is at Calle Hermanos Aguero 58.

VISITORS' CHECKLIST

Camagüey. **Road map** D3.
🏠 347,500. ✈ Ignacio
Agramonte, (32) 261 010.
🚌 Ave Avellaneda y Finlay, (32)
292 633. 🚍 Carretera Central
km 3, (32) 270 396. 🛈 Infotur,
Calle Ignacio Agramonte 448,
(32) 256 794. 🎭 Jornadas de la
Cultura Camagüeyana (first half
of Feb); Carnival (23–29 Jun).

🔒 Iglesia de la Merced

Plaza de los Trabajadores 4. **Tel** (32) 292 783. ☐ 8–11am, 4–5:30pm Mon–Fri, 8–11am Sat, 8–10am, 5–7pm Sun. 🛈 5pm Mon–Fri, 7am Sat, 9am & 6pm Sun.

The Iglesia de la Merced was built in 1601 but was rebuilt from 1748 to 1756, and now has a Baroque façade with a central bell tower. Inside are striking, almost Art Nouveau-style murals. The choir and catacombs are also of interest. Most famous, however, is the Holy Sepulchre with an 18th-century statue of Christ by Mexican sculptor Juan Benítez Alfonso. It was cast from 23,000 silver coins collected from the faithful by Manuel Agüero, a citizen who, after his wife's death in 1726, became a monk and devoted himself to restoring the church.

🎭 Teatro Principal

Calle Pedro Valencia 64. **Tel** (32) 293 048. First opened in 1850 and rebuilt in 1926 after a devastating fire, the local theatre is famous as the home of the Camagüey Ballet, one of the leading dance companies in Latin America (see p288).

THE *TINAJONES*

These symbols of the city can be seen everywhere – in parks and gardens and especially in the courtyards of the local colonial houses. *Tinajones* are large jars, which may be as much as 2 m (6 ft) tall, made of clay from the nearby Sierra de Cubitas. The jars were introduced by Catalonian immigrants in the early 1700s, and are used today to collect rainwater and to store food.

A *tinajón* in the central square

Key to Symbols *see back flap*

Exploring Camagüey

The vast historic centre of Camagüey, a complex 16th-century labyrinth of winding alleyways, dead ends, forks and squares, is not easy to navigate. The centre consists mainly of two-storey houses without arcades, pierced by large windows protected by wooden grilles. Each house has an inner courtyard. There are numerous old churches, most of them well attended, whose bell towers jut above the red tile roofs of the colonial houses. As with Trinidad, the well-preserved architecture is the result of the town's geographic isolation: the railway line only arrived in 1903, and the Carretera Central road in 1931.

The Cinco Esquinas (Five Corners), one of the town's more complicated junctions

Other City Centre Sights

Many interesting sights are just a short walk away from Parque Ignacio Agramonte.

Calle Martí runs west from the square up to Plazuela de la Bedoya, a delightful colonial square that has been restored and filled with statues. An old Ursuline convent stands here, as well as a church, the **Iglesia del Carmen**. Although not completed until 1825, it has a distinctly Baroque character.

Calle Cristo leads to Plazuela del Cristo, which is dominated by the Iglesia del Santo Cristo del Buen Viaje and the Cementerio General

Author Gertrudis Gómez de Avellaneda

(1814), the oldest cemetery in Cuba. Back near Parque Agramonte, there is a complex interchange, the **Cinco Esquinas** (five corners), near the top of Calle Raúl Lamar, which is a good example of the intricate layout of the city centre.

Another route to explore runs along or near Calle República, a narrow, straight street that crosses the entire city from north to south. At the northern end, beyond the railway line, is the Museo Provincial Ignacio Agramonte (see p203).

Further south, a right turn at the Hotel Colón leads eastwards across to Calle Avellaneda. Here, at No. 22, is the birthplace of Gertrudis Gómez de Avellaneda, the 19th-century author of anti-slavery novels.

Further south, on Calle República, stands the **Iglesia de Nuestra Señora de la Soledad**, built in 1776. It was here that local patriot Ignacio Agramonte was baptized and also married. The façade features pilasters and moulding typical of early Cuban Baroque architecture, but the real attractions here are the decoratively painted arches and pillars and the wooden *alfarje* ceiling inside.

By going south to the far end of this street you will reach Calle Martí, which will take you back to Parque Agramonte.

Plaza San Juan de Dios

This square is also known as Plaza del Padre Olallo, in honour of a priest who was beatified in 2008 because he dedicated his life to caring for the sick in the city hospital.

Today, the totally restored Plaza San Juan de Dios is a quiet, picturesque spot, but also a gem of colonial architecture. Around it are 18th-century pastel buildings, two of which have been converted into restaurants. One whole side of the plaza is occupied by an important group of buildings that include a church and an old hospital, which is now the home of the Dirección

The Iglesia del Carmen, on Plaza del Carmen

Provincial de Patrimonio and the Oficina del Historiador de la Ciudad, a body that takes care of the province's cultural heritage. Construction of the building began in 1728.

Despite its small size, the **Iglesia de San Juan de Dios** is one of the most interesting churches in Camagüey. It still has its original floors, ceiling and wooden choir, and, most importantly, the high altar with the Holy Trinity and an anthropomorphic representation of the Holy Ghost, the only one in Cuba. The church façade is simple and rigorously symmetrical.

The old **Hospital** was used in the 20th century as a military infirmary, then a teacher training school, a refuge for flood victims, a centre for underprivileged children and, most recently, as the Instituto Tecnológico de la Salud (Technological Institute of Health). The square plan with two inner courtyards (clearly of *mudéjar* influence) was modelled on Baroque monasteries. The enclosure walls are thick and plain; in contrast the window grilles and wooden balustrades in the galleries are elegant and elaborate.

The Holy Trinity high altar

🔒 Iglesia y Hospital de San Juan de Dios

Plaza San Juan de Dios. ⏰ 7–11am, 2:30–4pm Mon–Sat. 🚫 1 Jan, 1 May, 26 Jul, 25 Dec. 📷 🚫 📷

One of the cloisters in the old San Juan de Dios hospital

🏛 Museo Provincial Ignacio Agramonte

Avenida de los Mártires 2, esq. Ignacio Sánchez. **Tel** *(32) 282 425.* ⏰ *10am–1pm, 2–5pm Tue–Sat, 10am–1pm Sun.* 📷 📷 📷 *(with charge).*

The only military building in town was the head-quarters of the Spanish army cavalry in the 19th century. In 1905 it became a hotel, and since 1948 it has housed a large museum of the history, natural history and art of the city and its province. The prestigious small art collection is second only to that in the Museo de Bellas Artes in Havana, with three works by the famous Cuban artist Fidelio Ponce. There is also a fine collection of books, including some manuscripts by the Canaries writer Silvestre de Balboa, author of *Espejo de Paciencia,*

a poem (1608) regarded as the first literary work in Cuba *(see p28).*

🌿 Parque Casino Campestre

The largest natural park in any Cuban city, the Casino was for a long time used for agricultural fairs, and became a public park in the 19th century. The Hatibonico river flows through it. Besides the many statues of patriots and illustrious figures from Camagüey and Cuba, it has a monument to the Seville pilots Barberán and Collar, who on 10 June 1933 made a historic transatlantic flight from Seville to Camagüey in 19 hours 11 minutes.

Environs

The plains north of Camagüey are cattle country. **Rancho King**, a former cattle ranch, has a restaurant and rooms and offers horse-riding trips and rodeos. It is most easily accessed from Playa Santa Lucía, 26 miles (16 km) to the north.

Plaza San Juan de Dios, known for its well-preserved colonial architecture

A country road north of Camagüey, leading to Sierra de Cubitas

Sierra de Cubitas ⓫

Camagüey. **Map** D3.

The range of hills that lies 40 km (25 miles) north of Camagüey forms the largest local reserve of flora and fauna, with over 300 plant species. To date, however, this area has no tourist facilities on any scale.

The main attractions are caverns such as Hoyo de Bonet, the largest karst depression in Cuba, and the Pichardo and María Teresa grottoes, where cave drawings have been discovered. Expert speleologists, on the other hand, can visit the Cueva de Rolando, a cave 132 m (435 ft) long with a subterranean lake 50 m (165 ft) across, the bottom of which has not yet been explored.

In the neighbouring Valle del Río Máximo is the **Paso de los Paredones**, a long, deep ravine with holes caused by water erosion, some as much as 100 m (328 ft) deep and up to 1 km (0.6 mile) wide. The thick vegetation, through which sunlight penetrates for only a few hours, is home to a variety of native birds *(tocororo* and *cartacuba; see pp20–21)* and migratory birds, as well as harmless reptiles and rodents.

Playa Santa Lucía ⓬

Camagüey. **Map** D3. ⓘ *Cubatur, Ave. Turistica, Playa Santa Lucía, (32) 336 291 or (32) 365 303.*

The most famous beach resort in the province offers 21 km (13 miles) of fine white sand lapped by turquoise waves. The large coral reef only 3 km (2 miles) from the shore is a scuba diver's paradise *(see p293).* It shelters the coast from the currents of the Canal Viejo de Bahamas, thus safeguarding calm swimming conditions for adults and children alike, as well as creating a good area for practising all watersports.

There are more than 30 dive sites along the reef, which can be reached with the help of the international diving centres, while Shark's Point offers dives full of romance, exploring the wrecks of pirate and Spanish vessels. For the brave there is also the chance to observe the bull shark, *Carcharinus leucas,* at close range from February to March and from July to September.

At the bay of Nuevitas, 6 km (4 miles) west of Santa Lucía, near the tiny seashore village of La Boca, is **Playa Los Cocos**. This lovely unspoilt beach has fine white sand and clear water, and is a must for visitors to Santa Lucía.

A beautiful beach on Cayo Sabinal

Cayo Sabinal ⓭

Camagüey. **Map** D3. 🛳

Together with Cayo Romano and Cayo Guajaba, this small island forms part of a protected area. It is the home of deer and the largest colony of flamingos in Cuba, as well as a nesting area for four species of sea turtle. Cayo

A pier at Playa Santa Lucía, departure point for boats going out to the coral reef
◁ Playa Los Cocos, near Playa Santa Lucía

Sabinal can be reached via a causeway from Playa Santa Lucía, and a planned *pedraplén* causeway will link it with Jardines del Rey.

In the past Cayo Sabinal was home to permanent residents: first the natives, then pirates and Spanish coalmen. Today, the key is visited mostly for its three beautiful beaches, Playa Bonita, Playa Los Pinos and Playa Brava. The Colón Lighthouse dates from 1894.

South of Cayo Sabinal is the Bay of Nuevitas, where the city of Camagüey was first founded. The three small islands in the bay, known as **Los Ballenatos**, are popular destinations for boat trips.

Las Tunas ⓮

Las Tunas. **Map** E3.
🏛 *198,000.* ✈ 🚉 🚌
ℹ *Hotel Las Tunas, Ave. 2 de diciembre, (31) 345 014; Ecotur, (31) 372 073.* 🎪 *Jornada Nacional Cucalambeana (end of Jun).*

Until 1975, Las Tunas was just one of the cities in the old Provincia de Oriente. Then administrative reform made it the capital of an autonomous province. The town was founded on the site of two native villages that were razed to the ground by the *conquistador* Alonso de Ojeda in the early 1500s. However, the town only really began to develop three centuries later, progressively taking on the character of a frontier town between central and eastern Cuba. The historic centre has some colonial buildings but no major monuments of note. However, the city does have many artists' studios.

The **Museo Histórico Provincial**, in the town hall, has archaeological finds and documents relating to the history of the province. The Memorial a los Mártires de Barbados commemorates a terrorist act against Cuba carried out in 1976: a bomb exploded on a Cubana aeroplane headed for Havana, killing 73 passengers and the entire crew.

Every year Las Tunas springs to life on the occasion of the Jornada Nacional Cucalambeana, dedicated to Juan Cristóbal Nápoles Fajardo, known as El Cucalambé, a farmer and poet born here in 1829. Local and other Cuban artists, as well as foreign scholars, take part in this festival of music and folk traditions.

Environs
Near Las Tunas are many sites linked with the wars of independence. They include the **Fuerte de la Loma**, now a national monument, built by the Spanish to halt the advance of the Mambí, and the city of **Puerto Padre**, the scene of major battles in the Ten Years' War (1868–78).

The best beach here is **Playa Covarrubias**, which is near Puerto Padre, on the Atlantic coast.

The town hall of Las Tunas

Jardines de la Reina ⓯

Ciego de Ávila, Camagüey. **Map** D4.
🚢 *Júcaro, Embarcadero Avalón, (33) 498 104.*

This archipelago in the Caribbean Sea was discovered by Christopher Columbus and called Jardines de la Reina in honour of the queen *(reina)*, Isabel of Castile. Established as a National Park in 1996, it is one of Cuba's largest protected areas. These islands can be reached by boat from the pleasant fishing village of Júcaro.

The great number of unspoilt *cayos*, the secluded pristine beaches, mangroves and palm groves with rich fauna consisting of crocodiles, iguanas, turtles and tropical birds, and a 200-km (125-mile) coral reef make this archipelago a paradise for nature lovers.

Near Cayo Anclita, only about 100 m (328 ft) from the coast, is a floating hotel reserved for fishermen, divers and photographers. The waters abound with groupers, snappers, barracudas and sharks, among many other fish. Tours of the area can be booked via the floating hotel.

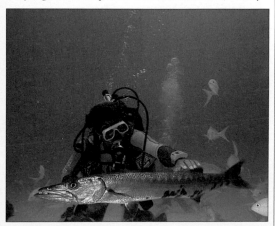
A scuba diver with a barracuda

EASTERN CUBA

GRANMA · HOLGUÍN · SANTIAGO DE CUBA · GUANTÁNAMO

Cubans refer to the eastern part of Cuba as the Oriente, giving it an exotic, magical appeal. The landscape, stretching out towards Haiti and other Caribbean islands, is varied, with majestic mountains, magnificent coastlines and an area of arid desert, unusual in Cuba. The eastern cities, often rich in history, include Santiago de Cuba, host to one of Latin America's most famous carnivals.

From the 17th to the 19th centuries, thousands of black slaves were brought to Cuba from Africa, men and women who became the ancestors of the multi-ethnic mix visible in Eastern Cuba today, part African, but also part Spanish, part French and Chinese. In this cultural melting pot, African and European, Roman Catholic and pagan traditions are blended, sometimes inextricably.

The area is full of apparent contradictions: there is the combative Oriente, rebellious and indomitable; and yet there is also the laid-back Oriente, an oasis of pleasure, and the sonorous Oriente, the cradle of great musicians. It is true that the people of Eastern Cuba have always fought with great fervour. One eloquent example is the Indian chief Hatuey, who was burned at the stake in the 16th century for organizing resistance against the Spanish. Then, in the 19th century, local nationalists led the wars of independence. The citizens of Bayamo even burned down their town rather than hand it over to the enemy. In the 20th century, there were the *rebeldes* (many of whom were from Eastern Cuba, including Fidel Castro himself), who launched the struggle against Batista's dictatorship by attacking the Moncada barracks in Santiago.

Yet the people of eastern Cuba also know how to have a good time, adore music, rhythm and dance of all kinds, and each July put on a colourful Carnival and Fiesta del Caribe at Santiago de Cuba; the carnival is one of the most celebrated in Latin America.

Cacti growing along the Costa Sur, the only arid zone on the island, east of Guantánamo

◁ The steps on Calle Padre Pico, in the heart of Santiago de Cuba

Exploring Eastern Cuba

The classic starting point for touring the eastern
provinces is Santiago de Cuba, a city rich in history,
with lovely colonial architecture and sites associated
with the 1959 revolution. To the west rises the
majestic Sierra Maestra, also with its own associations
with the guerrilla war of the 1950s. The Sierra is most
easily reached, in fact, from the north, near Bayamo.
To the east, the Parque Baconao has all kinds of
attractions, ideal for families with children, while
more adventurous souls can head further east, to the
province of Guantánamo, famous for its US naval
base, and Baracoa, Cuba's oldest city. The province
of Holguín, further north, has some fine beaches,
and Cuba's most interesting archaeological site.

The small islands of the Bahía de
Naranjo national park

SEE ALSO

- *Where to Stay* pp266–9
- *Where to Eat* p283

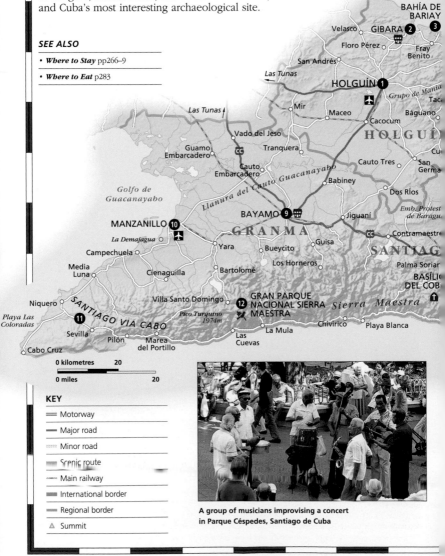

A group of musicians improvising a concert
in Parque Céspedes, Santiago de Cuba

KEY

═══ Motorway

─── Major road

┄┄┄ Minor road

▓▓▓ Scenic route

╌╌╌ Main railway

▬▬▬ International border

─── Regional border

△ Summit

SIGHTS AT A GLANCE

Bahía de Bariay ❸
Banes ❻
Baracoa pp242–3 ⓴
Basílica del Cobre ⓭
Bayamo ❾
Boca de Yumurí ㉔
Castillo del Morro
  pp232–3 ⓯
Cayo Saetía ❽
Chorro de Maíta ❺
Costa Sur ⓲

El Yunque ㉑
Gibara ❷
Gran Parque Nacional
  Sierra Maestra ⓬
Guantánamo ⓱
Guardalavaca ❹
Holguín pp212–13 ❶
La Farola ⓳
Manzanillo ❿
Mayarí ❼
Parque Baconao
  pp234–7 ⓰

Parque Nacional Alejandro
  de Humboldt ㉓
Río Toa ㉒
Santiago de Cuba
  pp222–31 ⓮

Tour

Towards Santiago via
  Cabo Cruz pp218–19 ⓫

The *azulejos* decoration in the
Colonia Española in Manzanillo

GETTING AROUND

Although sights on the outskirts of Santiago
can be reached by bus or taxi, by far the
best way to get around Eastern Cuba is
to hire a car. Some journeys are among
the most picturesque in Cuba, especially the
drive to Baracoa via "La Farola" *(see
p239)*. Another option would be to fly to
the main eastern towns. Various organized
tours are also available, starting off
from Santiago or from the beach
resorts of Holguín province, especially
Guardalavaca. These tours can be
booked through travel agencies.

**A perfectly restored Neo-Classical building
in the centre of Baracoa**

Holguín ❶

Called the city of parks because of its many leafy squares, Holguín is a modern town built on a grid layout and situated between two hills, Cerro de Mayabe and Loma de la Cruz. The people of Holguín took an active part in the wars of independence under the leadership of Calixto García, the famous general who liberated the city from the Spanish in 1872. The house he was born in is now a museum; the square named after him marks the centre of the city and is dominated by a statue of the heroic general.

A peanut vendor in Parque García

San Isidoro Cathedral, in the spacious Parque Peralta

Exploring Holguín

Calle Maceo and Manduley – two parallel streets with shops, hotels, bars and clubs, including the Casa de la Trova – cross three squares: **Parque San José, Parque Calixto García** and **Parque Peralta**. Parque García, always buzzing with people, is the site of the town's chief monuments and museums including **Casa Natal de Calixto García**.

🏧 La Periquera (Museo Provincial de Historia)

Calle Frexes 198, e/ Libertad y Maceo. *Tel* (24) 463 395.
⬜ 9am–4:30pm Tue–Sat, 8:30am–noon Sun. ◼ 1 Jan, 1 May, 26 Jul, 10 Oct, 25 Dec.
📷 📹 📱 (with charge).
This large Neo-Classical building with a courtyard overlooks Parque Calixto García. It was built in 1860 as a ballroom and casino for the local upper middle class. In 1868, at the beginning of the Ten Years' War *(see p44)*, the building was occupied by the Spanish army and converted into a barracks. Hence the building's nickname, *La Periquera*, which translates as "parrot cage", a reference to the brightly coloured uniforms of the Spanish army.

Today, the building is the home of the Museo Provincial de Historia, where five rooms illustrate the main stages of the cultural development of Holguín. Also on

display are archaeological relics of the Taíno Indians, who lived here from the 8th to the 15th centuries. The most famous item in the collection is the Hacha de Holguín, a stone axe head carved as a human figure. It was discovered in the hills around Holguín, and has become the symbol of the city.

🏛 Museo de Historia Natural Carlos de la Torre y Huerta

Calle Maceo 129, e/ Martí y Luz Caballero. *Tel* (24) 423 935.
⬜ 9am–noon, 12:30–5pm Tue–Sat, 9am–noon Sun. 📷 📹 📱 (with charge).
One of the most interesting natural history museums in Cuba has 11 collections with many specimens of Cuban and Caribbean flora and fauna. There is an outstanding collection of birds and shells, including *Polymita* snails from Baracoa *(see p245)*, and a 50-million-year-old fossil fish, found in the Sierra Maestra.

Hacha de Holguín

🛐 Catedral de San Isidoro

Calle Manduley, e/ Luz Caballero y Aricochea, Parque Peralta. *Tel* (24) 422 107. ⬜ 5:30–7pm Mon, 7am–noon, 3–5:30pm, 7:30–8:30pm Tue & Fri, 7am–noon Wed, Thu, Sat & Sun. 🛐 daily.
Consecrated as a cathedral in 1979, San Isidoro was built in 1720 on the site of the first mass held to celebrate the city's founding: Parque Peralta. It is also known as Parque de Flores because a flower market used to be held here.

The church contains a copy of the popular Madonna of Caridad, the original of which is in the Basilica del Cobre near Santiago de Cuba *(see p221)*. On 4 April there is a celebration in honour of the Virgin.

Loma de la Cruz

There are marvellous, far-reaching views from the top of the Loma de la Cruz (Hill of the Cross). The engineers who founded Holguín used this site to plan the layout of the town, but it was only much later (from 1927–50) that the 458-step stairway was built to the top. Every year on 3 May, the people of Holguín

Parque Calixto García, with La Periquera; behind, the Loma de la Cruz

For hotels and restaurants in this region see pp266–9 and p283

A panoramic view of Holguín from the top of the Loma de la Cruz

VISITORS' CHECKLIST

Holguín. **Road Map** E4.
342,500. 13 km (8 miles)
south. Calle V Pita, (24) 422
331. Carretera Central y
Independencia, (24) 422 111.
Cubatur, Guardalavaca, (24)
430 170, 430 171. Romerías
de Mayo (2–8 May).

climb up the hill for the Romerías de Mayo, a celebration of Spanish origin. The top of Loma, about 3 km (2 miles) northwest of Parque Calixto García, is marked by a Spanish lookout tower and by a cross placed there on 3 May 1790 by friar Antonio Alegría.

Plaza de la Revolución
Situated east of the city centre, behind Hotel Pernik, this vast square contains a monument to the heroes of Cuban independence, the mausoleum of Calixto García and a small monument to his mother. The square is the main venue for political rallies and popular festivities.

Environs
Another, more distant viewing point over the city is the **Mirador de Mayabe** on the Cerro de Mayabe, which is about 10 km (6 miles) southeast of the city centre.

From the mirador there is a view of the valley with its fruit orchards and of Holguín in the distance. This spot is also home to an *aldea campesina* (country village), with simple lodgings and a restaurant, as well as an open-air museum. This illustrates the lives of Cuban farmers living in a small village, with various examples of a *bohío real*, a typical rural home with a palm-leaf roof

and earth floor, a hen-house and a courtyard containing jars for transporting water.

At No. 301 on the road leading to Gibara, a mile or so north of the centre, is the small **Fábrica de Órganos**, the only factory in Cuba that manufactures mechanical organs. Sadly, it is no longer open to the public.

A mechanical organ made in the Holguín factory

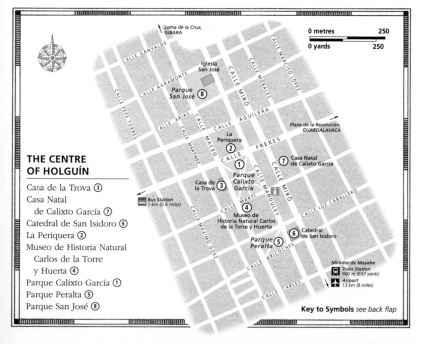

THE CENTRE OF HOLGUÍN

Casa de la Trova ③
Casa Natal de Calixto García ⑦
Catedral de San Isidoro ⑥
La Periquera ②
Museo de Historia Natural Carlos de la Torre y Huerta ④
Parque Calixto García ①
Parque Peralta ⑤
Parque San José ⑧

View of Gibara, an appealing seaside town with a colonial centre

Gibara ❷

Holguín. **Road Map** E3.
👥 71,500.

South of the bay that Columbus named Río de Mares (the river of seas) is the picturesque town of Gibara. In the 19th century this was the main port on the northern coast of the province of Oriente, and it has the most important colonial architecture in the area. Gibara is sometimes known as "Villa Blanca" (white town) because of its white houses.

The shady Malecón (seafront) has a statue of Columbus shown gazing at the horizon, a ruined garrison and views of the small fishing harbour. From here, narrow streets lead to the main square, overlooked by the **Iglesia de San Fulgencio** (1854), and an old theatre. The **Museo de Ciencias Naturales** (Natural

Façade of the Iglesia de San Fulgencio at Gibara

History Museum) has one of the best butterfly collections in Cuba, and the **Museo de Artes Decorativas** (Decorative Arts Museum) is housed in a magnificent 19th-century mansion. The museum has been closed since 2008 after the town suffered extensive hurricane damage. It is not known when it will reopen.

🏛 **Museo de Ciencias Naturales**
Calle Maceo 131, e/ Martí y Luz Caballero. **Tel** (24) 844 458.
⏱ 9am–4pm Tue–Sat, 9am–noon Sun. ⬛ 1 Jan, 1 May, 26 Jul, 10 Oct, 25 Dec. 📷 🎫 🎫 📷 (with charge).

🏛 **Museo de Artes Decorativas**
Calle Independencia 19. **Tel** (24) 844 687. ⏱ currently closed for restoration. 📷 🎫 📷 (with charge).

Bahía de Bariay ❸

Holguín. **Road Map** E3.

East of Gibara is a bay with a spit of land in the middle called Cayo de Bariay. Most historians (but not Baracoans, *see p242*) agree that Columbus first landed here in 1492. With its abundant flowers and trees laden with fruit, it looked like paradise to the explorer. In 1992, on the 500th anniversary of Columbus' landing in Cuba, a monument called *Encuentro* ("Encounter"), dedicated to the Taíno Indians, was erected here. The site is relatively remote if travelling by car, but boat trips can be arranged from Guardalavaca (*see p215*). East of Cayo de Bariay is the beautiful **Playa Don Lino**.

COLUMBUS IN CUBA

Christopher Columbus, explorer of the New World

On 28 October 1492, when he first set foot on Cuban land, Columbus wrote in his travel journal: "I have never seen a more beautiful place. Along the banks of the river were trees I have never seen at home, with flowers and fruit of the most diverse kinds, among the branches of which one heard the delightful chirping of birds. There were a great number of palms. When I descended from the launch, I approached two fishermen's huts. Upon seeing me, the natives took flight and fled. Back on the boat, I went up the river for a good distance. I felt such joy upon seeing these flowery gardens and green forests and hearing the birds sing that I could not tear myself away, and thus continued my trip. This island is truly the most beautiful land human eyes have ever beheld."

Guardalavaca ❹

Holguín. **Road Map** F3.

Converted in the mid-1980s into a holiday resort, the beaches of Guardalavaca are the most popular holiday destination in Cuba after Varadero *(see pp162–3)*. Although the resort is within easy reach of Holguín, which lies 58 km (35 miles) to the southwest along a road through curious conical hills, the location still feels remote.

The 4-km (2-mile) crescent-shaped main beach, enclosed at either end by rocks, is backed by abundant vegetation. The sea is crystal-clear, the sand is fine, and there is a coral reef quite close to the shore. To the west are several developed beaches.

The name "Guardalavaca" (watch the cow) derives from the Spanish word for the cattle egret *(see p20)*, a bird which is common throughout Cuba, and especially prevalent here.

West of the beach is **Bahía de Naranjo**, a natural park that comprises 32 km (20 miles) of coastline and 10 sq km (3.9 sq miles) of woods, with karst hills covered with thick vegetation. There are three small islands in the bay; on one, Cayo Naranjo, there is an aquarium featuring shows with sea lions and dolphins. Boat tours, diving and fishing trips are also organized here.

Skeletons found in the necropolis of Chorro de Maíta

Chorro de Maíta ❺

Cerro de Yaguajay, Banes (Holguín). **Road Map** F4. *Tel* (24) 430 201. ☐ 9am–5pm Mon–Sat, 9am–1pm Sun. ● 1 Jan, 1 May, 26 Jul, 10 Oct, 25 Dec. ▨ ☑ ◙ (with charge).

Near the coast, just 5 km (3 miles) south of Guardalavaca, is Chorro de Maíta, the largest native Indian necropolis in Cuba and the Antilles. At this unmissable site archaeologists have found 56 skeletons and a number of clay objects, bone amulets, funerary offerings and decorated shells.

All this material can be seen from a boardwalk inside the museum. Across the road is an *aldea taína*, a reconstruction

of a pre-Columbian rural village, built for entertainment, but historically accurate. Visitors can buy souvenirs and sample food that the Amerindians used to eat. In front of the huts are life-size statues of natives.

Banes ❻

Holguín. **Road Map** F4.

This country town, 32 km (20 m) southwest of Holguín, is located in the middle of a vast and rich excavation zone (the province of Holguín has yielded one-third of the archaeological finds in Cuba). Banes is the home of the **Museo Indocubano Bani**, Cuba's most important archaeological museum outside Havana. The museum has over a thousand objects on display, including axes, terracotta vases, flint knives and, most notably, a 4-cm (2-in) high figure of a woman in gold, known as the Ídolo de Oro. It was found near Banes, and dates from the 13th century.

Ídolo de Oro, Museo Indocubano Bani

🏛 **Museo Indocubano Bani**
Calle General Barrero 305, e/ Martí y Céspedes. *Tel* (24) 802 487. ☐ 9am–5pm Tue–Sat, 8am–noon Sun. ▨ ☑ ◙ (with charge).

The lovely clear turquoise sea at Guardalavaca, Eastern Cuba's Varadero

The coves at Cayo Saetía, known for their fine white sand

Mayarí **⑦**

Holguín. **Road Map** F4. 🏛 60,000.

Mayarí, 100 km (62 miles) southeast of Holguín, was founded in 1757 and, together with Gibara *(see p214)*, is the oldest city in the province.

Nearby are the **Farallones de Seboruco**, caves where objects left by the Taíno people have been found. Nearby is the **Meseta de Pinares de Mayarí**, a large forest cloaking the hills up to an altitude of 1,000 m (3,280 ft).

Southwest of Mayarí is Birán, where Fidel Castro was born. His parents' house, **Finca Birán**, is now a museum.

🏛 **Finca Birán**
Tel (24) 286 102. ⏰ 9am–3pm Tue–Sun (except when raining).
🚫 📷 📷

Cayo Saetía **⑧**

Holguín. **Road Map** F4.

Lying at the mouth of the Bay of Nipe, this small island covering 42 sq km (16 sq miles), with wonderfully fascinating coves, is connected to the mainland by a drawbridge. It was formerly a private hunting reserve, and in the woods and meadows, antelopes and zebra still live side by side with species native to Cuba. On safaris, led by expert guides, visitors travelling on horseback or in jeeps can observe and photograph the animals. The few tourist facilities on this island are for paying guests only and were designed with every care for the environment. A boat trip to Cayo Saetía from Guardalavaca is a highlight.

Bayamo **⑨**

Granma. **Road Map** E4. 🏛 230,000. ✈ 🚉 *Saco y Línea, (23) 423 034.* 🚌 *Carretera Central y Jesús Rabí, (23) 424 036.* 🛈 *Havanatur, Parque Céspedes, (23) 427 664.*

The second oldest town in Cuba after Baracoa, Bayamo was founded in 1513 by Diego

The statue of Carlos Manuel de Céspedes at Bayamo

Velázquez. Until 1975 it was part of the large Oriente province, but after administrative reform it became the capital of a new province, Granma. It is a pasture and livestock breeding area, but has also been the home of nationalists and the cradle of political revolts and struggles.

In 1869, rather than surrender their town to Spain, the citizens burned Bayamo down. As a result, the centre is relatively modern. Daily life revolves around **Parque Céspedes**, the main square, dominated by a statue of local plantation owner and war of independence hero Carlos Manuel de Céspedes (1955). The square is home to almost all the important buildings in town: the Cultural Centre, the Royalton Hotel, the offices of the Poder Popular, and the historic Pedrito café.

Adjacent to the main square is **Plaza del Himno** (Square of the Hymn). It gained its name after *La Bayamesa*, the Cuban national anthem, was first played in the church here on 20 October 1868. Marking this event is a sculpture that includes a bronze plaque on which are engraved the words and music by Perucho Figueredo. His bust stands next to the nationalists' flag. In the smaller **Parque Maceo**

Relaxing in the shade at Parque Céspedes, in Bayamo

BAYAMO "THE REBELLIOUS"

Bayamo has a long tradition of rebellion. In the early 1500s, the native Indians, led by their chief, Hatuey, fiercely resisted the Spanish *(see p219)*. A few years later an African slave killed the pirate Gilberto Girón, displaying his head as a trophy in the central plaza. This episode inspired the epic poem *Espejo de Paciencia* by Silvestre de Balboa, the first major work of Cuban literature *(see p28)*. But the most dramatic episode in the history of Bayamo concerns the struggles for independence, during which, on 10 October 1868, a group of local nationalists and intellectuals – Juan Clemente Zenea, Carlos Manuel de Céspedes *(see p43)*, Pedro Figueredo, José Fornaris and José Joaquín Palma – organized an anti-Spanish revolt. They entered the town on 20 October, and declared it the capital of the Republic in Arms. On 12 January, faced with the fact that Bayamo would be recaptured by colonial troops, the citizens decided to set fire to their own town, an act which later led to the choice of *La Bayamesa* as the national anthem.

The monument dedicated to the national anthem, *La Bayamesa*

Interior of the Parroquial Mayor de San Salvador

Osorio, formerly Parque de San Francisco, north of Parque Céspedes, is the Casa de la Trova Olimpio La O, one of the town's few 18th-century buildings. The courtyard is used by local groups for concerts.

🏛 **Casa Natal de Carlos Manuel de Céspedes**
Calle Maceo 57, e/ Marmol y Palma. **Tel** *(23) 423 864.*
⏰ *9am–5pm Tue–Fri, 9am–1:30pm, 8–10pm Sat, 10am–2pm Sun.* 📷 *(with charge).*
The house where the leading figure in the first war against Spain in the 19th century was born on 18 April 1819 is a handsome, two-storey Colonial building facing Parque Céspedes. Architecturally it is the most important building in the city.

The rooms on the ground floor, which open onto a courtyard with a fountain, contain the heart of the collection, with Céspedes' documents and personal items, including his steel and bronze sword.

Upstairs are several furnished rooms, one of which has a bronze bed with mother-of-pearl medallions, a fine example of Colonial furniture. A gallery leads to the old kitchen, which still has its original ceramic oven.

Façade of the birthplace of Carlos Manuel de Céspedes

🛈 **Parroquial Mayor de San Salvador**
Plaza del Himno esq. José Joaquín Palma. **Tel** *(23) 422 514.* ⏰ *9am–noon Mon–Fri, 9–10:30am Sun.*
When the nationalists of Bayamo chose to burn down their own town rather than leave anything for the Spanish, they put the holy images kept in the Parroquial Mayor (the Cathedral) into safekeeping. That was the plan, at all events. Unfortunately, the only things spared by the fire were the font (which had been used for the baptism of Carlos Manuel de Céspedes) and the Capilla de los Dolores, a chapel built in 1740, which contained an image of the Virgin Mary and a Baroque altarpiece made of gilded wood. The altarpiece has a particularly fine frame decorated with tropical motifs and representations of local fruit and animals, an unusual and very Cuban element in the art of the 18th century.

In 1916, Bishop Guerra commissioned the reconstruction of the old Parroquial Mayor, dedicated to Jesus the Saviour, the patron saint of Bayamo. The original building had been finished in 1613 and in the course of time had been transformed into a large three-aisle church with two choirs, nine altars and a finely wrought pulpit.

The new church was opened on 9 October 1919, with the old image of Jesus the Saviour salvaged from the fire, a new marble altar, a patriotic painting by the Dominican artist Luis Desangles, and plastered brick walls frescoed by Esteban Ferrer.

Manzanillo

Granma. **Road map** E4.
✈ "Sierra Maestra", 8 km (5 miles)
south of town. 🚌 🚉 Bayamo,
Camagüey, Havana, Pilón, Yara.

Built along the Caribbean Bay
of Guacanayabo, Manzanillo
is a charming seaside town. It
was founded as Puerto Real
in 1784, and reached its
apogee in the second half of
the 19th century, thanks to
sugar and the slave trade.
 Memories are still strong
of the feats of Castro's rebel
forces in the nearby Sierra
Maestra, especially those of
Castro's assistant Celia
Sánchez, who organized a
crucial rearguard here. She
is honoured by a striking
monument in the town.
 In Parque Céspedes, the
central square, a brickwork

The Glorieta Morisca de Manzanillo, where the municipal band plays

bandstand for concerts by
local bands was opened on
25 June 1924. The so-called
Glorieta Morisca gained its
name because of its Arab-
influenced decoration,
designed by José Martín del
Castillo, an architect from
Granada. Other monuments

in town, all near the Parque
Céspedes, include the Neo-
Classical Iglesia de la Purísima
Concepción, built in the
1920s; the atmospheric Café
1906, the 19th-century town
hall, now the Asamblea
Municipal del Poder Popular;
and the Colonia Española, a

Towards Santiago via Cabo Cruz ⓫

This fascinating route by road to Santiago skirts the
high slopes of the Sierra Maestra which, along the
south coast, forces the road into the sea in places,
especially after hurricanes. The scenery is unspoiled
and at times wild, and conceals several places of
historical significance. The route can be covered in a
long day, but for a more relaxing drive visitors could
consider staying in Marea del Portillo or Chivirico.

La Demajagua ①
Céspedes's estate still has
sugar-making equipment,
such as these *calderas* used
for making molasses.

Playa Las Coloradas ③
It was near here that 82 rebels
landed aboard the *Granma*
in December 1956 (*see p48*).

Media Luna ②
This is the birthplace of the
revolutionary Celia Sánchez
(*see p51*). The house is
now a museum.

**Parque Nacional Desembarco
del *Granma*** ④
This park is rich in
local flora, including
some extraordinary
orchids. There are also
various sites commemm-
orating the journey of the
revolutionaries following
their arrival on the *Granma*.

Niquero

Punto Nu

Bélic

③

④

Cabo Cruz

El Guafe ⑤
This archaeological site has pre-
Columbian finds displayed in caves.

social club for Spanish immigrants that was completed in 1935. The club is located in a building with an Andalusian courtyard and a panel of painted tiles representing Columbus's landing in Cuba.

Environs
10 km (6 miles) south of Manzanillo are the remains of **La Demajagua**, the estate belonging to Carlos Manuel de Céspedes (*see pp42 & 217*). On 10 October 1868, he freed all of his slaves, urging them to join him in fighting the Spanish.
    Yara, 24 km (15 miles) east of Manzanillo, is where Céspedes proclaimed Cuban independence, and where the Indian hero Hatuey was burned at the stake. There is a small museum in the central square, Plaza Grito de Yara.

HATUEY'S SACRIFICE

Over the centuries, the sacrifice of Hatuey acquired great patriotic significance and gave rise to numerous legends, including *La Luz de Yara* (The Light of Yara), written by Luis Victoriano Betancourt in 1875. The author relates that from the stake on which the Indian hero was being burned, there arose a mysterious light that wandered throughout the island, protecting the sleep of the slaves who were awaiting their freedom. This light was the soul of Hatuey. Three centuries later, the wandering light returned to the site of the Indian's sacrifice, and in a flash all the palm trees in Cuba shook, the sky was lit up, the earth trembled, and the light turned into a fire that stirred Cubans' hearts: "It was the Light of Yara, which was about to take its revenge. It was the tomb of Hatuey, which became the cradle of independence. It was 10 October" – the beginning of the war of independence.

The Indian chief Hatuey being burned at the stake

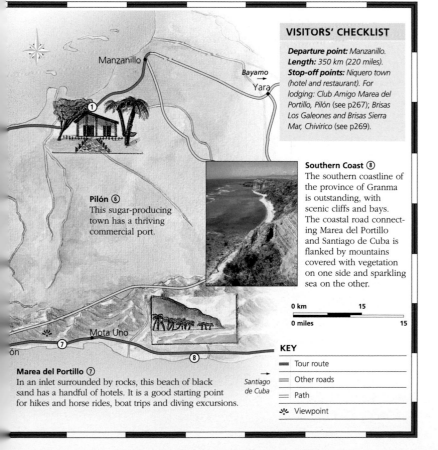

Manzanillo

Bayamo →
Yara

Santiago de Cuba →

ón

Mota Uno

VISITORS' CHECKLIST

Departure point: *Manzanillo.*
Length: *350 km (220 miles).*
Stop-off points: *Niquero town (hotel and restaurant). For lodging: Club Amigo Marea del Portillo, Pilón (see p267); Brisas Los Galeones and Brisas Sierra Mar, Chivirico (see p269).*

Southern Coast ⑧
The southern coastline of the province of Granma is outstanding, with scenic cliffs and bays. The coastal road connecting Marea del Portillo and Santiago de Cuba is flanked by mountains covered with vegetation on one side and sparkling sea on the other.

Pilón ⑥
This sugar-producing town has a thriving commercial port.

```
0 km                    15
0 miles                 15
```

KEY

━━ Tour route
══ Other roads
── Path
☆ Viewpoint

Marea del Portillo ⑦
In an inlet surrounded by rocks, this beach of black sand has a handful of hotels. It is a good starting point for hikes and horse rides, boat trips and diving excursions.

Gran Parque Nacional Sierra Maestra ⑫

Granma, Santiago de Cuba.
Road Map F4.
ℹ️ *Islazul, General García 207, Bayamo, (23) 423 273; Villa Santo Domingo, (23) 565 568.*

This national park, which covers an area of 38,000 ha (95,000 acres), spans the provinces of Granma and Santiago de Cuba. This is where the major peaks of the island are found, including Pico Turquino (at 1,974 m/ 6,390 ft, the highest in Cuba), as well as sites made famous by the guerrilla war waged by Fidel Castro and the *barbudos*.

The main starting point for exploring the Sierra Maestra is **Villa Santo Domingo**, about 35 km (22 miles) south of the Bayamo–Manzanillo road (there is simple accommodation in Santo Domingo).

From Santo Domingo, you can make the challenging 5-km (3-mile) journey – on foot or in a good off-road vehicle – to the **Alto del Naranjo** viewpoint (950 m/ 3,120 ft). With a permit (obtainable from the visitors' office north of Villa Santo

View from the Pico Turquino, the highest mountain in Cuba

Domingo), you can go on to **Comandancia de la Plata**, Castro's headquarters in the 1950s. Here there is a museum, a small camp hospital and the site from which Che Guevara made his radio broadcasts.

Comandancia de la Plata is accessible only on foot – an hour's walk through lovely, though often foggy, forest. The area was made into a national park in 1980, and is not only important historically.

The *gavilán del monte*, common in the Sierra Maestra

The dense, humid forest conceals many species of orchid and various kinds of local fauna. The mountains of the Sierra Maestra are excellent hiking territory, and also attract mountain climbers. The scenery is spectacular but be prepared for spartan facilities. A limited number of treks can be organized from the visitors' office, where guides must be hired. Overnight accommodation in the mountains is available either at campsites or in simple refuges. Note, however, that since much of this area is a military zone, lone trekking is not permitted.

At present, it is possible to do a three-day guided trek across the park, beginning at Alto del Naranjo and ending at Las Cuevas, a small town on the Caribbean Sea. Hikers do not need to be expert mountaineers in order to take part in this walking tour, because the path is equipped with ladders, handrails and rock-cut steps. However, it is still advisable to do a certain amount of training beforehand. The final descent from Pico Turquino onwards is fairly strenuous and walkers need to be reasonably fit.

It is important to take proper mountain gear with you: walking boots, thick socks, a hat to protect you from the sun, as well as a sweater, a windproof jacket, perhaps even a waterproof groundsheet and a good tent. The humidity in the Sierra, which is often enveloped in mist, is very high, and showers are common.

The coast at the southern edge of the Sierra Maestra, known as the **Riviera del Caribe**, is spectacular. The coastal road runs close above the waters of the Caribbean Sea and offers excellent views of coastal stacks and coves.

View of the splendid coastline south of Sierra Maestra

For hotels and restaurants in this region see pp266–9 and p283

Basílica del Cobre ⑬

Santiago de Cuba. **Road Map** F4.
🚌 *Carretera Central 21, (22) 346
118.* 🕐 *6:30am–6pm daily.* ✝ *8am,
10:15am Mon–Sat, 8am, 10am, 4pm
Sun.* 🎆 *procession (8 Sep).*

The village of El Cobre, about 20 km (12 miles) west of Santiago de Cuba, was once famous for its copper *(cobre)* mines. A great number of slaves worked here up until 1807. Nowadays the village is best known for Cuba's most famous church, the Basílica de Nuestra Señora de la Caridad del Cobre. Here the main attraction is a statue of the Virgen del Cobre. This black Madonna is richly dressed in yellow, and wears a crown encrusted with diamonds, emeralds and rubies, with a golden halo above. She carries a cross of diamonds and amethysts. The statue is kept in an air-conditioned glass case behind the high altar.

It is taken out every year on 8 September when a procession takes place to commemorate the Virgin's saint's day. The Virgen del Cobre was proclaimed the protectress of Cuba in 1916 and was blessed and crowned by Pope John Paul II in 1998 *(see p64).*

The Basílica del Cobre, surrounded by tropical vegetation

This fine three-aisled church, built in 1926, stands on a hill, the Cerro de la Cantera, which is linked to the village by a flight of 254 steps. The elegant central bell tower and two

The austere interior of the Sanctuary of the Virgen del Cobre

side towers crowned by brick-red domes are a striking sight above the light-painted façade.

The basilica is the object of pilgrimages from all over the island. In the Los Milagros chapel, thousands of *ex votos* left by pilgrims are on display. Some are rather curious, such as the beards left by some of the rebels who survived the guerrilla war in the Sierra; an object belonging to Castro's mother; and earth collected by Cuban soldiers who fought in Angola. There is a guest-book for visitors to peruse through and sign.

THE VIRGEN DEL COBRE

The statue of the Virgen del Cobre

According to legend, in 1606 three slaves who worked in the copper mines of El Cobre were saved in the Bay of Nipe, off the north coast of Cuba, by the statue of a black Virgin Mary holding the Holy Child in her arms. They had been caught in a storm while out in a boat and would have drowned had not the Virgin, whose image was floating among the waves, come to their aid. In reality, it seems that the statue arrived in Cuba by ship from Illescas, a town in Castile, upon the request of the governor Sánchez de Moya, who wanted a Spanish Madonna for the village of El Cobre. Whatever the truth, in 1611 the Virgen de la Caridad was given a small sanctuary and immediately became an object of veneration for the locals, who continued to attribute miraculous powers to her. The devotion for this Madonna has always been very strong, even among non-practising Catholics. Her

figure is associated with the Afro-Cuban cult of Oshún *(see p22)*, the goddess of rivers, gentleness, femininity and love, who is also always depicted as a beautiful black woman wearing yellow. Now that the *Santería* religion is widespread in Cuba, the sacred image of the Virgin of El Cobre and the more profane, sensuous image of the beautiful African goddess are often combined in prayers and discussion, and set beside each other on rustic home altars, often without any apparent awareness of contradiction.

A group of *ex votos* offered by the *barbudos*

Santiago de Cuba ⑭

Sign for the Rum Museum

This is perhaps the most African, the most musical and the most passionate city in Cuba. In 1930 the Spanish poet Federico García Lorca likened it to "a harp made of living branches, a caiman, a tobacco flower". Except for the cars and some modern buildings, Santiago has not altered much. This is a city where the heat – and the hills – mean that people move to a slow rhythm. It is a lively, exciting place where festivities and dancing are celebrated with fervour, never more so than during July's Carnival. Santiago's citizens also take pride in the fact that Santiago is called the "Cradle of the Revolution". Sandwiched between the Sierra Maestramountains and the sea, this is the second city in Cuba in population size. In 2012, Hurricane Sandy tore through Santiago causing much devastation.

A restored Neo-Classical building in the historic centre

Parque Céspedes

The city centre spreads out in chaotic fashion around Parque Céspedes in a maze of narrow streets. Any visit to the historic centre of Santiago must start in Parque Céspedes, the main square. From here, visitors are inevitably drawn along **Calle Heredia**, the most famous, popular and festive street in the town. Every house bears signs of the city's great passions: music, dancing, carnivals and poetry. At certain times, including the first half of July when the Fiesta del Caribe is held, this street becomes a stage for amateur artists. Traditional *son* music, on the other hand, can be heard in the courtyard of the

Calle Heredia, the liveliest street in Santiago de Cuba

Patio de Artex at No. 304, while No. 208, the former "Cafetín de Virgilio", became the Casa de la Trova in 1968, and local and foreign bands can be heard playing here day and night. Photographs of great Cuban musicians past and present such as El Guayabero and Compay Segundo cover the walls.

West of Parque Céspedes

The picturesque area west of Parque Céspedes, called Tivolí, and the deep bay can be seen from the **Balcón de Velázquez**, a wonderful viewpoint situated at the corner of Calle Mariano Corona and Bartolomé Masó. The viewpoint was named after the Spanish conquistador Diego Velázquez, who founded the city in 1515. A small fort was built here in the 16th century

SIGHTS AT A GLANCE

Ayuntamiento ②
Balcón de Velázquez ⑪
Café La Isabelica ⑨
Casa de Diego Velázquez ①
Casa de la Trova ⑤
Casa Natal
  de Antonio Maceo ⑭
Casa Natal de José María
  Heredia ⑥
Catedral de la Asunción ④
Cuartel Moncada ⑮

Hotel Casa Granda ③
Museo de la Lucha
  Clandestina ⑬
Museo del Carnaval ⑧
Museo del Ron ⑩
Museo Provincial
  Bacardí Moreau ⑦
Parque Histórico
  Abel Santamaría ⑯
Plaza de Marte ⑰
Steps of Padre Pico ⑫

VISITORS' CHECKLIST

Santiago de Cuba. **Road Map** F4.
🏃 490,000. ✈ 7 km
(4 miles) south of town.
🚉 Ave. Jesús Menéndez, esq.
Hechevarría. 🚌 Ave. de los
Libertadores, esq. Yarayó, (22)
628 484. 🛈 Infotur & Cubatur,
Calle Lacret 701, esq. Heredia,
(22) 669 401/666 033.
🎭 Festival del Caribe (early Jul),
Carnival (late Jul).

0 metres   200
0 yards   200

Key to Symbols see back flap

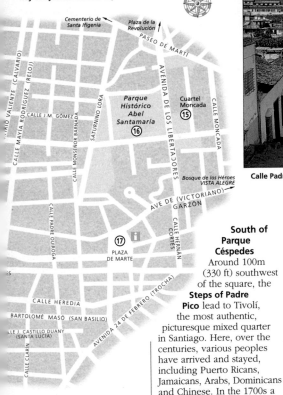

Calle Padre Pico seen from the top of the steps

South of Parque Céspedes

Around 100m (330 ft) southwest of the square, the **Steps of Padre Pico** lead to Tivolí, the most authentic, picturesque mixed quarter in Santiago. Here, over the centuries, various peoples have arrived and stayed, including Puerto Ricans, Jamaicans, Arabs, Dominicans and Chinese. In the 1700s a colony of French people from Haiti also settled here, setting up shops, music schools, theatres and hotels.

East of Parque Céspedes

To the east of the square, at the corner of Calle Bartolomé Masó and Calle Hartmann (San Félix), is the **Museo del Ron** (Rum Museum), housed in a late 19th-century building. Displays illustrate how rum is distilled and matured (see p75), alongside the history of the Bacardí factory, with an exhibition of labels from bottles of rum, new and old.

Another place to visit is Parque Dolores, a leafy square surrounded by buildings with wrought-iron balconies. A small old café on the square's corner, **La Isabelica**, serves excellent coffee.

Customers at La Isabelica, an atmospheric historic café

to house artillery to be used in the event of an attack. Today, only fragments of the original walls remain. Inside the viewpoint area itself are some attractive bronze tondos (circular relief carvings) with portraits of Diego Velázquez, Hernán Cortés, Bartolomé de Las Casas and the Indian chief Guamá. Cultural events are sometimes held at the Balcón de Velázquez.

Street-by-Street: Parque Céspedes

The former Plaza de Armas in Santiago is the heart of the city, both geographically and spiritually. Renamed Parque Céspedes in honour of the nation's founding father (see p44), this square is a place for socializing, relaxing, chatting and celebrating. At all hours of the day and night, the benches are filled with people, young, old, women, children and visitors. No one is alone here for long. Everyone sooner or later gets involved in a conversation or entertainment of some kind, because this square's other role is as an open-air venue where music – live, recorded, or improvised – takes the leading role. Restored in Neo-Classical style in 1943, the square consists of four areas, each with greenery, divided by lanes.

Casa de la Trova
Live music is performed here daily.

★ **Museo Provincial Bacardí Moreau**
The oldest museum in Cuba, housed in an elegant Neo-Classical building, is also the most eclectic. Items on display range from an Egyptian mummy to mementoes of the wars of independence and works by living artists (p228).

The house where the poet José Heredia was born is a fine 18th-century building around a leafy courtyard (p227).

CALLE GENERAL LAC
CALLE HARTMANN
CALLE HEREDIA
CALLE AGUILERA

KEY

— — — Suggested route

STAR SIGHTS

★ Casa de Diego Velázquez

★ Museo Provincial Bacardí Moreau

★ Catedral de la Asunción

Hotel Casa Granda
One of Cuba's historic hotels (see p269), the Casa Granda opened in 1920. Graham Greene (see p87) described it in Our Man in Havana *as a hotel frequented by spies. Its terrace overlooks the park.*

★ Catedral de la Asunción
The Cathedral façade is Neo-Classical, but the original church is four centuries old. It is believed that Diego Velázquez is buried somewhere beneath the building, but there is no proof of this (p227).

Balcón de Velázquez
This spacious viewing terrace, built over the site of a Spanish fortress, offers a magnificent view of the picturesque quarter of Tivolí, as well as the port and the bay of Santiago.

CALLE BARTOLOMÉ MASÓ

CALLE FÉLIX PEÑA

CALLE HEREDIA

Seafront

CALLE MARIANO CORONA

★ Casa de Diego Velázquez
Built in 1516–30, the residence of the Spanish conquistador Diego Velázquez is considered by some to be the oldest building in Cuba. Restoration was carried out in 1965, and it is now the home of the Museo de Ambiente Histórico Cubano (p226).

PARQUE CÉSPEDES

0 metres   50
0 yards   50

The Casa de la Cultura Miguel Matamoros, an eclectic building (1919) housing the sumptuous Salón de los Espejos, is a venue for artistic and cultural events.

Ayuntamiento
The Ayuntamiento (town hall), a symbol of the city, was built in 1950 according to 18th-century designs found in the Indies Archive. It was from this building's central balcony that Fidel Castro made his first speech to the Cuban people, on 1 January 1959.

Exploring Parque Céspedes

Ceramic plate, Casa de Velázquez

One of the liveliest squares in Cuba, Parque Céspedes is not only a place for socializing, but also has sites of cultural and architectural importance. Allow half a day to visit three of the most important monuments around the park: the house of Diego Velázquez, the impressive cathedral and the residence of the great 19th-century poet José María Heredia.

The courtyard in the 19th-century wing of Diego Velázquez's house

A room with Colonial furniture in Diego Velázquez's house

The building now houses the Museo de Ambiente Histórico Cubano, covering the history of furniture in Cuba. It contains superb examples from all colonial periods. Among the mostly austere Creole furniture, dating from the 16th and 17th centuries, are a splendid priest's high-backed chair and a finely wrought coffer – two excellent examples of Moorish-style objects.

The basement has 18th-century "Luis Las Casas" furniture, a style peculiar to Cuba which combines English influences and French Rococo motifs. These pieces of furniture are massive, lavish and intricately worked, often finished at the base with feet shaped like claws. The 19th-century section includes a dining room with stained-glass windows and French furniture, including rocking chairs, a console table and a Charles X mirror.

Another important item is a tapestry with the coat-of-arms of the Velázquez family, the only piece in the museum that is directly related to this Spanish *conquistador*.

🏛 Casa de Diego Velázquez (Museo de Ambiente Histórico Cubano)

Calle Félix Peña 612, e/ Heredia y Aguilera. **Tel** (22) 652 652.
🕐 1–5pm Fri, 9am–5pm Sat–Thu.
📷 🚫 📷 (with charge).

This building, constructed in 1516–30 as a residence for the governor Diego Velázquez, is the oldest home in Cuba, according to architect Francisco Prat Puig, who restored the house in 1965. (Other scholars have disputed this assertion, however, and not everyone has praised the restoration.) Whatever the truth, this splendid residence is still a fascinating place to visit.

In the 1600s it was the so-called House of Transactions (the ground floor still has an old furnace in which gold ingots were made). In the 19th century it was joined to the building next door. The upstairs gallery facing the courtyard is closed off by a Moorish wooden blind, to screen residents from the eyes of strangers. Also upstairs, some of the original *alfarje* ceilings survive.

THE 16TH-CENTURY MUDEJAR-STYLE HOUSE

Considered the oldest private building in Cuba and declared a national monument because of its historic value, the 16th-century section of Velázquez's house is a fine example of the Cuban version of the *mudéjar* (Moorish) style – although much of what is there is the result of restoration.

The courtyard, *in* mudéjar *style, is narrow and long and runs around a central well.*

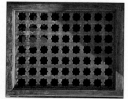

Wooden screens *protect the gallery and balconies from the sun and public gaze.*

Frescoes, *known as* cenefas, *decorate the lower part of the walls, but they are not original.*

Cedar ceilings *with geometric patterns, called* alfarjes, *were common in the 16th century.*

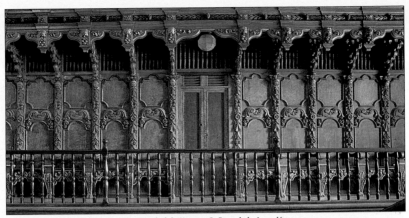

The lovely wooden inlaid choir in the Catedral de Nuestra Señora de la Asunción

⛪ Catedral de Nuestra Señora de la Asunción

Calle Heredia, e/ Lacret y Félix Peña. **Tel** *(22) 628 502.* ☐ *8:30am–12:30pm, 5–7:30pm Tue–Sat, 8–10am, 5–6:30pm Sun.* ✝ *6:30pm Tue–Fri, 5pm Sat, 9am & 6:30pm Sun.*

The cathedral of Santiago has a basilica layout, with a central nave and four aisles, an apse and a narthex or vestibule at the back. The church has been rebuilt several times over the centuries. The original was built in 1522, but in the early 17th century a series of

Interior of the cathedral's dome

pirate raids caused so much damage that the church was rebuilt in 1666–70. In the 18th and 19th centuries it was further damaged by earthquakes.

Today the cathedral, which has been declared a national monument, displays a mixture of styles, the result of a series of changes made in 1922 by the architect Segrera, who added the bell towers, had the interior painted, and also reworked the façade. A marble angel was set over the main entrance and statues of Christopher Columbus and Bartolomé de las Casas were placed in side niches.

The cathedral also has a museum, the **Museo Eclesiástico**, which displays frescoes by the Dominican friar Luis Desangles, liturgical objects, statues and an important collection of ecclesiastical music scores.

🏛 Casa Natal de José María Heredia

Calle Heredia 260, e/ Hartmann (San Félix) y Pío Rosado (Carnicería). **Tel** *(22) 625 350.* ☐ *9am–7pm Tue–Sat, 9am–1pm Sun.* ● *1 Jan, 1 May, 26 Jul, 10 Oct, 25 Dec.* 🖼 📷 📷 *(with charge).*

This is the modest but elegant 18th-century house where the nationalist poet José María Heredia (1803–39) was born. Heredia, highly regarded for his odes to nature *(see p28)*, should not be confused with his cousin, a French Parnassian poet, who was also born in Cuba but spent practically all his life in Europe.

The well-preserved house contains period furniture and objects, wooden ceilings and tiled floors, and is well worth a visit. From the large entrance hall, with a coffered ceiling and paintings of the poet's ancestors on the walls, a large arch leads into the central peristyled courtyard. Here there are wooden columns, a stone well and abundant vegetation.

Other rooms in the house include Heredia's bedroom with its impressive mahogany bed and elegant antique lamps.

Cultural events and poetry readings are often held in the museum's large porticoes. In addition, every year literary seminars and workshops are held here as part of the Fiesta del Caribe, or Fiesta del Fuego. This summer cultural event takes over the entire city of Santiago *(see p35).*

Entrance hall of Heredia's house, its arch leading to the courtyard

Around Calle Heredia

This street is one of the liveliest in Cuba. It buzzes with music and street stalls, and the sound of guitars, maracas, percussion and voices can be heard at all hours of the day, not just in the Casa de la Trova or the Patio de Artex, but also in the Museo del Carnaval, where concerts are held in the courtyard. The nearby Museo Bacardí is devoted to Cuban history.

Decorated *tumbadoras (see p31)* in the Museo del Carnaval

***Techos de Santiago de Cuba* by Felipe González, Museo Bacardí**

☷ Museo Provincial Bacardí Moreau

Calle Pío Rosado (Carniceria), esq. Aguilera. *Tel* (22) 628 402.
⬤ 1–4:30pm Mon, 9am–4:30pm Tue–Sat, 9am–12:30pm Sun.
🖐 📷 📷 *(with charge).*

This is the oldest museum in Cuba. It was founded in 1828 and is a rich source of relics dating from the Spanish conquest to the wars of independence. The objects were collected and organized in the late 1800s and early 1900s by Emilio Bacardí, founder of the famous rum distillery. Bacardí was also a famous patriot and the first mayor of Santiago when Cuba became a republic. His aim was to display the origin and development of the Cuban nationalist movement from a cultural point of view, and he asked the architect Segrera to design a building for the objects and works of art he had collected.

The statue of Liberty in the foyer

The museum is housed in an eclectic building with a broad staircase and an atrium dominated by two large statues of Minerva and Liberty. On the ground floor is a large collection of arms used by nationalist generals and heroes such as Antonio Maceo, Máximo Gómez and José Martí. There is also an important collection of works by 19th-century Cuban painters, including Felipe López González, Juan Emilio Hernández Giro, José Joaquín Tejada Revilla and Buenaventura Martínez. Twentieth-century artists represented here are Wifredo Lam and René Portocarrero *(see pp26–7)*. The archaeology section includes the only Egyptian mummy in Cuba.

☷ Museo del Carnaval

Calle Heredia 303, esq. Pío Rosado (Carniceria). *Tel* (22) 626 955.
⬤ 9am–5pm Tue–Sun. 🖐 📷
📷 *(with charge).*

This lovely late 18th-century building was converted into an elementary school in the mid-1900s, then into an office building, and eventually became the offices of the Carnival Commission. The Museo del Carnaval was opened here on 7 June 1983. The six rooms contain photographs with some explanatory captions in Spanish, chronologies, banners, musical instruments, costumes and papier mâché masks – a survey of the Carnival festivities held in Santiago. Carnival here differs from the traditional Spanish model and combines many African and Franco-Haitian elements.

The courtyard is used for folk events and concerts, as well as for rehearsals by bands preparing to perform during Carnival.

☷ Museo de la Lucha Clandestina

Calle Rabí 1, e/ San Carlos y Santa Rita. *Tel* (22) 624 689.
⬤ 9am–5pm Tue–Sun. 🖐 📷
📷 *(with charge).*

The Museum of the Clandestine Struggle overlooks a pleasant square in the district of Tivolí, southwest of Parque Céspedes. The building was the headquarters of Batista's police from 1951 to 1956. On 30 November 1956 it was burnt down by revolutionaries, led by Frank País *(see p50)*.

The four rooms in the restored building commemorate the activities of the Movimiento 26 de Julio, the movement headed in Santiago by Frank País up to 30 July 1957, when the young rebel leader was assassinated by Batista's police.

Part of an elaborate float in the Museo del Carnaval

Carnival in Santiago de Cuba

The roots of the Carnival in Santiago are religious: since the end of the 17th century there have been processions and festivities from 24 June to 26 July in honour of the city's patron saint, Santiago Apóstolo. At the end of the parade, slaves who were members of the *cabildos* – societies that kept alive African languages, traditions and beliefs – were allowed to go out into the streets, where they sang to the accompaniment of drums, rattles and other instruments. These were the forerunners of the *comparsas*, the soul of Carnival: groups of people wearing masks or costumes, dancing to the rhythm of the *conga* and carrying streamers, banners and *farolas* (brightly coloured paper street lamps). In the second half of July the whole town celebrates, every district taking part in the parades, each with at least one *comparsa*.

Playing the trompeta china

The young people *in each quarter meet every evening except Monday in the focos culturales, places where they prepare for Carnival by rehearsing the dances and music they will perform in July.*

The type of **tumbadora** *used in the conga*

Parades *go through the streets of Santiago. Some of the comparsas, such as the Carabalí Izuama (see p289), date from the 19th century.*

The musicians in each group are dressed alike. They are followed by a crowd swaying to the rhythm of the music.

THE CONGA
The chief dance for Carnival is the *conga* (also a genuine musical genre). People form a procession and dance through the streets, following a band playing various instruments, including different kinds of drums, and led by the *trompeta china*, introduced to Cuba in the late 1800s.

The Tropicana de Santiago *joins the procession with the other* comparsas, *and also presents open-air performances in lavish costumes.*

The *bombo*, a drum with a deep sound

Papier mâché masks *or* gigantes *are an essential part of a Carnival float. Huge and brightly coloured, they often represent animals or caricatures of human faces.*

Beyond Santiago's Historic Centre

Calle Saco (also known as Enramada), Santiago's main commercial street, links the heart of the old city with the port. After passing through a working-class quarter, with early 20th-century wooden houses, the street ends at Paseo Marítimo. Laid out in the colonial era as a seafront promenade for the city's high society, this broad street retains echoes of its former beauty and still has its original 1840 paving, stretching out along the port, where cruisers and yachts are moored. An alternative route to explore is to go in the opposite direction, east of the centre, where there are important historic sites, including the Moncada barracks.

🏛 Casa Natal de Antonio Maceo

Calle Los Maceo 207, e/ Corona y Rastro. *Tel (22) 623 750.*
⬜ *9am–5pm Mon–Sat.* 🎫 🅿
📷 *(with charge).*
The house where this great general was born on 14 June 1845 (he died near Havana on 7 December 1896; *see p44*) is a modest place. Visitors can see some of the hero's personal belongings and family photographs, including one of his brother José, who was also a general, and one of his mother, Mariana Grajales.

🏛 Cementerio de Santa Ifigenia

Avenida Crombet. *Tel (22) 632 723.*
⬜ *7am–6pm daily.* 🎫 🅿
📷 *(with charge).*
This monumental cemetery (1868) is the second most important in Cuba after the Colón cemetery in Havana *(see pp104–5)*. It was originally laid out with a Latin cross plan and divided into courtyards, the most important of which were

The mausoleum of Martí in the Santa Ifigenia Cemetery

reserved for those of higher social status. A visit to the Santa Ifigenia cemetery evokes two centuries of Cuban history, past the tombs of such illustrious 19th-century figures as José Martí, Carlos Manuel de Céspedes, Emilio Bacardí and the mother of Antonio Maceo, as well as the 20th-century revolutionaries of the Movimiento 26 de Julio such as Frank País, who was killed in 1957 *(see p50)*.

The funerary monuments themselves are fascinating. The Neo-Classical tombs nearest the entrance are the oldest, followed by the eclectic and then Modernist tombs. The Rationalist tombs built from the mid-20th century on include Martí's large octagonal mausoleum.

🏛 Museo Histórico 26 de Julio – Cuartel Moncada

Calle General Portuondo (Trinidad), e/ Moncada y Ave de los Libertadores.
Tel (22) 661 157. ⬜ *9am–12:30pm Mon & Sun, 9am–4:30pm Tue–Sat, .*
🎫 🅿 📷 *(with charge).*
On 26 July 1953, at the height of the Carnival festivities, Fidel Castro led about 100 rebels in an attack on the Moncada barracks *(see p48)*. Capturing Moncada, the second largest garrison in Cuba, built in the 19th century, would have meant securing a large stock of weapons and thus triggering a general revolt. Abel Santamaría was to attack the Saturnino Lora hospital, a strategic site on a promontory overlooking the barracks, and Raúl Castro was to capture the law courts building. This bold attempt failed, but it did succeed in increasing public awareness of the activity of the young revolutionaries. Eight of them died during the attack, while 55 were taken prisoner; some were tortured and executed.

Since January 1959 the barracks, which still bears bullet holes, has housed the Ciudad Escolar 26 de Julio school. Part of the building houses the Museo Histórico 26 de Julio, which in fact

The impressive façade of the former Moncada army barracks, now a school and museum

The monument to General Antonio Maceo in Plaza de la Revolución

illustrates the history of Cuba from the time of Columbus, but devotes most space to the guerrilla war of the 1950s. There is a model reproducing the attack on Moncada. There are also possessions which belonged to Fidel Castro, his brother Raúl and Che Guevara when they were waging war in the Sierra Maestra.

🏛 **Museo Abel Santamaría Cuadrado – Parque Histórico Abel Santamaría**
Calle General Portuondo (Trinidad), e/ Trinidad y Carretera Central. *Tel (22) 624 119.* ⬜ *9am–5pm Mon–Sat.* 📷 🎫 📷 *(with charge).*
The Moncada barracks, former Saturnino Lora hospital and law court buildings, form part of the Parque Histórico Abel Santamaría. In the 1953 raid, the former hospital was the target of a group of rebels led by Abel Santamaría, who was captured and killed by the police after the failed attempt.

The remaining hospital buildings now house a museum with documents and photographs relating to the trial of Fidel Castro and the other rebels, which was held a few days after the attack on the barracks in one of the rooms.

Besides the photographs illustrating the difficult social and economic conditions in Cuba during the 1950s, there is the manuscript of Castro's landmark self-defence in court, later entitled *History Will Absolve Me (see p149).*

Plaza de Marte
East of Plaza Dolores is the third largest square in Santiago, laid out in the 19th century. It is of great historic importance: here capital punishment was meted out both in the colonial period and under General Machado. At its centre is a 20-m (65-ft) column (1902) celebrating Cuban independence.

🏫 **Bosque de los Héroes**
East of the centre, behind the unmistakable Hotel Santiago, lies a small, unobtrusive hill. A white marble monument was erected here in 1973 to honour Che Guevara and the comrades-in-arms who died with him in Bolivia. Their names are engraved here.

The column in Plaza de Marte

Plaza de la Revolución
In the northeastern part of Santiago, beyond the Moncada barracks, is Plaza de la Revolución, a large, rather soulless square at a crossroads of three major avenues. The square is dominated by a vast monument executed in the early 1990s by the Santiago sculptor, Alberto Lezcay, representing General Maceo *(see p44)* on horseback, surrounded by 23 stylized machetes.

Plaza de la Revolución marks the start of the modern, residential area of the city, where the architecture shows a marked Soviet influence.

Vista Alegre
The Vista Alegre quarter has fine eclectic-style buildings constructed in the 1920s and 1930s. The quarter also has two important institutions: the **Centro Africano Fernando Ortíz**, with African masks, statues and musical instruments on display, and the **Casa del Caribe**, which houses a historical archive, library, alfresco music venue and centre for conferences, workshops and events *(see p290)*. During the Fiesta del Caribe, the Casa del Caribe presents examples of Yoruba, Congo and voodoo rites.

Bosque de los Héroes, honouring Che Guevara and comrades

Castillo del Morro ⑮

At the entrance to the Bay of Santiago, 10 km (6 miles) southwest of the city centre, stands an imposing castle, declared a World Heritage Site by UNESCO in 1997. The Castillo del Morro combines medieval elements with a modern sense of space, adhering nonetheless to classical Renaissance principles of geometric forms and symmetry. The fortress was designed in 1637 by engineer Giovanni Bautista Antonelli for the governor Pedro de la Roca, who wanted to defend the city against pirate raids. Construction of the citadel, large enough to house 400 soldiers, took from 1638 to 1700. The castle was converted into a prison in 1775, becoming a fortress once again in 1898 during the wars of independence, when the US fleet attacked the city. Today it houses a naval and piracy museum.

A cannon, part of the old battery used to defend the bay

In the casemates a display of prints illustrates the history of Santiago's forts.

Artillery area

★ **View of the Bay**
The parapets and lookouts on the upper parts of the fortress were used by the sentries to keep watch. Visitors today can appreciate the setting and enjoy a marvellous view over the bay.

Underground passageways link the various parts of the castle. This one leads to the artillery area.

The stone stairway on the side of the castle facing the sea is part of an open-air network of steps leading to the upper levels.

STAR SIGHTS

★ View of the Bay

★ Central Square

Plataforma de la F (*morrillo*, or bluff)

Triangular Lunette
*Built in 1590–1610 as the main
protection for the fortress
gate, this structure
originally stood separately
from the castle. It was
later incorporated into
the main structure.*

VISITORS' CHECKLIST

Santiago de Cuba.
Carretera del Morro, km 7.5.
Road Map F4.
Tel (22) 691 569.
☐ 8am–7pm daily.

Drawbridge
*This bridge passes over
a dry moat that runs
alongside the fortification
on the inland side. It is
well preserved, and still
has the original winch
which was used to raise
and lower the bridge.*

Dry moat

★ **Central Square**
*This square, the nerve
centre of the castle, was
used as an area for
organizing daily activities.
The square provides access
to the chapel, barracks,
garrison and
underground rooms.*

THE BAY OF SANTIAGO

About 8 km (5 miles) southwest of the centre of Santiago, at
the end of the Carretera Turística, is Marina Punta Gorda.
From here ferries cross over to a small island in the middle of
the bay. This is Cayo Granma,
home to a picturesque fishing
village made up of multicoloured huts and small houses.
Many of those on the island's
margins are built on piles or
pontoons extending over the
water. This island is a peaceful
place off the beaten track,
with only one restaurant and
abundant greenery – a good
place to relax in and round off
a visit to Santiago de Cuba.

**View of Cayo Granma from
the Carretera Turística**

**Three separate main
structures**, built on five
different levels, form the
skeleton of the castle.
This unusual construction
is a result of the uneven
terrain of the headland.

Parque Baconao ⑯

Lying between the Caribbean Sea and the eastern fringes of the Sierra Maestra, and straddling the provinces of Santiago and Guantánamo, Parque Baconao has been declared a biosphere reserve by UNESCO. The largest and most original amusement park in Cuba (80,000 ha/197,600 acres) combines mountains and beaches with old coffee plantations and an unusual range of attractions. The park was developed in the 1980s thanks to the voluntary work of students and labourers, and has been updated periodically. Today, visitors can appreciate a wide range of cultural and outdoor activities and attractions, and there is plenty of hotel accommodation.

Gran Piedra
This is an enormous monolith, from the top of which, at an altitude of 1,234m (4,048 ft), you can even see Jamaica and Haiti on clear days (see p236).

The Cafetal La Isabelica, the oldest coffee plantation in the province, has been converted into a museum *(see p236)*.

Jardín Botánico (Botanic Garden)

Siberia

La Isabé

Perseverancia

Tres Arroyos

Prado de las Esculturas
This sculpture garden, with 20 works by Cuban and foreign artists, was laid out in the late 1980s. The display extends for 1 km (0.6 mile) and can also be viewed by car.

Abel Santamaría

El Palenque

Las Guásimas

Damaiayabo

El Oasis

Juragu

Siboney

Granjita Siboney
This farm, once a key operational base for the Cuban rebels, is now a museum of revolutionary artifacts *(see p236)*.

At the Oasis, a centre managed by artists, visitors can go horse riding and watch rodeo shows.

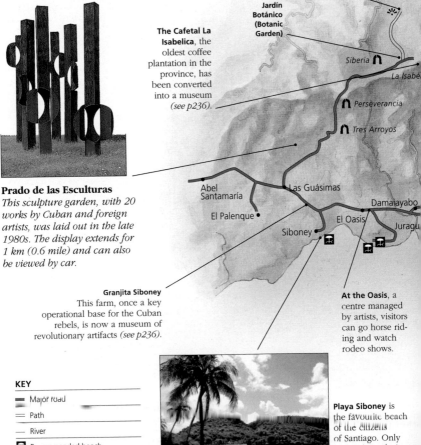

KEY

▬	Major road
═	Path
─	River
🏖	Recommended beach
⚶	Viewpoint
⋔	Ruins of old *cafetales*

Playa Siboney is the favourite beach of the citizens of Santiago. Only 19 km (12 miles) from town, it can be reached by regular bus service or taxi.

For hotels and restaurants in this region see pp266–9 and p283

Laguna Baconao
At this lagoon boats can be hired for trips around the lagoon or up the Baconao river. There is a crocodile farm near the Casa de Rolando restaurant at the lakeside.

VISITORS' CHECKLIST

Santiago de Cuba.
Road Map F4.
Tours in the park
Cubatur, Ave. Garzón e/ 3ra y 4ta, Santiago de Cuba, (22) 652 560 or (22) 687 010.

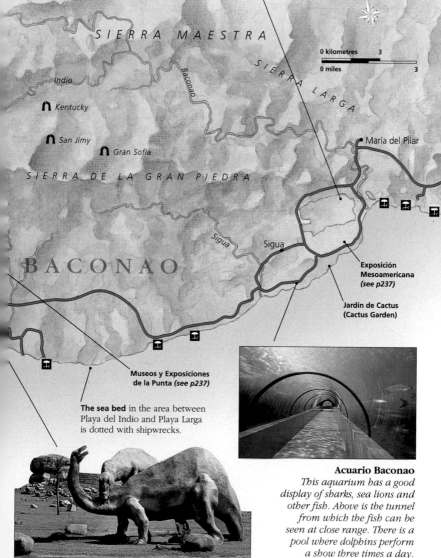

SIERRA MAESTRA

SIERRA LARGA

0 kilometres 3
0 miles 3

Indio

Kentucky

Baconao

San Jimy

Gran Sofia

María del Pilar

SIERRA DE LA GRAN PIEDRA

BACONAO

Sigua

Sigua

Exposición Mesoamericana
(see p237)

Jardín de Cactus
(Cactus Garden)

Museos y Exposiciones de la Punta *(see p237)*

The sea bed in the area between Playa del Indio and Playa Larga is dotted with shipwrecks.

Acuario Baconao
This aquarium has a good display of sharks, sea lions and other fish. Above is the tunnel from which the fish can be seen at close range. There is a pool where dolphins perform a show three times a day.

Valle de la Prehistoria
This children's park features huge sculptures of dinosaurs and there is also a Natural History Museum.

Exploring the Parque Baconao

The 1960 Maya Cuba car, a museum piece

It is possible to explore the park by car or taxi in a day, although accommodation is available. Heading east from Santiago, along Avenida Raúl Pujol, you will pass the zoo (Parque Zoológico), and, nearby, the Arbol de la Paz (Tree of Peace), a ceiba tree beneath which the Spanish signed the surrender agreement in 1898. The entrance to Parque Baconao is not far beyond the confines of the city. Most of the attractions are suitable for families and can be reached by car, but the peak of the Gran Piedra and the easternmost beaches are only accessible on foot.

A strelitzia in flower at the Gran Piedra Jardín Botánico

The spectacular view from the Gran Piedra

species of orchid and multi-coloured strelitzias (flowers more commonly known as bird of paradise), a flight of 459 steps leads up to the top of the Gran Piedra (1,234 m/4,048 ft asl). This gigantic, 25-m (82-ft) monolith rests on the crater of an extinct volcano.

It is best to make the climb in the morning, because the afternoon can bring foggy weather and you may not see far into the distance. However, on clear days the view is simply superb: it stretches from the mountains to the coast, and even as far as Haiti.

🚩 Granjita Siboney

Carretera Siboney km 13.5.
Tel (22) 399 168. ⏺ *9am–1pm Mon, 9:15am–4:45pm Tue–Sun.*
🖼️ 🎫 📷 *(with charge).*

By the roadside 16 km (10 miles) east of Santiago, this is the farm rented by Abel Santamaría in 1953 as a base of operations in the run-up to the assault on the Moncada barracks. It was from here, on 26 July, that the young rebels drove into Santiago to launch the attack. Their attempt failed and Granjita Siboney itself was later attacked by Batista's men. The (reconstructed) bullet holes can be seen around the door.

Granjita Siboney is now a museum with the uniforms and some of the weapons that the revolutionaries wore and carried that day. Next door is the Generación del Centenario gallery, with paintings honouring the rebels who died during the attack on the barracks, as well as photographs, documents and the car Castro used in the attack.

🌿 Gran Piedra

Jardín Botánico ⏺ *8am–4pm daily.*
🖼️ 📷

Heading west from Granjita Siboney, you come to a turn-off to Gran Piedra: this 12-km (7-mile) road with hairpin bends provides one of the best panoramas in Cuba and views of the intense green of the tropical and mountain forests. Beyond the Jardín Botánico, with its many

🏛 Cafetal La Isabelica

Carretera de la Gran Piedra km 14. ⏺ *8am–4pm daily.* 🖼️ 📷 🎫

There are numerous old coffee plantations around the Gran Piedra, all of which have been added to the World Heritage Site list by UNESCO. Almost all of the plantations are in ruins, but one exception is the Cafetal La Isabelica,

Granjita Siboney farm, showing the signs of the July 1953 attack

which can be reached easily via a path from the foot of the Gran Piedra. This plantation belonged to Victor Constantin, a French landowner who, together with many others, fled from Haiti in the late 1700s following a slave uprising there. He brought with him numerous slaves and his mistress, Isabel María, after whom he named his plantation.

The largest structure is the manor house, which has been reconstructed following a fire that burned it down. The ground floor was partly for the labourers and partly used to store tools and implements. The first floor consists of a bedroom, living room, dining room and studio, all with 18th-century furniture and furnishings.

Reproductions of pre-Columbian objects, Exposición Mesoamericana

Interior of the Cafetal La Isabelica owner's manor house

The house overlooks a terrace where coffee beans were left to dry – actually the roof of a large storehouse. Nearby are the kitchens, behind which is the water tank; the whole area is surrounded by coffee plants. Visitors to the *cafetal* museum are offered a demonstration of how coffee is grown and processed for consumption. There is a small café on the premises.

🏛 Conjunto de Museos y Exposiciones de la Punta
Carretera de Baconao.
🕓 *daily.* 📷 📷
A cross between a museum and a trade fair, this collection of buildings contains displays of all kinds of things from stamps and dolls to ceramics and archaeological finds.

Of particular interest is the Salón de Historia del Transporte Terrestre por Carretera, which houses a fascinating collection of 2,000-plus miniature cars and an array of old vintage cars, including a local Maya Cuba – a tiny, one-cylinder car. The oldest is a 1912 Model T Ford. There are also vehicles of historical significance, including cars that once belonged to Fidel Castro and Benny Moré.

🏛 Exposición Mesoamericana
Carretera de Baconao.
🕓 *daily.* 📷
This series of sea caves along the road are showcases for reproductions of Central American pre-Columbian works of art.

THE ORIGINS OF COFFEE GROWING IN CUBA

Coffee was introduced to Cuba at the end of the 18th century, by which time it had been a fashionable drink among the European aristocracy and bourgeoisie for some time. The French coffee growers who had fled to Eastern Cuba from Haiti in 1791 were well aware of this: they were the ones who brought the "new" plant to the island. The hills around Santiago and the valleys between Baracoa and Guantánamo were ideal for coffee growing, because they offered both water and shade. Coffee was an immediate success, and demand increased so much that it was planted along the coast too. In 1803 there were 100,000 coffee trees; by 1807

Coffee growing beneath the trees in the mountains

this figure had increased to four million, cultivated on 191 plantations. The French growers became very wealthy, building palatial manor houses on their plantations. As the cultivation of coffee required plenty of manual labour, and there weren't enough workers from Haiti, there was a "boom" in the slave trade in the early 19th century. Cuban archives mention 7,654 "dead souls" at the beginning of the century, and 42,000 in 1820. While this immigration contributed to the economic fortune of the island, it proved to be the end of the landowners. It was not long before the slaves, increasingly numerous and organized, began to rebel against their condition (see p42).

Guantánamo

Guantánamo. **Road Map** F4.
👥 243,600. ✈ 🚌 🚂 ℹ *Infotur,
Calle Galixto García el Crombet y
Emilio Giró, (21) 351 993.*

If it were not for the US
naval base and the famous
song *Guantanamera* (girl
from Guantánamo), this town
would probably only be
known to Cubans and music
experts. Its name, in fact, is
linked with the *changuí*, a
variation of *son* music that
developed in the coffee
plantations in the mountains,
music made famous by the
musician Helio Revé.

The Parroquial de Santa Catalina de Riccis in the Parque Martí

Guantanamera was com-
posed by Joseíto Fernández
in the 1940s almost for fun,
drawing inspiration from a
proud local girl who had not
reacted to a compliment he
paid her. Later, some "literary"
verses from the *Versos
Sencillos* by José Martí were
adapted to the music.

The town of Guantánamo
was founded in 1796 to take
in the French fleeing from
Haiti and developed during
the 19th century. The capital
of a varied province where
desert areas studded with
cactus alternate with green
mountains, Guantánamo has
few sights of note. A tour of
the small historic centre is
little more than a walk around
Parque Martí, dominated by
the **Parroquial de Santa
Catalina de Riccis** (1863).

Opposite the church is a
statue of General Pedro A
Pérez, sculpted in 1928. Nearby, on Calle Pedro A Pérez,
stands one of the town's most
impressive buildings, the

Palacio de Salcines. Designed
by architect José Leticio
Salcines in 1919, this building's eclectic architectural
style features a decorative
façade of cornices and columns. A Neo-Classical cupola
crowns the building, on top
of which stands a statue of La
Fama – the messenger of
Zeus, in Greek mythology –
by Italian architect Américo J
Chini. The Palacio is also
home to the **Museo de Artes
Decorativas**, in which antique
furniture and decorative
objects dating from the late
19th and early 20th centuries
can be seen.

An interesting colonial building facing Parque Martí is the
old Spanish prison, which is
now the home of the modest
Museo Provincial.

The Plaza de la Revolución
is one of the largest and
probably most austere in the
country. The kitsch 1960s
Hotel Guantánamo dominates
the vast, concrete Plaza
Mariana Garajales, which itself
is dominated by a towering
brutalist sculpture, *Monument
to the Heroes*, that honours
Cuba's independence fighters,
including Frank País.

🏛 **Museo de Artes
Decorativas**
Calle Pedro A Pérez 804, e/ Prado y
Aguilera ⬤ *closed for restoration.*

🏛 **Museo Provincial
de Guantánamo**
Plaza Marti, esq. Prado.
Tel (21) 325 872. ⬤ *8am–4:30pm
Mon–Fri, 8am–noon Sat.*
⬤ *1 Jan, 1 May, 26 Jul, 10 Oct,
25 Dec.* 📷 📹 📷 *(with charge).*

Environs

Around 20 km (12 miles) east
of Guantánamo, on the road to
Lomas de Yateras, a coffee-
growing area, is an unusual
open-air museum, the **Museo
Zoológico de Piedra**. It was
founded by Angel Iñigo, a
farmer and self-taught sculptor.
Since 1978 he has produced
sculptures of about 40
animals in stone, including
lions, boa constrictors, tapirs,
buffaloes, rhinoceroses and
gorillas. All are on display.

At the mouth of Guan-
tánamo bay, some 20 km
(12 miles) south of the city are
two Cuban ports, **Caimanera**
and **Boquerón**, both close to
the US naval base. The former
is within a Cuban military zone
and is off-limits to everyone
except those who live there
and those with a special pass.

It used to be possible to
"spy" on the US naval base
from a viewing point, or
mirador, on a hill off the
Baracoa road, but this is now
closed to the public. However,
the base can be seen from
another viewing point, at the
Hotel Caimanera in Caimanera
town. Staying overnight at
Hotel Caimanera *(see p267)*
is allowed with Ministry of the
Interior permission, or you can
arrange a visit as part of a day
trip via Havanatur in Santiago
(Calle 8 No. 56 e/Ave 1 & 3,
Vista Alegre, tel. (22) 641
125/), or in Baracoa (Calle
Martí 202, tel. (21) 645 358).

🏛 **Museo Zoológico de Piedra**
Boquerón de Yateras. ⬤ *8am–5pm
Mon–Sat.* ⬤ *1 Jan, 1 May, 26 Jul,
10 Oct, 25 Dec.* 📷 📷

**Joseíto Fernández, composer of
the song** *Guantanamera*

For hotels and restaurants in this region see pp266–9 and p283

Costa Sur ⓲

Guantánamo. **Road Map** F4.

Travelling eastwards from Guantánamo, visitors will pass through the most barren part of Cuba, where the climate is desert-like because of the hot winds blowing here. This is a unique area on the island where cacti and succulents are the main vegetation. The coast road, tucked in between the mountains and the blue sea, is spectacular. The rocky coast has tiny coves with pebble beaches, home to an assortment of seashells and *Polymita picta* snails *(see p245).*

La Farola ⓳

Guantánamo. **Road Map** F4.

Cajobabo – a southern coastal town where José Martí and Máximo Gómez landed to begin the 1895 war against Spain – marks the beginning of La Farola, a spectacular 49-km (30-mile) road that wends its way upwards over the mountains to Baracoa, through vegetation that becomes more and more luxuriant as the coast is left behind.

Until 1959 Cajobabo could only be reached by ship. In order to connect it to the rest of the island, in the 1960s engineers excavated sections of mountainside in the Sierra

del Purial in order to create a kind of "flying highway". The road acquired its name *(farola* means beacon) because in some stretches it looks like a beam, suspended in air. It is regarded as one of the great engineering feats of recent Cuban history.

This highway and the periodic viewing points offer incredible views of the peaks of the Sierra Maestra, lush valleys, tropical forests, pine groves, banana plantations, rivers, waterfalls and royal palm trees. The luxuriant vegetation seems to swallow up the road in places. Along the road, people sell local produce such as coffee, red bananas and chocolate.

THE AMERICAN NAVAL BASE

In 1903 the US – the victors, together with the Cubans, in the war against Spain – obliged the Cuban Republic to accept the Platt Amendment *(see p45),* whereby the latter had to grant the US Navy the right to install a naval base in the bay of Guantánamo. The US was granted a lease of a minimum of 99 years in 1934. For this occupancy, the American government pays $2,000 per year, though it is said that the Cuban government has regularly returned this sum to the US since 1959. In the past the situation has taken on the dramatic overtones of the Cold War and highlighted a difficult state of co-existence. Inside the base, menial jobs are done by Puerto Ricans, the wives of the servicemen do their shopping in supermarkets stocked with food flown in from the US, and there are two English-language radio stations and one TV station. The base, US territory in Cuba, covers 110 sq km (43 sq miles), and has two runways for military planes. The whole area is surrounded by 27 km (17 miles) of fence.

The American base at Guantánamo

View from one of the observation points along La Farola road

Baracoa ⑳

Cocoa beans, a local crop

The oldest city in Cuba lies at the far eastern tip of the island. Its name in the Arauaca language, spoken by the former inhabitants of the area, means "the presence of the sea". Nuestra Señora de la Asunción de Baracoa villa was founded on 15 August 1511, on a curved bay that had been discovered some 20 years earlier by Columbus, and immediately became the political and ecclesiastical capital of Cuba. However, this status was short-lived. In 1515, the city founder Diego Velázquez transferred his residence to Santiago, marking the beginning of a long period of social and economic isolation for Baracoa.

The Cruz de la Parra, perhaps brought to Cuba by Columbus

A street in Baracoa, dominated by lush vegetation

Exploring Baracoa

"Baracoa means nature", the Cubans say, and it is certainly true: enclosed by tropical forest and the sea, for four centuries this town has managed to live by fishing, cultivating cocoa, coconuts and bananas, and by gathering wood. While the isolation has created inconveniences, it has also allowed the locals to maintain their traditions and preserve the ecosystem.

The historic centre of Baracoa is not Colonial, but a mixture of styles, with some Neo-Classical and French influences. Thick vegetation towers over the buildings and has even invaded some houses, many of which are built of wood.

The best view of the town is seen from the terrace of an 18th-century fortress on a hill above the town: the **Castillo de Seboruco**, now El Castillo hotel *(see p267)*. From here you can see the roofs and the bay of Baracoa, dominated to the west by the mountain of El Yunque *(see p244)*.

Parque Independencia

In the main square, overlooked by the cathedral, is a famous bust of the Indian leader Hatuey *(see p219)*. Nearby are the **Casa de la Trova**, the **Fondo de Bienes Culturales**, which exhibits works by local painters, sculptors and craftsmen, and the **Casa de la Cultura**, an eclectic building with colonial elements that hosts evening performances and events.

At No. 123 Calle Maceo is the **Casa del Chocolate**, which serves excellent hot chocolate. Baracoa cocoa is famous throughout Cuba.

🔒 Catedral de Nuestra Señora de la Asunción

Calle Maceo 152. *Tel (21) 643 352.* 🕐 7–11am, 4–7pm Mon–Sat, 7–11am Sun. ✝ 7:30am Tue–Wed, 5:30pm Thu–Fri, 8pm Sat, 9am Sun.

This modest cathedral, built in 1512 and restored in 1833 and 2010–12, is most famous as the home of the Cruz de la Parra, a wooden cross that is said to be the oldest symbol of Christianity in the New World. According to legend, the cross was brought to Cuba by Columbus on his first voyage to America, and on 1 December 1492 it was placed on the spot where Baracoa was later founded. It is said that the cross disappeared one day and was then miraculously found under the climbing vine *(parra)* in a settler's garden, hence its name. The four tips of the cross are now covered with metal sheets, because in the past worshippers used to pull off splinters and keep them as relics. Scientific analysis of the wood proves the cross is some 500 years old, but the discovery that it is made from indigenous Cuban wood disproves the legendary connection to Columbus.

A typical single-storey wooden house in Baracoa

◁ **The bay of Baracoa viewed from the Castillo de Seboruco**

🏛 Fuerte Matachín (Museo Municipal)

Calle Martí y Malecón. **Tel** *(21) 642 122.* ⏰ *8am–noon, 2–6pm Mon–Sat, 8am–noon Sun.* 🎦 📷 *(with charge).*

This small museum, which provides an interesting overview of local history, is housed in a military fortress built during the colonial period to defend the city from pirates. (Piracy was particularly active in the 18th and 19th centuries.) Along the fort walls, a battery of cannons faces seawards.

Statue of Columbus, Museo Municipal garden

The displays start with archaeological finds of the pre-Columbian era, and are followed by documents, maps, paintings and prints related to Spanish domination, pirates, slaves and the plantations.

There is an interesting natural history section with specimens on display, including the *Polymita* snails *(see p245).* The museum is also a historical and geographical research centre and fosters initiatives to preserve and develop local culture; city tours are available.

El Malecón

This is the seafront that connects the two 19th-century forts in Baracoa: Fuerte Matachín to the east, and **Fuerte de la Punta** to the west, which is now a restaurant. The Malecón is ideal for a quiet stroll during the week. On Saturdays a bustling food market is held here in the morning, and in the evening the road is prepared for the *noche baracoesa* – "Baracoan night" – a lively folk festival during which people gather to eat, drink and dance along the seafront.

Hotel La Rusa

Halfway along the Malecón is Hotel La Rusa, a historic hotel, refurbished in 2009, that once belonged to the Russian princess Magdalena Rowenskaya, who fled her country with her husband in 1917 after the October Revolution. She eventually settled in Baracoa, where she ended up opening a restaurant and giving singing lessons. Much later, she became active in the

VISITORS' CHECKLIST

Guantánamo. **Road Map** F4. 🏘 *81,950.* ✈ *4 km (2 miles) W of town, (21) 645 376.* 🚌 *Ave. Los Mártires, esq. Martí, (21) 643 880.* ℹ *Cubatur, Calle Maceo 149 esq. Pelayo Cuervo, (21) 645 306; Ecotur, Calle Maceo 120, (21) 643 627; Infotur, Calle Maceo 129-A, (21) 641 781.* 📅 *Sun.*

26 July Movement and entertained Castro, Che and other revolutionaries. The hotel foyer and bar contain photographs and relics belonging to this eccentric figure, who was later immortalized by the novelist Alejo Carpentier *(see p29)* in his work *The Consecration of Spring.*

The renovated exterior of the Hotel La Rusa

THE CENTRE OF BARACOA

The mountain of El Yunque, dominating the bay of Baracoa

El Yunque ㉑

Guantánamo. **Road Map** F4.
🛈 Ecotur, Calle Maceo 120, Baracoa,
(21) 643 627.

A limestone formation, 575 m
(1,885 ft) high, covered with
thick vegetation, El Yunque
was a sacred site for the
Taíno Indians for many
centuries. Later it became a
natural landmark for naviga-
tors about to land at the port
of Baracoa. The Spanish
called it "El Yunque" (the
anvil) because of its
unmistakable outline. The
outcrop's shape has led to
local misapprehension that
this was the rock that
Columbus described as "a
square mountain that looks
like an island" in 1492. In fact,
he was referring to a similarly
shaped rock at Bariay near
Gibara (see p214).

The slopes of
the mountain,
which has been
declared a bio-
sphere reserve
by UNESCO, are
home to botanical
rarities, including two
carnivorous plants and
Podocarpus, one of the oldest
plant species in the world, as
well as an endemic palm tree,
Coccothrinax yunquensis.

El Yunque is also the
habitat for some endangered
species of bird such as the
carpintero real (Campeophilus

principalis) and the *cagua-
rero* hawk *(Chondrohierax
wilsonii)*, as well as for the
smallest amphibian in the
world, the *Sminthillus limba-
tus*, less than 1 cm (0.4 inch)
long, and another very
ancient species, the *almiquí
(Solenodon cubanus)*, a rare
mammal similar to a rat.

Río Toa ㉒

Road Map F4.

The valley fed by the Río
Toa, Cuba's biggest river, has
been made into a nature
reserve, the **Parque Natural
Río Toa**. Still lacking in roads
and facilities, this park is part
of a wide-ranging project to
create refuges and camping
sites that will not interfere
with the local ecosystems.

Local farmers still use an
old-fashioned craft to
travel upstream –
the *cayuca*, a flat
canoe of Indian
origin. From the
river, visitors
can admire the
majestic Pico
Galán (974 m/3,200 ft) and
the great waterfalls that
cascade into the river from
steep cliffs. Enquire at Ecotur
if you are interested in
exploring the area.

Going up the Río Toa
in a rowing boat

Environs
Northwest of Baracoa, 21 km
(12 miles) past the mouth of

Playa Maguaná, one of the unspoilt beaches near Baracoa

For hotels and restaurants in this region see pp266–9 and p283

Río Miel, flowing through virtually virgin tropical forest between Baracoa and Boca de Yumurí

the Río Toa, is **Playa Maguaná**, the most beautiful beach in the province, with dazzling white sand. The beach's Indian name refers to the presence of a nearby archaeological site. A 2-km (1-mile) coral reef lies only 500 m (1,640 ft) from the shore. Be warned though that the sea can often be rather choppy in this area.

There is an attractive rustic hotel hidden among the coconut palms, where villas can be rented, but this place is still delightfully unspoilt.

Parque Nacional Alejandro de Humboldt ㉓

Road Map F4.

This mountainous rainforest 56 km (35 miles) north of Baracoa is Cuba's most richly biodiverse park and a UNESCO World Heritage Site. Named after the 19th-century German naturalist and explorer Alexander von Humboldt, it is

home to a variety of birds, snails, scorpions, frogs, birds, and the rare Cuban solenodon (*Solenodon cubanus*), which looks like a giant shrew with an extraordinarily long snout. At the edge of the park is the stunning Bahía Taco bay, home to a small group of manatees. The Ecotur office in Baracoa (*see p295*) can help with arranging walks and boat trips in the bay.

Boca de Yumurí ㉔

Road Map F4.

Around 30 km (18 miles) east of Baracoa, this village of *bohíos* (traditional dwellings with palm-leaf roofs) takes its name from the Yumurí river, which flows into the sea here. Its inhabitants live by fishing, but earn a little extra by taking tourists on river boat rides.

A short boat ride across the Yumurí river will take you to an enchanting beach. Another interesting trip is to go upstream, where the river course reaches an impressive canyon with walls as much as 180 m (590 ft) high.

The Río Yumurí flows through an area interesting for its ecology. Colourful tropical birdlife abounds, including the *zunzún*, the *tocororo* and the *cartacuba* (*see pp20–21*).

POLYMITA SNAILS

A genus endemic to the Baracoa area, the *Polymita* is a snail with a brilliantly coloured shell. According to the colour, six species of *Polymita* can be identified: *P. picta, P. muscarum, P. sulphurosa, P. versicolor, P. venusta* and *P. brocheri*. All these species live on trees and plants, and feed on mushrooms and lichens, contributing to the health of the plants, especially coffee trees. *Polymita* snails can be easily recognized, because the shell with coloured stripes looks as though it has been painted, and stands out clearly against the bright green vegetation.

Patterned Polymita shells

Legend has it that the snail acquired its colours from a young Indian who had no pearls or jewels to give to his beloved. He painted a snail shell with the yellow of the sun, the green of the woods, the red of the flowers, and the white from the foam of the waves. But when he decided to take the blue from the sky, it was too late in the day, and he had to be content with the black of night. Today this snail, highly prized for its shell, is an endangered species. Selling or gathering *Polymita* is not permitted.

TRAVELLERS'
NEEDS

WHERE TO STAY

Carro de la Revolución,
ceramic piece by Sosabravo *(see p27)* Habana Libre hotel, Havana

Since 1980, when Cuba decided to open its frontiers to foreign visitors, the growth in tourism has obliged the government to invest heavily in the hotel industry. Many old historic hotels have been restored and equipped with international standards of comfort, and new infrastructure has been created, often through joint ventures involving the Cuban Ministry of Tourism and foreign companies. Today, visitors can choose from a variety of accommodation, with choices ranging from modern luxury hotels with swimming pools and good sports facilities to colonial, city centre hotels and all-inclusive holiday villages on small uninhabited islands. The cheapest hotels are still decidedly spartan and rarely meet international standards. Cubans are allowed to let out rooms in their own homes or even entire apartments; this arrangement has proved to be popular with tourists.

Airy hotel interior in Havana

HOTEL CHAINS

Most visitors to Cuba come on package holidays and a number of hotel chains cater for this type of tourism. All hotels are state-owned, although many are managed by joint venture agencies.

One upmarket chain is the Cuban **Gran Caribe**, whose hotels include the historic Hotel Nacional in Havana *(see p98)*, an architectural gem built in 1930, the Hotel Plaza and the Hotel Inglaterra *(see pp81–2)* in Havana's Parque Central, and the elegant Casa Granda in Santiago. Gran Caribe also manages several more modern hotels, such as the Hotel Riviera in Havana and the Hotel Jagua in Cienfuegos, and well-equipped residences in seaside resorts such as the Hotel Internacional in Varadero.

High standards are also guaranteed by the Cuban chain **Cubanacán** and the Spanish

Meliã and **Iberostar** chains; all of these companies have hotels throughout Cuba. Cubanacán manages good hotels of its own and others affiliated to international chains, including several good-value three-star hotels, such as the Versalles in Santiago de Cuba *(see p269)*, and the Club Amigo Atlántico in Guardalavaca *(see p256)*. The Meliã chain manages the elegant Meliã Cohiba in Havana *(see p255)*, and the modern Hotel Santiago in Santiago de Cuba.

Gaviota, the tourism arm of the military *(see p251)*, offers comfortable accommodation in the main coastal resorts, on the *cayos* and in mountain areas. Gaviota runs the only holiday village at Cayo Saetía.

The hotels forming the **Islazul** chain are of a lower standard, but are still on an international level, offering basic levels of comfort at lower prices.

Another quite different style is offered by **Habaguanex**, a Cuban company founded under the auspices of the Oficina del Historiador de la Ciudad in Havana, which restores old buildings in the La Habana Vieja quarter, converting them into shops, cafés and hotels. Habaguanex hotels include historic buildings such as the Hostal Conde de Villanueva, a converted 17th-century mansion; the San Miguel; the Hotel Ambos Mundos *(see p253)*, a Hemingway favourite; and the Hotel Santa Isabel *(see p253)*, in a splendid restored colonial building facing the Plaza de Armas *(see p67)*.

A fountain in the elegant foyer of the Hotel Meliã Cohiba, Varadero

◁ **Interior of the historic El Floridita bar in Havana**

GRADING

Cuban hotels are classified according to the international star system, from one star rising to five stars. However, visitors are likely to find that standards within a particular star rating can vary considerably. Some mid-range hotels may have been good quality in the 1950s, but have since become rundown and not brought into line with modern needs. One-star hotels are generally to be avoided; a better choice would be a private house.

The Meliá Cohiba in Havana, a five-star luxury hotel *(see p255)*

PRICES

Hotel rates in the capital and in the more famous seaside resorts such as Cayo Largo, Varadero, Cayo Coco and Playa Guardalavaca, are higher than in the rest of the country and correspond more or less to international levels.

The terrace at Hotel Casa Granda in the heart of Santiago de Cuba *(see p269)*

Whatever the star rating of a hotel, prices will be higher in peak season, which runs from Christmas to 1 April, and from the beginning of July to the end of August.

BOOKING

It is best to book accommodation well ahead of your visit through a travel agency in your home country or online to ensure that you will get a room and date to your liking. Your tour operator may also be able to offer special package deals. In high season, in particular when there are special events such as Carnival in Santiago, or one of the many local and cultural festivals in Havana, it may be difficult to find a room.

Visitors taking part in trade events such as the Feria Internacional de Turismo (Tourism Fair), held in May, or the February Book Fair, will find there are special pricing agreements with hotels in Havana.

TIPPING

It is customary to leave a tip *(propina)* for the hotel staff at the end of your stay. The amount of the *propina* is at your discretion and will vary according to the type of hotel, how long you stay and the type and quality of service. It is, however, useful to remember that a tip in convertible pesos or euros may amount to the equivalent of a month's salary in Cuban *pesos (see p306).*

A percentage of the tips is often donated to charities. The national fund for cancer research is one of the main causes to benefit in this way.

HOLIDAY VILLAGES

These are ideal for people who want a relaxing, sunny holiday by the beach or surrounded by unspoiled landscape, with comfortable rooms and all meals and facilities provided.

All-inclusive packages offer a complete deal, with lodging in bungalows or apartments with bathroom, phone, air conditioning and TV. The price typically includes breakfast, lunch and dinner (usually buffet), and all drinks. Sports activities of all kinds (sailing, snorkelling, scuba diving, swimming, surfing) are provided, some at extra cost. Other options include a snack bar and pool bar; games rooms, playgrounds and baby-sitting services; freshwater pools for children and adults; car rental service; shops and beach equipment. In some parts of Cuba, these all-inclusive holiday villages are the only option available.

The pool and tennis courts at the Hotel Sol Palmeras in Varadero

The Hotel Moka, in the Sierra del Rosario reserve, a favourite with "eco-tourists"

CAMPING

Besides some modest camping sites reserved for Cubans, there are other sites *(campismos)* run by **Cubamar Viajes**, located in or near nature reserves and along the coast. Despite being categorized as camping sites, accommodation is in fact in bungalows *(cabañas)*. The sites usually have a restaurant and a pool.

The quality of the *cabañas* varies, but they are usually simple and clean. However, this type of accommodation does not suit everyone, and not all sites are open to foreigners. These camping sites often operate more like a holiday village, with daytime and evening recreational activities.

Casual tent-pitching or sleeping out on beaches is not permitted in Cuba.

SPECIALIST HOLIDAYS

Many tour operators specializing in holidays in Cuba also offer specialist tours for those interested in a particular activity. Many all-inclusive resorts offer diving lessons for beginners, but qualified divers have a wider range of options. People planning more advanced diving need to provide proof of their qualifications and must take out fully comprehensive travel insurance. Many operators recommend that divers should be able to demonstrate a minimum of ten logged dives. Some dive sites such as María La Gorda *(see p146)* and Isla de la Juventud *(see p150)* require skill and experience. Keen divers can stay in hotels and tourist villages near dive sites.

The best place to learn salsa is, of course, in Cuba, and UK-based **Caledonia** arranges all-inclusive holidays with salsa tuition by expert teachers and visits to the best dance venues.

Conservation-conscious holidays in unspoiled landscape are available from a few hotels that operate as ecological tourism centres. These are found in the Pinar del Río area and in the Sierra del Rosario, near Marea del Portillo (in the Sierra Maestra) and Baracoa. Many centres also organize excursions, such as birdwatching and fishing trips.

There are also health centres, combining relaxation and medical or beauty treatments. The fairly modern, comfortable clinics and beauty centres are run by well-trained staff. Health provision for foreign visitors is provided in these centres by **Servimed**, the government organisation that runs state healthcare in Cuba *(see also p303)*, while accommodation is organized by **Turismo y Salud**.

There are many mud and mineral therapies on offer in Balneario Elguea and Villa Clara, and a range of other therapeutic treatments at Varadero and Cayo Coco.

A cabin in pinewoods in Las Terrazas village

DISABLED TRAVELLERS

Only the more recently built hotels have rooms purpose-built for disabled people, including bathrooms with wheelchair access. Unfortunately, the majority of Cuban hotels are not equipped with such facilities. Nonetheless, in general hotel staff will do everything they can to be of help to disabled clients.

Accommodation in the María La Gorda hotel, particularly popular with divers

PRIVATE ROOMS

Renting rooms in private homes *(casas particulares)* is an excellent arrangement for visitors who want to experience everyday Cuban life at first-hand and meet local people. To make the best of the opportunity, it will help to have a smattering of Spanish.

There is no longer a limit on the number of people per room. Besides single rooms, you can also rent small apartments. You can often find very comfortable living quarters in historic buildings, particularly in old cities like Trinidad.

Interior of a private home in Gibara, in Holguín province

The proverbial Cuban hospitality makes this type of accommodation particularly pleasant: after all, living in a private home is the simplest and best way to feel part of the place. Another advantage is that the home owners and their families can provide ideas about what to see, where to eat and how to spend the evening.

If you are interested in this type of arrangement, it is best to get addresses from someone you know who has already done this. On the whole, avoid taking advice from strangers, and do not allow someone you have met casually on the street to take you to a private home, as he/she may simply be an unreliable "hustler". These people usually receive a commission of your room rent from the owners, which is added to the room price.

The sticker used for *casas particulares* licensed for rental

If you are pleased with the accommodation in a private home, ask the owners for recommended addresses in other places that you intend to visit: this should provide some guarantee of similar standards. Houses legally authorized to let out rooms can be recognized by the sticker on the door. When you take up your room, the owners will request a passport, as they are obliged by law to register your personal data with Cuban Immigration.

The taxes paid for room rental in the *casas particulares* are used by local authorities to build homes for young couples. Proposed higher taxes may see many *casas* close across the country. It is advisable to call ahead to any *casa* you hope to stay at.

The amenities, cleanliness and charm of these homes will of course vary and there are no cut-and-dried standards. There are no official lists of home owners offering rooms, but more information can be obtained by visiting: www.cubacasas.net.

DIRECTORY

HOTEL CHAINS

Cubanacán
Calle 23 #156 e/n N y O,
Vedado,
Havana.
Tel (7) 833 4090 ext. 251.
www.hoteles
cubanacan.com

Gaviota
Edificio La Marina,
Ave. del Puerto 102,
Havana.
Tel (7) 867 0404.
www.gaviota-grupo.com

Gran Caribe
Calle 7 no. 4210,
e/42 y 44, Miramar,
Havana.
Tel (7) 204 0575.
www.gran-caribe.cu

Habaguanex
Tel (7) 867 1039.
www.habaguanex.
ohc.cu

Iberostar
Lonja del Comercio,
Plaza San Francisco,
La Habana Vieja.
Tel (7) 866 6069.
www.iberostar.com

Islazul
Tel (7) 832 0571.
www.islazul.cu

Meliã
Ave. 5 no. 2008,
Miramar,
Havana.
Tel (7) 204 3449.
www.meliacuba.com

CAMPING

Cubamar Viajes
Calle 3e/ 12y
Malécon,
Vedado, Havana.
Tel (7) 833 2523.
Fax (7) 833 3111.
www.cubamarviajes.cu

SPECIALIST TOURISM

Caledonia
Tel (0131) 621 7721 (UK).
www.caledonia
languages.com.uk

Servimed – Turismo y Salud
Ave. 43 no. 1418,
esq.18,
Miramar,
Havana.
Tel (7) 204 4811.
www.servimedcuba.com

Choosing a Hotel

The accommodation in this guide has been selected across a wide price range for its character, facilities and location. The prices at many establishments, particularly the national hotel chains and the big beach resort hotels, are subject to frequent change. Entries are listed by region, beginning with Havana. For details of restaurants, see pages 276–83.

PRICE CATEGORIES (IN CUBAN CONVERTIBLE PESOS – CUC$)

Standard double room per night, with breakfast and all taxes included.
$ Under 50 CUC$
$$ 50–100 CUC$
$$$ 100–150 CUC$
$$$$ 150–200 CUC$
$$$$$ Over 200 CUC$

HAVANA

LA HABANA VIEJA Casa de Amalia
 $

Prado 20, 7mo piso, e/ San Lázaro y Cárcel **Tel** (7) 861 7824 **Rooms** 2 **Map** 4 D1

There are fantastic views out over the ocean and across to the lighthouse and fortress complex on the eastern side of the bay from this seventh-floor flat. One of the guest rooms is very small, and the furnishings are quite basic, but the hosts are attentive.

LA HABANA VIEJA Casa de Humberto Acosta
$

Compostela 611, 2do piso, e/ Sol y Luz **Tel** (7) 860 3264 **Rooms** 3 **Map** 4 E3

The Casa de Humberto Acosta's large first-floor terrace, on which breakfast and *mojitos* are served, is the highlight here, but the common rooms of the whole house are a delight, with bags of colonial character. The guest rooms are rather basic but cool and clean, with private bathrooms.

LA HABANA VIEJA Casa de Sergio y Miriam
$

Luz no.109, apto 5, e/ Inquisidor y San Ignacio **Tel** (7) 860 8192 **Rooms** 2 **Map** 4 F3

This is deep in southern La Habana Vieja and provides an authentic taste of old town life away from the tour groups. Both rooms here have two single beds (one with en-suite bathroom), and both are a bit cramped but very clean. Breakfast is charged at 4 CUC$ per person.

LA HABANA VIEJA Chez Nous
$

Brasil (Teniente Rey) 115 esq. Cuba **Tel** (7) 862 6287 **Rooms** 2 **Map** 4 E3

An exceptional *casa particular* and one of the most distinctly furnished in the city. There's genuine original colonial-era furniture all over the high-ceilinged house and an extraordinary Romanesque-style bathroom. One of the rooms is on the roof, accessed via a spiral staircase and, in contrast to the rest of the house, is very modern. Lots of comfort.

LA HABANA VIEJA Hotel Park View
$$

Colón 101 esq. Morro **Tel** (7) 861 3293 **Fax** (7) 863 6036 **Rooms** 55 **Map** 4 D2

The most modern of La Habana Vieja's renovated hotels, with a character distinct from all the others. The lobby area with its small bar is smart and shiny but also down-to-earth with comfy cushioned armchairs. There are great views from the seventh-floor restaurant and rooms are homely, with small TVs. **www.habaguanex.ohc.cu/hotels**

LA HABANA VIEJA Hostal del Tejadillo
$$$

Tejadillo 12 esq. San Ignacio **Tel** (7) 863 7283 **Fax** (7) 863 8830 **Rooms** 32 **Map** 4 E2

An intimate, refined hotel but the least distinct of the colonial conversions in La Habana Vieja. The restaurant is very small, though it spills onto a tiny, walled-in patio. Rooms are of the same high standard as all the hotels, and some are gathered around a second patio brimming with potted plants. **www.habaguanex.ohc.cu/hotels**

LA HABANA VIEJA Hostal Los Frailes
$$$

Brasil (Teniente Rey) 8, e/ Oficios y Mercaderes **Tel** (7) 862 9383 **Fax** (7) 862 9718 **Rooms** 22 **Map** 4 F3

Something of a novelty hotel, the staff in this moody little place all dress as monks. This seems to have engendered an appropriately subdued vibe. The communal areas, such as the lobby lounge with its low wood-raftered ceiling and the intimate patio with a quietly flowing fountain, are deliberately dark and shady. **www.habaguanex.ohc.cu/hotels**

LA HABANA VIEJA Hostal Mesón de la Flota
$$$

Mercaderes 257 e/ Amargura y Brasil (Teniente Rey) **Tel** (7) 863 3838 **Fax** (7) 862 9281 **Rooms** 5 **Map** 4 E2

One of the least expensive hotels in La Habana Vieja, Hostal Mesón de la Flota has a distinct rustic tavern character and a vague Spanish theme. Don't expect any early nights here as the tapas restaurant has nightly flamenco performances with amplified music. **www.habaguanex.ohc.cu/hotels**

LA HABANA VIEJA Hostal Valencia
$$$

Oficios 53 esq. Obrapía **Tel** (7) 867 1037 **Fax** (7) 860 5628 **Rooms** 14 **Map** 4 E2

Rural chic and rustic charm characterize this down-to-earth hotel. There's a paella restaurant whose tables spill out from its intimate interior onto the central patio, rich in potted plants. All rooms are located up the wide staircase on the first floor and are very comfortable. **www.habaguanex.ohc.cu/hotels**

Key to Symbols *see back cover flap*

LA HABANA VIEJA Hotel Ambos Mundos $$$

Obispo esq. Mercaderes **Tel** *(7) 860 9530* **Fax** *(7) 860 9532* **Rooms** *52* **Map** *4 E2*

Hotel Ambos Mundos is famous for counting Ernest Hemingway among its guests. His room, still much as he left it, is now a tourist attraction. The spacious lobby and its refined bar is a classic La Habana Vieja hangout, as is the lovely rooftop-garden restaurant and bar. The original cage-elevator is a great touch. **www.habaguanex.ohc.cu/hotels**

LA HABANA VIEJA Hotel Armadores de Santander $$$

Luz esq. San Pedro **Tel** *(7) 862 8000* **Fax** *(7) 862 8080* **Rooms** *32* **Map** *4 F3*

This is the only La Habana Vieja hotel right on the harbour with views out across it from the first-floor restaurant. With little else of note in the immediate vicinity it feels a touch isolated, but this is a good thing for those looking to avoid the hustle and bustle surrounding most hotels in this neighbourhood. **www.habaguanex.ohc.cu/hotels**

LA HABANA VIEJA Hotel Florida $$$

Obispo esq. Cuba **Tel** *(7) 862 4127* **Fax** *(7) 862 4117* **Rooms** *41* **Map** *4 E2*

A magnificent colonial conversion with an enchanting central patio surrounded by Neo-Classical arches and pillars. The guest rooms are excellent – large and sumptuously furnished in a colonial style with wrought-iron beds. The hotel is located on La Habana Vieja's busiest street, but once inside you barely feel it. **www.habaguanex.ohc.cu/hotels**

LA HABANA VIEJA Hotel Palacio O'Farrill $$$

Cuba 102-108 esq. Chacón **Tel** *(7) 860 5080* **Fax** *(7) 860 5083* **Rooms** *38* **Map** *4 E2*

Another impressive colonial restoration, this stylish hotel is located on a street in a residential neighbourhood. Though just a couple of blocks from the cathedral and close to the most touristy sections of the city, it feels strangely removed from them. The highlight here is the jazz-club bar, with live music at weekends. **www.habaguanex.ohc.cu/hotels**

LA HABANA VIEJA Hotel Raquel $$$

Amargura esq. San Ignacio **Tel** *(7) 860 8280* **Fax** *(7) 860 8275* **Rooms** *25* **Map** *4 E2*

The superbly stylish lobby with its ornate ceiling, marble pillars and stained-glass skylight roof, is a great place to sit and read, drink and generally relax. Cordoned off in one corner is the city's only Jewish-themed restaurant. The rooms upstairs, gathered around a set of interior balcony corridors, are top-notch. **www.habaguanex.ohc.cu/hotels**

LA HABANA VIEJA Hotel San Miguel $$$

Cuba 52 esq. Peña Pobre **Tel** *(7) 862 7656* **Fax** *(7) 863 4088* **Rooms** *10* **Map** *4 E1*

Set on a wide avenue with traffic passing by (as opposed to the narrow, historic streets characteristic of most of the old town's hotels), there are great views from the rooftop bar of the fortifications across the bay. This is also one of the few hotels in this area with a solarium. Bedrooms are large and comfy. **www.habaguanex.ohc.cu/hotels**

LA HABANA VIEJA Hotel Palacio del Marqués de San Felipe $$$$$

Oficios no.152 esq. Amargura **Tel** *(7) 864 9191* **Rooms** *27* **Map** *4 F2*

Hotel Palacio del Marqués de San Felipe y Santiago de Bejucal is part of the Habanaguex chain. Fully restored and facing the Plaza San Francisco de Asís, the façade of this magnificent building is baroque, but in contrast the rooms are modern and super-stylish. Nothing is too much trouble for the friendly staff. **www.habanaguex.ohc.cu/hotels**

LA HABANA VIEJA Hotel Santa Isabel $$$$$

Baratillo 9 e/ Obispo y Narciso López **Tel** *(7) 860 8201* **Fax** *(7) 860 8391* **Rooms** *27* **Map** *4 F2*

At the foot of the Plaza de Armas, this refined colonial building is larger than most hotels in La Habana Vieja. It is a shrine to "high art", with Neo-Classical furniture and evocative paintings. The guest rooms really stand out, their furnishings beautifully and authentically in keeping with this historic building. **www.habaguanex.ohc.cu/hotels**

CENTRO HABANA AND PRADO Casa de Miriam y Sinaí $

Neptuno 521, e/ Campanario y Lealtad **Tel** *(7) 878 4456* **Rooms** *2* **Map** *3 C2*

A fabulous first-floor flat with a surprisingly large central patio full of rocking chairs. The two spacious rooms, one with streetside balcony, are spotlessly clean and have top-drawer en-suite bathrooms. The hosts are extremely friendly and Sinaí speaks English, German and Italian.

CENTRO HABANA AND PRADO Casa de Ricardo Morales $

Campanario 363, apto 3, e/ San Miguel y San Rafael **Tel** *(7) 866 8363* **Rooms** *1* **Map** *3 C3*

A great option for those who want complete independence, since the owner is often out working and allows guests the run of this entire first-floor flat. Tastefully furnished, neat and compact, the living room is particularly fetching, with a little dining table, a large comfy sofa and artwork from Mexico. There's also a balcony.

CENTRO HABANA AND PRADO Casa Yamelis Elizalde $

Calle Jesús María 58, apto 8, e/ Calle San Ignacio y Cuba **Tel** *(05) 331 9498* **Rooms** *1* **Map** *4 F3*

Federico and Yamelis Llanes are long-term casa owners and run a highly professional service. This renovated casa on the fourth floor of a 1959 property offers a light and airy room with its own balcony and a partial sea view. A safety deposit box is available. The property is near several churches, the main crafts market and the harbour.

CENTRO HABANA AND PRADO Hotel Caribbean $

Prado 164, e/ Colón y Refugio **Tel** *(7) 860 8233, 860 8210* **Fax** *(7) 860 9479* **Rooms** *35* **Map** *4 D2*

A small hotel on the promenade section of the Prado, but with more of a backstreet flavour. Rooms are half the price of what you'd pay up the road on the Parque Central. Ask for a room facing the street as the others are quite dingy. Internet access available. **www.islazul.cu**

CENTRO HABANA AND PRADO Hotel Lincoln

🗺 🍴 🗒 🛇 ⬜ 　　　　　Ⓢ

Virtudes 164 esq. Avenida de Italia (Galiano) **Tel** *(7) 862 8061* **Rooms** *134*　　　　　**Map** *3 C2*

One of the cheapest hotels in Centro Habana, on the edge of one of the most residential and least touristy of the borough's neighbourhoods. The building itself dates from 1926 but the decor inside is pure 1970s kitsch, with flowered curtains and garish three-piece suites in the lobby. Certainly not lacking in character. **www.islazul.cu**

CENTRO HABANA AND PRADO Hotel Deauville

🗺 🍴 🛏 🗒 🛇 ⬜ 　　　　ⓈⓈ

Avenida de Italia (Galiano) esq. Malecón **Tel** *(7) 866 8812* **Fax** *(7) 866 8148* **Rooms** *144*　　　**Map** *3 C2*

A plain, unexceptional high-rise hotel located on the Malecón, a fact which enhances its appeal considerably, as does the small second-floor swimming pool and the great views. There's a basement nightclub and a standard issue restaurant. Friendly staff are keen to help. **www.gran-caribe.cu**

CENTRO HABANA AND PRADO Hotel Inglaterra

🗺 🍴 🗒 🛇 ⬜ 　　　　ⓈⓈⓈ

Prado 416 esq. San Rafael, Parque Central **Tel** *(7) 860 8594 to 97* **Fax** *(7) 860 8254* **Rooms** *83*　　　**Map** *4 D2*

A focal point for this part of Havana, the pavement-porch café of this austere building, founded in 1875, is always alive with chatter. The interior is a model of elegant austerity, particularly in the large restaurant with its columned arches. Rooms vary in size but are all decorated with restrained refinement. **www.gran-caribe.com**

CENTRO HABANA AND PRADO Hotel Plaza

🗺 🍴 🗒 🖼 　　　　ⓈⓈⓈ

Ignacio Agramonte 267 **Tel** *(7) 860 8583* **Fax** *(7) 860 8592* **Rooms** *188*　　　**Map** *4 D2*

This grand old hotel near the Parque Central has touches of grandeur, although the communal areas lack character. The main restaurant is a kind of Neo-Classical cafeteria and the lobby is very elegant but feels like a waiting room. Hotel Plaza also has a cheap pizza restaurant with an a la carte menu. **www.gran-caribe.cu**

CENTRO HABANA AND PRADO Hotel Telégrafo

🗺 🍴 🗒 🖼 　　　　ⓈⓈⓈ

Prado 408 esq. Neptuno **Tel** *(7) 861 1010* **Fax** *(7) 861 4844* **Rooms** *63*　　　**Map** *4 D2*

Established in 1911, Hotel Telégrafo is part of the Parque Central hotel chain. It combines modern and colonial-style architecture to great effect, particularly in the ground-floor bar with its brick arches and in the top-floor glass ceiling. **www.habaguanex.ohc.cu/hotels**

CENTRO HABANA AND PRADO Hotel Sevilla

🗺 🍴 🛏 🖼 🗒 🛇 ⬜ 　　ⓈⓈⓈⓈ

Trocadero 55, e/ Prado y Zulueta **Tel** *(7) 860 8560* **Fax** *(7) 860 8875* **Rooms** *178*　　　**Map** *4 D2*

Uniquely for this part of the city, Sevilla has a garden terrace outside the hotel itself, the site of its swimming pool. The majestic building also possesses a spectacular top-floor restaurant serving up some of the fanciest cuisine in Havana. Fitness centre, sauna and solarium. Very comfortable rooms, with mock colonial furniture. **www.accorhotels.com**

CENTRO HABANA AND PRADO Hotel Parque Central

🗺 🍴 🛏 🖼 🗒 🛇 ⬜ 　ⓈⓈⓈⓈⓈ

Neptuno, e/ Prado y Zulueta, Parque Central **Tel** *(7) 860 6627* **Fax** *(7) 860 6630* **Rooms** *278*　　**Map** *4 D2*

The least historically authentic of the old hotels on the Parque Central, but by far the best equipped and most luxurious. There's a swimming pool on the roof, a business centre and a gym, and the lobby bar is encircled by a balustraded interior balcony, all bathed in a warm glow from the skylight. **www.iberostar.com**

CENTRO HABANA AND PRADO Hotel Saratoga

🗺 🍴 🛏 🖼 🗒 🛇 ⬜ 　ⓈⓈⓈⓈⓈ

Prado 603 esq. Dragones **Tel** *(7) 868 1000* **Fax** *(7) 868 1002* **Rooms** *96*　　　**Map** *4 D3*

Outlandishly posh, with resplendently stylish interiors, this is the classiest hotel in this part of the city. A rooftop pool, restaurant and bar, solarium and gym, and rooms with DVD players, Internet connection, satellite TV and minibar reflect the levels of comfort all over this amazing hotel. Breakfast is not included. **www.hotel-saratoga.com**

VEDADO Casa Lilly

📝 🗺 🗒 🖼 　　　　Ⓢ

Calle G (Av. de los Presidentes) no.301 (apto 13), e/ 13 y 15 **Tel** *(7) 832 4021* **Rooms** *3*　　　**Map** *2 D2*

Located in a 1950s tower block with a balcony on each floor, this is one of Havana's finest *casas particulares*. Three quiet rooms are comfortably furnished in colonial style. Breakfast is served by the friendly family around the enormous dining table or on the balcony with stunning sea and city views. **www.casalilly.com**

VEDADO Casa de Melida Jordán

📝 🗒 🛇 　　　　Ⓢ

Calle 25 no.1102, e/ 6 y 8 **Tel** *(7) 836 1136* **Rooms** *2*　　　**Map** *1 C4*

Surrounded by a wealth of plant life, this magnificent two-floor house has distinguished black railings on the exterior and a gorgeous interior. Both guest rooms are very comfortable, with good beds. One even has its own separate entrance for complete privacy.

VEDADO Casa de Mercedes González

📝 🗺 🗒 　　　　Ⓢ

Calle 21 no.360, apt. 2A, e/ G y H **Tel** *(7) 8325846* **Rooms** *2*　　　**Map** *2 E2*

On the second floor of a 1950s building, this spacious apartment has two very well-equipped, large rooms with fridge, TV and en-suite bathrooms. The house has a library of books for guests to use, and a lovely terrace balcony where you can sit and read.

VEDADO Casa Teresita

📝 　　　　Ⓢ

Paseo 28, e/ Linea y 11 **Tel** *(7) 830 2649* **Rooms** *3*　　　**Map** *1 C2*

This large, plush mansion in the heart of Vedado, and a few blocks from the sea, is run by two friendly sisters. Two of the large bedrooms share an adjacent bathroom with a stunning painted glass window. It is a great place to meet fellow travellers over the hearty communal breakfasts. Good transport links.

Key to Price Guide *see p252* **Key to Symbols** *see back cover flap*

VEDADO Hotel Habana Riviera $$

Avenida Paseo e/ Malecón y 1ra **Tel** *(7) 836 4051* **Fax** *(7) 833 3739, 834 4225* **Rooms** *352* **Map** *1 B2*

A classic from the pre-Revolution years, this upmarket seafront high-rise hotel was once controlled by the US Mafia. There's a wealthy 1950s-chic look about the place, in the rooms and particularly in the Art Deco lobby. The pool is one of the largest in urban Havana, and the Copa Room Cabaret is one of the city's most renowned. **www.gran-caribe.cu**

VEDADO Hotel Saint John's $$

Calle O e/ 23 y 25 **Tel** *(7) 833 3740, 834 4187* **Fax** *(7) 833 3561* **Rooms** *86* **Map** *2 F2*

There's always a buzz, day or night, outside Saint John's, on one of the busiest corners in the city and sharing the same space as a trendy jazz club. The restaurant has a slight canteen feel about it, though the food isn't bad. There's a simple cafeteria bar on the roof with great views along the seafront. **www.gran-caribe.cu**

VEDADO Hotel Vedado $$

Calle O 244 e/ 23 y 25 **Tel** *(7) 836 4072* **Rooms** *203* **Map** *1 C1*

Though a somewhat tired-looking tower block in the heart of Vedado and lacking in character, this is more affordable than almost all the other hotels in the district, with a cosy, private pool area. A nice touch is the series of photos of Havana landmarks and architecture spread around the hotel. There's also a fitness centre. **www.gran-caribe.cu**

VEDADO Hotel Victoria $$

Calle 19 esq. M **Tel** *(7) 8333510* **Fax** *(7) 833 3109* **Rooms** *31* **Map** *1 C1*

One of Vedado's smallest hotels, the charming, unpretentious Hotel Victoria is the area's best lower-end option. The communal areas are intimate and quite chic, with a handsome and cosy bar, wood-panelled restaurant room and a miniature pool. Rooms are on the small side. Not far from restaurants and nightspots. **www.gran-caribe.cu**

VEDADO Habana Libre Tryp $$$

Calle L e/ 23 y 25 **Tel** *(7) 838 4011, 834 6100* **Fax** *(7) 834 6365, 834 6177* **Rooms** *572* **Map** *2 F2*

Life in this part of the city revolves around this swish hotel, a Havana landmark, known as the Havana Hilton before the Revolution. Its rooms are some of the largest in the city, many with unbeatable views. The small pool is on a first-floor terrace, and there are several excellent restaurants, including the rooftop Sierra Maestra. **www.meliacuba.com**

VEDADO Hotel Presidente $$$

Calzada 110 esq. Avenida de los Presidentes **Tel** *(7) 838 1801 to 04* **Fax** *(7) 833 3753* **Rooms** *158* **Map** *1 C1*

This classy hotel stands in its own secluded corner of residential Vedado, with a dashing, gentlemanly look and feel. The marble-floored lobby is accented with elegant colonial furniture and antiques, and the pool is flanked by balustraded terraces. Comfortable rooms, many with ocean views. **www.gran-caribe.cu**

VEDADO Hotel Nacional de Cuba $$$$

Calle O esq. 21 **Tel** *(7) 836 3564* **Fax** *(7) 836 5054* **Rooms** *426* **Map** *2 F1*

No other hotel presents regal elegance and grace on such a grand scale as the palatial Nacional, built in the 1930s. Among the highlights are a swanky banquet-hall restaurant divided by arches, two more restaurants in the moody basement, sweeping lawns on low cliffs above the Malecón and a garden-terrace bar. **www.hotelnacionaldecuba.com**

VEDADO Meliã Cohiba $$$$$

Avenida Paseo e/ 1ra y 3ra **Tel** *(7) 833 3636* **Fax** *(7) 834 4555* **Rooms** *462* **Map** *1 B2*

Meliã Cohiba is a sleek ultra-modern high-rise, a block from the seafront. One of the best equipped hotels in the city, it has five restaurants, nine meeting rooms for business guests, squash courts, a Jacuzzi and sauna, and one of the ritziest clubs in the city – the Habana Café. A large, two-part pool caps it all off. **www.meliacuba.com**

GREATER HAVANA (KOHLY-PLAYA) Hotel El Bosque $$

Calle 28A e/ 49A y 49C **Tel** *(7) 204 9232 to 35* **Fax** *(7) 204 5637* **Rooms** *62*

Perched just above the Parque Almendares, Havana's only archetypal big-city park, this location is pleasantly green and suburban. You don't get the kind of luxury found at many of Miramar's hotels, but the more down-to-earth, intimate vibe will better suit some tastes. Shares facilities with its neighbour, the Hotel Kohly. **www.gaviota-grupo.com**

GREATER HAVANA (KOHLY PLAYA) Hotel Kohly $$

Calle 49 esq. 36A **Tel** *(7) 204 0240 to 42* **Fax** *(7) 204 1733* **Rooms** *136*

Less attractive but better equipped than its sister hotel, the Hotel El Bosque, this parkside building features a small pool, a tennis court, a diminutive gym and a sauna. The enclosed, terraced pool has a relaxing aura of privacy and you can wander directly into the wooded park from the hotel grounds. Bright rooms. **www.gaviota-grupo.com**

GREATER HAVANA (MIRAMAR) Casa de Mauricio Alonso $

Calle A no.312, apto 9, e/ Ave. 3ra y Ave. 5ta **Tel** *(7) 203 7581* **Rooms** *1*

Just over the river from Vedado, this *casa particular* is much closer to the livelier parts of the city than most lodgings in Miramar. The spacious accommodation, in a penthouse apartment, is well equipped and there are great views both of the city and of the ocean.

GREATER HAVANA (MIRAMAR) Residencia Miramar $

Avenida 7ma no.4403, e/ 44 y 46 **Tel** *(7) 202 1075* **Rooms** *2*

A delightful *casa particular* in a classic Miramar residence à la 1950s suburban Miami. Room facilities include phone and fridge, and the whole house is kept spotlessly clean. There's a lovely patio garden and the host is very friendly, with plenty of experience in the room-renting business.

GREATER HAVANA (MIRAMAR) Chateau Miramar ⑤⑤

1ra y 62, Miramar **Tel** *(7) 204 1951 to 57* **Fax** *(7) 204 0224* **Rooms** *50*

Right on the waterfront, this hotel looks like a cross between a castle and a multi-storey car park. It's aimed at the business market and this shows in the shiny, well kept but essentially soulless environment here which pervades the rooms as well as the restaurant and bars. **www.hotelescubanacan.com**

GREATER HAVANA (MIRAMAR) Occidental Miramar ⑤⑤⑤

5ta e/ 72 y 76 **Tel** *(7) 204 3584* **Fax** *(7) 204 8158* **Rooms** *427*

This upmarket hotel looks a bit like a conference centre but has sports and activity facilities unrivalled in the city. Six tennis courts, an indoor squash court, a fitness centre, sauna, Jacuzzi and even tennis lessons are on offer, as well as outdoor and indoor playgrounds for children. Generic but very comfortable rooms. **www.occidental-hoteles.com**

GREATER HAVANA (MIRAMAR) Meliã Habana ⑤⑤⑤⑤

3ra. e/ 76 y 80 **Tel** *(7) 204 8500* **Fax** *(7) 204 3902, 204 3905* **Rooms** *397*

A swish, top-class business hotel in the heart of Miramar's commercial district with a knockout lobby, a huge curving corridor of polished floors, rising columns and an army of sofa suites. There are 12 meeting rooms and offices for rent, plus 3 pools and 4 restaurants. **www.meliacuba.com**

GREATER HAVANA (PLAYAS DEL ESTE) Aparthotel Las Terrazas ⑤

Avenida de las Terrazas e/ 10 y Rotonda **Tel** *(7) 797 1344* **Fax** *(7) 797 1316* **Rooms** *247*

Though there are three restaurants on site, the apartments are sufficiently equipped for self-caterers, with ovens and fridges, and some with three bedrooms. There's a grocery store but you'll need to go further afield to buy enough provisions for a proper meal. Large, split-level pool. **www.islazul.cu**

GREATER HAVANA (PLAYAS DEL ESTE) Mirador del Mar ⑤

Calle 11 e/ 1ra y 3ra **Tel** *(7) 797 1262* **Rooms** *79*

Spread around a hillside looking down onto the beach, this hotel neighbourhood is made up of houses of varying sizes, some of them bungalows, some with first floor balcony terraces, some sleeping as many as five people. There are two small pools, two restaurants, three bars and a modest nightclub. **www.islazul.cu**

GREATER HAVANA (PLAYAS DEL ESTE) Hotel Atlántico ⑤⑤⑤

Avenida de las Terrazas 21, Santa María del Mar **Tel** *(7) 797 1085, 797 1532* **Fax** *(7) 797 1263* **Rooms** *92*

An old shell but a newer, renovated interior with upbeat colours make this one of the smarter hotels in the Playas del Este, operating as an all-inclusive resort. There are two tennis courts, an entertainment programme which includes a cabaret, a buffet restaurant and a pizza parlour. **www.gran-caribe.cu**

GREATER HAVANA (PLAYAS DEL ESTE) Villa Los Pinos ⑤⑤⑤

Avenida de las Terrazas 21, Santa María del Mar **Tel** *(7) 797 1361* **Fax** *(7) 797 1263* **Rooms** *70*

Here you will find roomy two-, three- and four- bedroom houses, some with their own pool and all with their own kitchen (including microwave ovens and all the usual mod cons); one house even has its own squash court. This is the most upmarket accommodation in this area, and is located on a good section of beach. **www.gran-caribe.cu**

WESTERN CUBA

CAYO LARGO DEL SUR Villa Marinera Cayo Largo del Sur 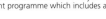 ⑤⑤⑤

Marina Cayo Largo del Sur, Isla de la Juventud **Tel** *(45) 248 137* **Fax** *(45) 248 213* **Rooms** *12*

An attractive wood-cabin complex on a great patch of beach. The roomy cabins have porches and a natural feel inside with wood-panelled walls and subtle furnishings. They all face the sea, just a few metres from the shore. The small pool, simple restaurant and marina all enhance this lovely little complex, which is in tune with its surroundings.

CAYO LARGO DEL SUR Hotel Sol Pelícano ⑤⑤⑤⑤

Cayo Largo del Sur, Archipiélago de los Canarreos, Isla de la Juventud **Tel** *(45) 248 333* **Fax** *(45) 248 265* **Rooms** *304*

Looking a bit like a Wild West village outpost (but painted pastel blue), this unusual luxury resort has slightly haggard, sandy grounds and two- and three-storey concrete ranch-house buildings. There's a ranchon beach eatery, an intimate gourmet restaurant and a large buffet restaurant. The large pool has a fountain in the centre. **www.sol-pelicano.com**

CAYO LARGO DEL SUR Playa Blanca ⑤⑤⑤⑤

Cayo Largo del Sur, Archipiélago de los Canarreos, Isla de la Juventud **Tel** *(45) 248 080* **Fax** *(45) 248 088* **Rooms** *306*

The majestic lobby is vaguely reminiscent of Tony Montana's mansion lobby in the film *Scarface*, with staircases on either side leading up to indoor balconies. From here a walkway lined with palms leads to one of the three pools. Dotted around are paintings and sculptures by local artists. Rooms are gracefully decorated. **www.gran-caribe.cu**

CAYO LARGO DEL SUR Hotel Sol Cayo Largo ⑤⑤⑤⑤⑤

Cayo Largo del Sur, Archipiélago de los Canarreos, Isla de la Juventud **Tel** *(45) 248 260* **Fax** *(45) 248 265* **Rooms** *296*

On a great stretch of beach and featuring a magnificent swimming pool, a well-equipped fitness centre, a beach-front restaurant and two other indoor restaurants. This hotel specializes in weddings and honeymoons, with lovely romantic spaces like the gazebo overlooking the beach and the raised poolside arbours. **www.meliacuba.com**

Key to Price Guide *see p252* **Key to Symbols** *see back cover flap*

CAYO LEVISA Hotel Cayo Levisa $$$

*Carretera a Palma Rubia, La Palma, Pinar del Río **Tel** (48) 756 501, (48) 756 505 **Rooms** 33*

Hidden from the mainland behind the thick scrub that covers the low island (cay) on which it nestles, this offshore cabin retreat can't be beaten for peace and tranquility. Watersports provide the only entertainment, with excursions to more remote cays. Prices are all-inclusive. **www.hotelescubanacan.com**

ISLA DE LA JUVENTUD Hotel Rancho del Tesoro $

*Carretera La Fe Km 2.5 **Tel** (46) 323 085, 323 035 **Rooms** 34*

This is a very basic countryside hotel consisting of a box building with a three-storey turret tower and a simple restaurant and bar. It is an unfussy, restful place to stay but don't expect to be pampered here. Guest rooms have satellite TV and mini-bar. **www.gran-caribe.cu**

ISLA DE LA JUVENTUD Villa Mas $

*Calle 41 no.4108, apto. 7, e/ 8 y 10, Nueva Gerona **Tel** (46) 323 544 **Rooms** 1*

This *casa particular* in a dusty apartment complex away from the centre may not look like much from the outside but the accommodation here is sprucely decorated and well equipped, featuring TV and fridge. There's a home-made bar on the inviting rooftop terrace.

ISLA DE LA JUVENTUD Hotel Colony $$$

*Carretera Sigüanea Km 42 **Tel** (46) 398 282 **Fax** (46) 398 420 **Rooms** 24*

The closest hotel to the beach on the Punta Francés peninsula, this modest coastal resort is aimed predominantly at scuba divers (dive packages can be arranged from here). There are rooms in the original, rather plain 1950s building and slightly better ones in the bungalows. The highlight is the bar and grill at the end of a long pier. **www.nauticamarlin.com**

LAS TERRAZAS Hotel Moka $$

*Las Terrazas, Autopista Nacional Habana-Pinar del Rio Km 51, Candelaria **Tel** (48) 578 600 **Fax** (48) 578 605 **Rooms** 31*

Few hotels in Cuba are as harmonious with their environment as this superb hillside sanctum. Shrouded in woodland, the graceful main building, with its outdoor corridors, has a lobby built around a large tree that rises through the roof. Paths and steps wind through the trees to the village below. Comfortable rooms. **www.lasterrazas.cu/dormir.html**

LAS TERRAZAS Hotel Moka Villas $$

*Las Terrazas, Autopista Nacional Habana-Pinar del Rio Km 51, Candelaria **Tel** (48) 578 600 **Rooms** 4*

The eco-community of Las Terrazas focuses around the small Lago de San Juan lake. In addition to the Hotel Moka accommodation *(see above)*, very attractive family villas (one with an alfresco shower) are dotted around the slopes that tumble down to the lake. Guests live with families from the community. **www.lasterrazas.cu**

PENÍNSULA DE GUANAHACABIBES Hotel María La Gorda $$

*María La Gorda, Península de Guanahacabibes, Pinar del Rio **Tel** (48) 778 131 **Fax** (48) 778 077 **Rooms** 55*

A real end-of-the-line beach resort, this is one of Cuba's most isolated mainland hotels. Rooms are in comfortable wood cabins on the edge of a forest thicket or in concrete villas on the beach. There's an excellent dive club and the buffet breakfast and dinner are included. The whole resort is cash only. **www.gaviota-grupo.com**

PENÍNSULA DE GUANAHACABIBES Villa Cabo San Antonio $$

*Carretera a Cabo de San Antonio, Península de Guanahacabibes, Pinar del Rio **Tel** (48) 757 655 **Rooms** 16*

These attractive bungalow cabins on stilts are scattered around parkland in the most remote spot in the country. This accommodation is for those who love diving, deep-sea fishing, rugged landscapes and isolation. The wild sea is just a few minutes' walk away. **www.gaviota-grupo.com**

PINAR DEL RÍO CITY Casa de Maribel Pérez Madera $

*Isabel Rubio 4 (bajos), e/ Marti y Adela Azcuy **Tel** (48) 753 217 **Rooms** 1*

Located right in the heart of Pinar del Río City is this freshly furnished, pocket-size ground-floor flat with one guest room. It is clean, cosy and comfortable, with a homely atmosphere. Although basic and small, the flat has a snug rather than cramped feel to it.

PINAR DEL RÍO CITY Hotel Pinar del Río $

*Marti y Final **Tel** (48) 755 070 to 74 **Fax** (48) 771 699 **Rooms** 149*

Though much better equipped than the city's other hotel, this unattractive building is past its prime. Guest rooms are small, and the furnishings are old-fashioned. It does, however, possess the only pool in Pinar del Río and the best nightclub in the city. **www.islazul.cu**

PINAR DEL RÍO CITY Hotel Vueltabajo $$

*Marti 103, esq. Rafael Morales **Tel** (48) 759 381 to 83 **Rooms** 39*

Right in the centre of town, on the bustling main street, this small-scale hotel is in a handsome balconied two-storey building fronted by simple high arches. The lobby, bar and rooms are all smart, small and refined but the restaurant lacks character and its food is unremarkable. **www.islazul.cu**

PINAR DEL RÍO PROVINCE Hotel Aguas Claras $

*Carretera a Viñales Km 7.5 **Tel** (48) 778 427 **Fax** (7) 860 5628 **Rooms** 40*

This hotel, with small villas scattered around a pool and situated in rural grounds, is an idyllic spot just a short drive out of Pinar del Río. A river flows along the edge of the property and horseback riding is available, making this an attractive option for families with older children. **www.cubamarviajes.cu**

SAN DIEGO DE LOS BAÑOS Hotel Mirador ⑤

Calle 23 y Final, San Diego de los Baños, Los Palacios **Tel/Fax** *(48) 778 338* **Rooms** *50*

Tucked away in the corner of tiny San Diego de los Baños village, just over a river from dense woodlands, is this picturesque two-storey hotel with canopied corridor balconies. It has well-tended terrace gardens with a pretty little pool, complete with its own mini-bridge. **www.islazul.cu**

SOROA Villa Soroa ⑤⑤

Carretera de Soroa Km 8, San Cristóbal **Tel** *(48) 523 534, 523 556, 523 512* **Rooms** *49*

Surrounded by looming hills in its own compact valley, this villa complex has a wonderful natural setting. With modest facilities but a large pool, it is a real chillout spot and popular with package tourists. There's a hilltop restaurant nearby. The reasonably comfortable villas surround the pool. **www.hotelescubanacan.com**

VIÑALES Casa Déborah Hernández ⑤

Calle C Final no.1 **Tel** *(48) 796 207* **Rooms** *1*

Located in the heart of the small town of Viñales but set back off the main street, this peaceful casa offers one room with an en-suite bathroom in a flourishing garden set behind the family home. Guests can enjoy breakfast under a canopy in the garden.

VIÑALES Casa Oscar Jaime Rodríguez ⑤

Calle Adela Azcuy 43 **Tel** *(48) 793 381* **Rooms** *2*

Oscar runs a great *casa* that's popular with the camping fraternity. It's slightly unusual in that the communal areas are focused around the central dining area, creating a "hostel" atmosphere rarely found in Cuba. The house has been built in colonial style, in a peaceful part of town. Fantastic cocktails too.

VIÑALES Villa El Isleño ⑤

Carretera a Viñales Km 25 **Tel** *(48) 793 107* **Rooms** *2*

The first house in the village on the road from Pinar del Río, this very well-kept *casa particular* has a backyard with great views of the Mogote hills. With TV and fridge and sparkling clean bathrooms, these are among the most comfortable guest rooms in Viñales, especially the one in its own block out the back.

VIÑALES La Ermita ⑤⑤

Carretera La Ermita Km 1.5 **Tel** *(48) 796 071, 796 100, 796 122* **Fax** *(48) 796 069* **Rooms** *62*

Up a small hill from the village, this neat and tidy cabin complex is the most relaxing place to stay in Viñales. The panoramic views of the valley can be enjoyed equally from the balcony restaurant, the pool, the well-trimmed lawns or the rooms themselves – in villas or in the graceful two-storey buildings with red-tile roofs. **www.hotelescubanacan.com**

VIÑALES Los Jazmines ⑤⑤

Carretera a Viñales Km 23 **Tel** *(48) 796 411* **Fax** *(48) 796 215* **Rooms** *70*

Most photos of Viñales are taken from the lookout platform of this magnificently situated hotel. The main building is a splendid 1950s pink neo-colonial provincial mansion, where the average-quality restaurant is housed, and there are modern blocks housing the most comfortable rooms. **www.hotelescubanacan.com**

VIÑALES Rancho San Vicente ⑤⑤

Carretera Puerto Esperanza Km 33 **Tel** *(48) 796 201, 796 221, 796 222, 796 111* **Fax** *(48) 796 265* **Rooms** *54*

Down in the valley, set on wooded, grassy slopes leading down to the quiet road, this wood-cabin refuge is a well-priced option. The delightful cabins, in their natural setting, have porches and glass-panelled front walls. There's also a pretty pool and an arched restaurant building. **www.hotelescubanacan.com**

CENTRAL CUBA – WEST

CAIBARIÉN Brisas del Mar  ⑤

Carretera Playa final, Caibarién **Tel** *(42) 351 699* **Rooms** *12*

Brisas del Mar is a good budget alternative to the resorts on the nearby cays, and well placed for day trips. Right at the end of town on a secluded little jut of land, this low-key hotel has rooms facing out to sea and its own small patch of beach. Guest rooms are kept in good condition with the standard modern conveniences. **www.islazul.cu**

CAYO SANTA MARÍA Villa Las Brujas ⑤⑤

Cayo Las Brujas, Villa Clara **Tel** *(42) 350 199* **Rooms** *24*

The least expensive place to stay on Villa Clara's north coast cays is hidden away at the end of a road cutting through the island scrub. The comfortable cabin accommodation faces the sea, and there's a simple rustic restaurant next to the beach in a circular building. **www.gaviota-grupo.com**

CAYO SANTA MARÍA Sol Cayo Santa María ⑤⑤⑤⑤

Cayo Santa María, Villa Clara **Tel** *(42) 350 200* **Fax** *(42) 350 205* **Rooms** *301*

Of the four all-inclusive Meliá resorts on the cays, this is the smallest yet still boasts two tennis courts, a gym, three bars and four restaurants. Standard double rooms in one- and two-storey villas are brightly furnished with ceiling fans, satellite TV, mini-bar, hair dryer and breakfast table and chairs. **www.meliacuba.com**

Key to Price Guide *see p252* **Key to Symbols** *see back cover flap*

CAYO SANTA MARÍA Iberostar Ensenachos  $$$$$
Cayo Ensenachos, Villa Clara **Tel** *(42) 350 300* **Fax** *(42) 350 301 to 03* **Rooms** *506*

This enormous all-inclusive resort is awesomely well equipped and its setting jaw-droppingly gorgeous. Split into three sections, the Royal Suite area features garden villas on their own peninsula at the far end of the hotel's two private beaches. State-of-the-art spa, four restaurants, six bars and CD/DVD players in all rooms. **www.iberostar.com**

CAYO SANTA MARÍA Meliã Cayo Santa María $$$$$
Cayo Santa María, Villa Clara **Tel** *(42) 350 500* **Fax** *(42) 350 505* **Rooms** *358*

Beautifully built into and around the cay's dense vegetation, this high-class all-inclusive resort counts two swimming pools, an amphitheatre, and Mediterranean, Italian and buffet restaurants among its extensive facilities. Guest rooms are exquisitely furnished and quite homely, with balconies or terraces. **www.meliacuba.com**

CIENFUEGOS Casa de la Amistad $
Avenida 56 no.2927, e/ 29 y 31 **Tel** *(43) 516 143* **Rooms** *2*

Run by an elderly couple whose set of guestbooks attest to both their friendliness and the popularity of this eclectic old house in the centre. A spiral staircase to the roof, a little bar installed in the entrance hall, stained-glass windows and period furnishings makes this place a fascinating and enjoyable place to stay.

CIENFUEGOS Casa Piñeiro $
Calle 41 no.1402, e/ 14 y 16, Punta Gorda **Tel** *(43) 513 808* **Rooms** *2*

An enthusiastic cook and an astute host, Jorge Piñeiro runs one of the best-known *casas particulares* in the city and is a great source of information for visitors. The house has a spacious outside eating area with a banquet-length picnic table and a built-in brick barbecue. Rooms are large and come equipped with TVs.

CIENFUEGOS Club Amigo Rancho Luna $$
Carretera Rancho Luna Km 15 **Tel** *(43) 548 012, 548 020, 548 026* **Fax** *(43) 548131* **Rooms** *225*

Hogging the only decent section of beach here, this patchy all-inclusive resort has a huge rectangular pool and a family atmosphere. Scuba diving lessons are offered, as are various other watersports. The long buildings accommodating guest rooms have a weathered look; about half of them have sea views. **www.gran-caribe.cu**

CIENFUEGOS Hotel Faro Luna $$
Carretera de Pasacaballo Km 18 **Tel** *(43) 548 030* **Fax** *(43) 551 686* **Rooms** *46*

A cosy little all-inclusive complex with a small main building and pool, and an attractive set of cabins lined up above and along the rocky shore. This is a good place for divers, with an excellent dive-club on site as well as a dolphinarium, located in a natural pool nearby. Rooms are comfortable but nothing special. **www.gran-caribe.cu**

CIENFUEGOS Palacio Azul $$
Calle 37 e/ 12 y 14, Punta Gorda **Tel** *(43) 555 828* **Rooms** *7*

Standing proudly on its own modest patch of bayside real estate, this pastel blue 1921 mansion has a down-to-earth atmosphere and is a great place to stay if you're looking for character. The guest rooms are well equipped and very spacious, some with bay views. The restaurant is only open for breakfast. **www.hotelescubanacan.com**

CIENFUEGOS Hotel Jagua $$$
Calle 37, e/ 0 y 2, Punta Gorda **Tel** *(43) 551 003* **Fax** *(43) 551 245* **Rooms** *149*

With the most attractive setting in town, at the tip of the peninsula reaching out into the bay waters, is this unremarkable block building containing a well-appointed four-star hotel. The interior is easier on the eye, with a light and airy lobby, and a pool area looking out over the bay. **www.gran-caribe.cu**

CIENFUEGOS Hotel Unión $$$
Calle 31, esq. 54 **Tel** *(43) 551 020* **Fax** *(43) 551 685* **Rooms** *49*

This 19th-century building has been wonderfully restored to its former Neo-Classical glory and is now the best hotel in Cienfuegos. Luxury and style combine comfortably, so that the sleek glass elevator and the pool, which is intimately enclosed within the hotel walls, blend in with the Old World decor and ambience. **www.hotelescubanacan.com**

LAGO HANABANILLA Hotel Hanabanilla $
Salto del Hanabanilla, Manicaragua, Villa Clara **Tel** *(42) 208 461* **Fax** *(42) 203 506* **Rooms** *125*

A hulk of a main building in a glorious natural setting in lush green hills and by the side of a large, twisting lake, this hotel attracts a large number of fishing enthusiasts. It is well set up for making the most of what the lake has to offer, with daily boat trips and watersports facilities. Rooms are basic. **www.islazul.cu**

PENÍNSULA DE ZAPATA Casa Luis $
Carretera a Cienfuegos, e/ Carretera a Playa Larga, Playa Girón **Tel** *(45) 984 258* **Rooms** *4*

At the best *casa particular* in the Bay of Pigs, Luis and his wife offer an exceptional service in their modern home. Rooms are furnished in modern style and the nightly communal dinners are outstanding. Luis offers excursions in his beautiful polished antique Ford. Horseriding and scuba diving trips can be arranged.

PENÍNSULA DE ZAPATA Hotel Playa Girón  $$
Playa Girón, Península de Zapata, Matanzas **Tel** *(45) 984 110* **Rooms** *123*

The peninsula's largest all-inclusive resort is spread around a grassy patch of land. Guest rooms are housed in simple concrete bungalows, some quite large, and are reasonably well equipped. The beach here is somewhat spoiled by a concrete wave-breaker, which obscures the view out to sea. **www.hotelescubanacan.com**

PENÍNSULA DE ZAPATA, MATANZAS Casa Alma

Calle Milanés (C/83) 29008 e/ 290 y 292, Matanzas **Tel** *(43) 290 857* **Rooms** *3*

In the heart of downtown Matanzas, this grand Spanish colonial home with attractive tiles, antique furniture and beautiful *mediopuntos* (stained-glass arches) makes a welcoming and convenient place to stay. It is run by Mayra, who has her finger on the pulse of Matanzas' cultural life.

PENÍNSULA DE ZAPATA, MATANZAS Finca Don Pedro

Península de Zapata, Matanzas **Tel** *(45) 912 825* **Rooms** *12*

This rustic set of wooden lodges offers excellent value – the most affordable on the peninsula, though the coast is a 20-minute drive away. The farmland setting is a bit rough and ready, but the lodges are spacious, comfortable and have satellite TV, mini-bar, ceiling fans, porches and rocking chairs. Great place to relax. **www.hotelescubanacan.com**

PENÍNSULA DE ZAPATA, MATANZAS Guamá

Laguna del Tesoro, Península de Zapata, Matanzas **Tel** *(45) 915 551* **Rooms** *44*

Wonderfully isolated out on the huge Laguna del Tesoro lake on a series of interconnected little islands, this mini-complex is modelled on a pre-Columbian Taíno settlement. Guest rooms are housed in round, wooden lodges hovering over the lake on stilts. **www.hotelescubanacan.com**

PENÍNSULA DE ZAPATA, MATANZAS Hotel Encanto Velasco

Calle Contreras, e/ Santa Teresa y Ayuntamiento **Tel** *(45) 253 880* **Rooms** *17*

Located in the heart of Matanzas, facing the central Parque de la Libertad, is this hotel in a handsome restored 1902 colonial building. It is the only hotel – and the most luxurious state-run accommodation – in town. The alfresco terrace makes a quiet haven in which to enjoy a drink or snack. **www.hotelescubanacan.com**

PENÍNSULA DE ZAPATA, MATANZAS Hotel Playa Larga

Playa Larga, Península de Zapata, Matanzas **Tel** *(45) 987 294* **Fax** *(45) 987 294* **Rooms** *60*

At the foot of the bay and at the edge of the nature reserve, this is the best located hotel on the peninsula for those wanting to combine scuba diving, bird watching, fishing and nature trailing. Accommodation is in bungalows facing the sea on somewhat tired-looking landscaped grounds. **www.hotelescubanacan.com**

REMEDIOS Hostal Villa Colonial Frank y Arelys

Antonio Maceo 43, e/ Av General Carrillo y Fe del Valle **Tel** *(42) 396 274* **Rooms** *3*

This beautiful 1839 colonial home is an exceptionally well run *casa particular*. Owners Frank and Arelys are very hospitable hosts and a mine of information on local culture and history. There is a small *paladar* on the top terrace, but it does not affect the privacy of house guests. **http://www.cubacasaparticularvillacolonial.com/**

REMEDIOS Hotel Encanto Mascotte

Máximo Gómez 114, e/ P Margal y A del Rio, Plaza Martí **Tel** *(42) 395 144* **Fax** *(42) 395 327* **Rooms** *10*

A plain yet refined and tastefully refurbished colonial period building, the town's only hotel is the focal point for most visitors whether or not they're staying here. Hotel Mascotte is a lovely, uncomplicated and comfortable place to stay for a few days. Rooms have satellite TV and mini-bar. **www.hotelescubanacan.com**

SANTA CLARA Casa de Consuelo Ramos Rodríguez

Independencia 265, apto 1, e/ Pedro Estevez (Unión) y San Isidro **Tel** *(42) 202 064* **Rooms** *2*

This ground-floor flat looks small and ordinary from the outside, so the wide corridors and large double rooms come as quite a surprise. The sizeable patio in the back garden is embellished with trees, shrubs and a green canopy shading the benches. There's a piano in the dining room, which is flanked by two more tiny patios.

SANTA CLARA Casa de Martha Artiles Alemán (Adriano's Hostel)

Martha Abreu 56 (altos), e/ Villuendas y Zayas **Tel** *(42) 205 008* **Rooms** *4*

A large first-floor flat with a half-colonial, half-modern look and feel. There are two three-piece suites in the caverous, pristinely furnished living room with its streetside balcony. A huge roof terrace with table and chairs provides sweeping views of Santa Clara. Impressive rooms, one with leather couch, TV and video.

SANTA CLARA Casa Mercy

Eduardo Machado (San Cristóbal) 4, e/ Cuba y Colón **Tel** *(42) 216 941* **Rooms** *2*

Just one block from the central square, there's an unpretentious family vibe at this well-run house. Both rooms are located upstairs, with their own terrace area overlooking the tiny central patio. Rooms have well-stocked mini-bars, and one has a small balcony. Mercy is a fantastic cook and does everything with a smile. Cocktails also available.

SANTA CLARA Florida Center

Maestra Nicolasa (Candelaria) 56, e/ Colón y Maceo **Tel** *(42) 208 161* **Rooms** *2*

This stunning house has an almost overwhelming number of notable features. The spellbinding central patio is a jungle of potted plants, palms and bushes; the bedrooms are an original mix of colonial-era and Art Deco furniture with modern, spotless bathrooms; and the front room is crammed full of colonial furniture and pictures. A unique option.

SANTA CLARA Santa Clara Libre

Parque Leoncio Vidal 6, e/ Tristá y Padre Chao **Tel** *(42) 207 548* **Fax** *(42) 202 771* **Rooms** *143*

An ugly high-rise hotel in a great location, right on the lively Parque Leoncio. Most rooms are small, but many have fantastic panoramic views of the city. There's a roof-top bar and nightclub, but the other communal areas are unremarkable. A budget option if you don't want to stay in a *casa particular*. **www.islazul.cu**

Key to Price Guide *see p252* **Key to Symbols** *see back cover flap*

SANTA CLARA Villa La Granjita
Carretera de Malezas Km 2.5 **Tel** *(42) 218 190* **Fax** *(42) 218 149* **Rooms** *71*

A large ranch in the middle of farmland beyond the city limits, this wooden cabin complex has an organic feel, the extensive grounds only partly landscaped, with a lot of it left in a natural state. The unusual accommodation units are multi-sided, two-storey, matted-roof huts with satellite TV, minibar and balcony or terrace. **www.hotelescubanacan.com**

SANTA CLARA Hotel Los Caneyes
Avenida los Eucaliptos y Circunvalación **Tel** *(42) 204 513, 218 140* **Fax** *(42) 218 140* **Rooms** *90*

Just beyond the southern outskirts of the city, a three-peso car ride from the centre, this hotel nestles in its own woodlands and feels isolated and tranquil, though the peace is occasionally disturbed by the hotel's entertainment programme. Good buffet restaurant in a reconstructed traditional Taíno circular lodge. **www.hotelescubanacan.com**

VARADERO Hotel Herradura
Avenida de Playa, e/ 35 y 36 **Tel** *(45) 613 703* **Fax** *(45) 667 496* **Rooms** *75*

A semi-circular building that couldn't be any closer to the beach, with steps down from the terrace area leading virtually into the ocean. Guest rooms come in twos, and each pair shares a communal living room and balcony, all of which face the sea. The hotel restaurant is not recommended. **www.islazul.cu**

VARADERO Hotel Los Delfines
Avenida 1ra, e/ 38 y 39 **Tel** *(45) 667 720* **Fax** *(45) 667 727* **Rooms** *103*

One of the only all-inclusives in the town section of Varadero, this is made up of a set of modern apartment blocks. The compact landscaped grounds and small circular pool are modest by the standards of all-inclusives on the peninsula, but this is one of the few places you can get the all-in treatment without being completely isolated. **www.islazul.cu**

VARADERO Hotel Pullman Dos Mares (formerly Hotel dos Mares)
Calle 53, esq. Avenida 1ra **Tel** *(45) 612 702* **Rooms** *34*

One of the most likeable budget options, this is not a classic beach-resort hotel at all. A pastel-yellow and white building looking something like a large and expensive Mediterranean townhouse, the rooms here are on the small side, but there's a cool and cosy sunken bar, just below street level. **www.islazul.cu**

VARADERO Hotel Pullman Dos Mares (formerly Hotel Pullman)
Avenida 1ra, e/ 49 y 50 **Tel** *(45) 612 702* **Rooms** *16*

Sharing services with the Dos Mares at Calle 53, this quieter hotel has more of a town than a beach feel. A single castle-like turret gives it a toytown look, and there's a simple garden terrace around which the rooms are located. It's worth paying the extra 10 CUC$ for one of the larger rooms with a balcony. **www.islazul.cu**

VARADERO Hotel Acuazul
Avenida 1ra y 13 **Tel** *(45) 667 132* **Fax** *(45) 667 229* **Rooms** *78*

Hotel Acuazul is an all-inclusive apartment block high-rise with little architectural merit, but lending great views to most rooms, which are surprisingly spacious. Guest rooms come equipped with satellite TV, balcony and bath tub and have a 1970s look about them. The swimming pool is quite small. **www.islazul.cu**

VARADERO Hotel Mar Del Sur
Avenida 3ra y 30 **Tel** *(45) 612 246* **Fax** *(45) 667 881* **Rooms** *366*

Closer to the main road than to the beach, this dated-looking all-inclusive complex has a reasonable set of facilities for the price and, unlike most hotels, receives as many Cuban visitors as foreign tourists. The gardens linking it all together help to soften the look of the clumsily designed concrete blocks. **www.islazul.cu**

VARADERO Hotel Varazul
Avenida 1ra y 13 **Tel** *(45) 667 132* **Fax** *(45) 667 229* **Rooms** *69*

Guests here have access to all the facilities at the Acuazul next door, including the pool. Like its neighbour, this is a high-rise all-inclusive hotel with little charm, but its apartments have large guest rooms with balconies and are set up for self-catering. Fourteen of the rooms are available for long stays. **www.islazul.cu**

VARADERO Hotetur Sun Beach
Calle 17, e/ Avenida 1ra y Avenida 3ra **Tel** *(45) 667 490* **Fax** *(45) 614 994* **Rooms** *272*

Two towering blocks, dominating the immediate surroundings, make up this all-inclusive hotel. Among the several high-rise hotels in this part of town, Hotetur Sun Beach has by far the best set of facilities and the largest communal areas in this price category. **www.hotetur.com**

VARADERO Villa La Mar
Avenida 3ra, e/ 28 y 30 **Tel** *(45) 614 525* **Fax** *(45) 612 508* **Rooms** *264*

This is one of the least expensive but certainly not the worst hotel in Varadero. Though firmly rooted in the old school of Cuban beach architecture, it has more soul than some of the alternatives elsewhere, thanks in part to its large gardens. There is also a games room, two restaurants and a discotheque. **www.islazul.cu**

VARADERO Villa Sotavento
Avenida 1ra y 13 **Tel** *(45) 667 132* **Fax** *(45) 667 229* **Rooms** *36*

Blending into the local neighbourhood, Villa Sotavento consists of a variety of different houses, no different in outward appearance to local domestic residences, split into two or three units each and spread around a five- or six-block area. Guests have access to the all-inclusive facilities at the Hotel Acuazul *(see above)*. **www.islazul.cu**

VARADERO Be Live Las Morlas

$$$

Avenida Las Américas y A, Reparto La Torre **Tel** *(45) 667 230* **Fax** *(45) 667 215* **Rooms** *148*

One of the most intimate all-inclusives, here almost everything is on a smaller scale, lending Las Morlas an endearing appeal. The pool (an artificial stream forming a figure of 8) is enclosed by the semi-circular main building, making the main outdoor area feel something like a secret hideaway. Guest rooms are also small. **www.belivehotels.com**

VARADERO Bellevue Palma Real

$$$

Avenida 3rd y 64 **Tel** *(45) 614 555* **Fax** *(45) 614 550* **Rooms** *466*

Only a couple of blocks from the beach but backing onto the main road of Varadero, the location of Palma Real is not as good as that of the other upmarket area hotels. It has two large pools, and rooms are of a good standard, though many are in an older building that predates the rest of the complex. **www.bluebayresorts.com**

VARADERO Club Kawama

$$$

Avenida Kawama, e/ 0 y 1 **Tel** *(45) 614 416 to 20* **Fax** *(45) 667 334* **Rooms** *336*

Hugging a long stretch of beach, this is one of the more interesting all-inclusives, thanks to the grey stone, fort-like constructions which were the original resort buildings. In one of these is housed a marvellous basement restaurant-cabaret. In a separate section of the complex, along the beach, are newer holiday mansions. **www.gran-caribe.com**

VARADERO Cuatro Palmas

$$$

Avenida 1ra, e/ 60 y 64 **Tel** *(45) 667 040* **Fax** *(45) 667 208* **Rooms** *312*

A town hotel with optional all-inclusive plans, bridging the gap between the mega resorts up the road and the budget hotels down the other way. Facilities are good, with a gym and sauna, a large buffet restaurant and a more intimate Cuban cuisine restaurant. **www.accorhotels.com**

VARADERO Sol Sirenas Coral

$$$

Avenida Las Américas y K, Reparto La Torre **Tel** *(45) 668 070* **Fax** *(45) 668 075* **Rooms** *718*

Sol Sirenas Coral was once two separate all-inclusive resorts, and there are two distinctly different sections that feel quite remote from one another (one in need of an injection of life and colour). It also means there are twice the number of facilities as at most comparable hotels, including three swimming pools. **www.meliacuba.com**

VARADERO Blau Varadero Hotel

$$$$

Carretera Las Morlas Km 15 **Tel** *(45) 667 545* **Fax** *(45) 667 494* **Rooms** *395*

Inspired by Mayan architecture, Blau Varadero Hotel has a vast pyramidal atrium lobby, a spectacular pool complex, a state-of-the-art theatre, several watersports and tennis. Guest rooms feature stylish contemporary furnishings in subdued colours, king-sized beds and marble-clad bathrooms. **www.blauhotels.com**

VARADERO Breezes Varadero

$$$$

Avenida Las Américas Km 3 **Tel** *(45) 667 030* **Rooms** *270*

At this over-18s only SuperClubs all-inclusive resort all rooms are suites, with a high level of comfort and lots of space. The usual amenities come as standard in all suites, while those in the 11 two-storey buildings have separate living rooms. Extensive grounds, fitness centre and three restaurants. **www.hotelescubanacan.com**

VARADERO Club Barlovento

$$$$

Avenida 1ra, e/ 10 y 12 **Tel** *(45) 667 140* **Fax** *(45) 667 218* **Rooms** *296*

This smart and stylish (though relatively small) all-inclusive is framed around pseudo-colonial architecture that underwent refurbishment in late 2006. It lies within walking distance of the western end of the town and a number of local restaurants. Rooms have a balcony or terrace, kitchenettes and all the usual gadgets. **http://hotelesc.es**

VARADERO Mansión Xanadú

$$$$

Autopista del Sur Km 8.5 **Tel** *(45) 667 388* **Fax** *(45) 668 481* **Rooms** *6*

This unique hotel is housed in the millionaire mansion that belonged to the Dupont Family before they left it with the Revolution (see p163). The guest rooms are huge, the restaurant is one of Varadero's finest and there are special deals for guests using the golf course next door. Breakfast and dinner are included. **www.varaderogolfclub.com**

VARADERO Villa Cuba

$$$$

Avenida Las Américas Km 3 **Tel** *(45) 668 280* **Fax** *(45) 668 282* **Rooms** *365*

The multi-level lobby area, a network of platforms and staircases with a bar at the halfway point, is one of the most captivating hotel interiors in Varadero. From here the grounds stretch down to the beach and feature small groups of villas, each with their own little pools. Two restaurants, a gym, sauna and Jacuzzi. **www.gran-caribe.com**

VARADERO Barceló Solymar Arenas Blancas

$$$$$

Calle 64, e/ Avenida 1ra y Autopista del Sur **Tel** *(45) 614 450* **Fax** *(45) 614 490* **Rooms** *358*

A family all-inclusive at the very top of the town, Arenas Blancas is the most luxurious hotel in town. The huge main building is otherwise unremarkable but the pool is one of the largest in Varadero, snaking its way around a large part of the landscaped gardens. The guest rooms are very large, with all modern conveniences. **www.barcelo.com**

VARADERO Meliã Las Americas

$$$$$

Autopista del Sur Km 7 **Tel** *(45) 667 600* **Fax** *(45) 667 625* **Rooms** *336*

Run in conjunction with the golf course that stretches out either side of this superb hotel, Meliã Las Americas is one of the few all-inclusives where most of the rooms are in the main building and the area occupied by the complex is comparatively small. The gardens are fabulous, with undulating paths up to the split-level pool. **www.meliacuba.com**

Key to Price Guide *see p252* **Key to Symbols** *see back cover flap*

VARADERO Meliã Paradisus Varadero

Punta Francés **Tel** *(45) 668 700* **Fax** *(45) 668 705* **Rooms** *429*

An "ultra all-inclusive" in the parlance of the Meliã chain that run this staggeringly extensive and expensive complex, with no less than eight restaurants as well as two pools, tennis courts, gym, sauna and Jacuzzi. If you want your own pool, sauna and Jacuzzi you can pay the extra for the Garden Villa, which also comes with a butler. **www.meliacuba.com**

VARADERO Meliã Península Varadero

Punta Hicacos **Tel** *(45) 668 800* **Fax** *(45) 668 805, 668 808* **Rooms** *591*

The top choice for families, this massive resort has a fabulous kids' zone with its own pool that features a little castle on an island, and various other facilities for the under-12s. The standard double rooms would be considered suites in most hotels, with walk-in closets, couch and coffee table, as well as Internet access. **www.meliacuba.com**

VARADERO Meliã Varadero

Autopista del Sur Km 7 **Tel** *(45) 667 013* **Fax** *(45) 667 012* **Rooms** *490*

This sumptuous shrine to holiday architecture has an unforgettable lobby patio, with hanging vines dropping down six storeys of balconies to encircle a little maze of waterways and plantlife. One of its four restaurants is located on a small clifftop with waves lapping down below. Wi-Fi is available throughout the hotel. **www.meliacuba.com**

VARADERO Sandals Royal Hicacos Resort and Spa

Carretera de las Morlas Km 15 **Tel** *(45) 668 844* **Fax** *(45) 668 851* **Rooms** *404*

On one of the most secluded sections of the peninsula, this resplendent all-inclusive, couples-only resort has some of the best rooms in Varadero, each with a king-size bed. The impressive facilities include squash courts, a fitness centre, a mini basketball court and three tennis courts. **www.sandalshicacos.com**

VARADERO Sol Palmeras

Autopista del Sur Km 8 **Tel** *(45) 667 009* **Fax** *(45) 667 008* **Rooms** *407 (plus 200 bungalows)*

Dense in plantlife, the grounds around the pool and the various sports courts invite exploration, with paths weaving around the vegetation from the main four-storey building. There are different types of rooms, with standard doubles in the large main building, and over 100 bungalows and four grades of suites. All-inclusive. **www.meliacuba.com**

CENTRAL CUBA – EAST

CAMAGÜEY Casa de Alfredo Castillo

Cisnero 124 esq. Raúl Lamar **Tel** *(32) 297 436* **Rooms** *2*

A few blocks away from the centre, this is one of the city's more modern *casa particulares* with two spacious rooms offering an above-average level of comfort within the private home market. Casa de Alfredo Castillo is astutely well run, and the owners speak English and French.

CAMAGÜEY Casa Lucy

Alegría 23, e/ Ignacio Agramonte y Montera **Tel** *(32) 283 701* **Rooms** *2*

This reassuringly clean house has a delightful patio garden with a fountain, seven bird cages and even a little bar counter. The rooms are large, one of them actually more of a mini-apartment with a living room and cooking facilities, and they both have security boxes. There is parking for two cars. Good food here, too.

CAMAGÜEY Hotel Colón

República 472 e/ San José y San Martín **Tel** *(32) 251 520, 254 878* **Fax** *(32) 283 346* **Rooms** *47*

This medium-sized town hotel is in a beautifully restored 1926 gem of a building. The majestic lobby, with its shiny dark wood, marble and tiled surfaces, is a highlight and sets the tone for the rest of the classy interior spaces, including a lovely central patio and bedrooms which are a bit small – ask for one of the matrimonial rooms. **www.islazul.cu**

CAMAGÜEY Hotel Plaza

Van Horne 1, e/ República y Avellaneda **Tel** *(32) 282 457, 282 435* **Rooms** *67*

The oldest and least refined of Camagüey's three neo-colonial hotels, this is still a smart-looking place and certainly doesn't lack character. Guest rooms vary considerably in size and are located either around the central patio or looking onto the street outside. There is a bar in the lobby and a stylish restaurant. **www.islazul.cu**

CAMAGÜEY Gran Hotel

Maceo 67 e/ Ignacio Agramonte y General Gómez **Tel** *(32) 292 093, 292 094* **Fax** *(32) 293 933* **Rooms** *72*

Built in 1939, this is a real classic and has maintained the look and feel of refined decadence that would have characterized it prior to the Revolution. There's a rooftop bar and top-floor restaurant, both with great views, and a dimly atmospheric piano bar. Throughout the building are hallmarks of this marvellous hotel's vintage. **www.islazul.cu**

CAYO COCO Hotel Colonial

Jardines del Rey, Cayo Coco, Ciego de Ávila **Tel** *(33) 301311* **Fax** *(33) 301384* **Rooms** *342*

The arch-laden main building of this distinctive all-inclusive is modelled on classic colonial Cuban architecture and centres around a beguiling garden patio. The elegant rooms feature wrought-iron beds and refined wooden furniture in keeping with the colonial theme. **www.hotelescubanacan.com**

CAYO COCO Hotel Playa Coco
$$\$\$\$$

Jardines del Rey, Cayo Coco, Ciego de Ávila **Tel** *(33) 302 250* **Fax** *(33) 302 255* **Rooms** *307*

Not as impressive as other resorts on Cayo Coco, the colonial theme here could have been taken much further. Nevertheless there are three pools, two Jacuzzis (one large enough for 20 people), numerous sporting facilities and Japanese and Italian restaurants. **www.gaviota-grupo.com**

CAYO COCO Tryp Cayo Coco
$$\$\$\$\$$

Jardines del Rey, Cayo Coco, Ciego de Ávila **Tel** *(33) 301 300* **Fax** *(33) 301 386* **Rooms** *508*

A family all-inclusive with an enormous sprawling pool and extensive ocean front grounds smothered in palm trees. There's a playground, babysitting services and a kids' club for 5-13 year olds. Adults wanting to escape can enjoy the smaller "ecological pool". Six restaurants, gym and night-lit tennis courts. **www.meliacuba.com**

CAYO COCO Iberostar Cayo Coco & Iberostar Mojito
$$\$\$\$\$\$$

Jardines del Rey, Cayo Coco, Ciego de Ávila **Tel** *(33) 301 470* **Fax** *(33) 301 498* **Rooms** *690*

Iberostar, who run well-regarded all-inclusives, have taken over the management of an established hotel and divided it into the Cayo Coco and the Mojito. Rooms include bungalows over water in a tranquil lagoon close to the beach as well as those set in villa blocks arranged around the pool. Excellent range of facilities. **www.iberostar.com**

CAYO COCO Meliá Cayo Coco
$$\$\$\$\$\$$

Jardines del Rey, Cayo Coco, Ciego de Ávila **Tel** *(33) 301 180* **Fax** *(33) 301 195* **Rooms** *250*

This exceptional all-inclusive resort, aimed at couples (over-18s only), goes for quality over quantity with its facilities. Most outstanding are the 62 rooms suspended over a saltwater lagoon on stilts. Three excellent restaurants include the airy Arena Real, perched just over the water's edge with serene views. **www.meliacuba.com**

CAYO COCO Sol Cayo Coco
$$\$\$\$\$\$$

Jardines del Rey, Cayo Coco, Ciego de Ávila **Tel** *(33) 301 280* **Fax** *(33) 301285* **Rooms** *270*

The most family-oriented all-inclusive resort on Cayo Coco has all sorts of facilities for kids, including a playgroup centre and a kids' pool area. There's an impressive list of watersports, such as water basketball, canoeing and water polo while the excellent nautical club has catamarans, sailing boats and pedal boats. **www.meliacuba.com**

CAYO GUILLERMO Villa Cojímar
$$\$\$\$$

Jardines del Rey, Cayo Guillermo, Ciego de Ávila **Tel** *(33) 301 712, 301 725* **Fax** *(33) 301 727* **Rooms** *280*

The oldest resort on Cayo Guillermo, Villa Cojímar is less luxurious than modern neighbouring hotels but it's also one of the least expensive. The guest rooms have been renovated and are well equipped. Facilities include a gym, sauna, and games room. **www.gran-caribe.cu**

CAYO GUILLERMO Iberostar Daiquirí
$$\$\$\$\$$

Jardines del Rey, Cayo Guillermo, Ciego de Ávila **Tel** *(33) 301 650* **Fax** *(33) 301 645* **Rooms** *312*

Iberostar Daiquirí is not as widely spread out as some of the other all-inclusives on the cays, though it is still a large resort. The rooms here are arranged in several long three-storey buildings enveloping the pool area. There are three restaurants, a beach barbecue grill, gym, tennis courts and watersports. **www.iberostar.com**

CAYO GUILLERMO Meliá Cayo Guillermo
$$\$\$\$\$\$$

Jardines del Rey, Cayo Guillermo, Ciego de Ávila **Tel** *(33) 301 680* **Fax** *(33) 301 685, 301 684* **Rooms** *301*

Though it isn't a couples-only resort, Meliá Cayo Guillermo specializes in romance with a wedding gazebo, hammocks in their own hut suspended over the water and a long wooden walkway extending into the sea where covered platforms offer seclusion and tranquility. Four restaurants, fitness centre and two tennis courts. **www.solmeliacuba.com**

CAYO GUILLERMO Sol Cayo Guillermo
$$\$\$\$\$\$$

Jardines del Rey, Cayo Guillermo, Ciego de Ávila **Tel** *(33) 301 760* **Fax** *(33) 301 748* **Rooms** *268*

There's a relaxing, harmonious feel around this neatly designed hotel complex. The scattered bungalows and two-storey villas blend in with the palm-shrouded gardens, all with traditional red brick-coloured roofs, polished tile floors and pastel interiors. There's an attractive pool and decent stretch of beach. **www.meliacuba.com**

MORÓN Casa Xiomara
$$\$$$

Calle 8 no.2C, e/ Sordo y C **Tel** *(33) 504 236* **Rooms** *1*

The guest accommodation at this *casa particular* is a small independent apartment in the plant-filled patio of the main house, which is just minutes' walk from the bronze statue of the cockerel of Morón. The advice and hospitality at this modest family home is wonderful. Both English and Italian are spoken.

MORÓN Hotel Morón
$$\$$$

Avenida Tarafa, Morón, Ciego de Avila **Tel** *(33) 502 230* **Fax** *(33) 502 133* **Rooms** *153*

This is a conveniently located transit hotel and although the building isn't attractive it is one of the province's largest hotels outside of the cays, making it a reliable place to get a room if you're driving through Cuba or out to Cayo Coco. There is a decent sized, clean swimming pool, too. **www.islazul.cu**

PENÍNSULA ANCÓN Club Amigo Ancón
$$\$\$$$

Playa Ancón, Península Ancón, Trinidad, Sancti Spíritus **Tel** *(41) 996 120* **Fax** *(41) 996 121* **Rooms** *279*

At the tip of the peninsula, on the best section of beach, renovations have brightened up this multi-storey building. There's plenty to do here, with a large swimming pool, hidden from the beach behind the hotel, two tennis courts and pool tables. **www.hotelescubanacan.com**

Key to Price Guide *see p252* **Key to Symbols** *see back cover flap*

PENÍNSULA ANCÓN Hotel Costasur $$

Playa María Aguilar, Península Ancón, Trinidad, Sancti Spíritus **Tel** *(41) 996 174* **Fax** *(41) 996 173* **Rooms** *132*

The beach here is inferior to those found nearer the other hotels on the peninsula, but the attractive bungalows lining the seafront lawn and resanded beach are as appealing a place to stay as anywhere else on this stretch of coastline. There's an airy lobby bar, a tennis court and standard pool. **www.hotelescubanacan.com**

PENÍNSULA ANCÓN Brisas Trinidad del Mar $$$

Península Ancón, Trinidad, Sancti Spíritus **Tel** *(41) 996 500* **Fax** *(41) 996 565* **Rooms** *241*

The most upmarket resort on the peninsula is dotted with architectural touches meant to mimic the colonial buildings up the road in Trinidad. These touches do add some character to what is otherwise a standard all-inclusive with all the usual comfort and facilities, such as tennis courts and a gym as well as a kids' club. **www.hotelescubanacan.com**

PLAYA SANTA LUCÍA Club Amigo Mayanabo $$

Avenida Turística de Tararaco, Playa Santa Lucía, Camagüey **Tel** *(32) 336 184* **Fax** *(32) 365 295* **Rooms** *225*

This all-inclusive hotel is a mixed bag. The landscaped grounds are a tad patchy in places and the main buildings a little dated but it does have the biggest pool in Santa Lucía and there's a captivating water-bound beach bar at the end of a mini-pier. Guest rooms are clean but would improve with refurbishment. **www.hotelescubanacan.com**

PLAYA SANTA LUCÍA Gran Club Santa Lucía $$

Avenida Turística de Tararaco, Playa Santa Lucía, Nuevitas, Camagüey **Tel** *(32) 336 129* **Fax** *(32) 365 147* **Rooms** *252*

The rooms here and the resort in general are as well equipped as any hotel in the area. There are several restaurants, tennis courts, a beauty parlour, a gym and a games room. Be sure to ask for a room away from the road (some rooms are disappointingly close to the road) or pay extra for a suite. **www.hotelescubanacan.com**

PLAYA SANTA LUCÍA Hotel Brisas Santa Lucía $$$

Avenida Turística, Playa Santa Lucía, Nuevitas, Camagüey **Tel** *(32) 336 317* **Fax** *(32) 365 142* **Rooms** *412*

Admittedly there is a long list of facilities here, among which are four bars, tennis courts, a gym and a host of water-sports apparatus, but the hotel really qualifies as a three-star rather than a four-star facility. Some of the rooms are in need of refurbishment. **www.hotelescubanacan.com**

SANCTI SPÍRITUS Casa de Martha Rodríguez Martínez y Miguel $

Plácido 69, e/ Calderón y Tirso Marín **Tel** *(41) 323 556* **Rooms** *2*

One of the most professionally run *casas particulares* in the city. Its guest rooms, which have ceiling fans as well as a/c, TV and top-quality en-suite bathrooms, are cleaned daily and the owner produces a menu for meal times. There's an intimate terrace where food is served, and a roof terrace with modest views over the city.

SANCTI SPÍRITUS Hotel Zaza $

Finca San José Km 5.5, Lago Zaza **Tel** *(41) 327 015* **Fax** *(41) 328 359, 325 490* **Rooms** *65*

Another of Cuba's shrines to concrete, this heavy-set four-storey hotel is completely out-of-sync with its natural surroundings and the man-made reservoir (the largest of its kind in Cuba) stretching before it. Fishing is the focus here, and although there's a pool most visitors bring a rod rather than a swimsuit. **www.islazul.cu**

SANCTI SPÍRITUS Los Richards $

Independencia 17 (altos), Plaza Serafín Sanchez **Tel** *(41) 326 745* **Rooms** *1*

Of all the houses renting rooms in the city, this is the most centrally located. There's a huge space exclusively for the use of guests with a living-room, bedroom and bathroom as well as a balcony looking out onto the plaza. Up on the roof the owners have constructed their own *bohío*-roof open-air dining area.

SANCTI SPÍRITUS CITY Villa Los Laureles $

Carretera Central Km 383 **Tel** *(41) 361 056* **Fax** *(41) 323 913* **Rooms** *76*

This roadside villa complex on the outskirts of the city on the island-wide Carretera Central is used predominantly by weary motorists. The basic layout, with inoffensive-looking bungalows gathered around a medium-sized, oblong pool, adds to the straightforward appeal of the place. Rooms have satellite TV, radio and minibar. **www.islazul.cu**

SANCTI SPÍRITUS CITY Hotel del Rijo $$

Honorato del Castillo 12 **Tel** *(41) 328 588* **Fax** *(41) 328 577* **Rooms** *16*

Considerably underpriced compared to numerous other town hotels in Cuba, this delectable little colonial conversion on a tiny square in the heart of the city is a wonderful place to stay. Rooms are surprisingly spacious, well equipped, subtly decorated with dark-wood furnishings and high-quality bathrooms with marble touches. **www.islazul.cu**

SANCTI SPÍRITUS CITY Hotel Plaza $$

Independencia 1, esq. Avenida de los Mártires, Plaza Serafín Sánchez **Tel** *(41) 327 102* **Fax** *(41) 326 940* **Rooms** *25*

Right on the main square, this is the city's other excellent-value hotel. All the spaces are full of character, from the graceful lobby with its wicker furnishings to the intimate restaurant and the attractive rooms with colonial-style furnishings, many with balconies looking over the square. **www.islazul.cu**

SANCTI SPÍRITUS CITY Rancho Hatuey $$

Carretera Central Km 383 **Tel** *(41) 361 315* **Fax** *(41) 328 830* **Rooms** *74*

Spread thinly around its spacious, grassy, gently undulating grounds, this simple hotel complex melts into the surrounding countryside to the extent that you can't really see the joint. Rooms are in boxy, two-storey concrete cabins and there's a pool area in the centre. The best place in town for peace and relaxation. **www.islazul.cu**

TRINIDAD Casa Font

Calle Gustavo Izquierdo 105, e/ Piro Guinart y Simón Bolivar **Tel** *(41) 993 683* **Rooms** *2*

The vast 18th-century home run by the Font family is stunning. The building features beautiful Spanish colonial furniture and heirlooms, and one of the bedrooms is graced with an elegant bed decorated in mother of pearl. Breakfast is served in the patio garden by the friendly host Beatriz.

TRINIDAD Casa Margely

Piro Guinart 360, e/ Fernando Hernández Echerri y Juan M Márquez **Tel** *(41) 996 525* **Rooms** *2*

The rooms in this fairly opulent colonial residence are walled off at the back of the central patio in a private little section of the house with its own garden gate and dining room. Both rooms have two double beds, but only one has an en-suite bathroom; the other bathroom is at the end of the leafy outdoor corridor linking it all up.

TRINIDAD Casa Muñoz

José Martí 401, e/ Fidel Claro y Santiago Escobar **Tel** *(41) 993 673* **Rooms** *3*

Julio Muñoz and Rosa Orbea offer guests three airy, spacious en-suite rooms in this delightful colonial house. Julio is a mine of information on the town's colonial heritage; a published photographer, he also offers photgraphy workshops. The family are animal-lovers and pets include a horse stabled in the garden. **www.casa.trinidadphoto.com**

TRINIDAD Casa Santana

Maceo 425, e/ Fco. J. Zerquera y Colón **Tel** *(41) 994 372* **Rooms** *1*

Casa Santana is run by an enthusiastic host who hands you a book on the history of Trinidad when you arrive. The whole of the upstairs of the house, three rooms in all, is given over to guests. The backyard patio is spacious, and a well is one of the many original colonial artifacts found all over the house. **www.particuba.net/villes/trinidad/santana**

TRINIDAD Hostal Las Mercedes

Camilo Cienfuegos 272, e/ Maceo y Francisco Cadahía **Tel** *(41) 993 107* **Rooms** *1*

On one of the busier streets just outside the historic centre of Trinidad, the room here looks onto the open backyard patio full of plants and trees, including a huge cactus. The high-ceiling guest room has a huge colonial style bathroom, a bronze bed and an imposing wardrobe. Run by an exuberant owner and her son.

TRINIDAD Hotel Las Cuevas

Finca Santa Ana **Tel** *(41) 996 133, 6434* **Fax** *(41) 996 161* **Rooms** *114*

Laid out on a hillside just above the town, there are great views wherever you are in this very relaxing and secluded cabin complex. The serenity is disturbed only by the nightly shows of traditional Cuban music and dance that take place on the terrace outside the restaurant. The unique hotel disco is in a cave deep in the hillside. **www.hotelescubanacan.com**

TRINIDAD Iberostar Grand Hotel Trinidad

José Martí 262, e/ Lino Pérez y Colón, Parque Céspedes **Tel** *(41) 996 073* **Fax** *(41) 996 077* **Rooms** *40*

This sumptuous small-scale five-star hotel has an enchanting central patio and some great touches, like the giant pineapple lampshade and the memorabilia encased in the glass-topped lobby coffee tables. The restaurant is one of the most expensive in Trinidad. Rooms have either a balcony or terrace. **www.iberostar.com**

EASTERN CUBA

BARACOA Casa Daniel

Calle Céspedes 28 e/ Rubert López y Maceo **Tel** *(21) 641 443* **Rooms** *1*

Casa Daniel is a friendly *casa particular* that offers a quiet room with an en-suite bathroom in a modern family home. Breakfasts are served in the interior courtyard. Daniel, the host, works at Baracoa's museum and is a fount of all knowledge on the history and culture of the city.

BARACOA Casa de Nancy Borges Gallego

Ciro Frias 3 esq. Flor Crombet **Tel** *(21) 643 272* **Rooms** *1*

An agreeable place run by hospitable owners, one of whom – René Frometa – is the adopted son of local legend La Rusa, an immigrant Russian who gave shelter to the rebel army during the Revolution. One of the rooms in the house is set up as a kind of museum in homage to the lady. Rooms are clean and comfortable.

BARACOA Hostal La Habanera

Los Maceos 124 e/ Maravi y Frank Pais, Baracoa, Guantánamo **Tel** *(21) 645 273* **Rooms** *10*

Occupying a beautifully refurbished colonial residence built in 1867, this charming hotel is right in the heart of Baracoa. For the price, rooms are of an excellent standard: spacious with high ceilings and smart, tiled floors. Some of the rooms share a veranda that overlooks Calle Maceo. Tour booking available. **www.gaviota-grupo.com**

BARACOA Hotel la Rusa

Máximo Gómez no. 161 e/ Pelayo Cuervo y Ciro Frías, Baracoa, Guantánamo **Tel** *(21) 643 011* **Rooms** *12*

On the seafront, this simple, refurbished three-storey building has small rooms, modestly furnished, with tiny bathrooms. Some have pleasant sea views. The restaurant tables are along a narrow terrace. The former owner was a Russian immigrant (hence the name) who gave refuge to Fidel and his men during the Revolution. **www.gaviota-grupo.com**

Key to Price Guide *see p252* **Key to Symbols** *see back cover flap*

BARACOA El Castillo $$

Loma de Paraíso, Baracoa, Guantánamo **Tel** *(21) 645 194, 645 165* **Fax** *(21) 645 339* **Rooms** *62*

The best place to stay for postcard views of Baracoa and the bay, this laid-back hotel is part-housed in a converted 18th-century fort. The historic theme extends to the rooms, which are furnished in a smart, refined colonial style. The whole hotel is imbued with a soothing sense of calm. Great views from the small pool. **www.gaviota-grupo.com**

BARACOA Porto Santo $$

Carretera del Aeropuerto, Baracoa, Guantánamo **Tel** *(21) 645 106* **Fax** *(21) 645 339* **Rooms** *83*

Secluded and right on the edge of the bay, the location is where Columbus is said to have planted the Cruz de Parra, a cross declaring the European arrival in the Americas. The hotel has its own private patch of beach and is gracefully spread around neatly trimmed lawns. Guest rooms are average. **www.gaviota-grupo.com**

BARACOA Villa Maguana $$

Playa Maguana, km 20, Baracoa **Tel** *(21) 641 204* **Fax** *(23) 427 389* **Rooms** *16*

Located 20 km (12 miles) north of Baracoa, on the road to Moa, are four rustic, two-storey villas sitting among tropical trees and foliage. Rooms are simply but comfortably furnished and the setting, close to a private beach cove belonging to this beach hideaway, makes for a peaceful retreat. **www.gaviota-grupo.com**

BAYAMO Casa Olga Celeiro Rizo $

Parada 16, e/ Martí y Mármol **Tel** *(23) 423 859* **Rooms** *2*

Olga lets out two rooms, sharing a bathroom, in a small house right on the Francisco Maceo Osorio plaza. Reclining on rocking chairs on the balcony, you can enjoy music drifting up from the Casa de la Trova, but the rooms are quiet enough at night. The couple are very hospitable, and the home cooking is excellent.

BAYAMO Hotel Encanto Royalton $$

Antonio Maceo no.53, e/ General García y José Palma **Tel** *(23) 422 290* **Fax** *(23) 424 792* **Rooms** *33*

The smartest hotel in town, dating from the 1940s, is located on the main square. Its restaurant is one of the best in the city, with a veranda overlooking the square. All rooms have been decorated and furnished with a well-ordered restraint, featuring dark wood, TV and small but pristine bathrooms. Four have views of the square. **www.islazul.cu**

CAIMANERA Hotel Caimanera $

Loma Norte, Caimanera, Guantánamo **Tel** *(21) 499 415* **Rooms** *10*

This small, simple hotel has a unique claim to fame: it's as near as most people are allowed to get to the controversial US naval base at Guantánamo Bay and even has a designated lookout from where guests view the base through binoculars. Booking 72 hours in advance is obligatory. **www.islazul.cu**

CAYO SAETÍA Villa Cayo Saetía $$

Cayo Saetía, Mayarí, Holguín **Tel** *(24) 516 900, 516 901* **Rooms** *12*

A chilled-out, unpretentious little cabin complex on the coast, perfect for relaxation. The well-equipped wooden cabins are thoughtfully and harmoniously furnished, perfectly combining a good level of comfort with a rustic decor neatly in tune with the natural surroundings. Jeep safaris can be arranged. **www.villacayosaetia.com**

GRANMA PROVINCE Club Amigo Marea del Portillo $$

Marea del Portillo Km 12.5, Pilón, Granma **Tel** *(23) 597 008, 597 102* **Fax** *(23) 597 080* **Rooms** *238*

A serene natural setting between the mountains and the sea make this three-star all-inclusive a perfect place to escape. From the pool area, with its mountain views, sloping lawns lead down to a lovely, shrub-lined beach. There are programmes of entertainment, including showcases of traditional Cuban culture. **www.hotelescubanacan.com**

HOLGUÍN CITY Hotel Pernik $

Avenida Jorge Dimitrov y Plaza de la Revolución, Nuevo Holguín, Holguín **Tel** *(24) 481 011* **Fax** *(24) 481 158* **Rooms** *200*

From the 1970s school of Russian-influenced hotel architecture, this relatively well equipped but unspectacular town hotel has a large oblong pool, three restaurants and several bars. More uniquely, there are eight "gallery rooms" dedicated to personalities from the world of Cuban culture, though the quality of these rooms varies. **www.islazul.cu**

HOLGUÍN PROVINCE Villa Mirador de Mayabe $

Altura de Mayabe Km 8.5, Holguín **Tel** *(24) 422 160* **Fax** *(24) 425 498* **Rooms** *24*

Perched on a hillside covered in flourishing dense woodlands and overlooking a valley surrounding the city of Holguín, the view from this hotel is a large part of the attraction of staying here. The comfortable rooms have modern conveniences. Facilities include a restaurant and a pool with panoramic views. **www.islazul.cu**

PARQUE BACONAO Villa Gran Piedra $

Carretera Gran Piedra Km 14, Santiago de Cuba **Tel** *(22) 686 393, 686 147, 686 395* **Rooms** *27*

At over 1,200 m (3,940 ft) above sea level, this is Cuba's highest hotel. The breathtaking views from this mountainside resort, woven into the ruins of a colonial coffee plantation, make it a very special place to stay, even though the amenities and facilities here are only average. Rooms are in stone and brick cabins. **www.islazul.cu**

PARQUE BACONAO Club Amigo Carisol Los Corales $$

Carretera de Baconao Km 31, Santiago de Cuba **Tel** *(22) 356 122* **Fax** *(22) 356 177* **Rooms** *310*

The all-inclusive Club Amigo Carisol Los Corales has its own section of beach and accommodation is spread out around attractive tree-studded grounds. Decent pool and a lively entertainment schedule, but the standard of food is average. There's a kids' club, and watersports facilities include catamarans and kayaks. **www.hotelescubanacan.com**

PARQUE BACONAO Hotel Costa Morena

Carretera de Baconao Km 34.5, Sigüa, Santiago de Cuba **Tel** *(22) 356 135* **Fax** *(22) 356 160* **Rooms** *115*

Overlooking the Caribbean and surrounded by the hills of the Parque Baconao, this is a great all-inclusive place to stay if you like the outdoors. There's a natural swimming pool as well as a standard man-made one, and all rooms have sea views. Hiking and trekking around the park can be arranged from here. **www.islazul.cu**

PLAYA COVARRUBIAS Brisas Covarrubias

Playa Covarrubias, Puerto Padre, Las Tunas **Tel** *(31) 515 530* **Fax** *(31) 515 352* **Rooms** *181*

This waterfront all-inclusive with landscaped grounds leading down to the beach is located close to a fantastic coral reef. There are facilities for snorkelling and diving, while other available activities range from billiards, table tennis and bingo to basketball, archery and exercises in the aqua gym. **www.hotelescubanacan.com**

PLAYA ESMERALDA Sol Río de Luna y Mares

Playa Esmeralda, Rafael Freyre, Holguín **Tel** *(24) 430 030* **Fax** *(24) 430 065* **Rooms** *464*

On a fantastic, broad stretch of beach backing onto wooded, palm-dotted grounds, this family resort has a lively, upbeat feel. Rooms are colourful and all feature either a terrace or a balcony. Amenities include six restaurants, two pools and two tennis courts, plus a beach disco. Horseriding excursions can be arranged. **www.meliacuba.com**

PLAYA ESMERALDA Paradisus Río de Oro

Carretera Guardalavaca, Playa Esmeralda, Rafael Freyre, Holguín **Tel** *(24) 430 090* **Fax** *(24) 430 095* **Rooms** *356*

This ultra all-inclusive set on a bayfront nature reserve has an exclusive feel and is aimed predominantly at the adults-only market, with facilities for weddings and honeymoons. All rooms are luxurious and tasteful and the two Garden Villas have 300 sq m (3,230 sq ft) of private grounds and their own pools and gardens. **www.meliacuba.com**

PLAYA GUARDALAVACA Club Amigo Atlántico-Guardalavaca

Playa Guardalavaca, Banes, Holguín **Tel** *(24) 430 180 to 82, 430 121* **Fax** *(24) 430 200* **Rooms** *747*

A vast all-inclusive complex with a variety of different accommodation choices, some in the large main building, others in villas of varying shapes and sizes. Dance and Spanish classes are offered alongside all sorts of sporting facilities with football, basketball, tennis, volleyball and archery all catered for. **www.hotelescubanacan.com**

PLAYA GUARDALAVACA Hotel Brisas Guardalavaca

Calle 2 no.1, Playa Guardalavaca, Banes, Holguín **Tel** *(24) 430 218, 430 162* **Fax** *(24) 430 418* **Rooms** *437*

A hotel village made up of attractive tiled-roof apartment blocks. The under-12s are well-catered for here with a kids' club, games area and a full programme of entertainment. Adults don't do badly either, and all doubles come with king-sized beds. **www.hotelescubanacan.com**

PLAYA PESQUERO Blau Costa Verde Beach Resort

Playa Pesquero, Rafael Freyre, Holguín **Tel** *(24) 433 510* **Fax** *(24) 433 515* **Rooms** *309*

At the heart of this luxury resort is the impressive and alluring pool, snaking around trees and buildings and featuring a poolside bar and restaurant. Other facilities include a beauty parlour, Jacuzzi, gymnasium, a diving centre, a disco and a cigar shop. There's also a babysitting service for a fee. **www.gaviota-grupo.com**

PLAYA PESQUERO Hotel Playa Pesquero

Playa Pesquero, Rafael Freyre, Holguín **Tel** *(24) 433 530* **Fax** *(24) 433 535* **Rooms** *944*

A staggeringly large all-inclusive hotel complex on the beach. The endless list of facilities includes three swimming pools, three Jacuzzis, seven restaurants, six bars and three tennis courts with spotlights for night-time games. Rooms are luxurious and feature all the mod cons you would expect. **www.gaviota-grupo.com**

PLAYA PESQUERO Playa Costa Verde

Playa Pesquero, Rafael Freyre, Holguín **Tel** *(24) 433 520* **Fax** *(24) 433 525* **Rooms** *480*

A beachfront mega-resort featuring a great selection of outdoor areas including a huge pool, a set of four tennis courts and a multi-purpose sports pitch all linked together by immaculately landscaped gardens. Indoors there's an extremely well-equipped gym as well as Japanese, Italian and Cuban restaurants. **www.gaviota-grupo.com**

SANTIAGO DE CUBA Casa Colonial Maruchi

Hartmann (San Félix) 357, e/ Trinidad y San Germán **Tel** *(22) 620 767* **Rooms** *2*

One of the most professionally run and characterful *casas particulares* in the city. The front rooms are furnished with colonial period furniture, and the delightful central patio has plants everywhere. A rooftop terrace completes the picture. Gregarious Maruchi runs the place.

SANTIAGO DE CUBA Casa de Leonardo y Rosa

Clarín (Padre Quiroga) 9, e/ Aguilera y Heredia **Tel** *(22) 623 574* **Rooms** *2*

This early 20th-century residence offers two guest accommodations – a small double room with a large bathroom, and located at the back of the house beyond the patio with its attractive water feature is a separate little apartment with its own garden gate, kitchenette with classic 1950s fridge and stone steps leading up to the airy bedroom.

SANTIAGO DE CUBA Casa Mundo

Heredia 308, e/ Pio Rosado (Carnicería) y Porfirio Valiente (Calvario) **Tel** *(22) 624 097* **Rooms** *2*

A colonial house right in the historic centre of the city. Though there is no single definable style, inside there is a genuine sense of the past and some great pieces of furniture, like the ornate early 20th-century dresser in one of the bedrooms. Both rooms have their own bathroom, but only one is en suite.

Key to Price Guide *see p252* **Key to Symbols** *see back cover flap*

SANTIAGO DE CUBA Casa Pedro Guillermo Martí Vázquez   Ⓢ

Corona 805, e/ Santa Rita y San Carlos **Tel** *(22) 620 101* **Rooms** *2*

This enormous colonial house, a stone's throw from the central park, has two rooms for guests. The hosts are kind and friendly, often inviting their visitors to enjoy refreshing drinks in the large front room, which is decorated with original tiles. The couple's children offer another two rooms in their own *casa* a couple of blocks away.

SANTIAGO DE CUBA Gran Hotel   Ⓢ

José Antonio Saco (Enramada) 312, esq. Hartmann (San Félix) **Tel** *(22) 653020* **Rooms** *15*

An everyday town hotel and the least touristy in Santiago de Cuba. Located on one of the main shopping streets, a couple of blocks from Parque Céspedes, this budget option is surrounded by hustle and bustle. Rooms are basic but clean and comfortable, and some have small balconies. **www.islazul.cu**

SANTIAGO DE CUBA Hotel Libertad   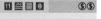 Ⓢ

Aguilera 658, Plaza de Marte **Tel** *(22) 627710* **Rooms** *17*

On the least touristy of the three central squares, this neo-colonial conversion has bags of character and is more stylish and refined than its price band might suggest. A dignified, columned, arched lobby leads onto wide corridors and a broad staircase ascending to the roof-terrace bar and sweeping vistas of the east of the city. **www.islazul.cu**

SANTIAGO DE CUBA Villa Gaviota Santiago de Cuba   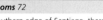 Ⓢ

Avenida Manduley 502, e/ 19 y 21, Reparto Vista Alegre **Tel** *(22) 641368* **Fax** *(22) 687166* **Rooms** *51*

Dotted around this enchanting neighbourhood that was home to the city's wealthy before the Revolution, the guest rooms here are in converted mansions, which have been divided into two or three apartments each. Some rooms share bathrooms. A purpose-built central building houses the pool and restaurant. **www.gaviota-grupo.com**

SANTIAGO DE CUBA Hostal San Basilio    ⓈⓈ

Bartolomé Masó 403 e/ Carnicería y Porfirio Valiente (Calvario) **Tel** *(22) 651702* **Fax** *(22) 687069* **Rooms** *8*

Tucked away on an old, narrow street a few blocks from the main square, this pleasant, tiny hotel is housed in a graceful colonial residence. It's the kind of place where you can't help getting to know the staff, with the receptionist doubling up as the waiter and the dinky kitchen and dining area occupying the same room. **www.hotelescubanacan.com**

SANTIAGO DE CUBA Hotel Casa Granda   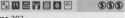 ⓈⓈ

Heredia 201 esq. San Pedro **Tel** *(22) 686600* **Fax** *(22) 686035* **Rooms** *58*

A magnificent colonial building on the main square in the heart of the city, this is ideal for anyone wanting to stay in the thick of the action. Rooms are in need of updating, but there is a roof terrace where you can eat and drink with sweeping views down to the bay. **www.hotelescubanacan.com**

SANTIAGO DE CUBA Hotel Las Américas   ⓈⓈ

General Cebreco y Avenida de las Américas **Tel** *(22) 642011* **Fax** *(22) 687075* **Rooms** *70*

The location on the aristocratic side of the city, with its broad, tree-lined avenues, provides what was formerly one of Santiago's most prestigious hotels with attractive enough surroundings to take the less attractive edge off this now dated-looking apartment hotel. As well as two restaurants and two bars, the hotel has its own cabaret. **www.islazul.cu**

SANTIAGO DE CUBA Hotel San Juan    ⓈⓈ

Carretera de Siboney Km 1.5 **Tel** *(22) 687200* **Fax** *(22) 687237* **Rooms** *110*

Right at the city limits, this is a laid-back place to stay set in attractive, verdant grounds with a large swimming pool around which many of the cabins housing the rooms are centred. The rooms themselves are nothing special but well equipped with satellite TV, radio, safety deposit box and en-suite bathrooms. **www.islazul.cu**

SANTIAGO DE CUBA Versalles    ⓈⓈ

Carretera al Morro Km 1, Altura de Versalles **Tel** *(22) 691016* **Fax** *(22) 686039* **Rooms** *72*

From this good-value cabin complex near the historic El Morro castle, beyond the southern edge of Santiago, there are fabulous views back over the city and out to the Sierra Maestra mountains. Facilities include tennis, basketball and volleyball courts. There is also easy access to the airport. **www.cubanacan.cu**

SANTIAGO DE CUBA Meliã Santiago de Cuba   ⓈⓈⓈ

Calle M el 4ta y Avenida Las Américas **Tel** *(22) 687070* **Fax** *(22) 687170* **Rooms** *302*

On a pleasant, leafy avenue away from the centre, this is the flashiest, most upmarket hotel in Santiago. The main building is a quirky, colourful high-rise block from which most rooms have stunning views. There are three good restaurants, and the impressive grounds feature a fantastic split-level pool, a basketball court and football pitch. **www.meliacuba.com**

SIERRA MAESTRA Brisas Sierra Mar   ⓈⓈ

Carretera Chivirico Km 60 **Tel** *(22) 329110* **Fax** *(22) 329116* **Rooms** *200*

A beach-front hotel in its own beautiful little woody enclave with the Sierra Maestra mountains as a backdrop. A great option for families with young children, as this all-inclusive has a play area and a series of entertainment programmes designed for 4- to 12-year olds. Many rooms have balconies with uninterrupted sea views. **www.hotelescubanacan.com**

SIERRA MAESTRA Brisas Los Galeones   ⓈⓈⓈ

Carretera Chivirico Km 72 **Tel** *(22) 326160* **Rooms** *32*

The sister hotel of the Brisas Sierra Mar *(below)*, this is the more intimate version of the impressive all-inclusive. All rooms have mountain and sea views. A minibus links the two hotels, 12 km (7.5 miles) apart, and guests can use the facilities at either, which include massage, jacuzzi, sauna, gym and tennis courts. Over 16s only. **www.hotelescubanacan.com**

WHERE TO EAT

In traditional Cuban cooking, rice and beans are the staples rather than bread, and the most common dishes are meat-based. Seafood also features heavily with shrimp, lobster and fish dishes found on a large proportion of restaurant menus. Different influences can be seen in Cuban cooking and there are local variations, especially in the east of Cuba. Food is rarely spicy. Besides international dish-

The neon sign at the historic La Zaragozana restaurant

es, local menus generally feature some specialities of *comida criolla* (Creole cuisine; *see p272)*. Places offering food range from state-run restaurants and hotel restaurants, usually comfortable and elegant, to *paladares* (ranging from informal to chic) that serve home cooking. In Havana there are also Chinese and Arab restaurants, and pizzerias are everywhere. Vegetarian restaurants are rare.

RESTAURANTS AND CAFES

Cuba's state-run restaurants used to have a bad reputation. However, standards have improved, partly due to competition from private *paladares,* and some state-run chains, for example **Palmares**, are well regarded.

Some of Havana's most delightful restaurants are housed in well-restored colonial buildings complete with period furnishings. Many have a view or a garden of some kind. Live music is often performed and makes for a lively atmosphere.

The restaurants in luxury hotels are usually high-quality and feature international dishes along with a good wine list. As an alternative to formal, à la carte dining, many hotels offer buffets, which in Cuba are called *mesa sueca* (smorgasbord), where, for a fixed price, you can eat anything from pasta to roast suckling pig with rice

The inviting dining room of the Tocororo restaurant in Havana

and black beans.

Some of Havana's most famous bars have a separately managed restaurant. Examples are the Bodeguita del Medio and El Floridita in Havana, and La Terraza in Cojímar. These are open all day serving snacks and cocktails, and offer a full menu for lunch and dinner.

PALADARES

The cheapest and best places offering Cuban cooking are called *paladares*. These are private restaurants offering a fixed price or à la carte menu inside Cuban homes. Dishes are often simple but can be surprisingly good – and often better quality than their state-run equivalents. However, be wary of people who accost you in the street and offer to show you a *paladar*: once there, your helpful guide will receive a commission and your bill will cost a few pesos more. Furthermore, your new friend may ask you to treat him to dinner!

Since Raúl Castro's moderate economic reforms in 2011, the private dining scene in Cuba has been transformed. Regulations that limited the number of tables per establishment were replaced by new rules allowing thousands of people to obtain licenses to run *paladares*. These are now also found in beach resorts such as Varadero where, previously, they had been banned. The greatest changes can be seen in Trinidad and Havana. In the capital, entrepreneurs have increased the range of dining options by opening chic, hip and elegant dining establishments, putting Havana on the culinary map.

Dining out at La Campaña de Toledo restaurant in Camagüey

Inside a typical *paladar*, which has traditional cuisine and live music

PRIVATE HOMES

It often happens that private homes offering rooms to let *(see p251)* also provide main meals as well as breakfast. Since the food normally eaten by the home owners is plainer than the food offered to guests, you will be asked to let them know in advance whether you intend to eat in or out. In general, the standards of cleanliness in authorized private homes are good. The quality of the food varies quite a lot: you may be lucky and eat extremely well, feasting perhaps on fresh lobster or prawns.

Sign of the Coppelia
ice-cream chain

SNACKS AND FAST FOOD

All kinds of snacks are widely available in Cuba. Virtually all *cafeterías*, inside and outside hotels, sell the classic Cuban sandwich, with cheese and ham, or hot dogs with mustard, ketchup and chips, to eat in or take away.

There is also an American-style fast food chain, **El Rápido**, where for a few convertible pesos you can get fried chicken with a side dish of *papas fritas* (chips), beer or *refresco* (soft drink). These places also offer *perros calientes* (hot dogs), *hamburguesas* (hamburgers), pizza and ice cream.

People eat either at tables or at the counter. This chain's standards of hygiene are usually high.

Along the major roads and on the motorways you will find the equivalent of small motorway cafés selling soft drinks, beer, fruit juice, pizza, ice cream and, sometimes, sandwiches. Some kiosks are set among trees, perfect for a relaxing stop in the shade.

The best ice cream is sold at the **Coppelia** parlours, which are found in many Cuban cities (the one in Havana is an institution, *see p98*). They are highly popular so be prepared to wait in a queue.

Lastly, you can buy food along the road from people who run small stalls in front of their homes. Food on offer may include pizza, sandwiches, fritters of corn or *malanga* (a local root vegetable), coconut sweets and peanut nougat. Around noon *cajitas*, cardboard boxes containing rice, beans, salad, pork or chicken, are a popular lunch option.

The same foods can be found on sale in the fruit and vegetable markets *(agromercados)* throughout the island. However, standards of hygiene may vary considerably *(see p302)*.

PAYING

In many restaurants and *paladares*, expect to pay in cash with convertible pesos. Only the better restaurants and hotels accept credit cards. At markets or on the road you can pay in Cuban *pesos*, although convertible pesos would also be accepted (change may be given in *pesos*). Restaurant bills should include a tip; add more to show appreciation.

WHEN TO EAT

Breakfast *(desayuno)* is served from 6 or 7am and, at most eateries, usually consists of a buffet offering fresh fruit, bread, butter, ham, cheese and eggs, yoghurt, milk, coffee and jam. Lunch is served from noon to 1:30pm, but many restaurants and *paladares* have adapted to tourists' needs and serve food well into the afternoon.

Dinner is eaten from 7 to 9pm. Don't expect to find a restaurant willing to serve you a meal after 10pm, except perhaps in Havana.

A branch of the fast-food chain, El Rápido, at Sancti Spíritus

Flavours of Cuba

Cuba's *mercados agropecuarios* (farmers' markets) are a cornucopia of fruits and vegetables fresh from the fields. Tomatoes, cucumbers and squash are staples, along with ripe *plátanos*, the humble yet ubiquitous plantain (a relative of the banana). Exotic fruits enliven stalls with their distinctive bouquets and hues. Poultry run around freely until ready for the pot, while home-fed pigs provide pork – the main meat. The government maintains a monopoly on the sale of beef, prawns and lobster, making them hard to find outside the state-run restaurants.

Guava paste and white cheese

A young Cuban farmer displays his harvest of plantains

COMIDA CRIOLLA

Traditional Cuban *comida criolla* (creole cuisine) is the main cuisine, based mainly on the frying pan and using simple ingredients, with little regional variation – not least due to national shortages of everything. It is a melding of Spanish, African and indigenous, pre-Columbian Indian influences. Local produce such as *calabaza* (a squash), yucca (cassava) and maize (sweetcorn), tomatoes, potatoes and bell peppers are combined with pumpkin and cabbage introduced by the Spanish. African vegetables include *malanga* (a root vegetable with a delicate flavour), *plátano vianda* (a variety of plantain that is eaten cooked) and *quimbombó* – okra, often called ladies' fingers.

Typically flavoured with peppers, onion, oregano and cumin, *criolla* dishes are usually served with boiled potatoes or other root vegetables *(viandas)*. Simple salads vary according to the time of year: in winter they might well feature lettuce, tomatoes, white cabbage and, at times, beets; in the summer they may include green beans, carrots, cucumber and avocado.

Custard apple   Plantains   Limes   Watermelon   Pineapple

Mango

Papaya

Some of the tropical fruits that add flavour and colour to Cuban cuisine

CUBAN DISHES AND SPECIALITIES

Cuba's zesty cultural mix has produced some superb national dishes, such as aromatic *ropa vieja*. Pork *(cerdo)* is a Cuban favourite, especially smoked loin *(loma ahumado)* roasted on a spit. The main accompaniment is white rice with black beans *(frijoles)*, often cooked together to form *moros y cristianos*, known as *congrí* or *congrí oriental* when the beans are red. Another common accompaniment is fried plantains, which are sometimes mashed and re-fried in patties *(tostones)*. Rice dishes, and even succulent roast chicken cooked in orange sauce, are often enlivened with *mojo*, a zesty sauce of garlic, oil and bitter orange. Main meals are usually followed by a fruit plate, or a relatively simple dessert such as flan or a fruit preserve served with cheese.

Black beans

Filete de pescado grillé *may be any grilled fillet of white fish, here served with tostones and white cabbage salad.*

Fruit and vegetable stall at a Havana farmers' market

The most ubiquitous meat on the island is ham; pork is also served roasted *(cerdo asado)* or as thin fillets *(chuletas)*. Chicken is usually coated with flour and fried in oil *(pollo frito)*, although it is also occasionally served fricasséed, accompanied by French fries. Fish and seafood, notably lobster and shrimp, is typically served in a tomato sauce *(enchilada)* or fried, grilled or baked with butter and garlic, as with sea bass and mahi mahi, which is almost always grilled. *Camarones* (meaty prawns) are served in many different ways – stewed, grilled, baked or boiled and garnished with mayonnaise. Breakfasts are usually limited to simple omelettes and a fruit plate, perhaps with bread and local white cheese (similar to Greek féta) plus yoghurt.

BARACOAN SPECIALITIES

Baracoan fare, from the far eastern side of the island, revolves around the use of coconut and cocoa, cultivated since pre-Columbian times

Cubans fishing in the evening on the Malecon in Havana

by the indigenous peoples. Coconut milk flavours *bacán*, a tortilla of baked plantain filled with spiced pork and cooked wrapped in a banana leaf. It is also used as a base in which to simmer spinach-like *calalú*. Red plantains, known as *plátanos manzanos*, are mashed with coconut milk to make *rangollo*. Cocoa forms the base of Baracoa's delicious chocolate and is the key ingredient of *chorote*, an ambrosial drink thickened with cornflour. Mixed with copious amounts of sugar (sometimes with the addition of grated orange peel and nuts), shredded coconut makes a delicious sweet.

ON THE MENU

Coco rallado Grated coconut in syrup, served with cheese.

Cucurucho Shredded coconut with orange, fruits, nuts and honey, pressed in a palm leaf.

Empanada Turnover pastries filled with minced meat, potatoes and other vegetables.

Filete uruguayano Pork or fish cutlet stuffed with ham and cheese, then baked.

Potaje Thick soup made from black or red beans with garlic, onions and herbs and spices.

Ropa vieja Shredded beef marinated and cooked with spices and onion, served with white rice.

Ajiaco *consists of vegetables, including plantains, which are simmered with meat and herbs to form a rich stew.*

Cerdo asado *is roast pork, usually served quite simply with rice and beans and often an orange sauce.*

Flan de huevos *appears on most menus. It is a typically Spanish dessert, similar to crème caramel but sweeter.*

What to Drink in Cuba

A wide range of drinks, both alcoholic and non-alcoholic, is available in Cuba. Imported wine is available in restaurants and *paladars*. Tap water is drinkable in many places but to avoid any health problems it is better to keep to bottled water. Visitors should be careful, too, about buying drinks such as fruit juice or fruit shakes from street or market stalls. In bars and cafés not up to international standards – especially in eastern Cuba – avoid ice in drinks like cocktails. In such places, it is advisable to stick to pre-packaged drinks, draught beer or rum.

Preparing refreshing *guarapo*, or sugar cane juice

BEER

Beer *(cerveza)* is the most widely seen and popular drink in Cuba. It is drunk very cold and at all hours of the day, as well as during meals. There are excellent bottled and canned Cuban lager beers, such as Cristal, Lagarto, Mayabe and Bucanero (the latter is also sold in a *fuerte* version, which is stronger and

Beer: Bucanero (strong) and Cristal (light)

drier). A drink similar to beer is *malta*, a very sweet, fizzy malt-based drink that is popular with Cuban children. *Malta* is sometimes mixed with condensed milk to be used as an energizer and tonic.

PACKAGED SOFT DRINKS

Soft drinks – lemon, orange and cola – called *refrescos*, either Cuban or imported, are sold canned. The Tropical Island range of fruit juices, packaged in cartons, is excellent. All kinds of fruits are used: mango, *guayaba* (guava), pineapple, apple, pear, orange, grapefruit, banana with orange, tropical cocktail, tamarind, peach and tomato. The most common brand of bottled water sold, still *(sin gas)* or sparkling *(con gas)*, is Ciego Montero.

HOT DRINKS

Hotel bars serve Italian espresso coffee or American coffee. The coffee served in private homes or sold on the streets is usually strong and has sugar already added. It is served in a tiny coffee cup. For a dash of milk, ask for a *cortado*; order a *café con leche* for a more milky coffee. *Sin azúcar* means "without sugar".

Black tea is generally not on any restaurant or café menu, nor can black teabags be found in supermarkets. It is best to pack your own. Herbal tea is more readily available; camomile tea *(manzanilla)*, for example, is easy to find.

SPIRITS

The most widespread and popular spirit in Cuba is, of course, rum. There are several different types *(see p75)*: the youngest – *silver dry* and *carta blanca* – are used in cocktails, while the aged rums *(carta oro*, five years old, and *añejos*, at least seven years old) are drunk neat. Besides Havana Club and Varadero, which are known worldwide, there are many other different brands of rum in Cuba. Among the best are Matusalém, an upmarket, aged rum from Santiago with a smooth flavour; and Mulata, which is very popular.

A "poor relation" of rum is *aguardiente*, which is stronger and quite sour, and drunk mainly by locals. *Guayabita* is a speciality of Pinar del Río, made from rum and guava fruit *(see p141)*. In addition, a range of very sweet flavoured liqueurs (such as coconut, mint, banana and pineapple) is available, usually served with ice or in cocktails.

A bottle of aged rum

FRUIT SHAKES AND SQUASHES

The most common fruit squash is lemonade, made with lime, sugar, water and ice. More nutritious drinks are the *batidos*, which are shakes made from fresh fruit, often mango and papaya. Milk, sugar and *guanábana*, not an easy fruit to find, make a drink called *champola*. Coconut juice with ice is a delicious, refreshing drink. Another typical Cuban drink is *guarapo*, which is made by squeezing fresh sugar cane stalks with a special crusher. It makes for a refreshing and energizing drink, but it is exceedingly sweet. To tone down the sweetness, Cubans add a few drops of lime or a dash of rum.

Coconut juice served in the shell

Cuban Cocktails

Cuba has been famous for its rum since the 1500s, although the rum the pirates loved so much was not the same as today's, but a bitter and highly alcoholic drink, at times sweetened with sugar and *hierba buena*, a variety of mint common in Latin America. This explosive mixture, jokingly called *draguecito* or "little dragon", is probably the ancestor of the *mojito*, one of the most famous Cuban cocktails. In the early 1900s a Cuban

Lime, used in all kinds of cocktails

engineer named Pagluchi and his American colleague Cox, while making an inspection near Santiago, mixed rum with sugar and lemon, and named the drink after the place they were in, Daiquirí. In the 1920s, during American Prohibition, Cuba, which had become an "off limits" paradise for drinkers, developed and refined these early cocktails and went on to create others. In parallel, the role of the professional barman (*cantinero*) acquired increasing importance.

Daiquirí frappé *is served in a chilled cocktail glass. White rum is placed in an electric blender and mixed with one teaspoon of sugar, five drops of maraschino, lime juice and crushed ice. Hemingway liked to drink this cocktail at El Floridita (see p277).*

Mojito *comes in a highball glass. White cane sugar is mixed with lime juice and a crushed stem of mint. To this is added white rum, and the glass is then filled with sparkling mineral water and chopped ice and the drink is stirred. The "temple" of the mojito is La Bodeguita del Medio (see p276).*

Cuba Libre *is made from rum and cola mixed with ice and lime juice. The drink was supposedly invented by US soldiers who took part in the Cuban wars of independence (1898). The name, Free Cuba, comes from the nationalists' motto.*

Havana Especial *is made with pineapple juice, silver dry rum, a dash of maraschino and crushed ice, mixed and served in a tall, slim glass. This cocktail has a very delicate flavour.*

THE *CANTINEROS'* CLUB

This club for professional barmen (*cantineros*) was founded in Havana in 1924 and sponsored by a group of Cuban distilleries and breweries. By the early 1930s the club had a central office on the Prado. The club's aims remain unchanged today: defence of the interests of its members, professional training for young people (who are required to learn the recipes for at least 100 cocktails), and English lessons. The club also currently promotes the Havana Club International Grand Prix.

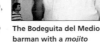

The Bodeguita del Medio barman with a *mojito*

Canchánchara *is made by the bar of the same name in Trinidad (see p182) with rum, lime, honey and water. It is served in an earthenware cup.*

Choosing a Restaurant

These restaurants have been selected across a wide range of price categories for their good value, quality of food and good atmosphere. In parts of Cuba, where there are no particularly recommendable restaurants, places that offer at least good value have been included. Alternatives are hotel restaurants (see pp248–69) and paladares (see p270).

PRICE CATEGORIES (IN CUBAN CONVERTIBLE PESOS – CUC$)

For a three-course meal for one including a cocktail, tax and service:
$ Under 10 CUC$
$$ 10–15 CUC$
$$$ 15–20 CUC$
$$$$ 20–25 CUC$
$$$$$ Over 25 CUC$

HAVANA

LA HABANA VIEJA Al Medina
$$$
Oficios no.12, e/ Obispo y Obrapía **Tel** *(7) 867 1041*   **Map** *4 F2*

The key to making the most of this Lebanese restaurant, whether in the lovely canopied courtyard or under the brick arches inside, is to not expect authentic Arabic food. *Pollo Musukan* or *Samac al Olivo* might sound like exotic dishes but are actually simply prepared meat and fish, grilled or fried without spices or sauces but with perfectly fresh ingredients.

LA HABANA VIEJA El Santo Ángel
$$$
Brasil (Teniente Rey) esq. San Ignacio, Plaza Vieja **Tel** *(7) 861 1626*   **Map** *4 E3*

There are original uses of standard Cuban ingredients at this highly respectable restaurant, producing dishes like chicken with a compôte of pineapple and spicy tomato. Choose from a table on the plaza, the pleasant central patio or the graceful dining rooms in this historic building.

LA HABANA VIEJA La Bodeguita del Medio
$$$
Empedrado no.207, e/ San Ignacio y Cuba **Tel** *(7) 866 8857*   **Map** *4 E2*

The most famous restaurant in the city, this is a tourist trap but at the same time has retained much of the alluring character that made it popular in the first place. Always packed, this grotto of narrow corridors and intimate corners is never short on sociable atmosphere. The Cuban meat and seafood dishes are good but don't quite match the ambience.

LA HABANA VIEJA La Casa de la Parra
$$$
Brasil (Teniente Rey) esq. Bernaza **Tel** *(7) 867 1029*   **Map** *4 D3*

One of the most inexpensive restaurants in La Habana Vieja, this *criolla* restaurant serves standard-fare meat and seafood dishes, all cooked in the usual Cuban way. Paella and lobster, both at half the price you'd pay elsewhere, also feature on the menu. A series of plain but intimate rooms make up the dining area.

LA HABANA VIEJA La Piña de Plata
$$$
Obispo esq. Bernaza **Tel** *(7) 867 1300 ext.134*   **Map** *4 D2*

This is the most conveniently located Italian and *comida criolla* restaurant in this part of town – you will almost certainly pass this place at some point, at the top of La Habana Vieja's busiest street. It serves average-quality pasta but generously topped pizzas, and is an inexpensive if somewhat soulless place to re-fuel.

LA HABANA VIEJA La Torre de Marfil
$$$
Mercaderes no.115, e/ Obispo y Obrapía **Tel** *(7) 867 1038*   **Map** *4 E2*

This Chinese restaurant in the most spruced-up section of the old city has a red and black colour scheme and some hearty, good-value chop sueys, including a vegetarian option. Soups are one of the specialities here, and all dishes are served up on fine Oriental china. There's an indoor pagoda and a simple central patio.

LA HABANA VIEJA Paladar Doña Eutimia
$$$
Callejón del Chorro 60c, Plaza de la Catedral **Tel** *(05) 281 5883*   **Map** *4 E2*

Old Havana's best *paladar* is, justifiably, always full. Dine on pork steaks, a mixed grill or a tasty *ropa vieja* (shredded beef) in an elegant dining room bedecked with wall clocks, fine prints, Art Nouveau lamps and small tables set with fresh flowers. It is worth trying to book a table in advance.

LA HABANA VIEJA El Baturro
$$$$
Egido no.661, e/ Merced y Jesús María **Tel** *(7) 860 9078*   **Map** *4 E4*

The waiters at this rustic restaurant usually offer a set-meal menu featuring a cocktail, black bean or chickpea soup, a main dish of lobster, shrimp, beef or chicken with *viandas*, rice and salad, dessert and coffee. Though not overpriced, you will be obliged to spend more than you would otherwise pay if you coax the à la carte menu out of them.

LA HABANA VIEJA El Templete
$$$$
Avenida del Puerto no.12-14 esq. Narciso López **Tel** *(7) 864 7777*   **Map** *4 F2*

This seafood specialist facing the harbour offers the best cuisine in La Habana Vieja. Significantly, the head chef is Mallorcan and breaks all the Cuban norms with plenty of flavours and variety. From an impressive set of starters like octopus *a la gallega*, to simple mains like lobster salad or fancier dishes like eel *a la vasca*, it's all top quality.

Key to Symbols *see back cover flap*

LA HABANA VIEJA La Dominica

O'Reilly 108 esq. Mercaderes **Tel** *(7) 860 2918*

There's a seafood slant at this decent Italian restaurant with smoked salmon on the starters menu, shrimp and lobster pasta among the specials and a number of shrimp and squid dishes. The laid-back pavement café is in contrast to the chandeliers and polished floors of the refined, rather formal interior. There's a good wine list here.

LA HABANA VIEJA La Mina

Oficios no.109 esq. Obispo, Plaza de Armas **Tel** *(7) 862 0216* **Map** *4 E2*

At the heart of the tourist circuit, this place is always buzzing with foreign clientele and is a lively place to experience Cuban creole cooking. The fish, pork and chicken meals are surprisingly well priced given the touristy location and there are seven dining areas to choose from, including the terrace on the square and a superior central courtyard.

LA HABANA VIEJA Café del Oriente

Oficios no.112 esq. Amargura **Tel** *(7) 860 6686* **Map** *4 F2*

This stylish café sits on Plaza San Francisco overlooking the handsome old stock exchange. Dine outside under parasols or enjoy the dark wood interior. Smartly dressed waiters serve some of Havana's most sophisticated cuisine. Rabbit, beef and plenty of fish are served.

LA HABANA VIEJA El Floridita

Avenida de Bélgica (Monserrate) esq. Obispo **Tel** *(7) 867 1299* **Map** *4 D2*

One of the plushest restaurants in this part of the city, beyond the classic bar where Hemingway famously used to drink, has soft furnishings and soft lighting but hard prices. Fancy dishes like shrimp in orange cream sauce or thermidor lobster characterize the menu, while the cocktail list is perhaps the most comprehensive in the city.

LA HABANA VIEJA El Jardín del Eden

Hotel Raquel, San Ignacio no.103 esq. Amargura **Tel** *(7) 860 8280* **Map** *4 E2*

The only Jewish restaurant in the city. In the elegant lobby of this fantastic hotel, this semi-formal place offers a distinctive eating experience. Parmentier potato soup and Milanese eggplant stand out among the starters, with *shashliks* (kebabs) featuring heavily in the main dishes. Unusual accompaniments like sweet and sour cabbage complete the picture.

LA HABANA VIEJA El Patio

San Ignacio no.54, Plaza de la Catedral **Tel** *(7) 867 1035* **Map** *4 E2*

A seemingly endless succession of bands keep the only restaurant on the Plaza de la Catedral lively day and night. This is a good place to try top-quality Cuban classics. The grilled lobster is expensive but very good, and the *Ropa Vieja* (shredded beef) is faithfully prepared. A choice of 11 rooms and a wonderful leafy patio.

CENTRO HABANA AND PRADO Casa de Castilla

Neptuno no.519, e/ Campanario y Lealtad **Tel** *(7) 862 5482* **Map** *3 C2*

The simple creole cuisine on offer at this restaurant in the heart of Centro Habana is fresh, well prepared and tasty, offering outstanding value for money. A sliding door at the back of a large entrance hall seals the dining room off from the noise and heat of the busy street.

CENTRO HABANA AND PRADO A Prado y Neptuno

Paseo del Prado esq. Neptuno **Tel** *(7) 860 9636* **Map** *4 D2*

Some of the best, most authentic pizzas in the city are served up on large wooden plates at this popular, down-to-earth Italian eatery. There are some seafood main dishes and 14 pastas, but the real focus is on the 21 different pizzas. Dimly lit, with a clubby vibe, this place is almost always bustling, even when neighbouring restaurants are dead.

CENTRO HABANA AND PRADO Casa Miglis

Calle Lealtad 120, e/ Animas y Lagunas **Tel** *(7) 864 1486* **Map** *3 B4*

A welcome addition to Havana's culinary scene, Casa Miglis is an uber-stylish Nordic-influenced *paladar* inside a colonial terraced house. Delicious meatballs, seafood casserole and grilled fish are just a few of the tantalising dishes on the regular changing menu. The funky bar is a great place to enjoy a few *tragos* of rum.

CENTRO HABANA AND PRADO La Guarida

Concordia no.418, e/ Gervasio y Escobar **Tel** *(7) 866 9047* **Map** *3 B2*

This *paladar's* original claim to fame as the apartment where the film *Fresa y Chocolate* was shot has been superceded by the reputation of its food and ambience. Whether the tasty chicken in honey and lemon sauce, or the rabbit in with *Caponata* (aubergine stew), every dish is imaginative and flavourful. Three cosy, eclectically decorated rooms.

CENTRO HABANA AND PRADO Roof Garden

Hotel Sevilla, Trocadero no.55, e/ Paseo del Prado y Agramonte **Tel** *(7) 860 8560 ext.164* **Map** *4 D2*

This ritzy gourmet restaurant on the ninth floor of the Hotel Sevilla owes its sense of occasion to the regal decor and furnishings, featuring an ornately crafted high ceiling and panoramic views through its huge windows. The offerings, like rum lobster, are vaguely French but definitely out-of-the-ordinary by Cuban standards. Open from 7pm.

VEDADO La Casa

Calle 30 no.865, e/ 26 y 41 **Tel** *(7) 881 7000* **Map** *1 A5*

At this exceptional family-run *paladar* in the heart of Nuevo Vedado, guests can either dine alfresco on the patio or in the air-conditioned dining room. La Casa's extensive menu includes rabbit in mushroom sauce, smoked salmon, paella and risotto. Thursday nights feature a spectacular sushi spread served by staff wearing Japanese dress.

VEDADO La Roca
21 esq. M **Tel** *(7) 832 3619*
$$$
Map *2 E2*

The food here is good – the grilled fillet of fish is a good choice, as is the better-than-average-value lobster, and beef is prominent on the international and Cuban menu – but more of a draw is the distinctive environment. Formal black-tie service in an Art Deco dining space with coloured-glass panels that give off a soothing light.

VEDADO Café Laurent
Calle M no.257, e/ 19 y 21 **Tel** *(7) 832 6890*
$$$$
Map *2 E2*

The smart alfresco dining terrace with its rooftop views of Vedado is not the only draw at this penthouse *paladar*. The food is delicious (think Uruguayan beef or squid tails in ink), the 1950s retro feel is stylish, service is faultless and the lunchtime five-course set menu for 12 CUC$ is unbeatable.

VEDADO Calle Diez
Calle 10 no.314 e/ 5ta Av y 3ra Av **Tel** *(7) 209 6702*
$$$$
Map *1 C3*

One of Havana's best *paladares*, Calle Diez boasts the city's only female *paladar* chef. The sleek monochrome interior in the elegant villa is a little austere at first, but the surroundings warm up with the professional service and outstanding food. The beef steak in pepper sauce and the mamey mousse are exceptional.

VEDADO El Polinesio
Calle 23, e/ L y M **Tel** *(7) 834 6131*
$$$$
Map *2 F2*

Below the lobby of the Habana Libre hotel, but accessed from the street outside, there is a distinct basement flavour to this moody, low-ceiling, bamboo-bedecked, Tiki establishment that specializes in Cuban-Asian food. Barbecued chicken is the house speciality. There's a good wine and cocktail list to choose from.

VEDADO Habanachef
Calle 24 no.360, e/ Calle 21 y 23 **Tel** *(7) 830 1410*
$$$$
Map *1 A5*

Offering one of Havana's best eating experiences, Habanachef is a professionally run *paladar* with a daily changing menu. Diners are shown a blackboard listing tempting offerings such as battered sardines, pumpkin soup, grilled tuna and rabbit – all of which is cooked to perfection. Unusual in Cuba, it also serves wine by the glass.

VEDADO Le Chansonnier
Calle J no.257, e/ 15 y Línea **Tel** *(7) 832 1576*
$$$$$
Map *1 E2*

A culinary star in the Havana dining scene, Le Chansonnier is a chic French-themed *paladar* popular with expats, tourists and Havana's celebrity set. Mango and avocado salads plus succulent duck in orange reduction are some of the tantalising treats on offer. Save room for one of the delecatable desserts. It is best to book ahead.

GREATER HAVANA (COJÍMAR) La Terraza de Cojímar
Real no.161, Cojimar **Tel** *(7) 766 5151*

$$$$

This restaurant is renowned for its Ernest Hemingway associations, and held more allure when it was frequented by the late Gregorio Fuentes – on whom the author based the protagonist in *The Old Man and the Sea*. You can still enjoy seafood soup, shrimp and various fish dishes surrounded by photos of both men and some big local catches.

GREATER HAVANA (HABANA DEL ESTE) Los XII Apóstoles
Castillo del Morro, Parque Morro Cabaña **Tel** *(7) 863 8295*
$$$$

From the sun terrace of this restaurant at the foot of the El Morro fortress, there are pleasant views of La Habana Vieja on the other side of the bay. Traditional Cuban food is served behind a battery of 12 cannons (the 12 "apostles" in the restaurant's name), which once protected El Morro.

GREATER HAVANA (HABANA DEL ESTE) La Divina Pastora
Avenida Monumental, Parque Morro Cabaña **Tel** *(7) 860 8341*

$$$$$

Get a table out on the terrace from where you can enjoy the fantastic views of the city and bay – the main reason for making the trip here. The Cuban cuisine is reasonable but pricey, and there's a varied selection of seafood. The excellent live traditional music also makes a visit worthwhile.

GREATER HAVANA (JARDÍN BOTÁNICO NACIONAL) El Bambú
Jardín Botánico Nacional, Carretera Rocío Km 3.5, Calabazar **Tel** *(7) 643 7278*
$$

Looking down onto the beautifully landscaped Japanese section of the Botanical Gardens, outside the city proper, this excellent organic, vegetarian outdoor restaurant has one of the most serene settings in the whole of Havana. It operates a buffet service, with herbs from the gardens flavouring the salads, rices and soups. Open lunch only, Wed–Sun.

GREATER HAVANA (MIRAMAR) Don Cangrejo
Avenida 1ra, e/ 16 y 18 **Tel** *(7) 204 4169*

$$$$

This waterfront restaurant with outdoor tables right by the ocean is one of Havana's finest seafood specialists. The large variety of dishes includes crab cooked in several styles, shrimp, lobster and its Gran Mariscada house special – a huge mixed seafood platter. It is famous for its poolside music nights.

GREATER HAVANA (MIRAMAR) El Aljibe
Avenida 7ma, e/ 24 y 26 **Tel** *(7) 204 1583*
$$$$

With a reputation for up-to-the-mark creole cooking going back many years, this top-class ranch-style restaurant is a great place to sample some classic national dishes. *Ropa Vieja* (minced beef), *Masas de Cerdo* (hunks of pork) and the house special, *Pollo Asado El Aljibe* (roast chicken in citrus juices). Plenty of rustic charm.

Key to Price Guide *see p276* **Key to Symbols** *see back cover flap*

GREATER HAVANA (MIRAMAR) La Fontana

Calle 3 no.305, esq. Calle 46 **Tel** *(7) 202 8337*

A well-established, well-run *paladar* offering alfresco and interior dining with nightly live music. The grill area and pizza oven add choice to the already varied menu, which includes charcoal-grilled octopus and delicious pork chops in a succulent mango sauce. The subterranean bar is a popular haunt with Havana's celebrity set.

GREATER HAVANA (MIRAMAR) Río Mar

3ra y Final no.11, La Puntilla **Tel** *(7) 209 4838*

At this restaurant in a stylish modern mansion with a fabulous terrace overlooking the sea in Miramar, diners can either eat inside on Philippe Starck chairs under chandeliers or on the popular terrace. Well-executed dishes include a full range of shellfish, such as octopus in pesto, as well as Cuban favourites like *ropa vieja* (shredded beef).

GREATER HAVANA (MIRAMAR) Tocororo

Avenida 3ra y 18 **Tel** *(7) 204 2209*

This smart but laid-back eatery in a fabulously decorated Miramar mansion is a good place for foodies. The main emphasis is on creole ingredients, including live lobster, and there are good beef steaks. Save room for a delicious homemade dessert such as coconut flan.

GREATER HAVANA (PLAYA) La Ferminia

Avenida 5ta no.18207 esq. 184, Reparto Flores **Tel** *(7) 273 6786, 273 6555*

In the decadent surroundings of what was once a residential mansion, there are four elegant private dining rooms with windows onto the beautiful garden patio, which holds more tables. Topping the list of exquisitely prepared international and Cuban food is *La Espada Corrida*, a full-on mix of six different tasty meats.

WESTERN CUBA

ISLA DE LA JUVENTUD El Cochinito

José Martí esq. 24, Nueva Gerona **Tel** *(46) 322 809*

Cubans and foreigners alike are charged in local Cuban *pesos* here, so the creole cuisine works out extremely cheap. Right in the centre of Nueva Gerona, this is one of the best-known restaurants round these parts, but don't assume this translates to top-end cookery. Like at most *peso* restaurants the food is basic, but good value.

ISLA DE LA JUVENTUD La Ínsula

José Martí esq. 22, Nueva Gerona **Tel** *(46) 321 825*

The only place in Nueva Gerona that can justifiably claim to have a bit of class, this is the most popular restaurant with tourists and has the most reliable meals in town. Their take on traditional Cuban dishes includes *Pollo Ínsula*, a chicken dish in a sweet and sour sauce with butter, and *Lomo Ahumado* (smoked loin of pork).

PINAR DEL RÍO Nuestra Casa

Colón no.161, e/ Ceferino Fernández y Primero de Enero

A meal here in the city's only *paladar* feels like eating in a giant tree house, with several tables set out on a roof terrace in the shadow of overhanging trees. Set meals of simply prepared chicken, fish or pork make up the limited selection here. This is a basic operation but it still offers better food than in all the state restaurants in town.

PINAR DEL RÍO Rumayor

Carretera a Viñales Km 1, Pinar del Rio city **Tel** *(48) 763 007, 763 051*

The best state restaurant in the provincial capital of Pinar del Río is out of the way, on a woody patch of land on the northern outskirts of the city. The smoked chicken is the best dish on a short menu, but the rustic surroundings of this wooden lodge and its tribal imagery give it character. Ring ahead, as opening hours are sporadic.

SIERRA DEL ROSARIO Casa del Campesino

Comunidad de Las Terrazas, Las Terrazas **Tel** *(48) 578 555, 578 700*

For a traditional farm meal, surrounded by animals, fruit trees and beehives, visit this farmer's countryside house where guests can help with the cooking, share with the family and walk around the house while waiting for the roast pork or chicken to be served. A nice experience.

SIERRA DEL ROSARIO El Romero

Comunidad de Las Terrazas, Las Terrazas **Tel** *(48) 578 555 ext.129*

This organic, vegetarian restaurant perched over the back of the village in an apartment block is a rarity in Cuba, offering a comprehensive menu of genuinely tasty, imaginatively prepared and presented dishes, including purées, soups, salads, pastas, pâtes, egg dishes and more. Each dish comes in large, medium or small portions.

VIÑALES El Palenque de los Cimarrones

Cueva de San Miguel, Carretera a Puerto Esperanza Km 36 **Tel** *(48) 796 290*

You can drive or walk around the outside of the *mogote* hill, behind which are the *bohío* roofs of this tour-group lunch-only stop, but it's more fun to go through the rock itself to the hideout location on the other side. Juicy chicken dishes and other creole food make up the menu. Coincide with a tour group and you'll get an Afro-Cuban show of music and dance.

Casa de Don Tomás $$$

Cisnero, el Adela Azcuy y Carretera a Pinar del Río **Tel** *(48) 796 300*

The only state restaurant in the village at Viñales, and one of few places open after dark, this ranch building surrounded by attractive gardens is always full of guests. The house special, the *Delicias de Don Tomás* – a weighty combination of meats and rice – is not for the faint-hearted. For more delicate palates there's good-value lobster, fish, pork and chicken.

VIÑALES El Olivio $$$

Calle Salvador Cisneros 89 **Tel** *(48) 696 654*

Located on the main street in town, in the heart of the action, El Olivio offers alfresco dining at one of three tables on the tiny terrace out front or in the airy dining room. Choices on the Cuban creole and Italian menu include fresh salads, lasagna and other pasta dishes, and the chef's special – roast lamb's back with caramelized onions.

CENTRAL CUBA – WEST

CIENFUEGOS El Criollito $$

Calle 33 no. 5603, el 56 y 58 **Tel** *(43) 525 540*

There are only five tables at this centrally-located *paladar* in a colonial house. There isn't a menu so the waiter will offer you a choice of chicken, pork or fish cooked to your requirements, each accompanied by copious amounts of fried plantain chips, rice and salad. A guitarist sometimes entertains diners with Cuban music.

CIENFUEGOS Bouyon 1825 $$$

Calle 25 no.5605, el Calle 56 y 58 **Tel** *(43) 517 376*

At this *paladar* in the heart of the historic centre, the fixed-price Cuban creole menu features grilled meat and seafood dishes. Pork, beef, chicken, fish or shrimps are served with rice *congrí* and *tostones* (crispy fried plantains). The price includes a side order of bread, as well as a dessert and coffee.

CIENFUEGOS Café Cienfuegos $$$

Club Cienfuegos, Paseo del Prado, el Ave. 8 y Ave.12 **Tel** *(43) 512 891 ext.112*

In the palatial Club Cienfuegos building is this refined seafood restaurant with a classic saloon bar and high ceilings. It is one of the best restaurants in Cienfuegos, if you want a sense of occasion. Fish, shrimp and lobster dominate the menu but there's also vegetarian paella and several meat dishes.

CIENFUEGOS Palacio del Valle $$$

Paseo del Prado esq. Ave. 0 **Tel** *(43) 551 003*

The ornate dining room in the magnificent Palacio del Valle is in keeping with the intricate Moorish architecture that characterizes the whole building. The food isn't quite magnificent, but the seafood platter and the lobster are good bets. Climb the spiral staircase to the delightful rooftop bar for views of the bay and city.

CIENFUEGOS El Tranvía $$$$

Avenida 52 no.4530, el Calle 45 y 47 **Tel** *(43) 524 920*

At this popular *paladar* staff dressed in tram conductor uniforms busy about the old tram converted into a bar while diners enjoy platters of fresh fish or chicken. The favourite dish is the *Espada del Tranvía* cooked with a mixture of chicken, chorizo, beef and pork, accompanied by rice and salads. It's enough to feed two diners!

PENÍNSULA DE ZAPATA Caleta Buena $$

Caleta Buena, Playa Girón **Tel** *(45) 915 589*

Some 8 km (5 miles) down a bumpy track beyond the Playa Girón hotel resort is this seafront ranch-style restaurant on a plot of land known as Caleta Buena. It's a wonderfully secluded and tranquil place for a seafood lunch. The open-air grill sits just above a lovely, clear natural pool. The entrance fee to Caleta Buena will be deducted from your bill.

PENÍNSULA DE ZAPATA Doña Rosita $$

Playa Caletón, opposite old cematery, Playa Larga **Tel** *(45) 987 517*

Located in the heart of Playa Larga village this well-run, neatly furnished *paladar* offers good value meals and professional service. The freshly caught seafood is grilled on the spot and served with salad, *tostones* (fried plantains) and *frijoles* (beans). The *mojitos* are a must, as is a quick sundowner in nearby Tiki's, a bar owned by the same family.

SANTA CLARA La Concha $$

Carretera Central esq. Danielito **Tel** *(42) 218 124*

Consistently recommended by locals as the best state restaurant in the city, this billing is accurate but very much relative to the low standards set by the competition. Here you will find basic pastas, pizzas and reasonable *comida criolla* (creole food). A large school-style dining room with a tiled mural provides the basic setting.

SANTA CLARA Los Taínos $$

Hotel Los Caneyes, Avenida los Eucaliptos y Circunvalación **Tel** *(42) 218 140*

The 12 CUC$ buffet in a reconstructed Taíno lodge setting at this hotel is worth the trip to the low hills beyond the southern outskirts of the city. With dishes based around pasta, traditionally prepared meat or plates for vegetarians from the modest salad counter, it offers a selection of food way beyond anything on offer in the city centre.

Key to Price Guide *see p276* **Key to Symbols** *see back cover flap*

SANTA CLARA Hostal-Restaurant Florida Center
 $$$

Calle Maestra Nicolasa (Candelaria) no.56, e/ Colón y Maceo **Tel** *(42) 208 161*

Visitors to this charming *paladar* in a 19th-century colonial home dine alfresco on a flower-perfumed patio. The host ensures that guests receive excellent service and enjoy his homemade dinners of lobster and shrimp in tomato sauce, or roast chicken with potatoes, while listening to Cuban tunes.

SANTA CLARA La Casona Guevera
 $$$$

Calle San Cristobal no.58, e/ Juan Bruno Zayas y Villuendes **Tel** *(42) 224 279*

At this popular *paladar* in central Santa Clara, the friendly family who run it serve up generous portions of Cuban creole dishes and barbecued food. Try the grilled fillet of fish or splash out on the lobster. Either way, you won't be disappointed. There's a good selection of desserts and wines too, and the *mojitos* are excellent.

VARADERO Chong Kwok
$$

Avenida 1ra esq. 55 **Tel** *(45) 612 460, 613 525*

The floor-cushion seating and low tables at this Chinese restaurant are more authentic than the food, but there are at least some chop suey dishes and a choice of stir-fried rice, all of it very reasonably priced. On the menu alongside these are some remarkably Cuban-looking dishes, including grilled lobster at just under 20 CUC$.

VARADERO Dante
$$

Parque Josone, Ave. 1ra, e/ 56 y 58 **Tel** *(45) 667 228 ext.103*

Unusually for an Italian restaurant in Cuba, the pasta dishes here are superior to the pizzas. That said, there are some sauces to be avoided, like the carbonara which has a very odd kick to it, and others which are much more dependable, like the bolognese. Ask for a table on the balcony over the lake for a wonderfully relaxing meal.

VARADERO El Bodegón Criollo
 $$

Avenida de Playa esq. 40 **Tel** *(45) 667 784*

With more character than most other restaurants in the town, this grey and red fairytale-style cottage with a small collection of intimate spaces has more than a passing resemblance to the famous La Bodeguita del Medio in Havana, with walls full of scribbled signatures. Good-quality classic Cuban dishes.

VARADERO Esquina Cuba
$$

Avenida 1ra esq. 36 **Tel** *(45) 614 019*

An open-air venue by the side of the road serving standard tasty *comida criolla*, this place suffers slightly from its unexotic location but regains a little lost ground with the 1950s memorabilia scattered around, including a genuine white and pink Oldsmobile and an old jukebox.

VARADERO La Fondue (Casa del Queso Cubano)
$$

Avenida 1ra, e/ 62 y 63 **Tel** *(45) 667 747*

La Fondue offers a unique menu by Cuban standards, based loosely on French-Swiss cuisine. The simple formula here is to cook everything with cheese. There are also less experimental dishes based on more familiar Cuban recipes. The restaurant itself is in a pleasant roadside building with a Mediterranean villa interior.

VARADERO Mallorca
$$

Avenida 1ra, e/ 61 y 62 **Tel** *(45) 667 746*

The reputation of Mallorca as a Spanish restaurant is owed almost exclusively to the fact that its trademark dish is paella, but the rest of the menu is Cuban. The excellent-value paellas come with either vegetables, shrimp, squid, chicken or, for the house special, a mixture of all four. A smart but homely interior in a handsome villa.

VARADERO Pizza Nova
$$

Plaza América, Autopista del Sur Km 7 **Tel** *(45) 668 585*

A pizza chain restaurant in a shopping mall might not sound like a great place to eat, but with a lovely view of the sea over tree tops from the balcony, and a good selection of appetizing thin-crust pizzas, this is actually a great option. There's a decent range of pastas, too.

VARADERO El Retiro
 $$$

Parque Josone, Ave. 1ra, e/ 56 y 58 **Tel** *(45) 667 316 ext.102*

Housed in what was once the residence of wealthy financiers, there's still a slight air of class about this place. The speciality here is lobster, served whole or on skewers, garnished with garlic or lemon or, in the case of the *Gran Grillada*, cooked and served with shrimp, beef and pork. The staff are approachable and friendly.

VARADERO La Campana
 $$$

Parque Josone, Ave. 1ra, e/ 56 y 58 **Tel** *(45) 667 224 ext.104*

Inside this restaurant with its rustic interior and large fireplace, there's a sense of being in an alpine lodge rather than in the middle of Parque Josone, with the sweeping, wooded grounds laid out before it. It's also one of the better purveyors of authentic creole cooking in Varadero. The house speciality is the Cuban classic, *Ropa Vieja* (shredded stewed beef).

VARADERO Mi Casita
 $$$

Avenida 1 y Calle 36 **Tel** *(45) 612 545*

Objets d'art and antiques artfully clutter this fine-dining establishment with friendly staff on Varadero's main street. The menu features tasty *criollo* food, with the Cuban food platter, accompanied by rice, soup, bread and butter, and followed by ice cream and coffee, offering great value for 7 CUC$.

...RO Steak House Toro $$$

...ra esq. 25 **Tel** *(45) 667 145*

Mea... vers will not be disappointed at this Canadian-Cuban joint venture offering North American-sized steaks. Lying cellar-like, a few feet below street level, this is a stereotypical steak house with a wagon wheel and beer barrel central to the decor. From six-ounce filets to chateaubriand, all appetites and wallets are catered for.

VARADERO Casa de Al $$$$

Avenida Kawama **Tel** *(45) 668 018*

On a beautiful stretch of unspoilt beach at the western end of the Varadero peninsula, this house was said to be the home of Al Capone and the centre of his bootlegging operations. The attentive service, fine-dining atmosphere and decor are amusingly at odds with the gangster-inspired menu of such dishes as "Lucky Luciano" filet mignon.

VARADERO Mesón de Quijote $$$$

Carretera las Américas **Tel** *(45) 667 796*

This hilltop restaurant, next to a tower, is conveniently located for some of the all-inclusive hotels in the area. The long dining room is lined with windows, although there is not much of a view. Most diners opt for the seafood (including lobster) but a choice of meats in imaginative sauces is also available.

VARADERO Las Américas $$$$$

Mansión Xanadú, Autopista del Sur Km 7 **Tel** *(45) 667 388*

A high-class establishment in the refined antique-furniture dining rooms of what was once a millionaire's mansion, the Mansión Xanadú (*see p262*). Nowadays it's an exclusive hotel and one of the best restaurants on the whole peninsula, serving Cuban and international *haute cuisine* and with a fantastic wine list.

CENTRAL CUBA – EAST

CAMAGÜEY Don Ronquillo $$

Ignacio Agramonte no. 406 esq. República **Tel** *(32) 285 239*

In the touristy Galería Colonial complex, a bar, coffee bar, shops and cabaret share an immaculately restored colonial residence with this attractive restaurant in an airy, covered courtyard setting where you can sample a number of traditional Camagueyan recipes.

CAMAGÜEY La Campana de Toledo $$

Plaza San Juan de Dios **Tel** *(32) 286 812*

An 18th-century townhouse typical of the plaza where it's found, with a large and leafy courtyard out back where there are several tables. Chicken, pork and fish feature on one of the better menus in the city, but for something a bit different there's *Boliche Mechado* – beef garnished with bacon served with fries and *congrí* (rice and black beans).

CAMAGÜEY Restaurant Isabella $$

Calle Ignacio Agramonte e/ Independencia y Lopez Recio **Tel** *(32) 221 540*

This cinematic-themed restaurant in the heart of the old town is a breath of fresh air in colonial Camagüey. Diners at this state-run restaurant sit in director's chairs surrounded by an assortment of film posters, antique cameras and other memorabilia while enjoying expertly prepared thin-crust pizzas, pastas and lasagnas.

SANCTI SPÍRITUS Mesón de la Plaza $$

Máximo Gómez no.34, e/ Honorato y Cervantes **Tel** *(41) 328 546*

This rustic restaurant reminiscent of a Spanish *taberna* has long wooden tables with benches, a wooden raftered ceiling with wrought-iron hanging lamps, and earthenware bowls at each table. The food is Cuban with a Spanish twist; the house tipple is *sangría* and there's a delicious chickpea soup. The selection of main dishes features beef stewed with corn.

TRINIDAD La Nueva Era $$$

Calle Simón Bolívar no.518, esq. Juan M. Márquez y Fernando H. Echerri **Tel** *(05) 290 3791*

Located in a stunning 18th-century Trinidadian mansion embellished with sumptuous antiques, chandeliers and mirrors, as well as a stuffed crocodile perched on a piano, this *paladar* offers a full range of Creole cuisine along with Mediterranean alternatives such as kebabs and paellas. Live traditional Cuban bands accompany meal times.

TRINIDAD Vista Gourmet $$$$

Callejón de Galdós 2b, e/ Ernesto V. Muñoz y Callejón de los Gallegos **Tel** *(41) 996 700*

Situated on a hill affording spectacular views of the old city, this friendly *paladar* offers tasty Cuban creole and Italian cuisine, superb spicy *mojitos* and faultless service. Dinner is a buffet spread for starters and desserts, while the main course is chosen from a menu that includes chicken stuffed with tapenade and honey. Excellent choice of wines.

TRINIDAD Restaurante de Iberostar $$$$$

Iberostar Grand Hotel Trinidad, José Martí 262, e/ Lino Pérez y Colón **Tel** *(41) 996 073*

The most expensive food in the town can be found in the fantastically plush restaurant at the Grand Hotel Trinidad. The buffet dinner is the biggest treat – an opportunity to feast on international food such as beef *carpaccio* (raw beef with sauce), *serrano* ham (green chilli with ham) and tiramisu. Hotel guests enjoy a 20 per cent discount.

Key to Price Guide *see p276* **Key to Symbols** *see back cover flap*

EASTERN CUBA

BARACOA Duaba
  $$
Hotel El Castillo, Loma de Paraíso **Tel** *(21) 645 165*

Not to be confused with Finca Duaba in the nearby countryside, this restaurant in the wonderfully located Hotel El Castillo, gazing over the town, is one of the best places for local variations on traditional Cuban cooking. Among these are chicken with maize and bacon or the fish and coconut speciality, *Pescado a la Santa Bárbara*.

BARACOA La Libertad
 $$
Calle Felix Frenes 14, e/ Ciro Frias y Céspedes **Tel** *(05) 871 8500*

This *paladar*, set in a Spanish colonial home decorated throughout with old Swiss clocks, is a delight. The Cuban creole menu changes daily but the house specialities of bacon and pumpkin soup and octopus in coconut sauce feature regularly. All mains come with soup, salad and rice.

BARACOA La Colonial
$$$
Calle Martí **Tel** *(21) 645 391*

Baracoa's only *paladar* is run from an elegant colonial home on the main street. Diners can choose from a menu that changes daily but always includes freshly-caught fish and shellfish. Prawns and fish cooked in a sauce made with the local *leche de coco* (coconut milk) are always delicious.

HOLGUÍN Salón 1720
 $$$
Frexes esq. Miró **Tel** *(24) 468 150*

This standout restaurant in a magnificently refined colonial building offers the tastiest food in Holguín, a mixture of international and Cuban delicacies. The plush surroundings enhance the experience, as do the names of the dishes, such as *Tesoros del Mar* (Sea Treasures), a lobster, shrimp and fish combination, or *Tres Reyes* (Three Kings), a mixed meat grill.

SANTIAGO DE CUBA El Barracón
$
Avenida Victoriano Garzón **Tel** *(22) 661 877*

This homely state-run restaurant pays homage to Cuba's *cimarrones* (runaway slaves) with its rustic decor and paintings commemorating those that worked on slave plantations. Here, diners can sit at long wooden tables and enjoy creative dishes such as hearty *carne pa' chango*, a tasty lamb stew, and fried plantain patties.

SANTIAGO DE CUBA El Morro
 $$
Carretera al Morro Km 7.5 **Tel** *(22) 691 576*

This outdoor restaurant, nesting on the edge of green cliffs by the fortress of the same name, has a truly spectacular setting outside Santiago at the mouth of the bay. It's worth eating here for the superb mountain and sea views alone. There's a wide choice of seafood, chicken and pork and there are 12 CUC$ three-course set meals.

SANTIAGO DE CUBA La Taberna de Dolores
$$
Aguilera no.468 esq. Mayía Rodríguez, Plaza Dolores **Tel** *(22) 623 913*

The sombre, shadowy interior lends this place a distinct character. Downstairs is a bar and café from where a hidden staircase leads up to the restaurant on the first floor. The balcony seats, looking down on the Plaza Dolores, are the nicest place to sit and order from the limited pork and chicken menu.

SANTIAGO DE CUBA Salón Tropical
 $$
Fernández Marcané no. 310 (altos), e/ 9 y 10 **Tel** *(22) 641 161*

The tables at this impressive, professionally run *paladar* in suburban Santiago occupy a plant-filled rooftop patio from where there are splendid views of the city; there's also a cosy indoor dining room. The unusually long menu includes seven different pork variations, a couple of liver dishes, fish and chicken, all cooked with care and subtly garnished.

SANTIAGO DE CUBA El Holandés
$$$
Calle Heredia no.251, esq. Hartmann **Tel** *(22) 624 878*

This city centre colonial home and *casa particular* with unusual Mudéjar interior decoration presents classic Cuban creole dishes with faultless service. The huge portions of pork, fish and chicken are accompanied by rice, salad, fried plantain and warm bread. The few tables on the terrace make an excellent people-watching spot.

SANTIAGO DE CUBA Zunzún
 $$$
Avenida Manduley no.159 esq. 7, Reparto Vista Alegre Viejo **Tel** *(22) 641 528*

On a broad, tree-lined avenue, in what used to be a very rich neighbourhood before the Revolution, is the 1940s mansion housing this classy restaurant. Divided into five compact and well-appointed dining rooms, the same restraint shown in the decor characterizes the menu which has just six main courses, all original takes on traditional creole cooking.

SANTIAGO DE CUBA La Isabelica
$$$$
Meliá Santiago de Cuba, Calle M e/ 4ta y Avenida Las Américas **Tel** *(22) 687 070*

An intimate and formal little *comida criolla* restaurant on the edge of the central garden court in the Meliá Santiago de Cuba. Despite the high prices at the top end of the menu, you don't actually have to break the bank to eat here. The curried chicken breast with plum and pineapple, for example, is only just over the 10 CUC$ mark.

SHOPS AND MARKETS

Tourists do most of their shopping in state-run shops, often in the hotels. However, the legalization of limited private enterprise has given a boost to the handicrafts and food markets *(mercados agropecuarios)*. In the past there wasn't much to buy, but now an improving range of souvenirs is available. All the same, Cuba is not the

Hand-made cigars on display for customers

place to look for designer outlets. State-run shops offer goods at fixed prices, which tend to be on the high side, whereas market prices are lower and may be negotiable. Cigars of guaranteed quality are sold only in specialist shops and in hard currency shops. Be very wary of buying cigars – or anything else for that matter – on the black market.

Handicrafts for sale at La Rampa market in Havana *(see p98)*

OPENING HOURS

Opening hours in Cuba are erratic but as a guideline *tiendas* (convertible pesos shops) are open 9am–7pm in the summer and 9am–6pm in the winter, while small shops open 9am–6pm all year round. On Sundays, shops close at 1pm. The fruit and vegetable markets are open on Sunday mornings, closed on Mondays, then open Tuesday to Friday from 8am to around 6pm. Fast food chain El Rápido *(see p271)* is open 24 hours a day.

HOW TO PAY

Most tourists will not use the local currency, the *peso* *(see p307)*, at all during their stay. Most goods that tourists want to buy, from rum to CDs, are only available in hard currency shops (most of which accept credit cards). In the food markets, the locals use mainly pesos, but stall holders will happily accept convertible pesos

(change may be in *pesos*). To buy *pesos*, go to one of the bureaux de change, called CADECA, found in most city centres and often near the entrance to major food markets.

WHERE TO GO

In the cities and tourist resorts, *tiendas* and supermarkets sell everything from cosmetics and clothes to tinned food, but do not carry the range of items seen in European supermarkets. Tourist resorts and larger

The logo of a popular *tiendas* chain

towns often have shops specializing in clothes. Tourist *tiendas*, especially in hotels, sell T-shirts printed with Cuban images including the inevitable portraits of Che Guevara, as well as *guayaberas*, typical Caribbean cotton shirts.

In the El Rápido *(see p271)* chain, and in the Fotoservice shops where film is sold and processed, visitors can buy soft drinks, rum, biscuits, sweets, butter and milk, as well as small household utensils and articles normally found in perfume shops.

Fresh fruit, vegetables and fresh meat are to be found only in the food markets.

SPECIALIST SHOPS

Cigars should be purchased in the specialist shops, often known as **La Casa del Habano**, which sell cigars direct from the cigar factories (and which may, in fact, be attached to a factory), and keep them at the right temperature and humidity level. Do not buy cigars from people on the street, as they are almost invariably fakes made

An outlet of the hard-currency Tiendas Panamericanas chain

by machine, rather than handmade, or are badly preserved, bear signs of faulty workmanship, or contain banana leaves and other rubbish. In addition, street vendors will not be able to provide you with an official purchase receipt, needed to take goods out of the country.

Branches of the **ARTex** chain stock a good selection of CDs, records and cassettes. Another well-stocked music store is **Longina**, in Calle Obispo, La Habana Vieja. Note that recordings of local music may not be available outside Cuba.

Paintings, sculpture and prints in the art galleries (www.galeriascuba nas.com) and in the *tiendas* of the Fondo de Bienes Culturales are sold with official authenticity certificates, which are needed for export.

A squash stand in the Mercado de Cuatro Caminos, Havana

Shelves with cigars in a Casa del Habano

La Casa del Habano
Real Fábrica de Tabacos Partagás, Havana. *Tel* (7) 866 8060; Ave 1, esq. 63, Varadero. *Tel* (45) 667 843.

Club Havana, Ave 5, e/188 and 192, Playa, Havana. *Tel* (7) 204 5700.

Tienda ARTex
Ave. L, esq. 23, Havana.
Tel (7) 838 3162.
www.soycubano.com

HANDICRAFTS

Cuba does not have a long tradition of producing handicrafts. Today, however, market stalls are found everywhere, selling all sorts of things from wood carvings and ceramics to embroidery, papier mâché objects and musical instruments. In La Habana Vieja there is a daily handicrafts market in the Almacenes San José and a second-hand book market in Plaza de Armas *(see p69)*. There is also a market on La Rampa in Vedado.

The market in Trinidad, near the central square, is a good place to look for embroidered linen and cotton. Crafts are also sold in state-run shops, in the Ferias de Artesanía and in the Galerías de Arte throughout the island.

MARKETS

The fruit and vegetable markets *(mercados agropecuarios)* in Cuba are lively and entertaining places to stroll around. Stalls sell fresh fruit and vegetables, pork and sausages, sweets, traditional food and flowers.

In Havana, the most central food market is in the Barrio Chino *(see p90)*, but the largest and most famous is the Mercado de Cuatro Caminos, south of the centre at Máximo Gómez (Monte) 256. The market is housed in a building constructed in 1922 and originally occupied by stalls selling Chinese food. It takes up a whole block.

Today the market extends out into nearby streets and includes stalls selling everything from meat to dried fruit. There are also cheap restaurants and stalls selling fritters, fruit shakes and juice.

Mercado de Cuatro Caminos
Máximo Gómez (Monte) 256, e/ Arroyo (Manglar and Matadero), Havana. ☐ *8am–5:30pm Tue–Sat, 8am–1pm Sun.*

A SOUVENIR IN FRONT OF THE CAPITOLIO

Photographer with his old Polaroid camera

In front of the Capitolio *(see pp82–3)* in Havana, visitors can have their picture taken with an original 1930s Polaroid camera, for one convertible peso. The photos develop immediately and the resulting picture, in black and white, looks just like a convincingly old photograph.

Embroidered table linen at the Trinidad market

What to Buy in Cuba

Dancing rag dolls

Apart from the famous Cuban cigars and excellent rum, there are many other good things to buy in Cuba: gold and silver jewellery, and hand-crafted objects made from local materials: wood, straw, papier mâché, shells, seeds, terracotta and glass. Cuban musical instruments are also popular choices. There are also toiletries and pharmaceutical products that are to be found nowhere else in the world, on sale in the international pharmacies and shops in the airport, where you can also buy books, video cassettes, DVDs and CDs.

Rum
This classic brand of rum can be bought all over Cuba. Bottles are also sold in boxes (especially at the aiport) to make them easier to transport.

Bauza
Cigars that do not meet the rigorous standards of the cigar-makers are labelled Bauza. However, they are still of very good quality. They are sold at authorized outlets at very reasonable prices.

A box of Vegas Robaina cigars

CIGARS
Packaged in elegant cedar boxes, Cuban cigars make a luxury gift *(see pp32–3)*. Copies, however, can be convincing: make sure that the box has the branded label *"hecho in Cuba totalmente a mano"* (totally handmade in Cuba), the official government seal, a hologram and the "Habanos" band.

Local Handicrafts
Raw material from the Caribbean (bamboo, shells and seeds) is used to make decorative wall hangings and colourful necklaces. Do not buy black coral jewellery: the coral is an endangered species.

A seed necklace

A seed and shell necklace

Musical Instruments
Many traditional Cuban musical instruments (see p31) such as claves, bongos, maracas, güiro, and tumbadora drums are made by craftsmen. They are sold in music stores and markets. Some, such as guitars, can be made to order.

Bongos

Hats and Baskets
Banana leaves and other plant fibres are used to weave typical hats and baskets of various shapes and sizes: an affordable, classic souvenir.

BOOKS AND CURIOS

Cuba's largest second-hand book market, held daily in the Plaza de Armas in La Habana Vieja, also offers coins, badges, stamps, and other memorabilia – cigar cards, wrappers, comic books and Bacardí factory receipts, for example. Collectors will also find stallholders at Fin de Siglo in Calle San Rafael.

A cedar-wood cigar box

PAPIER MACHE

The *papier mâché* technique is popular in Cuba. It is used to produce many items including masks, models, toys and knick-knacks. These articles are always painted in bright, decorative colours.

African-style figures

A mask representing the sun

WOOD

Cedar and rosewood are used to make small wooden figures that often draw inspiration from African tradition. Carved cedarwood cigar boxes always display elegant craftsmanship. Wooden objects can also be found on sale in the Galerías de Arte.

Doll

Model vintage cars

PERFUMES AND MEDICINES

The Suchel Camacho company produces very good perfumes, including spicy Coral Negro, flower-scented Mariposa and elegant Alicia Alonso, as well as quality face and body creams, at reasonable prices. The pharmaceutical sector is also in the avant-garde: PPG, an anti-cholesterol drug obtained from sugar cane, is also good for arteriosclerosis; shark cartilage strengthens bones in children and older people; and spirulina is a food supplement derived from algae. Excellent honey, with royal jelly and propolis (bee-glue), is also available.

Naïf Paintings
Markets and the Galerías de Arte sell naïf paintings of Afro-Caribbean inspiration depicting landscapes and views of colonial towns, or Afro-Cuban divinities.

Eau de toilette

Moisturizing cream

ENTERTAINMENT IN CUBA

The possibilities for lively entertainment are diverse in a country where there is tremendous love of music, dance and theatrical display. Ballet, theatre, concerts, festivals and sporting activities are in full swing year round. In most major cities, there are theatres and concert spaces, and even in the smallest towns you will find a Casa de la Cultura

An Afro-Cuban dancer in Santiago

or Casa de la Trova, hosting performances of traditional music. Visitors opting for a vacation at Cuba's many all-inclusive beach resorts will find canned entertainment mostly performed by hotel staff. Beyond the resorts, any street corner may easily be turned into an improvised dance floor with just the help of a CD player, and discos abound everywhere.

Attractive façade of the Teatro Tomás Terry in Cienfuegos

INFORMATION & TICKETS

Major tourist hotels distribute brochures free of charge, but usually these refer only to the costliest tourist venues, and general information on cultural happenings and locales is scant. A good online resource is **Cubarte: The Portal of Cuban Culture** at www.cubarte-english.cult.cu; try also www.cubaabsolutely.com. Tickets for major cabarets and international events can be bought at hotel tour desks.

THEATRE

Regional theatre is more restrained than in Havana. An exception is Santiago – its more than a dozen theatre companies include several experimental ones that, for years, have boldly sought new forms of expression. These can be seen at the **El Mambí** theatre or the **Van Troi/Cabildo Teatral Santiago** hall. The **José Martí** theatre is more traditional. The modern and prestigious **José María Heredia** theatre is particularly active

during the Fiesta del Fuego in July *(see p35)*. The **Teatro Papalote** company, in Matanzas, performs in its own theatre and is acclaimed nationwide. The world-famous **Grupo Teatro Escambray** performs in rural communities. Other major venues include the **Teatro Tomás Terry**, in Cienfuegos; the restored **Teatro la Caridad**, in Santa Clara; and the **Teatro Principal**, in Camagüey.

BALLET AND CLASSICAL MUSIC

Founded in 1967, the acclaimed Ballet de Camagüey presents world-class classical dance productions in the Teatro Principal *(see Theatre)*. Camagüey is also home to the **Ballet Folklórico de Camagüey**, one of Cuba's foremost troupes. In the Oriente, **Ballet Folklórico Babul** is based at the Teatro Guaso in Guantánamo.

Most provincial capitals have theatres where classical music performances are hosted. Travelling symphonica can be heard at Santiago's **Teatro**

Heredia; the more intimate **Sala de Conciertos Dolores** is a venue for smaller ensembles.

FOLK AND TRADITIONAL MUSIC

Traditional Afro-based music and dance thrives in the provinces and is particularly strong in Oriente and Trinidad, where visitors should look for splendid African-derived performances by the Conjunto Folklórico de Trinidad, which also performs Bantu and Yoruba dances outside Cuba, as does Trinidad's Cocoró y su Aché, which performs at the **Palenque de los Congos Reales**. Trinidad holds a *Semana de la Cultura* (Culture Week) each January, when *madrugadas*, songs sung in the streets, are performed. Holguín's *Semana de la Cultura* is perhaps Cuba's most vibrant.

Santiago is the home of the **Conjunto Folklórico de Oriente** and the **Ballet Folklórico Cutumba**, who perform at Cine Galaxia. In the courtyard of the **Museo del Carnaval**, rehearsals of groups

Performance by the acclaimed Ballet Folklórico de Camagüey

A traditional *son* band performing in a Trinidad street

preparing for Carnival *(see p229)* are open to the public.

Don't miss the evening training sessions in the various *focos culturales* from Tuesday to Friday. The **Cabildo Carabalí Izuama** rehearses Carnival songs derived from African musical traditions, while in the *foco cultural*, founded by Haitian slaves in the late 1700s, 18th-century dances are accompanied by Bantu musical instruments. Here, too, both the **Casa del Caribe** and **Centro Africano Fernando Ortíz** hold *rumbas* on weekends *(see p290: Cultural Centres)*.

Guantánamo is the birthplace of many traditional dance forms, including *changüí*, and is home to the annual June Festival Nacional de Changüí. At other times, *changüí* and its derivative, *son*, are performed by the world-famous Orquesta Revé and other leading local proponents at the **Casa de la Música**, the Casa de la Trova *(see p290: Casas de la Trova)* and the **British West Indian Welfare Center**. Witness Haitian folkloric dance at the **Tumba Francesa**.

The **Casa de la Cultura** in Pinar del Río is known for its *controversias*, a form of song in which two singers pit themselves against each another in creative impromptu verse. The **Casa de la Cultura** in Nueva Gerona is a centre for the local music and dance form known as *sucusuco*, unique to the Isla de la Juventud. And Las Tunas has an annual **Jornada Cucalambeana**

folkloric festival where local songsters perform *décimas*, ten-syllable rhyming songs.

NIGHTCLUBS, CABARETS AND DISCOTHEQUES

Most tourist villages and large-scale hotels in Cuba have clubs that open until late. Customers pay in convertible pesos; depending on location, most Cubans cannot afford them, so don't expect to find a broad cross-section of Cuban society.

Outside tourist resorts, most nightclubs are associated with cabarets. The most important are the **Tropicana**, in both Matanzas and Santiago. Varadero also offers two excellent *cabarets espéctaculos*: the large-scale **Cabaret Continental**, and the **Cueva del Pirata**, where shows are held in an atmospheric natural cave. It also now boasts a **Casa de la Musicá**. Every other major town has at least one cabaret, which turn into nightclubs with dancing once the show ends.

Most discos are based in the tourist resorts, concentrated in Varadero. These are large, modern discos featuring loud music (usually a mix of salsa and other Latin sounds with world-beat), neon lighting and simple decor. The entry fee is in convertible pesos and is usually quite expensive. Several such discos are for hotel patrons only. For these reasons, the majority of the customers are foreigners. However, there is usually a sprinkling of young Cuban couples, as well as wayward singles waiting outside in the hope of partnering with a foreigner for entry (occasional police sweeps occur, when Cubans being too friendly with foreigners are arrested).

The best such clubs in Varadero are **Mambo Club** and **Palacio de la Rumba**. All three are popular with Cubans, who often travel many miles to party until dawn. The most unusual venue is Trinidad's Disco Ayala, deep inside a cave.

You can also listen to modern "música popular" in Casas de la Música in a few major cities. The principal venue, the **Casa de la Música de Trinidad**, hosts concerts by local groups. Several open-air ruins in Trinidad are also used as nightclubs. The **Patio de Artex** in Cienfuegos is also bursting with energy on weekends; and the **Club Benny Moré** is a 1950s-style nightclub with disco following comedy and cabaret.

Santiago's venerable hot-spots are the **Patio de Artex**, **Casa de la Trova** and **Casa de las Tradiciones**.

One of the Tropicana dancers in a typically exotic costume

Live music and dancing at an intimate Casa de la Trova

CASAS DE LA TROVA

The traditional and intimate Casas de la Trova are clubs where people can listen to live music, dance or just relax over a cocktail. First opened in 1959 in almost all Cuban provincial capitals, these were originally places where older musicians, interpreters of traditional *trova*, could perform and educate younger people in their musical skills. Today, Casas de la Trova are found in virtually every town and even in rural villages and are usually the most important musical venues. Many also organize lectures, conferences, poetry readings and art exhibitions, thus maintaining their original spirit as keepers of tradition.

In some places, such as in Santiago and Trinidad, Casas de la Trova have geared themselves to tourists, with a bar offering different Cuban cocktails, and a shop selling CDs, DVDs, books and souvenirs. Whatever the style, Casas de la Trova continue to be popular with Cubans of all ages and offer plenty of atmosphere.

The most important Casas de la Trova are in **Santiago**, home of *son*, and **Trinidad**, where the classical tradition of the *trova* prevails. The *trova* at **Bayamo** has a faster rhythm and stronger Afro-Caribbean overtones, while **Camagüey** focuses more on melodic tunes. Some Casas de la Trova are associated with venerated musicians, such as Casa de la Trova "El Guayabero" in **Holguín**, where the esteemed

Faustino Oramas "El Guayabero" Osorio performed.

In some towns, traditional *trova* activities are held in the Casas de la Cultura, charged with a more broadly based mandate to preserve traditional culture. In **Baracoa** and **Sancti Spíritus**, for example, they put on performances by *repentistas* (improvisers). The Casa de la Cultura in **Pinar del Río** hosts performances of *punto guajiro*, country-style music centred around improvisation.

A less touristy alternative to the Casa de la Trova is the Casa de las Tradiciones *(see Nightclubs, Cabarets and Discotheques)* in Santiago, a good place to see up-and-coming local groups.

CULTURAL CENTRES

The Casa de la Cultura is an institution in every Cuban city. These cultural centres foster various forms of artistic expression: the figurative arts, poetry and music. Trinidad and Santiago are the most active cities culturally.

In Santiago, those interested in anthropology and religion can visit the **Centro Cultural Africano Fernando Ortíz**, dedicated to the African influences in Cuba, and the **Casa del Caribe**, which organizes an annual Caribbean Cultural Festival. The eclectic fare at the **Ateneo Cultural** ranges from poetry readings to rap performances.

UNEAC (National Writers and Artists' Union), with branches in a number of cities, puts on exhibitions, conferences and concerts.

The Holguín and Santiago branches are particularly active and host cultural debates, art shows and music shows, as well as poetry readings.

CHILDREN

Cuba has plenty of children's playgrounds, including rather basic fairgrounds in Santiago and other major cities. The most complete fairground is Varadero's basic **Todo En Uno**, which has a tiny roller-coaster, *carros locos* (bumper cars) and other attractions. Nearby, Parque Retiro Josone *(see p162)* has a miniature train among its attractions for children. At the **Delfinario de Varadero**, daily dolphin shows delight children; swimming with these creatures is also permitted.

Cuba has four other provincial dolphin shows: at **Delfinario de Rancho Luna**, near Cienfuegos; **Delfinario Cayo Santa María**, located near Cayo Ensenachos; **Acuario Cayo Naranjo**, at Guardalavaca; and Acuario Baconao *(see p235)*.

Several cities – notably Santa Clara and Bayamo – have goat-drawn cart rides for children in the main squares.

The **Teatro Guignol** is a noted children's puppet theatre founded in 1959. All year round, plays and puppet shows are performed, as they are in many other Cuban cities. Holiday villages provide safe play areas for small children, as well as shallow swimming pools and children's activity programmes.

Swimming with a dolphin at the Acuario Cayo Naranjo

DIRECTORY

THEATRE

El Mambí
Calle Bartolomé Masó 303, Santiago de Cuba.

Grupo Teatro Escambray
La Macagua, Manicaragua. *Tel (42) 491 393.*

José María Heredia
Ave. las Américas, Santiago de Cuba. *Tel (22) 643 178.*

José Martí
Calle Santo Tomás, Santiago de Cuba.
Tel (22) 620 507.

Teatro la Caridad
Calle Marta Abreu e/ Máximo Gómez y Lorda, Santa Clara. *Tel (42) 205 548.*

Teatro Papalote
Calle Daoíz y Ayuntamiento, Matanzas. *Tel (45) 244 672.*

Teatro Principal
Padre Valencia 64, Camagüey.
Tel (32) 293 048.

Teatro Tomás Terry
Plaza Martí, Cienfuegos.
Tel (43) 511 026.

Van Troi/Cabildo Teatral Santiago
Calle Saco 415, Santiago de Cuba. *Tel (22) 626 888.*

BALLET AND CLASSICAL MUSIC

Ballet Folklórico Babul
Paseo 855 e/ Cuartel y Ahogados, Guantánamo. *Tel (21) 327 940.*

Ballet Folklórico de Camagüey
Calle Pobre esq. Triana, Camagüey.
Tel (32) 298 512.

Sala de Conciertos Dolores
Aguilera esq. Mayía Rodríguez, Santiago de Cuba.
Tel (22) 652 356.

Teatro Heredia
Ave. las Américas, esq. Ave. de los Desfiles, Santiago de Cuba.
Tel (22) 643 178

FOLK AND TRADITIONAL MUSIC

Ballet Folklórico Cutumba
Cine Galaxia, Calle Trocha esq. Santa Ursula, Santiago de Cuba.
Tel (22) 655 173.

British West Indian Welfare Center
Serafín Sánchez 663, e/ Paseo y Narciso López, Guantánamo.
Tel (21) 325 297.

Cabildo Carabalí Izuama
Calle Pío Rosado, e/ San Mateo y San Antonio, Santiago de Cuba.

Casa de la Cultura
Calle 24 esq. 37, Nueva Gerona. *Tel (48) 323 591.* Marti 65, Pinar del Río.
Tel (48) 752 324.

Casa de la Música
Calixto García e/ Crombet y Gulo, Guantánamo.
Tel (21) 327 266.

Conjunto Folklórico de Oriente
Calle Hartmann 407, Santiago de Cuba.

Jornada Cucalambeana
Las Tunas, late June (see p35).

Museo del Carnaval
Heredia 304, Santiago de Cuba. *Tel (22) 626 955.*

Palenque de los Congos Reales
Echerri 146, esq. Jesús Menéndez, Trinidad.
Tel (41) 994 512.

Tumba Francesa
Calle Serafín Sánchez 715, Guantánamo.

NIGHTCLUBS, CABARETS AND DISCOTHEQUES

Cabaret Continental
Hotel Varadero Internacional, Varadero.
Tel (45) 667 038.

Casa de la Música de Trinidad
Calle Rosario 3, Casco Histórico.
Tel (41) 996 622.

Casa de la Música de Varadero
Av. Playa e/ Calle 42 y 43.
Tel (45) 668 918.

Casa de las Tradiciones
Calle Rabí 154, Santiago de Cuba.
Tel (22) 653 892.

Club Benny Moré
Avenida 54 2907, e/ 29 y 31, Cienfuegos.
Tel (43) 551 674.

Cueva del Pirata
Autopista Sur, Km 11, Varadero.
Tel (45) 667 751.

Mambo Club
Club Amigo Varadero, Carretera Las Morlas.
Tel (45) 668 565.

Palacio de la Rumba
Hotel Bella Costa, Ave. las Américas, Varadero.
Tel (45) 668 210.

Patio de Artex
Ave. 16 y Calle 35, Cienfuegos.
Tel (43) 551 255.
Heredia 304, Santiago de Cuba. *Tel (22) 654 814.*

Tropicana de Matanzas
Autopista Varadero Km 4.5. *Tel (45) 265 380.*

Tropicana de Santiago
Autopista Nacional Km 1.5. *Tel (22) 642 579.*

CASAS DE LA TROVA

Baracoa
Calle Maceo 149.

Bayamo
Calle Martí esq. Maceo.
Tel (23) 425 673.

Camagüey
Calle Cisneros y Martí.
Tel (32) 291 357.

Holguín
Calle Maceo 174.

Pinar del Río
Gerardo Medina 108.
Tel (48) 754 794.

Sancti Spíritus
Casa de la Cultural, Zerquera esq. Ernest Valdes.

Santiago
Heredia 208.
Tel (22) 652 689.

Trinidad
Calle Echerrí 29.
Tel (41) 996 445.

CULTURAL CENTRES

Ateneo Cultural
Félix Peña e/ Castillo Duany y Diego Palacios, Santiago de Cuba.
Tel (22) 623 635.

Casa del Caribe
Calle 13 154, Santiago de Cuba. *Tel (22) 643 609*

Centro Cultural Africano Fernando Ortíz
Manduley esq. Calle 5, Santiago de Cuba.
Tel (22) 642 487.

UNEAC de Holguín
Libertad 148.
Tel (24) 474 066.

CHILDREN

Acuario Cayo Naranjo
Carretera a Guardalavaca.
Tel (24) 430 445.

Delfinario Cayo Santa María
Carretera Cayo Santa María. *Tel (42) 350 013.*

Delfinario de Rancho Luna
Carretera a Pasacaballo.
Tel (43) 548 120.

Delfinario de Varadero
Autopista Km 11. Varadero. *Tel (45) 66 8031.*

Teatro Guignol
San Basilio e/ San Felix y San Pedro.
Tel (22) 628 713.

Todo En Uno
Autopista Sur y Calle 54, Varadero.

Spectator Sports

After the revolution, the government abolished professional sports and invested large amounts of money in physical education and amateur sports, and as a result some outstandingly successful sportsmen and women have emerged. Baseball and boxing are by far the most popular sports (baseball is virtually a national obsession), but volleyball, basketball, football and athletics are also widely practised. Major sporting events are held in Havana and televised throughout the island.

The Cuban national women's volleyball team in action

INFORMATION AND TICKETS

It is both easy and cheap to go to a baseball game; in fact, tickets cost only a few Cuban *pesos*, which is less than a dollar. Tickets can be purchased directly at the stadium box office just before the game.

The major stadiums have specially reserved seating areas for foreign spectators.

MULTI-PURPOSE SPORTS ARENAS

A new stadium, the **Estadio Panamericano** sports complex, was built in the Habana del Este quarter of the capital for the 1991 Pan-American Games. It is now a major venue for athletics. Cuba has produced some great athletes, including Javier Sotomayor, Ana Fidelia Quirot and Ivan Pedroso (*see p19*). The centre also has pools for swimming competitions, water polo and synchronized swimming, tennis courts and a velodrome.

The **Sala Polivalente Ramón Fonst** in Vedado specializes in volleyball and basketball, while the **Coliseo de la Ciudad Deportiva** in the Boyeros district hosts national and international volleyball, basketball, boxing and fencing matches.

BASEBALL

This is the national sport. It has been a passion here for over a century, and today's teams are world-class. The first baseball stadium in Havana was built in 1881 and the first amateur championship was held in 1905. The official baseball season is from November to March, and games are played on Tuesdays, Wednesdays, Thursdays and Saturdays at 1:30 and 8pm and on Sundays at 1:30pm.

Watching a game is fun; many families attend and there is always a good atmosphere. Games are played in the **Estadio Latinoamericano**, inaugurated in 1946, which has a seating capacity of 55,000.

BOXING

Cuba has won several Olympic boxing titles. The founder of the modern school of boxing is Alcides Sagarra, a trainer who has been active in the profession since 1960, producing such greats as Teófilo Stevenson (1852–2012), the Olympic heavyweight champion, who set up his own school.

At the annual Girardo Córdova Cardín tournament, expert boxers fight against emerging ones; this is part of the selection procedure for the Equipo Cuba, one of the best boxing teams in the world.

Fights can be seen at the **Sala Kid Chocolate**, located opposite the Capitolio in Centro Habana.

DIRECTORY

MULTI-PURPOSE SPORTS ARENAS

Coliseo de la Ciudad Deportiva
Ave. de Rancho Boyeros y Via Blanca, Havana.
Tel (7) 648 7047.

Estadio Panamericano
Carretera de Cojímar, km 4.5 y Ave. Monumental.
Tel (7) 870 6526.

Sala Polivalente Ramón Fonst
Ave. Independencia e/ 19 de Mayo y Bruzón, Havana.
Map 2 E4.
Tel (7) 882 0000.

BASEBALL

Estadio Latinoamericano
Calle Zequeira, El Cerro, Havana.
Tel (7) 870 6526/6312.

BOXING

Sala Kid Chocolate
Paseo de Martí (Prado) y Diablí, Havana. **Map** 4 D3.
Tel (7) 861 1546.

Cuba's national baseball team during a game

Outdoor Activities

The logo of Cubadeportes

The varied Cuban landscape allows for a wide range of outdoor activities. Facilities for a variety of water sports along the coast are increasingly good, particularly in the north, and mountain ranges and nature parks have just as much to offer. Tourist centres are equipped with exercise gyms, swimming pools and tennis courts, and also organize trekking and horse riding excursions. For athletes and fitness fanatics who want to stay in good shape, the state-run Cubadeportes organization makes it possible to experience Cuban sports at first-hand by arranging meetings with local athletes and the provision of special courses.

Beach volleyball at a tourist village on Cayo Largo

DIVING

With 5,746 km (3,570 miles) of coastline and over 4,000 small islands, Cuba is one of the supreme places in the Caribbean for diving enthusiasts. The crystal-clear water (with a temperature ranging from 23–30° C, 70–85° F) and variety of sea beds in particular make the Cuban sea a paradise for scuba divers at any time of year. Thanks to the coral reef and numerous offshore islands *(cayos)*, there are no strong currents along the coast and the horizontal visibility under water is hardly ever less than 40 m (130 ft).

There is an abundance of sites along the coral reef for both wall and platform dives. Punta Perdiz, in the Bahía de Cochinos (Bay of Pigs) is a spectacular wall dive. Besides all kinds of coral, on the sea bed divers can see gorgonian fans and sponges, all manner of multi-coloured fish *(see p147)*, tarpons, barracuda, sea turtles, large lobsters, beautiful anemones, and perhaps even sharks. A family of bull

sharks lives in the Boca de Nuevitas (near Playa Santa Lucía), and the area can be visited with the instructors from the **Shark's Friends** diving centre.

There are also fascinating shipwrecks to explore. In the past the island's bays were used as refuges for pirate galleons, and in some areas, such as Playa Santa Lucía, divers can still see anchors and cannons – relics from the 19th century – lying on the sea floor. Military enthusiasts can see Soviet vessels and aircraft among the more recent sunken craft. Underwater tunnels and grottoes add to the attractions.

Tourism has spurred the number of diving centres and the modernization of existing clubs that can be found spotted all over Cuba's coastline and located in every holiday resort.

Scuba centres have all the latest facilities as well as trained international-level instructors, and offer courses for all levels of ability. Some,

such as the Hotel Colony on Isla de la Juventud *(see p150)*, also have decompression chambers. Divers can hire all the equipment they need on site; however, it is advisable to bring along indispensable items such as a depth gauge and a knife.

The most important diving centres *(centros de buceo)* are **El Colony** on Isla de la Juventud (best suited to experienced divers), **Avalon** at Jardines de la Reina, the **Centro de Buceo María La Gorda** and **Green Moray** at Cayo Guillermo. It is possible to dive from the shore at Playa Santa Lucía and Playa Girón. Other operators can be found at Varadero and Guardalavaca.

The Jardines de la Reina islands are also wonderful places to dive, although they can only be reached by sea. Cruise yachts take scuba divers to sites with unspoiled sea floors, where sea turtles can be seen.

For information concerning diving in general, contact **Marlin Náutica**.

SURFING AND WINDSURFING

At the main seaside resorts (Varadero, Guardalavaca, Cayo Largo, Cayo Coco and Marea del Portillo) conditions are ideal for surfing and windsurfing, and at the larger holiday villages all the necessary equipment can be hired.

A scuba diver exploring a shipwreck off the Playa Santa Lucía *(see p206)*

Enjoying the sea on a catamaran hired from a tourist marina

SAILING AND MOTORBOATS

Thanks to its position at the entrance to the Gulf of Mexico, Cuba makes an ideal stopping-off point for yachts and sailing boats. The tourist marinas, many of which belong to the **Marinas Marlin** chain *(see p250)*, provide a series of facilities and services, including motor-boats and catamarans for hire and yacht excursions.

Most sailing is done around the Archipiélago de los Canarreos, south of the main-land. The best season for sailing is from December to April, because the climate is mild, the winds are not too strong, and storms infrequent. However, Cuba is surrounded by generally tranquil waters, and there are plenty of bays if shelter is needed.

FISHING

Fishing enthusiasts will be in their element in Cuba. The northwestern coast is marvellous for deep-sea fishing, where the catch might include swordfish, tuna or mackerel, while fish such as tarpon can be caught off the southern coast.

Fishing is often one of the activities provided by marinas and holiday villages. Holidays tailor-made for fishermen are organized by Marlin Náutica and **Cubanacán**.

In June, the Marina Heming-way, along the north coast west of Havana *(see p137)*, is the venue for the Ernest Hemingway International Billfishing Tournament, a com-petition reserved for expert marlin fishermen *(see p35)*. The original rules were established by the author, who had a passion for deep-sea fishing.

The freshwater lakes and rivers around the island are very good for trout fishing.

TENNIS AND GOLF

Almost all the holiday villages and large hotel complexes have tennis courts. Non-residents usually make use of them by paying a fee.

The island also has two good golf courses: the nine-hole **Club de Golf Habana** and the 18-hole **Club de Golf de Varadero**.

The sport is increasingly popular and there are plans to lay out even more golf courses in the main tourist resorts in the near future.

CYCLING

Touring the island by bicycle is an excellent way to enjoy the landscape and meet local people. The bicycles offered for rent to tourists (by larger hotels and most holiday villages) are of better quality than those the locals have to use. Cycling is not usually dangerous, particularly outside the towns where traffic is light. Beware, however, of potholes in the road. Fortunately, there are plenty of roadside workshops *(talleres)*, where repairs can be carried out.

Bikes should always be locked or left in supervised places (thefts are common), and remember to wear a helmet. Mountain bikes are best for rough terrain.

Hikers on a path near Topes de Collantes *(see p191)*

HIKING, EXCURSIONS AND BIRDWATCHING

Trekking on horseback is another very enjoyable way to see the Cuban landscape. In Havana the only horse riding centre is in Parque Lenin *(see p116)*, but hotels in the main resorts, eco-tourist centres and camping sites can provide horses as well as organized excursions. Both experienced and inexperienced riders are catered for.

Until recently, the only opportunities for hiking – either with official guides or on well-marked trails – were in the areas of Viñales, Topes de Collantes and Sierra Maestra (from Alto de Naranjo to Las Cuevas).

Varadero's golf course, close to the sea

However, eco-tourist principles have since spread to all parts of Cuba and programmes have been devised to cater for a wider range of interests, such as speleology, botany and birdwatching. The Península de Zapata *(see pp164–7)* is a particularly good area for birders, since the marshland ecosystem is a haven for hundreds of different bird species. Further east around Baracoa are the biosphere reserve of El Yunque and the Parque Nacional Alejandro de Humboldt *(see pp244–5)*, both home to rare species.

For information on nature tours and programmes, contact **Gaviota Tours** and **Ecotur**; the latter organization oversees the upkeep and improvement of the trails.

HUNTING

Cubans enjoy the thrill of hunting *(cinegética)* and the island has a number of hunting reserves *(cotos de caza)*, where people are allowed to hunt birds and small animals within rigorously defined limits and under the supervision of the forest rangers. The reserves are usually sited near lagoons, lakes or cays, and hunting is for wild duck, snipe, guinea fowl and pigeons, among other birds. In general, it is possible to hire all the equipment needed for hunting at these reserves, although prices can be high. The hunting season is from the end of October until the middle of March.

Cuba's specialist hunting trip agency is Ecotur.

Horse riding among the *mogotes* in the Valle de Viñales

DIRECTORY

DIVING

Avalon
Jardines de la Reina, Júcaro. *Tel (7) 204 7422.*

Centro de Buceo María La Gorda
La Bajada, Pinar del Río. *Tel (48) 778 131.*

El Colony
Carretera de Siguanea, km 41, Isla de la Juventud. *Tel (46) 398 181.*

Green Moray
Cayo Guillermo. *Tel (33) 301 627.*

Marlin Náutica
Marlin Jardines del Rey, Cayo Coco. *Tel (33) 201 221.* www.nauticamarlin.com

Shark's Friends
Hotel Brisa Santa Lucía, Playa Santa Lucía, Camagüey. *Tel (32) 365 182.*

SAILING AND MOTORBOATS

Marea del Portillo
Marea del Portillo, Pilón. *Tel (23) 597 081.*

Marina Cayo Coco-Guillermo
Cayo Guillermo, Archipiélago Jardines del Rey. *Tel/Fax (33) 301 737.*

Marina Cayo Largo
Cayo Largo. *Tel (45) 248 212.*

Marina Chapelin
Autopista del Sur km 12.5, Varadero. *Tel (45) 667 550.*

Marina Dársena Varadero
Carretera de las Morlas km 21, Varadero *Tel (45) 614 448.*

Marina Hemingway
Ave. 5 y 248, Santa Fe, Playa, Havana. *Tel (7) 204 5088.*

Marina Internacional Vita
Bahia de Vita, Holguin. *Tel (24) 430 445.*

Marina Santa Lucía
Playa Santa Lucía, Camagüey. *Tel (32) 365 182.*

Marina Santiago
Ave. 1, Punta Gorda, Santiago de Cuba. *Tel (22) 691 446.*

Marina Tarará
Via Blanca km 18, Playa Tarará, Havana. *Tel (7) 796 0242.*

Marina Trinidad
Carretera María Aguilar, Playa Ancón. *Tel (41) 996 205.*

FISHING

Cubanacán
Carretera Playa Girón, km 1.5, Matanzas. *Tel (45) 912 825.*

GOLF

Club de Golf Habana
Carretera de Vento km 8, Capdevila. *Tel (7) 649 8918.*

Club de Golf de Varadero
Ave. Las Américas, Varadero. *Tel (45) 668 482.* *Fax (45) 668 481.* www.varaderogolf.com

HIKING, EXCURSIONS AND BIRDWATCHING

Ecotur
Ave. Independencia 116 esq. Santa Catalina, Havana. *Tel (7) 641 0306.*
Antonio Maceo 121, Baracoa. *Tel (21) 643 627.* www.ecotur.co.cu

Gaviota Tours
Edificio La Marina, level 3, Ave del Puerto 102 e/ Jústiz y Obrapía, Havana. *Tel (7) 869 5588.* *Fax (7) 866 1879.* www.gaviota-group.com

SURVIVAL
GUIDE

PRACTICAL INFORMATION

In the last 20 years Cuba has made great strides in the field of tourism and can now provide visitors with modern, international-level facilities. It is now possible for tourists to move about much more easily on the island, although advance planning is still essential, especially as regards transport around the island. An effective approach is to contact one of the many travel agencies in Cuba, which may have their own offices or be based in the major hotels. The latter also function as tourist offices, providing practical information and often a booking service. However, although Cuban tourist operators are very good, visitors still need to be adaptable and flexible. The pace of life here is slow, as is the bureaucracy, so be prepared to waste a certain amount of time when trying to get things done. Whatever happens, try and remain optimistic. With a bit of patience and a lot of perseverance *"todo se resuelve"*, as they say in Cuba: a solution can always be found.

Logo of the Cuban
tourist bureau

One of the Playas del Este at Havana, crowded with tourists and locals

WHEN TO GO

Apart from September to November, prime hurricane months, and July and August, when the torrid heat can make touring quite tiring (unless you spend your entire holiday at the seaside), any time of year is good for a visit to Cuba. It is possible to relax on the beach all year round, thanks to the mild climate.

The best period for visits is December to March, when the climate is warm without being unbearable and there are more cultural events, such as the Festival Internacional del Nuevo Cine Latinoamericano and the international jazz festival *(see p37)*. This is also a popular time of year to get married in Cuba. However, be aware that getting married here is bureaucratic and requires that all necessary documents be translated into Spanish and notarised. Contact the Consultoria Jurídica in Cuba for more information.

Consultoria Jurídica
Tel (7) 204 2490.

VISAS AND PASSPORTS

To enter Cuba, European travellers must have a valid passport, a return ticket, valid health insurance, and a tourist visa *(tarjeta de turista)* issued by a Cuban consulate, or the travel agency or the airline you bought your ticket from. This visa is a form which you have to fill in with your personal data. Visas are valid for one month and can be extended for another 30 days: in Havana, go to the **Vedado Immigration Office**. In other cities, you must go to the local Dirección Provincial de Inmigración. If, however, you are going to Cuba on business or to work as a journalist, you should apply to the Cuban embassy or consulate in your home country well in advance for a special visa.

For US-passport holders, special regulations apply *(see p308)*.

Vedado Immigration Office
Calle 17 No. 203 e/ J y K, Vedado, Havana.

CUSTOMS INFORMATION

Besides their personal belongings, tourists are allowed to take into Cuba new or used objects whose overall value is no more than CUC$1,000, plus 10 kg (22 lb) of medicines in their original packaging. Small appliances such as electric razors are allowed, but not objects such as walkie talkies. It is forbidden to import fresh food such as fruit and plants of any kind, as well as explosives, drugs, and pornographic material. Hunters with firearms must present their permits at customs.

If you intend to take more than 50 cigars out of the country you must be able to produce a receipt declaring their purchase at a state-run shop. If you take out more than 50 you may well need to pay duty when you get home. Visitors can take no more than three bottles of liqueur and 200 cigarettes out of the country.

In order to export works of art that are part of the national heritage, you must have official authorization from the Registro Nacional de Bienes Culturales del Ministerio de Cultura.

Avoid purchasing items made from endangered species such as tortoiseshell, or bags or belts made from non-farmed reptile skins. These are covered under the Convention on International Trade in Endangered Species (CITES). The import and export of vaccinated domestic animals is allowed.

Rum for sale in a *tienda*, three per person for export

LANGUAGES

The official language in Cuba is Castilian Spanish, which is spoken with a distinctive local inflection and vocabulary *(see p335)*.

English is spoken fairly widely in Havana and in some main hotels and resorts.

FORMS OF GREETING

The most common greeting in Cuba is a kiss on the cheek, while shaking hands is common among men only in formal circumstances. It is polite to use proper titles when speaking to Cubans - *señor, señora, señorita, doctor, ingeniero* (engineer) and *profesor*. The word *compañero* (comrade) is not used as much as it once was and in any case is used only among Cubans, or at the very most with foreigners who are part of volunteer organizations on the island.

WHAT TO WEAR

The most suitable clothing for tourists is light and generally casual attire. In the winter a cotton or woollen sweater is useful in the evening, and may be useful at other times of year in places with air conditioning. A waterproof may come in handy all year round because of the tropical showers. Sunhats are recommended to protect the skin from the burning sun.

Two tourists in casual summer clothes

Except for evenings out at cabarets and nightclubs, there is usually no need for evening dress. However, Cubans do appreciate elegance and cleanliness. For a formal meeting or interview, men should not wear shorts or T-shirts, but trousers and a light shirt instead; and women should wear a dress or a skirt and blouse, but nothing too revealing.

LOCAL CUSTOMS

Cuba is a tolerant country but attitudes are still rather conservative. Nudism and topless sunbathing are not allowed on most beaches.

Despite the macho traditions in Cuba, the taboo concerning homosexuality has virtually disappeared, provided that common sense and modesty are respected. Cuban men feel virtually obliged to pay compliments *(el piropo)* to women passing by on the street: it is almost a

form of chivalry, a ritual, even if it is not always expressed with good taste. In any case, these kinds of comments should not be misinterpreted; no reaction is seriously expected, or at the very most a smile.

Women travelling alone should not experience problems, although they may be obliged to deal with frequent offers of assistance and compliments from men. The best way to put an end to undesired flirtation without offending is simply to say that you are married; this should be enough for most men to take the hint and leave you alone.

HITCHHIKING

The lack of fuel and consequent scarcity of public transport has forced Cubans to resort to hitch-hiking *(pedir botella)* both in the towns and in the countryside. Everyone hitch-hikes, young and old, to get to work, run errands or travel to other towns and villages, but it is never completely reliable. Students sometimes have to walk for miles and miles to get to their schools.

Although locals are used to picking up hitchhikers, it is not recommended for tourists who are driving to do this. Cubans always pick up their fellow countrymen, but if they offer a foreigner a ride they may be fined by police unless they have a permit. Some drivers may expect payment.

Hitchhiking is a popular form of transport for Cubans in rural areas

JINETERISMO

The tourist boom and the economic crisis have given rise to a particular form of hustling and prostitution known as *jineterismo*, which consists of living off foreign tourists, not only through prostitution proper, but also by selling counterfeit goods (especially cigars), finding rooms for rent or *paladares* and receiving a commission from the owners. The *jinetera* (*jinetero* if male) accosts the tourist, and initiates a relationship that may last a night or several days. Sometimes the aim is not just to make money, but also to get an invitation to go abroad.

At first this social phenomenon was underestimated, but now the Cuban authorities are trying to limit its spread with severe measures, not against tourists but against Cubans acting in this way. To avoid difficult situations, be wary of "chance" meetings, above all outside hotels or in discos.

This mainly affects Havana and cities and resorts popular with tourists. Cubans are very friendly people so don't dismiss everyone as a *jinetero*.

CUBAN LAW

In Cuba camping and sleeping in sleeping bags on the beach, or in areas not specifically used as a camping site, is strictly forbidden.

Cannabis may be offered on the street or outside a disco, but purchasing even a tiny amount of marijuana is illegal and could lead to immediate expulsion from the country.

TOURIST INFORMATION

State-run tourist bureaux such as Infotur, Cubatur or

Plaque at entrance to the Colonial Art Museum, Sancti Spíritus

Sign indicating a disabled access bus stop

Cubanacán have offices in major cities, at airports and in many hotels, offering basic information, ticket booking and trips. Maps, guides and brochures are also available. The Cuban publisher Ediciones GEO produces particularly good maps.

OPENING HOURS

Normal weekday working hours are 8am to 5:30pm; banks open at 8am and close at 3pm. Museum opening hours vary, but in general they are from around 9am to 5pm, with a half-day on Sunday. If a visit is important to you, it is best to telephone ahead.

An entry fee is always charged at museums. Children pay half-price, Cubans pay in national *pesos* and tourists, on average, pay 1–5 convertible pesos. The same amount may be charged for permission to take photos in museums.

DISABLED TRAVELLERS

Only major airports, hotels and restaurants have wheelchair access for the disabled. José Martí International Airport is wheelchair-accessible throughout, and is equipped with ramps, lifts, accessible toilets and adapted telephone boxes. A programme is under way to gradually add such facilities to other airports and stations, as well as public buildings, museums, offices and streets.

ELECTRICAL ADAPTORS

The electric current in Cuba is 110 volts AC (the same as in the US), and plug sockets take two flat prongs. For European-type appliances

and plugs you will need a voltage converter and an electric adaptor plug, although some of the up-market hotels have sockets that accept round-pin Continental-style plugs and three-pin British plugs. Many modern buildings and hotels also have 220-volt AC current.

CUBAN TIME

Cuba is five hours behind Greenwich Mean Time (GMT), like the US east coast. There is daylight savings time in summer, exactly as in Europe.

DIRECTORY

EMBASSIES

United Kingdom
Calle 34 No. 702y, esq. Ave. 17, Miramar, Playa, Havana.
Tel (7) 214 2200.
Fax (7) 214 2268.
http://ukincuba.fco.gov.uk

Canada
Calle 30 No. 518, esq. Ave. 7, Miramar, Playa, Havana.
Tel (7) 2042 516.
Fax (7) 2042 044.
www.canadainternational.gc.ca/cuba

USA
Interests Section, Calle Calzada, esq. L, Vedado, Havana.
Map 2 E1. *Tel* (7) 833 3551–59.
http://havana.usint.gov

TOURIST BUREAU

Infotur
Obispo 524, e/ Bernazay Villegas, Havana.
Map 4 D2. *Tel* (7) 866 3333.
www.infotur.cu

WEBSITES

General
www.cubatravel.cu
www.cubaupdate.org
www.dtcuba.com
http://havanajournal.com

Cuban Culture
www.afrocubaweb.com
www.cubaabsolutely.com
www.cubarte-english.cult.cu

In Spanish
www.cubasi.cu

Personal Security

Compared with any other part of North, Central or South America, Cuba is a peaceful and safe place to travel in. However, in recent years, the great development of tourism, combined with the economic crisis, has triggered an increase in petty crime, especially in Havana and Santiago. Although the situation is under control, it is wise to take a few precautions: leave your valuables, documents and money in the hotel safe; never carry a large amount of money with you; do not wear showy jewellery; and keep an eye on your camera. If you have a hired car, it is always advisable to park near hotels or in pay car parks if possible, and do not leave any belongings open to view in the car.

A traffic policeman

CUBAN POLICE AND THE FIRE BRIGADE

Policemen in Cuba are usually polite and willing to help tourists. The officials who check passports in the airports, who belong to the Inmigración y Extranjería and wear green military uniforms, do their job slowly and with what might be considered excessive meticulousness, but problems are not common. Tourists' luggage is often not checked, but it is best to adhere to the customs regulations to be on the safe side.

The policemen of the PNR (Policía Nacional Revolucionaria) wear blue trousers and a light grey shirt. Their role is to maintain public order, and they seldom stop foreigners. In some tourist areas such as Varadero and La Habana Vieja, you may see policemen in dark blue uniforms; they belong to a special corps that was created expressly to protect tourists from pickpockets and to check the documents of

A fire engine at Matanzas

suspicious individuals. They speak some English and can also provide information.

Different uniforms are worn by the traffic policemen (policía de tránsito) and firemen (bomberos). Traffic police wear very dark navy blue uniforms, sunglasses and motorcycle helmets. They may stop you for speeding; do not ignore them.

Guards from the relatively new SEPSA organization provide security for banks and tiendas and also see to transporting valuables.

Road sign indicating a dangerous stretch of road

ROAD SAFETY

There are not that many cars in Cuba, even though traffic is increasing. While driving in the cities, watch out for cyclists, who do not always observe traffic regulations. The greatest potential dangers while travelling on roads and motorways through the countryside (see p313) are the animals grazing on the side of the road, the railway crossings without gates, and the vast areas of unlit roads. The road surface is often bumpy, with sometimes deep potholes, so speeds should be kept down.

When it rains for several days in a row, the roads may easily become flooded.

THEFT AND LOST PROPERTY

To report the loss or theft of personal documents and belongings, either find a policeman, who should take you to the nearest police station, or ask for directions. Once there, be prepared for a long wait to make your report.

NATURAL DISASTERS

The greatest natural danger in Cuba is the possibility of being caught in a hurricane. Hurricane season runs from June through November. The autumn months are when hurricanes are most likely, with most occuring in September. Nowadays hurricanes are forecast well in advance, leaving plenty of time for adequate security measures, so the risk involved should not be that great. Should a hurricane occur, follow the instructions given by hotel staff. You will probably be told to wait in the hotel until it passes, and asked to keep away from windows.

DIRECTORY

EMERGENCY NUMBERS

Ambulance
Tel 104.

Fire Brigade
Tel 105.

Police
Tel 106.

Health and Medical Matters

A pharmacy sign

Thanks to the good health services, and the absence of most tropical diseases, a trip to Cuba should pose no unusual health risks. All the international hotels have a doctor on 24-hour call, and the first visit, as well as first-aid service, is free of charge. However, owing to the present economic difficulties in the country and the embargo, everyday pharmaceutical items are in very short supply. Normal pharmacies are rarely well stocked, but the well-supplied *farmacias internacionales* – international pharmacies which charge in convertible pesos – are now found in many towns. However, it is best to bring your own supply of usual medicine – pain relievers, fever reducers, antibiotics and stomach treatments – as well as strong sunscreens and insect repellents.

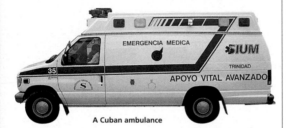

A Cuban ambulance

VACCINATIONS

No vaccinations or inoculations are required for visits to Cuba. Remarkably, almost all tropical diseases have been eliminated, and it is quite safe to travel around the entire island.

Malaria has also gone, thanks to a successful eradication campaign. There are restrictive sanitary regulations only for those arriving from countries in which yellow fever and cholera are endemic diseases.

MEDICAL TREATMENT

Cuban public health care is free of charge, efficient and superior to that offered in any other Latin American country, though it has been put under severe pressure by the US embargo.

The national service is reserved for Cuban citizens. Foreign visitors are treated in international clinics or in public hospitals, where they will have to pay for treatment in convertible pesos. On the plus side, they are given more comfortable rooms.

HEALTH INSURANCE

Cuba requires that all visitors to Cuba and non-Cuban residents hold a valid health insurance policy. Those who do not may be required to purchase insurance at the airport. This is provided by **Asistur**, Cuba's travel emergency help organisation. US-issued medical insurance policies are not valid in Cuba. Citizens holding these must seek extra cover through **Havanatur Celimar**.

PHARMACIES

The national pharmacies are not well stocked and generally reserved for Cubans. Medicines are sold only upon presentation of a prescription. In these pharmacies foreigners can only purchase medicines made from natural ingredients, including syrups, tinctures and vegetable essences, which are made on the premises. They are excellent, effective and cost virtually nothing (they can be paid for in *pesos*). On the other hand, the international pharmacies, which are located in Havana and a few tourist resorts, stock various medicines that can be bought with or without a prescription, as well as over-the-counter products not found in the *tiendas*.

PUBLIC WCS (RESTROOMS)

Public toilets are hard to find, and they are often dirty and without water. Toilet paper is limited and it is wise to carry a good supply with you.

ILLNESSES

Summer colds are quite common in Cuba and it is a good idea to carry a light sweater or jacket for these occasions.

Asthma sufferers may find that the humid climate could trigger an attack; visitors to Cuba with respiratory problems should always carry their usual medicine (packaged) and an inhaler with them. All the hospitals and *policlínicos* (the neighbourhood out-patient

Entrance to the historic Taquechel pharmacy in Havana (see p72)

Wearing a hat and using sunscreen to avoid burns and heatstroke

clinics) are well-equipped for these problems. Another fairly common nuisance in Cuba is diarrhoea, or worse, dysentery. This can generally be prevented by always drinking bottled water, or water that has been purified with tablets; another useful precaution is to avoid food and drinks sold on the street. It is best to avoid ice in cocktails as well.

All these measures should also be enough to ward off giardiasis, a disease caused by a parasite that attacks the intestine and causes dysentery, nausea, fatigue and weight loss.

Rare cases of yellow fever and dengue fever may occur in the summer in the marshy zones of Eastern Cuba (although in practice few tourists visit these areas). However, since these two diseases are spread by mosquitoes, it is advisable to use plenty of insect repellent when planning to tour marshy areas, and to burn mosquito-repellent coils in the evening.

PROTECTION FROM THE SUN

The sun in Cuba is very strong and protection is necessary, especially in July and August. Wear a hat, whether in town or in the countryside, and use a strong sun lotion with a high screen factor. This should be reapplied regularly, particularly after swimming. It is also advisable to drink plenty of water to prevent dehydration. High humidity and heat may cause heatstroke, with symptoms of thirst, nausea, fever, and dizziness. If this occurs, keep up fluid intake and take cold baths.

INSECTS

Mosquitoes are the main irritant in Cuba (and can cause disease). In swampy or lagoon areas, such as the Zapata swamp, pay particular attention to applying insect repellent, cover up in the evening and sleep with the fan or air conditioning on.

DIRECTORY

EMERGENCY NUMBERS

Ambulance and First Aid
Tel 104.

HEALTH INSURANCE

Asistur
Tel (7) 866 4499. **www**.asistur.cu

Havanatur Celimar
www.havanaturcelimar.com/servicios.asp

INTERNATIONAL HOSPITALS AND CLINICS

Havana
Clínica Cira García, Calle 20 n. 4101, esq. 41, Miramar, Havana. *Tel* (7) 2042 811. **www**.cirag.cu

Santiago de Cuba
Ave Raúl Pujol y Calle 10. *Tel* (22) 642 589.

Varadero
Calle 61 y 1. *Tel* (45) 667 226.

INTERNATIONAL PHARMACIES

Farmacia Internacional Habana Libre
Hotel Habana Libre, Ave. L, e/ 23 y 25, Vedado, Havana. **Map** 2 E2. *Tel* (7) 831 9538.

Farmacia Internacional Miramar
Ave. 41 esq. 20, Miramar, Havana. *Tel* (7) 204 4350.

HEALTH TOURISM

Servimed – Turismo y Salud
www.servimedcuba.com

HEALTH TOURISM

Thanks to its favourable climate, Cuba has long been regarded as an effective sanatorium, popular with an international clientele. By the 19th century, the first hotels had been built near springs of therapeutic mineral water. Beside the spas, there are now international clinics which provide general medical care and also specialize in anti-stress and skin treatments, as well as hospitals for the rehabilitation of alcoholics and drug addicts. These centres are located throughout the country and are in great demand: the waiting lists are not long, the prices are competitive and the results are good. They are run by the state-run **Servimed** organization.

Dermatological treatment in one of the specialist clinics

Communications

An unusual letter box

The telephone is by far the most widespread system of communication in Cuba. Unlike the postal service, which is not all that efficient, the telephone network run by ETECSA has improved considerably. Today there are public telephones that work with pre-paid phone cards. The use of e-mail is highly restricted for Cubans. Cuba also has five national television channels and several national, regional and municipal radio stations. Many hotels have a satellite dish and broadcast a TV channel especially for tourists. The leading daily newspaper is *Granma*, while the weekly *Granma Internacional* is printed in various languages.

TELEPHONE NUMBERS

If you are calling from abroad, dial the international access code of your country (eg 00 in the UK), followed by the Cuba country code (53), the local area code, and lastly the local phone number you want to reach. The local area codes, which may have one or two digits, are given in brackets in front of all phone numbers listed in this guide. For local calls, for example within towns and cities, there is no need to dial the area code. The number of digits of local numbers varies, since the phone network system is in the process of being updated.

PUBLIC TELEPHONES

You can make local, long-distance, and international calls from hotels, but while this is certainly the easiest way, since the operator does everything for you, it is also the most expensive. Throughout the country there has been an increase in the number of public telephones that can be used to make direct-dial international calls without the help of the operator. Telephone cards *(tarjetas propias)* with scratch-off codes can be purchased at hotels, post offices and ETECSA telephone centres for $5, $10 and $20. To make a call, lift the receiver and wait for the dialling tone. Either press the button marked 166, or dial 166 and wait for instructions; you will be offered an English-language option if needed. You will then be asked to enter the 12-digit number on your scratch card, followed by the hash (#) key; then dial the number as below.

Telephone card

There are also coin-operated phones that take Cuban *pesos*. These are useful for local calls. You must insert at least one 5-*centavos* coin (also known as a "*medio*"), or use a 20-*centavos* coin (a "*peseta*") to talk for a few minutes.

5- and 20-*centavos* coins

PRIVATE TELEPHONES

The only direct-dial calls that can be made from private telephones are to numbers within Cuba; international calls must be made through an operator. Calls to foreign countries are always reverse charge, unless you use an ETECSA telephone with a contract specifying payment in convertible pesos. This type of phone can be found in hotels, in travel agencies, in some public offices and in the homes of foreigners who work in Cuba, rarely in Cubans' private homes. Telephone cards can be used from private lines.

MOBILE PHONES

There are four main GSM frequencies (Global System for Mobile Communications) in use around the world, so if you want to guarantee that your phone will work, make sure you have a quad-band phone. Tri-band phones from outside the US are also usually compatible. Phones with US SIM cards do not work in Cuba. Contact your service provider for clarification.

To use your mobile phone abroad you may need "permission" from your network operator as often they need to enable "roaming" for your phone. Remember, at the moment, you are charged for calls you receive as well as calls you make, and you have to pay a premium for the international leg of the call.

Another option may be to purchase a local SIM card – the electronic chip that links your phone to a particular network – that can be topped

---

DIALLING CODES

- Directory inquiries 113.
- To make a long-distance call via the operator, dial 00.
- To make a reverse charge (collect) international call via the operator, dial 180.
- To dial long-distance within Cuba from a public or private phone, dial 01 then the area code, except when calling to and from Havana: add 0 before the area code.
- To make a direct-dial international telephone call from a public telephone with a phone card, dial 119, followed by the country code (Australia 61; Ireland 353; New Zealand 64; UK 44; USA and Canada 1), the area code and then the local telephone number.

up with credit and uses the local mobile phone networks. You can only do this if your handset is "unlocked" – some operators lock their phones to specific networks. However, this is not particularly cheap in Cuba, costing CUC\$3 a day through the only provider, **Cubacel**. Cubacel works with TDMA and GSM phones. The cheapest international calls start at CUC\$1.40 per minute; international texts are CUC\$1. For most travellers this will mean using their own phone in Cuba may work out cheaper.

Check your insurance policy in case your phone is stolen, and keep your network operator's helpline number handy for emergencies.

POSTAL SERVICE

The Cuban postal service is slow, but generally no worse than in any other Latin American country. Stamps *(sellos)* can be purchased in *pesos* in hotels or in post offices *(oficinas de correo)*. Whatever the postage, letters take a long time to arrive; it may help a little to post mail in the *oficinas de correo* postboxes.

The safest, and comparatively the fastest, way to post documents, letters or parcels that are important or urgent is via international courier services: **DHL** or **Cubapack Internacional SA**.

Entrance to a post office *(oficina de correo)* in Havana

ADDRESSES

In Cuba the street number, preceded by "N." or "#", comes after the name of the street or square, followed by "*esq.*" *(esquina* = corner) and the name of the cross street,

or by "*e/*" *(entre* = between) and the name of two streets *(see p118)*. This is followed by the number of the apartment, if it has one, or by "*altos*" (first floor) or "*bajos*" (ground floor) if it is a private house, followed by the name of the "*reparto*" (quarter) or district, and then by the locality.

RADIO AND TELEVISION

There are five main Cuban television channels. Cuba-visión broadcasts soap operas, films, news, music and US drama series around the clock. Tele Rebelde specializes in news and sports programmes and airs school lessons during the day and documentaries in the evening, as do Canal Educativo and Canal Educativo 2. Multivisión also screens documentaries. Each province has its own local channel.

Hotels have a selection of channels such as CNN, Discovery ESPN, Cinemax, HBO and The Cartoon Network, all of which are not allowed in family homes.

There is also a tourist channel which can be viewed in hotels. *Canal del Sol* features mainly films and sports.

A good radio station is *Radio Taíno*, with music and information in English and Spanish (1180 AM in Havana and 1100 AM in Varadero). *Radio Rebelde* has news, music and sports; *Radio Habana Cuba* broadcasts for an overseas audience; and *Radio Reloj* broadcasts news 24 hours a day.

NEWSPAPERS AND PERIODICALS

The daily newspaper with the widest circulation in the country is *Granma*, the official organ of the Cuban Communist Party, published in Spanish. The party also publishes a weekly version for foreigners, *Granma Internacional*, in multiple languages. There are also several provincial dailies: *Trabajadores* (Monday to Saturday only) and *Tribuna de La Habana* in Havana; *Guerrillero* in Pinar del Río; *Girón* in Matanzas; *5 de*

Septiembre in Cienfuegos; *Adelante* in Camagüey; *Ahora* in Holguín; *Sierra Maestra* in Santiago de Cuba; and *Victoria* in Isla de la Juventud.

Among Cuba's magazines, *Bohemia* is a well-respected cultural weekly. In Havana, the weekly *Cartelera* provides information on the latest arts and culture in English.

A few hotels offer Internet access

INTERNET AND FAX

Although the use of personal e-mail is highly restricted for Cubans, it is being used increasingly in offices. Surfing the Internet however, is still limited to the "privileged few". You can log on in many hotels, and a few cyber cafés, by buying an ETECSA scratch card for CUC\$6 per hour. Wi-Fi is available from CUC\$8 per hour in a handful of hotels in Havana, Varadero and at the Meliã in Santiago *(see p269)*.

Fax services are available in all the international post offices in the large cities, as well as in all the major hotels.

DIRECTORY

MOBILE PHONES

Cubacel
www.etecsa.cu

COURIER SERVICES

Cubapack Internacional SA
Calle 22 n. 4115, e/ 41 y 47, Playa, Havana.
Tel (7) 204 2817, (7) 204 2134.

DHL
Calle 26, esq. 1, Playa, Havana.
Tel (7) 204 1876.

Banking and Local Currency

Cuba's currency is the *peso cubano* (CUP), but most visitors primarily use the *peso convertible* (CUC), or convertible peso. You can buy and pay for everything in convertible pesos. The US dollar was valid in Cuba until 2004 when the law changed, and it is now the least desirable major currency to bring to the country as, although exchangeable in banks, it is subject to a 10 per cent surcharge. Credit cards and travellers' cheques issued by US banks are not accepted anywhere in Cuba. Euros are now widely accepted in hotels in Varadero, Jardines del Rey, Holguín, Santa Lucía and Cayo Largo del Sur.

BANKS AND BUREAUX DE CHANGE

Banks are usually open from 8am to 3pm from Monday to Friday. Among those that carry out foreign currency transactions the best prepared are the **Banco de Crédito y Comercio** (BANDEC) and the **Banco Financiero Internacional** (BFI), with branches in the major tourist resorts and provincial capitals. Bank commissions on travellers' cheques is 2 or 3 per cent and more at weekends.

Bureaux de change, especially those located in hotels, have longer opening hours than banks. The commission for cashing travellers' cheques is around 4 per cent. The **CADECA Casas de Cambio**, often located near shops or markets, are the only places to buy *pesos cubanos*. Rates at hotel exchange desks are higher than those on the high street. Money can also be

The logo of the Banco Financiero Internacional

withdrawn using a credit or debit card (VISA or Master-card). Tell your bank about your travel plans to avoid any problems. Most Automated Teller Machines (ATMs) accept foreign cards, and can be easily found in cities and near popular tourist destinations.

CREDIT CARDS

The vast majority of hotels, some restaurants and many convertible peso-charging shops accept credit cards, though only those issued by non-US banks and never American Express. If you encounter a problem using a credit card, contact the **Centro de Tarjetas de Crédito in Havana**.

In many small towns, and even in some remote tourist resorts, credit cards will be useless, so it is wise to carry a certain amount of cash with you (this is essential outside of the major cities and tourist resorts). Wherever you are cash will be needed for tips and small purchases.

CURRENCY

The dual economy of the *peso cubano* and the *peso convertible* (convertible peso) can be confusing, especially as both currencies are often referred to as *pesos*. Even the symbol ($) used to denote them is the same. The most

The handsome Neo-Classical façade of a bank in Santa Clara

common terms to differentiate them are *"moneda nacional"* or CUP for the *peso cubano*, and *"divisa"* or CUC for the convertible peso.

There are currently 24 *pesos cubanos* to the convertible peso. Visitors will use the convertible peso almost exclusively, while the *peso cubano* is used mostly just by Cubans. However, it is the only valid currency on local buses, at most cinemas and sports stadiums, so it may be a good idea to carry a small amount with you. Some services, such as museum fees, are charged to Cubans in *pesos* and to foreigners in convertible pesos.

DIRECTORY

BANKS

Banco de Crédito y Comercio
Amargura 158, e/ Aguiar y Cuba
La Habana Vieja, Havana.
Tel (7) 860 4911.

Banco Financiero Internacional
5ta Ave. no.9009 esq. 92,
Miramar, Playa,
Havana.
Tel (7) 267 5000.

BUREAUX DE CHANGE

CADECA Casa de Cambio
Aeropuerto José Martí, Terminal 3, Havana. ▢ 24 hours daily.

CADECA Casa de Cambio
Aeropuerto de Varadero.

CADECA Casa de Cambio
Hotel Nacional, Calle 0 esq. 21,
Vedado, Havana.
▢ 8am–noon, 1–11pm Mon–Sun.

CADECA Casa de Cambio
Obispo no.257, e/ Aguiar y Cuba,
La Habana Vieja, Havana.
▢ 8am–8pm daily.

CREDIT CARD ASSISTANCE

Centro de Tarjetas de Crédito
Calle 23 (La Rampa), e/ L y M,
Vedado, Havana.
Tel (7) 835 6444.

Coins
*There are 100 centavos (cents) to a national
peso. Cuban coins come in 1 centavo ("kilo"),
2 centavos, 5 centavos ("medio" – used for calls),
20 centavos ("peseta", also used for phone calls);
and 1 and 3 pesos (the latter bearing Che
Guevara's portrait).*

3 pesos

1 peso

20 centavos

5 centavos

Pesos Cubanos
*Cuban bank notes come in units of
1, 3, 5, 10, 20, 50 and 100 pesos.
Each note has a different colour.
Twenty-four pesos correspond to one
peso convertible: be careful not to
confuse the bank notes.*

5 pesos

10 pesos

20 pesos

Pesos Convertibles
(Convertible Pesos)
*Bank notes of the peso convertible
circulate in units of 1, 3, 5, 10, 20, 50
and 100 pesos. The coins come in units
of 1, 5, 10, 25, 50 cents and 1 peso.
These pesos convertibles are not valid
anywhere outside Cuba.*

1 peso convertible

25 centavos

10 centavos

5 centavos

1 centavo

10 pesos convertibles

TRAVEL INFORMATION

The majority of foreign tourists arrive in Cuba by aeroplane. Charter and regular scheduled flights arrive from Europe, Canada, Central and South America, and there are even some special flights from the US. The internal connections within Cuba are good, and there is at least one airport in every Cuban province; 10 are international and 21 domestic. Taxis are available at the airport for hotel transfers, if these have not been previously arranged, or cars may be hired (driving is the most efficient way of getting around Cuba). Do not, however, expect any of the big international names in car rental: hire firms are Cuban (see p313). On Cayo Largo, one of Cuba's most well-known island resorts, there is an airport with international links, and Isla de la Juventud is linked to the rest of Cuba by a domestic airport as well as by ferries and catamarans.

Logo of Cuba's national airline

ARRIVING BY AIR

Cuba is connected to Europe and the rest of the world by flights operated by several major airlines, with scheduled and charter flights.

Most arrivals from Britain are charter flights. **Thomas Cook** offers package deals to Cayo Coco, Varadero, Holguín and Cayo Santa María, and **Thomson** offers flights to Holgúin, Varadero and Santa Clara. The Cuban national airline, **Cubana de Aviación**, has regular flights between European cities, including Paris and Madrid, and Havana.

Most scheduled routes from Britain involve a stopover in a third country, though **Virgin Atlantic** flies direct from Gatwick to Havana. **Air France** flights depart from Heathrow and other UK airports to Havana via Paris. **Iberia** flights (from London and Manchester)

Entrance to the José Martí airport in Havana

go via Madrid in Spain. **Air Europa** flies via Madrid; **KLM** via Amsterdam.

From Canada, there are flights with Cubana de Aviación and **Air Canada**. Cubana de Aviación and **Interjet** also operate flights from Mexico – with services departing from Cancún and Mexico City airports.

US TRAVELLERS

American law means that it is illegal for US-passport holders to spend money in Cuba as tourists or on business – hence the "travel ban" – but it is possible to apply for a licence from the **US Treasury Department**. These can be given for religious or humanitarian

CITY	AIRPORT	ℹ INFORMATION	DISTANCE FROM CITY OR TOURIST CENTRE
Havana	José Martí	(7) 266 4133	Town centre: 25 km (15 miles)
Varadero	Juan Gualberto Gómez	(45) 247 015	Town centre: 6 km (4 miles)
Cayo Largo del Sur	Vilo Acuña	(45) 248 141	(in the middle of the cay)
Camagüey	Ignacio Agramonte	(32) 261 010	Town centre: 9 km (5.5 miles)
Holguín	Frank País	(24) 335 487	Town centre: 13 km (8 miles)
Santiago de Cuba	Antonio Maceo	(22) 698 614	Town centre: 5 km (3 miles)
Manzanillo	Sierra Maestra	(23) 577 401	Town centre: 8 km (5 miles)
Cayo Coco	Jardines del Rey	(33) 309 165	(in the east of the cay)
Cienfuegos	Jaime González	(43) 552 047	Town centre: 5 km (3 miles)

interest trips, to freelance journalists (full-time journalists need no specific licence), and to students whose university has applied for a licence. Regulations tend to change, so check the current situation.

Since 2011, it has also been possible for US citizens to visit Cuba on a "people-to-people license". These educational tours are offered by official US Travel Service Providers. The US Treasury Department website lists the regulations.

Many US travellers choose to go without a licence, flying via Mexico, Canada or the Caribbean. These trips cannot be arranged through US travel agents.

> **Aeropuerto Internacional
> José Martí-La Habana
> Terminal Internacional**

Sign for the international airport at Havana

AIRPORTS

Cuba has 10 international and 21 domestic airports. The main international airport is José Martí, 18 km (11 miles) south of Havana. Charter flights land at Terminal II, scheduled flights at Terminal III, while Terminal I is reserved for domestic flights.

Most of the other international airports (other than in Havana) are for charter flights for tourists en route to holiday resorts. Of these, Varadero is the busiest.

ARRIVING BY SEA

Because of the US embargo, Cuba is not connected to North and South America by ferries, and few cruise ships dock here. But private yachts are welcome at Cuba's many harbours, including Marina Hemingway in Havana (special rules apply for US passport holders – see above). The following documents are needed: the passports of all those on board, the ownership documents, the name and registration

number of the boat, and the customs document (*zarpe*) issued at the last port the ship called at. The *Cruising Guide to Cuba* by Simon Charles is a good source of information.

ORGANIZED TOURS AND PACKAGE HOLIDAYS

Air fares vary depending on the airline and time of year. Fares tend to be higher at peak periods, that is in July and August and at Christmas and Easter. The best value is often to buy a package including charter flights from a tour operator; your travel agent can help you decide which is the most suitable for your needs. There are usually reductions for children under 12 years. From the UK, charter flights are available to Cuba from both Gatwick and Manchester.

Mainstream UK tour operators include Thomas Cook and **The Holiday Place**. Specialist operators, who can help independent travellers plan a tailor-made visit, include **Captivating Cuba, Cuba Direct, Journey Latin America** and **Esencia Experiences**. Caledonia *(see pp250–51)* offers arrangements including music and dance tuition.

Special interest holidays, especially those involving diving, watersports and salsa are particularly popular, and eco-tourism is also a developing area *(see p250)*. Among the tour operators offering special interest holidays are **Scuba en Cuba** and **Cubania**.

An aeroplane landing at Cayo Largo, an international holiday resort

DIRECTORY

ARRIVING BY AIR

Air Canada
Tel 0871 220 1111 (UK).
www.aircanada.com

Air Europa
Tel 0871 423 0717 (UK).
www.aireuropa.com

Air France
Tel 0871 663 3777 (UK).
www.airfrance.com

Cubana de Aviación
Tel 020 7538 5933 (UK).
www.cubana.cu

Iberia
Tel 0870 609 0500 (UK).
www.iberia.com

Interjet
Tel 1866 858 307 0870 (US).
www.interjet.com

KLM
Tel 0871 231 0000 (UK).
www.klm.com

Thomas Cook
Tel 0845 308 9442 (UK).
www.thomascook.com

Thomson
Tel 0871 231 4691 (UK).
www.thomson.co.uk

Virgin Atlantic
Tel 0844 209 7777 (UK).
www.virgin-atlantic.com

US TRAVELLERS

US Treasury Department
www.treas.gov/ofac
Tel (202) 622 2000 (US).

ORGANIZED TOURS AND PACKAGE HOLIDAYS

Captivating Cuba
Tel 0800 171 2150 (UK).
www.captivatingcuba.com

Cuba Direct
Tel 0800 056 0576 (UK).
www.cuba-direct.co.uk

Cubania
Tel (53) 7207 9888.
www.cubaniatravel.com

Esencia Experiences
Tel 01481 714 898 (UK).
www.esenciaexperiences.com

Journey Latin America
Tel 020 3432 1551 (UK).
www.journeylatinamerica.co.uk

Scuba en Cuba
Tel 01895 624 100 (UK).
www.scuba-en-cuba.com

The Holiday Place
Tel 020 7644 1755 (UK).
www.theholidayplace.co.uk

Getting Around Cuba

If your time is limited, one way to get around the island on public transport is by aeroplane, because this is the only really fast means of transport in Cuba. The network of domestic flights is good and connections are made via Cubana de Aviación, code-shared with Aerocaribbean airlines. Trains are much cheaper, but they are also much slower and very unreliable. Tourist coach services, on the other hand, are a good option. They are numerous, comfortable and provide services to all the tourist resorts and provincial capitals.

and young people under 18 years pay only 33 per cent of the normal fare.

The aeroplanes are not always new, the domestic flight safety record is dubious, and the service may lack frills, but the staff are experienced and reliable.

SHIPS AND FERRIES

If time is not an issue, it is possible to travel to Isla de la Juventud by sea rather than by air. Departure is from the port of Batabanó, on the southern coast, 60 km (37 miles) from the capital. Nowadays a catamaran built by Damex Shipbuilding & Engineering does the journey in about two and a half hours. Tickets for the catamaran can be bought at the quay or as part of a combination ticket at Havana bus station. Book ahead at all times.

In the cities of Havana, Santiago and Cienfuegos, you can also find waterbuses or ferries called *lanchas* or *lanchitas*, which operate around their respective bays, linking towns or providing a crossing to the opposite side.

Nueva Gerona national airport, Isla de la Juventud

BOOKING AND CHECK-IN FOR DOMESTIC FLIGHTS

There are flights from Havana to Baracoa, Bayamo, Camagüey, Cayo Coco, Cayo Largo, Cienfuegos, Guantánamo, Holguín, Las Tunas, Manzanillo, Moa, Nueva Gerona, Santa Clara and Santiago de Cuba.

It is not necessary to go in person to the **Cubana de Aviación** or **Aerocaribbean** airline offices to book a domestic flight; any travel agency will contact these airlines for you and make your reservation without

any extra charge. However, bear in mind that you should book very early, especially for flights in high season. Check-in is 60 minutes before take-off, and the maximum luggage weight allowance is 20 kg (44 lbs).

Domestic flights cost about twice as much as trains or coaches, but if you book one together with an international flight with Cubana, there is a saving of 25 per cent. Children under the age of two travel free of charge,

A Cubana de Aviación plane for domestic flights

Small ferries connect the coast north of Pinar del Río with the island of Cayo Levisa.

TRAINS

Cuba has 4,881 km (3,030 miles) of public railway lines, serving all the provincial capitals. Over time, the service has severely deteriorated and the carriages are by no

A *lanchita*, a waterbus connecting the various towns around the bay of Havana

means modern and clean. Refreshments may not be available, so take supplies.

There is at least one train per day on each of the main lines, but do not count on it arriving on time.

The trains known as "*especiales*", which cover long distance routes such as Havana-Santiago, have air conditioning (though it may not always function as it should), reclinable seats and a refreshment service.

Information on timetables and tickets (tourists have to pay in convertible pesos) can be obtained at the **LADIS/ Agencia La Coubre** agency, which sells tickets to foreigners. It is open for business from 8am to 3pm Monday to Friday.

The advantage in travelling by train is that it is almost always possible to find a seat without booking in advance, even in high season. If you have time, patience and are on a tight budget, railway travel can be a very pleasant and sociable way of travelling around Cuba.

COACH SERVICES

A minibus for tourists

The modern coaches operated by the **Víazul** company provide transport to the main cities and towns and tourist resorts in Cuba. They connect Havana with Santiago (passing through Santa Clara, Ciego de Ávila, Camagüey, Las Tunas, Holguín and Bayamo), Varadero, Trinidad and Viñales. There is also a direct service between Varadero and Trinidad, and a daily link between Santiago and Baracoa.

On the positive side, Viazul coaches are very comfortable and arrive on time – the

Façade of the railway station in Morón

disadvantage is that, at least on the stretch between Havana and Santiago, the frequent intermediate stops in all the provincial capitals make for rather a long journey. The seats can be reclined (a little), and there are toilets for passengers (but be sure to bring some toilet paper with you). The air conditioning is always turned on full, so that if you do decide to use this means of transport, always carry on board a sweater or jacket. Now that Cubans use this service, demand, especially in high season, is great. Always book in advance during these times. In July in Santiago, up to a week's advance booking is required.

Cubanacán also runs Conectando Cuba, which is a similar service to that offered by Víazul with the addition of a hotel door to hotel door service. Ask about booking this at your hotel reception.

Travel agencies also supply hotels with minibus shuttle services to take guests to nearby tourist resorts.

Tickets can either be booked in advance from a travel agency or bought on the day from a bus station.

DIRECTORY

AEROCARIBBEAN

Havana
Calle 23 no. 64, Vedado.
Map 2 F2. *Tel* (7) 879 7524 or (7) 838 1039.

CUBANA DE AVIACIÓN

Baracoa
Calle José Martí 185.
Tel (21) 645 107.

Camagüey
Calle República 400.
Tel (32) 291 338.

Holguín
Calle Libertad esq. Martí.
Tel (24) 468 556.

Santiago de Cuba
Calle Enramada esq. San Pedro.
Tel (22) 651 578.

Varadero
Ave 1ra e/ 54 y 55.
Tel (45) 611 823–5.

LADIS/AGENCIA LA COUBRE

Havana
Estación La Coubre,
Desamperados, La Habana Vieja.
Map 4 E4. *Tel* (7) 860 3163.

VÍAZUL

Havana Main Office
Ave 26 y Zoológico, Nuevo Vedado. *Tel* (7) 881 1413 or (7) 881 5652. **www**.viazul.com

Santiago de Cuba
Ave de los Libertadores esq. Yarayó. *Tel* (22) 628 484

Varadero
Calle 36 y Autopista.
Tel (45) 614 886.

A Víazul line coach

Travelling by Car

The best way to see a lot of Cuba's hinterland is to travel by car. With a car it is possible to discover places and scenery that it would be difficult to see on an organized tour, and even more so if you travel by air. It is best to plan an itinerary and stopovers in advance, and a good road map is essential. A few precautions should be taken. Keep speed down and always park in supervised car parks. In summer, because of the heat, it is advisable to travel early in the morning. You will see many people hitchhiking on the road; you are not obliged to pick them up, but it is a normal way of life in Cuba and the lift will be appreciated (*see p299*).

Example of a new road sign seen outside cities

A lorry picking up hitchhikers on the Autopista Nacional (motorway)

THE HIGHWAY CODE

In Cuba traffic drives on the right. The speed limits for cars are 20 km/h (12 mph) in parking areas, 40 km/h (25 mph) near schools, 50 km/h (30 mph) in town, 60 km/h (37 mph) on dirt roads and in tunnels, 90 km/h (55 mph) on asphalt roads and 100 km/h (62 mph) on the motorway.

Every so often on the *Autopista* (motorway) you will see signs telling you to reduce your speed to around 50 km/h: do not ignore these instructions, as they are often followed by road blocks. In general, the police are quite tolerant with tourists, but speeding may invalidate car hire insurance.

In town, headlights should be kept dipped. Seat belt use is both recommended and compulsory.

The road signs, of which there are very few, are the usual international ones, but there are also others on the country roads that warn drivers they are approaching a junction or a stretch of dangerous road (*see p317*).

THE ROAD NETWORK

The carretera central is an old, narrow and not particularly comfortable road linking Pinar del Río to Guantánamo, via all the provincial capitals. The only motorway in Cuba is the Autopista Nacional, or "Ocho Vías"; it goes from Pinar del Río to Jatibonico, near Sancti Spíritus (the Holguín–Santiago de Cuba stretch is under construction) and is toll-free. It is in good condition but should be used as if it were an ordinary road, without exceeding the speed limit, because every so often the road is crossed by unmarked railway lines or wandering animals.

The worst roads, with potholes and bumps, are found in Eastern Cuba, but the surfaces of city streets are by no means perfect either.

PETROL

Fuel is distributed through the many Servi-Cupet and Oro Negro service stations throughout the island. They sell petrol for convertible pesos and are open 24 hours a day. However, there are fewer stations outside the towns, so keep the tank topped up, just in case.

Ask the car hire company for a free *automapa*, which shows where the Servi-Cupet service stations are located across the island.

ROAD MAPS

A good road map is essential. The *Guia de Carretera* published by Limusa is very informative but unfortunately not widely available. **Infotur** in Havana and some car rental companies may stock copies.

Maps and brochures are also distributed free of charge by Infotur, in travel agencies and by car hire companies.

A hire car at a Servi-Cupet service station

NUMBER PLATES

Cuban car number plates come in different colours, indicating the type of ownership. Above the number is a word indicating the category of the vehicle: *"estatal"* means it belongs to a state-run organization, *"particular"* means it is a private car, *"turismo"* is used for cars rented by tourists and *"empresa"* for joint venture companies.

Official plate

Private plate

Tourist plate

ROAD SAFETY

The most serious danger on Cuban roads is posed, in fact, by slow vehicles: carts and carriages, tractors and cyclists tend to occupy the middle of the road, and before over-taking them it is a good idea to sound the horn.

It is also a good rule of thumb to sound the horn before making a sharp turn or when passing a lorry (they often do not have rear-view mirrors).

It is forbidden to keep your car lights on during the day, unless there is heavy fog. It is advisable not to drive outside town at night unless absolutely necessary, because of poor visibility and lack of road signs. Roads are

not lit and you may run into animals, pedestrians and even cyclists, whose bicycles are rarely equipped with front lights and rear reflectors.

At any time of day, take extra care after rainy weather, because road surfaces may become flooded (*see p301*). In mountain areas there may be some danger of falling rocks.

Tourists on a scooter

CAR HIRE

In order to hire a car in Cuba visitors must have a valid driver's licence from their own country or an international licence, be over 21 years of age, and have a valid passport to show to the car rental company. The three main agencies are **Havanautos**, **Cubacar** and **Vía Rent a Car**. Chauffer-driven cars are available from **Rex**. These have their own offices, and a number of branch offices in hotels throughout the island and in Servi-Cupet service stations, so that they are able to provide a good network of support.

Cars can also be picked up and dropped off at most of the airports, but it is advisable to book them well in advance, especially in high season, when the smaller and cheaper models are very much in demand. Payment is made in advance, and you must either leave a cash deposit (which is refunded) or leave an imprint of your credit card. You must also pay a minimum of CUC$10 insurance per day. A car may

be dropped off at a different office from the one where it was hired, but there will be a charge. A penalty will also have to be paid if the contract for car hire is lost. There are two kinds of optional insurance for hire cars. Plan A covers accidents but not theft, and Plan B covers all risks except for loss of a tyre.

In the event of an accident you must obtain a copy of the police report that states that you are not culpable (if you are not); this should then be handed over to the car hire company.

For exploring certain parts of the island, including the extreme west and far east, it may be best to hire a four-wheel drive (off-roader) to negotiate the pitted roads.

Larger groups of visitors might prefer to rent a minibus from **Transtur**. It is also possible to hire scooters.

DIRECTORY

ROAD MAPS

Infotur
Obispo 524, e/ Bernazay
Villegas, Havana.
Map 4 D2. **Tel** *(7) 866 3333.*
www.infotur.cu

CAR HIRE

Cubacar
Calle 3rd y Paseo, Vedado, Havana.
Tel *(7) 833 2164.*

Havanautos
Hotel Sevilla, Trocadero 55,
La Habana Vieja, Havana.
Tel *(7) 866 8956.*

Rex
5 ta Avenida y 92 , Playa.
Tel *(7) 209 2207.*

Transtur
3 y Paseo, Vedado, Havana.
Tel *(7) 833 2164.*
www.transtur.cu

**Vía Rent a Car
(Transgaviota)**
Calle 9na y 98, Playa.
Tel *(7) 206 9935.*

**A hired four-wheel drive: a good choice of
vehicle for the road conditions in Cuba**

Getting Around Havana

In Havana, road traffic is on the increase but is still nowhere near the levels of a normal European or American city. Getting around using public transport can be a major undertaking, unless you use the local tourist bus service, HabanaBusTour. On the other hand, there are plenty of taxis, which offer a safe and fast way of getting around town. In La Habana Vieja and Centro Habana, the most pleasant way to explore is to hire a bicitaxi or to stay on foot.

HabanaBusTour, the best and cheapest way to explore Havana

A bicitaxi near the Capitol building

WALKING IN HAVANA

Havana is an immense city and every district *(municipio)* extends for miles. However, if you are staying in the city centre (the area described on pages 56–105) then it should be quite feasible to do a lot of exploring on foot. Besides, walking along the Malecón seaside promenade, or through the tree-lined streets in the Vedado quarter, or the old colonial section of town, is a very pleasant occupation. Visitors have the chance to discover hidden corners and details of buildings that would not be noticed in a car.

Should you begin to tire, it's easy enough to flag down a taxi or bicitaxi *(see opposite)*; there are more of these on the streets since the government confirmed a relaxation of the rules limiting self-employment. The best places for hailing taxis are the main arteries such as Calle 23 in Vedado. Should you get lost, ask a local passer-by for help; Cubans are usually very courteous and helpful with foreign tourists

BUS SERVICES

Travelling by bus in the city can be something of an adventure. However, it is made easier by the hop-on/hop-off air-conditioned tourist bus service, HabanaBusTour, with two different routes around town. Route 1 starts in Parque Central and travels west to Plaza de la Revolución; Route 2 heads east to Playas del Este. A daily ticket costs five convertible pesos for Route 1 and three convertible pesos for Route 2.

Take the local buses to visit the areas not covered by the

tourist buses, but be prepared to devote plenty of time and patience to each journey. The ability to speak Spanish will help, and be sure to make a note of the number of the bus you have to take as well as its route, because there are no route maps at the bus stops to indicate the various stops. At any bus stop you must generally ask who is the last *(último* or *última)* in line for the *ruta* (destination) you want. There is a queue even though you may not be aware of it, which will re-form in an organized way once the bus arrives.

Passengers get on the front of the bus, where the conductor or driver should be paid the fare in small change in national *pesos*. The cost is usually 40 Cuban cents, though you can also pay 5 centavos convertibles per journey. Buses are usually very crowded, so feel lucky if you find an empty seat. The heat can often be suffocating. Allow plenty of time to get out, because passengers tend to block the exit door. Hold wallets and bags close to deter pickpockets.

The metrobus service has now replaced the old *camellos*. The buses are more comfortable and run more often.

The modern Metrobus has replaced the old *camello*

TAXIS

Certainly the safest and most comfortable way of getting about in Havana is by taxi. There are many cars bearing the word TAXI, but not all of them are authorized to pick up tourists. Official taxis can be recognized easily because they are new and well-kept, comfortable, and usually have air conditioning. Avoid illegal taxis, which have no accident insurance and may be more expensive. The official taxi company is **Cubataxi**.

Taxis can be summoned by phone or hailed in the street. Taxi ranks are found in front of hotels, at the airport and in the following two places in La Habana Vieja: by Plaza de Armas behind el Templete, and at the corner of Calle Empedrado and Tacón. A quirky alternative is to hire an old American convertible car, which are also official taxis; easily recognisable because they have the Gran Car sign and logo on both sides. These can usely be found outside the Hotel Nacional (*see p254*).

Tourists can also legally ride in local taxi *colectivos* – old American cars, which bear the sign TAXI in the window. Each journey within Havana costs 10 Cuban pesos. Foreigners may pay in convertible pesos and will be given change in *moneda nacional*.

COCOTAXIS

An original and unusual means of transport is the *cocotaxi*, an egg-shaped yellow scooter

A state-owned taxi, the best way to travel direct between districts

that can carry two passengers as well as the driver. It costs more than a taxi and doesn't have a meter. The driver does not give receipts, however, it is very useful for short rides.

The yellow *cocotaxi*, an unusual three-seater scooter

HORSE-DRAWN VEHICLES

In La Habana Vieja it is possible to go on an enjoyable sightseeing tour in horse-drawn carriages – perfectly restored old carts or Colonial-style carriages, quite unlike those used by Cubans outside of town. These vehicles are not cheap, but can be a romantic and picturesque way of exploring the city.

The carriage and gig rank is located in the square between Calle Empedrado and Calle Tacón, at one end of the handicrafts market.

BICITAXIS

A more environmentally friendly but slower alternative to taxis is to use a bici-taxi, as bicycle rickshaws are known in Cuba. These are used by Cubans and tourists for short rides in the centre.

They circulate mostly in La Habana Vieja, or can be found outside hotel entrances.

DRIVING IN HAVANA

People who are used to heavy traffic in big cities will not find driving in Havana too difficult. But it is important to stay alert at all times and watch out for the many cyclists, pedestrians and even dogs, which often run free in the streets. Keep speeds low in order to be able to spot and avoid the many potholes and bumps. The road signs and markings are reasonably good.

In the city centre there are three tunnels. Two pass under the Almendares river, connecting Vedado and Miramar (*see p109*). The other, which begins in Plaza Mártires del 71, behind the Castillo de la Punta, takes you rapidly to the other side of the bay and the Morro and Cabaña fortresses (*see pp110–11*). The latter is especially useful for those heading for the beaches in Habana del Este (*see p113*). The alternative is the long, winding port road, though it is easy to get lost.

DIRECTORY

TAXIS

Cocotaxi
Tel (/) 8/3 1411.

Cubataxi
Tel (7) 855 5555-59.

Gran Car
Tel (7) 855 5567.

A horse-drawn carriage in Calle Obispo, La Habana Vieja

General Index

Acknowledgments

Fabio Ratti Editoria would like to thank the following staff at Dorling Kindersley:

Map Co-Ordinator
Dave Pugh.

DTP Manager
Jason Little.

Managing Editor
Anna Streiffert.

Managing Art Editor
Jane Ewart.

Director of Publishing, Travel Guides
Gillian Allan.

Publisher
Douglas Amrine.

Dorling Kindersley would like to thank all those whose contribution and assistance have made the preparation of this book possible.

Main Contributor
Irina Bajini, a scholar who specializes in Hispanic-American languages and literature, lives in Milan and Havana. Among her publications are a conversation handbook, a Cuban-Italian dictionary published by Vallardi, and a book on the santería religion: *Il dio delle onde, del fuoco, del vento* (The God of the Waves, Fire and Wind), published by Sperling&Kupfer. She has also translated a number of Cuban books.

Other Contributors
Alejandro Alonso, an expert in Cuban art, is a journalist and critic who has published essays and curated exhibitions in Cuba and abroad. The former deputy director of the Museo de Bellas Artes, Alonso now heads the Museo Nacional de la Cerámica (National Ceramics Museum) in Havana, which he founded in 1990.

Miguel Angel Castro Machado, the second *historiador de la ciudad* of Baracoa, teaches Hispanic-American literature at the University of Santiago de Cuba.

Andrea G Molinari is executive director of Lauda Air Italia airline and a passionate smoker of, and expert on, Cuban cigars. He is the author of *Sigaro. La guida per l'apprendista fumatore di sigari cubani* (Cigars. A Guide for Newcomers to Cuban Cigar Smoking), published by IdeaLibri.

Marco Oliva is a diving instructor and an expert on diving in the Caribbean. He holds various specialist licences, including those for underwater photography, scuba-diving on wrecks, and marine biology.

Francesca Piana, a journalist and specialist on Latin America, has written numerous travel articles as well as guides to Greece, Mexico, Ecuador and Chile for the Touring Club.

Revisions Team
Alejandro Alonso, Marta Bescos, Claire Boobbyer, Walfrido La O (Academia de la Historia de Cuba, Havana), Maite Lantaron, Jude Ledger, Hayley Maher, Lucy Richards, Ellen Root, Juan Romero Marcos.

For Dorling Kindersley: Louise Abbott, Monica Allende, Claire Baranowski, Julie Bond, Claire Boobbyer, Ernesto Juan Castellanos, Conrad van Dyk, Emer FitzGerald, Juliet Kenny, Kathryn Lane, Maite Lantaron, Carly Madden, Alison McGill, Catherine Palmi, Naomi Peck, Helen Peters, Rada Radojicic, Marisa Renzullo, Ellen Root, Mary Scott, Susana Smith, Helen Townsend.

Proof Reader
Stewart J. Wild.

Special Thanks
Archivo fotográfico e histórico de La Habana; Archivo ICAIC; Laura Arrighi (Lauda Air Italia); Bárbara Atorresagasti; Sandro Bajini; Freddy L Cámara; Casa de África, Havana; Aleida Castellanos (Havanatur Italia); Pedro Contreras (Centro de Desarrollo de las Artes Visuales, Havana); Vittoria Cumini (Tocororo restaurant, Milan); Juan Carlos and José Arturo de Dios Lorente; Alfredo Díaz (Tocororo restaurant, Milan); Mariano Fernández Arias (Gaviota); Cecilia Infante (José Martí publishers, Havana); Jardín Botánico del Parque Lenin; Lien La O Bouzán; Manuel Martínez Gomez ("Bohemia" archives); Adrian Adán Gonzalez (Tocororo restaurant, Milan); Guillerma López; Chiara Maretti (Lauda Air Italia); Stefano Mariotti; François Missen; Annachiara Montefusco (Cubanacán Italia); Jorge A Morente Padrón (Archipiélago); Orencio Nardo García (Museo de la Revolución); Eduardo Núñez (Publicitur); Mariacarla Nebuloni; Oficina del Historiador de la Ciudad, Havana; Sullen Olivé Monteagudo (Arcoiris); Angelo

Parravicini (Lauda Air Italia); Milagros Pérez (Havanatur Italia); Alicia Pérez Casanova (Horizontes); Josefina Pichardo (Centro de Información y Documentación Turísticas); Richard Pierce; Poder Popular de Isla de la Juventud; Carla Provvedini (Ufficio Turistico di Cuba, Milan); Quinta de los Molinos, Havana; Gianluca Ragni (Gran Caribe); Celia Estela Rojas (Museo de las Parrandas de Remedios); Federica Romagnoli; Aniet Venereo (Archipiélago); Yoraida Santiesteban Vaillant; Lucia Zaccagni.

The Publisher would like to thank Andrea G Molinari in particular for the enthusiasm and willingness with which he supported the preparation of this guide.

Picture Sources
Geocuba, Havana; Habanos SA.

Reproduction Rights
The Publisher would like to thank all the museums, hotels, restaurants, shops and other sights of interest for their kind assistance and authorization to photograph their premises.

Specially Commissioned Photos
Drinks: Paolo Pulga, courtesy of the Tocororo restaurant, Corsico (Milan).

Additional Photography
Julie Bond, Ernesto Juan Castellanos, Maite Lantaron, Ian O'Leary, Tony Souter, Daniel Stoddart.

Picture Credits
key: a = above; b = below/bottom; c = centre; l = left; r = right; t = top

Works of art have been reproduced with the permission of the following copyright holders: Augustín Cárdenas *Figure 1953* © DACS, London 2011 95c; Wilfredo Lam *Third World* 1966 © ADAGP, Paris and DACS, London 2011 26c.

ALAMY IMAGES: 1bestofphoto 305tr; John Birdsall 273tl; Rolf Brenner 288cl; George Brice 185t; Adam Eastland 125clb; isifa Image Service s.r.o. /PHB 212tr; Mike Kipling Photography 124br; LOOK Die Bildagentur der Fotografen GmbH / Holger Leue 198tr; Sergio Pitamitz 125tr; Robert Harding Picture Library Ltd/Bruno Morandi 290tl; Tribaleye Images/Jamie Marshall 290br. ALEJANDRO ALONSO, HAVANA: 93cl, 95c. ARCHIVIO MONDADORI, MILAN: Andrea and Antonella Ferrari 153t. ARCHIVIO RADAMÉS GIRO, Havana: 30br, 30bl.

PIERFRANCO ARGENTIERO, SOMMA LOMBARDO: 32bl (all the photos), 33br, 33b, 286cla, 286clb.

MARCO BIAGIOTTI, Perugia: 19bl, 27cl, 87t, 91c, 110c, 132, 139c, 139clb. CLAIRE BOOBBYER: Front endpapers lbc, 78, 131cra, 202bl, 238tr, 243cr, 287tl.

CAPITAL CULTURE: James Sparshatt 125br.

CASA DE ÁFRICA, Havana: 9 (insert), 40bl, 42–3c, 42cl, 42bl, 73b. CASA PARTICULAR CUBA: 251c.

CENTRO DOCUMENTAZIONE MONDADORI, Milan: 46tr, 47bl, 49tr, 49tl, 52b, 87br, 114cl, 114cr, 114b, 117bl, 167b.

CENTRO HISTÓRICO DE LA CIUDAD DE LA HABANA, Havana: 28c, 28br, 29tr, 40, 41, 43t, 44, 45, 46bl, 47b, 48tr, 48b, 49bl, 50cl, 59b, 151cl, 219t.

GIANFRANCO CISINI, Milan: 57bl, 80tr, 111br, 165b, 173tl, 174c, 175t, 176t, 188c, 221clb, 231c.

CORBIS: Jose Fuste Raga 10cl, 11tl; Reuters/Claudia Daut 126bl; Reuters/Susana Vera 124tc; Reuters/Mark Wilson 239cr.

4CORNERS IMAGES: Sime/Schmid Reinhard 11br.

RAÚL CORRALES, Havana: 50–51c.

CUBANACÁN, Milan: A Cozzi 303b.

MARTINO FAGIUOLI, MODENA: 24cra, 24clb, 51tl, 86cr, 182tr, 220b, 224c, 225tl, 225tr, 225c, 226tl, 227b, 226br, 228tl, 229 cla, 229c, 229br, 233tl, 233b, 234c, 235c, 236t, 236b, 242c, 242b, 243t.

FARABOLAFOTO, Milan: 49cr, 50tr, 51tr, 52tr, 53bl, 57tl, 66cl.

GETTY IMAGES: National Geographic/Steve Winter 11clb; Photogapher's Choice/Louis Quail 272cl.

PAOLO GONZATO, Milan: 14tl, 18c, 20crb *(aura tiñosa)*, 20crb (ox), 29c, 30tr, 31tr *(claves)*, 31tr *(güiro)*, 53cb, 75br (all the photos), 155, 160t, 163t, 172t, 172b, 173cb, 173bl, 173br, 178, 180b, 182tl, 182clb, 184tl, 184tr, 184c, 188cra, 188clb, 188crb, 188b, 189t, 192b, 194c, 201b, 212tl, 213t, 220t, 231t, 234t, 236c, 248b, 272tl, 275clb, 284t, 286tl, 286tr, 286clb, 287b (all the photos), 289t, 302c, 312t, 312b.

GRAZIA GUERRESCHI, Milan: 23ad, 23bd, 37as.

HOTEL HABANA LIBRE, Havana: Sven Creutzmann 248t. HOTEL PLAZA CUBA: 81br.

Icaic, Havana: 27bl, 29bl, 29br, 37b. Image Bank, Milan: 21 clb (flamingo), L Abreu 5t, 215b, C Ansaloni 156b, 165ca, 166tr, 166b, G Bandieri, 58cra, A Cavalli 16c, 18t, 21tra, 23bd, 23bl, 53br, 54–5, 58cla, 59tr, 59cr, 67tl, 81c, 88t, 102tl, 113br, 116t, 134c, 152c, 153c, 154, 157t, 170b, 176c, 177tr, 185t, 192t, 193t, 198tl, 216tl, 235b, 249c, 287cl, 298c; M Everton 294b; GW Faint 126t; L King 303t; A Mihich 294t; A Pistolesi 21cra, 144–45, 148b, 150c, 211b, 244b, 245t; GA Rossi 4b, 14, 20tr, 20cra, 33tr, 57tr, 58br, 61t, 65b, 66b, 72tr, 72cr, 75cb, 85ca, 85b, 87bl, 96, 105b, 110t, 111b, 115tr, 115b, 130bc, 131tl, 133, 152t, 152b, 156t, 162t, 163b, 168c, 179, 198c, 232t, 233c, 249b, 270t, 270c, 293ca, 309b; E Vergani 113t, 165c.

Infotur: 298tc.

Lonely Planet Images: Doug McKinlay 273cb.

Stefano Mariotti, Milan: 32br. Stephan Mittas: 108cla.

Museo Nacional De Bellas Artes, Havana: 26, 27tr, 27cr, 38, 92, 93, 94, 95. Paolo Negri, Milan: 80cla, 80b, 148tl, 148c, 150b, 274t, 275b, 275br.

Marco Oliva, Milan: 75cla, 89c, 134b, 136b, 137tr, 137c, 137b, 138t, 138bl, 146t, 147 (all the photos), 150t, 173tr 191t, 207b, 232c, 250c, 250b, 293b.

Olympia, Milan: 19cr, 53t, 64b, 292t, 292b.

Photoshot: Deborah Benbrook 103tr.

Prensa Latina, Havana: 28tr, 30bc, 31tl, 31bl, 31bc, 36c, 47tr, 50bl, 51br, 51bl, 52c, 124b, 171b, 202c, 238b.

Laura Recordati, Milan: 118t, 118b, 271c. Reuters: Oswaldo Rivas 288br.

Lucio Rossi, Milan: 3, 18b, 20tl, 20cla, 20clb (woodpecker), 20clb (cartacuba), 20bl, 21tl, 21trb, 21clb (gavilán), 21crb (zunzuncito), 21crb (lizard), 21bl, 21 br, 22ca, 22cb, 23tl, 25br, 33cra, 34t, 35tr, 59cl, 69b, 72tl, 72b, 87crb, 98cl, 109b, 114t, 131tr, 131b, 136tr, 136c, 139tl, 142t, 142c, 143t, 146c, 146b, 153b, 164tl, 164tr, 164bl (all photos), 165tl, 166tl, 167t, 167c, 180t, 192c, 193b (all photos), 197t, 197c, 197b, 198tr, 198b, 199c, 199b, 209, 210b, 218b, 220c, 221t, 222tr, 224tr, 229t, 229cra, 230b, 237c, 237b, 239b, 240–41, 242tl, 242tr, 244t, 244c, 245c, 245b, 248c, 249t, 250t, 271t, 295, 301b, 315b.

Alberto Salazar, Havana: 31c.

South American Pictures: Rolando Pujol 124cl.

Studio Falletti, Milan: 33tr, 33cla, 33cr, 33clb, 138cr, 139tr, 139crb.

Wikipedia, The Free Encyclopedia: NASA 36bl.

JACKET
Front - Alamy Images: Jon Arnold Images Ltd./ Jon Arnold. Back - Alamy Images: Lonely Planet Images/Rhonda Gutenberg clb; AWL Images: Nadia Isakova bl; Dorling Kindersley: Lucio Rossi tl; Rough Guides/Lydia Evans cla. Spine - Alamy Images: Jon Arnold Images Ltd./Jon Arnold t.

All other images © Dorling Kindersley.
For further information see:
www.dkimages.com

SPECIAL EDITIONS OF DK TRAVEL GUIDES

DK Travel Guides can be purchased in bulk quantities at discounted prices for use in promotions or as premiums. We are also able to offer special editions and personalized jackets, corporate imprints, and excerpts from all of our books, tailored specifically to meet your own needs.

To find out more, please contact:
(in the United States) **SpecialSales@dk.com**
(in the UK) **travelspecialsales@uk.dk.com**
(in Canada) DK Special Sales at **general@tourmaline.ca**
(in Australia) **business.development@pearson.com.au**

Phrase Book

The Spanish spoken in Cuba is basically the same as the Castilian used in Spain with certain deviations. As in the Spanish-speaking countries in Central and Southern America, the "z" is pronounced like the "s", as is the "c" when it comes before "e" or "i". Among the grammatical variations, visitors should be aware that Cubans use *Ustedes* in place of *Vosotros*, to say "you" when referring to more than one person. It is notable that some Indian, African and English words are commonly used in present-day Cuban Spanish. This basic phrase book includes useful common phrases and words, and particular attention has been paid to typically Cuban idioms in a list of Cuban Terms.

Cuban Terms

apagón	apagon	black-out, power cut
babalawo	babala-wo	a priest of Afro-Cuban religion
bohío	bo-ee-o	traditional rural house with palm leaf roof
carro	karro	car
casa de la trova	kasa deh la troba	club where traditional music is played
batey	batay	village around sugar factory
cayo	ka-yo	small island
chama	chama	child
criollo	kr-yo-yo	Creole (born in Cuba of Spanish descent)
divisa	deebeesa	convertible peso (slang)
guagua	gwagwa	bus
guajiro	gwaheero	farmer
guarapo	gwarapo	sugar cane juice
ingenio	eenhen-yo	sugar factory complex
jama	hama	food, meal
eva	eba	woman
jinetera	heenetaira	prostitute, or female hustler
jinetero	heenetairo	male person hustling tourists
libreta	leebreta	rations book
moneda nacional	moneda nas-yonal	pesos ("national currency")
moros y cristianos	moros ee krist-yanos	rice & black beans (Moors & Christians)
paladar	paladar	privately-owned restaurant
puro	pooro	authentic Cuban cigar
santero	santairo	santería priest
tabaco	tabako	low-quality cigar
tambor	tambor	Afro-Cuban religious musical feast
tienda	t-yenda	shop that only accepts convertible pesos
trago	trago	alcoholic drink
tunas	toonas	prickly pears
zafra	safra	sugar cane harvest

Emergencies

Help!	¡socorro!	sokorro
Stop!	¡pare!	pareh
Call a doctor	Llamen a un médico	yamen a oon medeeko
Call an ambulance	Llamen a una ambulancia	yamen a oona amboolans-ya
Police!	¡policía!	poleesee-a
I've been robbed	Me robaron	meh rrobaron

Communication Essentials

Yes	sí	see
No	no	no
Please	por favor	por fabor
Pardon me	perdone	pairdoneh
Excuse me	disculpe	deeskoolpeh
I'm sorry	lo siento	lo s-yento
Thanks	gracias	gras-yas
Hello!	¡hola!	ohlah
Good day	buenos días	bwenos dee-as
Good afternoon	buenas tardes	bwenas tardes
Good evening	buenas noches	bwenas noches
Night	noche	nocheh
Morning	mañana	man-yana
Tomorrow	mañana	man-yana
Yesterday	ayer	a-yair
Here	acá	aka
How?	¿cómo?	komo
When?	¿cuándo?	kwando
Where?	¿dónde?	dondeh
Why?	¿por qué?	por keh

How are you?	¿qué tal?	keh tal
It's a pleasure!	¡mucho gusto!	moocho goosto
Goodbye, so long	hasta luego	asta lwego

Useful Phrases

That's fine	está bien/ocá	esta b-yen/oka
Fine	¡qué bien!	keh b-yen
How long?	¿Cuánto falta?	kwanto falta
Do you speak a little English?	¿Habla un poco de inglés?	abla oon poko deh eengles
I don't understand	No entiendo	no ent-yendo
Could you speak more slowly?	¿Puede hablar más despacio?	pwedeh ablas mas despas-yo
I agree/OK	de acuerdo/ocá	deh akwairdo/oka
Certainly!	¡Claro que sí!	klaro keh see!
Let's go!	¡Vámonos!	bamonos

Useful Words

Large	grande	grandeh
Small	pequeño	peken-yo
Hot	caliente	kal-yenteh
Cold	frío	free-o
Good	bueno	bweno
Bad	malo	malo
So-so	más o menos	mas o menos
Well/fine	bien	b-yen
Open	abierto	ab-yairto
Closed	cerrado	serrado
Full	lleno	yeno
Empty	vacío	basee-o
Right	derecha	dairecha
Left	izquierda	isk-yairda
Straight	recto	rrekto
Under	debajo	debaho
Over	arriba	arreeba
Quickly/early	pronto/temprano	pronto/temprano
Late	tarde	tardeh
Now	ahora	a-ora
Soon	ahorita	a-oreeta
More	más	mas
Less	menos	menos
Little	poco	poko
Sufficient	suficiente	soofees-yenteh
Much	mucho/muy	moocho/mwee
Too much	demasiado	demas-yado
In front of	delante	delanteh
Behind	detrás	detras
First floor	primer piso	preemair peeso
Ground floor	planta baja	planta baha
Lift/elevator	elevador	elebador
Bathroom/toilet	servicios	sairbees-yos
Women	mujeres	moohaires
Men	hombres	ombres
Toilet paper	papel sanitario	papel saneetar-yo
Camera	cámara	kamara
Batteries	baterías	batairee-as
Passport	pasaporte	pasaporteh
Visa; tourist card	visa; tarjeta turistica	beesa; tarheta tooreesteeka

Health

I don't feel well	Me siento mal	meh s-yento mal
I have a stomach ache	Me duele el estómago	meh dweleh el estomago
headache	la cabeza	la kabesa
He/she is ill	Está enfermo/a	esta enfairmo
I need to rest	Necesito decansar	neseseeto dekansar
Drug store	farmacia	farmasee-ya

Post Office and Bank

Bank	banco	banko
I want to send a letter	Quiero enviar una carta	k-yairo emb-yar oona karta
Postcard	postal tarjeta	postal tarheta

| Stamp | sello | se-yo |
| Draw out money | sacar dinero | sakar deenairo |

Shopping

How much is it?	¿Cuánto cuesta?	kwanto kwesta
What time do you open/close?	¿A qué hora abre/cierra?	a ke ora abreh/s-yairra
May I pay with a credit card?	¿Puedo pagar con tarjeta de crédito?	pwedo pagar kon tarheta deh kredeeto?

Sightseeing

Beach	playa	pla-ya
Castle, fortress	castillo	kastee-yo
Cathedral	catedral	katedral
Church	iglesia	eegles-ya
District	barrio	barr-yo
Garden	jardín	hardeen
Guide	guía	gee-a
House	casa	kasa
Motorway	autopista	owtopeesta
Museum	museo	mooseh-o
Park	parque	parkeh
Road	carretera	karretaira
Square, plaza	plaza, parque	plasa, parkeh
Street	calle, callejón	ka-ye, ka-yehon
Town hall	Ayuntamiento	a-yoontam-yento
Tourist bureau	buró de turismo	booro deh tooreesmo

Transport

Could you call a taxi for me?	¿Me puede llamar a un taxi?	meh pwedeh yamar a oon taksee?
Airport	aeropuerto	a-airopwairto
Train station	estación de ferrocarriles	estas-yon deh fairrokarreeles
Bus station	terminal de guagas	tairmeenal deh gwagwas
When does it leave?	¿A qué hora sale?	a keh ora saleh?
Customs	aduana	adwana
Boarding pass	tarjeta de embarque	tarheta deh embarkeh
Car hire	alquiler de carros	alkeelair deh karros
Bicycle	bicicleta	beeseekleta
Insurance	seguro	segooro
Petrol/gas station	estación de gasolina	estas-yon deh gasoleena

Staying in a Hotel

Single room/double	habitación sencilla/doble	abeetas-yon sensee-ya /dobleh
Shower	ducha	doocha
Bathtub	bañera	ban-yaira
Balcony	balcón, terraza	balkon, tairrasa
Air conditioning	aire acondicionado	eye-reh akondisionado
I want to be woken at…	Necesito que me despierten a las…	neseeseeto keh meh desp-yairten a las…
Warm water/cold	agua caliente/fría	agwa kal-yenteh/free-a
Soap	jabón	habon
Towel	toalla	to-a-ya
Key	llave	yabeh

Eating Out

What is there to eat?	¿Qué hay para comer?	keh I para komair?
The bill, please	la cuenta, por favor	la kwenta por fabor
Glass	vaso	baso
Cutlery	cubiertos	koob-yairtos
I would like some water	Quisiera un poco de agua	kees-yaira oon poko deh agwa
Have you got wine?	¿Tienen vino?	t-yenen beeno?
The beer is not cold enough	La cerveza no está bien fría	la sairbesa no esta b-yen free-a
Breakfast	desayuno	desa-yoono
Lunch	almuerzo	almwairso
Dinner	comida/cena	komeeda/sane-a
Raw/cooked	crudo/cocido	kroodo/koseedo

Menu Decoder

aceite	asayteh	oil
agua mineral	agwa meenairal	mineral water
ajo	aho	garlic
arroz	arros	rice
asado	asado	roasted
atún	atoon	tuna
azúcar	asookar	sugar
bacalao	bakala-o	cod

café	kafeh
camarones	kamarones
carne	karneh
congrí	kongreh
cerveza	sairbesa
dulce	doolseh
ensalada	ensalada
fruta	froota
fruta bomba	froota bon
helado	elado
huevo	webo
jugo	hoogo
langosta	langosta
leche	lecheh
marisco	mareesko
mantequilla	mantekee-ya
pan	pan
papas	papas
postre	postreh
pescado	peskado
plátano	platano
pollo	po-yo
potaje/sopa	potaheh/sopa
puerco	pwairko
queso	keso
refresco	refresko
sal	sal
salsa	salsa
té	teh
vinagre	beenagreh

Time

Minute	minuto
Hour	hora
Half-hour	media hora
Monday	lunes
Tuesday	martes
Wednesday	miércoles
Thursday	jueves
Friday	viernes
Saturday	sábado
Sunday	domingo
January	enero
February	febrero
March	marzo
April	abril
May	mayo
June	junio
July	julio
August	agosto
September	setiembre
October	octubre
November	noviembre
December	diciembre

Numbers

0	cero	sairo
1	uno	oono
2	dos	dos
3	tres	tres
4	cuatro	kuatro
5	cinco	seenko
6	seis	says
7	siete	s-yeteh
8	ocho	ocho
9	nueve	nwebeh
10	diez	d-yes
11	once	onseh
12	doce	doseh
13	trece	treseh
14	catorce	katorseh
15	quince	keenseh
16	dieciséis	d-yeseesays
17	diecisiete	d-yesees-yeteh
18	dieciocho	d-yes-yocho
19	diecinueve	d-yeseenweb
20	veinte	baynteh
30	treinta	traynta
40	cuarenta	kwarenta
50	cincuenta	seenkwenta
60	sesenta	sesenta
70	setenta	setenta
80	ochenta	ochenta
90	noventa	nobenta
100	cien	s-yen
500	quinientos	keen-yentos
1000	mil	meel

Road Map of Cuba

Gulf of Mexico

Archipiélago de los Colorados

Marina Hemingway   HAVANA
Mariel   ARTEMISA   MAYABE
Soroa   Batabanó
Viñales
PINAR DEL RÍO   Golfo de Batabanó
San Juan y Martínez   San Luis
Nueva Gerona
La Fé
María La Gorda

Isla de la Juventud

Archipiélago de

0 km   90   90
0 miles

PROVINCES OF CUBA

LA HABANA
ARTEMISA   MAYABEQUE   VI   CL
PINAR DEL RÍO   MATANZAS   CIENFUEGOS
ISLA DE LA JUVENTUD

CARIBBEAN

0 kilometres   200   200
0 miles